Elizabeth Warne was born in Bristol and has since moved north via Oxford and Salford to Scotland. She now lives with her husband in a Regency gatehouse situated in the beautiful wooded valley of the West of Girvan in south-west Scotland. She sold her first short story at the age of nine and has since written a number of historical novels under pseudonyms.

Ragtime Girl

Elizabeth Warne

KNIGHT

First published in 1989
by HEADLINE BOOK PUBLISHING PLC

First published in paperback in 1990
by HEADLINE BOOK PUBLISHING PLC

This edition published 1997 by
Knight an imprint of Brockhampton Press

10 9 8 7 6 5 4 3 2 1

ISBN 1 86019 6373

Typeset in 10/11¼ pt Plantin
by Colset Private Limited, Singapore

Printed and bound in Great Britain by
Mackays of Chatham PLC, Chatham, Kent

Brockhampton Press
20 Bloomsbury Street
London
WC1B 3QA

My grateful thanks to my mother, Vera Warne, my aunt, the late Alice Jefferies, and the many senior citizens of Bristol, who so generously shared their memories with me.

Also to Agnes Hay, Audio Librarian of Kyle and Carrick District Libraries, whose musical assistance I enlisted so often.

Chapter One

Laura Blackford clutched at her hat as a gust of the strong March breeze threatened to lift it from her head. This morning it had fitted perfectly.

Every step was taking her nearer home. The thought of what her grandmother would say when she saw her hair was terrifying. Lesser sins had often turned Granma into a frightening judge, jury and executioner. Many times Laura had spent hours in her room, hungry, red-eyed from tears shed from the thrashing she had been given with a slipper, or, for really naughty deeds, like laughing in chapel, the crook-handled cane that hung beside the kitchen fireplace. At seventeen, almost eighteen, in fact, she was too old to beat now, but Granma's tongue was fiercer than the cane.

Her pace as she hurried up the long hill from inner Bristol to the suburbs was not easy to keep up with. Her plump companion was inches shorter than Laura's five feet eight and her face was red and damp with exertion. 'Where's the bloody fire?' she gasped, perspiration trickling down her forehead.

Laura turned her head so quickly that the beige felt hat tipped sideways. 'What? Oh, sorry, Betty, I have to rush. I'll be late home.'

'I know that. I work in Gregory's, too, don't I? We can't help a last-minute rush of customers. I believe old man Gregory would keep open all night if he could.'

'Yes, but it's not that the shop closed late – after all, it was only ten minutes – it's having to walk home.'

'Well, that's bound to take time!'

Laura made no answer. She was supposed to walk to work and take a penny tram ride home. Today she had spent her

1

tram money and she was broke until payday.

Laura mercifully slowed her steps for Betty. She was in for trouble, so what difference could a few more minutes make? And the reprimand would be mild set against the one she would get when Granma saw her hair.

'If I was as thin as you,' explained Betty, breathing more easily, 'I dare say I could run all the way home.'

'I don't run,' Laura protested.

'Well, as near as makes no difference. Surely your folks won't call out the police because you're a bit late.'

'No, of course not. It's just that Granma always has tea ready on time.'

Betty giggled. 'What'll she say when she sees your shingle?'

Laura went cold. She must have been crazy to have her head shorn, but today the spring sun had warmed her and there had been a touch of mad March in the air. And anyway she had wanted for ages to look like the other girls. Bobbed and shingled hair had been the fashion since at least 1922, about five years ago, and even little girls didn't wear their hair long. Laura had felt freakishly out of style.

Betty had a curly bob. She had started only last Monday in the hardware department of Gregory's Department Store, where Laura worked in millinery, and Laura had instantly liked her cheeky cheerfulness.

'Well, your Gran can't eat you an' she can't put your hair back,' Betty said. 'An' as for bein' late, you can tell her we were kept workin' an hour or more, can't you?'

'But it's not true!'

'It might be.'

'I've never told Granma a lie!'

Betty tossed her head, and a street light glistened on the bunch of shiny red cherries on her blue hat. 'Huh! There's nothin' wrong in a lie now an' then. It makes life much easier.'

'Does it?' Laura was doubtful. 'Surely it makes things more complicated.'

'Well, if it does, you can tell another one to cover up. An' anyway, I don't call fiddlin' the time you left work tellin' a lie.'

Betty was beginning to sound miffy and Laura said, 'She'll

forget the time when she sees my hair.' For all her attempt at nonchalance her voice cracked.

Betty looked at her, her eyes filled with curiosity. 'When she sees it gone, you mean, don't you?' she joked feebly. She had quickly forgotten her irritation. She was a good sort. 'She's sure to like it. It gives you a kind of elegant look, you bein' so thin.'

'I'm too thin,' said Laura automatically.

'Huh! That's all right for you to say. You got to admit the fashion's for skinny women. You always look kind of right, even if your clothes –' Betty stopped.

Laura hurried to put her at ease. 'Granma is a bit old-fashioned. She won't hear of my skirts up to my knees and I have to wear this big hat because of my hair.'

'Not for much longer,' cried Betty in a sing-song voice.

'No-o,' faltered Laura.

She often felt rebellious at the strict regime imposed by Granma and today some of the other girls had persuaded her to visit a hairdresser in her lunch break. For once she had been surrounded by an admiring group who applauded as every one of her long, light brown tresses floated to the floor. She had taken one look in the hairdresser's mirror and gasped as she saw how much her appearance was altered. When she was back at work she sneaked numerous looks in the shop mirrors and each time it was a shock to see her shorn head, but as the day passed people complimented her and the unexpected approval of Miss Pringle, head of millinery, had been comforting.

'You've got a nice shaped head, Miss Blackford,' she had said, in her prim way, 'very neat and small. You may be able to model the hats when Miss Handley is busy.'

Miss Pringle seldom gave praise. But Miss Pringle wouldn't be around to defend her when she got home. Laura would stand alone to face Granma's displeasure.

To call Granma old-fashioned was an understatement. She was antediluvian. Laura liked the word; she rolled it around her mind, taking pleasure in it. She enjoyed reading Grampa's dictionary.

'You're not listening,' protested Betty.

'Sorry, I was thinking.'

3

'You think too much! I was askin' why you lived with your Gran? Someone told me you've got a family near the top of Warmley Hill.'

Laura felt the familiar tightening of her stomach. 'It's – convenient.'

'Who for?'

'Everyone. I've got two brothers and five sisters and they need all the room they can get.'

'Well, why didn't your Gran and Gramps take some more of the family? Why only you?'

It was a question Laura would like answered, too. She used to question her elders, but was always put off with an excuse or a rebuke and had not mentioned it for years. She tried to sound nonchalant, 'There was a flu epidemic twelve years ago. I was only five – in hospital with scarlet fever. When I got better they wanted my bed and I couldn't go home because the family were in quarantine, so I went to Granma's.'

'An' never went home again.'

'That's silly!' said Laura. 'Of course I go home. I go every weekend.'

'Well, don't tell me anythin' if you don't want to!' Again Betty tossed her head and the cherries danced. 'I don't bloody care!'

'Sorry, I didn't mean to be rude.'

'Well, you bloody well sounded it!'

Laura saw her new friendship was in danger; she could lose Betty, as she had lost others because they found her 'different'. 'I'm ever so sorry.'

'Oh, it's all right. I'm know I'm a bit nosy.'

'Don't say that. It's natural for a friend to be interested. My mother had the flu. Really ill she was and she couldn't look after my little brother properly when he caught it, and he died. She thought the world of him and they say the shock nearly killed her. She never mentions his name. I was told I had to wait until she felt better and then, well, it just became a kind of habit to stay with Granma.'

'Perhaps you remind her of your brother dyin'.'

4

Laura was startled. Who would have expected Betty to arrive so quickly at such a conclusion? She had wondered about it herself. 'I don't know. Mum always favours the boys. Anyway, I stayed on with Granma.'

'I shouldn't like that. I've got a nice Gran, but I'd rather be home. Still, as long as you're happy.'

The two hurried past the Regent Picture House where folk were queuing, stamping their feet and blowing on ungloved hands in the spring chill. Laura looked at the garish poster. '*Ben Hur*,' she said.

'Funny name!' Betty squinted at the poster through short-sighted eyes. 'Wonder what it's about?'

'It's from a book. I read it,' said Laura eagerly. 'It's in Grampa's library.' The word sounded grand, but that's what he called his few shelves of books. Granma complained that they trapped dust, but for once Grampa was firm. 'They're my chief pleasure in life, my dear,' he argued in his mild way.

Laura enthused, 'I should love to see the picture. They say the chariot race is something wonderful.'

'My boyfriend will take me to see it,' said Betty in a casual manner that Laura envied. 'We go twice a week to keep up with the serial. They always leave the heroine in awful danger. It's really tantalisin'. Last time she was tied to railway lines with a train comin'. I don't read, myself. Except magazine stories. Mam gets *Peg's Paper*. This week there's a story about a girl who's havin' a baby and she doesn't know who the father is.'

'Isn't it her husband?'

'She's not married – that's what makes it so interestin'. Her picture's painted on the front. She's really lovely. Blond hair and lips like – like rosebuds. And there's a tear rollin' down one of her cheeks.'

'That's dreadful! She must have been very wicked. Only fallen women have babies if they're not married.'

'God, Laura, you're a bloody scream! She's not wicked. She fainted and a man took advantage.'

Laura's hazel eyes opened wide. 'Took advantage! When she was unconscious? What did he do?'

'Well, if she's havin' a baby it's bloody obvious.'

'Oh, yes.' Laura was blushing, not because of the fictional girl's predicament, but because at seventeen she still wasn't completely sure of what the man had done. Here and there she had picked up snippets of information and a year ago she had borrowed a book called *The Sheik* from her eldest sister and read it surreptitiously, her eyes starting. A girl had been kidnapped and carried into the desert by a handsome sheik. Laura had pored over some of the phrases until she knew them by heart. 'Terror, agonising, soul-shaking terror . . . the flaming light of desire burning in his eyes . . . his warm strong body had robbed her of all strength, of all power of resistance . . . brutal hands that forced her to compliance'. The book never made clear what had been done to the heroine, but in the end she had enjoyed the hero's love. As Laura had read, latent feelings stirred inside her, filling her with a dissatisfied craving, drawing a half pleasurable, half worrying, tingling from her loins. When a girl at work had whispered to her what really happened between a man and a woman she had found it difficult to credit. She tried to imagine the minister, or the Sunday school superintendent engaged in such activity and her imagination faltered. When she thought of Granma and Grampa it failed completely. Someone had got it wrong somewhere. Granma's only advice was, 'Keep yourself to yourself. If you bring trouble here, out you go.' Trouble, as everyone knew, meant an illegitimate baby.

Bewildered by the imperfect knowledge which inhibited her understanding of her own body she had once tentatively asked her mother how babies were made. Mum had stared at her. 'You'll find out when you're married. That's soon enough for any woman. If I'd my time over again, I'd sure as hell be a man.'

Her older sisters went into fits of mirth whenever they spoke of girls ignorant of what they called the facts of life and Laura had no wish to give them a stick to beat her with. She felt as if she were standing on the edge of awareness, looking through thick glass, longing to be one of the crowd.

Betty stopped at the fish and chip shop beneath the tall clock tower. 'I've got to get five sixpenny lots for supper tonight. Mam's out cleanin' today and she'll be too tired to cook. You comin' in?'

Laura should have scurried on, but it was tempting to postpone the confrontation at home. Drawn by the comradely invitation, the steamy, friendly warmth and the smell of frying food that made her empty stomach gurgle, she followed Betty inside. There were a dozen people waiting to be served including several young men whom Betty greeted loudly. Laura had been to school with most of them. She smiled in their general direction and a couple of them nodded.

A man detached himself from the group. 'Well, if it isn't little Betty Cooper!' His accent was a curious mixture of Bristolian, Cockney, and Oxford English, as if he had been taking elocution lessons he couldn't master.

'Not so much of the little,' said Betty in a flirtatious voice. 'This is my friend, Laura Blackford. Laura, Rick Merriman. He used to live next door to my aunty out Hanham way. What're you doin' here then, Rick? I thought you lived in London now.'

'We did. We're back now, more's the pity. London's the place to have a good time. There's loads of picture houses and dance halls and the sights in the West End would knock your eyes out. Talk about the idle bloomin' rich.'

Betty tossed her head. 'Huh! Why move back then?'

'Mum went to London to nurse my Gran. She died and Mum wanted to come home. I thought I'd best stay with her.'

Rick's words might have provoked jeers and teasing from the other young men – 'Mummy's boy' being the least insulting – but his tone forbade them, not to mention his broad frame, his big muscles and the quick, aggressive glance he shot his listening fellows.

'Yes, well, she needs you I expect,' vouchsafed Betty. 'You bein' the only one. Where're you livin'?'

'Hotwells. Got a job in the office in Wills Tobacco Factory. I'm just over to visit some of my mates.'

'Oooh, what 'tis to be educated,' teased Betty. 'A job in the office at Wills!'

'Mum went back to the packin' room and my uncle is an office manager there and spoke for me. Any fool can add a few figures and write them in a ledger.'

7

'Why didn't your mam come back Kingswood way to live?'

Rick raised his dark, heavy brows. Laura liked his quizzical expression. 'Because we've got rooms with her aunty in Hotwells that's why. Want to know anythin' else?'

Betty half turned her back on him, her full lips pouting. 'Please yourself! See if I care!'

Rick ignored her and his eyes travelled over Laura. 'You've got a nice name. Bit fancy, but nice.'

'Lots of her family have got nice names.' Betty couldn't resist an opportunity to chat. 'Her mam called them after posh people she's read about. And the young 'uns have got stars' names.'

'You mean the heavenly bodies?' Rick's voice had an inflexion that brought hot colour to Laura's face.

'Oh, go on with you.' Betty made a gesture towards his ear.

Rick ducked, his hands raised. 'Don't hit me.'

There were guffaws and giggles all round. The sweating friers had just tipped a fresh load of batter-coated fish into the sizzling, spitting fat and the shoppers welcomed anything that enlivened the hungry wait.

'You know perfectly well I was speakin' of the film stars,' said Betty. 'One of Laura's little brothers is called Valentino. He was named after –'

'Don't tell me, let me guess,' grinned Rick. 'Rudolph, the great lover. I bet your brother's glad he's called that.'

'No, he isn't,' admitted Laura. 'In fact, I think he's having to fight every boy in the neighbourhood to stop them tormenting him, and he's only six. He calls himself Val and won't answer to anything else.'

'I don't blame the poor little sod.'

There was a general laugh in which Laura joined. She felt suddenly happy and at ease. The steamy atmosphere reminded her a bit of Mum and Dad's house where, on wet days, the endless washing taken in by Mum hung steaming on pulleys near the ceiling and on clothes-horses wherever there was a fire.

Rick stepped nearer. 'You've got a nice smile,' he said to Laura.

'Teeth too big,' Laura muttered, and wished she hadn't. Her

family ragged her unmercifully about her teeth, calling them tombstones, or piano keys. She couldn't blame them. Sometimes when she looked in the mirror she thought she was all facial bones and eyes and teeth. All the heroines in books and films had soft rounded faces, and displayed small, shining pearls when they smiled.

'They're not,' said Rick. 'They're straight and white. You should eat a few more fish and chips then your face would fill out a bit and kinda fit round them.' He studied her face as if she were a painting. 'Though that might spoil the lines.' He lit a cigarette from a stub which he ground beneath his foot. His shoes were black and shiny and his grey suit had pointed lapels and turned up trousers. He looked really grown-up. Twenty, at least. He offered the cigarette packet to Laura.

She shook her head. 'I don't smoke.' Granma hated to see a woman smoke at all, let alone in a public place. 'Lips that have touched cigarettes shall never touch mine,' was one of her favourite sayings.

'She's only keepin' me company,' said Betty. 'Her Granma never comes here.'

Rick's eyes opened wide, his eyebrows climbed again. 'Don't she like the food they sell? I thought everyone did.'

He was staring at Laura. 'Oh, she likes it,' she said, 'but she cooks it herself.'

'Fancy!' Rick turned towards the counter. 'You gonna be much longer? My belly thinks my throat's been cut.'

'You can have it now if you want it half raw,' snorted the vendor. 'Sir,' he added in exaggerated tones.

'Well give us a few chips to be goin' on with.'

The man frowned, then lifted half a dozen chips from the heated rack with a scoop and tipped them on to a piece of newspaper. Rick shook salt and vinegar over them liberally and bit into one. 'God, that's hot!' he exclaimed, and held out the paper to Laura who picked up a chip. She blew on it in a way that Granma would have deplored, then sank her teeth into it. The combination of fried potato, and salt, and tangy vinegar burst on her taste buds.

'Thanks, Rick, that was lovely,' she ventured.

He grinned. 'Have another.'

'I'd like to, but I can't wait any longer. Sorry,' she said softly to Betty, 'I'll have to go. Granma's sure to be cross.' Her voice quavered a little.

Rick stationed himself across the doorway. 'Not so fast. How do I get to see you again?'

Laura looked up at him. She was five feet eight and he was about three inches taller. He wasn't handsome. His face was broad and his nose only just escaped being stubby. His black curly hair sprang from his head, only partially tamed by a liberal application of hair cream, but his dark eyes were filled with teasing mirth and his liveliness made her forget his looks. She felt unexpectedly attracted to him.

'I don't know. I never go out – except to chapel.'

'Not even to the pictures?'

'Well, yes, sometimes with Mum or my sisters and brothers.'

'You mean there's lots more of you at home.'

Laura made a noncommittal sound and Rick bent forward and asked confidentially, 'Would you like to go out with me?'

Laura was too thrilled to be subtle. 'Oh, yes,' she breathed. 'I honestly would, but –'

'Where do you live?'

'It's no good giving you my address. You can't come there,' she blurted in sudden alarm.

'Why not? Is this Granma of yours a dragon? Does she' – he breathed in cigarette smoke and blew it out in two long streams from his nostrils – 'do that even when she's not enjoyin' a gasper?'

'Granma would never smoke,' protested Laura.

'Why not?'

She could hardly say that Granma considered it common to smoke cigarettes when Rick apparently chainsmoked and half the folk in the shop were puffing away. Even the fish frier had an ash-tipped Woodbine hanging from a corner of his lower lip. 'Common' was one of Granma's favourite words. All Laura's friends so far had been pronounced common. Short skirts, silk stockings and shingled hair were all common. Laura had

10

no doubt at all that Rick would be filed under the same label.

'It makes her cough.' Laura was astonished to hear herself mouthing the lie without so much as a blush.

'Smoking makes everybody cough. I sound like a factory hooter first thing in the mornin'.' Rick got another laugh from the audience.

'I'll have to go. Honest, I must! Please let me pass.'

'I like you, baby. What's your hurry?'

'We've got visitors coming for supper.' Another lie. She was paving the road to Hell, Granma would say, but she had to get away and she'd never had the opportunity of learning the art of flirting with words.

Actually, Granma only ever entertained her cronies in the afternoons in the front room, with its superior bay window, in which stood a highly polished table that supported a pot of green foliage and a statuette of a crinolined lady. The guests were safely concealed behind snow-white net curtains as they drank tea and ate little cakes and thin brown bread and butter from the best Coronation tea service. It had pink and green flowers on a white background and was kept in the front room cabinet when not in use. With it had come the free gift of a white bust of King George the Fifth, which was displayed on the mantelpiece. At those times Granma's hearty laugh would ring out, causing Laura and Grampa to grin at one another as they sat by the kitchen range enjoying a respite from her watchful domination. Sometimes Granma called Laura to play hymns on the piano on which she had taken lessons twice a week.

Rick gave her a mock salute and stepped aside. 'Be seein' you, baby.'

Laura hurried from the shop, his words ringing in her head. He probably didn't mean what he said. And if he did Granma would never let her go out with him. According to her you had to be at least eighteen before you could accept a date, or, as she called it, a social invitation; and no girl or boy ever brought home a member of the opposite sex unless they were firmly committed to marriage, engagement ring and all. Granma had her eyes on a boy from the chapel for Laura. Reggie Prewett was tubby, short-sighted and devout. Behind his back he was known to the young, irreverent members of the congregation as Prissy Prewitt, but he was the son of one of Granma's ladies' circle, his father was a prosperous grocer, and Reggie, as the only boy, stood to inherit.

'I mean it!' Rick had left the shop and was shouting after her. Heads turned. She tried to pray that no one who knew Granma was watching, but her silent appeal was suddenly lost in excited giggles.

Chapter Two

Laura half ran down the main road, the words of a popular song zinging round her brain. 'Shall I have it bobbed or shingled?' she sang inwardly over and over again.

She wished she dared whistle, but Granma said that ladies didn't and you never knew who was watching and listening, ready to tell on you. Kingswood people seemed to know everybody's business, almost like one big family, though not like hers, she thought, with a wry twist of her mouth. Granma and Mum detested one another.

A gust of wind set her clutching at her hat. It was big enough to encompass the big bun of hair that had twisted atop her head until today, but now the hat swamped her.

Oh, my God, she thought, I've done it now. And she had told lies and was adding blasphemy to her wickedness. Perhaps shingled hair, and short skirts, and dancing, and dresses cut low at the back did provoke evil thoughts and deeds, just as Granma said. She passed the grim, grey, Victorian-built school she had attended from the age of three to thirteen when she had passed the labour exam. She had written an essay and had later stood in front of the members of the Board of Education and answered questions and been pronounced ready to leave school and go to work. For once Mum and Granma had been in agreement about a girl not wasting time with books when she could be earning money. She waited while a tram rattled along the tracks out of the Tramway Terminal, her mind trying to grasp some coherent argument with which to confront Granma.

From her twelve shillings a week earnings she was allowed two shillings for pocket money and a penny a day for the tram fare home. This week she had needed to spend money on new lisle stockings and some garter elastic. What was left, including her tram money, had gone today on her hair cut.

She knocked on Granma's door; she had never been given a key. She wasn't even sure if Grampa had one. He greeted her, smiling tentatively, nervously, and she followed him into the small brown-papered hallway. There was a strong smell of polish and the dark green lino reflected the gaslight like a still pool of water.

'You're late, my girl,' Grampa whispered. 'Your Granma says the shepherd's pie's all dried up and ruined.'

At the thought of what a catastrophe as huge as a ruined pie would do to Granma's temper Laura forgot, for a moment, her hair. Grampa hung her serviceable grey coat on the hall stand then, as Laura lifted her slender arms to remove her hat, memory returned. She paused, staring at Grampa, then with a swift, resigned movement she swept her hat off and plonked it on a coat hook.

Grampa goggled at her. 'You – you're different – your hair – oh, dear – Granma –'

'Will you two be all night?' called Granma. 'This pie's hardly worth eating. A ruin of good food. You should be ashamed. There's plenty out of work and hungry would be glad of it.'

The two in the hall moved like automatons to the living-room door and walked silently in. The fire in the range burned brightly; the flames were reflected in the highly polished furniture and danced on the cups which hung on hooks on the dresser. The gas lamp hissed, a copper kettle sang, ready to make the after-supper tea, and Granma, her well-fleshed body rigidly corseted, gowned in bottle-green marocain, was plopping steaming savoury portions of minced lamb from yesterday's roast, topped with creamed potatoes on to willow pattern dinner plates, beside which the cutlery was placed with precision. The pie had not really suffered from being kept hot. An unmistakable smell of treacle sponge and custard came from covered dishes keeping warm. Granma was a good, plain cook and Grampa's wages as a foreman in a local boot factory enabled her to buy the best ingredients.

'Ruined!' said Granma. 'But good food will never go to waste in *this* house. Now get it down you. Laura, you can explain why you're so late after we've eaten. Mr Gregory never kept you till this time on a midweek day.'

She glanced up and stopped moving, the spoon poised. Her mouth dropped open. Laura had read about this, but had never actually seen it. The thought, coupled with her nervous agitation, made her want to laugh hysterically.

Granma's lips moved several times before she produced a sound. 'Your hair,' she whispered, then with rising inflection, 'Your hair! You've had it cut. It's *shingled*!' She made it sound like a bad word.

Laura swallowed hard. 'Don't be cross, please, Granma. All the girls have short hair these days.'

'They most certainly do not! The two Misses Cranford have their hair pinned up. And so do the daughters of the minister.'

Laura bit her lips. These women were years older than she and all unmarried.

Granma dropped the serving spoon into the pie and sat down heavily. 'That I should live to see such ingratitude.'

'It's not ungrateful to have your hair cut,' protested Laura, 'and I'm not ungrateful, Granma, truly I'm not –'

Granma continued as if the girl hadn't spoken. 'I take you in, at a time of life when I was expecting peace and quiet, and this is the way you repay me.'

This was an old, often-used refrain and Laura could have spoken the words along with Granma. She felt suddenly angry. 'I didn't ask to be "taken in",' she flashed. 'I'd sooner be home where I belong.'

Granma looked at her as if she had thrown a bible on the fire. 'I always knew it,' she rasped. 'You're a sneaky thing, aren't you? You look so good, as if butter wouldn't melt in your mouth, but you're sly. Always quiet. Always listening to older folks' conversation. I shouldn't wonder at it if you had your ear at the keyhole when my friends visit.'

Laura gasped at the injustice of the accusation.

Grampa said hesitantly, 'Amy, my dear, that's not fair. Laura sits with me when you entertain your friends.'

'You!' Granma's fury was directed at her husband. 'You'd say anything to shut me up. Don't think I don't know. All you've ever wanted was a quiet life and, thanks to me, you've always had it. I'm the one that's had to bring up the daughter of the slut our son married.'

Laura sat seething with rebellion. She hated to hear her mother maligned, but any defence she tried to make would be drowned, as always, in a stream of facts about her mother's way of living that could not be denied. Phyllis had never been forgiven for capturing Granma's only son. Laura was sick at heart at realising yet again that she had never been truly accepted by Granma. She belonged nowhere.

Granma's eyes were fixed on Laura's head as if stuck by glue. 'Well, miss, your hair's gone. What next? Skirts showing your underwear! Running after the boys! Well, there's bad blood in you. Not from my side, thank Heaven, but it's there all right.'

Grampa courageously ventured, 'I rather like her hair, Amy. It's –'

'It's terrible,' pronounced Granma, cutting across him. 'Absolutely terrible. Well, there's one thing about hair, it grows again, and the sooner the better. Meanwhile, you owe me an apology.'

Laura felt like yelling, It's my bloody hair! She wondered what would happen if she did. Instead she said, 'I'm sorry to have upset you, Granma. Well, in a way I'm sorry. I didn't mean to deceive you – but the style is modern and I like it. Long hair's just not the thing these days.'

'Not the thing!' Granma's voice oozed scorn. 'I suppose you got egged on by the girls from hardware. After all the trouble I went to get you taken on in millinery, you have to mix with common girls.'

'They're quite nice, some of them,' said Laura. 'Anyway it's done now –'

'I can see that for myself. You've upset me. I don't know if I can eat my supper.'

'Oh, Amy, you must –' said Grampa.

'God will punish you,' said Granma shaking her finger at Laura. 'He sees all and knows all. You'll be punished for defying me.'

16

Laura swallowed, then said steadily, 'Miss Pringle likes it. She even said I might be able to do a bit of modelling for our customers.'

'Clients,' corrected Granma automatically. 'Miss Pringle likes it?' At last she looked away and picked up the serving spoon. 'She wouldn't be so pleased if she knew you had gone against my wishes.'

She slapped pie on to Laura's plate and added a spoonful of carrots and peas. 'Hair that short only makes your face look thinner and your teeth bigger. I would have thought that's the last thing you wanted.'

Laura flinched. Granma knew exactly where to place her barbs.

After a grace said by Grampa they ate in silence, Granma stopping often to gaze at Laura's head, inhibiting Laura's appetite, but she managed to finish the plateful. Not to do so would attract more wrath.

When Granma spoke both Laura and Grampa jumped. 'Did you say Miss Pringle might ask you to model the hats?'

'Yes, Granma.'

'Flaunting yourself in front of a lot of people with more money than sense! I'm not sure I'll allow it. I'll have to think about it.'

Laura felt a gleam of hope. Granma might come round. Perhaps she would even let her go out with Rick. Pigs might fly! And anyway he'd probably forgotten her already. Hotwells was two long tram rides away and Wills Tobacco Factory was full of girls on the look out for a likely man.

After she had washed the dishes at the brown stone sink in the cold, stone-flagged scullery, Laura sat near the living-room range, toasting her feet on the high brass fender, sewing. She and Granma made their clothes, treadling away on a sewing machine, and Laura usually did the finishing by hand in exquisitely tiny stitches. Granma was fastening black bugle beads to a new black moiré silk best dress and Grampa was smoking his pipe – Granma did not mind a pipe – and reading *Bleak House* by Charles Dickens. He had read every book in his miniature library several times over and never seemed to tire of them.

Laura thought of Rick. He didn't look much like a movie hero, but how many men did? She sewed prayers into her stitches that Rick would ask her for a date.

At ten o'clock Granma made cocoa, filled the hot water bottles, and they all retired to bed. Her grandparents' room was at the back – where the garden joined those of a parallel road of houses – because Granma couldn't abide the street noises. Laura slept in the larger front room. She undressed quickly and slid between the cold, heavy linen sheets. She drew up her feet into her long flannelette nightie and cuddled her arms around the big stone bottle. She was just growing sleepy when a sound made her sit up.

Down in the road someone was singing. Not in the drunken, raucous tones that were habitual after pub turning-out time, but in a smoke-hoarse and pleasing tenor that warbled a popular song. *I'd climb the highest mountain, if I knew that on that mountain, I'd find you-o-o-o*. Several home-going folk shouted good-humoured insults.

Laura slid out of bed and pulled a crack in the heavy chenille curtains. Her hand flew to her mouth. Out on the pavement Rick was on one knee, arms outstretched, facing the house, singing soulfully. She was overcome by a fit of laughter in which amusement, trepidation and hope were equally mixed. Surely he couldn't be serenading her! How could he know where she slept? Then she caught sight of other forms in the shadows. Betty, two men, and Sally Whiteley, daughter of the respectable family who lived next door. She had undoubtedly been persuaded to tell Rick where Laura's bedroom was. Who would have thought such an ordinary man as Rick could be so romantic? She wished she had a flower to throw him. She'd seen a film star do that. Across the street, lights were appearing. Laura was horrified. The neighbours would make the most of this when they told Granma. She slid up her window and leaned out.

'Go away,' she said in a loud stage whisper. 'You'll get me shot.'

Rick's reaction was to slap both his hands on his heart and increase the volume.

'Please,' Laura begged, before she began to giggle helplessly.

Curtains were being pulled back and Laura hastily closed her window and peered once more through a crack. Sally said something urgently to Rick who stood up.

A man flung up his window and yelled, 'Stop that caterwaulin'. There's workin' folks here tryin' to sleep.'

Rick dusted his knees, bowed in the direction of the man, then made a deeper obeisance to Laura's window and sauntered off, whistling in ear-piercing tones.

Laura was overcome by her nervous, crazy laughter and lay in bed, a handful of sheet stuffed into her mouth so that the sound could not assault Granma's ears.

The next day she walked to work, exhilarated by the hope that a man admired her and decided that when she got her wages she would buy something pretty to trim a hat. On the way, she was joined by three of her sisters; Lillian, at eighteen, the eldest girl still living at home, and little Iris, just thirteen, both worked in Gregory's haberdashery, though Iris was so small she needed a box to stand on to serve. Freda, whose flat, plain face was usually dotted with pimples worked as a machinist in a corset factory not far from Gregory's.

'How are Mum and Dad?' asked Laura. She always asked.

Freda's good-natured grin creased her pudgy face as she made her usual reply, 'Mum's all right. So's our Dad.'

Lillian snapped, 'No different from usual.'

But Iris contradicted, 'That's not true, our Lillian. Mum's feelin' bad.'

'What's the matter with her?' asked Laura.

'Too much washin',' said Lillian, and tossed her head and walked off to join a group of her friends.

Iris said, 'Mrs Wilson sprained her wrist so Mum brought her lady's washin' home and did it so Mrs Wilson'll get paid. She's a good sort, our Mum.'

'I know. Is she really ill?'

'She says it's nothin'. She's got a pain inside. She says it's from all the liftin' of the sheets and the manglin'. Today she's got all the ironin' to do. I offered to help tonight, but she said

19

the washin' has to go back today or Mrs Wilson's lady will complain and probably sack her.'

Freda said, 'Our Joyce is helpin'. She's playin' with the kids and keepin' them away from the kitchen.'

'Mum's mindin' four now as well as our lot,' said Iris. 'Someone's husband just died and their mother's got a job at Carson's, dippin' chocolates.'

'Joyce is gettin' quite good at housework.' A tender smile creased Freda's face as she spoke of her twin who had been born second, after a struggle which had left Mum fearfully weak, and Joyce a little 'slow'. Freda loved Joyce more than anyone in the world.

The three miles seemed quite short as the girls chattered and greeted friends, and flirted with young men, all striding towards Bristol and work. At Gregory's Laura hung her hat and coat in the cloakroom and smoothed down her black dress with the white collar and cuffs worn by the millinery ladies upstairs in fashions. Lillian scowled. She had to wear dark green with brown cuffs and had been jealous from the first when Granma had persuaded Gregory's that Laura should grace one of their best departments.

The morning was busy but, during an afternoon lull, Laura could not resist trying on a sky-blue felt hat that was as close fitting as a helmet, and sported a burst of feathery plumes at the top. Yesterday it would not have fitted over her hair. Today she approved of the way it hugged her head and framed her face. She sighed. She would never be called pretty, but fine feathers could help. Not the ones on this hat, though. There were too many. The girl who was supposed to be keeping watch was so interested she forgot her task, and suddenly Miss Pringle was there, back early from her lunch break. Laura saw her reflection in the mirror, whipped off the hat and whirled round, waiting for the storm to break. To her surprise, it didn't. She received quite a mild reproof, followed by a reiteration of the promise that she should model some time.

Laura was thrilled. The assistants who acted as models dressed up and sauntered through Gregory's top floor restaurant to tempt the customers to buy new clothes. They considered themselves very superior – and she might join them. Doors of opportunity were opening to her. And today was pay-day. Things were going almost too well. She was not superstitious, but all the same she crossed her fingers and touched wood.

Gregory's stayed open late on Fridays and Saturdays to tempt as much as possible from the pay packets of the weekly wage earners. As the long day passed, Laura looked in every mirror and had to make a conscious effort not to keep smoothing her gleaming hair. She tried not to think of Rick, but it was impossible to keep him from her mind. She prayed that he would ask her out. Even though she'd have to say 'no' she just wanted to be asked. It might be the longed-for passport into the groups of giggling girls who compared notes about their boyfriends.

Closing time was eight o'clock and at five minutes to the hour, when the staff were reaching for dust covers and thinking longingly of supper, a tall woman, elegantly dressed in a midnight blue coat of softest wool fastened by a diamanté buckle at her hip, and a cloche hat with a diamanté hat-pin shaped like an arrow, swept into the millinery department.

'There's always one!' muttered Dolores Handley, the senior shop assistant-model in millinery. 'Oh, God, it's Lady Mallender.' She stepped forward, fixing a smile to her lips. 'Can I help you, modom?' she enquired in the 'posh' voice she kept for high-spending customers.

'I have absolutely no idea. Where is Miss Pringle? She always attends to me.'

'She was called upstairs to speak to Mr Gregory senior. Shall I send word?'

'I've no time to waste. She should be here when she is needed. I want a hat for a special occasion. A greeny-blue hat in silk or satin. It must not have a brim. I want to see and be seen.'

'Have you brought a colour swatch, modom?'

'No, I have not. I shall know what I want when I see it. That is if you ever intend to show me anything,' she snapped.

Dolores was flustered. 'I'm sorry, modom. If you would wait one moment, I believe I have just the thing.'

She took up an eau-de-nil hat from a stand. Laura thought it was beautiful, but the customer drew back and eyed it as if it had been stinking fish.

'I said a green-blue hat, you stupid girl. That is not at all what I require.'

'Is it the shape that's wrong, modom, or – ?'

'The colour is quite, quite impossible. I want turquoise. Really this place is becoming almost unbearable. I do trust I shall not have to take my custom elsewhere.'

'Miss Pringle has it listed as turquoise, Lady Mallender.'

'Indeed! Well I disagree. Take it away and bring me something better.' She glanced at her watch with its jewelled bracelet. 'And hurry!'

Laura said quietly to Dolores, 'I think her ladyship might care to see the turquoise turban that came in today.'

'Where is it?' hissed Dolores.

'In the drawer. It was going on display tomorrow. I'll get it for you.' Laura pulled open the deep heavy wooden drawer beneath the display stand and handed out a swathe of shining satin.

Lady Mallender actually produced a thin smile. 'That is much more like it. Fit it on me. No, not you!' She waved Dolores away. 'The one who had the sense to look in the drawer.'

She sat as Laura placed the hat on her head, twisting this way and that so that the sheen picked up the light. A bow perched on the front like a butterfly gave out small sparkles from a scattering of marquisites.

Laura held a mirror behind her to give an all-round view.

'It's really rather pretty,' decided Lady Mallender.

Laura smiled professionally. She was held by a fascination that filled her with resentment even as it captivated her. Many of the shoppers were dears, but the ways of some of the wealthy were an enigma. This woman and her bad manners made her angry. Lady Mallender wasn't pretty, but her skin was flawless, her brows plucked to a dark line, her hair permanently waved, and she gave off the air of elegant superiority that only money could buy, and which seemed more than mere good

22

looks. The hat cost more than Laura's mother made in weeks of washing other folks' clothes and her proud ladyship didn't even seem to appreciate it all that much. Her mouth, heavy with bright red lipstick, was pursed and she frowned at her image. She produced a small enamelled powder compact and dabbed some Rachel powder on her nose, sending out small clouds that floated to the fixture and settled on the soft felts. Now they would have to dust the shining surfaces and brush the hats all over again.

'I think I shall take it. Have it sent round tomorrow. Early! I need it for the afternoon and wish to try it with my outfit. I've no time tonight.'

'Yes, modom. Of course, modom. Thank you, modom,' murmured Dolores, only just managing to keep the sarcasm from her tone.

Miss Pringle, having been alerted, arrived in a rush, yet still managing to retain her dignity. 'So sorry, Lady Mallender. I was detained. I do hope you have found something you like.'

'I have. Good evening.'

'Old bitch!' said Dolores. Her lips moved, but there was no sound. A girl could get sacked for swearing at all, leave alone about a customer, however difficult.

They had almost finished clearing up when Dolores's young sister, Milly, a junior in accessories, came rushing up to tell them of a scene being made by Lady Mallender on the ground floor. 'She wants a small turquoise bag and she's not sure we've got one to match her hat. She's on her way here with a couple to try –'

'What are you doing here, Millicent Handley?' Miss Pringle's tones were etched in ice and Milly scampered away, almost bumping into Lady Mallender as she swept back into the department.

'Miss Pringle!' Her ladyship's voice was shrill. 'I wish to see the hat I just purchased. I need a purse to match. I wish to compare these.'

She dropped the purses to the counter hastily uncovered by Dolores and sat down in front of the dust-sheeted display stand.

'My God, you don't even wait for clients to leave the store to pack up. It's as if you don't really want us at all.'

'If I had known your ladyship was returning I would have waited,' said Miss Pringle. Laura admired the way she spoke. Although she must have been quaking at the threat of losing such a wealthy and distinguished customer she sounded only apologetic and soothing.

She snapped her fingers and Dolores removed the turquoise turban from a hatbox marked 'sold'.

'Where's the other girl?' asked Lady Mallender petulantly, and Laura stepped forward. Another thing women like this did was to create a havoc of resentment among the staff.

Laura took the hat and held up each of the evening purses against it. They clashed and Lady Mallender stood up so abruptly she almost tipped over the small gilt chair used by customers and *never* by staff.

'As I thought! Hopeless! That means I shall have to try elsewhere. Really, it's too vexing. Keep the hat to one side, Miss Pringle, though it is highly probable I shall telephone to cancel my purchase.'

Laura watched the woman walk away. Her stockings were of sheer silk, the seams at the back a perfectly straight line, her feet were turned out very slightly in her suede shoes with elegant heels.

'Miss Blackford!' Miss Pringle allowed full rein to the irritation she did not dare use on Lady Mallender. 'Perhaps you would not mind replacing the dust covers. Miss Blackford! Have you gone to sleep?'

Laura remained quite still. She scarcely heard. Afterwards she put her reckless action down to yesterday's unsettling excitement. An idea which she only later recognised as preposterous had leapt into her head.

'Please, Miss Pringle, may I leave the floor for a moment?' This was the euphemistic phrase used when there was a need to visit the lavatory.

'Can't you wait? We shall be finished in a few moments.' Miss Pringle looked at her watch. 'Oh, well, we are rather late tonight. Lady Mallender –' She stopped, her lips pressed together. 'What are you staring at, Miss Handley? Finish the dusting. Hurry back, Miss Blackford.'

Laura hurried down the narrow, uncarpeted staff stairs which led to the street outside. There was no sign of Lady Mallender. She waited in agonised impatience. Her ladyship couldn't have reached here before her, could she? No, there was her large car, the uniformed chauffeur leaning nonchalantly against it, watching the passersby. Laura stood, twisting her hands. She would have to return to the shop floor. And it had seemed such a good idea.

Laura peered through the glass front doors. Lady Mallender had stopped at the cosmetic and perfume counter. Ethel was wrapping something in fancy pink and blue paper and Dolly was taking the money. She jerked petulantly at the pull which sent the metal cannister swinging along wires above their heads to accounts. Both girls wore professional smiles, but inside they would be seething. Accounts would be furious, too, at having to reopen the cash. The cosmetic sales assistants wore white tunics with pink belts that fastened on their hips with a blue bow, and were always exquisitely groomed, their bobbed hair shining, their faces expertly painted. Men came into the store to try to date them. Mr Gregory turned a blind eye as long as the girls succeeded in selling something to their admirers. Undoubtedly there were eager boyfriends waiting for them outside.

Just as Laura had decided that she couldn't possibly wait any longer, Lady Mallender walked out and, as the doors swung together behind her, Laura stepped forward. A swift glance showed her that Dolly and Ethel had spotted her and were staring at her curiously.

Laura said urgently, 'Please, your ladyship –'

Lady Mallender turned. She was about as tall as Laura, but her heels gave her added height so that she looked down on her. Her aristocratic nose was thin, a blade fashioned for cutting the pretensions of those she considered her inferiors, her pale blue eyes were cold. 'What on earth – ? Oh! The girl from millinery!'

'Yes, madam. I know where I can get an evening purse to

match your hat exactly. That is if you wish –'

Laura's voice trailed off as her ladyship's eyebrows were raised. They were incredibly thin. In fact, Laura wondered if they were all pencil, with no hairs left at all.

'Do you mean to tell me that Miss Pringle allowed you to *chase* after me? Well, all I can say is –' The memory of her need overcame her indignation. 'You can get me a purse? Where? Tell me. I'll send for it myself.'

'I'm sorry to contradict you, my lady, but I have to get in touch with – with a lady who runs a small private business. I'm sure she has just what you want. I'll bring it to your home tomorrow evening.'

'That is useless. I want it for an important luncheon engagement tomorrow. My fool of a dressmaker has made me a gown that doesn't match the hat I originally chose – it's too late to get a new gown, but I thought I would have no difficulty with a hat and matching bag. I shall probably change my dressmaker, though much good it may do me. One simply cannot depend on a certain class of women –'

Laura bit back her temper. 'Tomorrow is Saturday –'

'Well? What of it?'

'I only meant that it's a working day so I'll have to come early – before work.'

'Very well, if you can guarantee –'

'Oh, I can, my lady, I promise –'

'First thing tomorrow. Hand it in at the servants' entrance.'

Without waiting for an answer Lady Mallender stepped into her car, not even glancing at the uniformed chauffeur who held open the door.

Laura made her way back inside and upstairs, suddenly overcome by the enormity of what she had done. The whole planned exercise was fraught with problems.

Miss Pringle greeted her return frostily. 'You took your time. Now, for heaven's sake help with the clearing up and we can all go home.'

Outside on the pavement, as the porters were bolting the big doors, the girls hurried in various directions, most of them, thought Laura enviously, to meet boyfriends; Ethel and Dolly were actually stepping into cars. She was on her way to the tram stop when there was the sharp toot-toot of a horn and a voice called her name. She whirled round to see Rick Merriman sitting astride a motor cycle coasting towards her. He stopped beside her, cutting the engine. 'Hello, baby. I told you I'd see you again.'

Laura was awkward with nerves. 'Fancy singing in the road like that last night! Goodness knows what the neighbours thought.'

'Neighbours! You can't live your life worryin' about other folk. Do what you have to do and enjoy it.'

Laura began to pace slowly along the pavement, desperately trying to think of something to say. If only she was quick and witty like Lillian. Rick let his motorcycle roll beside her, propelling it with his feet.

'You don't always do what you want,' she blurted. 'You said you'd rather be in London, but you came back to Bristol with your mother.'

'Yes, well, that's a bit different. She's not in good health.'

'I think that's wonderful of you, Rick, I really do.' Laura smiled at him.

'Say, baby, your eyes are really pretty. Grand colour and nice lashes and eyebrows, though they need a bit of pluckin'. Don't tell me. Granma don't like plucked brows!'

Laura was pink with pleasure at his compliment. 'No, she doesn't.'

'Strikes me that Granma is a shockin' killjoy. Doesn't she like anythin'?'

'She likes tea parties with her friends and going to chapel. She reads the *Christian Herald* and *Woman's World*. She can sew and she keeps her home spotless and cooks good food. Do you want more, or is that enough for you?'

'Oho, showin' our claws are we? Our Laura's not so cool and collected after all. Well, I like a girl with a bit of spirit.'

'I'm not your Laura.' Her heart was racing. Some of the girls from Gregory's passed and couldn't resist staring at Rick who looked splendid in his leather jacket and boots, his goggles pushed up over his leather helmet.

He laughed. 'How about a lift home?'

Laura stopped. 'A lift? How?'

'Sit on the luggage rack. I'll pad it with my jacket and you'll be comfy.'

'There's nowhere to put my feet.'

'Just let 'em hang. Keep 'em away from the wheel. I won't go too fast. I'm always careful.'

'With other girls on your luggage rack, I suppose.'

Rick grinned, and shrugged.

'Huh!' Laura tossed her head. 'Go and find one of them. If you think I'm going to make a show of myself on that contraption you can think again. Offer me a lift in something decent and I'll consider it. Tonight, I'll get the tram.'

'Suit yourself,' said Rick cheerfully. 'Be seein' you, baby.' And he revved up the engine and roared away leaving blue exhaust smoke in his wake. Laura watched him disappear round a curve with a mixture of regret and exasperation. Also with a sense of surprise at the sudden ease with which she had conducted her first attempt at flirtation.

On the jolting tram she sat upstairs on the seats open to the sky. Travel sickness had been the plague of her life and although she was growing out of it she had come to enjoy the fresh air after spending so many hours in the store.

Every Friday, with Granma's approval, she visited a friend. And tonight, as usual, she got off the tram at the church stop and made her way to a small row of terraced houses similar to her parents'. She climbed the stairs to the top flat and Miss Morton came out to greet her.

'There you are, my love. Supper's all ready.'

Miss Edith Morton had lived in her two upstairs rooms since she began work forty years ago. This evening Laura saw her in a different light, one cast by a new awareness of herself as a woman. Miss Morton might once have been quite tall, but she was stooped from years of bending over her work, and she had been good-looking too. There was a faded sepia photo of her on the mantelpiece. For the first time Laura wondered if she had ever been in love.

Miss Morton was a milliner and Laura had liked her from

the day she had seen her on the stage at a chapel concert, giving a humorous but kindly monologue about her customers, using different hats to illustrate it. She had served an apprenticeship and worked in a fashion house before setting up a modest business of her own. Furniture crowded her rooms and every surface was covered by the tools of her trade and rainbow-hued materials. Although retired now, she still made hats and sold them at easy rates to the local women. Granma would have thrown up her hands at the clutter, but Laura liked it. This was the only place in which she felt cosy and confident. She took off her hat and coat.

'Laura! You've had your hair shingled at last! I never thought your Granma would let you.' Miss Morton's blue-veined hands were clasped in admiration.

Laura shrugged. 'I did it without telling her.'

'Oh, my! Was she very angry?'

'Yes, dreadfully. But she cooled down a bit when she heard that Miss Pringle had approved and said I might even model hats one day.'

The two ate their supper in companionable silence amidst the clutter. As Laura munched her ham she gazed around, never tiring of looking at the hat blocks with their various shapes and names: Dome, Shaped, Espartie, and the Dolly Head that had a face to show off a finished hat. The two women, far apart in years but close in friendship, finished their meal with the custard slices Miss Morton had bought. She said she had no time to cook. Granma would have been disgusted. 'Boughten food!' Laura could hear the scorn in her voice.

The dishes were gathered on to a tray and deposited on the draining board in the tiny curtained-off space that was the kitchen.

'We'll leave them, tonight, Laura. I've got an idea for a sweetly pretty hat for you. You don't want to keep that old beige thing, do you?'

Laura shook her head. 'But Granma won't let me get rid of it. She said it would be a wicked waste.'

Miss Morton fluttered her hands. 'I'll make something else of it. Or you can. You're good enough now at the millinery.'

'Thank you, Miss Morton, I'll be glad of that, but tonight I have a special favour to ask.'

Laura told her friend about Lady Mallender and her promise of an evening bag by next morning.

Miss Morton laughed. 'The cheek of you! What colour is it to be?'

Laura's fingers scrabbled about on the table, sliding among the slippery heaps of organza, chiffon and silk and drew out a piece of satin, holding it up triumphantly.

'This is it.'

'A lovely shade, and I know how well you carry a colour in your head. That's a gift, Laura. Never lose it. It'll stand you in good stead if you go into a fashion trade. So her ladyship wants a special purse. Describe the hat to me.'

She listened with her head cocked on one side like a sparrow. 'I see. Well we'd best get started. A soft one is fashionable for special occasions and they cost the earth in the shops. We'll ask a good price. Fifteen shillings isn't too much. We'll share the money between us, my love. Half each.'

'But the materials are yours.'

'And the bulk of the work will be yours. I can't sew hour after hour like I used to. Do you know what I shall do with my share, Laura?' Miss Morton's smile stretched wide. 'I've been saving for weeks to spend a few days in Weston. I've been feeling peaky and the sea air will do me good. A friend asked me to go, but I had to say no.' Her eyes grew dreamy. 'Long ago my parents took me there every year, but I haven't been for ever so long.'

'Good idea,' said Laura. 'I shall buy myself some material for a coat. A nice golden brown weave. A fashionable *short* coat just touching my knees. Perhaps you'd let me sew it here? I'll have to do it all by hand, but once it's made Granma will have to let me wear it. She won't stand for my owning a garment I can't wear, though she'll nag for ever,' she finished, sighing.

Laura thought of Rick's face when he caught sight of her in something pretty. 'Or maybe I'll make a dress. Yes, a dress. Almond green – I've always wanted a crêpe de Chine dress in almond green. We've got a beautiful one in Gregory's I can copy. It's got a buff jabot, but I may not bother with that. It's forty-nine and sixpence. Fancy paying that for one dress!'

'Fancy being able to,' said Miss Morton drily. 'But don't get carried away, my love. It's only one little fifteen-shilling bag we're talking about. We'd best get started. We'll use satin to match her hat with buckram for stiffening, moiré silk for the lining.'

They talked while they worked, but never lost their concentration. By ten o'clock they had the basis for a purse and Laura had pleated the satin turquoise in a mirror image of the pleating on Lady Mallender's hat.

She glanced at the clock. 'Oh, golly! Gone ten o'clock! It's past bedtime. Granma will be looking for me. I'll take the bag home. When Granma's gone to sleep I'll light a candle and finish it.'

She hurried along the street, meeting boys and girls her own age who were strolling and talking as if they had all night. She felt a surge of rebellion. Why should she be subjected to so rigorous a routine? Lillian waved to her from across the road where she sat on a low wall with a friend and a couple of boys. She said something that made them giggle and Laura bent her head, biting her lips. She was sure it would have been some sneering remark about herself. Boys whistled and clicked their tongues at her, but not because she was pretty. They did it to all the girls. Granma had told her often enough that she was plain and had better make sure she had a good trade behind her. The pubs were turning out the last lingering customers and she glanced back to see her parents, each carrying bottles of beer, walking a trifle unsteadily towards home. Granma maintained that her son, William, had never so much as tasted a drop of liquor until he had met Phyllis. Well, he could certainly put it back now. So could Mum. Especially on a Saturday night when they had a few extra shillings and Sunday morning to sleep it off. On Saturday nights they rolled home singing together, arms about one another, like a pair of lovers. Granma seldom spoke of Phyllis, but when she did the bitterness in her voice had a tangible quality.

Granma and Grampa had already drunk their cocoa. Laura's

was only just warm and she swallowed it hastily, apologising for her late arrival.

Granma's lips were thin with disapproval, but she asked as politely as ever after Miss Morton's health. A woman who could increase Laura's knowledge of millinery was to be encouraged.

Laura sat up in bed well after midnight putting tiny stitches into Lady Mallender's bag. She heard the church clock strike two as she finished and, sighing with relief, blew out her candle.

Granma had to call her three times before she woke properly, then her heart began to race. She had intended to leave extra early, making some excuse about cleaning the fixtures at work. To get her ladyship's bag to her in her big house overlooking the Downs would mean a long journey right into the Tramway Centre, up Park Row and the steep Blackboy Hill in the slow, jolting tram. Then she'd have to run over the grassy Downs. If she were very late for work she would be turned away and lose a day's money.

She arrived in the bustling Centre where she needed to change trams, with hope of getting to work on time rapidly vanishing. She was wondering which would be the greater evil; to risk a terrible row with Granma, or to disappoint Lady Mallender who would then storm into Gregory's and demand to know what had happened. The consequences of either disaster were terrible to contemplate. Dismissal perhaps. She wished she had never started this mad escapade. A tram to the Downs arrived and filled up just before Laura reached the step. She was shaking with nerves when one of the roaring motor-cycle engines slowed and a voice said, 'Hello, baby, aren't you in the wrong place?'

She turned to see Rick, astride his bike, grinning at her. His grin faded as he saw her expression. 'What's to do? Somethin' wrong?'

Laura glanced at the luggage rack. 'You offered me a lift the other day. Could you give me one now?'

Rick laughed. 'Sure can.' He slid his jacket off and padded the rack with it. 'Hop aboard, kiddo. Hang on to me and keep your legs away from the wheel. Where to?'

Laura directed him and clung to him as they roared away, weaving in and out of the traffic in a way that would have terrified her if she had not been so frantic. Rick gave a long, low whistle as they stopped in front of the large stone-built Mallender residence. 'Some joint they've got here!'

Laura jumped off and raced round the back to the servants' entrance, and banged loudly on the kitchen door.

It was opened by a fat woman in a white apron. 'For the love of fortune, what's all the racket? Oh, you must be the girl from Gregory's. Her ladyship wants you to take the bag up yourself.'

'I can't. I'll be late for work.'

'Well, they'll understand, won't they? After all, you're on an errand for the store, aren't you?'

'No, it's a private arrangement.'

'Well, I don't know nothin' about that. All I know is her ladyship wants to see you and if you want to stay in her good books you'd better go up.'

A male voice called, 'Shut that door. It's blowin' cold in.'

'That's Mr Renton, the butler. I can't do with him startin' off on the wrong foot. Come on, don't make me stand here all day.'

Laura followed the cook who led her through a large kitchen where some servants were eating at a table while others were hurrying about following the orders of a black-gowned woman who, Laura guessed, was the housekeeper. She was handed over to a housemaid who led her through a green baize door to the wooden backstairs, then through another into a thickly carpeted corridor. A door opened to her knock and a middle-aged woman with a heavily lined face peered out.

'Good morning, Miss Gardner,' said the housemaid. 'This girl's brought her ladyship's bag.'

'Well, don't stand gawping,' snapped the woman to Laura. 'Come in.'

'Who is it, Gardner?' asked a languid voice.

'The girl with the bag from Gregory's, my lady.'

'It's not –' began Laura, then gave it up as a bad job. Even if she had time to explain no one would bother to listen. These people cared only for their own concerns.

'I have your bag, my lady.'

'I expected you earlier. Come here. Show it to me.'

33

Laura walked forward, her lips pressed together. 'Here it is, my lady.'

Lady Mallender took the tissue-wrapped parcel and opened it horribly slowly, pausing once to yawn, her fingers with red-tipped nails, covering her mouth. She inspected the bag closely. 'Pretty. Quite pretty. And you're sure it will match my hat.'

'Yes, my lady.'

'Good. Tell them to send the hat to me as soon as you arrive at work.'

'But, my lady, I can't –'

'Can't! What do you mean, can't?'

'You can give a message, girl,' snapped Gardner. 'You're not dumb, are you?'

'Lady Mallender,' broke out Laura desperately, 'I believe I explained that this transaction is a private one. I don't know what Mr Gregory would say if he knew about it.'

Her ladyship's brows rose. She yawned again. 'Oh, God, preserve me from the proletariat. Yes, I do remember something of the sort. In that case, Gardner, you can telephone Gregory's.' She picked up a magazine and started to read.

'My lady –' Laura started desperately.

Lady Mallender looked up with an expression of amazement. 'Are you still here? What do you want? Oh, payment, I daresay. I'll see you next time I come into the store. I cannot concern myself with trivialities today. I have a terrifyingly full programme ahead.'

Laura thought of Miss Morton's little holiday at the seaside, of her own plans to stun Rick with her new clothes and felt she could have strangled her arrogant ladyship with her feather bed-jacket. But she had no time to argue. She walked from the room, rebelliously ignored the servants' door, and down the carpeted stairs into a tiled hallway. A long-case clock proclaimed the time. Eight-fifteen, and Gregory's expected their staff to be neat and in place before the store opened at eight-thirty. It was impossible. She would lose a day's pay and Granma's wrath would descend on her.

She glanced back at the imposing house behind whose

windows lounged people who neither knew nor cared about working folk, not even the servants who toiled to make their useless lives easier, if Lady Mallender's attitude to Gardner and her chauffeur was anything to go by. She walked through the small side gate, suddenly weary, close to tears of tiredness and frustration.

'Come on, baby, you'll be late.'

The mist in her eyes cleared as Laura saw that Rick had waited for her. He stubbed out the inevitable cigarette and patted the rack where his jacket still lay. Laura laughed with relief and jumped on to the back of the motor cycle. She slid her arms round Rick's waist, sniffed at the male tobacco smell of him, and brushed a soft, secret kiss along his turned-up collar.

'You looked miserable. What did they do to you?' Rick shouted above the engine noise.

'Lady Mallender called me a member of the proletariat.'

'Well, so you are! You should be proud of it.'

'I am. But I don't like being spoken to as if I was a dog.'

Rick laughed. 'That's the ticket. Give 'em hell!'

Now the need for haste had passed Laura was aware of the speed they travelled, of the hard road slipping beneath the wheels, of what could happen if they had an accident. But it was odd how safe she felt. Safe and bubbly with happiness. Rick liked her a lot. He must do.

When they stopped outside the employees' entrance to Gregory's Laura was gratified to know that many eyes watched her slide from the motor cycle. She pulled her crumpled hat from beneath her arm where she had shoved it for safe keeping.

'Thank you, Rick, thank you very much. You've really saved my bacon this morning.'

'It was nothin'.'

Laura moved away reluctantly, hoping, praying that Rick would say something about seeing her again. 'Won't you be in trouble for being late, Rick?' she asked.

'Nah! I'm not due in until nine.' He revved up the engine. 'Be seein' you, baby.' He roared off down the street and Laura stared after him. To her delight he suddenly made a turn and drove back, half skidding to a halt.

'I almost forgot. My mind was on other things. Will you come dancin' with me tonight?'

'Oh, yes,' breathed Laura.

'Fine. I'll pick you up at your place. What time do you finish?'

'Not till nine on Saturdays.'

'Store-owners! Bloody slave-drivers! See you about ten then at your place.'

'Not there,' said Laura hastily. 'At the end of the road. I may be a few minutes late. I hope you don't mind.'

'I'll wait.'

This time Laura watched until Rick disappeared down the road and round a bend.

Chapter Three

After work Laura raced round to Miss Morton's to break the news of Lady Mallender's casual meanness.

Miss Morton was disappointed but resigned. 'That's great folks for you. How should they know what life's like for us at the bottom? Well, there's many worse off than us, Laura. With unemployment getting higher all the time, some don't get enough to eat.'

At work, she had been so overcome by the reckless promise she had made to Rick she could scarcely concentrate. How on earth would she be able to keep the date? The hours dragged on until nine o'clock when Gregory's Department Store was locked and left to the caretaker and the rats.

The tram seemed to jolt up the long hills for ever. Granma quickly fried potatoes to go with the plate of cold meat she had put by and Laura ate her way through it with determination. She groaned inwardly at the sight of an apple pie with thick yellow custard, but managed a portion and at ten o'clock Granma and Granpa retired to bed and she was alone in her room.

She pulled out her best summer dress of plain beige crepe de Chine, belted round the hips. She had no time to mourn the lack of dancing frocks in her wardrobe. With fingers that almost lost their nimbleness through nerves she pleated a length of golden-brown ribbon into a flower and sewed it with big stitches to her belt. Round her neck went the yellow beads bought her by her father in a generous mood after a win on the Derby. Feeling like a scarlet woman, she touched eau de Cologne, the only perfume Granma allowed because of its medicinal use, to her throat and wrists, patted powder on her face, coated her lips with a sixpenny pink lipstick she had bought that day, and smoothed Vaseline over her brows and eyelashes, and upper lids. The only full length mirror in the house was on Granma's wardrobe and Laura had to stand on her bed and twist and arch herself to try to gauge the result of her efforts in her small wall mirror. She pulled on her coat, tied a scarf over her head, then paused and stood perfectly still, listening. Grampa's snores came faintly from the back bedroom and she thought she could just detect a fainter snore.

She opened her door a crack, stuck out her head, then crept downstairs, avoiding the steps that creaked. She felt like a thief as she took the house key from behind the clock on the mantelpiece. Outside she shivered in the night air, more from nerves than cold.

A voice behind her made her jump and sent her heart racing. 'What kept you, baby?'

'Oh, Rick!' she whispered. 'It's you.'

'Why all the cloak and dagger stuff?'

'They don't know I'm out.'

'Lord! You're a right little devil, aren't you? Is this how you always keep dates?'

Laura was too tense to think up a flirty response. 'You're my first,' she said, then waited for Rick to laugh.

He didn't and she was grateful. 'I'm honoured, baby. Come on. Let's go.'

Laura followed him to the end of the road and exclaimed with amazement when Rick gestured to a small open-top car. 'Hop in, baby.'

'Oh, Rick, is it yours? Fancy having a bike and a motor car.'

'I haven't. I borrowed this. It's more suitable for takin' a lady to a dance.'

Laura sat back in the leather seat, sniffing the unfamiliar smell of petrol and hot oil. She snuggled under the blanket Rick handed her and revelled in the wind blowing through her hair. She felt like Cinderella on her way to the ball.

Rick drove into town and stopped outside a public hall from which the sounds of a jazz band splintered the air. Laura's heart began to pound with excitement.

In the cloakroom she saw herself full length and was pleased with the result – until she saw the other girls. The ballroom was vivid with reflections that radiated from satin and silk and taffeta dresses, all of them shorter than hers, several barely reaching to the knees, and with the glitter from thousands of shiny beads sewn to hems and sashes that swung with the girls' bodies in time to the music, and from bracelets and necklaces and hair ornaments. She felt like a buff-coloured hen in a farm-yard full of paradise birds.

Rick waited for her, looking unfamiliar in a pale grey suit and a snowy shirt. His hair was plastered to his head with a fresh application of hair cream. She felt reassured at once and her excitement increased. She had no idea why this man should have taken a fancy to her, but she glowed with gratitude to the fates.

He held out his arms. 'Come on, kiddo! Let's do the Black Bottom.'

Laura had learned the steps of the new dances from watching the girls at Gregory's practising in their lunch breaks. She had copied them in her bedroom in stockinged feet, humming what she could recall of the slick new tunes, but performing the energetic gymnastics needed for the dance in public was scary. At first she had to concentrate until the music, the lights, the smoky heat and the company combined to send a surge of excitement through her blood and she forgot her inhibitions and flung herself recklessly into dance after dance. A grinning Rick mirrored her movements.

Someone's long necklace snapped and dozens of beads were scattered across the floor. There were screams of mirth as they caused skids. A girl fell over and showed her daringly red-gartered stocking tops and a glimpse of pink camiknickers and a great roar of appreciation rose to the ceiling. When the musicians finally paused for breath Laura was panting and laughing with the thrill of it all.

Rick led her from the floor, a hand beneath her elbow. 'Great, kiddo. I didn't know you could dance like that.'

'Neither did I! I never have before.'

'Wow! You're a natural. Let's have a drink.'

There was beer and cocktails, but Laura accepted only lemonade. 'Well, you don't need booze to get you goin',' Rick said. 'Your eyes really are pretty. They shine like a couple of full moons.'

Laura attempted to flutter her lids like a film star, but found they were glued up by the melting Vaseline and she took out her hanky and wiped some of the grease away. Rick laughed and held out a packet of cigarettes. Laura began to shake her head, but most of the other girls were smoking and she reached out and took one. Rick lit it and she breathed back the smoke. It hit the back of her throat and she coughed violently.

Rick grinned. 'Don't inhale yet, baby. Get used to smokin' first.'

Laura nodded. She puffed a few more times before asking to be excused. In the ladies' room she stubbed out the cigarette. She scarcely recognised her reflected image. Her cheeks were flushed over her high cheekbones, her eyes shone brilliantly, she looked almost pretty. She patted her face with powder and renewed her lipstick, wishing she'd had the courage to buy a deeper colour. Most of the girls' mouths were pillar-box red, just like Gregory's rich clients.

The band struck up for a slow foxtrot and the lights dimmed. Laura slid into Rick's arms as if she belonged there. He held her so close she could feel the strong beat of his heart. All around them other couples were snuggled together, some were even kissing. Rick's arms tightened round her and moulded her to his body. They moved in unison and Laura had never felt so happy. Rick was a dream-man. No, better because he was real flesh and blood. She inhaled the maleness of him, the scent of his hair-cream, a clean soapy aroma from his body, the smell of tobacco, of freshly laundered clothes, of a new suit. Everything about him excited her and aroused the unfamiliar sensations she'd got when she read *The Sheik*. She wished he would try to kiss her.

As if reading her mind he bent his head and touched his mouth to her cheek. She turned towards him and his lips found hers. They were gentle and warm and her mouth clung to his in a hungry way that would have been unthinkable so short a time ago.

'Hey, now, baby –' he murmured. 'You're really somethin'.'

When the music stopped Laura was still held in an ecstatic trance. Rick took her arm and gently propelled her from the floor and she sank into one of the small chairs and fanned herself with her tiny vanity bag. He stood gazing down at her with a smile that sent her weak at the knees. His face was smeared with lipstick and she wiped it away. Laura, modelling herself on the other girls, behaved nonchalantly as she took a tiny mirror from her bag and applied another coat of lipstick.

People greeted Rick as they sauntered past. 'Hi, Rick, how about a drink?'

'How about it, baby?' Rick asked.

Laura nodded. In the bar she watched the barman mixing ingredients and shaking them in a silver flask.

'Try a cocktail,' urged Rick.

'I signed the Temperance Pledge,' said Laura.

One of the girls overheard and shrieked raucously. 'How's about that? She signed the pledge.'

There was general mirth. 'Who didn't!' Rick drawled. 'We can't be held to something we were made to do when we were kids.'

Laura smiled at him, her thanks written in her eyes. 'What should I have, Rick?'

'I've invented a Bristol Special,' said the barman.

'Oh, yeah! What's in it?'

'That's my secret.'

'It's great, Rick,' shouted a red-haired girl in a shiny pink dress.

Rick nodded. 'Give me two.'

Laura looked at the thick green concoction and sipped. It was minty. Really it tasted much like Granma's indigestion remedy. She drank it in several gulps.

'Take it easy, kiddo,' grinned Rick. 'Like another?'

Laura nodded and Rick led her to a small table. There wasn't much room and they sat close together on an upholstered bench. Laura emptied her glass again. 'I could manage another of those.' A giggle surprised her.

'You've had enough for now, baby. You can run through the whole repertoire in time.' He brought her tea and insisted she drink it. 'It'll help keep you sober.'

Who wants to stay sober? thought Laura, as she swayed in Rick's arms in another foxtrot. If this was getting tipsy she was all for it. She floated in a haze of utter bliss. She, Laura Blackford, who had never had a boyfriend in her life, had attracted one who was popular and fun to be with.

The band stopped and the band leader held up his hand for silence. 'Ladies and gentlemen, you're dancing to the music of Cyril Bateman and his Hot Shots. I'm Cyril.' There was a burst of applause and a few mock-derisive noises. Undismayed, Cyril bowed and continued, 'We have with us tonight one of Bristol's best amateur singers. None other than Mr Rick Merriman. Come on up, Rick, and give us the benefit of your talent.'

There were claps, whistles and hoots of encouragement. Laura was startled and even more so when the voice continued, 'Bring up the lovely little lady, too. Let's see if she can sing.'

A spotlight played on them and Laura panicked. Rick grabbed her hand as she was about to flee. 'Come on, kiddo, show them what you're made of.'

Her legs trembling, Laura was urged on to the stage, and Cyril said, 'Right, folks. *Ain't She Sweet*.'

'I don't know it,' gasped Laura.

'I thought everybody – what do you know?' asked Cyril.

'N – nothing modern.'

The band leader was staring at her as if she were a being from another planet. 'Sorry, Rick, I thought for sure she'd – well, not to worry.'

Rick was undismayed. 'Can you read music, baby?'

Laura nodded.

The band leader handed her a piece of sheet music and she scanned it quickly. 'I can manage this.'

'Fine, honey,' said Cyril and announced a charleston.

Rick sang, *Ain't she sweet/As she's walkin' down the street* – his voice was strong and his pitch good. After a moment Laura joined in. She had always loved singing and her voice, too, was strong after years of hymns and sacred songs. As she blended with Rick her confidence grew. She briefly hoped that no one in the hectic crowd recognised her or, if they did, that they didn't tell Granma. At the idea her voice faltered, then euphoria took control again. At the end of the song she and Rick were applauded loudly and Laura felt thrilled as they rejoined the dancers.

Too soon the band struck up a waltz and Rick murmured in her ear, 'Last dance.'

'Oh, why can't it go on all night?'

'Because in another five minutes it'll be Sunday.'

'Is it midnight? It can't be! We've hardly begun.'

'We didn't get here until way past ten.'

'No,' sighed Laura, 'that's true. Do they have later dances?'

'On Friday nights. Would you like to come to one with me?'

'Oh, yes,' breathed Laura.

She snuggled up to him in the car driving home. The effect of the cocktails lingered and her hand crept out daringly and smoothed his cheek. Her fingers rasped over new stubble and she shivered with delight.

Rick stopped the car at the end of her road. Laura could not bear to move. She wished the night could go on for ever. Rick turned and pulled her to him and kissed her, slowly, taking his time to savour the fullness of her lips, and her blood turned to liquid fire and she poured all her suppressed instincts into her response.

The kiss went on until they were breathless. Rick stared down at her. He had his back to the street lamp and she could not see his expression. 'God, baby, you're a dark horse. Who'd have thought it?' He kissed her again and his hand moved to her breast and teased a nipple which was hard with her arousal. Laura was drowning in an instinctive need that amazed her. She ached for him to caress her in ways that were utterly wrong. With a desperate effort she pushed him away and slumped back against the car seat, her breathing short and jerky.

'Laura,' whispered Rick, 'you're wonderful.'

He leaned over her and his mouth claimed hers again and this time she did not offer resistance when his fingers played lightly over her. His hand was moving slowly down her body. She should stop him, but her just-discovered raw sensuality held her captive and she cried out, part in pleasure, part in frustration.

43

She hugged him to her. 'Please – please –' was all she could say.

'Laura, honey, you're incredible, but any minute now some nosy copper will be along with his flashlight.'

His words brought Laura to her senses as if someone had thrown a bucket of ice-cold water over her. Reality suddenly impinged. Granma! What if she had awakened and gone into Laura's room? She never had, but what if – ? Now she felt horribly embarrassed by her own passion. Rick would think she was a right little madam. Someone who could swing her hips, as her mother once described a girl who was said to be too free with boys.

'Rick –' she said, with a sob in her voice. 'I shouldn't – I mean –'

He touched her mouth with fingers that were gentle. 'Don't worry, sweetheart. I'll be seein' you.'

It was unbelievably easy to get back into the house. She slid Granma's key behind the clock and within minutes was in bed, but not to sleep. Her heart would take a long time to stop its pounding and her body was alive with a new, hot appetite which flooded over her in waves. Once she would have been too terrified of the consequences to let a man even kiss her, but over their sewing of the purse she had taken a deep breath and had asked Miss Morton several pertinent questions that had been answered in a sensible way.

There were pleasures of the body that could be enjoyed without danger, Laura had learned. Miss Morton didn't reveal how far she had gone with her only boyfriend who had died of diphtheria when he was twenty, but clearly she had not been a prude.

Laura could not forget the touch of Rick's hands. Rick! Rick! His name ran through her like a refrain. She was in love and she exulted in it.

In the morning she was still too thrilled to be tired. She attended morning worship. In chapel she supposed she should feel shame and guilt at allowing a man to make love to her so soon after their first meeting but, according to Granma and the preacher, God dictated all things, so He must be responsible for sex, too. She assured herself she couldn't be blamed for having feelings. She ate the large dinner that was obligatory at midday on Sunday, and went over the programme for the afternoon when she took a Sunday school class of a dozen small boys and girls.

Sunday teatime she always visited her parents. It was something she both looked forward to, and dreaded. She never knew how she would be greeted. Sometimes she thought her mother disliked her; at others she treated her with absent-minded kindness. Dad was a perpetual enigma. He seemed cocooned in his own comfortably lined world, one created by his mother and perpetuated by his adoring wife. If ever he singled out Laura for attention she felt so choked by her inborn love for him she became awkward.

She walked up the short front path. The small patch of ground held a few ferns and scuffed grass, the bare patches showing impressions of children's feet in the mud. A battered tin train lay in the damp shadow of the straggly hedge that reinforced the low brick wall and rusty railings. The front door was never locked and she pushed her way in, stepping over the three youngest girls and the toys which were strewn along the narrow passage. Except for Granma's superior bay window the house was almost the same design as hers, but it was very different in fact. There was a smell compounded of cooking, washing, ironing, the latest baby and the cats, all overlaid by the cheap scent her sisters splashed on lavishly. There had almost always been babies, when Mum was either pregnant or nursing an infant at her breast, and the family now numbered thirteen. Others had died at birth and there had been miscarriages, an experience common to overworked women. There was a gap of seven years between Iris and the next when Mum had been ailing. As soon as her health picked up she fell pregnant again with Valentino and he was followed by three girls, Priscilla, Virginia and Greta, all named after film stars.

Laura greeted the infants who took little notice of her after they had received their usual sweets. Why should they? She was just someone who visited.

She was startled by a sudden blare of music and she followed the sound to the front room. There had never been money to furnish it and all it held was a scratched cupboard and a couple of wonky-legged chairs. The floor was bare boards. Lillian, Freda and Joyce were swaying in time to a very scratchy recording played on a gramophone with a horn.

Lillian looked Laura up and down. 'Well, if it isn't Lady Muck on her weekly visit to the slums! Been on any motor bikes lately?'

Laura flushed, but she had given up answering her elder sister's taunts. When she was younger she had tried to explain that she would willingly leave the superior accommodation and food at Granma's for the noisy companionship of her family, but Lillian hadn't wanted to know. Laura certainly wasn't going to discuss Rick with her.

Freda, with her pudgy, spotty face, small eyes and thickset body, was the only plain one in the house, but she was invariably kind. 'Lay off her, our Lillian,' she said. 'Look what we've got, Laura. An old gramophone. Ralph took it off the cart and brought it home. You have to wind it up. And there's a tin of needles that goes with it. You have to keep changin' them or the music sounds funny.'

Joyce smiled her beautiful smile that barely reached her deep blue eyes. 'If you don't wind enough the voices go slow. It sounds funny. Fancy someone throwin' away a whole gramophone! They must be ever so rich, mustn't they, Laura? Ralph's kind, isn't he?'

'Huh! It's old-fashioned,' sneered Lillian, gyrating and singing to *Fascinatin' Rhythm*. 'Rich folks! They've bought themselves a better one.'

Laura gave Joyce a kiss; she was the younger twin by an hour, and complications at her birth had affected her brain. She was gentle and sweet and dearly loved by the whole family. When she was small, already showing the promise of great beauty, Mum had often expressed her bewildered worry. 'Why couldn't Joyce have been the plain one? Poor old Freda's got a face like the back of a tram. It'll have to be a desperate boy who'll want her. But Joyce –' She always ended at this point, racked by her vision of some future disaster. Laura had not understood at the time, but now she was aware that Joyce had been granted a face and figure that would tempt men, but not the wisdom to fend them off, or the intelligence that would invite marriage.

Laura walked through to the kitchen, where Dad sat by the range fire reading *The Pink 'Un*, his favourite sporting paper. He glanced up and smiled absently. 'Hello, chick. Sunday again?' And retired again behind the paper which he held awkwardly, having lost a large part of three fingers of his right hand in an accident in a boot factory four years before. After a fight by the union he had been given three hundred and fifty pounds compensation. It had seemed a fortune and Dad had not since looked for another job, though the money had long gone. A finger on his other hand was bandaged.

'You've cut yourself, Dad?'

He peered at her, then at his finger. 'Oh, yes. I was helping with the outwork yesterday. The knife slipped.'

William – his name was never shortened, not even by his wife – sometimes joined two of his sons who did outwork in the back shed. He said it was so as not to be a burden on his family. Somehow he always managed to cut himself after a short time. It was the fault of having lost so much of his fingers, he explained. His wife, Phyllis, always agreed and never pointed out that many a man, and woman too, worked on in the Kingswood boot factories after similar accidents. In fact, it was said locally that you weren't a proper boot-maker until you'd lost part of a hand. Laura expressed concern, then waited for a moment, until she saw she would get nothing more from him.

Mum was in the scullery poking some sheets into a tin bath with a wooden stick. They would soak all night and she would wash them in the morning. Enid, the eldest girl, was on her knees stoking the boiler fire, over which more washing bubbled. She was married and six months gone with her first child.

'Laura,' said Mum, sounding neither glad nor sorry.

Laura felt the recurring stab of pain. She should be used to her reception by now, but she wasn't. Every Sunday she hoped for a miracle. She pictured her mother holding her close one

47

day and kissing her as she sometimes did the others. She loved Mum so much it hurt. She loved both her parents. Enid gave her a nod and a smile. She still worked in a chocolate factory, ran her two-roomed home and helped Phyllis when she could. She had been pink-cheeked, with a softly rounded body; now, apart from the bulge in front, she was thin and her face was wan. Marriage to an ordinary man played havoc with a woman, Laura thought. Rick wasn't ordinary. Life with him would be endlessly thrilling.

Phyllis had turned back to her task. The gramophone blared out *Ain't She Sweet* and Laura heard the voices of her sisters, joined now by the boys. In an instant she was transported back to the dance hall, beside Rick, singing with him. She was in his arms, experiencing his thrilling caresses. There *was* someone who cared for her. She wanted to tell the family. They might value her more then. But she must wait until Rick had made a proper declaration, then she could show him off. Granma couldn't stop her. It was up to Mum and Dad to give the go ahead for her marriage. Perhaps with a gold ring on her finger people would take more notice of her.

Phyllis joined in the scratchy rendering of the song in a wavering, thin voice. She was very pale and Laura was suddenly afraid for her.

'Mum, you don't look well. Let me do that for you.'

'I'm capable of lookin' after my own work,' Phyllis snapped. 'I've got a heavy period, that's all.'

As she spoke her eyes flickered over to Enid. They were keeping secrets from her and abruptly Laura felt unable to bear it. She walked away and back into the front room and, ignoring Lillian's exaggerated expressions of amazement, threw herself into a frenzied dance. Alfred and Harold, the outworkers, applauded. They were fourteen and fifteen and, like thousands of others, unable to get jobs. They dragged a home-made trolley to a boot factory and brought home uppers and leather for soles and heels, then sat for hours in the shed spitting out the nails they held in their mouths and hammering them into the boots which they would take back to the factory for finishing, and return with another load. The work was tedious and ever-lasting and poorly paid.

Lillian stopped dancing to watch Laura with burning eyes. 'Get you,' she said, when the music stopped. 'I suppose you think you can dance. You're like a beanpole with corns.'

For once Laura could rise above the insults. Enid came to tell them that tea was ready and they trooped in a disorderly fashion to the kitchen which was steamy from freshly mangled sheets hanging over their heads. The day was fine and quite warm but, in common with her neighbours, Phyllis would never dream of hanging out washing on a Sunday. The table was laid with a blue and white cloth which was marked by cigarette burns and tea stains. Phyllis was sitting down, a loaf held to her chest, spreading bread with margarine, then slicing it thickly with a long knife, its blade slender and wicked-looking from much sharpening on the back stone step. The small children joined Laura, Lillian and the twins at the table, squashing together on a wooden bench. Dad remained in his chair and the boys sat on the worn leather fender seats. Enid smeared plum jam thinly on the bread, while Iris got out an old biscuit tin and filled a cracked plate with cake-waste – broken and slightly stale cakes bought for threepence a big bag. Nothing matched, the knives were the cheapest it was possible to buy, the tea was dark brown and stewed, the acrid smell of leather off-cuts being burned to eke out the fuel filled the air, infiltrated clothes and hair, and added an odd dimension to the taste of food, but Laura would have given years of her life to feel that she rightly belonged here.

A call from the front door was followed by footsteps and their cousin, Marion, walked in. She was welcomed and she seated herself, half shoving an amiably grinning Harold from his perch.

She accepted a hunk of bread and jam and took an enormous bite. For a moment there was peace, then Marion spoke through a mouthful of food. 'Guess who I saw last night at a dance hall down town!'

Lillian stared at Marion and mumbled through a mouth similarly full of food, 'How should we know? We were all at the church hall dance. What were you doin' in town, anyway? Too toffee-nosed for Kingswood now?'

'Don't be daft! Of course I'm not. I've got a new chap and he took me there.'

'It's all right for some!' Lillian licked jam from her fingers. 'So what's the mystery?'

'Laura can tell you.'

'Laura!' Lillian derided. 'Granma never lets her one little chicken out of her sight. How would *Laura* know?'

'Because it was her I saw,' said Marion, stretching out for a slightly squashed mock-cream cornet.

Lillian pushed the plate closer, her eyes wide with disbelief. 'Laura! That's impossible. She must have a double.'

'It was her! Tell them, Laura. She sang with the band, too. You did, didn't you, Laura?'

Lillian shrieked with raucous laughter. 'Come off it, Marion! I know when I'm bein' kidded!'

'You were there and you did sing, didn't you, Laura,' pleaded Marion.

Laura nodded, and waited for the onslaught.

'*Laura*! At a dance, an' *singin*'! Well, wonders never cease. She must have been goin' with a duke at least for Granma to let her out.'

'It wasn't a duke,' said Marion. 'It was Rick Merriman. Used to live Hanham way. Do you know him?'

Lillian shook her head, frowning. 'Never heard of him. Does he ride a motor bike? Some of the girls said they saw Laura on one. I thought they were just kiddin' me on.' Her voice was angry, uncertain.

'What's he like?' asked Enid, shifting her swollen stomach into a more comfortable position.

'Well, he's not exactly handsome –'

Lillian shrieked again. 'I bet he's not! Imagine Laura with a film-star type!'

'For heaven's sake, our Lil, give someone else a chance to speak,' said Freda. 'What's he like, Laura?'

Marion answered, 'Quite tall – near six feet I'd say. Nice face and black hair. A real snazzy dresser. He wore a new suit and proper dancing shoes, and he wasn't short of money, either. He bought drinks for people and paid with a five-pound note. I watched him and Laura leave in a car.'

'What?' Lillian flushed with jealous rage. 'You sly bitch!' she spat at Laura. 'You never said a thing.'

'I wasn't aware you were interested,' said Laura.

'Wasn't aware!' Lillian mocked her tones. 'Speaks posh, don't she? I suppose that's what got you a rich man.'

'Shut up, Lillian,' said Phyllis wearily. 'You're always goin' on at Laura.'

'So are you, when you feel like it,' retorted Lillian.

'I'm entitled. I'm her mother. Did you have a nice time, Laura?'

Laura looked at her mother with a rush of love. 'I did, Mum, I had a lovely time. I don't think he's really rich. He borrowed the car. He said he couldn't use his motor bike to take out a –' She stopped. The word 'lady' could only further inflame Lillian's temper.

'A girl like you,' said Phyllis, her smile revealing gaps she couldn't afford to fill in her front teeth.

'When are you seein' him again?' asked Freda.

'Soon.' Laura crossed her fingers for luck.

'Yes, but when?' demanded Lillian.

'Be quiet,' said William. 'A man likes a bit of peace when he has his tea. Is there any ham, Phyllis?'

His wife stood up. 'There's a bit, love. I was keepin' it for your supper. Do you want it now?'

'A dab of mustard with it,' said William.

Laura felt resentful. Couldn't Dad see that Mum looked exhausted? Perhaps he never really looked at her. To offer help would be to criticise him if only by implication, and Mum wouldn't stand for it.

Enid left to feed her husband, and all the young adults, except Iris, went out to meet friends, Joyce with Freda who guarded her like a mediaeval dragon. Laura offered to help with the clearing up and for once Phyllis let her. She must be feeling much worse than she pretended.

In the scullery Iris washed dishes while Laura wiped with a thin, ragged teatowel. The door to the kitchen was shut and they could hear the faint creaking of Phyllis's rocking chair.

Another useful item from Ralph's cart. He was twenty-one, the eldest in the family, and spent his days going round the better parts of Bristol collecting throw-away items which he later sold. He insisted on giving Phyllis money for housekeeping, though he often slept on the cart, and sometimes he brought home stuff that he could easily have sold. His ambition was to open an antique shop.

'What's up with Mum, Iris?' Laura asked quietly.

'I think she's had a miss.'

'What? Do you mean a miscarriage?'

'Yes. I overheard her and Enid talkin'.' Iris stopped work and looked up at her tall sister. 'Laura, I know I shouldn't be sayin' this, but I think Mum did somethin' to bring the baby on.'

Laura stared at her sister, only half comprehending. Lillian would have made a feast out of tormenting her ignorance.

Iris said, 'I suppose Granma hasn't told you much about the facts of life.'

Laura began to wipe the cracked cake plate vigorously. 'She never says a thing, but I've found out for myself, don't you worry.'

'So you know that women can make a baby come early if they don't want it.'

Laura was too shocked, too hideously fascinated, to lie. 'Not really. I know what a miscarriage is, of course, but –'

'What Mum had is really called an abortion. You stick a knittin' needle, or a bit of twig, ever so far up. I think it breaks open the bag the baby's in and then you get a dreadfully heavy period and the baby goes with it.'

'Mum did that?'

'I'm sure she did.'

'She killed a baby!'

'Don't say that,' begged Iris. 'She was cryin' when she talked to Enid. Said she'd never done it before and she felt so guilty it was makin' her sick. Poor Mum. She's got too much to do. There's too many of us and never enough money.'

Laura said bleakly, 'Yes! Poor Mum. I wish I could help her.'

'So do I.' Iris concentrated on cleaning crumbs from the

bottom of the cake tin. 'I wish someone would speak to Dad –'
She flushed and began to make enough noise with the cake tin
to deter an answer.

'It's a crazy world,' said Laura. 'I should be explaining
things to you, not you to me.'

'Don't matter who says it to who,' said Iris matter-of-factly.
'It isn't your fault if you've been kept in the dark. But don't be
hard on Mum.'

'I never would! Never! I –' Laura could not say the word
'love'. It was totally foreign to her. It had never been used to
her, or by her. 'I think a lot of her.'

'I know. And, Laura, don't take on about the way Lillian
treats you. She's got a sharp way with her, but she can be nice.'

Laura said nothing. She saw no point in arguing, but the day
Lillian was nice to her she'd do a striptease at Gregory's!

All day Monday Laura was troubled by her experience with
Rick. Snippets of overheard conversations plagued her. 'Once
you let a man take liberties you've lost him, he'll look for
another girl' was a favourite saying. She kept her smile bright,
her conversation lively, so that no one should guess at her inner
anxiety. The day seemed to drag on for ever, but at last the store
closed and she hurried outside. Rick was not there and she was
worried. He probably thought she was cheap and easy. That's
how she had behaved. Cheap and easy. All the way home on the
tram the words rang through her head. She squirmed at the
memory of how quickly she had permitted Rick to caress her,
and the shaming thing was she wanted him to do it again. A fine
rain began to spray her face. The other occupants of the
upstairs deck turned their reversible seats and faced the back,
pulling up collars. Laura dragged off her hat and let the rain
soak her face and hair and the paper bag in which she had
trimmings for the new hat. What use would a new hat be if Rick
didn't see it?

When she got home, Granma made things worse. 'You've
remembered it's the Sunday school Anniversary practice
tonight,' she said.

It had gone clean out of Laura's head. The last thing she

wanted to do was go to chapel and rehearse a lot of children in the pieces they were going to sing and recite next Sunday.

By the time she got to bed she was exhausted by her efforts and her futile longings.

On Tuesday evening Rick was waiting outside Gregory's and her heart soared with joy. All memory of her suffering was wiped out. This time he had acquired a motor cycle with side car and he helped Laura into it as if he had been an old-time squire and she his lady. Laura could feel dozens of eyes boring into her back and she rejoiced. There was a protective canopy on the sidecar and, although in one way it was heavenly to be inside the small compartment while Rick braved the weather and veered in and out of the traffic, she couldn't talk to him. He stopped at the end of her road and opened the canopy.

'Go and tell your Granma you've got a date,' he said.

Laura stared up at him, eyes dilated. 'I can't! I just can't!'

'Why can't you? What's wrong with me, baby?'

Laura said fervently, 'There's nothing wrong with you, Rick. She doesn't let me go out with anybody.'

Rick lit a cigarette and blew the smoke out in a long bluish stream. 'How old are you?'

'Seventeen. Almost eighteen.'

'That's old enough. Go and tell her. Assert yourself.'

Laura tried to picture herself being assertive to Granma and failed.

Rick was watching her closely. 'Would you like me to come and ask her permission to take you out?' He dismounted and gave her a hand out.

'Rick, I know it sounds crazy, but it's impossible for me to introduce you to Granma. She treats me like a child. If she found out about you –!'

Rick waited a moment, then shrugged and glanced about him. 'She'll probably know soon, anyway. I can see the neighbours' curtains twitchin'.'

'I do want to go out with you, Rick, I really do. Could you pick me up after ten like last time?'

'I could, but I don't want to. It's twenty past six. We could have a great evenin'.'

Laura was twisted inside with indecision and her longing to be with Rick. 'I'll make an excuse. I'll find a way out. Will you wait for me.'

'All right, baby. I'll come back in an hour.' And he roared off.

Laura waited ten minutes. To arrive home before the tram could have brought her would arouse Granma's suspicions.

She ate her supper, then said casually, 'Granma, may I go round to see Miss Morton? I've bought some bits and bobs to go on a hat for myself.'

'You've got yourself a new hat?' Granma's voice was sharp.

'Not new. I bought a shape and I'm going to do it up ready for the Sunday school Anniversary.'

Granma frowned. 'Not too fancy, mind.'

'No.'

'No dangling cherries or shiny bows, or rubbish like that.'

'No.'

'All right. Be home by ten.'

Rick was waiting and Laura hopped into the sidecar and they were off. This time he headed out of town and stopped at a tiny country pub. Laura walked nervously into the lounge bar and looked round. It was her first time in a public house and she hardly knew what to expect. Lewd pictures and erotic carvings, perhaps. The blue plush seats and small round tables, the sporting prints on the wall, the big glowing fire and the three or four locals who sat discussing farming were so innocent that she laughed.

When she explained her mirth to Rick he grinned. 'Did you expect the devil with horns?'

'I think so.'

'What's your poison?'

'My drink, do you mean? I've heard a lot about gin, but never tried it.'

'Now's as good a time as any.'

The drink tasted lemony and pleasant and Laura swallowed it quickly and demanded another. 'I'm thirsty, Rick.'

He grinned and obeyed. 'Take this one slower, baby. That's strong stuff for a little girl. If you're thirsty you should have a beer.'

Laura was shocked. 'Not beer!' she blurted. 'Granma says that it's bad enough women drinking at all and those who drink beer are common.'

Rick's eyebrows rose. 'In that case, honey, there must be lots of common women. My mother and aunt for two.'

'Oh, Rick, I'm sorry. Granma's so –'

'Prudish,' he supplied. 'Bossy? A killjoy?'

'Yes, she is.' Laura hesitated. 'My mother likes beer. It's just one of the things Granma hates her for.'

'God, what a dragon!'

'Well, Mum does go to public houses and she gets quite tiddly.'

'She must give poor ole Granma a fit!'

Laura grinned. 'I'll have a beer, Rick.'

'That's my girl!'

Laura watched him walk to the bar, enjoying the movement of his muscular thighs beneath the leather trousers. My girl, he had said.

She drank deeply. The beer was slightly bitter, but not unpleasantly so. She placed the glass carefully on the table. She was beginning to feel light-headed. 'Rick, you must have a very good job at Wills.'

His eyebrows climbed. 'What are you gettin' at?'

Laura flushed. It simply was not done to mention money, not in Granma's way of thinking. 'Sorry, that's not polite.'

'It's all right, kiddo, I was only teasin'. You want to know how I can afford things. Am I right?'

She nodded.

'Well, the motor bike and sidecar are borrowed, like the car we used the other night.'

'You must have good friends.'

'It's tit for tat. I oblige them; they oblige me. Then on top of my job I do a bit of this and that.'

'Fat lot that tells me! And why do you call me "baby" and "kiddo" and "honey"? I've never heard anyone talk that way?'

'You would if you lived in London and got into the jazz scene. That's the place to be. Or America, where all the new things seem to come from. They talk that way out there and the show-business people here catch it. I've had my eyes well and truly opened. You should see the theatres, the music halls, the cinemas and dance halls. I've got ambitions.'

'To be a singer?'

'Hell, no! I sing with a band if it gets me to see the people I want to know. I play piano sometimes, too. I make extra that way.'

'I play, too, but only hymns,' Laura said regretfully.

'I quite like a hymn with a good rousing tune,' admitted Rick. 'Surprised? I take my Mum to chapel sometimes.'

Laura drank again. She felt happy, free. 'What do you want to do, Rick?'

'I aim to become an impresario.'

'A what?'

'The man behind the scenes. The one who controls the performers for the stage, and dance halls. I want to find talent and sign it up, draw up contracts, then take a percentage of everythin' from everybody.'

'Is that allowed?'

'Anythin''s allowed, if you're clever enough. In London I had a good look round and the fattest cats were always the men who arranged things. The sky's the limit.' He held up his glass to her, Laura clicked hers on it and wished him luck and they drank.

Rick strolled to the bar and ordered a beer for himself and a lemonade for Laura. She sipped it cautiously. She was feeling definitely odd. The room was swaying. Or was it she who swayed? They finished their drinks and Rick guided her out, his strong hand under her elbow, laughing as she stumbled. The fresh air hit her and she, too, began to laugh, crazily.

Rick opened the tiny door of the sidecar and eased her inside. Then they were driving along a dark road, the lights of the bike glancing off hedges and trees and fences. Laura had no idea where they were going and she didn't care. She was happy just to be with Rick.

They stopped beneath trees in a wood carpeted with last year's leaves. A sliver of moon floated from behind clouds and gleamed between branches clad in spring shoots. Rick extracted a blanket from a box on the carrier and laid it on the ground. He pulled Laura down beside him. It all seemed so right and natural to her and she lay close to him, sniffing him, adoring him. Her arms went round him and he held her tight as his mouth began to explore hers. He pushed his tongue between her soft lips and all admonitions and warnings were forgotten. Her senses were swamped with a longing that permeated her whole body which was responding in ways that made her loins ache. She grew weak with ecstasy beneath Rick's lips and when his hands began to roam over her she had no power, or wish, to stop them. He slid his caressing fingers beneath her dress and she cried out in her unimaginable pleasure, invaded by an overpowering longing to pull off the old-fashioned elasticated drawers that were preventing Rick from actual contact with her flesh. She struggled from his arms.

'Rick,' she murmured.

Her hands were at the waistband when nausea rushed up and overpowered her. She leapt to her feet and raced behind a bush, where she vomited, listening to the ghastly sound she made, smelling the horrible stench. When she had finished she stayed on her knees in the damp grass, tears pouring down her face. Surely no girl had ever ended an evening in such humiliation.

Rick came to her and helped her up. He was as gentle as a woman as he wiped her face with a handkerchief dipped in rain water from an old tree stump.

'I'm sorry,' she gasped. 'I'm sorry.' She couldn't think of anything else to say. No words could wipe out her misery.

Rick was laughing. Actually laughing. Was there anything that didn't amuse him? 'It's all right, baby. All my fault. I shouldn't have let you have the beer. I wasn't thinkin' straight. I'm used to girls who can knock back half a dozen assorted drinks and still walk the line.'

The only word that really registered with Laura was 'girls'. He was comparing her with other girls. Unfavourably, of course. He didn't have to bother with someone who got drunk and became horribly sick on only their second date, who had to resort to lies to get away from her grandmother.

'I've disappointed you in every way,' she said.

'In every way?' Rick still had a note of laughter in his voice. Was he mocking her?

'I got drunk. And – you wanted to – I wanted to – and I spoiled everything. I wish –' She stopped. She had no words to explain how she felt.

'You're very sweet, honey. Nothing's spoiled.'

'Didn't you want to – you know?'

Rick pulled her towards him and held her gently in his arms. 'Of course I did, baby. I still do, but you've never been with a man, have you?'

'No!' Laura was shocked. 'A girl keeps herself for someone special.' Her voice was ragged.

'Someone special? Laura, you're so sweet. Well, I don't go in for seducin' innocent girls.' He laughed. 'I guess I agree with Granma there.'

'How did you know?' demanded Laura.

'I can tell from experience. A good kid like you should keep herself for marriage.'

Laura's heart sank. He must have had lots of girl friends to be so experienced. She felt suddenly cold and shaky. 'What time is it?' she asked.

'Nine-forty. Why? Is it bedtime?'

Did she imagine the note of derision in his voice? 'I have to get back by ten,' she said bleakly.

'Don't worry, baby. We'll make it.'

Laura asked him to drop her near Miss Morton's. Before he drove off he lent her a comb and handed her a small paper of mint sweets. 'Suck one of these,' he grinned. 'It'll keep Granma's suspicions away.'

As he left she could hear him whistling. The tune floated back to her on the breeze and she stood for a moment, watching the receding tail lights. If she had not been sick what would have happened? Not much, according to Rick. Could a man exercise such control? Her thoughts slid to Dad, and Mum's pregnancies, then darted away. She was scared to realise that she felt no sense of shame at the way she had offered her body, but only a deep unhappiness at her failure. Perhaps Rick would go and find another girl, one who stayed out late and held her drink, who could release his sexual tension. The thought gave her a physical pain and she hurried down the street, head bent, arms clasped around her body to ease its anguish.

She had almost forgotten her lie to Granma and when she was asked about her hat it took a moment for her to get her wits together.

'It's not quite finished. I'll need to make another visit. I'll take my cocoa up with me, thank you.' She was gone before Granma could protest and later that night she crept down and poured the cocoa down the sink.

She must have an excuse to meet Rick again and she must also find time to make a new hat. She was getting deeper into a vortex of deceit which appalled her, but her longing to be with Rick overcame all sense of honour and caution.

She ran round to Miss Morton's again the following morning and gabbled out a story about Rick, about being in love, about having to deceive Granma.

Miss Morton took it all calmly. 'Would you like me to steam a shape for you? I've got some nice bronze-coloured velvet.'

'Oh, thank you. I don't deserve –'

'Nonsense! Get along to work now.'

Miss Morton's understanding gave Laura a warm glow, but it faded in the humiliating memory of herself last night, on her knees, spewing out her drink, stinking and weeping. And she had trusted Rick in a reckless way that could have rebounded on her. She could even have got a baby. The idea of falling for Rick's baby filled her with a thrill of wonder and horror. No respectable girl started a baby unless she was married. And what if he kissed and told? Some men did. She had heard the girls at work talking about them. Reputations could be torn to miserable shreds by words. By tomorrow she could be known as a girl who offered herself freely.

She had worked herself into such a state she was surprised to find herself walking normally to work with the usual crowd, the usual banter and laughter tossed between the men and women.

Of course everything would be all right. Rick wasn't the kind to tell tales, and he approved of girls remaining virgins until marriage. That showed he was good. As she worked through the day her imagination kept transporting her into a dream in which she was married to Rick. The dream wiped everything else from her life. It was the only thing that held significance. She had forgotten that Wednesday was another practice night for the Sunday school children. Never had it been so difficult to keep her irritation in check as they wriggled, squirmed, forgot their lines, dropped their bibles and hymn books.

On Thursday emotion took its toll and after the lunch break she felt lethargic. She was snapped back into full consciousness by the sight of Lady Mallender arriving in millinery. She came straight to Laura, walking past the indignant Miss Pringle and the open-mouthed Dolores.

From her purse she withdrew two halfcrowns which she held out to Laura with a parting of her lips which could, Laura supposed, be taken for a condescending smile. 'For the purse. It matched my hat. One or two of my friends quite admired it.'

Laura glanced round hastily. Fortunately three voluble customers arrived and kept the others busy. She began to hold out her hand, then stopped. Miss Morton had told her to ask fifteen shillings and she was being offered five for a purse that had taken her half the night to finish. If her ladyship had found one in Gregory's she would have paid a great deal more. Discretion urged her to take the money, but her sense of justice was outraged.

She looked Lady Mallender straight in the eye and said, 'The price is fifteen shillings.'

Lady Mallender raised her brows. 'For a home-made purse?'

Laura glanced round, glad to see that the customers were still being difficult. 'It's a professional piece of work, my lady,' she said quietly. 'It took a long time to make. You said it was admired.' She prayed that Lady Mallender would hand over the money and go.

The loud customers departed, their voices fading down the stairs and Laura began to regret not taking the five shillings.

Miss Pringle hurried over. 'Good afternoon, Lady Mallender. Can I be of assistance?'

In explaining the scene later to Miss Morton Laura said that Lady Mallender looked at Miss Pringle as if she were something the cat had dragged in and discarded. 'The matter is between myself and this girl. She is endeavouring to overcharge me for a purse.'

'But she has nothing to do with our accessory department –'

'I could not get what I wanted here, so this chit offered to make me one.'

'Miss Blackford! You offered to make her ladyship a purse?'

Laura was quaking inside. She wished to God she had just taken the money. If she lost her job she could not even imagine the depth of Granma's wrath, but she kept her head up. It wasn't as if she'd committed a crime. 'Yes, Miss Pringle, but not just offered. I made one with the help of a professional lady. Lady Mallender doesn't wish to pay the proper price.'

'I've never heard of such a thing – I beg your pardon, Lady Mallender. Miss Blackford had no right –'

'Her ladyship was delighted with the purse,' persisted Laura, feeling the heat as her boats burned behind her.

Lady Mallender pulled out a ten-shilling note which she added to the coins. 'Take the money! What a profiteer! I must say, Miss Pringle, I am astonished at the class of girl Gregory's employs these days.'

She turned and stalked away. 'No sale,' called Miss Pringle. It was the code used to alert a higher being to action and the floor-walker, young Mr Arthur Gregory, came hurrying and followed Lady Mallender who slowed her steps as they walked down the wide stairway, Arthur's head on one side as he listened to the valuable client's stream of words.

Miss Pringle stared at Laura. 'What an extremely foolish thing to do, Miss Blackford.'

'I suppose it was. I didn't think so at the time. She wanted the purse and I knew I could get one. The lady who helped me needs the money. If only Lady Mallender had paid me when I delivered it to her house. She's so nasty! With all her money she ought to be kind and understanding of people with little.'

Miss Pringle said, her tone bleak, 'It doesn't work that way.'

Dolores asked, 'Do you think Mr Gregory will be very angry?'

'I should think he will; such a thing has never happened before to my knowledge. I'll put in a word for you, Miss Blackford, though you don't deserve it. The dress show next week will be showing off the new spring range ready for the Whitsuntide holiday and I've set my mind on you as a model. Perhaps he'll forgive you.' She didn't look hopeful.

Chapter Four

To Laura's intense relief Mr Gregory did not dismiss her. This was her first visit to the large office on the top floor, job interviews being conducted in the small room used by Mr Arthur Gregory, the boss's son. She walked through upholstery and linens, her heart thumping, wearing the obligatory look of indignation at the customary tongue clickings and mock kisses sent her way by the junior salesmen. It was difficult to keep a fixed expression when her nose wanted to wrinkle at the delectable smells drifting from the restaurant. Laura caught a glimpse of the lucky ones who could afford to eat out expensively and heard their chatter and laughter, mostly feminine, as they lingered over coffee while smoke drifted from their cigarettes.

Her employer's office was richly carpeted and furnished with heavy dark oak furniture bought years ago by the founder member of the family firm. Mr Gregory senior sat behind a desk so large it seemed to swamp him. Perhaps it was that which gave Laura the sudden courage to hold up her head and walk across the room in the way she had seen Dolores move when she was practising her modelling.

Mr Gregory frowned at her. 'Now, Miss Blackford, explain what you have done to upset one of our chief clients.'

'Hasn't Mr Gregory junior told you?'

'Don't be impertinent, girl.' Mr Gregory paused. 'Miss Blackford, you have been a model employee and, as such, are entitled to have your say. Some employers would not tolerate as much.'

Laura knew this to be true. 'I didn't mean to be impertinent, sir.' She explained what had happened, including Miss Morton's need for money.

'I see. But leaving out, for the moment, the question of your disloyalty to the people who employ you, Lady Mallender offered you a fair sum for something made in a hurry by an amateur and you have offended her by demanding more. We cannot afford to have our client's upset, especially one as rich and influential as Lady Mallender. You must know that!'

'The bag was beautiful! My friend, Miss Morton, who is a skilled milliner, saw to that.'

'That is hardly the issue in question! And Lady Mallender says otherwise.'

'She told me it was admired, and paid what I asked – in the end. Would she have done that if the bag was amateurish?'

'She leads a very busy life. She has no time to argue with salesgirls, and she needed the bag urgently enough to overlook any shortcomings.'

Laura pressed her lips together. The word 'urgently' infuriated her. There were many women who needed things urgently, like a husband with a job, and medical attention, and money, and food, and a decent home.

'Is that *all* you have to say, Miss Blackford? No regrets that you could have lost us a valued client?'

'I'm sorry if what I did is bad for the store, sir, but I still think Lady Mallender behaved wrongly.'

'What a way to speak of her! I will not permit insolence from my staff towards their superiors.'

Again Laura controlled her tongue. If she spoke she knew that indignant words would pour from her and they could only make the situation worse. Her employer was one of *them* – the ones who always knew where their next meal was coming from, who could always pay their bills.

Mr Gregory, who could be terrifying when he chose, looked grim as he sat and tapped his fingers on the desk. He stood and walked over to the window and looked down into the busy street. His short body was thick from good living, his striped trousers and black coat a trifle strained over his flesh. 'This company, Miss Blackford, is almost a hundred years old.'

'Yes, sir.' For all his wealth he looked insignificant. Rick would tower over him. In fact, she could almost look down on him herself. It occurred to her for the first time, that, in the upper-class world which Mr Gregory inhabited, a lack of muscular power was no bar to wealthy success. All you needed was a good head for business. Of course, an inheritance like Gregory's Department Store wouldn't come amiss! A touch of cynicism twisted her lips.

Her employer returned to his chair, shuffled a few papers, put on a pair of round gold-rimmed spectacles. 'Miss Pringle tells me she wants you to model some hats next Saturday. The fashion department is co-operating, of course, and our girls will be wearing the latest styles. It's a big day for us, you know. We may not be one of the largest stores in Bristol, but our clients are among the most exclusive. Most of them come to see our Whitsuntide offerings. It's a good opportunity for you.' Laura was silent as he continued. 'Your record here is a good one so I have decided to overlook your offence. But it must never happen again. Loyalty, Miss Blackford, that's what we at Gregory's ask of our staff. It was *disloyal* of you to sell an item that Lady Mallender could have purchased here. If you had called upon Miss Pringle, or Mr Gregory junior, they would undoubtedly have satisfied her ladyship's requirements. You may go, but remember all that I have said.'

He arrived at the door before her and held it open. She was gratified, until he raised his hand to pat her cheek and followed with a smack on her bottom before closing the door behind her.

Laura stood fuming, her face burning. Just because she was an employee he thought he could paw her! He was no better than his lecherous son whom the girls tried to avoid being alone with. She marched back to millinery, raging because her employer was able to insult her with masculine impudence and she had no way of retaliating. Then a small smile crept over her face. She had won quite a victory over both Mr Gregory and her arrogant ladyship, and it felt good.

Saturday arrived. Laura had not seen Rick and she was seething with worry.

The atmosphere at Gregory's was now one of frenzied

excitement. Laura had washed her hair the night before and had risen early to brush it until the chestnut tones gleamed among the brown. The display was to begin at twelve and she spent the morning in the fitting rooms of the fashion department trying on clothes and hats. She and the three other models were given a lunch which had been brought down from the restaurant.

'It's all we'll get in the way of payment,' hissed Dolores, 'so make the most of it.'

At one o'clock precisely Laura nervously took her place on the third floor where screens draped with furnishing materials had been used to improvise a changing room. Because of her tall slenderness she had been allotted formal gowns and sports outfits; she needed no binding corsetry to wear the straight, boyish shapes.

Her turn arrived. She took a last glance in the mirror and saw an elegant woman wearing primrose yellow organza – a garden-party dress with pale violet braiding and a hem that just brushed her knees – and a cloche hat which matched the fine braid, and for the first time in her life she knew the feel of soft silk stockings. There was a collection of costume jewellery laid out on a small table and at the last moment she pinned a bold slash of a red shiny brooch to the hat. The brilliance of the scarlet against the pale violet excited her. She carried lace gloves and a tiny bag; light yellow shoes with the slenderest heels she had ever worn completed her ensemble. A girl from cosmetics had made up her face and she had even been sprayed with a luscious French perfume which floated around her like an aura. She decided she looked as good as any of Gregory's rich clients. She had never before appreciated the difference clothes could make.

Just as she was about to make her entrance Miss Pringle noticed the red brooch and flung up her hands, her mouth emitting a whoosh of horror.

Laura pretended not to notice. She entered the restaurant where the three-piece orchestra had been playing softly. As she pushed her hips forward in the exaggerated manner demanded by today's styles and began her walk, fingers of one hand

67

splayed on her hip, a second piano tuned into the music and a man's voice sang, *A pretty girl is like a melody,* in lingering, husky tones that exactly suited the occasion. She could never mistake that voice. Rick was on the small stage at the end of the cat walk.

She never knew afterwards how she kept going. She swung along the length of pale beige carpet that stretched before her like an endless path between the clients on their little gilt seats, twirled round as she had been taught, and walked back and out to a round of applause. Dolores passed her in a pair of lounging pyjamas.

Laura was shaking with tension as the dressers dragged off her finery and pulled on the next outfit. Miss Pringle glared at her over their heads. 'I'll thank you, Miss Blackford, not to tamper with the exhibits! That red brooch looked out of place. Don't dare do such a thing again!'

'This attractive garment,' the voice of the fashion-department head announced fruitily as she went back through the curtains, 'is for beach wear in the sun of Cannes, or Nice, or maybe the Venice Lido.'

During the rehearsals Laura had not been bothered by the low neckline, the deepcut back, the inches of thigh her beach costume displayed. She had pictured herself parading only in front of ladies. But she now realised some men from the leisured classes had accompanied their women. And any male who could get away from his counter for a few moments was peering happily at the models. And Rick was out there. She had to push herself on, knowing his gaze would make her feel almost naked after the passion she had revealed to him, and which, it seemed humiliatingly, he had no use for.

It took all her courage to move. Her chin was up, her posture one of unbelievable hauteur. One glance only she permitted herself towards the musicians. Rick was staring straight at her and gave her a slight, teasing grin that almost destroyed her poise. The applause was louder this time and as the show went on it was clear that she was the hit.

Even the words of Rick's song were a teasing background – *Oh, sweet and lovely lady be good* – as she appeared in a bathing suit that would have given Granma a seizure, but she cleared her mind of everything save the wish to make her first public appearance a success. Forget men! They were fickle. The only person she could trust was herself. She saw herself rising to glorious heights. After this she would surely become a regular model. She might even some day become head of a department.

Her last gown was of gold and silver lamé, the upper part – what little there was of it – cut so that it fitted like a second skin. The elongated back of the skirt trailed on the ground, the front hem rose above her knees. She carried an enormous feather fan which she fluttered coquettishly. On her head, in her ears, and around her wrists, diamanté jewellery glittered in the lights. She was clapped all the way out and back.

The show was over by three-thirty and the girls felt dreadfully flat. The clothes and accessories were returned to the various departments, except the stockings which the models were allowed to keep. Dolores congratulated Laura on her success and if she sounded a bit put out one could hardly wonder at it.

Miss Pringle was pink with delight. 'Miss Blackford, you were *professional*. Who taught you to walk like that? I believe the clients thought we had imported you from London. I should scold you for sticking that red brooch in your hat, only it appears the ladies liked it. They said it was different. Original, one said. We have a very satisfactory number of orders and several people complimented you.'

They did not include Lady Mallender, decided Laura. She had given her the frostiest glare each time she passed by.

When the store closed at nine Laura was drained of energy, but thoughts of Rick insisted on impinging on her every moment. He had looked so debonair and had sung so well in his sensual voice. She loved him more than ever; it was useless to try to deny it. That night, in her room, she stared a long time in her mirror. She looked exactly the same as always, long face, high cheekbones. She smiled. Her teeth had not shrunk. Yet something about her had impressed women who were accustomed to fashion shows in London, and probably Paris. She wondered if Rick had been equally impressed.

On Sunday the Anniversary celebrations went on all day, her class performed creditably, and in the evening Grampa was granted the honour of giving the sermon. In the pulpit he came into his own. He made statements, expounded on them, aired his opinions, and for once Granma could not argue with him. Only Laura knew that on his return home she would spend an hour or so pointing out where he was wrong. The only sermons Granma approved of were those that lashed the air with imprecations against the devil and his works, and lingered on punishments from above. Grampa presented a sweeter God.

Back at work on Monday Laura felt washed out, depressed and then, at the end of the day, there was Rick, grinning at her, holding open the door of a car, expecting her to step in, just as if he had not neglected her for days after making love to her, had not left her to wallow in self-disgust. And the degrading thing was she wanted to go with him.

But she did not. She played to the avid audience, pulling herself up, standing as she had when modelling; she even put a hand on her hip. 'Are you asking me to get in?'

Rick's grin grew wider. 'I sure am, baby. You were a wow at the show. I've been tellin' Mum an' aunty all about you. They said they'd like to meet you. Come home to supper with me.'

Laura was suddenly in turmoil. She stared at him. Surely he wouldn't be suggesting she visit his mother unless he had serious intentions? Yet how could a man who was really interested in her keep her dangling in cruel suspense, awaiting his next summons? And he knew her problem with Granma and her lack of freedom. He seemed to think he could ride roughshod over everything and everybody.

'Granma's expecting me,' she said coolly. 'I'm sorry to disappoint your mother –'

'Oh, that's all right. She didn't set a date.'

'Didn't set a date? To meet me? I don't understand you, Rick Merriman! What kind of a game are you playing?' And she began to stride down the road towards the tram stop.

Rick hurried after her. 'Don't be mad at me, baby.'

She turned her head aside. She could not endure it if he saw the gleam of angry tears. 'Go away! You're impossible!'

Rick seized her arm and when she attempted to shrug him off he simply squeezed tighter.

'I'll have a bruise!'

'Then stop fightin' me.'

Some of Gregory's girls stood and watched open-mouthed. Good, thought Laura, breathing more easily as she calmed down.

'That's better,' approved Rick. 'I suppose it's difficult for you to understand the way I operate. See, Laura, I told you I want to make somethin' of myself. I must!' His face darkened for a moment. 'I must! In show business you have to be ready to go anywhere at any time. Everythin' else has to take second place.'

'Has it?'

'Shall I come and see Granma and ask her –'

'No!'

'For God's sake, woman, she's got to let you have a date some time.'

'She will, provided she approves of the boy.'

'And you don't think she'd like me?'

Laura stared at him. At his snap-brim hat (Grampa always wore a black bowler), his two-tone shoes, his nicotine-stained fingers and the trailing cigarette smoke. His face was rugged, his eyes bold. She thought of the pale-faced, plumpish Reggie Prewett in his dark Sunday suit, or in the long white coat he wore behind his father's grocery counter. 'No, I don't think she would.'

'I'll make her like me. Just let me meet her.'

Laura sighed. 'Give me some warning. If I know beforehand you want a date I can make an excuse to escape.'

'Sounds like a prison.'

'Granma's always been very kind to me.'

'Some jailers are kind, I've heard tell.'

Laura did not respond.

'Righto,' said Rick, 'I'll try to get in touch, but I may have to

71

let you down at the last minute. Show business is like that. I *know* I'm free tonight.'

She turned away and he caught her arm. 'Laura,' he begged, 'can't you come? Make up some story or other for your Granma. Other girls manage.'

'I'm not other girls. My life is different.'

Rick dropped her arm. 'It certainly is. Why is your Granma so suspicious? What have you been up to?'

'Nothing!' Laura was horrified. She whirled round and saw that Rick was teasing, his dark eyes filled with laughter and she was assailed by relief. She smiled at him and made up her mind. She should meet his mother as soon as possible, then her status in his life would be clear to everyone. Even Granma.

'Rick,' she said, 'I'll see you on Wednesday. I'll ask Miss Morton to cover for me. She's a good sort and thinks Granma is too strict.'

But Miss Morton was worried when Laura asked her. 'It's wrong of me really to back you, Laura. Deceit doesn't come naturally to me.'

Laura felt guilty, but her desire to see Rick, to stabilise their relationship was overpowering. 'If Granma was reasonable I needn't go behind her back.'

'You're only seventeen – I hope you know what you're doing.'

'I do,' Laura assured her. 'Honestly, I do. Rick is wonderful. And don't forget I'm eighteen in May.'

'Does he love you?'

Laura hesitated. 'He's not exactly said so, but he's told his mother about me. He says the nicest things and he acts as if he does.'

Miss Morton looked startled. 'I hope he behaves like a gentleman with you.'

'He treats me beautifully,' said Laura, pretending to examine a piece of ecru lace.

Rick met Laura from work on Wednesday. He was driving the borrowed two-seater car again and she found it difficult not to stare back at the envious girls and see the expressions on their faces. She was uncharitably glad that Lillian was among the watchers.

Rick smiled at her. 'So Granma let you out, after all.'

'No! I'm supposed to be helping with a rush order of hats.'

'Is that what you like doin'? Makin' hats?'

'Mmmm. It's a very satisfying occupation. I feel triumph-ant every time I design one that adds to some woman's appearance.'

Rick's home was on the top floor of a grey stone three-storey building next to Brandon Hill, whose lower grassy slopes still displayed lines of washing pinked by the last rays of the sun. When they reached the flat Rick opened the front door and showed her into the living-room kitchen where an elderly woman was taking a pie from the oven.

'Aunty Mabel, this is Laura. Laura meet my aunty. Well, she's really Mum's aunt.'

The woman straightened, smiled, and held out her hand. 'Pleased to meet you, Laura. Sit yourself by the fire. The days are still nippy.' Laura felt warmed by her eager friendliness and the smell of cooking made her feel hungry. The door opened and another woman walked in carrying a basket of dry washing. A little dried leaf of a woman, small and pale.

Rick leapt to his feet, 'Mum, you should have waited for me. You knew I'd be home.' There was a tender, concerned note in Rick's voice.

'Fiddlesticks!' Her voice was stronger than she looked. 'This is woman's work, and how do I ever know when you'll be here? You and your show business.'

Mrs Merriman welcomed Laura without the warmth that Aunty Mabel had shown. Laura had an impression that she had been drained long ago of emotion. She carefully hung the wash-ing on a clotheshorse which Rick carried into one of the two bedrooms. Later it would be put near the fire to finish drying. Tomorrow was ironing day. The routine was the same in every house, unless they took in washing when it became a grindingly endless task.

'How was work today, Mum?'

'Like it always is. One pack of cigarettes looks the same as any other.'

'Wills wouldn't like to hear you say so.'

73

'Well, they're all alike to me,' said Mrs Merriman shortly.

Rick winked at Laura. 'Mum doesn't smoke.'

'I'd be a fool when it hurts my chest and makes me cough.'

'Haven't you been well today, Mum?'

Mrs Merriman smiled. 'I'm all right, son. Take no notice of my grumbles.' She turned to Laura. 'You work in Gregory's millinery, don't you? Must be nice. I expect you have some superior conversation. All the girls round me go on and on about boys, pictures, dances – or else it's grumbles about their families. I'm always glad to come home. I don't believe in talkin' about private things.'

'We're not allowed to say anything on the shop floor, Mrs Merriman, except to clients. In the cloakroom the workers sound pretty much the same as in your place.'

'Fancy. And with their advantages, too. There's no accountin' for folks.'

'Sit yourselves down,' said Aunty Mabel and dished out plates of steak and kidney pie. It was delicious and Laura began to enjoy herself. She was eating with people unknown to her in a strange house yet she felt at home. Rick was beside her and it seemed so right. Mrs Merriman grew more expansive as she was revived by food and the strong tea that Aunty Mabel kept pouring from a pot which simmered permanently on the hob. The curranty suet pudding was served with a dish of jam large enough to be described as wasteful luxury by Granma.

Afterwards Laura offered to help with the dishes, but was refused. Then the two women went into one of the bedrooms from which came the murmur of their conversation over the whirring of a sewing machine.

'Would you like to walk on Brandon Hill?' asked Rick.

Laura nodded and they climbed the steep slopes to the tall monument raised in honour of John Cabot, who had sailed from Bristol with his sons to North America in 1497, and gazed out over the town where the street lights created chains of brightness.

'It's beautiful,' said Laura. 'I've never seen Bristol like this.'

'Your Granma keeps you like a woman in a harem,' said Rick. They were seated on a small wooden bench. He was leaning with his arms along the back. Laura was sitting forward staring at the scene below.

'She means well.'

'Means well! They're the worst. We stayed a while with another aunty who meant well. She was always pokin' and pryin' and criticisin'. Nearly drove Mum mad. We were thankful to come and live with Aunty Mabel.'

'They're both very nice,' said Laura.

She waited, quivering inside, for Rick to say something significant about their relationship, but he seemed content just to sit by her, his cigarette glowing in the darkness. Laura smoked, too. She was getting the hang of it and had begun to enjoy it. She searched her mind for something to say that would jolt Rick out of his placid mood. She ached for him to touch her.

When he spoke, suddenly, her body arched with expectation. 'Laura, it's after nine. It'll soon be time to take you home. We don't want to upset Granma.'

Tears of disappointment stung behind her eyelids and she threw down her cigarette and moved close to him. 'Aren't you going to give me a goodnight kiss?' The provocative words were flung out from the torment of her senses.

Rick ground his cigarette beneath his heel. 'Always happy to oblige a lady!'

There was a laugh in his voice, but his kiss was slow and passionate. Her hands took on a life of their own, holding his head close to hers, touching his body.

He gasped and pulled away. 'Miss Blackford!' he exclaimed in mock indignation. 'What do you think you're doin'?'

'Don't tease me, Rick. I can't stand it. You must know how I feel –'

'You like me – quite a lot, I guess.'

'Like you! I –' She stopped, the barriers of convention up again. A woman always waited for a man to declare himself before she revealed her feelings.

Rick put his arms about her and held her gently. 'Don't fall in love with me,' he warned. 'I'm goin' places, doin' things – I need to be free.'

Laura shook him from her. 'Have you been seeing other girls?'

Rick gave a soft laugh of genuine amusement. 'A typical female reaction. I've got lots of friends, fellows and girls. I see them in the way of business and we go out to pubs and restaurants. It'll always be that way with me.'

Laura felt sick. She must make him understand. 'I wouldn't ever stop you doing what you want, Rick.'

He tipped her chin and kissed her lips lightly. 'You're such a sweet little innocent, Granma's right to look after you properly. Laura, be careful in future. You'll meet men who'll take advantage of you. You led me on too far, you know. You made it difficult for me to stop –'

She was on her feet, outraged, shaking with anger. 'Led you on! Led you on!' Words stuck in her throat.

'Laura, please –' He held out his hands.

'Don't touch me! You had no right to make love to me. You don't care about me.'

She ran down the dark hill, almost falling as she stumbled over grassy tufts. He was right behind her and caught her just before she reached the road. 'Laura, for God's sake – I've never said a word out of place to you. And I haven't hurt you –'

'Haven't hurt me?'

'I was careful. I'm sorry you took me so seriously. I guess I'm just not used to your kind. Showgirls are mostly well able to look after themselves.'

She struggled, but he would not let go and his strength was too much for her and she became still and quiet. She felt ill with misery.

'What time is it?' she asked in a flat voice.

Rick looked at his watch. 'Half past nine. Time to get you back, baby.'

'Don't baby me!' She knew she sounded childish, but her nerves were jangling. She sat beside Rick in the car and refused to answer him when he spoke. For the last mile not a word passed between them. He stopped near Miss Morton's lodging.

'Laura, I want to see you again. Can't we stay friends?'

She sat twisting her hands in her lap. 'I don't know. I don't know.'

She opened her door and fled.

Chapter Five

On Friday of the following week Thelma and Daphne Charlton, Lady Mallender's nieces, strolled into the millinery department. Dolores groaned. They were as demanding and as thoughtless as their aunt.

As she brought out the eleventh hat for them to try she muttered furiously to Laura, 'They haven't got any intention of buyin' a thing. They're probably just bored. Bright young things! The ones that call them that should watch them now.'

The two women, surrounded by discarded model hats, wore expensive afternoon dresses and fur capes, their earrings and bracelets glittered in the shop lights. They were both under twenty and had never done a day's work, and their pretty, heavily made-up faces were petulant. Miss Pringle intervened without success. More hats were brought out and rejected. Then Daphne demanded that the tall girl should serve them. Laura walked forward beneath the resentful gaze of both Dolores and Miss Pringle.

'How may I help you?' she asked.

'How do I look in this?' demanded Thelma. She was wearing a pale-blue straw with three feathery pink pompoms.

'Charming, madam,' said Laura. It was true. Both girls could have worn almost any hat attractively.

'What about me?' demanded Daphne who was trying on a yellow straw helmet with pale-green feathers.

'Very becoming, madam,' said Laura.

Miss Pringle and Dolores turned aside to attend to a mother and daughter.

'Thank God,' whispered Thelma. 'We thought they'd never go away, didn't we, Daphne?'

77

'The thing is,' said Daphne, 'we've come to order evening purses from you, but Aunt Maud said something about you doing it behind old Gregory's back so we decided we'd better do a bit of the cloak-and-dagger stuff.'

'That's right,' agreed Thelma. She opened her bag. 'Look, I've brought some bits of stuff to match. Mine's gold lamé and Daphne's is mauve georgette. We want the purses by the week-end after next, please.'

Laura was appalled. 'I can't,' she said desperately. 'I was nearly sacked last time.'

Thelma pouted her scarlet-rouged lips. 'Don't be such a spoilsport, Miss – what's your name?'

'Blackford,' whispered Laura. 'Please keep trying on hats. Miss Pringle will wonder –'

'I'm absolutely *wrecking* my *lovely* new Marcel wave,' grumbled Daphne, but she pulled on a grey felt hat with scarlet feathers and regarded herself in the mirror, twisting her head from side to side and demanding a mirror at the back. 'I'll take it,' she said unexpectedly.

Laura breathed a sigh of relief which was premature.

'Now, we've done you a favour you must do one for us?' said Daphne.

'What favour, Miss Charlton?'

'We've bought one of your hats.'

'They're Mr Gregory's, madam, not mine.'

'Well, yes, but you sold it. Don't you get commission or something?'

'No, madam.'

'Mean old skinflint! However, that's beside the point, what about our evening purses?' asked Daphne.

'I thought you understood. I can't possibly –'

'Thirty shillings each,' tempted Thelma, 'if they're as good as Aunt Maud's.'

Laura paused. A whole one pound ten shillings for both her and Miss Morton.

Thelma pulled out the two swatches and Laura hesitated, then transferred them swiftly to her pocket. 'What day do you want the purses?'

'Next Saturday week – bring them in the morning. Deliver them to this address and we'll pay at once. We won't get you into trouble like aunty did, promise!'

They left, talking loudly.

Granma didn't raise objections to Laura making extra visits to Miss Morton to help with orders which included a number of hats in time for Whitsuntide.

Laura began to notice that people were eyeing her with new respect. Somehow the word had run round the store that Laura Blackford had told Rick Merriman to push off. It also crept out that she had made a private deal with a client and had got away with it, and she had been the undoubted success of the fashion show. Betty, her eyes wide with appreciation, kept her informed of any store gossip she might have missed.

If they only knew how much she longed to see Rick. She kept a bland expression, but she ached from wanting him. She wished she had not revealed her feelings to him so blatantly. She had scared him off, just as Granma always warned. Men were dominant and must always take the initiative, she said. Laura looked at Grampa sometimes and tried to picture him being dominant with Granma.

Although Miss Morton had plenty on her hands making new hats, or refurbishing old ones for Whitsuntide, she was delighted by the extra well-paid work. Between them she and Laura made the purses, both as dainty and pretty as could be bought in any store and, moreover, specially designed. Miss Morton said they should charge more than thirty shillings for originals and Laura knew she was right. She had looked around the shops and found evening purses on sale for five pounds or more and not one whit better than theirs.

Leaving work on Friday night, tired by the long day and the late hours with Miss Morton she was, for once, not thinking of Rick. But when she heard his voice she smiled delightedly, then she frowned. If he thought he could drop her and pick her up when it suited him he was about to discover his mistake. He was driving the two-seater and had climbed out to open the passenger door. He was grinning confidently.

'Step into my automobile, madam. I'll give you a lift home.'

'That won't be necessary.'

'No, but it'll be nice.'

'I dare say you've other more important things to do than drive me around. I'll get the tram.'

'Laura, honey, please. Don't be cruel to me.'

'Cruel! Where have you been since last week?'

'Playing the piano to earn some extra money.'

'Every night for over a week?'

'Sure. I've been fillin' in for a pal in a picture house in town. He was sick. He's got a wife and four kids.'

'Do you mean you've given him the money you earned?'

'Why not? A pal's a pal.'

Laura stared at him. He was dressed in a dark jacket and trousers, a white shirt and black bow tie. 'What are you all dressed up for? I can't come out. I'm doing some work with Miss Morton.'

'I can't come out either. I've got a date.' Laura's eyes flashed and he put out his hands. 'With a dance band, not a girl.'

'I'm sure it's nothing to me if you want to date other girls.'

'That's all right then. Now, about the lift home, honey lamb.'

Laura smiled in spite of herself and having done so could not keep up a front. She weakly capitulated and climbed in the car. She was thankful to lean back and be driven. She really did feel tired.

'Why are you so exhausted?' demanded Rick.

She told him and he whistled through his teeth. 'So you've been helpin' Miss Morton. For no pay, I presume. Looks like we're birds of a feather. Would you like me to deliver the purses to the spoilt bitches for you tomorrow?'

'Oh, Rick, would you? They promised to pay at once.'

Laura ran up the narrow staircase to Miss Morton's room and was told to bring the young man in. Rick seemed to dwarf the living room. He admired several of the hats, especially the one Laura was making for herself, looked around the room cluttered with shapes, materials, ribbons and lace, and sniffed at the unique scent of damp-ironed felt. 'It's a regular beehive,' he said, then he took the tissue-wrapped purses carefully and left, driving off with a cheerful wave to the women at the window.

After supper Laura and Miss Morton put the finishing touches to several new hats. Laura worked on hers to have it ready for Sunday. Whitsuntide Sunday. A great event in the local calendar.

She had copied a pattern for a dress from an exclusive in Gregory's, adapting it so that it became an original. It was a simple shape falling straight from the shoulders to her hips, where box pleats allowed for walking. She added crimson silk georgette panels to the grey wool marocain. More georgette was swathed in a band around her neat cloche hat. Miss Morton was lending her some drop pearl earrings that had belonged to her mother.

When she left Gregory's on Saturday, she found Rick outside waiting for her with four pound notes in his hand.

'That's more than I asked. I hope you're not offering me your charity!'

He grinned at her. 'I'm too busy lookin' after Mum and myself. I told the toffee-nosed maid who came to fetch the bags that you hadn't asked enough. I got the extra pound – eventually.'

'I hope you didn't upset them?'

'The Misses Charlton? Who cares for their feelings?'

'I do. Not because I think they're particularly nice, but I don't want trouble at work.'

Rick frowned. 'A pound doesn't mean that much to them. Don't worry, baby.'

He said he was sorry he couldn't run her home, but he was working and had left a dance hall during the interval and must rush back. He made an incongruous figure riding his motor cycle in dinner jacket and bow tie. Laura watched him disappear, wishing she was seated behind him, smiled brightly at the ogling men and girls and set off with Betty for home.

Monday dawned clear and sunny, much to everyone's relief. It was a public holiday and Granma and Grampa, dressed in their new black Sunday best, indistinguishable from any other year's, walked with Laura to a rendezvous where all the churches at their end of Kingswood were gathering to begin the procession of witness that took place each Whitsuntide Monday. Granma was even more upright than usual because her new, extensively-boned corsets were not yet broken in. She was not noted for optimism and carried her long black umbrella, while Grampa had his best, silver-knobbed walking stick. They swung them with vigour dangerous to any who came too close.

The conversation and laughter almost drowned the various bands as they tuned their instruments. When a signal was given they moved off. Sunday schools, tiny Brownies and Cubs, the older Guides and Scouts, the Boy's Brigade.

Strong men carried the twin poles of the heavy church banners with their pictures and religious inscriptions. There were gaily decorated carts for the smallest children, drawn by massive dray horses sporting rosettes and ribbons on their manes and tails and on their harnesses which jingled with shiny brasses.

The streets were lined with people, many in new outfits, others down at heel and poorly clothed, their decent things waiting unclaimed on the pawnbroker's shelves after too many workless months, but who were nevertheless out to get as much fun as possible from the day. They called greetings to their friends. The irreverent shouted good-humoured insults.

When the Boy's Brigade behind their distinctive whistle and drums marched past, some children chanted *Here comes the Boy's Brigade,/All covered in marmalade,/a twopenny-halfpenny pill-box,/And half a yard of braid.* The Brigade's leader, a well-fleshed woman with a walk like a sergeant major, kept her eyes sternly in front.

Laura walked with her Sunday school class, tall and easily noticed among the tinies. Iris was the only other member of the family to join in and Laura knew where the rest of her brothers and sisters would be; they always positioned themselves near a sweet shop where they could sit on a low wall and buy oversweet yellow icecream, lollipops and cigarettes. They gave a special cheer to Granma and Grampa who ignored them.

'There she is, there's our Laura,' called the boys and the little girls demanded to be held higher so that they could wave.

As usual they drooled icecream and sugar. Lillian in a bright pink frock and a blue straw hat festooned with large pink artificial flowers made a point of calling her name in a shrill voice. 'You're right! It's our Laura, the Sunday school mannequin!' She had sensed long ago that it was quite easy to embarrass her sister.

The procession grew longer as it was joined by other churches round about, each with its own banner and band. At the end of the march the churches retired to separate fields where they held races and games for the children, each of whom ended the day with a paper bag containing a bun and an orange. For some it was one of the few treats in the whole year.

Laura had always felt self-conscious about walking because it set her apart once again from her family. She was thankful when the field was reached and she could relax. Just before she entered the gate she heard a soft whistle. Rick was standing half concealed by a tree. She stopped so abruptly that someone behind cannoned into her. She shook her head, but he refused to leave. Granma and Grampa were already in the field so Laura hurried over to him.

'What do you want?' she hissed.

'That's not a nice way to greet me after I've driven over from Hotwells just to see you. How about comin' for a spin? I've got the two-seater parked down the lane.'

'I can't possibly –'

'Who's goin' to miss you in this crowd?'

'Strange though it may seem to you, quite a lot of people. I have to organise my class for the races.'

Rick's eyebrows climbed. 'Is that so? Do you take a Sunday school class then?'

'What's wrong with that?'

'Did I say there was somethin' wrong? It's a good thing to do, but then you're a good girl, aren't you?'

Laura went hot. Was he being serious or sarcastic? Impossible to tell. He was infuriating!

'I'm fed up with you,' she said crossly.

'No, you aren't, baby. What time do the races end?'

'About three o'clock. The little ones run first.'

'See you here at three then.'

Rick sauntered off just as Laura heard her name being called by the Sunday school superintendent.

She had made up her mind that Rick would wait in vain for her, but three o'clock found her standing near the gate none the less, trying to look nonchalant. He arrived on time and her longing to be with him overcame all doubts as she hurried to the car and jumped in. The sweep of air was refreshing and she took off her hat and held it on her lap, letting the breeze blow through her hair.

'How did the races go? Did the good ones win and the bad ones lose?'

'Unfortunately, no.'

'Well, that's life. So often the baddies come out on top. Except in films, of course.'

'You seem to know a lot about it.'

'About goodies or baddies?'

Laura looked at him. He was perfectly at ease, his broad, strong hands on the steering wheel, his eyes watchful. 'How should I know?' she said.

'You don't.'

'Well, which are you?'

'A bit of each, honey. Aren't we all?'

Laura thought of the way she had been deceiving people lately. 'Yes, that's perfectly true. I try to be good, but –'

'But your naughty devils drive you down the wrong road.'

Rick had been driving for the open country and now he stopped near a field. 'Let's enjoy ourselves,' he said.

'What? Here?'

'Why not here?' Rick grinned. 'I've brought a picnic, that's all I meant.'

Laura blushed with mortification. 'Is that supposed to be funny?'

'I wouldn't know. Aunty made it up for me.'

This drew a laugh from her and she sat on a blanket, the sun warm on her face, the scent of clean earth and young vegetation sweet in her nostrils, while Rick unwrapped a white napkin containing meat-paste sandwiches. The bread and paste were home-made and delicious, the butter thick. Rick produced a bottle of wine and began to open it. The cork left the neck with an expert pop and he held out a tumbler of golden liquid to Laura. She sipped it, then drank deep. It had a fruity flavour and sent a glow of well-being through her.

Sated, she lay back, her hands behind her head. 'That was the best picnic I've ever had.'

'Out of how many?'

'Not too many.' She smiled , then grew serious. 'I remember picnics before I lived with Granma. Mum was different in those days. She used to take us down the lane to a field full of moon-daisies and cowslips. Sometimes the grass was short and there were tiny daisies and we made chains. I wish I knew –'

'What?'

'Nothing.'

'Nothin' couldn't make you sound so sad.'

'Sorry, I didn't mean to be sad, especially after the lovely picnic –'

'To hell with the picnic! What memories give you such a little girl lost look?'

She turned startled eyes on him. 'Is that how I look?'

'Yes, and sound, too. Come on, Laura, out with it.'

'It's all in the past.'

'It isn't! Whatever happened still affects you.'

'No one has ever understood that. It's just that I've never really known why no one at home wanted me.' Rick listened intently as Laura told him of her past. 'I had terrible nightmares.' Laura paused, 'I'd forgotten that! Those awful nightmares about death. And about Mum smiling at me, holding out her hand for mine, then running away just as I was about to touch her. I often woke in tears. Granma said I was a crybaby. I decided I wasn't loved by anyone because my brother died. I felt guilty, though I couldn't understand why I should.'

Laura sat up, hugging her knees, dark shadows in her mind clouding the day. 'There was something else.' She fell silent.

'Go on, baby, get it all out of your system.'

'I'll never be able to do that. This problem won't go away. It'll just get worse.' She spoke slowly, with a great effort. 'The twins – Freda and Joyce – were born only about ten months after me. For some reason Mum had a bad time with me.' She paused again, remembering. 'When I was very small I once heard her tell a neighbour that she was too weak after having me to cope with another birth so soon. She hadn't the strength to get Joyce born fast enough. She was the second to arrive and she was blue and didn't breathe for ages. Freda's all right, but Joyce is slow – very slow – her brain –'

Rick laid his hands over hers.

'Mum's fonder of the boys than the girls, but Joyce is different. Mum cares a lot for her. More than she does the rest of her daughters. Sometimes I think she loves her best of all of us.'

'You can't be blamed for the way you were born, honey.'

'No! But I think I am. And now Joyce is so pretty, the prettiest in the family. Mum is afraid for her. She's sixteen. Old enough for boys –'

Rick said seriously, 'I can understand your mother's worry. Some men are swine. Does Joyce go to work?'

'Yesterday I heard she's been promised a job as a kitchen maid in our landlord's house when the present one leaves to get married. Mum says she'll be safe there because there are only girls in the family. She'd keep Joyce home if she could, but she needs all the money she can get. My family's so big – I've ten brothers and sisters still at home – and Dad hardly ever earns anything.'

'Is he ill?'

'He was in the boot trade and lost the tops of three fingers of his right hand.'

'Lots of boot workers do. That shouldn't stop him workin'.'

'You know nothing about it!' Laura flared.

Rick caught her by the shoulders and turned her gently to face him. His kiss was soft, almost compassionate. She put her head on his shoulder.

'Rick, oh Rick, I do –'

He put his fingers over her lips. 'Don't say something you'll regret.'

She pulled herself away and sat stiffly upright. 'Oh, no, I

forgot. You've big plans, haven't you, and they don't include girls.'

'Oh, they include girls all right.'

'But not a commitment to one.'

'Sometimes you talk like a dictionary!'

She laughed, her good mood restored. 'It comes from all the reading I do. I'd better get back.'

'Will Granma be cross with you?'

'Probably not. I did my duty, as she calls it, and she'll think I'm with friends, but if I'm not home in good time for supper there'll be ructions. I'll have to tell her lies again. I seem to have done that a lot since I met you.'

Rick shrugged. 'Is it my fault your Granma's an old-fashioned dragon?'

When Laura got into work on Tuesday a grinning Arthur Gregory was waiting for her at the foot of the stairs. 'Well, if it isn't our little purse-maker.'

Laura froze, then turned to face him, her body rigid with the effort to keep from shaking. 'What are you talking about?'

'It's no good acting the innocent with me. Daphne and Thelma Charlton were at a dance on Saturday showing everyone the purses you made, and telling how some ghastly man had turned up on Saturday demanding two pounds each, when the deal had been for one pound ten.'

'They promised –' began Laura, then stopped.

'So, prisoner at the bar, you admit your crime.'

'Crime? Don't be silly. And please let me pass. You're making me late.'

He moved to one side. 'On you go. We'll continue our little discussion later. In private. It wouldn't do for my father to find out, would it? He's given you one chance and I don't think he'll put up with your disloyalty twice. But he need never know.' He took a quick step which brought him close and one hand roughly fondled her breast through her coat. 'You be nice to me and I'll be nice to you.'

Rage and disgust filled her. 'Go to hell!' she flung at him, and ran on up the stairs.

Chapter Six

There was a brief flurry of chattering as the girls compared notes about their day off.

'No more talking,' ordered Miss Pringle. 'We must work all the harder today to make up for any lost sales yesterday.'

Dolores made a face behind her back and jumped when Miss Pringle said, 'Miss Handley, polish the counter with furniture wax. It looks as if it has been neglected for days.'

'I polished it only last Friday when you were with Mr Gregory, Miss Pringle.'

Laura knew this to be untrue, but who was she to criticise? She seemed to be building an edifice of deceit around herself that could come crashing down on her at any moment. She had always hated lies. Now they were necessary if she was to keep on seeing Rick. If Granma wasn't so strict they wouldn't be needed, if Mum had taken her back home she would be as free as her sisters to follow her inclinations, if –

'Miss Blackford, you're dreaming again. We need the new hats out on display. Whitsuntide may be over, but our clients will be thinking of their spring holidays.'

'Spring holidays!' muttered Dolores. 'I'm lucky if I get a weekend in Weston-on-the-mud.'

Laura put the hats on the dolly heads which wore their finery with chilling detachment. Their cool, perfectly chiselled features with their colourless eyes looked dead. There was little difference in millinery styles from the winter. Felt was still popular. The few straws were larger, designed for beach wear.

'If I was rich I'd wear a straw cloche hat,' said Laura to Dolores.

'Then you'd be out of fashion,' snapped Miss Pringle who

had come up behind them in her soft-footed way.

'Rich women can *make* fashion,' protested Laura.

'Nonsense! They are slaves to the big designers, as are we all.'

'Well, if I was a designer –'

'Be quiet, Miss Blackford. I don't know what's got into you lately. You've always been so quiet, ever since you began working here.'

Four years ago that was, thought Laura, no, nearly five. Five years in the millinery and I'm still only second saleswoman and my wages are hardly enough to feed me. The extra money she had begun to make by working with Miss Morton was a boon. She had been able to add small touches of glamour to her outfits. She chose everything now with an eye to pleasing Rick. True, he had said nothing about them. Maybe he would only notice when something fashionable was missing. And maybe he never thinks about you at all, she admonished herself. She was scared at the way Rick constantly invaded her mind, and the way her senses craved him. And for some reason he had lately become the perfect gentleman; it was as if the passionate embraces had never happened. She tortured herself with speculation. Had she disappointed him in some way? Was he put off by her too eager response? Was he seeing another girl and making love to her?

'Miss Blackford!'

Laura suddenly realised that someone had been calling her name more than once.

Miss Pringle was standing in front of her, looking pink with irritation. 'Mr Gregory wants to see you, Miss Blackford. You'd best not keep him waiting.'

Laura was brought back abruptly to reality.

'What do you think he wants?' asked Dolores.

'It's no business of yours,' snapped Miss Pringle.

Laura climbed the stairs and knocked on Mr Gregory's door. Her employer was seated behind his desk and watched her walk across the expanse of carpet. She hoped he couldn't see how she was shaking. Her faint hope that he had sent for her for some matter to do with her work was banished quickly. 'So, Miss Blackford, you have been *deceitful again*.'

Laura felt incensed. 'Oh, no, sir, not deceitful! That's a horrible word.'

'It's the only one applicable in the circumstances. I am sure you know why you are here.'

Laura did not speak.

'You add mute insolence to your bad conduct. My son has told me that you were informed as soon as you arrived this morning that he knew you had made evening purses for two of our clients.'

Your son is an evil, lecherous, small-minded pig, thought Laura.

'He did speak to you, didn't he?'

'Yes, sir.'

'I warned you what would happen if you dealt privately with Gregory's clients again. I am very disappointed in you. I had high hopes for your future here. To discover that you have gone out of your way to undercut our prices shocks me. I cannot condone it.'

Laura realised with horror what was coming and the idea of telling Granma she had been dismissed terrified her. 'The young ladies were very insistent, sir,' she said. 'They told me they couldn't have bought their purses in Gregory's because they had spent all their pin money.'

'Nonsense! The Misses Charlton can, if they wish, obtain credit. You can't tell me you didn't know that.'

'Oh! Yes, I did know. I just didn't think. They persuaded me.'

'They could not have persuaded a *loyal* employee. There is no help for it. I cannot continue to employ a girl who is not to be trusted. Go to the cash office where you will find a week's wages. It's more than you deserve. That will be all.'

Mr Gregory bent his head over a pile of papers and began writing. Laura stood for a moment, staring at him, hating him for his smug pomposity.

Her voice was unsteady as she asked, 'Will you give me a reference, please?'

Mr Gregory looked up and goggled at her. 'A reference? After what you've done. Certainly not!'

'But, I'll never get another job without one. Surely, after I've given Gregory's five years of faithful service –'

'*We* have given *you* five years of excellent training and have been repaid by unbelievable disloyalty. Now, go! I am very busy.'

Laura turned and left. She walked slowly to the cash office where she received her money from a sympathetic-looking cashier. She fetched her hat and coat and within minutes was outside, standing on the pavement among the shoppers, with nowhere to go. She certainly couldn't endure the idea of returning home. At least, not without another job. And there was increasing unemployment. She wandered along the street, then stopped suddenly as a thought struck her. Perhaps Rick could help. He was so clever and seemed to know lots of people. Before she could change her mind she had boarded the first of the trams which would take her to Hotwells.

She sat on top alone, where a cool breeze fanned her hot face, and relaxed a little in her high isolation. Why shouldn't she make a little extra money? It would have been all right if the Charlton girls had kept their word, though she should have known better than to trust two empty-headed flappers. They had even boasted about their evening purses. Laura could just imagine them. 'Look, darlings, what we bought. Made by a little woman round the corner. No, darlings, we shan't give you her name. She's going to be exclusive to us.' The unspeakable Arthur Gregory had put two and two together and questioned the girls and they had given him the information he sought, willingly no doubt, enjoying his chagrin at knowing that one of his father's employees was undercutting him on purses that were every bit as good as the ones he sold.

It wasn't until Laura was actually standing outside the block of flats where Rick lived that she came to her senses.

What on earth was she doing here? Rick would be at work and, in any case, he was under no obligation to help her. All he seemed to want at the moment from her was friendship. She turned away and began to climb up Brandon Hill. White sheets, tinged with blue from the blue-bags that all washerwomen used, flapped gently against a background of fresh green grass and early flowers which were still damp from the morning dew. She arrived at the Cabot Tower, where she looked out over the city. So many buildings containing so many people, most of them busy doing something. There must be a place for her. The fresh air had made her hungry. She had money with her and decided to find some food and start looking for work. She never had before and was hazy about how to begin. As she descended the hill she saw a small figure she knew. Rick's aunt was obviously waiting for her. She smiled at Laura. 'Did you want Rick? He's not home yet. I saw you climbin' the hill. It's a pretty place, isn't it? Could you do with a cup of tea?'

'Oh, thanks, but – you'll be busy.'

'I'm always busy. Rick tells me to take things easy, but I can't seem to. He's a good boy. He gives me more housekeepin' than he should. Yes, Rick's a good 'un, all right.'

Laura sat in the spotless living room while Rick's aunt tended to washing which bubbled gently in a boiler in the scullery. The aroma rising from the cup of strong tea she was given mingled with the scents of soap and starch, and the faintly acrid smell of the black irons that stood on the hob.

'Every day's washin' day, here,' said Rick's aunt. 'I take it in for a few rich folk.'

'So does my mother, though she takes in a lot. It's good of you to stop work, Mrs –?'

'It's *Miss* Merriman, I'm Rick's great-aunt Mabel. One of nature's unclaimed treasures,' she said, chuckling, 'and I'm due for a cup of tea.' She pushed a plate of queen cakes towards Laura. 'Help yourself. They're good. Rick's mum makes them. She's never still, though she's not strong, you know. Not strong at all. She should give up workin', but she says she won't be a burden. I know how she feels, but our Rick gets cross with her at times. He wants her to live like a lady with her hands folded in her lap, but that's a sight he'll never see. He's a good sort, is our Rick. I'm glad he's got a nice girl like you.'

Laura drew a sharp breath and coughed on a morsel of cake.

Miss Merriman patted her back before she turned to the hob and the ironing. 'Went down the wrong way, did it?'

Laura sipped her tea and nodded, but Mabel Merriman was obviously not a woman who was easy to deceive. 'Why don't you tell me what's botherin' you, my love. You look as if you've lost a shillin' and found a farthin'.'

'I've been sacked,' burst out Laura desperately, waiting for the words of censure.

'Well, that's a pity, to be sure, but a smart girl like you will soon get another job. What awful crime did you do?'

She smiled as she spoke and her gentle reaction gave Laura strength. She explained, finishing, 'I've been such an idiot and I can't think what Granma will say.'

'I don't agree you've been an idiot. Anybody would be pleased to have extra cash comin' in. You shouldn't have told lies to get out to see Rick, but I can understand it. Our Rick's worth takin' a few risks for. Granma's very severe, isn't she?'

'Terribly. I can't tell her about Rick,' said Laura, the very idea terrifying her. 'She'll call me everything under the sun.'

'Truth's best in the end, my love. Words won't hurt you and she can't eat you.'

Miss Merriman would never understand. 'I thought I'd go looking for a job before I went home,' explained Laura. 'I really shouldn't have come here, but Rick's so clever and knows lots of people and I thought he'd be able to help me. If I could tell Granma I was suited, she might not be so upset. She apprenticed me in millinery when I was thirteen and she's always been very proud of that.'

The iron slid back and forth over a white sheet and Miss Merriman sighed. 'You know best, I dare say. I don't know anythin' about shops, but there's sometimes vacancies in the factories. Our Rick might know of one.'

'A factory!' Granma always stuck her nose in the air when she spoke of 'factory girls'.

Miss Merriman gave her a quizzical look. 'Rick's mum works in Wills Cigarette Factory. They're good to their people. They'd treat you better than that Mr Gregory did.'

'I didn't mean to sound –' Laura stopped. Rick's aunt, who seemed to be at complete peace with the world, only smiled as she rose and picked up a hot iron, protecting her hand with a wad of cotton, and placing the cooling one on the hob. She spat on the iron to test its heat and wiped away the sooty smuts with a damp cloth that sent up a small sizzling cloud of steam, then started on a pile of starched pillow-slips.

'Can I help you do that?' asked Laura.

'Bless you, no. To tell you the truth I enjoy the ironin'. I swear I can smell the grass and flowers the things were dried over and it's the end of a job well done. And goin' back to jobs I reckon your instinct brought you to the right place. Our Rick's sure to think of somethin'. We can't have you goin' on the dole.'

Laura's eyes opened wide. The dole. She'd forgotten the dole. According to Granma it was charity and only the most feckless, witless, no-gooders ever signed on the dole. 'Taking money for nothing,' she declared in her deepest, most censorious tones. Laura had not even contemplated such a fate. She had seen the lengthening queues of depressed people waiting for their meagre dole money, but they were strangers and nothing to do with her world. She'd never join them, never. She watched Miss Merriman. The pillow-slips had been taken from the line when they were exactly damp enough to yield their creases to the iron which was wielded with long, even strokes. She wished she could stay here for ever. She had never before been with anyone who combined gentle bustling activity with such an air of tranquillity.

After a while she rose to go, but Miss Merriman waved her back. 'Rick'll be in for his dinner soon, my love. You can have a bite to eat with us. I reckon he'll be able to help you.'

When Rick had brought Laura here before she had been too excited to notice much, but now she looked around curiously. There were pretty blue-flowered curtains at the window that matched the coverings on the two easy chairs. Each chair held a cushion in an embroidered cover.

'Do you like them?'

Miss Merriman's eyes seemed to miss nothing. Laura blushed a little as she remembered Granma's diction that it was as common to stare at other people's things as it was to watch them eat. But this small lady looked genuinely enquiring.

'They're pretty?' said Laura. 'Did you do them?'

'Me and Rick's mum, though she can't work like she used to. Her chest is bad; every winter she gets bronchitis and bendin' over for hours makes it worse. Do you like to sew?'

'I don't care much for embroidery, but I make my own clothes and help Granma with hers. What I love best is making hats. There's something about the way they change the shape of heads and faces. A good hat can sometimes make quite a plain woman look almost pretty.' Laura's eyes shone.

'Would you make one for me? At the proper rates, of course.'

Laura was embarrassed. 'You don't truly need a hat! You're asking to make me feel better.'

Miss Merriman laughed. 'Credit me with a bit more sense than that, my love. There's no money to spare here.'

'Then I'd like to. What kind?'

'What do you think my old face needs?' Miss Merriman held her head still for a moment.

Laura sized her up professionally. 'I think I know. Will you trust me? You don't have to buy it if it's not what you want.'

There was the sound of feet and voices on the stairs leading to the flat.

Miss Merriman put the iron on the hob. 'That's Rick's voice and he's got someone with him.'

Laura's heart beat faster. She was suddenly afraid. What a cheek she had coming here like this. Most men would be furious to find a girl had invited herself to his home. She had no more time for such distressful imaginings as the door opened and Rick was preceded into the room by a small, vivacious girl whose hair and eyes were almost as dark as his own. She was pretty, with a softly rounded figure. A frightening intensity of jealousy flared in Laura. He brought other girls here!

'Come in, Christine,' said Miss Merriman. 'Nice to see you. You'll have a bite to eat.'

Laura stood up, horribly conscious of her angular body, chagrined to find herself caught in such a situation by Rick and this girl. 'Hello, Rick, I'm just leaving.' She could not keep a tremor from her voice.

'Laura!' He looked pleased to see her. 'Sit down. You can't

leave when I've just arrived. This is Christine Somers, my cousin. Chrissie, meet Laura, a good friend.'

'A good friend', noted Laura, not 'my girl'. Cousins could fall in love and marry. The brittle edifice she had built around Rick shuddered.

Christine stuck out her hand. 'Any friend of Rick's and all that. I've heard of you. You'd better watch out. My baby cousin's a wolf.'

'Call me baby cousin again and I just might bite you,' said Rick.

'And I just might enjoy it.'

'That's enough!' ordered Miss Merriman, but with humour in her voice. 'What'll Laura think of such talk?'

Laura was bemused as she kept swinging from one assumption to another. If that wasn't flirting she'd just heard she'd like to know what was.

Miss Merriman quickly pulled the thick ironing blanket off the table and substituted a white cloth on which she laid bread, butter, cheese and pickles, and a dish of jam tarts. She kept filling their cups with her own strong brew of tea which reminded Laura of her mother's. Granma's tea was always freshly made, a delicate light brown, poured on to the milk. It would be unthinkable for her to drink stewed tea from a metal pot from the fire and add milk to taste.

Christine was giving news about some sick member of her family to Miss Merriman, and Rick turned to Laura and asked her softly, 'What brought you to us, baby? You look really blue.'

'I've been sacked.'

Rick's eyes opened wide and he grinned. 'Never! Not you!'

She felt angry. 'If you're going to mock me, I'll leave.'

'Sorry, honey, I shouldn't tease. What happened?'

Laura explained and he whistled softly. 'That pair of bitches!'

'Language!' said Miss Merriman reprovingly.

'Sorry, Aunty Mabel, but some women are enough to make a saint swear. I've seen them when the band's had a stint at some swell's ball. They've more money than they know what to do with and they've got tongues like snakes. They'd kill anyone with gossip.'

'I dare say Laura knows that by now,' said Miss Merriman drily. 'What she needs is a bit of advice about a job.'

'I'll ask around. There's sure to be somethin'.'

'Laura wants to tell her Granma tonight that she's not out of work.'

'There's a vacant place just come up in the strippin' room at Wills Tobacco Factory, Laura,' said Christine. 'My friend's left to get married. Her future husband's the old-fashioned sort who thinks a woman shouldn't work. Lucky thing! Laura could come back with me this afternoon. The place won't stay open for long. Wills are good employers.'

'That kind of work wouldn't suit Laura,' said Rick quickly.

Christine looked affronted. 'Oh, and why not? If it's good enough for me it's good enough for her. And what about your own mother? She works in Wills, too, and Aunty Mabel was a corset machinist all her workin' life.'

'I'll take the job if they offer it,' said Laura.

'I should think so!' said Christine.

'Cool down, Chrissie,' advised Rick.

He offered Laura a cigarette. She shook her head and he lit one for himself and gave one to his cousin, holding a match for her. He blew the smoke at Christine in a long blue stream which she returned with interest.

Rick grinned. 'You should know me better than to think I'd be toffee-nosed about your job, Chrissie. For a start Mum's been given light work on account of her health and if I remember rightly you soon moved to the packin' department. All I mean is that Laura's never done anythin' but sellin'. Look at her hands.'

'Huh! Mine were lilywhite once.'

'Rick, please,' begged Laura. 'I won't mind anything as long as I can go home with a job.'

He frowned. 'Why not wait until I see Mum. She might know of somethin' easier for you.'

'No, Rick. Christine, please take me with you.'

'Good for you,' said Christine, sticking out her tongue at her cousin. Rick shrugged and Christine got up, kissed her aunt, and within moments she was pushing Laura to the middle of the front seat of an open-topped car, then squashing in beside her. Rick cranked the engine which sprang into life and seated himself behind the wheel.

'Every time I see you you're drivin' somethin' different,' remarked Christine.

'You complainin'?' growled Rick.

'Don't be daft! Whose car is this?'

'Mine. Like it? It's a bull-nosed Morris.'

'It's a bit battered,' said Christine.

'Sure, it needs some work on it. But I got it for eight pounds plus my good old Douglas motor bike. I was sorry to see it go, but a car's more convenient.'

'Oh, yes,' said Christine. 'What for? Takin' girls out?'

'You bet,' said Rick. 'My lady friends will be much more comfortable.'

'And there's a nice lot of room in the back for a kiss and a cuddle,' said Christine cheekily.

Rick only grinned and Laura's heart sank. 'Lady friends'. In the plural. And Rick planned to enjoy himself in the back of the car. He swerved to avoid a dog, cursing under his breath, and Laura was squeezed against him for a moment. Even as she welcomed this involuntary intimacy she couldn't bear it when she didn't know from one day to the next just how many girls Rick was dating. Her jealousy ran through her like a sharp sword thrust.

'One day I'll have a Rolls Royce,' Rick said calmly.

'That'll be the day,' mocked Christine.

Chapter Seven

Laura wondered how on earth she would stick the new job. The other girls – they were all 'girls', though many were quite old – sat in rows facing each other across a table. They were not unfriendly towards Laura; in fact, she received encouraging smiles, but they talked in the verbal shorthand of those who have been companions for a long time so that she was among them, but not part of them. The thought of spending months, even years, just sitting doing the same thing over and over appalled her. She had never before realised how she had enjoyed working where she was on her feet and able to move about freely. A woman next to Laura was quite elderly and she sang almost inaudibly as her quick, stained fingers stripped the stem from the tobacco leaves. She told Laura she had worked in Wills for twenty years.

As well as having to cope with boredom Laura felt increasingly nauseated by the heavy, clinging smell of the raw tobacco leaves. There was a never-ending supply and already her back ached and her hands were sore.

She realised now that in finding a place for her in Gregory's millinery department Granma had been far kinder than she had ever appreciated.

The scene with Granma when she had broken the news that she had been dismissed from Gregory's and would be starting work the following Monday in Wills Tobacco Factory was one that kept pushing itself to the front of her mind.

Both Granma and Grampa had been so astonished by Laura's flat statement of what had happened that for a moment even Granma had been rendered speechless.

'I'm sorry, Granma,' Laura had said, adding quickly, 'but

there's one good thing, I shall get more money.'

'Money! Is that all you can think of?' Granma finally burst out. 'It was greed that set you on this downward path. And the extra money you earn in the *factory* will just about pay for your tram rides, unless you think of walking all the way to Bedminster and back each day.'

Grampa was silent. In fact, he could not have got a word in edgeways had he wished to do so.

'Ungrateful, deceitful, *wicked* girl,' Granma said, her face flushed with anger, her tones bitter. 'Fancy going behind Mr Gregory's back to steal his customers. Yes, miss, *steal*. It's your bad blood. I should have known that nothing good could come from *that woman*.'

'Don't call Mum that woman,' cried Laura, goaded to retaliation.

'I shall call her what I choose. She set out to trick my son into marriage and she succeeded only too well. I suppose no one's ever told you –'

Grampa put out his hands in protest.

'Be quiet, Wilfrid!' Granma was more angry than Laura had ever seen her, but to her amazement Grampa would not give in.

'No, Amy, I won't be quiet. Some things are best left unsaid. The girl's misbehaved and had her punishment and she'll soon realise what a fool she's been.'

Granma went red, her mouth opened and closed and she breathed hard through her nostrils. Then she said dogmatically, 'Your father married far beneath him. I've been strict with you because you must be protected from the evil you inherited. You've seen how that woman – Phyllis – keeps house. She's a slut. She spends good money on going to picture houses to stare at rubbish. She drinks and smokes, she uses bad language, and only sees the inside of a chapel when she's got another baby she wants christened – and she's got far too many of those.'

Laura, as shocked as she was by the vindictive outburst, still sensed that Granma had not said all she had intended. She reached behind her for a chair. As she sank into it Grampa could not resist giving her shoulder a squeeze.

'You're not sympathising with her, are you?' demanded Granma.

'Enough, Amy. Enough.'

Laura's head was spinning. She ached to defend her mother who worked unremittingly and uncomplainingly and completely accepted her husband's inflated view of himself. Nothing was too good for him. He lived a life of ease, going to the pub with Mum on Friday and Saturday nights, smoking his good tobacco, eating the food supplied by Mum and the rest of the family. He seemed to dwell on a plain removed from ordinary living, but Laura loved him dearly. She hated being in the position where to defend one parent she must denigrate the other. Why should she have been singled out to be the rope in a tug-of-war between warring family members? Of course her parents had flaws. Who didn't? But there was deep, abiding love in that disordered home. Her mother shrieked and swore and slapped indiscriminately at times, but she never stopped loving. So why had she rejected her? Laura's sorrow filled her.

'Wake up, Miss Blackford. It's time for dinner.'

Laura got up automatically and followed the others to the canteen where she ate the sandwiches that Granma cut for her. 'Never say that I don't do my duty by you,' she had said gratingly.

Of course it had been impossible to hide the truth from her family. She had to set off much earlier now to reach work on time. She missed the comradeship, she missed Iris and her gentle reports of what went on at home and last Sunday Lillian's tormenting tongue, fuelled by such an amazing piece of news, had become so unkind that even Dad had noticed and had told her to shut up. Sheer surprise kept Lillian quiet. When Dad intervened in family life it was as if a god had condescended to mortals. But later, in the front room, away from his restraining influence, Lillian had begun another mocking tirade. This time she was halted by Mum. 'Shut your bloody mouth, our Lillian. Dad's fed up with the way you carry on at Laura.'

It was the first time in her life that Laura had been defended by her mother and although it was on Dad's behalf she had felt warmed and comforted.

101

Miss Morton had been kind. 'I suppose it was wrong,' she said reluctantly, 'but it wasn't so terrible. Gregory's can easily afford to lose a couple of small sales.'

'If I had let that worm, Arthur Gregory, paw me about he wouldn't have told his father about me. I'd like to get even with him.'

'Don't get bitter, my love. It'll do you harm and it won't matter a jot to Arthur Gregory.'

'It'd do me a lot of good to see him squirm. It's awful at home now. Granma never misses a chance to get in a dig. She moves away from me because she says I stink of tobacco, and I do. It's in my hair and clothes. I sometimes think it's in my skin. And look at my hands.' Laura spread them. 'I have to use pumice stone to get the tobacco stains out. Twice Granma's sent me away from the table like a child to wash my hands again. They're terribly sore and rough.'

Miss Morton had produced a soothing cream. 'I'm afraid it might not be enough for your poor hands. You need smooth skin to make hats.'

Two weeks passed like a month and she had not seen Rick since he had driven her and Christine to the factory. He had left his job in the office and no one seemed to know where he was. She pushed away the thoughts that made her ache with the torments of jealousy. Her love for him was bewilderingly mingled with anger at the casual way he picked her up and dropped her as it suited him. Laura felt desperate. Life had become nightmarish. A dozen times she had reminded herself that Rick's aunt had invited her to call and had walked to the tram stop that would begin a journey to Hotwells, but she had lost her nerve. She asked Christine about him, trying to sound nonchalant.

Christine shrugged. 'Who knows? He could be anywhere. Rick's goin' to succeed and the only one he'll stop and think about is his mother. And Aunty Mabel, perhaps, though she's never asked anyone for help. There've been a few girls who've wanted our Rick, but the minute they start gettin' wedding bells in their heads he drops them. I shouldn't pin any hopes on him, if I were you.'

'Oh, no, it's nothing like that,' Laura assured her. 'I just wondered.'

'That's all right then. You should look about you for a good man. I'm goin' to. I want to get married and when I do I'm givin' up work. I can't wait for a life of leisure. My mother's lived like a lady for years.'

Laura thought of Mum and her frequent pregnancies, of her endless toil for small reward. Christine, she had learned, was an only child.

When the factory girls discovered that Laura could make hats and renovate old ones they were delighted. The extra money from these small commissions was not great, but it was welcome. Laura had looked forward to the creative activity which might lessen the pain of wanting Rick, and of her job, but after her roughened fingers had pulled snags in a piece of silk georgette and a length of satin she was obliged to accept the fact that she would have to stick to steaming the felts. Adding the final touches which made each piece of millinery a unique work of art was the part that Laura loved best and the frustration was another blow.

Miss Morton was disappointed, too. 'I've never seen anyone turn an ordinary hat into something really special the way you can, Laura. You've got a gift. It's such a shame you can't use it.'

On the second Saturday of her new job Laura left at lunchtime to find Rick outside in his car.

'Hi, baby. Did you miss me?'

Laura stood still. She wanted to tell him to go to hell, but her tongue wouldn't form the words. She felt boneless with joy and climbed into the car. The workers pouring out of the factory stared at her curiously, and many waved and greeted Rick.

Christine appeared. 'So you decided to come back, did you? Poor Laura's been miserable.'

Laura flushed. 'I have not,' she said firmly. 'Rick can come and go as he pleases. I'm not his keeper.'

'That's the stuff, baby.' Rick lit a cigarette 'Want a lift, our Christine?'

'Take me to the Centre. I'm meetin' someone there.'

'A chap? Yes, it must be. You've got your good coat on and a new hat.'

Christine touched the pink rose on her hat which exactly matched her complexion. 'Laura made it. It's nice, isn't it?'

'I had help,' said Laura. Her tone was sharp and Rick glanced at her, but made no comment.

They dropped Christine in the busy Tramway Centre and Rick parked near the docks.

'How's the job goin', baby?'

'I hate it,' burst out Laura. 'And before you say anything it's not because I'm in a factory, though I can't bear sitting all day. It's this.'

There was a sob in her voice as she held out her hands. 'I can't sew the fine materials any more and I miss it more than I could have believed. And, of course, Granma's even more irritable because she's having to make our summer dresses without me. I wish I could get a different job.'

Rick took her hands in his and unexpectedly lifted them to his lips. Joy spread through her. He asked, 'Did you miss me?'

His voice was soft and cajoling and she responded. 'Yes, I did. I missed you a lot.' And then wondered if she had said too much. Would he hear wedding bells? She couldn't deny to herself that they were in her head. She was a fool to fall headlong for a man who made it obvious that he was not ready to be tied down and wasn't even attracted to her. She pulled her hands away and began talking fast about hats.

Rick broke in impatiently. 'Is Granma expectin' you? What a dumb question! Of course she is. Was she cross about you gettin' the sack?'

'Cross? That's an understatement. She was livid and still is. No one else I know can keep up a grudge longer than Granma.'

'By all accounts she's kept one against your mother for more than twenty years.'

'Yes! She hates her.' Laura stopped abruptly. 'How do you know that?'

'Gossip gets around,' said Rick nonchalantly, steering the car out into the traffic.

'About my mother!'

'About everyone. Stop frettin'. Will you come to a theatre with me tonight?'

'A theatre?'

'Yes, you know, actors, music, singin'. Haven't you ever been to one?'

'Not for a long time.' Laura paused. 'When I was very small, before I lived with Granma, Mum and Dad took us to the pantomime at the King's every Christmas. They still take my brothers and sisters. The younger ones, anyway. I can remember I loved it.'

'Didn't Granma take you?'

'No! She says that theatres and cinemas are corrupting influences.'

Rick laughed and the sound startled Laura who could never find anything amusing about Granma's attitude to a world she considered basically wicked.

'Will you ask her if you can go?'

'No,' said Laura firmly. 'I shall tell her. Or maybe I won't,' she added reflectively. 'Granma hardly speaks to me now. She knows I spend a lot of time with Miss Morton and she'll just assume I'm going there.'

Rick raised a hand in mock astonishment. 'What if she doesn't? What if she questions you?'

'I'll think of something and I shall come out anyway.'

'Attagirl!'

'You use some amazing expressions, Rick.'

'I do, don't I?' His face split in a grin. 'I've been in London. I always meet American musicians there. They're a long way ahead of us in the jazz field, and their language is full of interestin' words.' He slowed as a horse and coal cart trundled across the road, then put his foot down again. 'The time will come when there won't be any horses on the streets,' he said.

'That's silly,' said Laura. 'Horses are cheaper than motor vehicles.'

Rick shrugged. Laura sometimes felt as if she were pitting herself against an illusion. Rick scarcely ever bothered to argue, leaving her off balance. Sometimes she was afraid that all he would ever care for would be cars and music.

'Tell me what jazz is, Rick.'

'It's a great sound – different from anythin' else. It began with the black people in America when they jazzed up everything, even hymns. Then the Dixieland Jazz Band made a record. I've got a copy I bought from a friend. It's pretty scratchy, but it's swell.'

Rick's voice was semi-worshipping, his mind and his heart given over entirely to his music. He wasn't talking about another girl and it was absurd of Laura to feel so envious.

'We're still learnin' from the early jazzmen. I hardly went to bed at all in London.' Rick was only partly informing her, mostly he was thinking aloud. 'After the clubs and dance halls and hotel ballrooms close for the night lots of the musicians get together anywhere they can – a cellar usually – and play all the things they love best. It's marvellous. That happens in Bristol a bit, too, but I'm goin' to try to make it big.'

'You won't live in London?' Laura dreaded the answer.

'Not while Mum needs me.'

She was both relieved and miserable. She would give anything to hear him say such words about her. She knew she should stop seeing him; what had begun as pleasure was disintegrating into splinters of pain. Yet when he dropped her at home she agreed to meet him in a couple of hours.

Granma was looking particularly grim. 'My back aches with sitting at that sewing machine. If I'd known you were going to treat me with such ingratitude –'

She left the sentence unfinished, but Laura ended it mentally – I'd never have taken on the job of bringing you up.

'I'm sorry, Granma,' was her automatic response.

'You don't sound it!'

'I don't know what else to say,' burst out Laura. 'Whatever I say or do is wrong now.'

'Don't raise your voice to me, miss. Everything is the result of your deceitful behaviour. You see what happens when you begin to tell lies? The ripples spread and heaven only knows where they'll end up.'

'I'll start looking round for another position where I won't spoil my hands. Perhaps one of the corset factories –'

'You'll do no such thing! Going from job to job is something I don't hold with. Your Grampa started in the boot trade with his firm when he was fourteen and look at him now. A foreman – respected and looked up to.'

'I've always liked what I do,' said Grampa. 'Would it matter if Laura did try to find other work? She's got such pretty hands. It's a shame to spoil them.'

'I'm surprised at you! After getting the sack with no references, she's lucky she's got anything.'

Grampa subsided. 'You're right there. We've not taken anyone on for weeks, in fact, the company is getting rid of workers. They say the demand for boots and shoes is falling, with so many out of work.'

'Well, you're one they'll hang on to,' said Granma complacently, as she put a plate of beef stew in front of him. 'Get that down you. And here's yours, Laura. I swear you're thinner than ever. What with your short hair as well you look like a plucked chicken and you smell like a tobacco pouch.'

Laura ate steadily. 'I'll be going round to Miss Morton's later,' she said.

'What good are you there?' demanded Granma. 'If you can't sew our clothes, how can you do the hats?'

'I just steam the shapes. It saves time for Miss Morton.'

'Well, I suppose that's something,' said Granma grudgingly. 'She's a good chapel woman. You can't come to mischief there.'

Laura would have liked to bathe, but the noise of the geyser would have brought Granma upstairs in a fury at such a waste of gas. One bath a week was all any Christian needed, she insisted. Laura washed her body in cold water, scrubbing furiously at herself. She could smell tobacco in her hair, but there was no way she could wash it and sit for ages by the kitchen fire drying it. And, in any case, Granma never let anyone out with newly washed hair. 'All the pores are open and you'll catch your death.' She sprinkled eau de Cologne on her hairbrush and brushed her hair vigorously. She wondered what they were going to see. Maybe a repertory play in the Little Theatre, or a west end touring play at the King's or perhaps famous stars at the Hippodrome. She had seen the theatre advertisements in Grampa's newspapers.

Rick was waiting for her at the end of the street and greeted her with a smile. 'Good girl. You're on time. That's something too few women manage.'

'How many have you taken out?' she blurted out, surprising herself.

Rick touched the side of his nose. 'Now that's not a question I expect to be asked, baby. Have I poked my nose into your private affairs?'

'If you mean men I've never had any!'

'I believe you,' said Rick.

'Why? What is there about me that – that –'

She stumbled to a halt and Rick said, 'Stop worryin', kid. I can tell you're a good girl. I like you that way.'

Laura relaxed into her seat. Granma said that men picked their wives from good girls, not trusting the flirtatious kind. Wives! The word had slid smoothly into her mind. She stole a surreptitious glance at Rick. To her disappointment he drove to the Empire, off Old Market, famous for twice-nightly spectaculars.

Rick held her elbow as he piloted her into the theatre. He knew everyone: the man in the box office, the girls showing people to their seats, the manager, Colonel Harry Day who greeted him expansively.

'We've got some good stuff on tonight, Rick, dear boy. *Spangles*. How's that for a name? Good, eh? And your little girl is in the first house.'

'Fine,' said Rick. As he led Laura into a seat in the stalls she was trembling. 'Your little girl,' the manager had said. What little girl? Surely Rick hadn't brought her here to watch one of his girlfriends perform? He was standing, answering greetings from several quarters. Mostly male; in fact the audience contained a lot more men than women.

The orchestra filed in and struck up with melodies from the London hit, *Boodles* in a deafening wave of sound, defeating all speech within a radius of ten yards, then the music changed and a line of scantily dressed girls paraded along the 'joy plank', the walk which ran round the edge of the orchestra pit. They were greeted by a cacophony of whistles and shouts of appreciation.

'The show's about due to go on the road,' said Rick in her

ear. 'Lovely girls, aren't they? The colonel has a good eye for pickin' them and his wife vets them, too.'

'His wife?' Laura was startled. The idea of a man's wife collaborating in choosing twenty or so chorus girls was a new concept to her.

'Kitty Colyer,' explained Rick. 'She sometimes plays the lead in the revues.'

Laura subsided. She knew what Granma's word would be for every aspect of this red-plush theatre and its gaudy show, but she found she was enjoying herself and certainly Rick was. She would worry about his little girl later.

The tympanist was kept busy with clashing cymbals and drum rolls accompanying jokes, some of which Laura only dimly understood, and some were so crude she was thankful for the dark which hid her blushes.

Rick, his eyes vivid with mirth, glanced down at her after an especially outrageous comedian had finished his act and was bowing to hearty applause and shrill whistles. Rick put his mouth close to her ear, 'Do you like the show, honey?'

'Most of it,' said Laura, hearing with annoyance the tone of slight distaste that tinged her voice. Would Granma's influence never depart?

Rick laughed loudly at her response. 'There's nothin' bad about it, Laura. It's just a bit naughty. Good old bawdy comedy has been on the stage for centuries.'

'Rick what did the manager mean when he said your little –?'

The man on tympany went suddenly berserk, banging and clanging everything in sight as the spotlight fell on a woman who, although no longer young, strolled on to the stage in stockings, and suspenders and a costume that barely covered her bulbous breasts. She launched into an incredibly loud rendering of *Ain't We Got Fun*, and followed it with Sophie Tucker numbers, not neglecting a single place where an innuendo could be stressed, or a leering wink could be inserted. The audience joined in the choruses with verve. The sheer ebullience of the act got to Laura and she wished she knew the words, and even found that she clapped as enthusiastically as the others.

Rick grinned. 'I knew this would grow on you, baby. You're no prude. You've shown me that.'

His sudden, oblique reference to her early display of passion for him shocked her.

During the interval they went out for refreshments. Laura watched Rick edge his way to the bar, the inevitable cigarette hanging from his lips, apparently able to command the barman's attention where others failed. Why was that? And why did the eyes of women follow him? She knew it was because he radiated vitality; wherever he went the atmosphere tensed and sang like a stringed instrument. As she saw the number of women who greeted him joyfully she wished disconsolately that she didn't love him so much. It was clear he would never get the chance to be faithful. He returned with a double whisky for himself and a glass of orange juice for her.

'You're sure you wouldn't like a gin to go with it, honey?' he asked, laughing.

She shook her head. The bar was crammed to capacity by people drinking as hard as possible before the bell rang for the second half.

Rick raised his glass to a large woman, long past youth, with very yellow hair, in a low-cut red satin gown, glittering with sequins. 'She did monologues,' he said. 'She used to be good, but drink got the better of her and she can't often get work. No one knows if she'll turn up on time, or at all. Poor old cow. Ah! wait here! I want a word with someone. I've got an interestin' proposition for him.'

Laura was left alone with her juice and a cigarette, as Rick talked volubly to a friend, his hands moving expressively.

As they shuffled back with the crowd to the auditorium he said, 'Sorry I left you, Laura, I have to take every chance to do business. If Jenny is good tonight she'll get other engagements.'

'Jenny?'

'Oh, yes! Jenny Starr – I haven't told you. I brought her back from London. She'd been out of work for ages and had run out of money. Show business is tough.'

'You brought her back with you?'

'Sure. Hush now, the second half's beginnin'. She's on first.'

Laura sat fuming as the curtains swished back to reveal a slender girl with a shining blond helmet of hair, wearing a sparkly blue dress that was at least two inches above her knees. There was a roar of appreciation when it was realised that large expanses of skin could be seen beneath the flimsy material. So this was Jenny! Laura felt a thrill of envy at her petite beauty, then the band struck up and Jenny rendered a song medley: *I'm Sitting on Top of the World*; *Sleepy Time Gal*; *Lady be good*; and ending with *Moonlight and Roses*. She had a pretty voice, but it was the suggestive movements of her body that brought the applause and whistles. She seemed to keep her eyes fixed on Rick though it was unlikely that she could see him through the footlights. As she curtsied she blew kisses in his direction. He must have told her where he was sitting.

'They like her,' said Rick with satisfaction. 'Do you want to stay and watch the rest, or come and meet Jenny?'

Laura stood up and followed him along the row, her lips so stiff with anger and worry she could barely frame apologies as she stepped on toes and impeded the vision of howling customers. 'If the sketch, *A Night in Paris*, is anything like *One Hour at Midnight*,' she muttered to Rick as they made their way backstage, 'I certainly don't want to stay!'

Rick grinned. 'That stuff is mild.'

'Is Starr her real name?'

Rick raised his brows. 'Haven't any idea. Does it matter?'

He tapped on a door and Jenny yelled at them to come in. She had taken off the dress and was wearing a negligée. Close up she looked prettier even than on stage.

'That was great, honey, wasn't it, Laura?'

'Most enjoyable,' Laura said, trying not to sound censorious.

Jenny opened her green eyes wide. 'Didn't you like it, Miss – ?'

'Blackford,' supplied Laura.

'She's Laura,' said Rick, his voice suddenly grown cool.

Jenny began to cream the thick stage make-up from her face. 'Laura's got every right not to like my act, Rick. It's a bit naughty. Anyone can see she's a *nice* girl.'

111

Before Rick could speak Laura said, 'I'm sorry, Jenny. You sang well, and your words were really easy to hear. I can't stand singers who swallow their words.'

Jenny's eyes met hers in the mirror and a message passed between them, compounded of suspicion, speculation and hostility. It lasted for a fraction of a second, but it was the kind of look that was manifest to any woman. Each knew that the other wanted Rick and Laura feared that Jenny had far more chance than she of winning him.

There was a man waiting when they returned to the foyer whom Rick introduced as Frank Glass. The size of his stomach reminded Laura of Rick's claim that the fattest cats were the men in the middle, taking money from everyone. Frank led the way to the Woolpack Inn where he ordered drinks all round, ignoring Laura's assertion that she didn't want a double gin and lime. The pub walls were covered with photographs of performers and several actors were there in person, still in stage make-up ready for the second house, downing beers.

'You're doin' well,' said Rick to Frank, his eyes on a gold watch and several finger rings, two of which held precious stones.

Frank asked sardonically, 'How can you tell?'

'I've got my ways,' said Rick, grinning. 'One of these days I'll be up there with you.'

'Yeah? I won't hold my breath.' But he laughed as he spoke.

Jenny wasn't appearing again that night and Frank insisted that they all go to a restaurant he knew. It was small, quiet, with a three-piece band playing softly. Laura was nervous and drank a glass of sherry too quickly, which mingled with the gin and relaxed her almost too much.

The banter between the men continued. 'One day I'll have a bigger car than you,' said Rick.

'And a belly as big as a pregnant cow, like mine, no doubt.'

Jenny shrieked with mirth. Laura smiled.

'Sorry, Laura,' said Frank. 'You're probably not used to that kind of talk.'

'Please –' stammered Laura. 'It's all right. I mean –'

Frank laid a pudgy hand on her arm. 'Forget it, kid. When

you've been around with this ladykiller much longer you'll never notice the odd indelicate word.'

Their meal included a rich, clear soup, followed by beef and vegetables. On the rare occasions Laura had eaten out it had been in a small café with waitresses; here the food was brought by soft-footed waiters who made her nervous. She didn't eat much, but Jenny tucked in and and joined in the conversation between the men who were discussing her fate. Mr Glass definitely wanted her for a cabaret act in some club or other and it was agreed that a contract would be signed between her and Rick, acting as her agent, and Frank. There were smiles and toasts all round.

A waiter brought a mousse. Laura enjoyed the airy texture and the dark chocolate taste; it was so different from blancmange.

Frank tucked into his gargantuan portion, his appetite apparently undented by the previous courses. 'Good food here, eh, Rick?' he said.

'Sure is. And no stuffy rules about evenin' dress.'

Laura asked, 'Is that unusual?'

Jenny shrieked with mirth. 'Haven't you been anywhere? Some places won't let you past the front door unless you're in full evening dress.' She drank deeply of her wine and held out her glass for more. She winked. 'But there's some where the men open their shirts to the waist.'

'Not in restaurants,' said Rick.

Frank helped himself to cheese and biscuits. He laughed. 'No, she means musicians when they play after the shows in the cellars. They get so hot, see, Laura. The sweat rolls down them, but those boys play for hours and hours after they've packed up their regular jobs. They just love making music.'

'So do I,' claimed Jenny, batting her long eyelashes at Frank and Rick in turn. 'I'm part of it all, aren't I?'

'Sure are, kid,' agreed Rick.

They drank coffee. Rick smoked one of Frank's big cigars and Jenny a cigarette in a tortoiseshell holder that was all of eight inches long. She was wearing a georgette dress the colour of her green eyes. It was low in the back and dipped to her breasts in front. Long shiny green earrings flickered every time she moved her head and her hair was adorned by a band of silver lamé in which a brooch glittered. Laura could not have changed without a lot of questions from Granma and she was in a dark-brown day dress. She vowed she would make herself a frivolous dress and hide it, perhaps at Miss Morton's. It would be fashionable and pretty, though not, she assured herself, one that showed so much white skin and leg as Jenny's. She had actually caught sight of Jenny's suspenders as she seated herself, and Frank Glass had let out a small gasp of pleasure.

'What's the time?' she asked.

Rick glanced at his watch and rose. 'Nearly ten. I'll leave you in Frank's capable hands, Jenny. Cinderella has to be in by ten.'

Jenny's shrill laugh rang out, joined by a boom of mirth from Frank. 'I'll look after Jenny,' he said thickly. 'She'll be all right with me.'

Outside, Laura demanded, 'Did you have to mock me in front of them?'

'I thought it was better to make a joke of it,' said Rick. He hailed a taxi in a casual manner that impressed Laura and had it return them to his car.

On the drive to Kingswood Rick said, 'I've no need to ask what you thought of Jenny. It was written all over you. I suppose you go by Granma's definition.'

'What do you mean?'

'Jenny's common in your eyes.'

'That's Granma's expression, not mine!'

'Well why were you lookin' so snooty?'

'I wasn't! I certainly didn't mean to.'

'You've got a face that shows what you're thinkin'.' Rick handed her a pack of cigarettes. 'Light one for me, and have one yourself.'

She stuck the cigarette between his lips, but didn't smoke herself.

'What's wrong now? You've only smoked once all evening. I thought you enjoyed it.'

'I do, but a couple of times lately Granma's sniffed at me when I've come in.'

'You smell of tobacco anyway from workin' at Wills.'

'Well thank *you*. Thank you *very* much!'

'My God, Laura, what a mood you're in. I expected you to enjoy yourself.'

'Enjoy knowing that you brought Jenny back to Bristol. I suppose you were with her all those days in London. And here was I, wondering all the time what had happened to you.' Laura stopped, appalled by the tearful, nagging tone of her voice.

'You're a suspicious little devil! And what right have you got to criticise me? I'll stay with a hundred girls if I want.'

'So you did live with her in London!' Tears of irrepressible fury stung Laura's eyes. 'Men like you make me ill! You think you can get any girl you look at.'

'No, I don't! Though I manage quite well, as you should know.'

Laura felt as if she had been struck. She sank back into her seat and was silent with shock and misery.

'That's much better,' growled Rick.

She stared at him from beneath her lashes. He looked relaxed in his usual haze of smoke. Trying to pin him down was like trying to catch a darting eel with your hands. She would never understand him. Had she fallen for a man with no heart? There seemed no future for her where Rick was concerned and if he never loved her she felt her heart would break.

Broken heart, or not, the world still demanded tobacco in increasingly large quantities and Laura had to return to the stripping room, her back aching from the hours of sitting, her hands red and sore. The other girls were friendly since she had refurbished many of their hats. At least, she had carried them to Miss Morton, suggested what should be done, and had brought them back. Laura refused to take any of the money earned. She pointed out that with the state her hands were in she was now only capable of being a messenger girl.

A week had passed since her visit to the theatre. She felt like a condemned prisoner, compelled to sit forever tearing at raw tobacco, the smell of it permeating her body. She must find something better to do, whatever Granma said. And she must find the courage to tell Granma that she was old enough to choose her friends, male as well as female.

But decision-making was taken from her. She arrived home and Grampa opened the door, looking pale. When she tried to speak, he motioned her to silence.

He whispered, 'Your Granma's been in your room today. She found –' He stopped as Granma appeared.

'Are you whispering, Wilfrid? I'll not have it! I intend to speak to the brazen hussy myself.'

In the living room the table was set for tea, the furniture shone, the fire blazed bright, but the atmosphere was thick with suspicion and anger.

Laura stood and waited.

Granma stared at her, eyes dilated with rage. She put her hand in her apron pocket and pulled out a half pack of cigarettes. 'You've been smoking,' she accused. 'I suspected it, so I went through your things.'

'That was a sneaky thing to do!'

Granma's eyes darted to the cane, still hanging by the fireplace.

Laura said flatly, 'You won't beat me. I'm too old for that. And, yes, I have smoked a few times. Everyone does it. But I never have in the house because I know you don't like it.'

Granma breathed heavily. 'Don't like it? I forbid it! It's a filthy habit *and* takes hard earned wages.'

Laura sighed. 'Fivepence for ten cigarettes of that size.'

'And what about the people who smoke away a whole fivepence a day? Or more, for all I know. No wonder some women can't manage.'

Laura gazed at her steadily and waited for what she knew would come next.

'Your mother smokes, and your sisters, and your brothers. All of them buying cigarettes. And the little ones' clothes are a disgrace. Last time your father visited Joyce pushed them here in that dreadful old pram Phyllis has had since her first. They waited outside and I was ashamed for the neighbours to see them at my door.'

'You could have asked them in!'

'I most certainly could not. Oh, I used to have your parents to tea sometimes, but now there are too many children and they're not disciplined properly. I'll never forget the day when Harold broke a glass vase I was given as a wedding present. And things are worse now. Their clothes never fit, their shoes are always scuffed, the other day I felt that what they needed was a good wash – and their noses were running.'

'Mum hasn't been feeling well lately –'

'Oh! What is it? Another baby?'

'No,' said Laura coldly, 'not another baby. I don't know what's wrong. Overwork, I should guess.'

'If she didn't have so many children –'

'It takes two to make a baby.' Laura's voice was sharp with anger.

'What!' The red ran up under Granma's skin. 'Never did I think to hear filth in my own house and from a girl I've done my level best to bring up to be respectable. I suppose that's what your mother says.'

'Mum wouldn't dream of discussing such a thing with me.'

'You amaze me!'

'Mum does her best,' said Laura, backtracking from a line of conversation which could lead nowhere.

'Well, it isn't good enough. And whatever she does she can't stop the consequences of your bad blood.'

'Bad blood? Smoking a few cigarettes?'

'No!' said Granma almost triumphantly, as if she were gloating at having her worst fears realised. 'I found these several days ago and put them back until I'd finished my enquiries.' She paused dramatically. 'Yes, my girl. I've found out all about you. You wicked creature. You've been deceiving us, your Grampa and me, who've brought you up as if you were our own. You've been lying and conniving and all to see that man, Rick Merriman. If you had to lower yourself to sneak out and meet a man you might at least have picked somebody decent.'

Laura sat down, shocked.

'Stand up!' ordered Granma.

'Leave her be,' said Grampa. 'She looks done in.'

'I'll give her done in!' Granma's bosom beneath her grey

117

dress heaved. 'And don't try to side with her. You're as shocked as I am!'

Grampa subsided.

'If you had allowed me proper freedom,' pointed out Laura, 'I wouldn't have had to deceive you, Granma. I hated doing it, but Rick – he means a lot to me.'

'Don't tell me you care for him! No decent girl would give him the time of day.'

Laura flared, 'Well, I'm a decent girl and I – like him a lot.'

'Perhaps you'll change your mind when you hear about his mother!'

'I've met his mother. She's nice, but not very strong. And Rick looks after her as best he can.'

'You've met her? Nice, is she? Well, you could hardly expect him to tell you the truth. She's not nice. She's never been married! And your boy friend is illegitimate! Now will you listen to me?'

'Rick is illegitimate?' Laura's voice came out in a whisper.

Granma seated herself. 'You're shocked. You deserve to be. If you'd asked my advice you would never have –'

'Oh, poor Mrs Merriman. Poor Rick.' Sorrow for them both filled Laura.

Granma gasped. 'Are you sympathising with them? I can't believe it. And it's *Miss* Merriman.'

'What happened is not Rick's fault. He must know what he is and yet he loves his mother. And what about her? What she must have suffered! And Rick!' Laura thought of his driving ambition; he was determined to be a success. To show the world! Was this why?

'Are you listening to me, Laura Blackford?'

Laura turned to Granma who said, 'Promise me not to meet this man again.'

'I can't!'

'What!'

'I can't, and I won't! He's a friend and I'm old enough to choose my friends.'

'And old enough to lie and cheat. And you've dragged Miss Morton into this. She was trustworthy until she met you!

118

You're an evil influence, just like your mother.'

'Will you stop insulting Mum!' Laura cried. 'What's she ever done to you to make you hate her?'

'I'll tell you!'

There was a sharp exclamation from Grampa.

Granma waved him to silence. Her eyes were filled with a curious excitement.

'Your father was a God-fearing man until he met your mother. I warned him against her, but he wouldn't listen. The next thing we knew she was in trouble and you know what I mean. Your father needn't have married her. I told him at the time she'd probably had other men –'

Laura sprang to her feet, shaking all over. 'You've got an evil mind!' she shouted. 'You don't know any such thing! Mum loves Dad dearly, and if he wanted to marry her I don't see that it was your right to try to stop him. Any more than it's your right to stop me from going out with the man I choose.'

'Don't shout at me, miss! And I don't know if your father actually wanted to marry your mother. It's my belief we brought him up too well. He's a gentleman – always was, and married her out of honour. Marrying a woman out of honour who'd got none at all herself. My William –' Granma was stopped by a sob.

Laura stretched out a hand. It was the first sign of emotion she had ever detected in Granma, it was like seeing a stone shed a tear, and she found herself looking for an instant through her eyes and felt sorry for her. Her sorrow was soon dissipated.

'Are you thinking of getting married?' demanded Granma. 'Don't tell me you've let Rick Merriman mess about with you! Though it wouldn't surprise me with a mother like you've got.'

Laura's anger grew cold and quiet. 'I am not planning to marry. Not yet.'

Granma said, 'Well, don't expect us to let you wed from this house if you choose to marry a bastard. And if you go on seeing him you'd best find somewhere else to live.'

'Amy! You couldn't turn our Laura out!'

'I don't want to, but it's up to her. We put up with the disgrace of her having the sack from Gregory's, though how I held my head up in chapel I don't know, but I'm not having her here unless she promises never to see this man again.'

Laura said in low tones, 'I can never promise that.'

'Has he asked you to wed him?' Grampa's voice was gentle.

'No,' Laura was forced to admit, 'but he likes me – he likes me a lot, and I –'

'Yes, you?' asked Granma harshly.

'I like him.'

'You *like* him. Surely you're not prepared to leave a good home because you *like* a man. Laura,' Granma's tone became wheedling, 'We've always done our best for you. I've looked forward to your wedding. I'd got it planned. A white wedding in Zion Chapel, a good meat tea after, a honeymoon by the sea in Weston, or maybe even further away, Blue Anchor, perhaps. I was speaking only the other day to Mrs Prewett and –'

Laura jumped to her feet. 'I'll never marry Reggie Prewett, not if I live as an old maid until I'm a hundred! And no matter what you say, or do, I don't think I'd be comfy here after what you've said about Mum and Rick. You've never tried to understand Mum, or to help her though she works hard enough for two. She has to.'

'I hope you're not insinuating things against my son.'

'*Your* son, and *my* father. I love him, too, you know, but evidently I can see him more clearly than you. Dad could work if he liked –'

'Enough!' Granma cried. 'That's enough. I'll not have anyone speak ill of our William.'

'Please,' begged Grampa, 'make it up between you. If you could both say sorry –'

'Both!' Granma turned on him in a fury. 'Both! I'm not the sinner here. I've said nothing but the truth. And I stick to my guns. Either Laura gives up Rick Merriman or out she goes.'

Chapter Eight

Laura leaned disconsolately on the brick wall of the backyard. The weather had turned chilly and she shivered and wondered if Lillian would ever emerge from the lavatory. Squares of newspapers were threaded with string and hung on a nail for toilet paper; they made convenient, if sometimes frustrating, reading.

Laura had been living with her parents for a week and the dreadful final scene with Granma was still vivid in her memory. She had raged and stormed and finally, to Laura's horror, shed tears. 'After all I've done for you,' she sobbed. 'You've no gratitude in you.'

The unique sight of Granma weeping made Laura feel weak, but her words stiffened her resolve. Of course she was grateful for the good home she'd had, but it was not her fault that she had been uprooted and brought up so strictly by Granma, with her incessant talk of sin and her hateful restrictions, and she could not end her association with Rick.

Laura felt more sorry for Grampa. He had tried to intervene, only to have his wife turn her wrath on him. Grampa wilted immediately. He was weak-willed. So was Dad. The sudden realisation surprised Laura who was unused to forming opinions of her elders. Dad *was* weak. That was probably why he had married Mum. Phyllis was strong and domineering, just like Granma. Both would be disgusted to know themselves compared, but it was true all the same.

Phyllis had stared at Laura in astonishment when she had arrived with her few possessions in a bundle.

'What do you mean, you've come home to live?' she demanded. 'You live with your grandmother. There's no room here for you.'

'There never was, was there?' Laura exploded angrily. 'I won't annoy you too long, but I've nowhere else to turn.'

'You don't mean you've been chucked out! Not by dear Amy!' Phyllis looked faintly amused. 'You'd best come in and tell us about it.'

Laura followed her mother who sat herself down in the kitchen. The little ones were playing with rag dolls which Laura had made them last Christmas. Dad was in his usual place by the fire.

'Guess what, William! Laura's been chucked out by your mother.'

William peered at Laura. 'Good lord, chick, you must have done somethin' awful.'

'Is it awful to have a boyfriend?'

'So,' said Phyllis, hissing the word like a snake, turning her gap-toothed grin on her husband. 'I might have guessed it was somethin' to do with sex. Amy's obsessed with it.'

'That's enough,' William spoke automatically. He didn't sound particularly interested and as he spoke his eyes were on his book, lying open now on his knees.

Lillian bounced into the room. 'Did I hear right? Don't tell me dear little Laura's got the push! Well, well, first Gregory's, now dear old Granma. Who'd have thought it! Not expectin', are you?'

'None of that talk!' said Phyllis sharply.

'You're the one that mentioned sex,' replied Lillian cheekily.

'That's different!' snapped Phyllis. 'Now then, Laura, tell us what's gone wrong.'

'You know I've met this man. Rick Merriman. He's really nice –'

'He takes her out on a motor bike, or a *car*,' interposed Lillian, unable to keep the resentful envy from her tone.

'Shut up, our Lil,' said Phyllis.

'That's not why I – like him,' went on Laura. As soon as Rick heard what had happened he would surely tell her he loved her, and maybe offer to take her away from here. Lots of men said they weren't interested in marriage, but when they met the right girl . . . 'He's kind and gentle and makes good money and treats me well. Granma won't hear of my seeing him again because his mother was never married, but that's not his fault. Why should he suffer?'

'The sins of the fathers,' said William. 'You can't get away from that.'

'That's cruel,' said Laura.

'It's in the bible, chick.'

'Lots of things in the bible seem cruel,' said Laura. She waited for a thunderbolt from above. Granma would have called one down to hear her speak like that. 'I must have somewhere to stay,' she pleaded. 'I've only what's left of my money after paying Granma –'

'Didn't she give you any back?' Lillian snapped.

'If I'm not wanted here, I'll find lodgings as soon as I can – if you're not able –' Laura halted. She was damned if she would cry in front of Lillian, but she felt emotionally fragile. She swallowed hard. 'I won't give up Rick.'

'God, d'you mean you've left Granma's swanky home just because of a man!' said Phyllis.

'She made me choose.'

Lillian snorted disgustedly. 'I should have told her I'd give him up, then gone on seein' him. You're pretty stupid, if you ask me. Fancy all that happenin' to dear Laura. And all for Rick Merriman! He says he's not a marryin' man.'

'Shut up, our Lil,' said Phyllis again. Laura got the impression that she was simply too tired to argue.

'How about it, Phyllis?' asked William. 'We can find an odd corner for her, can't we?'

Laura had given her father a look of gratitude and love which he didn't see. She had wished she could stop loving him. She almost wished she had not fallen in love with Rick. Love made you vulnerable.

A cold breeze whipped sharply around the back yard. As she shifted from one foot to the other she groaned slightly, holding her sore stomach. A fine drizzle began to fall, but she dared not go indoors or someone else would make for the lavatory, and her insides were painful. There was no kitchen hygiene to speak of in this house and she'd had an upset stomach since yesterday. She dared not call Lillian or she'd stay longer, out of spite. At last the door opened and Lillian strolled out. She grinned mockingly as Laura rushed past, desperate to relieve herself.

Night times were the worst. Phyllis and William slept in the front bedroom with the two youngest girls in cots. The boys were in the small second room and the girls in the third. There was nowhere to put another bed, even if there was one, and Laura slept with Iris on her narrow, lumpy mattress and, although Iris was slender, they had to sleep curled around each other and turn together. But it was better than sharing with Lillian and Freda. Joyce and Priscilla slept in the third bed. Laura had never thought about privacy, but that was because she'd had it since she was five. Now she valued it highly. For a week there had not been a single time when she was alone. And the walls seemed thin, or else voices echoed because there were no carpets, or plush furniture, or wallpaper as in Granma's house, to absorb sound. The house was lit by gas lamps, provided someone had a penny for the meter. As often as not, candles were used.

The work in the stripping room had seemed to get harder, not easier, and she came home to greasy meals, constant noise and bickering, and little sleep. She realised how pampered she had been all these years and understood something of Lillian's jealousy. Perhaps she, too, disliked the crowded house. She never missed an opportunity to remind Laura of what she had thrown away.

Worst of all, Laura had not seen Rick since the night at the theatre, and she lay awake, torturing herself with images of him with Jenny. If Laura had retained any illusions about sex she had lost them in the past few days. Lillian and her girlfriends, who came and went as they pleased, seemed to discuss little else. The remainder of their talk was of dances, going to the pictures, and having a good time in any way they could.

She returned to the house and washed her hands in the wide, shallow stone scullery sink. Phyllis was turning the handle of the iron mangle with its huge wooden rollers. Laura purposefully grabbed the handle. She had learned another lesson; in this house, if you wanted to do something you pushed your way in.

Phyllis straightened her back, her hands rubbing her aching muscles. 'Thanks,' she said, the word ground out with difficulty. She lifted an armful of linen and dropped it into a tub of water where a blue bag had been soaking. After that the washing would be mangled again. Then the pillow cases, tablecloths, table napkins and anything else the rich folk wanted stiff would be put into the big bowls of starch, to be mangled for the third time.

Laura's arms ached after ten minutes, and her hands felt as if they were burning, but she gritted her teeth and kept going. If her mother could do it, so could she.

As the days had passed Laura had been recalling things held in her infant memory and found it had been clouded by nostalgia. She couldn't fool herself anymore that she had been wanted even before she had left home. However her mother tried to hide it, Phyllis didn't like her.

Laura had been visiting almost every week for twelve years, and had longed for the free and easy lifestyle, but that had been on Sundays. The work slackened off on Sundays, there was cake for tea, a little leisure. On weekdays when everyone came home for supper there was usually only a huge saucepan of sheep's head broth with vegetables and a bag of testers – half loaves cut randomly by bakers to test the quality of their baking and sold cheap. And that, as Lillian pointed out acerbically, was much better than many folk had. Occasionally the diet was varied by a boiled-in-the-basin pie made with offcuts of meat, bits of bacon and fat ham topped with potatoes and covered by a thick smooth layer of pastry which had almost a slimy texture. Laura hated it, but she ate everything she was given. Her determination to avoid Lillian's tongue-lashings was rivalled only by Lillian's ability to find something to lash her with.

When Freda was around she sometimes took over the burden of work, but her task in life, one that she cherished, was to look after her twin sister and see she came to no harm. If Joyce wanted to walk they walked; if she preferred to sit in a field chewing grass Freda was there. Plain, pimpled Freda was no target for Lillian. Apart from being stolidly difficult to annoy, she had been known, when sufficiently provoked, to hand out physical punishment like a boxer. More than one boy who had come too close to her lovely sister had fled as Freda advanced on him frowningly.

Yesterday Laura had wondered aloud if she could take up the hems of her small sisters' dresses. They had been bought second hand and fitted only where they touched, a fact which Phyllis ignored.

'Oh, sorry,' said Lillian, 'Don't you like what Mum buys for the kids? Mum,' she called, 'Laura don't like the kids' dresses. She wants to alter them.'

'She can please herself,' replied Phyllis from the scullery, 'as long as I don't have to do anythin'.'

That night when they went to bed it was Laura's nightgown that caught Lillian's attention. Lillian slept in an old petticoat.

'Look at her,' she sneered to Iris, keeping her voice to a whisper because of the sleeping Priscilla. 'A nice cotton gown with eyelets and pink ribbon. Did Granma make it for you? Or did you sew it yourself on the treadle machine? We haven't got a treadle machine. Oh, but you know that now, don't you. Poor Laura will have to sit and sew by hand, just like us. Don't spoil your pretty hands, will you. Oh, I forgot, your hands are spoilt already. By the way Gregory's have got a very pretty girl in your place. She was trained in London. Miss Pringle is ever so pleased with her. It was lucky really you got the sack. And you should see that girl's hands. Like white silk, they are.'

'Shut up, you bitch!' Laura snapped, goaded past enduring.

'Nice language from Granma's darling. And where's Rick then? Don't say you've given up your comfy home for a bloke that don't care two hoots about you.'

Laura could stand no more. She launched herself at her sister who was taken by surprise and the two fell between the beds, tearing, biting, scratching.

Iris tried to pull them apart. 'You'll wake the little one,' she hissed. 'Stop it. Oh, please, stop it.'

Laura and Lillian were past hearing. Years of anger were being fought out on the cold linoleum. The door opened and Freda peered in.

'What a bloody racket! What's goin' on? Who's that on the floor? Lillian, and *Laura*.'

Priscilla sat up, rubbed her eyes and stared sleepily at her sisters.

'You've woken Priscilla,' wailed Iris.

Freda climbed over beds and grabbed at Lillian's hair, tugging it hard. 'Get up, you stupid cow. What're you attackin' Laura for?'

'Leave my hair alone,' shrieked Lillian. 'And she attacked me.'

'You must have said somethin' vile then, because she's left you alone all week. I'd have smacked you in the mouth if you'd treated me the way you treat her.'

'Will you let go my hair?' yelled Lillian.

Freda's response was to pull harder until Lillian allowed herself to be dragged away. Laura got up, blood streaming from a gash in her arm made by Lillian's nails. She was glad to see that she had marked Lillian who was dabbing at her neck with a corner of a sheet.

'Mum'll kill you when she's sees blood on the sheet,' pointed out Iris. 'Blood's awful hard to get out.'

Freda said, 'If you're not careful, our Lillian, there'll be a corpse on our hands and you'll hang from the neck till you're dead as mutton.'

'It'd be worth it,' snarled Lillian, glaring hate at Laura.

'What have I ever done to hurt you?' demanded Laura.

'Oh, go to hell!' snapped Lillian.

Freda pulled out the china chamber pot for Priscilla, held her over it, and settled her again, her voice unbelievably soft and kind. Freda was a creature of extremes.

Laura climbed into bed, a handkerchief wrapped tightly over her wound. Iris snuggled up to her and put her arms round her, smoothing her face into her back like a kitten.

'Take no notice of our Lillian,' she whispered. 'She's just jealous. She thinks you've had life easy.'

It took a long time for Laura to relax enough to sleep. She felt stifled by the crowded room, the light adenoidal snores of Freda, the dreamy murmurings of Priscilla. She even resented

127

the forced intimacy with Iris. She vowed that somehow she must get out of this situation, but she wouldn't go back to Granma, even if she was asked.

On the following Sunday, after midday dinner, Dad dozed with his sporting newspaper over his face while Phyllis nursed a hangover with tea and aspirins. There was a commotion from the children playing in the street, the sound of a horse's hooves and a hearty laugh.

'It's Ralph,' said Phyllis, her thin face lighting up.

'Ralph.' The name sang through the house and moments later Laura's tall, handsome brother entered the kitchen, carrying a bulging sack, his legs festooned with his small brothers and sisters who gave him no peace until he produced a large bag of toffees, his intense blue eyes sparkling. Alfred and Harold watched him admiringly and stuffed their mouths with nougat.

'That'll stick their jaws together and give us a bit of hush,' Ralph said. 'Hello, Laura, I thought I'd find you here today. How're you doing?'

'You'll find her here every day, more's the pity,' snapped Lillian.

Ralph grinned, showing his excellent white teeth in his fine-boned, weathered face. 'Your temper doesn't change much. Here, cop this.' He threw a parcel at his sister who caught it and dragged it open to reveal a fashionable jumper suit.

'Gosh, thanks!' Lillian said.

'It needs a bit of mending. But it came from a swell's house,' said Ralph. 'I expect our Laura will sew it for you.'

His smile warmed Laura. She and Ralph had always got on well.

'*She* can't sew,' said Lillian. 'Her soft white hands ain't soft no mo'.' Lillian sang the words in imitation of a blacked-up singer.

'Oh, yes, I forgot. The tobacco stripping room. It's a pity you lost your job at Gregory's, our Laura. I was told you knocked 'em dead at the fashion show.'

'Well, that's all over,' said Lillian with satisfaction.

'How do you know about Laura?' demanded Freda.

'I've got a friend who told me. In fact, he'll be along any

minute. He stopped to have a word with a chap he used to know.'

Ralph reached into the sack and handed two opened packets of Egyptian cigarettes and a sealed envelope which chinked pleasantly with money to his mother. There was something for everyone and nobody minded that there were small flaws in their presents. Naturally Ralph had to sell the best stuff from his cart to customers who'd pay good money. There were also boxes of special things stored in the back shed waiting for the time when he realised his ambition to open a shop. He bent to kiss his mother and her love for him was so intense and so obvious in her eyes that Laura drew a sharp breath of envy.

Joyce came in and tugged at Ralph's sleeve. 'Where's my present Ralph?'

Her brother gave her a swift hug and kiss. 'I've something extra nice for you, my love.' He took a necklace from his pocket and fastened it around Joyce's throat. She squealed and ran to the mirror to admire herself decked in the multi-coloured beads, before she turned and threw herself at Ralph. He caught her. 'Hey, now, there's no need to go crazy.' He kissed her and she raced off to show the beads to the neighbours.

Ralph's eyes followed her and he frowned. 'She gets prettier every time I see her.'

'And that's not often enough,' grumbled his father. 'You ought to come home more often.'

'Here, Dad, this is for you.' Ralph handed William a half bottle of whisky.

'You never got that off the cart,' said Freda.

'It's amazing what you can find at the back doors of the idle rich if you make friends with the cook,' grinned Ralph.

Phyllis lit up a cigarette and shook her head in mock disapproval, blowing out a cloud of aromatic smoke. 'You'd best watch your step, my lad. Some of those servants think nothin' of pinchin' stuff from their masters. If they get caught they'll tell on you.'

'I'll deny everything, Ma.'

There was a knocking on the open front door and Ralph yelled, 'Come on in, mate, and meet the folks.'

Laura's heart nearly stopped beating when Rick appeared in the doorway and strolled in, looking as if he belonged here. He always looked like that, wherever he was, she thought, while she always felt the odd one out.

Rick greeted William and Phyllis then walked over to Laura and slid his arm round her. 'How's life, kid? Sorry I've been too busy to see you.'

Laura managed a shrug, though her heart was now racing and pleasure swamped her. Nothing could be better than to have Rick's affection for her openly displayed. She could have laughed at Lillian's temper-filled eyes. God, she was getting as vindictive as her sister.

Sunday tea was even livelier than usual. Ralph had brought a big cake which he assured Phyllis he had bought in a perfectly good shop. 'Even the swells don't throw out whole cakes, Ma.'

Rick produced a large pot of jam. 'My aunty made it, and she's an expert. You'll vouch for that, won't you Laura?'

Laura nodded, happiness covering her like a magic veil which made her impervious to the increasingly venomous glares Lillian sent her way.

'Have you been to Rick's house, love?' asked Phyllis, and Laura wanted to laugh aloud in joy at the real interest in her mother's voice. A girl wasn't invited to a man's house unless he was serious about her. Not in Phyllis's world. That was another thing she and Granma had in common.

Harold and Alfred were muddy from a game of football. 'Get some of that dirt off you,' ordered Phyllis, her long knife sawing away at the bread held to her chest.

When the boys returned they sat on the fender seats. Joyce came in a few moments later, her eyes shining from the compliments she'd received from the neighbours. Rick immediately rose to let her take his place. Laura felt proud of his gentlemanly gesture.

Then Lillian rose. 'Take my chair, Rick. I've got somethin' I need to do.'

Laura watched her sister leave suspiciously, and Phyllis's eyes narrowed.

Moments later Lillian returned and without warning

plonked herself on to Rick's lap. Laura gasped, waiting for Rick to move to give her his chair. He stayed where he was, grinning as he munched bread and jam.

'I hope you're comfy,' he said.

'As long as you are,' Lillian answered cheekily. She had raced upstairs and dabbed on rouge and powder and scent. Her hair shone and Laura suspected she'd been at the boys' hair cream.

Laura's appetite deserted her. She refused the cake, its layered jam and mock cream making her feel nauseous and Lillian watched her, triumph in her eyes.

After tea Rick and Ralph went off together.

'Wenching, I suppose,' guessed William uninterestedly.

For once Lillian and Laura shared an emotion, even if it was only angry resentment.

Ralph stayed the night. Rick, he explained, had gone home. His mother was unwell and he preferred to be near her when she had one of her 'turns'. 'Poor woman, I reckon she's not long for this world,' said Ralph.

Laura was ashamed of her reaction. Her strongest emotion was one of fear that if something happened to Rick's mother he'd no longer feel tied to Bristol. He'd be off to London like a shot. If he did she'd follow him, she vowed. She tried to push aside the memory of Lillian on his lap. Even Phyllis had told Lillian she was a brazen little sod and Dad had tutted. Fat lot Lillian cared. If she could take Rick from her sister she would.

Rick took Laura out three times, with long gaps between dates. Once dancing, when she had worn a dress borrowed from her sister, Enid, who was the same height and build. At least, she had been. Now her body was heavy with her child and her face was permanently anxious. Her husband, a good but unambitious man, had lost his job at the boot factory.

'Not because he's done anythin' wrong,' raged Enid, weeping, 'but because they're short of orders.'

'Typical of bloody bosses,' said Lillian.

'And the midwife says I should stay home and rest because of my legs.' Her ankles were swollen. 'How can I give up work?

Jack's on the dole which is bloody starvation money, and we've got to save to pay the midwife. And the baby's in the wrong place and I might even need the doctor.'

Phyllis had stared at her daughter helplessly. 'Oh, my love – I hope to God the midwife's wrong. Tell me if you need food. No one in this family will ever go short of food, if I can help it.'

Laura felt guilty. She was hoarding all the money she had left after paying Mum housekeeping, darning her stockings over and over, walking miles instead of using the trams. She had to get out of the tobacco factory before it drove her crazy and ruined her hands for ever. She had amassed four pounds and hidden it in a cloth, draw-string bag beneath the mattress she shared with Iris who was the only one who knew it was there. She ran upstairs and came down with a pound which she handed to Enid.

'Thanks, Laura. You're a good 'un,' said Enid, and for a few precious moments Laura had basked in her mother's approval.

Rick had loved the dress. It was shiny apple green and to go with it Enid had lent her a long string of green and red beads which swung almost to her knees, and a bandeau with a red feather for her head. She fitted in now with the other girls.

He had taken her to the Empire to watch more of his acts. 'It's all workin' out, Laura. I'm gettin' clients, though I'll need classier ones earnin' more money before I can make a good livin'.'

Laura and Rick were driving in an open-top car. He owned this one, he told her with a mixture of pride and self-mockery. It was, he informed her, a Renault, and he'd got it in payment of a debt, all of thirty shillings.

'One day, Laura, I'll have a Rolls. They're big and powerful. Meanwhile we'll have to make do with this, even if it is a bit the worse for wear. Better than a motor bike, though, eh?'

'Much,' agreed Laura, snuggling down happily behind the wind-screen, 'though I wouldn't care what you took me out in, Rick.'

He glanced down at her with a wry grin. 'I believe you, honey, but –'

Laura waited, but Rick changed the subject. 'Your hands are real sore, aren't they? Why don't you change your job? You haven't got Granma breathin' down your neck any more.'

'I'm going to, but it won't be easy. More and more people are being laid off work. Businesses are failing. Enid's husband –'

'Yeah, I heard about Jack. He's a good man, but not bright enough to be pushy. You need a lot of push to make the grade today.'

'Who told you about Jack? I only knew myself yesterday.'

Rick grinned and shrugged. 'Word gets around.'

'The doctor says Enid should stay home.'

Rick slowed for a bicycle turning right. He looked grim. 'If she leaves work they'll have to live on the dole and that's even harder than havin' a dead-end job. Most of the folk round here don't make enough to feed a family, in or out of work. You won't see me caught in the marriage trap.'

'You might fall in love,' blurted Laura.

Rick grinned. 'What's that got to do with gettin' shackled by marriage?'

'I've always thought love and marriage went together.'

'It ain't necessarily so. A man – and a woman, too – can move faster alone. Why don't you set up in business on your own?'

'What! How? You're talking rubbish and you know it!' Laura glared at Rick. He wore his snap-brim hat, pulled down to avoid the breeze, his hands were strong on the wheel.

'Suppose you had a choice, what would you like to do best?'

'Make hats.' The answer came from deep inside. 'I'd like to make hats. But there's not a lot of money in it. Women can't afford to pay much. As often as not I've been helping Miss Morton make over old ones that have been worn for years.'

'You're lookin' too low, honey.' Rick adroitly got out a cigarette and lit it with one hand.

'Too low?'

'How much does Lady Mallender pay for her hats? And her daughter and those two bright young bitches who helped get you fired?'

'Pounds,' said Laura. 'Sometimes, when they're off to Ascot, or to Henley, more money than I earn in a month. If I could work for the gentry –'

'What's to stop you?'

'For heaven's sake, Rick. I can't just ask rich people if I can make their hats!'

'Why not?'

Laura grew pensive. 'I don't know,' she said slowly. 'I did ask her fine ladyship if she wanted a purse, didn't I?' Excitement stirred her. 'I could ask about hats. Why not? Yes, I'll do it. But I need time to get my hands smooth and I'd have to leave home. There's not an inch of space to do anything there and as like as not Lillian would grab at anything I made. It's not so easy to find a place to live. They never seem to have caught up with building houses since the war ended.'

'Don't give in before you've even started!'

Their third date had been merely a couple of hours snatched from Sunday. They drove between meadows and trees and Rick pulled over and parked by a gate. The sun was warm on their faces, the dust lifted by the car settled, green shoots were covering the rich earth, and Laura sighed with pleasure. Now he would take her in his arms and kiss her. Her mind leapt ahead in optimistic bounds. He would tell her that he loved her. Surely, surely, he would? How could he be with her and not feel the deep emotion that tore her apart?

Rick lit a cigarette and gave Laura one, before resuming the conversation begun last time. 'The way I see it, baby, you get shoved into this world without askin' – Laura tensed. Was he about to tell her the circumstances of his birth? That would prove he really trusted her – 'and it's up to us all to make the most of what we've got. I've learned that nobody, well, almost nobody, cares a damn about you, but if you succeed you get respect. And that's what I'm aimin' for. Respect.'

'Is that all?'

'All? It's a bloody sight more than I've had in the past, and more than most men get. Think about it, kid. Last year we had the General Strike. And what did that gain? Nothin'! Worse than nothin'. We got rich men and women – the so-called bright young things – drivin' buses and trains and thinkin' it all a big joke. A big lark, they called it. Sods! So everyone, except the miners, went back to work after ten days, and the poor devils of miners stuck it out for six solid months, then it was down the mines again with lower wages, longer hours and the Mininum Terms Agreement abolished. Some of them couldn't return to work at all. And why? Because they'd had the cheek to question their masters. Because they had the infernal nerve to want enough money to live on! Well, I aim to be my own master, and if you've any sense, Laura, you'll not be beholden to anyone either. You've got brains, you've got a talent. Use them!'

Rick's voice had been vibrant with feeling. Now he stopped and grinned. 'God, hark at me. I sound like a bloody politician.' He lit another cigarette with fingers that, to Laura's amazement, were shaking slightly. For all his tough talk he cared about people. 'Anyway, think about it, Laura. If I can help you, I will.'

Laura did think. As she sat for hours stripping and hating the raw tobacco whose fumes filled her mouth and nostrils and permeated her with its smell, she thought. She added to the pennies hoarded beneath the mattress.

She visited Miss Morton every evening and in her two tiny rooms she learned the craft of millinery as never before. She steamed and blocked and shrank fur felts, she discovered how to sew the strips of felt in one direction to hide the joins, to apply liquid stiffener to the shapes when the steaming was finished, to make hats in sections with small pieces of material – ends of bolts of cloth bought economically in job lots from drapers. She sat in the cluttered room and watched Miss Morton, eyes and mind alert, her fingers itching to take hold of delicate materials and give shape to her design ideas.

'You'll need to make your own esparterie shapes to fit individual heads,' explained Miss Morton. 'I always had the measurements of my best clients to hand, and if they changed their hairstyle it often meant making a different size.' She showed Laura how to paint the stiffening agent on to the coarse straw, ending with a firm shape on which to design a hat. Espartie blocks, Laura already knew, would crack if fashioned while stiff, but became pliable when wet.

'You'll not need them much at present with the cloches,

Laura, but big hats will come back into fashion and no lady wants one with a saggy brim.'

They giggled at the picture Laura described of Lady Mallender opening a garden fête as her hat slowly collapsed over her eyes. 'But it wouldn't be funny, really, Laura. You'd lose all your customers. Really expensive hats may be made entirely by hand using bandeaux and wiring. You'll need well-off folk if you're to make your mark in millinery.'

'I intend to have them,' said Laura grimly.

She spent more and more time with Miss Morton, even part of Sundays, ignoring Lillian's taunts that she thought herself too grand to stay at home after living at Granma's. She learned the correct terminology, and the proper stitches for each process: millinery backstitch, catch stitch working from right to left, forming long zigzag joins between two pieces of material. The needles tortured her sore hands, but she refused to give in. She kept her mind off the pain by thinking of the wonderful materials she would one day use to cover the shapes, the twists and turns of ribbons she would make into flowers for those who wanted prettiness, and into the abstracts popular at present, using primary colours together in slashes of shocking brilliance.

But at times she thought of Rick, wondering what he was doing, who he was seeing. She tried to discipline herself, to keep remembering that he too intended to succeed and must have time to himself. She tried not to dwell on his assertion that he had no wish for a permanent relationship. One day she would change his mind and he would want her as much as she did him – she pulled herself back into order, pushing needles in and out of tough cloth that could withstand her scratchy fingers, blinking away tears of pain and frustration. She fell into bed each night, too exhausted to care about Lillian's sarcastic remarks as she taunted her sister with her so-called lover's neglect.

Once, unbelievably, Laura had to refuse an invitation from Rick so that she could help Miss Morton finish a big order brought home from the factory. After Miss Morton's goodness she could not let her down, but it hurt unbearably.

When she had explained to Rick why she couldn't come out with him he had bent and kissed her softly on the mouth. 'That's my girl.' And Laura's heart somersaulted in joy at his appreciation.

Somehow the day would come when she could once more handle the soft silks, the gossamer georgettes, the sleek satins that made hats into individual models. She would work for the Lady Mallenders of this world and she would make them pay. One thing she had discovered in Gregory's was that a woman would pay heavily if you offered her something that would make her the envy of other rich women. When she had enough money to survive for a while she would walk out of the tobacco factory, get her hands back to their former softness and then tout for custom.

Jack couldn't get a job and he joined Harold and Alfred, doing piece-work in the back shed. He never went to the factories to collect the leather for the boots, or told a soul outside the family that he was making a little money. If *they* found out he would lose his dole money, and maybe even go to jail. Some poor devils had and only because they needed to fill the bellies of their children.

Enid fainted at work and the works nurse called a doctor who diagnosed high blood pressure. She was forced to remain at home, spending much of her time in bed or on the sofa in her living room. Laura thought guiltily of her savings, small though they were, and gave Enid a little money. But she couldn't relinquish her dream; she couldn't. She must begin a new life and then, when she was successful, she would lavish money on all of them. For a few brief exhilarating moments she clung to a vision of being hailed as the benefactress of the family while Phyllis and William glowed with admiring love for her.

Joyce started work. Freda had raged against the plan when it was first brought up. Red-faced with anger she had said in her most aggressive voice, 'She can't work, Mum, she'll get in a muddle and likely injure herself. Factories are awful places. There are always accidents –'

'Shut up, our Freda,' said Phyllis. 'Of course I'm not

sendin' Joyce to a factory. Our landlord's wife – it's only a walk away – will be wantin' a kitchen maid. I took Joyce along and the cook said she'll do. She understands about her not bein' clever, but said she don't need to be to wash pots an' pans.'

'Our Joyce washin' other folks' dirty dishes!' said Freda. 'An' what about –' She stopped, her face redder, her pimples standing out in glowing beacons. 'I mean, you always said she was too pretty –'

'You must think I'm daft,' snapped Phyllis. 'Of course I checked who lives in the house. They've got two daughters and no sons. Our Joyce'll be safe enough an' you can fetch her on her time off an' take her back. The cook's a nice, motherly woman. She'll feed her well an' it won't matter that she's not earnin' the usual wage.'

'Why not?' yelled Freda. 'She'll be doin' the same bloody work as any other kitchen maid!'

'For God's sake don't shriek! It goes right through my head. You know Joyce'll never rise no higher than washin' up. She can't concentrate long enough. If Mrs Telford – that's the cook – is willin' to make allowances we ought to be thankful. And her wage is comin' straight to me and that'll help our Enid. And Joyce is to have every Sunday afternoon off.'

'Slavery! Bloody slavery, that's what you're sendin' Joyce into –'

Joyce had listened to all this with her usual sweet smile curving her beautiful mouth. She patted Freda's hand. 'Don't be cross, Freda, I want to work and help our Enid.'

Freda subsided muttering imprecations about the rich.

Joyce came home on her first afternoon off carrying a bag of stale buns donated by Mrs Telford, and a magazine passed on by the daughters of the house, Miss Ethel and Miss Irene.

Enid and Jack had come to tea and Enid riffled through the magazine. 'Look at this!' she cried. 'It's enough to make a saint swear. It's a piece called "Should married women work?" It says,' she continued, assuming an accent she considered posh: ' "Once a woman marries it is her duty – and should be her pleasure – to remain in her home, turning it into a sanctuary for her husband, a haven of rest and spirituality, away from the

138

pollution of the outside world of work. And, later, when her marriage is blessed, building a cosy nest for her little ones with the same innocent dedication as the tiny birds in her garden." I should like to see the woman who wrote that make a cosy bloody nest on twenty-four shillin's a week, with the rent for a two-roomed house just gone up to ten shillin's.'

'The gentry don't know anythin' about the likes of us,' said Lillian. 'and if they did, they wouldn't care.'

'Some of them care,' said Laura. 'Some do try to help the poor.'

Lillian shot her an angry look. 'You would have to think different, wouldn't you! Perhaps you'll let me know when Lady Mallender and those two toffee-nosed cows who got you fired come to find out if you're all right.'

'They've got lots of magazines in their big house,' said Joyce equably. 'Mrs Telford gets them when they're finished with them upstairs. There's one all about clothes called *Vogyew*.'

'That's a queer name,' said Phyllis.

'I think she means *Vogue*,' ventured Laura.

There was a shout of laughter in which Joyce joined, but Freda scowled. 'I bet they make fun of her in that house.'

'No, Freda, they don't,' said Joyce. 'They like me. There's an old lady lives upstairs nearly at the top of the house and the housemaid lets me take her tea up. She's Mrs Goodwin's mother – Mrs Goodwin's my boss – an' she mostly stays in bed an' she's got a nurse. She likes me – the old lady, I mean, – not the nurse – I think the nurse wishes I wouldn't come upstairs, – an' the old lady says I must see her jewels. I should like that. I bet she's rich enough to have lots of beads an' things. They've got different stairs for the servants and I go right to the old lady's room without bein' in the best rooms at all. Nobody sees me.'

'See!' said Phyllis triumphantly. 'I knew she'd be all right. What harm can she come to in that house? As far as the nobs are concerned she's invisible.'

'Old Mrs Goodwin, eh, Joyce,' said William. 'I hope you mind your manners.'

Freda bit savagely into a stale bun. 'Sendin' us their throw-aways as if we was beggars.' She added jam and took another bite. 'I bet they spend more on magazines then we do on bread.' She stuffed the last piece of bun into her mouth and snuggled closer to Joyce putting her short strong arms around her. 'You'll tell your Freda if anyone hurts you, won't you, Joyce?' she said quietly. Joyce nodded, but she wasn't really paying attention and Freda's scowl grew darker. 'She always minded me before she was sent out to work. She's different already.'

'Give it a rest,' said William, and that was that.

On payday Laura lifted the mattress and reached for the small cloth bag to add her wages to the meagre pile. She couldn't find it. It must have slipped back. She thrust her hand further until she touched the wall. She scrabbled frantically with both hands and tore off the sheets and blankets and lifted the mattress. The money had gone. She felt sick, physically sick. She sank on to the bed Lillian shared with Freda and breathed deeply to avoid vomiting. The mattresses were turned only by those using the bed. Iris? No, she'd stake her life on Iris's honesty. Then who? She considered the sly, triumphant looks Lillian had been giving her lately. She stood and walked downstairs into the front room where the record machine was blaring. Lillian was dancing round the room singing loudly; she was wearing new shoes and a new blouse. The two youngest girls were reeling around half drunk with the jazzy music, bumping into one another and laughing. One-year-old Greta was clinging to the chair and jogging up and down shrieking tunelessly.

Laura strode to the record machine and lifted the needle arm.

Lillian stared in amazement. 'You cheeky cow, put that back on.'

'You took my money,' said Laura flatly.

Lillian looked more surprised than anything. 'How do you know? What the hell are you talkin' about? What money? You haven't got any.'

'Not now I haven't.' Laura's fury impelled her forward and she stood near to Lillian, her hands clenched. Lillian took a step back. 'Hey, our Laura, don't –'

Laura's eyes were wide and dark with anger. 'Give me my money,' she hissed.

'Naughty Laura,' said Virginia.

'Naughty Laura,' agreed Priscilla. 'We want the music. Put it back on, Lillian.'

Laura turned swiftly to the two little girls. 'Be quiet!'

Phyllis entered in time to hear the rage-filled order. 'Don't you talk to them kids like that! What do you think you're doin', spoilin' everyone's pleasure. Just because you're miserable in the factory –'

'Oh, you actually *noticed*,' cried Laura. 'Well, that's a wonder!'

'Don't be cheeky to me, miss. I'll not have it. I've never stood for no cheek from any of you and if you can't live like the rest of us you can –'

'Leave, I suppose. Go on, say it! You don't want me here!'

'Well, I certainly don't,' said Lillian.

Greta began to wail and Phyllis took her up into her arms, rocking her, crooning gentle words to her. Laura wondered if she'd ever been held like that by her mother.

'What was it about, anyway?' asked Phyllis.

'Lillian stole my money –' said Laura.

'I borrowed it,' said Lillian.

'What money?' asked Phyllis.

'I was saving some –'

'How much?' William had left his chair and pipe in the kitchen; the word money always drew him like a magnet.

'Nearly six pounds,' said Laura.

'Six pounds!' shrieked Phyllis. 'You've got six pounds when our Enid can hardly afford to buy medicine!'

Greta whimpered.

'She's a mean bitch, Mum,' said Lillian.

Laura turned on her bitterly, now feeling the rift between herself and the others more keenly than the theft of the money. 'So what did you do with it?'

Phyllis rasped, 'I know where it's gone. It's on her back, and her feet. And the rest is in that dance frock and beads she came home with yesterday. She said she'd got them cheap off a friend. You're both as selfish as one another.'

William tutted and shook his head. 'I don't understand you girls. There's Jack and the boys out in the shed working their fingers to the bone and Enid sick. And you two squabble over money that should have gone to your mother.'

'I've paid Mum what she asked,' cried Laura. 'I've got to get out of that factory, Dad. I shall go crazy. Surely *you* understand. I've been walking nearly all the way to work and back, I've cut my own hair, darned my stockings until they're more darns than anything, I've –'

'Spare us,' said Phyllis wearily. 'Have you got any left, Lillian?'

Lillian shook her head and Laura glared at her. In that moment she knew the meaning of hatred. She turned and walked out of the room and out of the house. She had to get away before she yielded to an impulse to scratch Lillian's smug expression from her face. She felt disturbed by the strength of the anger she had been feeling since she left Granma's. It was as if a volcano which had been dammed for years was now throwing up molten lava. There was a fine drizzle falling, but she didn't notice it as she made her way to Miss Morton's.

'Why didn't you ask me to look after your savings?' asked Miss Morton.

'I should have. How could I know my own sister would steal from me?'

Miss Morton gave her a towel for her hair and brought her cake and tea.

'I'll have to start all over again,' wailed Laura. 'It'll be months before I can leave Wills.'

Laura left Miss Morton's with a borrowed umbrella. She turned the bend at the top of the street in time to see Lillian, wearing the new blouse and shoes to which had been added a new soft crêpe de Chine skirt, climb into Rick's car. As he drove away Lillian looked back and saw Laura. She flashed her a bright smile and waved surreptitiously over her shoulder until the car disappeared round the corner.

Chapter Nine

Laura faced Rick over the table in a small café. A week had passed since she had seen Lillian in his car, a week of despair that threatened to undermine all her striving for independence. Lillian had piled on the misery, describing the wonderful dance he'd taken her to, sparing her sister nothing, 'His kisses are nice too, aren't they, Laura? Or don't you know?'

When Rick had intercepted Laura today on her way to Miss Morton's she had wanted to refuse his invitation, but weakly, helplessly, she had climbed into his car.

'Things are going very well,' he enthused, as she poured out two cups of tea.

Damn him! He behaved as if nothing had happened. Well, to him, it hadn't, she supposed. He couldn't know that she had seen him with Lillian, or that her sister was making a feast out of it.

'More clients?' she managed to ask.

'Yes, but I've had a new idea. The talkies are comin'. Nothin' can stop them. The music hall is dyin', Laura. It's sad, but true.'

Laura in her resentment refused to be impressed. She passed him the cake dish. 'What about the people who'll lose their jobs playing the piano for the films? What will happen to them? Do you really think a talking picture will kill off all the lovely live acts?'

'They can entertain in the intervals.' Rick stared at her. 'I thought you'd be interested. You're the only one I feel like talkin' to about what I want in life.' He took a bite of fruit cake.

The compliment should have filled her with profound pleasure, but it made her coldly angry. 'What about Lillian?'

'Your sister?'

'How many Lillian's do you know? I suppose you take out so many girls it must be hard to keep track.'

'No, I don't, and I've never taken your sister anywhere.'

'What a liar you are! I saw her climbing into your car and she's told me about the good time you gave her dancing. She even mentioned your – kisses.' Laura only just managed to keep a break from her voice.

'Dancin'? Kisses? What an imagination she's got! I'm not a liar, Laura. Well, not to you, anyway.'

'But I saw Lillian in your car.'

'You must have seen me givin' Lillian a lift to the church hall. She dashed out of your house just as I got there to see you and said she was late for a date and begged a ride. Why didn't you yell?' He sounded aggrieved.

'I was coming round the corner as you drove off.' And I didn't yell because I'm always terrified that someone will take you from me and I couldn't bear being humiliated in front of Lillian. Why couldn't she find the courage to speak her mind?

And she wanted to believe him. 'Why didn't you come back then?'

'I intended to, but I met a chap who'd seen an act that might interest me. Good thing I listened to him. I've taken on a great comedy partnership.'

Laura looked into Rick's eyes and saw the truth there. Her anger died, leaving her shaky and cold. 'Sorry,' she muttered. 'Lillian –'

'Could do with a clout round the ear.'

That brought laughter which released tension and Rick said, 'That's more like it, baby. Now back to the subject.'

'Oh, yes, talking pictures. It sounds interesting, but surely it's impossible.'

'No, it isn't, Laura.' Rick's eyes glinted with excitement. 'A small American company called Warner Brothers has got hold of a star – Al Jolson – he's known as the greatest entertainer in the world – and they're makin' a film called *The Jazz Singer*. You'll really be able to hear the songs and there's a rumour that he says a few words, too. We'll hear what the actors are sayin', just like on the stage. And they can sing, and dance, and the music will come right out of the screen at you.' He helped himself to a doughnut.

'I'm sure it'll be great,' said Laura. She was so filled with relief that Lillian had been lying that she was scarcely listening.

'I reckon that we'll both end up successful, baby. You with your hats and me with anythin' in show business I can get into. When are you leavin' the factory?'

'Not for ages.'

'But you must have saved enough by now.'

'I had six pounds. Lillian – borrowed it.'

'She'll never be able to pay that much back.'

'I don't think that was the idea.'

'Fancy Lillian. She seems such a nice kid.'

Laura bit back angry words. 'Most of the family told me off because I hadn't handed over the extra money to Enid.'

'Well, I know Jack and Enid are havin' it tough, but we've all got to look out for ourselves. What did they say when you told them you were savin' to set up on your own?'

Laura shuddered. 'I haven't. I couldn't stand all the tormenting I'd get. Oh, Rick' – her voice was a cry of despair – 'I don't fit in there. I don't belong anywhere.'

Rick reached across the table and took her rough, sore hands gently in his. He stared down at them then lifted them to his lips and kissed each palm. 'When I was a kid Mum always kissed my bruises well. I wish I could do the same for you.'

Oh, you could, Rick, darling Rick, if only you'd love me. She was far too inhibited to say the words to him and if she had he would surely get wary and not see her any more. 'Miss Morton's keeping my savings now,' was all she said.

'I had a special reason for askin' you out, Laura. I've rented an old picture house near Old Market. It's in a poor district and a bit run down because the owner's been ill for ages. He's just died and the family can't be bothered with it. It's a smelly old flea-pit, but if I had enough money I'd buy it. As it is I've taken it on a year's hire. Cash in advance.'

'Surely that cost a lot!'

'All I had put by. But I'm earnin' some from the music-hall

acts and I've been speed testin' motor cycles for Douglas's.'

'Speed testing! That's dangerous, isn't it?'

'Only if you fall off,' Rick grinned. 'And I've too much to do with my life to have an accident. Honest, Laura, it's thrillin'. Some of the cycles do up to seventy miles an hour.'

Laura swallowed. 'Do you go that fast?'

'Sure I do. Why not?'

Again Laura's tongue was imprisoned; because I'd die if anything happened to you. 'You said you had a special reason for asking me out.'

'I need your help.' The words lifted her heart. 'I can't afford to pay for staff in the picture house at first. Later there'll be plenty of money when I've got the machinery to add sound. People will crowd in. The buildin' is solid but it's filthy. Dust and cobwebs everywhere and the rats have been in.' Laura shuddered. 'Some of my mates are willin' to help clean the place, but I wondered if you could be there when I open.'

'To do what?'

'Anythin' that's needed. Will you come?'

Laura nodded and Rick leant over and kissed the tip of her nose. 'Good girl.'

Rick's cinema opened three weeks later. Laura was impressed by its new appearance. There was an enormous, garish poster giving details of opening night and the promise of a live show in the interval and two other posters, one proclaiming that scenes of incredibly wild parties among the upper crust would be portrayed on screen in *The Mad Whirl*, and a second announcing Rudolph Valentino in *The Sheik*.

Laura was thrilled. 'Is it the same as the book?' she asked Rick.

He shrugged. 'I guess so.'

He was thinner, with dark shadows beneath his eyes, and he smoked more than ever as he laboured to make his cinema usable while earning money where he could. Fortunately his clientele were used to the old wooden benches in the front, while those with more pence to spare could lounge in modest comfort in chairs at the back.

As soon as Laura mentioned *The Sheik* at home Phyllis was interested. Along with millions of women she had mourned Rudolph Valentino ever since his untimely and unheroic death from a perforated ulcer the year before. 'I'll come to the opening,' she said. William had never set foot inside a cinema or theatre and never wanted to, but Iris, Lillian, Joyce, Freda and the boys all promised to patronise Rick's venture. When Rick heard he invited them for free, a gesture that lifted him even higher in their esteem.

On one of his flying visits home Ralph was enthusiastic. 'Rick Merriman will go far,' he predicted. 'He's not afraid to take chances. I'll come along, too.' He turned to Laura. 'You'll be helping out, I hear. Rick trusts you.'

Laura glowed inwardly with happiness.

Iris was roped in to take the money while Rick was busy inside the tiny over-heated room from which the hundreds of feet of highly inflammable nitrate film was projected. He had worked hard to understand the way the clumsy machinery was operated.

On the opening night the queue wound round the front of the cinema and snaked away into the back streets.

'I knew Valentino would bring them,' gloated Rick.

'Not to mention scenes of wild mad whirling,' said Laura drily.

He grinned. 'Give the customers what they want, is my motto.'

The doors were opened and the folk rushed in paying twopence for the benches and threepence for the chairs.

Laura hurried about showing the customers to their seats, dealing with unruly youngsters and confiscating catapults. The atmosphere soon became dense with smoke and redolent with the smell of pigs' trotters, chips, mints, oranges and sweat.

Rick checked on the live performers, amateurs who wouldn't expect pay and were glad to have a chance of getting their acts over to a big live audience.

He came charging up to Laura. 'One of the bloody acts hasn't turned up,' he said desperately, 'and I've promised them three. It'll have to be you and me.'

'What?'

'We'll sing. We'll be great, you'll see.'

Laura was too breathless to argue. It would probably be all

right. Rick had a way of carrying people forward on the waves of his obsessions and making them succeed.

He collected the tin money box and locked it in the safe and Laura took her seat at the piano to synchronise appropriate music with the films. She was joined by a budding violinist of fourteen who swore he could easily watch the screen and play at the same time.

The noise during the showing of the wild partying was incredible. Laura banged the music out as hard as she could and Tommy, the violinist, scraped and twanged his fiddle, but surely only a few notes here and there could be heard above the whistles, boos, and cheers of appreciation that filled the air? Phyllis said that the talkies would never catch on because everyone would have to stay quiet when what they mostly wanted was a bloody good night out and Laura decided she would be proved right and Rick wrong, for once. No one would ever hear a word over the raucous noise.

The lights went on, a signal for every small boy to hurl orange peel and sucked trotters at their friends and rivals. Laura tried to keep order. Rick staggered out of the projection room, almost purple-faced, sweat streaming from him, but he was grinning widely. 'Every seat filled, Laura. Every single seat.'

'More than filled,' pointed out Laura looking down to the front where people crammed the sagging benches dangerously.

Laura and Iris took round trays of sweets and chocolate. That had been Rick's idea. He had suggested they might like to wear extra-short skirts like chorus girls, but they refused, Iris crimson with blushes. The happy audience forked out more pennies for the mint humbugs, toffees and gob-stoppers.

The first of the variety acts walked on stage and began to dance to a gramophone record. This was followed by a pair of jugglers who kept dropping things to an accompaniment of boos, jeers and a hail of rubbish.

Then Laura, feeling very small and totally unsure of her ability to hold the audience, climbed on to the stage. She and Rick had decided on *Always* because Laura knew the words. Rick seemed to be able to sing every song published. To her

148

surprise the noise quickly died down. *I'll be loving you, always; With a love that's true, always* – her eyes flickered often to Rick as she poured out her longing. He sang equally soulfully. They received sincere applause.

'That was great, kid. You sounded as if you meant it,' Rick said.

'So did you, Rick,' was all she could manage.

He grinned. 'The jugglers didn't do so well. You'll need to sweep the stage. I'm going to have a word with the dancers. I might be able to get them some professional work; I could do with the commission.'

Laura found a broom and swept away the debris to deafening shouts of 'Show us yer legs', and 'Get off. Bring on Valentino'.

The audience was reasonably stilled when Rick went on-stage to thank everyone for their patronage and to hope that they would return on Thursday for the change of programme. 'We've got, at great expense' – An ironic cheer went up – 'Harold Lloyd in *Safety Last* and *Three Weeks*, with none other than Conrad Nagel. Don't miss the love scenes on a bed of roses and a tiger skin.'

There was a crescendo of whistles from the men, the women were ecstatic, and the small boys blew raspberries – a new, vulgar habit.

Then *The Sheik* began. The film flickered through tobacco smoke, a swirling haze in the projection beam. Any male who spoke above a whisper was verbally – and, in some cases, physically – berated by the women. During the forced seduction scenes Laura and Tommy produced discordant sounds of distress to match the tormented heroine. At the happy end the music was soft as silk and the sobs of the watching women rose to the ceiling as the sheik and Agnes Ayres, the poor abducted beauty, found true love.

Phyllis and the others crowded into the manager's office and Rick opened bottles of port with which they drank to his health and wealth. Phyllis's eyes were red with weeping as she begged Rick to put more Valentino films on.

'I will, but only until the talkies begin,' promised Rick.

'Talkies!' said Phyllis. 'They'll never beat the lovely pictures we've got now.'

Rick just laughed and gave her another glass of port.

Ralph lifted his glass high to Rick. 'Here's to success, mate. You deserve it. I'd never have believed the old place could have been got ready in time.'

Then the second house pushed and jostled their way in and there was no more time for talk. Phyllis stayed to watch her hero again.

The cinema, rechristened The Palace of Delights by Rick's aunt, played two shows a night and Laura and Iris were always there racing around, taking on any job that needed doing. The thought of being in this adventure with Rick was lightening Laura's life. As she sat stripping the endless tobacco she recalled the previous night's work and looked forward to tonight. At the end of the second week Rick handed her and Iris some money. Laura pushed it back at him. 'You can't afford to pay me!'

'Don't be a fool, Laura. You need money as much as I do. Never underestimate what you're worth. If you do, everyone else will and they'll treat you like dirt. The world's a tough place for people like us.'

After such a speech Iris pocketed her wage with a shy smile. 'It seems daft to be paid for havin' fun,' she remarked.

The three of them then began to clean up after the second house, Iris carrying a bucket and mop and a wash cloth to wipe off the sticky messes.

'We'll have to get the place fumigated some time,' said Rick. 'Our beloved patrons bring more in than themselves. And we'll need the rat-catchers.'

The girls looked round nervously. Rick reassured them, 'Oh, they'll not come out yet, but they're watchin' us. If we turned off the lights and waited we'd hear them all right.'

Rick dropped Iris off at home and took Laura on for a drink. They were both dog-tired and for while said little. Then they began to recall incidents from the night's shows.

'One man asked me if I had a twin,' said Laura.

'What did you say?'

'I said I was triplets.'

Rick gave a shout of laughter. 'I wish you were.'

'What, triplets?'

Rick turned to look at her. 'No! I didn't mean it. You're unique, Laura. I've never met a girl like you.'

Laura waited breathlessly, but Rick just leaned back and downed his gin and tonic. 'Another drink?'

'Yes, please. I reckon we've earned it.'

Driving home Rick stopped the car in a lonely road.

'The moon's racing behind the clouds,' said Laura.

'Or the clouds are racin' in front of the moon. Which is it?'

'A bit of each perhaps. Like life. Six of one and half a dozen of the other, like Granma says about quarrels.'

'Have you seen her since you left her?'

'No, but I intend to go back when I've set up in business. Perhaps she'll like me again.'

'Does it mean so much to you?'

'Yes, it does. I lived with her for twelve years and she was good to me in her way, and I miss Grampa a lot.'

'You're a good kid, Laura.' Rick slid his arm over the back of her seat. 'How about a kiss – for luck.'

Laura turned to him and he leaned forward and touched her ready mouth with his. Instantly desire ran through her blood. She put her arms around his neck and her lips moved under his. He gasped and pulled her to him. The kiss deepened as their tongues caressed. Rick's hands roved over her body, driving her to peaks of need. Her own hands moved in an instinctive wish to give pleasure, and touched him. His muscles were taut with his own need. Tell me you love me, she begged silently. Say you love me.

She was shocked when he pushed her hands away and drew back. He lit a cigarette. She refused one, trembling with her need to be part of him.

'Laura, we mustn't be alone together. It's too dangerous. I'm too attracted to you. You're not beautiful, not in an ordinary way –'

'Well, thanks, kid!' she mimicked him desperately.

He laughed. 'You've got somethin' the others haven't, but I won't make love to you. I've explained before, I must have freedom and you'd destroy it. You're meant for marriage, not for brief affairs.'

Laura breathed hard to quell the angry, frustrated sobs she was holding back. She said shakily, 'You're afraid to marry, but if you'd only look at it properly you would see I could be an asset to you. I've helped you already, haven't I?'

'Sure you have and I'm grateful –'

'I don't want your bloody gratitude –'

'Don't swear, Laura.'

'Why not? Everybody else does!'

'That's the point. You're different.'

'Which means that you can't care for me.'

'It means that I might fall for you and I dare not.'

Laura leaned over and put her hands on his shoulders. 'Oh, Rick, please, if you knew –'

'Don't!' He thrust her away. 'I don't want love and marriage and everythin' that goes with it. I want success. I'm not goin' to stop at one flea-pit picture house. I want a big one, more than one, with proper orchestras like they've got at The Regent, and a café where people can eat before or after the show. And no one's goin' to stop me, not even you.' And he climbed out to crank the car. They drove home and parted in silence.

Laura lay awake for a long time in the stuffy bedroom, listening to the sounds of her sleeping sisters. There was a smell of sweat. Keeping properly clean here was difficult. Once a week the tin bath was lifted down from the shed wall and filled with water. The girls bathed first, then the bath was topped up with hot water for the boys. Granma's house had a proper bathroom with a flush lavatory and a hot water geyser and she missed it. The sweat mingled with cheap scent. Laura had lately taken to washing herself in front of Miss Morton's fire using a bowl of water and a wash rag. One day she would have a bathroom and it would be luxurious. She had seen the baths sold in Gregory's, white porcelain, brass taps, soap dishes, special mats and towels. Just as she drifted into sleep her treacherous mind pictured herself and Rick sharing a bathroom – even a bath.

She and Iris worked for Rick until he could afford properly paid help. He always took the two of them home together and there was a barrier between Laura and him which she found unendurable, yet couldn't think how to tear down.

She had saved eight pounds when Miss Morton's landlady came forward with an offer of a bed-sitting room. But Laura felt a strange reluctance to leave her family, which she couldn't understand. Perhaps she still hoped that her parents would show that they loved her. Maybe she feared she would see relief on their faces when she announced she was leaving.

One Saturday evening she was sitting in Dad's chair in the kitchen drinking a cup of cocoa. Lillian was out, as were the boys, Freda and Iris were in bed, and the house was uncannily quiet, the only sound being one of the cats cleaning himself. Then the raucous noise began as the Saturday night drunks turned into the road. As they grew nearer Laura detected the singing of William and Phyllis. Laura wanted to go to bed, she hated to see them drunk, but she felt lethargic, tired, physically and emotionally. The front door opened and she heard her parents giggling and stumbling their way along the passage. They stared at her. Phyllis put a large jug of beer on the table.

'Y – you're in your f – father's – chair,' she accused. 'No one sh -shits there.' She shrieked with mirth. 'Did you hear what I said, William? No one shits there!' They doubled up with mirth, clinging to one another.

'Well, move,' said Phyllis, wiping her eyes.

Laura seated herself on the fender.

'Why don't you go to bed,' suggested William.

'Tha'sh a good idea,' said Phyllis.

'Why? Don't you want me?' Laura felt suddenly angry.

'Want you?' repeated Phyllis. 'Why should we?'

William was filling his pipe with fingers made clumsy by beer.

Phyllis said, 'I've got to go, an' when you've got to go, you've got to –' She tripped over the kitchen mat and swore loudly, before they heard the lavatory door close with a crash that shook the kitchen window overlooking the yard.

William lit his pipe and stuck it in his mouth.

'Mum doesn't want me here. What did I do?' Laura's voice was cracked.

William stared at her, too tipsy to dissemble. 'Ish not your fault, chick. No one could shay it was. But your poor Mum –'

He puffed and Laura waited, seething with impatience, praying that her mother wouldn't come back yet.

'Not your fault, chick. Ish a long time ago.'

'What is? What?'

'When you were five, thash a long time ago – long time –' William's eyelids drooped. Laura felt like shaking him.

'Dad, please –'

'What? Oh, yesh – when Mum had the flu your brother died. Phyllis likes boys better'n girls.'

'The flu wasn't my fault!'

'No more it was, chick, no more it was.'

Phyllis started to sing. She was still seated on the wooden seat in the lavatory.

'Listen to her,' said William, with a grin. 'She'sh a card, ain't she?'

'Why didn't you bring me back after the flu was over?'

'The flu? Yesh. It wasn't that. When you were born – you know about such things, don't you?' William peered at her. 'Yesh, you're a grown woman now. When you were born it was a breech birth. You made my Phyllis very ill.'

'Do you mean that's what she holds against me.'

'There're other things. She was ill for a long time, but she fell again for the twins. When it came time for them to be born Freda was all right, but she had no strength, you see. She'd never recovered from having you. I sent for a doctor, but it was too late. By the time Joyce came the baby was ruined for life. The doctor said she'd been too long in the birthing. No air, d'you see? Her poor mind was touched.'

Laura was aghast. 'Do you mean I've been shut out of my own family all these years because of that. I'm being blamed for Joyce's – slowness. For my brother's death!'

'Not exactly *blamed*. Not *blamed*. But your mum can't help connecting you with it all. The twins were born only eleven months after you.'

Laura stood and stared at her father while flames of resentful fury darted through her. It was his fault, if it was anybody's, that the twins had come along when they did. She wanted to shake him, strike him, shout at him, for sitting calmly in his chair, holding his pipe, breathing out beer fumes as he brought down the fragile edifice of her being.

Chapter Ten

Laura moved the following week into the bed-sitting room. The landlady, Mrs Anderson, was a thin woman with an angry twist to her mouth. She showed Laura the room without a smile. 'I've put your bed up in the corner. There was a time when I'd never have let this room to anyone, but livin's hard today.'

Laura made murmuring sympathetic sounds.

'Oh, you think you know what I mean, I dare say, but you don't. Aren't you the Blackford girl brought up by her grandmother? You didn't know when you was well off. And your grandmother's a real saint. Chapel twice on Sundays and meetin's in the week, too. And your Grandfather – he gives a real good sermon. He's preached at our chapel more than once. Fancy leavin' such a good home. And I've heard you've not been seen in your chapel for weeks, either. Well, there's no tellin' what folk'll do.'

Laura felt a surge of anger which she controlled. No good would come of antagonising Mrs Anderson. She needed this room. She remembered how timidly Miss Morton behaved whenever she had a need to use the kitchen. No wonder. Fortunately a box room had been sacrificed to an upstairs flush lavatory and wash-hand basin with a cold tap.

'I kept my Sunday school class going until the superintendent found another teacher,' said Laura evenly. 'I shall go to chapel again some time. I've been working hard lately.'

Mrs Anderson snorted. 'I suppose you think I haven't! And I don't hold with folk workin' on a Sunday.'

She appeared to have taken the remark as a personal attack. 'The room is lovely,' Laura said.

'Well, it isn't like your grandmother's. I went there once to tea when she was raisin' funds for the missionaries.' There was a note of pride in her voice. 'She gave me a lovely tea, and her front room's a picture. Of course it's all right for them as has husbands, I've had to manage as best I could. I'd have thought you'd never want to leave such a good home and such a lovely grandmother.'

'I must stand on my own feet,' Laura said, as mildly as she could.

Mrs Anderson looked curiously at her. 'That's not the way I heard it, but it's your own business. I never pry. I don't expect others to.'

She looked around the room. 'I've given you one of my best armchairs. It's got covers on, as you see. I had those made when my late husband and me bought it many years ago. Underneath it's still like new. I'd have it in the kitchen, but there's not much room and besides it might pick up kitchen smells. No cookin' is allowed in here, though you can make a cup of tea for yourself over the fire when you've a mind to. The lino is practically new. You'll keep it well polished, of course. You can buy coal from me, if you like. Miss Morton's got her own bunker in the yard.' She looked at the sepia-print religious pictures, at the photograph of the king and queen, and at the mantelshelf covered in dark green velvet with a tasselled fringe. 'Keep the room in good order and you and me'll get along, Miss Blackford. You'll get a key to the front door, but I'll expect you to be in by half past ten unless you tell me otherwise. I'd prefer it if you didn't stay out late. I'm a light sleeper. You can use my stove at seven-thirty in the mornin', twelve mid-day and seven in the evening. Otherwise I'd prefer to have the kitchen to myself.'

'I see.' Laura wondered how Miss Morton had borne this bossy woman for so many years. 'How do I get my washing done?'

'You can go through my room to the washhouse once a week. We'll arrange a convenient time.'

She took the first week's rent of two shillings and sixpence, in advance, and paused at the door. 'By the way I've taken the hearth rug for my own use. You can put one of your own down, if you like.'

Laura stared at the closed door. She could have fared a lot worse. The room was dark, but clean – and it was hers, paid for by her own money. She could enjoy precious time alone and she didn't have to stay here forever. One day she would be able to tell autocratic landladies to go to hell!

Miss Morton laughed at Laura's account of her reception. 'Did she tell you she never pries? She's one of the world's worst gossips. She's not so bad, really. She's honest and she's clean. She's bitter about being left a young widow. Only twenty-five she was when her husband died of a burst appendix. We always have a drink together at Christmas and she gets quite friendly.'

'That's hard to imagine. She was so cold and unwelcoming.'

'We rub along very well together.'

'But life is nothing without friendship, without –' Her tongue failed her again over the word 'love'.

'Love?' prompted Miss Morton gently.

Laura flushed. 'Yes.'

Miss Morton pulled Laura close and gave her a kiss. 'Love will come to you, never fear. You're such a sweet child.'

'Child?' Laura raised an eyebrow. She had reached her eighteenth birthday a week ago. The family had given her a few modest presents, and Rick, a box of chocolates. Granma had ignored it.

'No, not any more,' Miss Morton laughed. 'An independent woman now, with your destiny in your hands.'

Laura left the tobacco stripping room for good on the following Saturday with immense thankfulness, taking with her orders for hat alterations she had not the heart to refuse.

Her hands healed as she cosseted them until she could smooth them along a piece of the finest silk without pulling a thread. Now she must justify her stand. What better way of beginning than to tackle the only wealthy woman with whom she'd had any contact outside of Gregory's. Lady Mallender!

Miss Morton's eyes opened wide, then her face crinkled with mirth. 'Oh, Laura, it's wonderful to have you here so close. You're like –' She stopped, blushing.

'Like what?'

'The daughter I always wanted.'

Laura's throat contracted. She kissed Miss Morton, speechless with gratitude.

Laura dressed carefully in a sweater and skirt, knitted by Miss Morton, in a leaf-green silky yarn. It flowed over her slender figure which needed no savage breast-binding corset to achieve the current shape. Spring was yielding to summer so she could manage without a coat, but she chose her hat with care. She must look absolutely up-to-date and original to gain orders. She had spent hours over a dome block swathing a bottle-green felt with leaf-green satin, allowing the darker colour to show here and there like shade in a spring forest. She added a peacock-blue shiny enamelled brooch, its long thin shape pointing boldly downwards over her face, emphasising its fine-boned planes. She teased her hair out so that gleaming strands of chestnut-brown curved from the sides of the hat in two small wings. A dainty bottle-green purse and gloves were added to her ensemble. She needed smart shoes and couldn't afford more than one pair, so she had spent seven shillings and sixpence on a grey suede pair with small heels, which would go with anything.

She touched her face with powder, rouged her lips, and walked to the nearest shop where she could buy a notebook and pencil, passing Crackers' Corner by the Kingswood Hotel, where unemployed men lingered to talk and enjoy the companionship of others in trouble. There were new faces all the time; there were now two million unemployed. Impossible to visualise such a figure in terms of human beings. She must make a go of her life unless she wanted to join the ranks of the hungry. The older men touched their caps as she walked past. The younger ones whistled. Laura had not been the kind of girl to draw whistles and she enjoyed it. What a difference clothes made.

She could not risk her carefully arranged outfit on the open top of the trams and so sat inside, fighting the queasiness that still plagued her. She arrived at the wrought-iron gates of the Mallender house and was suddenly petrified with nerves. She forced herself to push open the gate. It clanged behind her with a noise that she was sure everyone in the big house must have heard. The front door was opened by the butler.

Laura swallowed and said in tones as well-modulated and precise as she could manage, 'I wish to see Lady Mallender.'

'Is she expecting you?'

'I'm not sure,' Laura dissembled.

'I'll enquire. If you would care to wait here.' He allowed her into the hall. 'I will inform my lady that you are here. May I take your card?'

'I have none with me, I'm afraid.' Laura tried to sound nonchalant. Another lesson learned; she must get some calling cards printed.

'What name shall I give?'

She said firmly, 'Miss Blackford.'

Renton left with a stately step and Laura heard the murmur of voices. He reappeared. 'Lady Mallender has no recollection of asking you to call, Miss Blackford, and does not remember your name. She wishes you to state your business.'

'I have completed commissions for her ladyship in the past,' said Laura carefully, her nerves now threatening her voice. 'I am a fashion designer. I have an offer that I believe will interest her ladyship.'

Renton went away and returned again. 'Lady Mallender still does not recollect you, miss. She is preparing for an *important* committee meeting of one of her *many* charities. She suggests that you return some other time.'

Laura felt sick. 'When?'

'I cannot say, miss. You'd best telephone first.'

Laura almost told him she had never used a telephone. Where did she go from here? Short of rushing past the butler and intruding on Lady Mallender she could think of nothing.

There was a loud knocking on the front door and Renton opened it. A wave of shrill sound preceded the entry of Lady Mallender's nieces, Thelma and Daphne Charlton. Renton took their up-to-the-minute light spring coats with a benevolent smile. 'Your aunt is in her sitting room.'

Thelma stared at Laura. 'Have we met? I'm sure I know you.

160

Are you here for Aunty's charity meeting? What fun! We're hoping she'll hold a fancy dress party. Daphne and I have a wonderful idea. We're going as Laurel and Hardy.'

'Miss Blackford is just leaving,' said Renton, glaring at Laura.

'Your hat!' shrieked Thelma. 'Where did you buy it. It's *too*, too gorgeous, isn't it, Daphne?'

'*Utterly*, utterly. Be a love! Do tell!'

'I am a millinery designer.' Laura's voice was even more prim and precise. 'I made it. I am here to try to interest Lady Mallender, but she's too busy to see me.'

'Nonsense! She'll die when she sees your hat.' The girls shepherded Laura into their aunt's private sanctum, giggling their way past the frustrated butler.

Lady Mallender glanced up and smiled. 'You've brought a friend. Good. The more the better. We must raise as much as possible for the missionaries.'

She's got the same values as Granma, thought Laura. They both ignored hunger and despair right on their doorsteps. 'Do sit down, Miss – I seem to recall your face, but where?' The smile was wiped away. 'You're the insolent girl from Gregory's. How dare you enter my house masquerading as someone else. Ring for Renton, Thelma.'

Thelma ignored the command. 'That's where we met. In Gregory's. And you made us ducky little purses. We still use them, don't we Daphne?'

'Absolutely,' said Daphne, flinging herself into an easy chair and inserting a cigarette into a long tortoiseshell holder.

'Don't you adore her hat, Aunty,' demanded Thelma.

Lady Mallender looked consideringly at it and Laura drew a deep breath. By whatever means, she was in her ladyship's presence and she would make the most of it. 'I have left Gregory's,' she began.

'Oh I know.' giggled Thelma. 'That *ghastly* Arthur Gregory told us you'd got the sack. Does the nasty Arthur keep his hands to himself at work? I bet he doesn't. He's like an octopus.'

'Thelma!' Lady Mallender thundered, her long nose quivering.

'Sorry, Aunty, but he is a lecherous swine, you know.'

Daphne said, 'Fancy getting sacked. Poor old you. What happened? Where do you work now? Where's Nancy, Aunty Maud? She'll be here, won't she?'

Laura lowered her eyes and held herself rigid to mask her anger. These two flappers, shallow and pleasure-loving, had been the cause of her dismissal and indirectly her break from her home, and they couldn't even bother to listen to answers to their questions.

'Of course Nancy will be here,' said Lady Mallender. 'I wish you girls would have a talk with her. She gets far too upset about the working classes. I keep telling her they don't feel things the way we do, but she insists –' Lady Mallender's eyes fell on Laura. 'You're still here! Will one of you please ring for Renton, or must I rise and do it myself?'

'Don't send her away.' The girls were vociferous. 'Do you know she made her darling hat herself? She's a milliner now.'

'A milliner? I thought you made purses.'

'Yes, your ladyship, but I feel that my vocation is for hats.' Laura heard her bold reply with a certain amount of awe. Vocation, indeed!

'And you made the one you are wearing?'

'Yes, your ladyship. I have set up a workroom and am looking for exclusive clients. You are, of course, the first lady I thought of. I know how meticulously you match up your accessories, and you have so much influence in Bristol. Your patronage would be very welcome.' Laura wondered why they couldn't sense the treacly flattery. That they couldn't was patently obvious. Lady Mallender actually smiled.

'I'll be one of your first customers,' cried Thelma, who seemed to be the bolder of the sisters. 'I want a hat just like the one you're wearing –'

'I'm sorry, Miss Charlton, but I never repeat a model. Each one is designed to suit the wearer's features and hair colouring and, of course, must match her garments.'

Thelma pouted her bright red lips. She was smoking with a

cigarette holder even longer than her sister's.

'As a matter of fact,' said Lady Mallender, ponderously, 'your hat would go beautifully with my new bottle green suit. It's a pity it isn't new.'

'I'm wearing it today for the first time.'

'My suit is almost finished. Ring for Gardner, please, Daphne.'

Daphne rose and sauntered languidly across the room and pressed a button near the fireplace.

Gardner came hurrying in. Her eyes fell on Laura and her skin grew blotchy. 'Is that girl pestering you, m'lady? Mr Renton told me –'

'Simmer down, Gardner, old thing,' said Daphne. 'She's here at Aunty's invitation.'

Lady Mallender chose to disregard the inaccuracy. 'Gardner, bring me the colour swatches of my new spring outfit.'

As the maid left Thelma said, 'It's no good, Aunty Maud, Miss – what's your name? Blackford! I must try to remember! Miss Blackford said she won't let anyone have her hat.'

'No doubt she will if I pay enough,' boomed Lady Mallender.

Laura fumed inwardly. They talked about her as if she weren't there. If her arrogant ladyship wanted this hat she could have it, but she would pay damned well for it!

Gardner brought the swatches and was dismissed. As she passed Laura she gave her a look of dislike.

'You see!' exclaimed Lady Mallender. 'I knew I was right. It matches beautifully. I can carry colours in my head.' She turned to Laura. 'That's a talent you would do well to develop, young woman, if you want to be successful.'

'Yes, my lady,' said Laura, outwardly meek. The cheek of the woman! Laura had been good with colours since she was a child.

Laura stared at her ladyship. She was seated and Laura, not having been invited to sit was able to look down her nose at her. Their eyes met and a challenge flashed between them. Laura lifted the hat from her head and handed it to Lady Mallender who peered inside and then at Laura's shiningly clean hair. She rose and walked to the mirror over the mantelpiece and pulled on the hat. It fitted and did indeed match exactly the dark green of the suit and the pale green of the silk of which the blouse was made.

'I shall take your hat,' announced Lady Mallender. 'It fits me perfectly.' She sounded slightly aggrieved, as if a mere milliner had no right to the same sized head as herself. 'How much?'

Laura said without a quiver in her voice. 'Four guineas, your ladyship.'

'Four guineas! Outrageous! I could buy a hat from a proper milliner in London for little more. And it's *second-hand*!'

Laura said nothing. She stood perfectly still and waited. Lady Mallender took another long look in the mirror.

'It suits you beautifully, Aunty,' said Daphne.

'I should buy it,' advised Thelma. She pouted childishly. 'But I still hold a teensy weensy grudge that you wouldn't sell it to me, Miss Blackford.'

Lady Mallender reached for her purse and counted out four pound notes and four shillings. Laura thanked her courteously, before taking out her notebook and pencil and recording her first sale.

'Give me your address,' demanded Thelma. 'You must make a hat for me.'

'Me, too,' said Daphne.

'My quarters are a little cramped at present,' said Laura. 'Until I move into new premises I prefer to call on ladies at home.'

Thelma scribbled a note. 'Here's our address. Will you come tomorrow morning?'

Laura agreed and moved to the door. As it opened a girl stood framed for a moment. She was quite short, not much above five feet, pale and slender, her curly bobbed hair was light brown, her eyes a little darker. She paused hesitantly, as if shy, before entering.

'Nancy!' squealed the Charlton girls. 'About time. We've lots to do and heaps of jolly larks to tell you.'

Nancy smiled at Laura, before walking over to seat herself beside her mother. She sat awkwardly, clasping her hands in her lap so tightly that the knuckles were white.

Laura was shown out by an obviously resentful Renton and stood on the pavement outside the Mallender residence shaking with reaction. She felt suddenly cold, then laughed aloud in triumph. Four guineas for a bit of felt and decoration! And she had designed it and made it herself. She had sold something that had been conceived in her brain and fashioned by her hands. She laughed again, seeing success stretching before her.

'What's so funny, baby?'

She whirled to see Rick. Somehow it seemed right that he was there. He had rescued her after her humiliation on her previous visit. He should share her triumph now. 'I've just sold my own new hat, Rick. To Lady Mallender. I walked right in and announced I had a vocation and she bought the hat off my head. For four guineas.'

Rick whistled, then hugged her and kissed her nose. 'Great stuff, kid. Let's celebrate.'

He handed her into his shabby car as if she were a lady, bowing extravagantly. 'Welcome Miss Blackford, milliner extraordinary.'

As they drove away, Laura asked, 'How did you happen to be here?'

'I called on you at home, then tracked you to Miss Morton's. She said you'd gone to see her snobby ladyship, but wouldn't tell me why. She looked as if she had a secret joke.'

'It was a joke,' Laura laughed. Then she sobered. 'Oh, Rick, that house of the Mallenders is so rich. They've got loads of servants. I was about to be thrown out when the two Charlton girls arrived.' She explained what had happened. 'I suppose I've them to thank for getting me in, but their lives are so empty, they're – they're –'

'Parasites on the body of the nation?' finished Rick.

Laura stared at him. His head was wreathed in cigarette smoke which floated from a Woodbine dangling from his lips.

He grinned. 'I saw that in a book. I bet you think I don't read. You'd be wrong. I'm goin' to make the big time and I'm discoverin' everythin' I can about people, especially the idle rich. They've got two things I want. Money and influence. You did quite right to stand up for yourself. Four guineas. My God, if you sell only one hat a week at that price you'll be in clover, but you'll do much better than that. You'll be rollin' in money in no time. What you need are premises not too far from the town centre, with workrooms, and a shop.'

'You're going too fast,' said Laura. 'So far I've got four guineas and a bit of money I've saved. How's the cinema business?'

'Packin' 'em in two shows a night. I've got hold of some of the older films. The women flock to see their heroes, especially –'

'Don't tell me! Rudolf Valentino! Who's playing piano for you now?'

'I do it myself. I've got a chap who understands about projectors, and a couple of sisters to take the money and try to keep order.'

'Are you making enough to pay so many?'

'Sure am. Those pennies mount up and it doesn't cost a lot to hire old films.' Rick became serious. 'I'm savin'. When the talkies arrive it'll be every cinema for itself. Some of the big ones are already gettin' set for sound.'

'You seem very sure people will want it.'

'They'll want it, all right, baby.'

Rick stopped the car at a pub on the outskirts of town. They sat in the lounge and Laura sipped at a Bristol Cream sherry. It was the first time she had tasted it and she enjoyed its smooth feel on her throat, the delicate flavour, and the warm glow it produced. 'I could get addicted to this,' she laughed.

To her surprise Rick became solemn. He put his hand over hers. 'Don't say that, baby, not even in fun. A drunk woman's not a pretty sight.'

Laura thought of her mother reeling down the road on a Saturday night. Dad didn't seem to mind.

Rick still held her hand and all other thoughts fled. She wanted to lift it to her lips. Her senses stirred, inviting her, tempting her, daring her to fling aside caution and kiss Rick.

There was no one else in the bar. Even the barman was talking to some men on the other side of the partition which divided the lounge area from the public bar. It took all her will to resist. She must be careful if she was not to scare Rick off. But one day, she told herself, he would love her as she loved him. One day, he would be hers.

Chapter Eleven

Laura's elder brother, Ralph, called on her one evening and she greeted him happily. He was dressed in a scuffed leather coat donated by some rich man to his scavenger's cart, and a pair of thick tweed trousers, but he had an air about him.

'The word is that you're doing fine, Laura.'

'Oh. And who's word might that be?'

'Guess.'

'Rick Merriman.'

'Give the lady a teddy bear,' said Ralph in a raucous fairground voice. That was another talent he possessed. The ability to imitate voices. Laura was struggling to match her accent to those of her clients. When Lillian heard her she was scathing about folk who thought they were better than they should be, but Laura ignored her. Life was hardening her rapidly as she dealt with the usually unconscious, unrelenting rudeness of some of her clients.

'I might have guessed, though how he knows – I've not seen him for weeks.' She thought she had kept her disappointment from her tone, but Ralph looked sharply at her.

'Don't fall for that one, love. He's strictly a loner.'

Laura laughed and shrugged. 'As if I would. And men aren't the only ones who put business first. I intend to succeed, too.'

Ralph grinned. 'You will, I'm sure of it, but you need a proper place to work and sell your stuff. That's why I'm here. I've rented a place quite near Gregory's. I've collected enough decent second-hand things to set up properly. There's a large shop and a smaller one.'

'Oh, Ralph, I'm so glad for you. You'll be an impresario, or is it an entrepreneur?'

'I thought I was going to be an antique dealer!'

'Idiot!'

'Impresario! Entrepreneur! Those words are Rick's, aren't they? But I didn't come here to talk about him. He's more than capable of carving out his own life. It's you I'm interested in, Laura. I can offer you the small shop. It's got its own doorway into the street and a display window that would just suit you. You'd have three floors and you could set up workrooms. They'd be small, too, but could give you a great deal more scope than you've got here.'

'Ralph, it sounds wonderful, but I don't earn enough yet to pay for a shop.'

Miss Morton knocked and came in with a tray of tea in time to hear Laura's last words. 'Nothing ventured, nothing gained,' she said.

'Do you think I should go, Miss Morton?'

'I'll miss working with you, I can't deny that, but I'll see you when you come home.'

Ralph said gently, 'I was assuming that Laura would move to the shop. There are quite decent living areas on the top floor. I shall be in a flat next door so she wouldn't be alone, and I mean to install a connecting door so I can look after her.'

'Take the chance,' said Miss Morton. 'It means that people can come to you. Think of the time you'll save when you don't have to call on the customers. You can come and tell me all about it.'

Ralph said, 'I had a notion that you might work with Laura.'

'She's retired,' protested Laura.

'No, I'm not!' Miss Morton smiled delightedly. 'I've just become unretired. Give me a job, please. I don't need much pay. In fact,' she looked thoughtful, 'I've got a bit of money saved. I should very much like to put it into your business.'

Laura was horrified. 'But you can't! What if I fail? I should feel dreadful about it.'

'You're not going to fail, my love. And I shall feel left out if you don't give me a share.'

Laura looked from Ralph to Miss Morton, her stomach churning. She had set herself up comfortably here. Daphne and

Thelma Charlton had bought several hats from her and had boasted of Laura's exclusivity and she was earning enough from them and their friends to feel safe. To step outside was a risk. Many people, thrown out of regular jobs as unemployment crept higher, had tried to make good on their own and failed. But she *would* succeed! She would! She took a deep breath. 'I'll move, Ralph. And I'll gladly let you help me, Miss Morton, but I'll pay interest on money I borrow. That must be firmly understood.'

The premises were in a sad state of dilapidation and Ralph worked long hours, cleaning and painting them. He refused Laura's help, insisting that she must keep her hands soft. Laura discovered that he had, for years, been renting a corner of a warehouse and from it he brought bits of furniture for them both. Her bedroom was spartan. A bed, a table, a chair and a cupboard. Iris turned up often to help and surprised Laura one day with a rag rug sent by Phyllis in a burst of generosity. And once Betty, on her way home from Gregory's, caught sight of Laura in the empty shop and became fascinated by the venture and proved she could wield a nifty paintbrush.

On the Friday before the weekend she was to move Laura went to visit her parents. Lately she had seen little of them. She took a box of chocolates to mother as an extra thank you for the rug, which had been washed and dried before being sent and Laura was touched. The rug was old; in fact, as a child, Laura had lain upon it often and traced the strands of material with a questing finger, seeing the remnants of several family garments, worn by too many children to be of further use. Seeing it had transported Laura back to her childhood like nothing else had ever done. It had acted as a catalyst, resurrecting snippets of conversation, detrimental to herself, which she had blocked from her mind. If, as a child, she had possessed the eye and ear of an adult she would have understood so much more. But there was no changing the past. It was the future that mattered, but remembrances of Phyllis sobbing, groaning, shrieking her misery at bereavement and childbirth, and her anger at fate, permeated Laura's dreams.

She walked past the little ones playing on the patch of grass and entered her parents' house. The smell of leather and steam and starch and hot, ironed linen came at her in a wave. Phyllis glanced round from her place at the scullery sink.

'Oh, it's you.'

'I've come to tell you I'm moving.'

Phyllis rubbed a pillow case vigorously on the wash-board. 'Covered in lipstick. The dirty madam can't even bother to wash before she goes to bed. Having bathrooms don't make you cleaner, it seems. Rick told us you're takin' a shop.'

'Rick? You mean Ralph.'

Phyllis paused and rubbed the back of her red hands on her sweating forehead. 'I know who I mean, thank you very much.'

She continued to work and Laura felt anger burst within her. 'Well, thank you, Mum, for your kind attention. I'll be on my way. I just thought –'

'Not so fast, Miss Hoity-toity. I must get this mess off before I can put it in the boiler with the sheets. Make us a cup of tea. I could do with it.'

Instantly contrite, Laura made the tea. She tipped a bag of mixed biscuits she had brought on to a plate. William, who was dozing over the range, woke and looked blearily at her. 'Hello, chick. I hear you've been busy. Setting up for yourself, eh? Just like our Ralph.'

Laura nodded. 'Can I pour you a cup, Dad? Would you like a biscuit?'

He ate the biscuit fast and held out a hand for more. 'Rick said you're already doing well. You'll soon be able to keep your old Dad in tobacco.'

'When did you see Rick?'

'What? Oh, the other day. Can't remember exactly when. He calls a fair bit. Give me a custard cream, chick. They're my favourite.'

Phyllis entered, wiping her hands on her coarse sack apron. 'Tea. And biscuits,' she said with satisfaction. 'Have you given your Dad a custard cream. They're his favourites.'

'Yes. Mum, how often does Rick call here?'

'Oh, not often. He's busy, like yourself.'

'Why does he come here?'

'Why shouldn't he?' demanded Phyllis belligerently.

'That's enough, chick,' said William. 'Can't have you questioning your mother like that. It's not respecful.'

The boys came through from the shed. Their joyful cries of 'Biscuits! On a Friday!' brought Priscilla and Virginia racing into the kitchen. Baby Greta tottered after them, newly walking, still wobbly on her chubby legs. Within seconds the plate was empty.

'Won't our Lillian be cross when we tell her we ate all the biscuits,' said Priscilla. 'She's got a new boyfriend, Laura. You know him. Have you got anythin' else to eat?'

Laura shook her head. 'What's her boyfriend's name?'

'You know his name. Haven't you brought us some sweets?'

'Not today. Why do I know his name?'

Phyllis who had fallen into a lethargic state over her tea started. 'That's enough, you kids. Out of the kitchen. Can't have you under my feet.'

'Wait!' Laura's voice was a command. 'Prissy, who's Lillian's new boyfriend?'

'Rick,' shouted Priscilla as she left with her sisters.

'He takes her out sometimes, that's all,' said Phyllis. Her voice was placating.

'Rick Merriman?' asked Laura. 'Rick is taking out Lillian?'

William nodded. 'Just friends, you know. He's not the marrying kind.'

Laura rose, unable to bear any more. She kissed them and hurried away, her feet beating a tattoo on the pavement in rhythm with the drumming of Rick's name in her head. She should have known. When Lillian saw her chance she would grab at anything Laura wanted. It was inevitable. And Lillian was pretty, and had experience with boys, and once her day's work was over was free to indulge herself. Laura wondered if she was also free with her body. Images of her sister locked in Rick's arms, kissing, caressing – it was unendurable. She had sworn to herself that she would not show jealousy if he had girlfriends as long as he came back to her, but it seemed she had been fooling herself. And to date Lillian, her own sister, and the one who lost no opportunity to taunt her, that was a different matter.

By Sunday tea time Laura's few possessions were in the shop. There were two signboards out front. One proclaimed simply *Ralph Blackford – Antiques*, the other *Hats by Laura*. Miss Morton had suggested the name of Laura's business. 'And just put it into small letters, my love. Rich folk are used to being dazzled by swanky displays. When I was learning my trade I had a teacher who said: "Be understated. It impresses people if they think you don't need your work." It didn't turn out that way for me, but that's because I just *make* hats. You *create* them. There's a world of difference.'

Upstairs the two work rooms were furnished with trestle tables holding Miss Morton's precious hat blocks, smoothing irons, boards, measures, paint brushes, tailor's chalk, kettles for steam, and all the other paraphernalia needed by a milliner. A sink with a cold-water tap had been newly plumbed in, and Ralph had fixed mirrors which would reflect the hats and help to keep their shapes properly balanced in the making. Materials were lying in coloured profusion on the shelves. Ralph, Betty and Iris had helped and at the end of the long two days Ralph produced wine and they all drank a toast to success.

On Monday morning the two shops opened. Ralph's friends had previously visited as many wealthy houses as they could, dropping cards through letter-boxes. On each card was a handwritten invitation to any lady or gentleman who would care to call into either of the shops on opening day. Laura, knowing she had already gained a reputation for her models, was filled with hope. Her small window contained a length of shimmering crimson satin and two hats. One was a felt in bands of soft greys with narrow wings of a brim which would almost conceal the wearer's eyes in a flirtatious way. It was finished with a black and grey ribbon and bow. The other was a severe black straw cloche embellished with a crimson diamanté hat pin at the front. They were on blocks on which Laura had painted blue eyes, half veiled by lashes, and a scarlet slash of a mouth. Draped from a hidden nail were long strands of multi-coloured costume beads which made a glorious swirl of pattern beneath the hats. Two small formal purses in crimson and black and two pairs of gloves completed the display. Laura took a final look from outside.

'Looks like a collection of jewels,' said Rick's voice.

Laura whirled round in a flare of joy she couldn't control. 'Does that mean you approve?'

'Sure do, baby. It's great. I dropped your cards round to all the richest people.'

'*You* did?'

'Well, me and a few mates.'

'Thanks.' Laura produced a strained smile.

'Don't get too excited!'

'I won't.' Laura walked back into the shop followed by Rick.

'What in hell's up with you?' he snapped.

Laura wanted to lie, to pretend, but she couldn't. 'Lillian,' she said, her mouth stiff with anger.

'Oh, so that's it. Is there a law that says I can't take your sister out?'

'You didn't have time to see me.'

'Right! I didn't have time.'

'Yet you had dates with her.'

'I'll go out with any girl I choose. What business is it of yours?'

'None!' Laura turned away to rearrange unnecessarily the hats in the shop.

'I thought we were friends, baby. I thought we agreed on that.'

'Yes, we agreed.'

'Have you nothing more to say?'

Laura turned slowly and stared coolly at him. 'Nothing. We're friends. All right.'

Rick walked out, obviously still annoyed, and Laura sat down abruptly on one of the two small chairs, carefully painted silver by Harold. She gazed round. The walls were white, a background for more costume jewellery, most of which Ralph had salvaged. He had renovated it and Laura understood for the first time that he had become skilled at all sorts of restoration work. The small counter was pale oak. The shop interior was hidden from the street by the back-window drapes, and there was a square of soft-gold-coloured carpet. The place exuded elegance and she should have been quivering with excitement. Instead her heart was thumping with anger and hurt.

The Charlton girls arrived with three of their friends. Laura poured wine into glasses provided by Ralph.

'No cocktails, darling?' cried Thelma. 'Oh, well. Here's to the new shop.'

Toasts were drunk and continued to be drunk throughout the day. Laura became expert at appearing to drink while sipping at nothing and remaining sober. Ralph was getting visitors, too, though not as many as his sister. 'It's not to be expected, Laura,' he said calmly. 'My stuff isn't yet the kind that'll bring them in, but it will be. I've sold a reasonable amount. The rent's covered, anyway, though I may have to come to you for a crust.' His grin took any worry from her mind.

Just before six when she was about to close, the musical chime on the door sounded and Lady Mallender walked in, accompanied by a young man.

'So you have your own shop,' said her ladyship, looking about her. 'Quite a nice decor – for a shop, of course. Quite nice. What do you think, Adrian?'

'Very attractive,' said the young man. 'Different.' His eyes were on Laura. They were brown and gentle. His brown hair looked soft, silky even, and a strand fell over his forehead. He brushed it back with a graceful gesture. He was not tall, about five feet nine, Laura reckoned.

'I've heard a lot about you, Miss Blackford,' he said. 'My cousins rave over your hats and purses.'

'I'm grateful to them for free advertising,' said Laura in her professional voice.

Lady Mallender pointed an imperious finger at a raspberry pink straw with a darker pink ribbon. 'I will try that one on, Miss Blackford. I suppose we had better call you Laura now. *Hats by Laura*. Quite a nice sound. The hat will be exactly right for Henley Regatta. The brim will shield my eyes from the sun.'

Laura seated Lady Mallender in front of a gilded mirror and

carefully placed the pink straw on her head. Her ladyship twisted her head this way and that as Laura held up another mirror behind her.

'I'll take it,' she announced.

'No, your ladyship,' said Laura gently.

'No! What can you mean? How dare you! The hat is for sale, is it not?'

'Yes, your ladyship, but it does not suit you.'

'Who are you to say? Why doesn't it?'

'It is too pink, your ladyship. Your complexion requires softer shades.'

'My complexion? You are criticising my complexion?'

'No, your ladyship. I am simply stating a fact. Your skin is excellent and you have a fine colour that will not be enhanced by the hat.'

Lady Mallender stared at her reflection, before snatching off the hat and dashing it down on to the shelf, knocking three others from their stands in her anger. 'Well, I shall think twice before patronising your shop again, Miss Blackford. The idea! Criticising a client.'

Adrian, who had been leaning languidly against the door, said, 'She's right, you know, Mother. The colour is entirely wrong for you.'

Lady Mallender subsided immediately and gazed at her son with eyes so full of love that Laura caught her breath. 'Not right, darling?'

Adrian shook his head. His hair slid over one eye again and he shook it back impatiently. 'Laura is being honest with you. Laura,' he turned to her, 'fit that one over there on my mother.'

Laura carefully placed a navy blue straw with a navy bow on Lady Mallender's head. Her ladyship nodded. 'It does suit me, Adrian. You are quite right, as always. How clever of you!' She said over her shoulder, 'I will buy it. How much is it?'

'It should be five guineas, your ladyship, but in view of your past help and because it is my first day I shall ask only three and a half.'

Lady Mallender looked as delighted as Laura felt. The hat had cost only shillings to make. She had to keep reminding herself of Miss Morton's words. 'They pay to be exclusive, Laura. Never forget it. The actual cost of making the hat is unimportant.'

Lady Mallender admired herself again in the mirror and Laura caught Adrian's eyes. He smiled and gave a tiny wink. He lifted the hat from his mother's head with hands that were as white as a woman's. Clearly he did nothing more manual than drive a car. Beside them Rick's hands were large and coarse, she thought, with a shaft of pain and anger that hurt her bitterly as she thought of him touching Lillian.

She fetched a hatbox from upstairs. It was white, silver and gold, to match the decor and Adrian looked at it approvingly.

She drew aside the drapes and peeped through the front window as he helped his mother into a brand-new car, took the wheel and drove off. She sighed, then saw Rick approaching again. She had an impulse to lock the door, but didn't. Never again would she let him think he could upset her.

He strode in, filling the shop with his presence, bringing a smell of smoke, petrol, oil, hair cream. 'Whose Bentley was that driving away?'

'Adrian Mallender's.'

'Typical. A three-litre sports four-seater Bentley and he's never done a day's work in his life. He was up at Oxford, but didn't bother with tuition and now he spends money like it was water.'

'How do you know so much?'

'I make it my business to know about people, especially the swells. They're the ones with the money.'

'Money! That's all you think of.'

'I deny it, m'lord. I mean, m'lady.'

Laura smiled reluctantly. 'Is there something you wanted? I'm about to close. I'm tired.'

His manner changed. 'Are you, baby? I'm not surprised you're worn out dealin' with rich bitches. I hope you've stung them for plenty. I've just been in to see Ralph. He's got some good stuff. He's clever, is your brother.'

'I agree. You still haven't said why you're here. Surely you'll be late for your date.' She didn't add 'with Lillian', but the words hung on the air between them.

'Haven't got a date. Ralph suggested we go out for a meal together – the three of us. To mark the openin' of the double Blackford empire.'

'I don't know. I'll need to wash and change. I'm not sure I've got the energy.'

'Ralph will be disappointed.'

'What about you?' she couldn't resist asking, and was immediately irritated with herself.

'I'll be disappointed, too.'

She stared at him. She compared his face with its broad planes and almost stubby nose with Adrian Mallender's fine-drawn features. And instantly forgot Adrian.

The three of them ate dinner in a small restaurant of the kind Laura had only read about. The lights were low, the small orchestra played modern tunes and people danced on a pocket handkerchief of a floor. She drank a cocktail – a Sidecar – before they were seated, and chose food she had never tasted before, mulligatawny soup which made her tongue burn so that she drank a glass of wine quickly. It joined the Sidecar with its mix of brandy and Cointreau and when the men laughed at her she laughed with them without knowing why. She ate quails and saddle of lamb and a sugary pudding, drinking the appropriate wines with each, and followed it all with coffee and an orange-flavoured liqueur. Her head was spinning and she remembered with horror the time she had vomited after too much drink. Then she relaxed. Tonight she felt fine. Perhaps the food soaked up the booze. She giggled for no reason and Ralph and Rick broke off their talk of money matters and smiled at her.

'Come on, little sister, time to get you to bed.'

'To bed,' she agreed.

The men held an arm each as they supported her from the restaurant and she sat in the back of Rick's jolting car while the world spun pleasantly around her head. Ralph saw her to her bedroom and removed her shoes. 'Come on, love. You need to sleep. Try to get your clobber off.'

She remembered no more and when she awoke to the harsh

ringing of the alarm clock she was lying on the bed, still dressed, covered with a blanket. She sat up and groaned. Her head ached, her mouth fell desert-dry and her eyes seemed full of dust. A wash in cold water, a couple of aspirins and lashings of tea brought her round and she was in the shop at nine o'clock, waiting for clients.

Chapter Twelve

One June morning Rick strolled into the shop. Although it was only just past nine the sun was hot and Laura had dressed for the day in cool green. She had decided from the beginning that there would be no shop uniform for her. Her hair was newly shingled and washed, her nails matched her lipstick, both the brilliant red demanded by the latest fashions. She was pleased with her appearance.

Rick whistled as he looked her up and down. '*Nice baby*,' he began to sing.

'Stop it!' she snapped.

Rick was taken aback, then he just shrugged. 'You're annoyed with me. We were friends on the night we had dinner.'

'That was different.'

'How?'

'It was a celebration for Ralph and me. You just happened to be there.'

'I see. I also just happened to help Ralph carry you upstairs and –'

Laura's face flamed, her nerves jumped. 'And what?'

'Lie you on your bed. What in hell did you think I was goin' to say? You had your big brother protectin' you.'

'Do you mean that if Ralph hadn't been there you would have –'

'Would have what?'

'You know bloody well what I mean!'

'Don't swear!'

'Why in hell shouldn't I?'

'Because I don't like it.'

'Oh! The great Rick Merriman doesn't like me swearing. Well, what's it got to do with you?'

'Laura, I thought we'd agreed to be friends and, just for the record, I would not have laid a wrong finger on you if Ralph hadn't been there.'

'No,' she agreed and turned away from him to re-arrange a perfectly arranged hat. No, you wouldn't, her thoughts spun on. You wouldn't even if I'd been in full possession of my senses and wanted you. She stopped. If she wasn't careful she would walk headlong into a quagmire of emotion. She would betray the fact that she had missed him, had longed for him and ached for his kisses. It was a pain that wouldn't go away, this wanting Rick. But he was not hers, and never would be, according to Ralph. He said Rick was a rolling stone and wouldn't change. He would take a woman out, coax what he could from her, then leave her. Rick had not treated her that badly. The Charlton girls and their friends would have taken him in their stride. Their conversations in the shop were stunningly revealing about themselves. Marriage to a man in their own social sphere with plenty of money was what they aimed for but, before they settled, they wanted a jolly good time. Virginity, it seemed, was a joke, but she suspected much of the young women's talk was bravado – merely fashionable. Though a few members of the young upper classes appeared to be astonishingly free in their behaviour. As long as no one got embarrassingly pregnant, their motto was 'anything goes'. She had never dreamed that owning an exclusive millinery shop would provide such an education.

Only yesterday Thelma Charlton had chattered to two of her friends about how some society girl had got married the week before. 'A hurried affair, darlings, and she had to carry a *disgustingly* large bouquet in front of her and pretend she felt too overcome to stand at the reception because her mama kept her seated until it was time to leave. Can you imagine that?'

The girls had shrieked and said what an idiot she was when there was such a thing as contraception. They talked as if Laura were not there – something she was getting used to. If you weren't 'one of them' you had no ears, eyes, or voice except to serve them.

As she busied herself about the shop Rick's large hands came down suddenly over hers. She stared at them. They had rough black hairs on the backs and they were coarse – no, not coarse, strong, very strong. She jerked her mind from thoughts of how gentle they could be and shook herself free.

'I didn't say you could paw me.'

'You didn't mind once.'

She was furious. 'You fling that at me. You have the nerve to take out my sister, then –' Her voice broke. 'You – you – bastard!'

He went white and she realised with sudden horror what she had called him. The word was bandied about so freely by her customers that she had forgotten it had a meaning of ghastly import for him. 'Rick, I'm sorry, I wasn't thinking –'

'Weren't thinkin' what?' His brows were a dark straight line above his angry eyes.

'Nothing, Rick.'

'Someone's told you the dread secret of my birth,' he said in a flippant tone that conveyed more to her than his restrained fury. She had no reply and he stared at her a moment longer, a muscle working in his jaw. 'I'll be seein' you,' he said, before he turned and left.

Laura cursed her loose tongue.

A moment later Miss Morton came down the narrow back-stairs from the workroom. 'I've engaged a girl for the job you advertised, Laura. Noreen Staines, her name is. I've offered her twenty-two and six a week to start with, and the prospect of eightpence an hour piecework when she's proficient and she's happy with that. She's a widow, still only thirty-one. Her husband was killed in France in 1918. One of the last shots fired. Somehow that makes it more terrible. She's had a good apprenticeship in the trade and is enthusiastic. She's also got ideas of her own.'

Laura hesitated. Being an employer was something so alien to her that she was not quite sure how to react. 'Ideas of her own? I'm supposed to be the creative one.' She softened her words with a rueful smile.

'Of course, Laura, my dear, but if trade goes on at the rate it's begun you'll not be able to cover everything yourself. Noreen will defer to you, of course. You've been working day and night to get the shop going and you can't keep on like that. You're thinner than ever, love, and I would have said that was impossible. You must have time to rest and think and plan, as well as look after the financial side.'

Laura kissed Miss Morton. 'You're so sweet. You once said I was the kind of daughter you wanted. You're more like a mother to me than a friend.'

Miss Morton flushed and hurried back upstairs. Laura thanked God once more for her. She squared her shoulders. She would succeed. She must!

She went to visit Granma that night, taking precious time off from work. Grampa opened the door and his face lit up with pleasure. He drew her into the little hallway and kissed and hugged her. It was the most spontaneous gesture of affection she had ever received from a member of her family and it tightened her throat.

'Who is it, Wilfrid?' Granma's imperious tones boomed out.

Grampa hurried to the living-room door. 'It's our Laura come to see us, love.'

'Laura!'

Laura waited for a swift dismissal. After a silence Granma said, 'Well, don't just stand there. Tell her to come through.'

Laura entered the kitchen and was surprised to find that it felt like coming home.

She ran forward. 'Oh, Granma, I'm so glad to see you again. I've missed you.' She dared to bend forward and brush a kiss on Granma's cheek.

'Glad to see me, are you. Huh! You were glad enough to leave me not so long ago. And you've come back a lot bolder than you left.'

'I had to go. I'm sorry I quarrelled with you.'

'How's the big romance going?' Granma's tone was sarcastic.

'It isn't,' Laura said flatly.

'I could have told you so. That Rick Merriman is no use to anyone. Fly-by-night, that's what he is. Going from job to job like a tramp. Has ideas above his station. The stage! Huh!'

Granma rose. In spite of the heat she wore a heavy dark-brown watered-grosgrain frock with a high neck and long sleeves. A cameo brooch was pinned at her throat. She stood a moment looking Laura up and down and Laura felt like a little girl again caught out in something naughty. She had put on a yellow pleated skirt and a blouse to match. Her hat was a pale violet and sported a yellow rose.

'You've not cut your skirts above your knees yet.'

'Not yet, Granma,' said Laura, daring to make her tone slightly humorous.

'That's a pretty dress, though it'll show the dirt. Did you make it yourself?'

'With help from Miss Morton and Iris.'

'I hear you've given Miss Morton a regular job. At her age. She's over sixty. Should be retired.'

'She wanted to work.'

'I like your hat. Is it one of your own make?'

'It is, and thank you, Granma.'

'I might let you make one for me. Perhaps for next Whitsuntide. It'll have to be black, mind. None of your fancy colours.' Granma slid the kettle from the hob to the fire. 'Wilfrid, bring out the cake tin. I could do with a bite to eat. And you,' she said turning to Laura and frowning, 'look as if you could do with a good meal. You're like a skinned rabbit.'

She sounded no less critical than always, but Laura thought she could detect a different note in her voice. Could it possibly be that Granma had begun to respect her? She hoped so. She realised that she actually cared for the stubborn old woman.

Grampa winked at her behind Granma's back as she bent to pour hot water into the brown earthenware teapot. He piled a fancy plate with home-made cakes and brought cups and saucers and teaplates from the dresser. Laura suddenly felt hungry for the first time for days and tucked in greedily, watched by Granma who actually appeared to approve. Not so long ago she would have made a remark about 'folk who stuff themselves like pigs'.

As she finished the last crumb and wiped her fingers on the

linen napkin, Laura sat back with a sigh. 'It's been a lovely visit, but I must get back. I've orders to fill. And I want –' She paused uncertainly.

'To visit your parents, I suppose,' said Granma. 'Don't worry, that's as it should be. I'm afraid nothing will change my mind about your mother and the sluttish way she lives, but your father –'

'Granma, please don't run my mother down to me.'

'I don't know why you bother. She doesn't care about you.'

Grampa held put a beseeching hand. 'Don't, Amy, please. We've had a grand time together.'

Laura bit her lip. 'We mustn't quarrel. I've missed you. Both of you.'

As Laura was leaving, with a tremendous effort of will, Granma said, 'Come and see us again.'

Laura heard Phyllis yelling before she turned the corner. A gaggle of neighbours were gathered at the gate and she was fearful. They stood back to let her pass.

'Bloody bosses! Bloody government!' shrieked Phyllis. 'They all live like lords and expect us to manage on starvation wages. If she hadn't needed to work –' The words were followed by loud wailing sobs.

Laura walked fearfully into the kitchen. Tears rained down Phyllis's face as she screamed her anger to the world. When she saw Laura she snarled, 'Look at her. Done up like a dog's dinner. Runs her own shop. *She's* one of them now.'

Laura felt sick at the malevolence directed at her. 'What's happened?'

'Only our Enid's lost her baby, that's all, as if you care!'

Laura's temper went. 'Why are you carrying on at me? Why are you always such a bitch to me? Enid's my sister and I'm as sorry as anyone that her baby has died, but nobody told me a damn thing about it. Perhaps you wouldn't mind telling me if Enid is all right?'

Phyllis stopped shrieking and her mouth fell open. Then she said, 'Sorry, love, I didn't mean –'

'You meant every word,' said Laura grimly.

'Enid's all right,' sniffed Phyllis. 'She had a bad birth. A boy.

Lovely little chap, but he died not long after he was born. The midwife did her best and we fetched the doctor, but somethin' was wrong with him from the start. The doctor told us off for lettin' her go back to work –'

'She went back to work? He forbade it!'

'It's all very well to tell people not to work, but it don't put food in their mouths. Would you believe it, the landlord put up the bloody rent?'

'Why didn't someone tell me? If I'd known things were so bad with Enid I'd have done my best to help. I've been frantically busy getting the shop going.'

William, who sat by his wife, occasionally patting her helplessly, said, 'Not your fault, chick. You didn't know. I did what I could.'

'That's true,' said Phyllis. 'Your dad's been workin' in the shed all hours with the boys.'

'You should have told me, you should.' Laura looked round at the ring of unhappy faces of her siblings and said bitterly, 'One of you could have let me know.' She stood up.'I'm going round to see Enid. Who's looking after her?'

'We are, as best we can,' said Phyllis. 'I took on another couple of kids to mind and gave her the money, but it wasn't enough. We told the landlord that Jack was out of a job and that Enid was expectin' and not well enough to work. Do you know what he said? "We all have our problems, Mrs Blackford. I, too, have mine." His only problem is getting his fat belly through the door of his swanky car. Bastard!' She began to cry. 'They're all bastards. Don't you get like them, our Laura.'

Laura pushed open the door of Enid's one up, one down terrace house, outside cold tap and shared lavatory. Jack came to meet her. 'Hello, Laura. Good of you to come.'

He looked utterly dejected, his shoulders stooped, his face pale. 'You'll have heard. She's takin' it bad. Very bad. An' she's got to lie up for ages. Lost too much blood. Doctor says to feed her plenty of liver an' fresh greens an' fruit an' eggs an' milk an' cocoa, an' when I asked him how I could buy all that stuff when I'm on the dole he said I must do what I can if I want her to get

186

well. He sent round a bottle of iron tonic – cost a shillin' it did – an' that's supposed to help, but what about all the food? Your ma's been ever so kind to us, but she's got her work cut out to feed her own. Black treacle the doctor said, too, an' –'

'I'll go up and see Enid,' said Laura, quelling a sudden unreasonable desire to shake him. Jack was unimaginative and stolid, but a good man as long as he had a job. Losing it had quickly sent him drifting into hopelessness and shame.

Enid was scaringly white, her closed eyes sunk in shadows. A crib, brought by Ralph, was covered with a grey blanket. She opened her eyes which, as soon as she saw Laura, filled with tears. They trickled down her face and Laura put her arms round her sister. 'Don't, love, oh please, don't. You need all your strength to get well.'

'My little boy died. He died. I killed him.'

'No!' said Laura, horrified.

'I did. Doctor told me to rest, but I went back to work. I had to.'

'I know, love. I'm so sorry. I wish you'd come to me.'

'Why? You've got to make your own livin'? All we seem to do these days is sponge off other people. How can we help it? The fifteen weeks you're allowed for dole money were up and it was stopped. Jack went to see the Board of Guardians for Poor Relief. They made him stand while they sat and looked at him as if he was somethin' dragged from a gutter. They asked him dozens of nosy questions. We had to sell everythin' they decided we didn't need for survival so most of our weddin' presents went, then they paid us thirteen shillings a week and gave us bread tokens. It mortified me to take them to the baker and there was nothin' left by Thursday. I went back to the factory without tellin' the Guardians. My ankles and feet swelled right up and the works nurse sent me home. Mum started givin' me Joyce's two and six and I couldn't ask her for any more and I minded a couple of kids and took in washin'. Jack helped me, but – I killed my little boy!' She broke into fresh weeping.

Laura nursed her sister helplessly in her arms, feeling renewed fury at the butterflies and drones of the world who thought nothing of spending as much on a hat or a gown as would save a life. By God, she'd make her business exclusive. She'd make them pay and pay and pay.

'Do you want to see him?' asked Enid.

'See who?'

'My baby, of course. I only had him yesterday. The parson came round and christened him just before he – we called him William after Dad. It's too early for the funeral yet.' Fresh tears welled. 'We couldn't even afford that if everyone hadn't chipped in a bit. We had to stop payin' the Friendly Society so we haven't got insurance.'

'Where is he?'

'Lift the blanket, love. He's so beautiful.'

Laura gritted her teeth. She had never looked on death before. The baby was lying in a tiny white coffin which was laid in the crib. Its small ivory face was framed by a frilled bonnet in appalling incongruity.

'He looks as if he's asleep, don't he?' said Enid. 'If only I could have rested like I was told, I'm sure he would have lived. I knitted stuff for him and sewed his clothes. They're all ready in the bottom drawer.'

Laura pulled the blanket back over the crib. 'I'm so sorry, Enid.'

'I'll keep the clothes. One day I may have another baby. But not for a long time. The doctor said I mustn't. In any case, I can't go through this again in a hurry. All the waitin', the sickness at the start, a big belly, then the pain – and all for nothin'. Nothin'!'

'It won't always be like that.'

'No more babies! Not till my Jack's in a job. I asked the doctor how not to have a baby and he said, "Abstinence. That's the thing". I asked him what that meant and he laughed! He laughed at me! He seemed to think it was a joke, and he said, "You can't have your cake and eat it". Can you believe it? He meant no more – you know – no more married love. Jack'll sleep down on the sofa in future and me up here. I can't think what it'll be like. I love my Jack. Givin' him his rights was a comfort. It's not so much the love, though that's good, but bein' cosy in bed together. I'll not dare have him near me. I won't feel I'm married any more.' She turned to stare at the wall which was patchy with damp. 'And how long's a man goin' to stand for it? He'll find someone to oblige him. I couldn't bear that –' She stopped, her voice choked. 'I'll have to give in and I'll get pregnant and be bad all over again. There's no help for the likes of me. You've got the right idea, Laura. I hope you get rich – real rich.'

'I intend to.' Laura paused, then said tentatively, 'Enid, Jack could stop babies if he wore a – preventative.'

Enid's pale face coloured. 'What a thing to say, our Laura. We can't afford those rubber things and anyway men say they take away the pleasure.' She shook her head. 'Jack wouldn't use them. None of the men will. And I've heard you can't always be sure of them. Sometimes they don't seem to work. Someone said they put a small slit in every few they sell so as the birth rate will stay high and there'll be enough factory workers and servants.'

Laura was doubtful. 'Surely not? That's a tale to frighten folk.'

'You don't really know, do you? You can't be sure.'

Laura said thoughtfully, 'Perhaps not. But there are other ways. I'll tell you when you're better and then you can sleep in the same bed as Jack and be safe.'

Laura's education on such matters had progressed swiftly. Her sister might be shocked at the idea of female contraception but, on the other hand, she might try if she was presented with the means. Laura had obtained books by the great birth-control reformer, Marie Stopes. She had asked Ralph to get them. He had grinned at her, his brows raised, but made no comment. The reading made excellent sense. It had also further infuriated her. First against hospitals and doctors who told over-burdened women, their health broken by too many pregnancies, not to have any more babies, then refused them the knowledge they needed. And against the rich who could afford all the medical help they needed, nursemaids, servants in plenty, as much food as they wanted, and who were able to gain this precious information with ease, and enlist medical help from private doctors.

She opened her purse and took out all it contained in cash and pressed the two pounds into Enid's hand. 'Get Jack to buy you what you need. I'll bring more.'

Enid clutched her hand. 'God, Laura, you're a pal. A real sister.'

The words rang in Laura's head in a refrain. A real sister. After so many years of being an outsider. Perhaps Mum might like her better when she heard about the money. Money opened doors, made friends, moved hearts, altered attitudes. The benefits might be superficial, the friendships ephemeral, the soft hearts dependent on status, but it oiled the wheels of life in a miraculous way.

Chapter Thirteen

Laura sat for a moment's rest in the shop. She had no cause to complain about sales. Work was now her life. At night she designed and made hats which she sold by day. Noreen was proving an excellent employee, quick to learn, with skilled fingers, and Miss Morton was unfailingly cheerful and helpful.

Ralph, too, was doing well, though he said an antique business took time to develop. The people who patronised his shop often went on to Laura's and sometimes chose a hat, or an accessory, and also the other way round. Customers often went home carrying a small vase, a delicate set of bone china, an oriental rug, its colours faded into pastel beauty, as well as a white, silver and gold hatbox with a twisted gold and silver cord handle and the name 'Hats by Laura' printed on the top in a facsimile of her own graceful, sloping handwriting. Miss Morton had insisted that money be spent on the boxes and had herself negotiated a contract with a local cardboard box factory.

When Laura had told Ralph about Enid he looked stricken. 'Damn! I haven't been home for ages. Why didn't they let me know?'

'Or me,' said Laura. 'It's a stubborn streak they've all got. They won't ask. They expect you to know.'

'I'll go along tonight to our Enid's and do what I can. Board of Guardians! Swine, all of them! God, I wish I'd known.'

Laura's musings were interrupted by the aggressive opening of the shop door and the soft jangle of the temple bell donated by Ralph. She sprang to her feet, but kept her professional smile with some difficulty when she saw Mr Gregory senior glaring at her. 'It won't work, Miss Blackford!' he stated baldly.

'What!'

'Opening a hat shop close to my store just because you're piqued at getting dismissed.'

Laura looked at him in astonishment. 'Surely you don't believe that I'm here just to annoy you. What a ridiculous idea.'

His face went red. 'Ridiculous, am I?'

Laura said placatingly, 'I meant the idea, not you. I didn't intend to be rude. My brother rented the premises for his antiques and I'm glad of a place to work.'

'You should have offered your skills as a designer to Gregory's. After all I did for you – to come and take my trade away.'

Laura's good humour faded. 'You did nothing for me I hadn't earned,' she said steadily. 'And I had no reason to believe you'd be interested in my affairs. I got sacked, if you remember, for a couple of small transactions outside shop hours.'

'They were not small in terms of customer goodwill! You deserved to go and it shows a spiteful spirit to steal away my trade.'

'Am I really taking your trade away?'

'No! How could you! A mere chit with a tuppeny-ha'penny shop. I meant you are endeavouring to take it. You will not succeed, of course. Oh, I know that our clients are buying a few hats from you, but they'll come back to me when the novelty wears off. And then you'll see where your disloyalty gets you.'

'Disloyalty! You sacked me without a reference after all the faithful years I'd put in. You knew how difficult it would be to get a job. I owe you nothing.'

'You most certainly do. You served an apprenticeship with me. We taught you all you know.'

Laura laughed. 'That's nonsense! I learned how to sell hats, that's all. I've been taking lessons for years from a proper milliner.'

'I employ proper milliners!'

'You employ women who sell. Your hats come from factories and outside milliners and it's damn little you pay them! We make our own merchandise. Each hat is a model.'

'And just how long do you imagine you'll be able to keep that up?'

It was a dilemma that had been worrying Laura. She was constantly weary, and needed more staff, but at present her money was being ploughed back into the business to buy more materials and pay wages. 'I'll manage,' she said firmly, 'and what's more,' she couldn't resist adding, 'I make sure the ladies have purses to match their hats.'

The indirect reference to the cause of her dismissal infuriated Mr Gregory even more. His eyes bulged, his breast heaved under his pinstripe suit. 'Such insolence –'

'No, Mr Gregory, not insolence. I'm your equal now.'

He waved his hand dismissively. 'You presume to believe you are equal to me, or that this silly little place is equal to my department store. We'll see who wins in the end.'

He stamped out and Miss Morton crept in holding a cup of tea. 'Here, love, I reckon you'll need it after that. You stood up to him splendidly.'

'I know. But I sometimes have nightmares about failing. I can't possibly outshine Gregory's.'

'Don't be a pessimist. You're not trying to outshine Gregory's. You're a model milliner. You have a gift. But you must believe in yourself. That's important.'

After closing the shop that evening Laura climbed the stairs to her flat. She looked in at the workroom. It had once been two rooms, but Ralph had knocked down the dividing wall. Under Miss Morton's watchful guidance, Noreen was working on a piece of brilliant pink duchesse satin, using fly-running stitches which gathered up the material. It was intended for a hat to be worn by a prominent young Bristol matron to wear at the fête and gymkhana at the Ranelagh Polo Club in London. Laura had made careful notes of all the season's events to make sure she had a selection of suitable designs to offer her clients.

'This is a gorgeous colour, Laura,' Noreen said, looking up.

Her hair was a nondescript fawn, her figure small-breasted and wide-hipped, but her eyes were large, dark brown and luminous in her pale face. She was not pretty, but Laura could imagine her late husband losing himself in the beauty of her eyes.

'It's time to go home, Noreen.'

Noreen smiled. Her teeth were good. 'I know, but I can't leave in the middle of this kind of sewin'.'

'You shouldn't have begun it tonight.'

'I wanted to. The hat's promised in two days.'

'I intended to work on it after I'd had a bite of supper.'

Noreen was unmoved. 'I shall finish it.'

'Then you'll be paid overtime.'

'No, I shan't. I'm here against orders.'

Laura laughed. 'We'll see. When you've done the gathering come upstairs.' She turned to Miss Morton who was grafting a small brim to a blue felt so that there would be no trace of stitchery on the right side. The hot smell of steamed material hung in the air and mingled with that of new cloth. The blocks stood in a row on a newly built shelf, each bearing a hat in varying stages of design. A neat pile of French berets was ready to go on display. Tape measures lay across the table with scissors and threads. Laura felt a surge of optimism. She really owned a business, she could afford rent and wages. To hell with Mr Gregory and his like! She laughed aloud. 'I'll get us all something to eat. And if you choose to work past your time, Noreen, I shall be grateful but I shall pay you.'

They were fine words, but Laura felt a stab of apprehension as she entered her small kitchen. There was so little money left over for food. The two pounds she had handed to Enid had been more than the weekly housekeeping for herself and Ralph. Well, neither she nor Ralph grudged that. She had bought a sheep's head and the broth from it, with vegetables added daily, was tasty and provided adequate nourishment. She opened the oven door to check a rice pudding with raisins. It had a golden skin on top, dotted brown with nutmeg, and smelt wonderful.

Miss Morton, Noreen and Ralph arrived and tucked in, happily mopping up the last drop of gravy with hunks of bread.

Ralph grinned. 'That stew is becoming as familiar as an old friend. Rice pudding? With raisins? And a nutmeg top. Laura, you're a genius.'

Miss Morton said, 'She is, indeed, but she can't go on working at her present pace. No, Laura, don't argue. I don't care if you are cross with me, I must say what I think.'

Ralph looked at his sister. 'She's right, love. You're looking peaky.'

'Thanks.'

'Peaky, but distinguished,' said Ralph. 'Have you any ideas, Miss Morton? I reckon you're a good judge of how to proceed.'

The elderly spinster blushed. 'I thank God that you young folk entered my life. I would get no compliments otherwise! I can't imagine being without you.'

'I'd be lost without you,' said Laura, with feeling.

'You can't include me in one of your young people,' sighed Noreen.

'You're young to me,' said Miss Morton firmly. 'Now Laura, I've had an idea. More than that, I've spent a few hours visiting friends from the old days. Milliners like myself who could do with an interest in life. Seven of them are prepared to work at home on piecework. Three had already heard of you and had peeped inside the shop. They were most impressed.'

Laura was incredulous. 'You've done all that without saying a word!'

'I didn't want to raise your hopes.'

Laura leaned forward and kissed Miss Morton's cheek. She felt close to tears. 'I don't know what to say. Thank you seems inadequate.'

'It's enough,' said Miss Morton, 'especially when it's goes along with tasty broth and rice pudding. And, I hope, a good strong cup of tea.'

Noreen made the tea while Laura sat with her elbows on the table, chin propped in her hands, her eyes dreamy. 'I can tell you now what I want to do. With extra hands it'll be possible much sooner than I thought. I'm going to have a hat show. With mannequins, just like they do at Gregory's.'

'Sounds a good idea,' said Ralph. 'And I know just where you can hold it. In my shop. I'll make a space and borrow chairs from some of my mates and we'll use the ones I've got for sale as well. Who knows, someone might get attached enough to her seat to buy it.'

The four of them drank their tea and the tiny room was redolent with hope.

On the following day, just before the shop closed, Rick walked in. 'Hi, baby.'

'Oh, Rick. Hello.'

'Well, you don't sound too happy!'

As always when Laura saw him her heart began to thud. He was wearing a dark suit and hat and he exuded prosperous confidence. He was smiling, but she knew his defences were up. 'I am glad to see you,' she said, wishing she didn't sound so prim. 'Is there anything I can do for you?'

'No, thanks. Just wanted to find out how life was treatin' you.'

'Very well. How about you?'

'Great, baby. Just great. I've got seven good acts signed up and workin'. There's a pair of exhibition ballroom dancers that I'm sure I can get London engagements for. They do the Charleston like it's never been done before. And I've got a jugglin' act that'll bring the house down.'

'I gather you've set up your own agency.'

'Sure have, baby. I've got an office near Old Market. *The Richard Merriman Theatrical Agency*. How does that strike you?'

'It's clear enough,' said Laura drily. 'Is it prospering?'

'I'm doin' fine. Just fine. The office is tiny, but I'll do better an' I'm not just goin' to be an agent. They're not at the top of the heap.'

'And that would never do for Rick Merriman!'

He ignored the note of sarcasm. 'You can say that again! I'm goin' to be one of the big boys. I'll own theatres, cinemas, there's no end to what a man can do if he tries.'

'Meanwhile what about the fleapit?'

He refused to be offended and grinned. 'Couldn't be better.' He gave his hat a jaunty slant towards his eyes. 'Full every performance. I've kept hirin' the old films and the people flock in. I've got a manager in there now *and* I've rented a place in St George.'

'Congratulations!' Laura meant it and Rick's eyes softened.

'It's no grander than the other, but folks who haven't got

much money can afford to go to my cinemas. And I know you'll be glad that I've given Enid's Jack a job. He's not brainy enough to be a manager, but he makes a good handyman. I can't pay fabulous wages yet, but it's a bloody sight more than he was gettin' from the Board of Guardians. Mean sods! Rich, well-fed men sittin' around deciding how much money a person needs to eat. One says seven and six, another five and six. Guess what figure they settle on.'

'Five and six, naturally. What do they know of hunger and babies born dead because their mothers are weak and ill? Rick, it's so good of you to give Jack a job.'

'He's a nice bloke. I've bought a better car, too. Come and see.'

Laura went outside. 'It's beautiful.' She stroked its bonnet as if she were stroking Rick.

'Baby, you really do like it! It's French. Some rich chap shipped it over and I got it for a song. The upholstery's gettin' frayed and it's got a few dents and scratches, but it goes well.

'I'm going to buy a car as soon as I can afford it.'

'Great, kid. I'll help you learn to drive – if you'd like me to.'

Laura said eagerly, 'Oh, I would, I would.'

After Rick had gone she felt slightly more hopeful of resuming their closer relationship. Then she faced facts. For all his friendliness he had erected a barrier that she might never breach. It took her hours of steady work to recover her balance.

Ralph drove her round to meet her new employees, greyhaired all of them, but happy to think they could earn money at home, pursuing a vocation they enjoyed.

'Your army of wrinklies,' Ralph called them, but with a lilt of sympathetic laughter in his voice. All the women had drooled over Laura's tall, handsome escort. Their lively feminine instincts warmed to a free, attractive male.

The preparations for the show were feverish. Laura had decided to display some straws. They were not as readily disposed of as felts, hot as the weather was, though the few she had made had eventually sold. It seemed that clients didn't know quite what they wanted until it was offered them. But Miss Morton was doubtful about the wisdom of showing straw so late in the season.

'I know they might not sell,' said Laura, 'but I want to display a sample of what we can do. We can use those few plaited straws I got from the church jumble sale. The colours have faded, but they're good quality Italian straw plaits. We can take them to pieces and turn them. And we'll have felt cloches with and without brims, in different colours and lots of trimmings. Ralph's promised to show me all the paste brooches and feathers that he's got.'

Miss Morton capitulated. 'Your head for business is better than mine.'

Laura sent to the Luton wholesalers for finely shredded satin straw, and Yedda plaits made from Chinese and Japanese straw, and rafia in natural and bright shades; and to Stockport for a supply of raw felt hoods, the ready-made basis for hats. She had thought she was well versed in the art of millinery, but she discovered she was an infant compared to Miss Morton, who carried an enormous mass of information in her head. Laura had bought a school exercise book and wrote down all that the little milliner taught her. The list of materials and types of sewing seemed endless, but Laura's powerful desire to learn gave her a rapacious appetite for facts.

Noreen sat in on the teaching sessions and was proving more each day that she could be left to work with little supervision. As they talked over their endless hot pressing, pattern-making, cutting, stitching, Laura gleaned an impression of a life lived with stern parents who didn't believe in showing their emotions. Then a few short weeks with her beloved husband while he was on leave from the war, followed by his early death.

When Noreen spoke of her husband she kept her head down as she worked on a swathe of millinery velvet for an evening headdress. 'I wanted to die, Laura. I thought of killing myself. But that's a sin, isn't it? I might not go to heaven and then I'd never see Andy again. I couldn't bear that.'

She and Laura had something in common. A cold childhood, a longing for love. But Noreen's man had adored her. Rick liked women. In the plural. He was incapable of adoring a single woman.

The next day Thelma Charlton burst into the shop. She was

escorted by Adrian Mallender who greeted Laura with a smile. Thelma prowled around like a cat in a cage, touching things.

'Miss Charlton,' said Laura gently, 'I must ask you please to allow me to handle anything you need.'

Thelma pouted. She was wearing lipstick that was almost purple to match her dress, a tubular affair barely covering her knees. Laura winced. The colour was wrong for her.

'Show me that hat,' Thelma demanded, pointing to a dark-purple cloche with a pale-pink bow.

Laura shook her head. 'Not that one, Miss Charlton.'

'But I want it. I must have it. It will go well with this new dress.' She dragged off her own bottle-green felt. 'See, this contrasts, but it isn't right.'

'No, but you shouldn't wear purple at all, Miss Charlton. The colour is not for you.'

Adrian gave a yelp of mirth. 'I told you, darling. I said it was wrong. Laura was just the same with Mummy.'

Thelma looked furiously at Laura. 'Does that mean you don't approve of my dress?' she demanded.

'Please, Miss Charlton, don't be cross with me,' Laura begged in a placating tone. 'The dress is elegant, but it simply doesn't suit you. I tell you only for your own good. You are so pretty, with your lovely white skin and titian hair, it seems a shame to wear colours that don't quite become you.'

Thelma's scowl faded. 'God, you're a scream, Laura, just *too*, too funny, but I must have that hat. No, you won't sell it to me. Damn it, what am I going to do?'

Laura said gently, 'Give the green hat to your maid and buy a new one from me.'

Again Thelma scowled, then she trilled with laughter. 'You really are the end, isn't she, Adrian? I'll leave it to you to make me a better hat and I want it just like the pale-lavender one in the window. You approve of that colour? All right, all right, you never repeat a hat. But I want something like it. I'll send my maid with a colour swatch tonight. I must have the hat tomorrow.'

If Laura could have afforded it she would have told the girl she could go and put her head in a bucket. Someone – herself probably – was going to have to work half the night to make a hat for a spoilt girl whose wardrobe was certainly over-stocked. She merely smiled. 'Don't come until the afternoon, please.'

An hour later Adrian Mallender returned alone. 'I've returned to apologise for my cousin's lack of consideration, Miss Blackford. She's used to having everything her own way.'

'It doesn't matter,' said Laura, 'though it's kind of you to think of me.'

'Kind be dashed! I wanted to see you. It made a good excuse.' His eyes travelled over the shelves. Ralph had fitted more and Laura now stocked filmy chiffon scarves, dainty gloves and boxes of face powder and lipsticks. She intended to expand further into the cosmetic and accessory market.

'I wonder at your patience,' said Adrian. 'I'm sure I would have told Thelma to push off.'

'I almost did,' admitted Laura, 'but I can't afford to lose her goodwill. She and her sister have a lot of influence. So has Lady Mallender.'

Adrian smiled. 'Oh, Mummy's a darling. An absolute pet. I say, Miss Blackford – Laura – I suppose you wouldn't care to come for a spin with me. Mummy's twenty-first birthday present to me was a four-seater Bentley. I've hardly driven it yet and I'd love someone nice to share it with.'

It was the most charming invitation Laura had ever received and she couldn't resist it. 'I'd like to, just for a little drive. But I've lots of work to do. Your cousin's hat for one thing.'

'I'll not keep you a second after you want to return. I'll call for you at seven. Is that all right?'

Laura nodded and Adrian gave her a small bow and left. His presence had a most soothing effect on her, especially after Rick's abrasive manners. She thought of Rick and his second-hand car and of Adrian and his gleaming Bentley for which he hadn't had to raise a finger, and felt a twist of resentment on Rick's behalf. Life wasn't fair. Every day she understood Rick's attitude better. If only he would share the struggle with her. She looked at herself in the mirror. It was difficult to assess her appearance. Adrian had regarded her with clear admiration.

She wasn't pretty. But there was something. She turned to answer the shop bell as three flappers entered all chattering at once.

Adrian held open the passenger seat door for Laura and she stepped into the car. It was the first time she had experienced real opulence and she loved it. Adrian started the engine and they drove off, watched from the upstairs windows by Miss Morton and Noreen. Laura felt guilty at taking time off work, especially before the millinery show, but both women had urged her to go.

Adrian drove skilfully, not talking much, through the tramway centre, up Park Street, with its rows of expensive shops, up Blackboy Hill and over the Downs to the Clifton suspension bridge which was a miracle of engineering beauty. Laura looked down at the road and river far below. The mud flats showed the tide was out. The people walking along the portway looked like midgets.

Adrian said, 'Do you know that a lady once jumped off the bridge and her crinoline acted like a parachute and floated her safely down?'

Laura laughed. 'Is that so?'

'Honestly, it's true. Someone else jumped and the thick mud saved them.'

'I'll believe you. Thousands wouldn't.'

'Cross my heart!'

Adrian's well-modulated public school tone was soothing. He drove well, if without Rick's dash. She sank further into the softly leathered seat.

'Happy?'

The question startled her, so did the real concern with which it was asked.

'Yes,' she said. 'I do believe I am happy.'

'Well, don't sound so surprised.'

'No,' Laura couldn't bring herself to explain how much his simple question moved her. How could he understand, he who was clearly adored by his mother.

Surprisingly Noreen knew all about Adrian and the

Mallenders. She had worked for a short time as a kitchen maid in the Downs house when he was young. He was Lady Mallender's only son and she worshipped him. She was inordinately proud of her husband's title. 'She's much more snobby than Sir Hugo,' Noreen had said. 'It's funny because he's a baronet and his title goes back to the sixteenth century, but her ladyship was only an ordinary person when they married.'

'What's an ordinary person?' Miss Morton had asked teasingly.

'Well,' grinned Noreen. 'Not ordinary like us. But her father was a plain mister. He owned a factory. He's dead now. Left most of his money to his sons. Lady M must have been glad to marry a rich bloke. All she can think about, it seems, is for the title to be carried on through her son.'

Laura glanced now at Adrian. He resembled his mother in a way, yet paradoxically he was nothing like her. A faint similarity lay in a turn of the head, a fleeting expression. He was slender, almost as finely boned as a woman, and his hands on the wheel were soft and white. He was so unlike Rick. Adrian's face was clean-shaven and pale-skinned – Rick's chin was shadowed by his strong dark hair by tea-time. Damn it! Why must Rick always intrude on her thoughts? Adrian's eyes were long-lashed, their expression benign. He really was handsome. The kind of man a girl could swoon over. One who wouldn't hurt her, who would cherish her.

He stopped the car just inside a small wood. A soft warm breeze stirred the leaves which sent sunny patterns dancing over the two in the car. Laura braced herself to repel him if he should try to kiss her. She prayed that he wouldn't. If he did she would feel intense disappointment in him.

'Why have we stopped?' she asked coolly.

'I love it here. It's only minutes away from the city, yet such a lonely, soothing spot. I come here on my own. Sometimes I bring a book, sometimes I just sit and enjoy the atmosphere. It restores my soul, as it says in the good book.'

Laura said softly, 'I think that's wonderful.'

Adrian turned his gentle smile on her. 'I'm glad. I sense that we have much in common, Laura.'

Laura thought often of Adrian in the hectic days that followed. He had asked her to go to a theatre with him, but very regretfully she had to decline, explaining about the fashion show, and he had understood. He was wonderful that way. There was no aggression of the kind that Rick sometimes inflicted on her. He had no air of invasive sexuality that made her feel weak with helpless longing, no long disappearances that perpetuated her insecurity. He often came into the shop. Sometimes he was with his cousins, sometimes alone. He always bought something, a gift for his friends or, more often, his mother. He had perfect taste in his selections, going to immense trouble to decide on exact colours and textures.

One day Laura offered to let him see the workroom and he gazed around with great interest, before he walked over to Miss Morton and Noreen and asked them to show him what they were doing.

Miss Morton was working on one of the fancy straws which were to be a feature of the collection. Adrian's head was close to hers, his hair falling over his forehead, as she said, 'You see, Mr Mallender, the satin straw is pliable. I have completed the brim on a net shape, and now the crown is being covered with a whirl of straw. I began in the middle and stitch each section as I go.'

'It's a simply splendid colour, Miss Morton. It would suit my mother admirably. She looks sweet in sage green.'

Laura caught Miss Morton's eye briefly as they both stifled their mirth at the notion of Lady Mallender looking sweet in anything. But he was right about the colour.

'Are you sure you are preparing the right shape?' asked Adrian, with real anxiety in his voice. 'I fancy that straw brims are not entirely fashionable.'

Laura said blandly, 'I intend to make it fashionable.' Then she unbent. 'I don't really believe I have that much influence, Adrian. Wider brims are quite popular for holiday wear. I'm hoping mine will sell for Henley, but whatever happens, the straws will be showpieces, something that will intrigue my clients.' She hesitated, then said, 'Will Lady Mallender attend the showing of my first collection?'

'I will make sure she does by coming with her. Who will do the modelling?'

'I intend to display some of the hats myself and I also have a friend I can approach. My brother, Ralph, will speak the commentary.'

'It all sounds tophole.'

Miss Morton went to the ironing table and lifted an iron from one of the small gas rings kept burning throughout the day. She spat on the iron and it sizzled, then she wiped it with a spotless cloth and steam pressed the new straw.

'What happens next?' Adrian asked her, intrigued.

'I shall finish with a simple band of olive-green ribbon with a flat bow at the back and one pink silk rose at the side.'

'Splendid. Absolutely splendid! I'm sure my mother will want it. Laura, you must give her first refusal, please, only she won't refuse because I shall insist she buys it. When is the show to be? In two weeks? Can you be ready in time?'

'We intend to be,' said Laura drily. 'The invitations are already being prepared. I have quite a number of completed hats already. They're stored in one of my brother's rooms.'

Laura took invitations home to her family, disliking herself for her nervous reluctance in asking them to come. They could scarcely make a good impression on her clients. And, because of her sense of guilt, she was effusive in her persuasion to attend.

Phyllis looked at her card. It was in white pasteboard with the lettering picked out in gold with small silver flowers in one corner. She read it: 'You are cordially invited to the showing of the first collection of model hats of *Hats by Laura* which will take place on Wednesday, the twenty-second of June, at three o'clock. Refreshments will be served. Hats may be purchased, and orders taken.'

She handed it to William. 'It sounds grand, chick,' he said, 'though I hope you won't expect me to come.'

'No, Dad, I didn't think you would.'

'And we're not comin' either,' said Harold and Alfred.

Laura looked at them, their hair roughly shorn, their hands ingrained with leather dirt. 'I'm counting on you boys to help behind the scenes, moving chairs, checking the screens where the models will change – that kind of thing.'

'Only pansy men go to a thing like that.'

'Not at all,' said William, unexpectedly. 'I believe gentlemen quite often accompany their womenfolk on shopping sprees these days.'

'How do you know?' demanded Freda.

'I read it in the newspapers. You two boys must help your sister. No one need see you and she might make all our fortunes.'

The boys left, laughing hilariously at the idea of making a fortune out of women's fancy hats.

Joyce was home for her Sunday afternoon off and Laura asked her how she was getting on as a kitchen maid.

'Not bad, thank you, Laura,' said Joyce. 'I have to clean an awful lot of pots and pans and things. You wouldn't believe the food they have. I've never heard of some of it. We eat a lot of what's left over in the servants' hall and what we can't eat gets thrown away.'

'Bloodsuckers!' said Freda. 'Throwin' out food when there're folk starvin' for want of a crust.'

'They gave me some nice things,' said Joyce eagerly. 'Look, a bag of macaroons – they're only a few days old and not really stale – and some buns and iced cakes and the end of a piece of ham.'

'Eatin' their servants' bloody leftovers as if we was a lot of dogs,' snarled Freda.

'Now then,' said William. 'Don't look a gift horse in the mouth.'

'I wish I could go there and chuck the whole lot back at them.'

Lillian sauntered in. She was wearing a softly pink dress with russet spots that matched her golden-brown hair. Her expressive brown eyes were filled with mischief and she was grinning widely. 'I hear you've been givin' advice to our Enid.'

Laura tried to continue her conversation with Joyce, but Lillian said loudly, 'I never thought you had it in you.'

'What advice?' Phyllis demanded.

'It's more than just advice. She paid for an appointment for

Enid to see a posh doctor privately and he –' Lillian bent her head and whispered to her mother.

Phyllis was half shocked, half fascinated. 'That's not natural.'

'What isn't?' shrieked Freda.

'I might tell you later,' said Phyllis in a tone which meant that nothing would let such words pass her lips. She was prudish in many ways. Laura felt hot with embarrassment. There was no need for Lillian to reveal how Enid had been fitted with a vaginal cap that would prevent conception. Enid and Jack had been grateful anyway.

'I hear our Jack's doin' well in his job,' said Phyllis, trying to diffuse the tense atmosphere.

'Who told you?' asked Laura, knowing immediately by Lillian's expression what the answer would be.

'Rick told us, of course,' yawned Lillian. 'I'm tired! Dancin' till all hours is wearin' when it keeps happenin'. Rick's a good dancer, isn't he, Laura?'

Laura braced herself to suppress the jealousy that came beating at her.

'Rick's a good sort,' said Phyllis. 'He brings us free tickets to the pictures every change of programme. We couldn't afford to go so many times otherwise. Thank the Lord Enid's much better. She'll be back at work soon and with them both gettin' wages we'll all be better off. Now come on, everybody get sat down. Tea's ready.'

The Goodwins' leftover food disappeared as fast as the thick hunks of bread and jam. After Phyllis had cut some lean ham for William, the fatty bits were spread with mustard and put between doorsteps of bread for Harold and Alfred.

As Joyce licked icing sugar from her fingers she said, 'The old lady asks for me to come and see her every day now, Laura. She's awful nice.'

'Joyce gets presents,' grunted Freda.

'What sort of presents?'

'Cheap beads,' said Lillian. 'Bits of worn out lace. A gauzy scarf with a tear in it. Miserable old cow.'

'One of my necklaces is lovely,' said Joyce. 'It's pale green and looks as if it's never been worn.'

'The Goodwin girls come into my shop,' said Laura.

'Well, fancy that,' sneered Lillian. 'She calls them the Goodwin girls, just as cheeky as you like. I bet they wouldn't be flattered.'

'No,' agreed Laura, 'they wouldn't. In the shop I refer to them as clients and I'm very respectful.'

She had inflected a note of humour into her voice and Lillian stared, then frowned. 'You makin' fun of me?'

'Of course not.'

Laura needed to keep sounding cheerful, or she might break down and weep at the idea of Lillian going out with Rick so often, of her sister dancing in his arms . . . she stopped herself and put on a bright smile. 'The old lady is the girls' grandmother,' said Laura. 'They say she's "gaga".'

William tutted. 'That's not a nice way to speak of their grandmother.'

'They're not particularly nice people,' said Laura 'and they're flighty, always changing their boyfriends.'

'And our Joyce has to go and work for nasty little turds like that.' Freda's pimples stood out red on her dark, angry face.'

Laura ventured, 'Some of the nobs are quite nice when you get to know them.'

'*You* don't have to clean their bloody pots an' pans an' wait on their crack-pot relations.'

Phyllis sighed. 'Oh, dear. Give it a rest, our Freda.'

'So some of them are nice are they, chick?' William lowered his newspaper. 'Which ones?'

Laura was so astonished by her father's sudden interest that she blurted out more than she wished. 'Adrian Mallender for one.'

'How do you know him well enough to tell?' demanded Lillian.

'He comes into the shop quite often.'

'What's a man doin' in a ladies' shop?' demanded Freda.

'He buys presents.'

'Has he asked you for a date?' Lillian's voice was sharp with suspicion.

'I've driven out with him. He's got a gorgeous new Bentley four-seater.'

Laura was regrettably pleased to see Lillian flush with rage.

She jumped up and left, calling back, 'I'm off. Can't keep the boyfriend waitin'.'

'It's all right,' said Joyce. 'She's got a date with a boy from Pratt's Boots. She's not goin' out with your Rick.'

'He's not mine,' snapped Laura.

Joyce's eyes filled with tears and Phyllis looked daggers at Laura who said, 'Sorry, Joyce, darling, I didn't mean to snap. Look, I've brought you a pretty lace hankie.' Joyce was placated immediately, tracing the embroidered flowers and fingering the silky lace.

Freda said, 'That selfish old bitch keeps our Joyce dancin' attendance on her so she's up to all hours finishin' the washin' up.'

'I don't mind,' Joyce assured her sister. 'It's nice going into the posh part of the house. I see all sorts of different people.'

'Who, for instance?' Freda lived with suspicion these days. She still thought her beloved sister should stay at home with Phyllis where she'd be safe.

'Just people,' said Joyce vaguely. 'Rich people. They're no different from us, really.'

Laura raised her newly plucked brows. Joyce had recognised a truth that cleverer folk couldn't accept.

When tea was cleared away Freda and Joyce joined the others in the front room and soon the gramophone was squeaking and creaking out a jazzed-up version of *The Japanese Sandman*. Laura's feet itched to dance, but she knew she must get back to the shop. She was sleeping fewer and fewer hours and what rest she did get was troubled by nightmares induced by the fear of failure and her hopeless love for Rick.

She had confided her business worries to Adrian and he had been soothing and bracing at the same time. 'You'll be a success, Laura, I know you will and nothing ventured, nothing gained.'

'Well, that's original.'

'There's many a good cliché spoken sincerely,' he grinned.

For a moment Laura had felt cocooned by his gentle kindness. She thought that so sympathetic and understanding a man was to be preferred as a companion to the unpredictable kind, like Rick.

That was until Rick asked her out to a dance. She stared at

him. 'Are you crazy? The show's only three days away and you expect me to waste time dancing.'

'It'll do you good, baby. You're far too pale, and skinnier than ever.'

'Always the complimentary gentleman!'

'I do my best,' grinned Rick.

'If that's your best I shudder to think what your worst is like!'

'Why don't you go, Laura?' said Miss Morton. 'A change is as good as a rest and you might sleep the better for it.'

Noreen joined her persuasion to Miss Morton's and Rick offered to give her a day of his time picking up the hats from the outworkers and helping Ralph to prepare the shop.

Rick handed her into the car exactly as Adrian had. Laura looked closely at him. His hair was cut expertly and the hair cream used judiciously. His dark suit had evidently not come from the Fifty-Shilling Tailors and his shirt was of fine white linen. He caught her staring at him and grinned. 'D'you like what you see, baby?'

Oh, how she liked it! She might be able to fool herself that she was getting over him when he wasn't there, but sitting close to him in the intimacy of his car she knew he held the same powerful attraction for her.

The ballroom was a grand one with glowing chandeliers, gilt chairs lining the walls and a stage where a dance band in white ties and tails played. 'You look very prosperous, Rick. You're moving up in the world.'

'So are you, baby, and I like your frock. And the little cape. They suit you. You must be in the money to afford clothes like that.'

Laura was wearing a chiffon dress in pale turquoise with a string of turquoise and yellow beads reaching almost to her knees and long tear-shaped matching earrings. She was gratified to notice that, when she entered the ballroom on Rick's arm, heads were turned her way.

She tried to look enigmatic. She wasn't prepared to tell Rick that the dress was a 'second', damaged goods she had bought from a little shop in Park Street and put right herself. Anita

Rodrigues, the young woman who owned the shop was tall, with black hair and snapping black eyes, and hated men. Or so she had told Laura on their first meeting. Laura didn't care if Anita lured them into the back room and murdered them if she was prepared to sell model dresses to her for a song, even if they were damaged. Anita had been fascinated by Laura's account of her business venture. 'Maybe we can do one another a good turn, Laura. I'll put hats in my window and you could perhaps show dresses to match your hats.' The idea excited Laura. But first she had to make a success of the show.

The little soft wool cape had been fashioned by Iris from the best parts of a coat she had picked up for a penny at a church jumble sale and had given to Laura with shy pride. 'You look really grand,' Iris had said, on inspecting the full finished outfit. 'Miss Pringle misses you in millinery. She didn't mean to let on, but the one they got in your place is awful lazy and careless, and Dolores said Miss Pringle was so cross one day she told Dolores what she thought. I miss you at work, Laura, but I'm ever so glad you've got your own business. They say Mr Gregory's fit to bust with rage.'

Rick slid his arm around Laura's waist. 'Though you're so thin, baby, you look – somehow better than pretty.'

Laura supposed she should take that as a compliment, but she wanted to be pretty like Lillian or, better still, like Joyce, whose loveliness increased as she grew older.

Taking to the floor with Rick was sheer heaven. In the frenzied whirl of the Charleston and the Black Bottom she revelled in simply being with him, but when the band slowed the tempo she slid into his arms as if she were coming home. He held her close and they moved in total unison.

'We make a good team,' she murmured.

'Sure we do, baby. In the interval I've got two acts in the cabaret.'

Laura almost kicked him. 'Can't you think of anything but work? Is that why we're here, just to watch a couple of your acts?'

'Must keep an eye on them. If you don't they sometimes slacken and the next thing you know the manager's on my neck for sendin' him lousy acts.'

Laura had to admit that the trio of singing sisters was good. Then a couple of youths tap-danced their way to prolonged applause. Rick, who seemed to know just about everyone in Bristol, was one of the few with a small reserved table near the stage and they sat drinking cocktails.

When the last waltz was announced Rick held her so close she could feel the beat of his heart. The lights were lowered, the music drifted around them and Rick began to sing softly, hoarsely, reminding her of a time when she had confidently expected to be offered his love. It was so short a time ago, yet it seemed like years. *It's three o'clock in the morning, We've danced the whole night through.* She looked up and to her dismay tears formed and trembled on her lashes and slowly trickled down her cheeks. His eyes were gentle as he tipped her chin and rested his lips on hers for a moment. 'Don't cry, baby. Don't cry.' Any other man would surely have asked why she was crying? But she wouldn't have been able to answer. She knew only that she was overwhelmed by melancholy. Rick touched her lips with his again and the tears were lost as waves of aching need rippled through her. She slid her hands behind his head and pulled it down. Her mouth opened to him and he answered her need with a long searching kiss. She was transported into a world where she and Rick were alone, lovers in an enchanted ballroom and was startled when the music stopped and the lights blazed again.

Rick held her beneath her elbow as they walked to the car. She was dazed and suddenly exhausted and sat in silence during the journey. He helped her out and waited until she'd unlocked the shop and had gone inside.

She slept that night without dreams.

Adrian brought his sister into the shop the next day. Laura was adding the finishing touches to a burgundy wool felt with a bright green feather pinned with a burnished copper clip.

'Hello, Miss Blackford,' said Nancy shyly. 'That's a very pretty hat.'

'Thank you. I shouldn't be sewing it in the shop. Everything I make is supposed to be secret, but there's never enough time.'

'Could I help?'

Laura was startled. She could imagine the outraged reaction of Lady Mallender if she discovered that her society daughter was working in a milliner's workroom.

'I don't think Laura believes it's quite the thing for you, darling,' said Adrian, smiling.

'Your mother –' said Laura helplessly.

'Oh, yes, but Mummy wouldn't have to know. Oh, Miss Blackford, I envy you. I long and long to do something interesting, but all I'm supposed to do is look decorative and make a good marriage.'

'Steady on, old girl,' said Adrian.

Nancy blushed. 'Sorry,' she muttered. 'I'm always putting my foot in it. I shouldn't be discussing Mummy with –' She went even redder.

'Outsiders?' suggested Laura.

'Oh, please –' Nancy was almost paralysed with nerves.

Laura put her out of her misery. 'I'm only teasing.'

Nancy said seriously, 'I wouldn't say those things to anyone else, but Adrian thinks such a lot of you and –' She stopped. 'I'm doing it again. Talking too much. Giving away secrets.'

'It's not a secret that I admire Laura,' said Adrian. 'Keep cool, old girl. Laura's a good 'un. You can trust her.'

'And please, won't you call me Laura? No more formality.'

'And I'm Nancy.'

'But perhaps not when Mummy's about,' warned Adrian. 'Not yet, anyway.'

Before Laura had a chance to ask him what he meant a customer arrived and, by the time she had left carrying a *Hats by Laura* box, the moment had passed. Nancy was trying on hats and bought a pale-grey with a pink aigrette that brushed her rosy cheek.

'I'm so looking forward to the show,' she said, as she paid. 'In fact, I wish I could help with the modelling.'

Laura fervently wished so, too. Although Nancy was shy, probably because of her domineering mother, she was pretty and her Swiss finishing school had given her elegance and a graceful carriage.

'Who are the models?' asked Adrian.

'Wait and see,' was all Laura would say.

That night she, Miss Morton and Noreen worked on the hats until midnight. Iris brought Betty along and the two of them ran round making themselves useful.

Betty was ecstatic. 'It's all gorgeous, Laura. God, you're so lucky to be out of Gregory's. It gets worse. They say that young Mr Gregory's got one of the haberdashery girls into trouble and she's only fifteen. She's been sent up north to stay with her aunty, for her health it's supposed to be, but she was awful sick in the cloakroom lots of mornin's before she went.'

Laura let the chatter flow pleasantly over her head. After everyone had left she went on her rounds. There was a door through to Ralph's premises on the top floor and Laura went to look at her storeroom. She had no real need to visit it, but it gave her pleasure to look at the hats so laboriously designed and manufactured for the show. She had her hand stretched to the handle of the storeroom door when she heard a sound that turned her blood to ice. A furtive scratching and movement came from inside. Ralph had gone to Weston-Super-Mare to attend a country-house auction, after which he was driving to inspect a load of furniture he'd been offered privately. He might not return until the early hours and Laura was sure someone had broken in. She turned and had begun to tiptoe away, intending to race out and call the police, when she heard a furious squeaking, and stopped. Mice! She almost laughed in her relief. She didn't care much for mice, but if she opened the door and shouted they'd disappear. Ralph had been saying they must get a couple of cats. Tomorrow she'd make sure they did. She opened the door and pulled down the fine chain that would bring up the gas jet from a tiny blue haze to a yellow glow. Then she turned.

Great grey forms crouched on the floor and shelves, eyes glaring malevolently red.

'God!' she moaned, beginning to shake.

The room was alive with rats! Huge, river rats that lived in the River Frome which flowed darkly beneath the Bristol streets – beneath her shop – on its way to join the Avon. She backed slowly away as the rats resumed their occupation. They were gnawing at something and when Laura realised just what

213

it was her terror burst into frantic fury. Her straw hats, her hats that had been so lovely, light and airy, so beautiful, were in jagged tatters. They were eating her hats! Blind anger took over. She darted towards the old fireplace and grabbed a rusty poker and lifted it, rushing at the nearest rat. Instead of scurrying away it leapt straight for her. In an instant's stark terror she expected its long yellow teeth to fasten in her jugular. Then she was felled and banged her head on the teak mantelpiece. A trickle of blood ran down her face. She mustn't stay here, not here, among the rats. They were attracted by blood. To them she would be food. Horror swamped her. She struggled to fight off the darkness that was enveloping her, then there was a rushing sound in her ears and she slid into unconsciousness.

Chapter Fourteen

Laura came to, screaming, fighting in terror as she felt something touching her hands, her face.

It took several moments to realise that human hands were stroking her, giving her a little shake, and a voice was soothing her.

'It's all right, my love. I'm here. It's Ralph. Stop it! Stop screaming! I'm here to take care of you.'

She opened her eyes and clung to her brother. 'Oh, God, Ralph, it was awful – dreadful. Rats. I thought they'd kill me. They were huge. River rats. One attacked me!'

Ralph said comfortingly, 'I'm not sure it intended to. They say cornered rats are dangerous, but the trouble is you were blocking their escape route.'

'But it pushed me over!'

'No, love, I shoved you to one side. I didn't expect you to fall. I'm sorry you were hurt.'

'It doesn't matter. Thank God you came home!'

'Amen to that.'

Ralph carried Laura through to her living room and she lay on the sofa, still weak from horror.

'I think the rats must have climbed up the chimney,' he said. 'We'll get a rat-catcher in tomorrow to have a look.'

Laura suddenly remembered and sat up so suddenly she felt giddy and held a hand to her head. 'My hats,' she moaned. 'My beautiful straw hats. All ruined. All our work gone for nothing. And the show's only two days away. I'll be a laughing-stock. Gregory's will have beaten me, and how they'll crow.'

'Calm down, love. And sit there. Sit there, I said! I'm going to get you a drink and we'll inspect the damage together. It may not be as bad as it looks.'

He brought her strong coffee laced with brandy, and left her to drink it. When she'd finished they returned to the store-room. Laura hesitated on the threshhold, a shudder rippling through her. 'Ralph –'

'I'll go first and check,' he said and disappeared. 'All right, you can come in. They've gone.'

Laura stared at the wreckage. She burned with rage and loathing at the grey monsters who had done this to her. Slowly she and Ralph sifted through the hats; some were damaged beyond hope, but others appeared not to have been touched. A few of the felts were spoilt by droppings, but most were fine. After rescuing what she could of the trimmings, Laura tossed the soiled felts on to the heap of chewed straw.

'Some of my best designs have gone,' she said miserably. 'And I was going to impress Bristol with my art.'

'You'll do it yet, love.' Ralph sounded confident.

'I don't think so.' She swayed. 'I didn't realise how tired I was until this.'

'Snap out of it, Laura! You *are* tired, and very slightly drunk. I put a double in your coffee. It's bed for you and we'll tackle the problems in the morning.'

'We?'

'Yes, we! I'll fetch a hammer and nails now and block up the fireplace with wood. It'll take even those buggers more than a night to get in again. I've had a scout round. The other fireplaces are all safe, that's why they came in here.'

Laura laughed shakily. It wasn't often Ralph used bad language.

Her brandy-induced sleep came mercifully fast and she was awakened by Ralph bringing her a cup of tea. He kissed the top of her head. 'Drink up. I've got breakfast on the go –'

'I don't want any –'

'You'll eat! You've a long day ahead. Two long days and possibly a night. You need strength.'

Noreen and Miss Morton arrived soon after. 'Rats!' said

Noreen with a shudder. 'Oh, Laura, how terrible. It makes me feel ill to think of it.'

Miss Morton was more phlegmatic, as usual. 'What's to be done?' she asked. 'We can't disappoint the clients.'

'Ralph's gone out. He said he's going to enlist help,' said Laura. 'I can't imagine how.'

She soon discovered. Within an hour Ralph was back. He brought with him a rat-catcher who prowled around, muttering to himself as he worked. He called them to the basement. 'Just thee listen to this!' He opened a small broken door to an old dusty cupboard. Sounds of squeaking at every pitch reached them. 'Hear that. They be talkin' to one another. That's what rats d'do. They'm clever, they be.'

Laura listened with a mixture of horror and amazement. They really were 'talking'. Beneath the bustling life of Bristol a huge grey colony flourished on the dank, dark banks of the river Frome.

'Can you stop them coming in?' she asked.

'I'll do me best, missus. They'd gnaw through anythin' after a time. Your best bet is to call on me regular an' I'll inspect the premises. I do that for some others. Gregory's is one of my customers.'

Gregory's. How Mr Gregory and his son would sneer at the disaster which had struck her all-important show. The rat-catcher's words stiffened her backbone more than anything and she resolved that if she had to work from now until the hour of the show she wouldn't fail.

Ralph had been home and had actually persuaded William to sit in his antique shop while he went round to the old ladies and collected new hats and left those with only small damage to be repaired.

A little later, as Laura, Noreen and Miss Morton were assembling materials and discussing designs Freda walked in. 'I've come to help,' she announced. 'I'm not much good at fancy gewgaws, but I can plain sew. Just tell me what to do. Mum would come, but she's got a double load of washin' and all the kids to mind. She said to tell the factory I was sick today.'

Never had Laura been so thankful to see her sister's plain

face. She might be unimaginative, but she could work. And work she did. Most of the felt hats were unspoilt and they were able to concentrate on the straws. Freda stitched under Miss Morton's guidance, but she was invaluable as she stood uncomplainingly, hour after hour, steam pressing the hats at different stages, making tea, bringing food.

'I like it here,' she informed Laura. 'It's a bloody sight better than makin' corsets. And I bet our Joyce could manage it. I'd give a lot to see her out of that Goodwin house.'

'She's happy there, Freda.'

'Too happy,' burst out Freda.

'What do you mean? How can she be too happy?'

'Don't know. It's just somethin' about her. She's hidin' things from me. She's got secrets. She never had before – not from me.' Freda's voice was bleak and her heavy brows knitted over her broad nose in a scowl.

Poor Freda's jealous, thought Laura. Joyce is branching out and losing her dependence. 'She'll be fine, love,' she said. 'The Goodwins sound nicer to their servants than some, and the cook's keeping an eye on her.'

Freda removed a hot iron from the gas and put on the cool one and continued working. But she was dark with suppressed anger.

At lunchtime Iris arrived with Dolores. They both looked excited and carried bags of hot meat pies. 'Food for the workers,' said Dolores.

'How did you know – I mean?' Laura hesitated. Dolores could gossip as well as most people.

Dolores winked, 'Iris told me. Don't worry. I'll not tell the boss you've had a setback. I want to see you make a real splash on Wednesday, if only to annoy him. And Betty's comin', too. I know she's your friend and she's determined to do somethin'.'

Laura felt alight with gratitude. With so much goodwill how could she fail?

By Wednesday afternoon she had backache, headache, and her eyes felt gritty. Miss Morton was pale and Noreen's eyes were bloodshot. Nevertheless they were triumphant. They would have fewer hats to show, but Laura decided that the new ones were even better. Ideas which had been formulating had taken swift shape. Her tired brain seemed to work feverishly and she knew she had produced a collection well worth the showing. She wished they had music, but one couldn't have everything. There wasn't a single musical instrument in the antique shop. Ralph, with Alfred and Harold, moved furniture and laid a roll of turquoise and brown Wilton staircarpet to act as a catwalk. It had been discarded by someone wealthy, but it was good for a few years yet. William issued instructions. Laura had never seen him so animated. Once or twice she caught him giving her an admiring glance and was ridiculously pleased.

The display was due to begin at three. At two thirty all was in place. Anita had left her own shop in charge of her assistant and was ready to join Laura in the modelling. With her blue-black hair and olive complexion she could wear red and crimson, cerise and flame, navy and olive. She was a perfect complement to Laura who would model the wine and chestnut, the emerald and mauve. Now they would see how many women had accepted their invitations. Laura kept praying, please, let them come. Please, don't let it be all for nothing.

At a quarter to three Noreen announced in a shrill, horrified voice, 'There's a horse and cart full of junk stopped outside.'

'What?' Laura was incredulous. 'It'll have to move. We want room for the clients' cars. And what will people think? I'll ask them to go.'

She opened the door in time to see Rick leap from the cart, followed by two men. He grinned and touched his forehead in a salute. He was wearing overalls and lifted a tarpaulin to reveal a piano.

'Where do you want it, baby? Ralph said it was needed.'

'For heaven's sake, Rick. I'm modelling. I can't play as well.'

'Who says you have to?' The piano was manoeuvred into place just inside the door. Rick paid off the men who trundled away with the horse and cart and Rick slid out of his overalls to reveal a new suit. 'Just tell me where to wash my hands and comb my hair and I'll be ready.'

Laura wanted to hurl herself on him and kiss him – and only

partly in gratitude. The sight of him gave her the lift she needed to cope.

At ten to three four chairs were occupied by stout matrons. At five to three the number had crept to seven. Laura was biting her nails. An antique chiming clock struck three and a large car pulled up outside and four flappers trotted in, all smoking and chattering volubly.

They were the first of the flood.

'At this rate there'll be standin' room only,' said Dolores, peeping from behind a large Chinese screen covered in beautifully faded silk pictures.

'Lady Mallender isn't here.' Laura was disappointed.

'Not yet,' said Ralph. 'I'm sure Adrian will get her to come, but she's too important to arrive early.'

Then the Daimler drew up, the chauffeur opened the back door and Lady Mallender, Nancy and Adrian alighted. The two women settled themselves in reserved chairs. Adrian walked behind the screens and informed Laura that he and Ralph had decided that Adrian would do the commentary. 'As Ralph pointed out,' said Adrian, grinning, 'I've got a posh voice.'

'What about your mother?' Laura was aghast. 'I can't afford to offend her.'

'She doesn't mind at all.'

Laura was puzzled, but had no time to ponder as Rick began to play softly: *If you were the only girl in the world, and I was the only boy* – and the show began.

Adrian's mellifluous speaking voice floated over the audience. 'First we have the designer herself, Laura, in a hat which could be worn at almost any occasion. Note particularly the line of its cut –' He clearly took a keen pleasure in colours and textures. He was better than Miss Pringle, decided Laura.

She was dressed in floating grey chiffon, pale silk stockings for which she'd paid the shocking price of seven and eleven pence, praying that she wouldn't ladder them, and her grey shoes. Noreen had placed the first hat on her head, a turquoise felt. It was an almost stark cloche, its simplicity relieved only by an emerald enamel pin. The rows of ladies, some of the cream of Bristol society, watched as Laura paraded along the carpet, a cloud of grey floating around her pencil-slim figure, her head up, looking at no one, behaving as if she were alone. There was a murmur of voices. As she reached the end of the catwalk she caught a movement from Rick from the corner of her eye and, as she glanced at him, he winked. It gave her a curious mixture of pleasure and annoyance and on her return to the Chinese screen she looked haughtier than ever.

Anita passed her wearing a brilliant crimson hat with a curled, gilded feather. Laura didn't know whether Anita's startlingly foreign appearance, or the hat, caused the involuntary gasp of appreciation.

As Anita returned Laura stepped out to show a helmet of white spots on a cerise background decorated with an ornament of blue and bronze. The murmurs were louder as she stalked proudly to the door and back, and they sounded appreciative.

People had stopped outside and were blocking the pavement as they peered through the windows at this free show. She could hear their 'ohs' and 'ahs'. Some of the ladies frowned and she made a mental note to erect screens at her next show. To make her way as a milliner she needed rich women who must be pampered.

The workers behind the screen were silently efficient and as the show continued Laura sensed the admiration wafting from the clients. When she and Anita paraded together in a series of original straws there was spontaneous applause.

Rick played throughout unobtrusively. Gentle tunes. *Won't you play a simple melody; Look for the silver lining*. He allowed his sense of humour full play, too. When Anita paraded in a hat with a flower motif he played *When you wore a tulip*. And as Laura presented a navy-blue felt with a sweeping multi-coloured feather he swung into *There's a rainbow round my shoulder*. Absorbed and anxious as she was, Laura noticed everything he did.

The show was over by four o'clock. Noreen and Miss Morton wheeled out tea-trolleys borrowed from Ralph's stock, with cups and saucers, teapots and milk, and plates of dainty home-made biscuits donated by Rick's Aunty Mabel. The ladies were served by Adrian and Ralph and clearly enjoyed the attentions of two such handsome men. Ralph returned several times to Nancy and when he walked away she watched him admiringly.

In happy mood the clients called for Laura and Anita many times, asking them to bring a hat which had caught their fancy. With their peers looking on they paid nonchalantly for their favourites with sums of money that amazed Laura. The most expensive was the straw which Adrian had assured her would be purchased by his mother. A stout woman with a florid face called for it to be brought. Laura hesitated, glancing at Adrian who made his way to the stout woman and bowed. 'So sorry, Lady Marjorie, but Mummy has already purchased it.' He removed the hat gently from Laura's hands and handed it to his mother. 'You were quite right to want it, darling. It'll be perfection on you.' Her ladyship paid seven guineas without a whimper.

Ralph benefited, too, and swore he'd made more money than on an ordinary day. By eight o'clock the front door was locked, the carpet rolled up and the shop restored to normal. Everyone trooped up to Laura's flat and she poured glasses of sherry. William raised his high in the air. 'To my clever daughter,' he said.

It was an incredibly happy moment for Laura as William smiled at her over his glass. 'Well done, chick. You're a clever child.' It wasn't much, but it was the most she'd ever had. She handed him an envelope containing five pounds for his help. He hadn't done a lot, but she was glad of the excuse to send money to her mother. Not so long ago such a sum would have been unthinkable, but already her mind had expanded to encompass new horizons.

Harold and Alfred received enough to cover the loss of their own potential earnings and a generous bit over.

Laura hoped that Rick would stay on, but she was unsurprised when he told her that his friends would be back soon for the piano, and he must leave to fulfil a playing engagement.

'I thought you were one of the bosses now,' said Laura,

trying unsuccessfully to keep her disappointment from her voice.

'So are you, baby. But still you make hats and I play when I can. Every little helps.'

'You can't build an empire on little.'

'Great houses are built with lots of small bricks,' he said. 'You'd best remember that, honey. I'll do anythin' to get where I want to be.'

'Where's that?' she asked waspishly.

'Where men like Adrian Mallender are because they're born to it. No one's goin' to lift a finger to give me anythin'.'

'Surely you're not jealous of Adrian!'

'That's a bloody silly remark. God forbid!'

'What's wrong with him?'

'Oh, nothin', nothin'.' He was irritated and Laura couldn't blame him. She was behaving badly, possessively.

Later, when everyone but Ralph had gone, Iris arrived, followed by Dolores and – Laura could scarcely believe her eyes – Miss Pringle, who sipped sherry delicately. They listened attentively as Laura described her success.

'Congratulations, Miss Blackford,' said Miss Pringle. 'I would have helped, Wednesday being our half-day also, but Mr Gregory suddenly decided we must have a stock-taking. I fear it was simply a ruse to keep us from attending your show. He is not a considerate employer.' She looked suddenly alarmed by her burst of honesty. 'To have a business of your own at such a young age is an achievement indeed,' she finished primly.

'I've had lots of help,' said Laura. 'I'll never be able to thank everyone enough.'

Dolores said, 'Mr Gregory junior had a look through your windows while the show was going on. He came back fuming. I overheard him talkin' about it. I bet his father will curse the day he sacked you, Laura.'

'No need to be vindictive, Miss Handley,' said Miss Pringle. 'That does no good to anyone.'

Much later, when she was alone, Laura's heart beat fast as her private doorbell was rung. Could it be Rick? She ran down the steps and opened the door to find Adrian there, smiling, his arms filled with pink and white roses.

'For you,' he said. 'Nancy sends her compliments. And Mummy was very impressed. I'll keep up the gentle pressure and make sure she talks about you. She's tickled pink to have snatched the best hat in the show from under Lady Marjorie's nose. You're brilliant, poppet, do you know that? Brilliant!'

Laura dropped a small curtsey. 'Thank you, sir. It's kind of you to say so.'

'Kind be bothered. It's true.'

Laura sniffed at the flowers. 'Lovely,' she said. 'I adore scented flowers.'

'So do I.' Adrian continued to stand at the open door.

'Well, goodnight,' said Laura.

He looked acutely disappointed. 'Can't I come in for a while.'

'I'm here on my own,' said Laura, some of Granma's teaching suddenly surfacing.

'Heavens, you can't believe I would embarrass you in any way. I just like being with you, Laura.'

She couldn't resist and stood back to let him in and he followed her upstairs and sat in the easy chair, and stood up instantly. 'You must sit here. You're tired.'

'Do I look that bad?'

'Stop flirting, Laura. It doesn't suit you.'

'What! I wasn't flirting.'

'You were fishing for compliments. That's flirting.'

'Goodness, anyone would think I'd just invented it.'

'No, everyone does it these days, but that doesn't make it right for you.'

Laura subsided. She had no wish to continue this crazy conversation. 'What did you want to say?'

Adrian looked surprised. 'Nothing special. I told you I just like being with you.'

Laura laughed. He was like a puppy, sure of a welcome. He puzzled her. In many ways he was a sophisticate; in others he seemed a boy. But he was likeable. Very much so. And he had a soothing effect on her. Being with him was comfortable. Rick was jagged. You never knew what he'd say, or where he'd be from one minute to the next.

'Would you like tea, or sherry, Adrian?'

'Sherry, please. You bought a good one.'

'Ralph chose it.'

'Your brother is different from the rest of your family – those I've seen, anyway. So are you, for that matter.'

'Do the rest of them look slummy?' said Laura, handing him his drink, feeling rather indignant.

'No, darling, but your brothers and Freda aren't hot on looks, are they? Iris is better. She and Ralph must take after your father. So must you.'

'You've never met my mother.' Laura's voice showed the anger that was creeping over her. How dare this wealthy young socialite criticise her family as if they were creatures in a zoo.

Adrian was unabashed. 'No, but I hope to some day.'

Laura gave up. There was no point in trying to understand Adrian. His background would remain an enigma to her. She had been inside his home which had enough space for a dozen families, and watched today as his mother and her acquaintances had paid over enough money for hats to keep those families in food for at least a month.

Adrian stood up. 'I'll say goodnight, Laura. You need your rest. Congratulations again on your success. It was a splendid triumph.'

She rose and without warning he slid his arms round her waist, drawing her to him. He brushed her forehead with his lips, then each cheek and finally her mouth with almost reverent tenderness. She realised abruptly how lonely she felt. Surrounded by friends and family as she was, she still felt unbearably lonely – and always had. Rick stirred her to passion, but even he did not give her this warm comfortable glow of togetherness. She returned Adrian's kiss equally softly and felt as if a strong friendship had been bonded. A little of her loneliness was soothed away.

She lay in bed on Sunday morning, enjoying a brief rest. There could be no true respite at present. Perhaps never. She was very tired and suddenly dispirited. She'd had a vision of herself as a designer, leaving others to handle the work, but what if she had to spend her life hunched over a work-bench, like Miss Morton, whose shoulders were bent from years of toil?

She sprang out of bed and fetched the leather bag into which she had poured the takings. It was pleasingly heavy and she poured the contents on to her bed and stared at the piles of coins and notes. The sight soothed her. She couldn't expect this sort of cash every week, but it was a good beginning. A very good beginning.

Chapter Fifteen

Laura carefully placed holly and ivy along the base of the glass.
In a month it would be Christmas and she was pleased with her
window-dressing. Six hats were on display in varying shades of
green and red – a mix of two of the bright colours that were all
the rage. A dainty black umbrella with a tortoiseshell handle
was displayed among the scarves and gloves and paste jewellery, all in reds and greens. The beads were strung in apparently haphazard sizes. It was said that Madame Coco Chanel
had broken her graded pearls and impatiently put them
together as she found them, and in doing so had set a new
fashion. Anita now supplied some of the accessories for Laura's
shop, and in her own displayed Laura's hats, picking the ones
that matched her gowns. Each had an elegant hand-painted
sign in the window advertising the other shop. Between them
they had boosted their takings.

'Ver-r-r-y nice,' said Rick as she drew back into the shop.

'Does it look Christmassy?'

'I wasn't lookin' at the window, baby.'

'Flatterer,' she said. Such responses came almost naturally to
her now. During the past five months Rick had not once asked
her out. There had been times when she felt too tired to worry
about it, others when she lay exhausted and sleepless thinking
about him, remembering their love-making which she had
ended with her ghastly bout of vomiting. She supposed that it
had put him off her for ever. But he had held her gently and
wiped her face and comforted her. That showed a man who
cared for a woman as a person, not simply as someone to be
seduced. She assumed, bleakly, that he just wasn't attracted to
her. As she tossed and turned in the narrow bed above the shop

she wondered why she wanted him so; why the ache in her was never assuaged. It wasn't as if she lacked male admiration these days. She studied magazines, watched women in the shop, drank in the sophisticates she saw sometimes on the cinema screen, and modelled her behaviour on those she admired. She held her head up now, using the tall slenderness of her body to good effect. Her clothes and hats were always models and she was up-to-date with all the paste jewellery which even the rich wore nowadays.

And, above all, Adrian was unfailingly attentive. He wined and dined her, took her dancing to ballrooms where most of the men wore evening dress and the women were richly gowned. He even helped in the workroom and shop when she had to catch up with the work which was still an endless process. When she was extra tired he made sure she got some rest. He was gentle and kind and she liked him a great deal.

'You're lookin' marvellous, baby,' said Rick. ' "Tophole", as your friend Adrian would say.'

She whirled round. 'What do you know about Adrian?'

'He's your boyfriend.'

'He's not!' Laura paused. 'Is that what people say? That he's my boyfriend?'

'Sure is!'

'He takes me out when I'm able to get away.' She was unaware of the wistfulness in her voice and eyes as she looked at Rick.

He moved away and slid his hands down the length of a jet bead necklace. His strong hands, capable of hard physical work, tuned to understand the wants of a woman's body. Her breathing quickened. Would she never be free of her consuming passion for him?

'Don't do that,' she said flatly. 'You're disturbing the arrangement.'

He stopped at once. 'Are you makin' a good livin', kid?'

The concern in his voice shook her. She would never understand him.

'Yes, thanks. I'm doing well. I've plans, Rick.' Her voice became animated. 'I'm going to open another shop some day.

In Park Street, or Whiteladies Road. Somewhere where I'll catch the wealthy passing trade.'

'You're gettin' plenty of customers by word of mouth, aren't you?'

'Yes, but I've got so many ideas. There isn't room to expand here. And I'd like to run a third shop and sell good well-made hats in the lower range of prices. So many women make over the same hat from year to year until it falls to pieces. I'd like to do something for them.'

'Really poor women will always buy their stuff at jumble sales and church sales,' said Rick.

'Oh, Rick, you understand! Adrian and his kind would never know a thing like that.'

'If they did, it wouldn't matter tuppence to them.' Rick was suddenly serious. 'Laura, never forget they see our sort as servants, shopkeepers, anythin' that panders to their vanity. Did you know that Adrian Mallender drove a tram in the general strike? He helped to break the miners. The poor devils returned to work with longer hours and less pay.'

Laura shook her head. 'Granma thought the miners were wrong and that anyone who supported them –'

'Good God, woman, surely you're capable of formin' your own opinions over what's right or wrong.'

'Don't yell at me.'

'Sorry, but honestly, baby, you should be on the side of the workin' classes. You're one of them.'

'I suppose I am, really, Rick. I've just not thought much about it. I'm not yet nineteen and won't even have a vote for years.'

'It may come sooner than you think. I hear that Stanley Baldwin is in favour of givin' women the vote at twenty-one.'

'Well, don't worry, I'll take advantage of it – if it happens.'

'And what will you vote?'

Laura was abruptly tired of Rick's badgering. 'I'll do as I bloody well please,' she said acidly. 'What have my beliefs got to do with you?'

'Nothin'. Nothin' at all.' Rick shrugged off his mood and grinned. 'Pardon me for gettin' serious.'

'How's business?' Laura asked.

'Goin' good, baby. I've got twenty-five acts now and most of them are workin', though three are dancing couples and don't earn a lot. I've rented another picture house in Clifton and I'm gettin' it ready for the talkies.' Rick began to pace up and down in the confined space, making the chiffon scarves float in the breeze he caused.

'For heaven's sake, stand still,' implored Laura. 'You'll wreck the place.'

'Sorry, kid, but I get excited when I see the way things are goin'. There's so much a man can do; especially one without ties. I mean, Mum and Aunty Mabel never make demands on me.' Laura winced, but he went on, oblivious of the effect his words were having on her. 'I've met people who've seen *The Jazz Singer* in America. They say it's like magic to suddenly hear a voice comin' right out of Al Jolson's mouth as he sings.'

'A lot of people don't think it'll catch on.'

'You bet it'll catch on. And that'll be an end to the sub-titles.'

'And the piano-players,' reminded Laura.

'They can amuse the audience between films,' said Rick impatiently. 'Do you know that half the time the authors of the sub-titles make up their own words? One guy who mouthed, 'Get that harlot out of here?' came on the screen as "I think the lady had better leave".'

'And you think people would rather hear the first version yelled at them?'

'They'd rather hear the truth. Mark my words, Laura, the talkies are comin' and nothin' will stop them.'

'I'll believe it when I see it.'

'God, you're a stubborn woman. If the fashions change are you goin' to stick to the same kind of hats?'

'That's different.'

'It's not different. I tell you, Laura, the old slow days went with the war and everythin' moves faster now. I intend to be in the front, not draggin' my feet behind.'

As always, Laura ended by being infected by his enthusiasm. If only she was a close part of it. Adrian was sweet, but too worldly to show excitement. She drew a deep breath. 'You're still sending Mum free tickets. She told me about an old Lillian Gish picture. *Way Down East* it was called.'

Rick reached in his pocket for his cigarettes, looked at them, then put them back. Laura didn't approve of smoking in the shop. She couldn't forbid her customers, but didn't encourage it.

'I remember.' He grinned. 'I happened to be there and her eyes were red with cryin' when she came out. She said she hadn't enjoyed anythin' so much for ages. It had Lillian Gish as an unwed mother, cast off by her family, baptisin' her dyin' baby alone in a room.'

'Pure melodrama,' said Laura.

'But it brings in the customers.'

'Will the talkies be the same?'

Rick looked thoughtful. 'At first, perhaps, but I think films will have to change. Get better. And some of the stars will go. I've read that some wonderful actors who only have to mime now have terrible voices and are bein' dropped.'

'That doesn't surprise me. It sounds like a tough world.'

'No more than fashion, as you'll discover.'

'Maybe.'

Rick kissed the tip of her nose as a brother might and walked to the door. He hesitated, his hand on the handle, then turned. 'Laura, how often do you see Adrian Mallender?'

'As often as I please.'

'How often?'

'What's it to you?'

'I wouldn't want to see you hurt.'

Laura gasped. 'That's fine, coming from you.'

'What's that supposed to mean?'

Laura ached to yell accusations at him. To remind him that he had awakened fiery emotions in her, then left her to cope with them as best she could. To tell him he had made her love him. Instead, she said caustically, 'You seem to have a harem of girls. Some of them must get hurt.'

'I never upset anyone intentionally.'

'Huh! That's what they all say.'

'Who says?'

'Men!'

'You've suddenly become an expert, have you? All right. Go out with the Mallender boy. I only had your interests at heart.'

'My interests! You haven't got a heart! Mind your own business! Go away!' cried Laura.

They stared at each other furiously. Then Rick walked out, slamming the door behind him, rattling the glass pane, and seconds later his car roared into the distance.

Laura's anger was not cooled by Rick's abrupt departure. The nerve of the man! He didn't want her himself and tried to run down a man who did. She was startled by the idea. Did Adrian Mallender want her? He obviously enjoyed taking her out. He had held her hands across a candle-lit table and paid her compliments. What did it all amount to? She had learned that society girls changed their boyfriends almost as often as they changed their lipstick. Did Adrian mean the nice things he said, or was she a passing amusement? She could imagine the comments of the Charlton girls if they knew. 'My dear, he actually takes a shop girl out. A man I know actually saw them together! *Too*, too hysterical!'

The sight of herself in the large floor-length mirror which Ralph had installed helped put Laura in a better frame of mind. She felt very smart in her pale-gold wool two-piece made after a Patou-inspired fashion. Anita had sold it to her at the wholesale price. 'Of course, it's not actually a Patou original,' Anita had said. 'Neither of us can afford that kind of thing.'

'Patou is a dress designer, isn't he?' Laura asked tentatively.

Anita rolled her eyes. 'My God, what a question. He's one of the best, perhaps the best. You must come with me on my next visit to Paris and I'll take you to his place.'

Paris! Laura was startled. No one in her entire family had ever been abroad, except the men who had fought in the Great War. Most of them hadn't returned, and of the few who had, three were so damaged physically and mentally that they might as well have died.

'It's impossible to keep ahead if you don't follow Paris designers,' said Anita impatiently. '*Maman* says it's rumoured that waists are about to rise.'

'What about hats?'

Anita smiled, her teeth white against her olive skin. 'No change predicted yet, but it's vital to keep up. Fat lot of good it would be if you spent your time on a spring collection, then found out no one wanted to buy.'

The thought gave Laura goose pimples. Anita, though born in England, was the daughter of a Spanish father and a French mother who had returned to Paris on the death of her husband. He had been a minor official in the diplomatic service. Anita was fluent in both her parents' languages and Laura had picked up a few phrases from her which sounded well. She had also begun to buy magazines read by the well-to-do, *Vogue* and *Good Housekeeping* and made discoveries about worlds far removed from Granma's and her parents'.

Granma was different these days, almost respectful. She had heard about the hat show from William. What had impressed her most were the prices paid for her grand-daughter's hats. Laura dropped in on her on her way to visit her parents.

Granma greeted her with a frown, though Laura sensed that she was glad to see her. 'You're nothing but skin and bone.'

Laura said calmly, 'In one of my magazines it says that rich women who eat too much visit Baden Baden and Orsier, to get slim. Then they eat and get fat all over again.'

'Disgusting! They should try working for a living. Their fat would vanish like magic and they needn't go jaunting off to foreign places. Can't you afford another assistant yet?'

'As a matter of fact I can. I've engaged an experienced girl to help me. I've spoken about her before. Dolores Handley.'

'That flighty wench who encouraged you to get your hair shingled!'

'And look what's come of it,' Laura couldn't resist saying.

'Yes, well, it was still an act of defiance.' Granma changed the subject. 'As long as you think she'll do.'

'Oh, she will. A lot of her silliness was brought on by having to work for men she didn't like. I've got plans for her that'll get her further than Gregory's, and I'm paying her slightly more.'

'What plans, Laura?' asked Grampa gently.

'I'm thinking of opening a shop with lower prices. I might ask her to manage it.'

Granma frowned. 'Let's hope she does it properly, though if she's in another shop it won't help you much, will it?'

Laura drank a cup of tea and reluctantly ate a wedge of Granma's chocolate cake. It was delicious, but she would be expected to eat a full mid-day dinner at her parents'.

As she hurried away a cold wind blew, but she was warmly cocooned in a wool coat with a fur collar and cuffs, a fur felt hat, and kid walking boots. She expected a burst of sarcasm from Lillian, but none came. She was standing in the narrow passage, leaning on the wall. She looked pale and frightened.

'What's up, Lillian? Are you ill?'

Her sister shook her head. The small children, usually so noisy, were playing quietly in the front room. There was no sign of food, no steam, no cooking smells. Nothing was right. Laura hurried into the kitchen where she found Phyllis sitting, staring into space. William was grinding his teeth on his pipe. They looked at her, but neither acknowledged her. The boys were crouched near the roaring fire and Iris was hurrying about carrying cups of tea. Freda was standing by the table, her face crimson, her eyes wild.

'What's happened?' asked Laura. No one spoke. 'Won't somebody tell me? I am family, you know.'

Freda spoke in a voice strangled by anguish. 'It's our Joyce. A dreadful thing's happened to Joyce.'

Laura felt sick with fear. Nothing must hurt that dearest of sisters. She was a child, to be cherished.

Freda ground out slowly, 'She's expectin' a baby.'

'Oh, my God.' Laura sat down heavily. 'Oh, no, that's not possible. No man could –'

'I said how it would be,' grated Freda. 'I said she shouldn't go into that house. No one would listen.'

'Don't,' begged William. Laura was shocked at his supplicating tone. For once he had been jolted out of his complacence. Phyllis moaned and Laura went to her and tried to put her arms round her, but she was shrugged off. Laura felt the familiar hurt at her rejection. Even in the midst of a family disaster of such magnitude her mother didn't want to be comforted by her.

Phyllis said in a low, shaking voice, 'Some bloody man has got at Joyce. Some filthy, rotten, disgustin' pig has done this to her. No one could think she was in full possession of her senses. He took advantage of her.'

'How did you find out?' breathed Laura. 'What's she told you? Where is she? How far – ?'

Freda said, 'I was the one that found out. I knew there was somethin' the matter. I could feel it. She *is* my twin, you know, though no one bothered to listen to me when I said she did ought to stay home. I took her to the district nurse. She said she's four months gone. My Joyce is upstairs asleep. Expectin' a baby makes her very tired. She brought a note home from the high and mighty Goodwins' ever-so-wonderful cook. It says that Joyce isn't keepin' up with the work an' if things don't improve she'll have to leave.'

'Bitch,' said Phyllis. 'My God, what's to become of her? What'll this do to her?'

'Have you any idea who it was?' Laura's voice was thick with anger.

'She doesn't know his name.' Again it was Freda who answered. 'It seems the gaga old woman sent her on errands in the house and she met one of the young ladies' boyfriends. I knew she was keepin' secrets from me. I just knew it. Laura, you said the Goodwin girls buy your hats. Have you any ideas about the men they know?'

'They see a great many and I've heard names. They talk as if I wasn't there, except when they want something.' She paused. 'The only name I recognised was Gregory.'

'That dirty little stinker!' exploded Iris, surprising them all. 'He's always tryin' to get his hands –' she stopped, blushing.

Lillian had come in and had no such inhibition. '– up the girls' skirts,' she finished bluntly. 'It could be him. God, what a father for anyone's baby.'

'You can't prove it,' said William. 'It's no good accusing people just out of the blue?'

'Who's soddin' side are you on?' shrieked Freda.

For once Phyllis did not reprimand her.

'Our Joyce's, of course,' said William. 'But saying such

things about people is slander and could end up in court. And what good would that do Joyce?'

'Your father's right,' said Phyllis hopelessly. 'He's quite right. We can't beat the likes of the Goodwins and their friends. We'll have to hide her from folk who'll only hurt her more. Oh, my poor baby, my poor baby.' She rocked herself to and fro.

Freda glared at them all for a moment, then stamped out and Laura and Lillian followed her. 'Dad's nothing but a lazy bugger,' stormed Freda. 'If he'd got himself a proper job Joyce could have stayed home where she'd have been safe and this wouldn't have happened.' She began to sob, great tearing sobs that sent tears streaming down her face. Her nose turned red and ran, her skin grew blotchy.

Lillian handed her a handkerchief. 'For heaven's sake wipe your nose. You look bloody awful.'

Freda snatched at the handkerchief and dabbed at her nose. 'You don't care about Joyce!'

'Don't you dare say that,' screamed Lillian. 'Just because I don't drop tears and snot everywhere doesn't mean I don't care. If I knew the man who'd done this I'd kill him.'

'I'd get to him first.'

Laura stared at Freda. Lillian's threat was the spontaneous kind people often made; Freda's, she was sure, was terrifyingly rooted in truth.

She went upstairs to look at Joyce. Her sister lay asleep, her lips slightly parted, her skin stained with rose. She looked so young and innocent, so angelically lovely, it seemed impossible that she should be carrying a child, that some man had taken her body and used it, careless of the consequences. Laura wondered if Joyce had suffered pain, or experienced any pleasurable sensations. Maybe she loved him in her own simple way.

For dinner Phyllis and Iris made cheese and pickle sandwiches, but only the boys ate heartily; they were always hungry.

Joyce awoke and came downstairs, smiling with delight at seeing Laura. The change in her body was scarcely noticeable, but a close inspection revealed that her tiny waist had slightly thickened. Phyllis and Freda jumped up and led her to a chair.

'What a funny dinner,' said Joyce. 'Where's the stew, our

236

Mum? I told Mrs Telford that you make lovely stew. Better than hers, I said.'

'I've been that busy,' said Phyllis, 'but you'll get some for your tea.'

'Stew for tea.' Joyce looked doubtful.

'Could you eat a meat puddin'?' asked Iris. At Joyce's nod she said, 'Right. Mum, I'll get one on the boil as soon as the table's cleared.'

Freda fixed Laura with her small eyes. 'Are you makin' money?' she demanded.

'I'm selling hats,' said Laura, 'if that's what you mean. I don't have much money to spare. It goes into paying wages and buying materials for more hats.'

'Well, you can afford to dress like a bloody dog's dinner.'

'I must if I'm to attract the rich people. And things aren't always what they seem, Freda. My coat was bought second-hand, Anita's alteration-hand turned it and Miss Morton sewed on the fur. I made my hat. The boots were a bit of an extravagance, but I get chilblains.'

'Oh, how dreadful,' sneered Freda. 'You've got chilblains and our Joyce –' she stopped, reddening.

'What were you goin' to say about me?' asked Joyce.

'Nothin', love. Eat your sandwich.' Freda turned again to Laura. 'I suppose you know that Rick Merriman's sacked our Enid's Jack!' She was determined to quarrel with someone and Laura was the most vulnerable.

'No, I certainly didn't.' Laura was appalled. 'That's awful. I'm going to see Enid before I go back. How are things?'

'How do you think?' demanded Phyllis. 'They get meal tickets now and a loaf of bread. Jack has to go to the Board of Guardians and beg for every penny, and every mouthful again. God, I'd like to see some of them starve. I'd like them to come and beg off me. I'd spit in their faces.'

'I can't understand Rick.'

Iris said quietly, 'Jack was smokin' in the projection room. Rick had warned him against it because the films are very inflammable. The place was packed with people. If the films had caught alight hundreds could have died. Mum, you were there that night, and Lillian and the boys. You could all have been killed.'

'That's true,' agreed William, lighting up his pipe. Between puffs he went on, 'Imagine my feelings if a copper had come to the door and told me my family had been burnt up. That Jack's a fool. Our Enid did herself no good by wedding him.'

Laura left a pound with Phyllis and went to her sister's house. Enid was ironing, taking linen from a huge pile in a washing basket. She looked pale and was sweating, though the fire was tiny.

'Hello, Laura. See what we're brought to. I can't get my job back so I'm helpin' out the local washerwomen and they pay me a bit.'

'I'm really sorry, Enid. I wish Rick hadn't been so –'

'Jack deserved the sack. Stupid bugger! Fancy smokin' and puttin' all those lives in peril. Mum and the family were there, you know. I could murder him. My only consolation is that, thanks to you, I know I'm not goin' to have a baby until I'm really well again and can afford to stay home.'

Laura's purse was opened again and she produced five shillings. Enid stared at the money, then took it. 'I bet you've given some to Mum as well. We're all spongin' off you. It's not fair. It's just not fair.'

Chapter Sixteen

Two days before Christmas Rick brought Laura a gift. She hesitated, glancing up uncertainly at him, before tearing off the coloured paper. 'Soap.' She sniffed. 'Lovely. Mitcham's Lavender. And from Harrods. That's in London, isn't it? Have you been shopping in London?'

'Not recently. Harrods send anythin' on an order over five pounds. They look after you from birth to death.'

'Like the Co-op,' said Laura.

Rick laughed. 'Not quite like the Co-op! More like a palace. It's a wonderful store. Of course, I can't afford their prices for most things. They've got a big selection of wirelesses and some marvellous gramophones. One was in a cabinet and cost forty-five pounds. Imagine that!'

'I can't,' said Laura. 'Fancy having that much money to spend on something you don't need, when there are people in this country who don't get enough to eat.'

'I know what you mean, but denyin' yourself decent things won't help them eat. In fact, the more money spent the more work there'll be.'

'Well, all the extra work doesn't seem to have arrived round Kingswood way. Lots of the boot factories are on short time, and they've been sacking workers.'

'I know all about that, and I'm sorry, but forget it, Laura, just for Christmas. You work hard enough to be allowed to enjoy yourself. I'm glad you like the soap.'

'Oh, I do, Rick, I do.' She took another ecstatic sniff. 'It's wonderful.'

'Here's somethin' from Mum and Aunty Mabel.'

'But I scarcely know them! I've not bought them anything!'

'That won't matter to them. They haven't forgotten you. In fact, Aunty Mabel is very interested in you. She's been several times to peep at the shop.'

'Oh, tell her to come in.'

'I'll tell her, but I don't think she sees herself among the prancin' flappers. Mum' – he paused and his face sobered – 'Mum isn't pickin' up in health. She's worse, if anythin', but she still insists on workin'. Aunty Mabel says that's best. If she stops she might fret herself to death.'

'Is your mother really so ill?'

'I don't know. She refuses to see a doctor. She's had weak lungs from as far back as I can remember. Open the parcel, Laura.'

Laura discovered a box of hand-stitched lawn handkerchiefs with a small lacy border. Each one was embroidered and her initials intertwined.

'Mum did the plain sewin'. Aunty put the lace on and the initials.'

'They're wonderful. How kind of them to think of me. You must take something back.' Laura prowled round the shop and settled on a fine wool scarf for Rick's mother and a pot of hand lotion for Aunty Mabel.

'You doin' cosmetics now?'

'Just a few good ones. Anita and I order together from the wholesalers and share the cost.'

Rick looked at the dainty leaf-green pot of lotion. 'I can't see Aunty usin' this.'

'That's because you're a man. A woman's hands can get awfully sore in this weather. My customers use no end of lotions and potions to keep their skin nice and all most of them do is hurry in and out of their houses and cars and the shops. They're spoilt. Honestly, Rick, you'd never believe the amount of money rich women are ready to spend on cosmetics. One day I'm going to market my own brand.'

Rick grinned. 'You've learned fast, baby. You're even beginnin' to talk like them. "Awfully sore!" But don't go too fast. A lot of businessmen are havin' one hell of a hard time since the gold standard fell.'

'Ralph said that. I'm afraid I don't know much about high finance, but I get a lot of advice and help from Ralph. He seems to understand everything.'

'Keep listenin' to him. He's the sort that gets ahead. Actually!' he added teasingly, in a pompous voice, with a wry twist to his mouth. 'Don't your customers ever irritate you?'

Laura was packing the gifts in soft tissue. 'No one irritates me who can open a handbag bulging with money and hand some of it to me.'

Rick laughed. 'That's my baby.' He bent to kiss her cheek. She jerked away.

'I'm not your baby. I only see you once in a blue moon. And besides, I'm angry with you.'

'With me?' Rick put both hands over his heart and looked astonished.

'Don't play the innocent, Rick Merriman. My sister, Enid, is taking in ironing and she's still not properly over the birth, and the doctor says she should be careful for a long time. And if the Board of Guardians finds out that she's earning money and getting stuff from them they'll prosecute her, and Jack, too, I suppose. God knows what would happen. A fine? Prison? At the least they'll get no more help. And the Guardians are sure to find out. One girl I heard of, just fourteen, is having to contribute to her father's upkeep. He's just out of the army after twenty-seven years. He went though the whole war, and now he can't get work. They discovered that she'd bought a sixpenny bangle and she got told off. And it's your fault for sacking Jack –'

'For heaven's sake, Laura, stop goin' on at me. Jack's a bloody fool. He could have burnt half your family to cinders.'

'I know! I know he's a fool. I can't think what Enid ever saw in him. But he's a decent chap. Couldn't you give him another chance?'

'I already have.'

'What? You let me go on and all the time –'

'Have you any idea how bossy you've got lately? I didn't dare interrupt.'

'Nonsense!' snapped Laura, then laughed.

'That's much better. Jack's workin' for me as a general handyman. I've bought him a second-hand bicycle and he does small repairs and paint jobs in my cinemas. He'll never be allowed near the projection room again. And if anythin' needs a blowtorch I'll hire an expert. Am I forgiven?'

He smiled down at her and impulsively she pulled his head down and kissed him on the mouth. For an instant, during which her heart seemed to miss a beat, she thought he was going to respond in the way she ached for, but he stepped back, wished her a happy Christmas, and left.

He'd been gone for several minutes before Laura realised she hadn't even asked if he was still dating Lillian. She was afraid she'd get an answer she dreaded.

'Oh, Rick,' she whispered, leaning her forehead on the cool glass of the mirror.

A customer entered and she turned with her professional smile of welcome. And tonight she was going out for a meal with Adrian. He had the power to cherish and soothe her.

Laura spent Christmas Day with her family. In the past she had visited them on alternate years and recalled former festivities with pleasure. Absolutely no work, other than cooking, was done on that one special day. There was laughter and warmth and she had felt part of her family, but this year she was apprehensive. The shock of learning about Joyce had affected them all and she certainly couldn't see Freda making much of an effort to be jolly.

She was right.

Enid and Jack had already arrived, Mum's mother and father had travelled down from Manchester the night before and had been fitted somehow into a bed. With Mum there was never any nonsense about not enough room. Except where I'm concerned, thought Laura bitterly. There was no room for me. She shook herself free from self-pity. That was in the past, in a different life.

Lillian couldn't hide her envy of Laura's cream and burgundy checked wool dress and silk jabot, or her jade-coloured earrings that swung almost to her shoulders. 'Look at our Laura,' Lillian cried. 'The ugly duckling and the swan have got nothin' on this.'

'Just for one day will you shut your soddin', grumblin' mouth,' said Phyllis, her face flushed from bending over the range. But she said it without malice and Lillian shrugged.

Laura put her gifts beneath the straggly Christmas tree, decorated with home-made paper chains, and wondered whose garden the boys had raided this year. Who cared? Her closer acquaintance with the rich had certainly made inroads into her conception of what was, or was not, acceptable behaviour. From the women's gossip she had gleaned that their men were ruthless in business and the women in their social lives and, if they thought of their employees at all, they regarded them as so much fodder to work in their offices, factories and houses. She vowed that she would never get like them. Oh, she intended to be tough, to succeed, but she would always care for the less fortunate.

'Where's Joyce?' she asked hesitantly.

'Freda's taken her for a walk,' said Phyllis. She appeared to be about to say more, then closed her lips tightly, her face twisted with grief.

Gran and Gramps Palmer welcomed Laura with true warmth and Laura kissed them. They were both small and grey-haired, both had been weavers and had met in Bristol and Gran had gone with her husband when she was newly-wed to live north, away from her family. Gramps still worked, sweating out his days in a weaving shed in Lancashire. He was very thin and had a permanent cough. He laughed at the little ones who clustered around the tree, fingering the gifts, shaking them to see if they rattled, and was seized by a paroxysm of coughing which brought blood rushing to his face and neck. He coughed until sweat stood out on his brow.

Laura watched helplessly.

'It's the floatin' cotton wool in the weavin' sheds,' explained Gran for the hundredth time. 'It gets everywhere. I'm lucky I could leave work when I got married and had my babies.' She waited with habitual patience for the coughing to die away, then handed her husband a glass of beer.

He drank gratefully and wiped his forehead with a green-spotted handkerchief. 'You'll never let any of the young 'uns go into the mills, will you, our Phyllis?' he croaked. 'They know the cotton wool kills us by inches but they don't care. Bloody bosses!' He added, almost dispassionately, as if he had long ago accepted that life at the bottom was incapable of improvement.

'You know I shan't, our Dad,' said Phyllis absently, as she basted a large joint of pork. Poultry was too expensive, but the pork was succulent and brown with deliciously crisp crackling, the sage and onion stuffing and sausages meltingly tasty, and the potatoes well roasted.

The boys dragged in a work table from the shed and a snowy sheet covered both tables so that everyone could sit together for once.

'All hold the elbows in and move together,' said Gramps, making the little ones giggle. Gramps was full of fun and tricks. At supper when someone took the top from a sauce bottle there was a loud bang and a jack-in-box shot into the air. The children screamed with joy.

'I wish it was Christmas every day,' sighed Val.

'Well, it isn't, and never will be for the likes of us,' said Gran, 'so make the most of it.'

Freda sat next to Joyce, offering her all the best bits of food from her own plate. Joyce accepted everything and smiled happily at her family.

Freda scared Laura. She had always been dour, but now her eyes were heavy with sorrow and anger and she seldom left Joyce's side.

After dinner the presents were opened. Laura had brought sherry, cigarettes and a box of luxury chocolates, as well as personal offerings.

Even Lillian couldn't hold back a gasp of pleasure at the sight of a small bottle of expensive scent nestling in a blue silk scarf. 'Thanks, Laura,' she said, impulsively. 'It's nice for you that you can afford stuff like this these days,' she couldn't resist adding.

Laura had moved beyond Lillian's petty criticism, at least,

over money. She smiled and thanked everyone for her presents. She was aware that most of them had been ordered from a catalogue and not yet paid for. The talleyman was a regular visitor, especially after Christmas, but that didn't stop her enjoying a glass ash tray, a length of ecru lingerie lace, an aluminium tray and a fluffy towel. There were satin ribbons from the boys and small packets of sweets from the infants. Gran's gift was a home-made cretonne work bag with covered handles, filled with needles and thread. 'You'll be glad of it when you're sewin' your hats,' said Gran.

Phyllis said, 'We didn't know what to give you, Laura, you can get most things for yourself now, so Dad an' I decided on this.' Laura unwrapped a small brass bowl, a wedding present that had been kept on the mantelshelf for as long as she could remember. She blinked back tears. 'You can't spare this, Mum.'

'It's only ever full of bits and pieces that people can't be bothered to put away,' said Phyllis. 'They'll have to be tidier in future.'

In the afternoon and evening they played games. Silly, funny old-fashioned guessing games and boisterous ones that involved bursting balloons. When their elders were tired the younger ones retired to the front room and played musical bumps to a scratchy record. Everything brought laughter.

The small children had their sticky faces and hands washed in the scullery and were put to bed, rosy from food and excitement, still clutching their new toys.

Freda took Joyce into the front room and put on a record given to the family by Rick and carefully guarded from the children. They danced, Freda taking the man's part, holding her sister in her arms with obsessive tenderness. Joyce loved to dance and sing. Laura's attention to the conversation in the kitchen wavered as the strains of *Three o'clock in the morning* came wafting through the air. Would she never recover from this sickness of wanting Rick which had the power to strike at any time?

Phyllis announced, 'We've decided – Dad and me – to send

Joyce up north with Gran and Gramps. She'll be well looked after and no one round here will be able to point a finger at her.'

'Oh, must you!' exclaimed Laura. 'We'll all miss her terribly.'

'Can you think of somethin' better?' snapped Lillian. 'You know what folk are like with an unwed mother. Some of them are vicious.'

'It's true,' said Enid. 'I shan't forget in a hurry a girl who used to work beside me. She threw herself in the Feeder Canal and drowned.'

Laura shuddered. 'What will happen to Joyce's baby?'

'Gran will keep it for a while, then I'll have it home,' said Phyllis. 'I can say I'm mindin' it for someone.'

'Won't Joyce be upset if she can't keep her baby with her?'

'I don't know.' Phyllis looked bleak. 'I don't know how she'll manage at all. We'll have to face that when we come to it. But if we bring them back together people will talk.'

'They're sure to talk anyway if you suddenly send Joyce away,' said Laura.

William said, 'That's enough, Laura. Your Mum's doing her best.'

'I know. I wasn't being critical. It's just so awful. What 'bout Freda? She'll hate it without Joyce.'

'She's goin', too,' said Phyllis resignedly. 'To be honest, I 'an't be sorry. She's impossible to live with these days.' She 'ned to Gran. 'I'm sorry for you, Mum.'

'Gran sat serenely, her small hands folded in her black 'ombazine lap. 'Don't you fret, our Phyllis. Dad and me'll 'ook after them both. I can understand Freda. Joyce is her 'win. She feels this deeper than most.'

'Ralph drove Laura back to the shop in his creaky van. 'Do you think sending Joyce away will work out well, Ralph?' Laura was sombre.

'I don't know. I'd like to get my hands on the swine that did this to her.'

'Hasn't anyone an idea?'

'I've been asking around discreetly. The Goodwin girls are

pretty and lots of men visit the house. Lillian's decided it was Arthur Gregory.'

'God, I hope not. I wouldn't want a child in the family from that slimy pig!'

'Who would? But however much we dislike him we can't be sure that he fathered Joyce's baby.'

'Hasn't Joyce *any* idea?'

'It seems not. Apparently she never knew the man's name. He was too clever for that. The father could have been any one of dozens of men who visited the house, and it's best for Joyce if it's all kept quiet.'

'Surely there can't be many who would take advantage of a girl like her. She's just a child!'

'That wouldn't deter some. In fact, it would give them a bigger thrill.'

'Ralph!'

'Face facts, Laura. You're out in the world now. The sooner you learn what filthy devils some men are the better.'

'Well, I still think it would have to be someone pretty low.'

'I don't deny that. Here we are, love. Got your key ready. I'll put the van away.' Ralph rented a lock-up garage in a nearby street. 'Shall I come and say goodnight?'

'Oh, yes, please. I'll make us a pot of tea.'

Trade was slow after Christmas, but Laura knew from her experience in Gregory's that it would pick up again in the January sales.

'Have you got much you can reduce?' asked Anita.

'Almost anything,' said Laura. 'Since not many of the hats cost much to make.'

She had already ordered invitations to be printed, silver lettering on white card with *Hats by Laura* in gold, and sent them to her most prosperous and prestigious customers. The card invited each lady to a private view of her sale models. Gregory's always did the same and it was a successful ploy. Anything that tickled the satiated vanity of the rich was worth doing.

She had been helped by Nancy Mallender to discover many

of the addresses she needed. After the hat show Nancy had visited Ralph's shop more than once and had bought many of her Christmas presents from him. She always visited Laura afterwards and tried on hats.

She had sighed as she handed back a pretty rose coloured felt with a dove grey ribbon. 'I like it very much, but I don't have the opportunity to wear all the hats I already have.'

Laura must have shown unprofessional surprise because Nancy laughed. 'Mummy insists that I keep my wardrobe full of clothes, but to tell you the truth I'm happiest in something plain and my favourite hat is the French beret.'

'Would you like to see some?' asked Laura.

Nancy laughed again. 'You and Ralph are good salespeople. I do so admire you, Laura. And I envy you.'

Laura stared at her. '*You* envy *me*? You don't realise how difficult it is to make a living.'

'You make it seem enjoyable.'

'I enjoy the work, that's true, but the hours are long and it's all a terrific gamble.'

'I know. That's what makes it so exciting. I find so much of my life deadly dull.'

Laura said impulsively, 'Come on upstairs to see the workroom. That is, if you'd like to.'

'Yes, please.' Nancy's delicate face was suffused by a rosy blush of pleasure.

Miss Morton and Noreen were astonished to see the daughter of one of their most distinguished clients enter. Noreen hurried down to watch the shop, and two young apprentices, recently engaged, stared wide-eyed at Nancy's fur coat. Nancy was interested in everything and her natural friendliness made them almost forget who she was as she sniffed at the aromas of steamed cloth and glue water, listened to Miss Morton's explanation of the different processes, and exclaimed at the hats in varying stages of completion.

'You've got bowler hats, too. Are you going to dress men?'

Laura grinned. 'No! We buy the bowlers cheap and use them as blocks. That was Noreen's idea. We have to watch every penny we spend.'

Nancy clasped her hands. 'One day, Laura, you'll have the best millinery shop in Bristol. I just know it. And Ralph will be a famous antique dealer.'

She had hesitated a little before saying Ralph's name and her eyes glowed brighter. Surely she wasn't attracted to him? There was no future there. Lady Mallender would set out to ruin both Blackfords if she caught a whiff of a romance between her daughter and Ralph, a one-time rag-and-bone man.

When Nancy heard of the sale she said eagerly, 'I'll get hold of Mummy's address book and telephone you. You haven't a telephone. Oh, but you must have one installed. All the best shops have them. All right, I'll either come back myself, or send someone.'

The list arrived that evening, carried by a maid, and Laura, Noreen and Miss Morton worked late addressing envelopes and sticking stamps and Ralph slipped out and posted the invitations in the early hours.

The January sale was another success for Laura. She wondered why people kept warning her to take care and make haste slowly. Business was easy. All you had to do was concoct something different and rich women would clamour for it. What could go wrong?

She rented a small shop in Kingswood and Dolores was delighted to be asked to manage it and Laura moved deeper into the world of millinery wholesalers. She studied their offerings, choosing ready-made hats which were fashionable, but strong, capable of being unstitched one day by poor women for turning. It was a simple matter to add some ornament to a few of the hats to put in the window to draw in the customers. Dolores let it be known to some of the better-off that an exclusive touch could be added for a small fee. Laura also bought basic 'raw hoods' on which Noreen enthusiastically practised her new skills.

Laura called her new place *The Hat Shop*.

'That's good!' said Ralph. 'It'll be easily remembered.' He hadn't been entirely in favour of her branching out so soon, but

Laura overrode his objections, chief amongst which was that Dolores Handley would not prove suitable as a manager. 'She's a nice enough, girl, Laura, but I don't see her getting down to real work.'

'I tell you she's always wanted a chance to be something better than a salesgirl at Gregory's. I'm giving her a small commission, as well as her salary.'

'Well, that might help, but I still don't –' He'd stopped. 'I shouldn't be talking against a girl I hardly know. Your judgement's been sound so far.'

Adrian was delighted at this sign of Laura's increasing affluence. She bought a second-hand Austin Seven car and he was full of praise. 'Laura, it's sweet, it's so tiny. Absolutely tophole. You must let me have a drive.' As they trundled rather rattlingly along, he said, 'I've never been in such a little motor before. It reminds me of a pedal car I had as a child.'

'It's not that little!' protested Laura.

'Just teasing, darling.'

He called her darling quite a bit lately, but she knew that in his sphere of society it meant little or nothing. She wished it did. She was growing increasingly fond of him and thoroughly enjoyed their times together. He was a comfort to be with; with him she never felt the tormenting heat of desire. He was not exciting, but he was an excellent companion. If she was too busy to go out he often begged to be allowed into the workroom where he watched all the different processes of hat making and charmed Miss Morton and Noreen by his admiration, while the two young apprentices fussed round him like a pair of bantam hens.

'You must have a thousand better places to be,' protested Laura.

'No, I haven't. Most of my chums are away hunting, or shooting. They're always shooting things. They like nothing better than to come home with blood-stained sacks of smelly animals for their chefs to skin, or pluck, and cook.'

'But you don't mind eating them?' said Miss Morton.

He grinned ruefully. 'No, I have to confess I have a double

standard there! Everything's dead in town at present. Even the theatres have got pantomimes on and, while I bow to none in my love of a good laugh, you can't watch them twice. I could go to the races, but it's been raining since New Year and I prefer to keep dry.'

'Poor old you,' said Laura. Her slightly satirical tone only amused Adrian.

He stayed in the workroom for hours, watching Laura as she matched colours and sketched out her ideas. He even displayed some artistic ability himself in suggesting designs and decorations. He made them cups of reviving tea and usually brought something tasty for them to eat, and often a box of chocolates. It was impossible not to like him.

'At this rate you'll make me fat,' protested Noreen, accepting another chocolate.

'Is that so important?' asked Adrian. 'I suppose it must be. Mummy's magazines go on endlessly about obesity, not that any one here is obese. They recommend the most ghastly diets. Too awful, really. Food is so wonderful.'

'Everythin' seems wonderful to you,' remarked Noreen.

'Do you know, I believe it is. Well, perhaps not everything.' He grew unexpectedly sombre. 'Some things one has to do are not enjoyable.'

'Like what?' teased Noreen.

Adrian stared ahead, his eyes troubled, then he said lightly, 'Oh, nothing, really. Mummy's most awfully strict sometimes. Now, Miss Morton, show me again how you plait those brilliant satin straws. It's so fascinating.'

Rick came to tell Laura that, instead of renting his third movie house, he had borrowed enough money for a deposit to buy it. 'I'll have to work like a dog to pay the instalments,' he said. 'I'll add to the agency and perhaps go out playing piano again, but it'll all be worth it in the end.'

Laura noticed that he'd given up the more expensive Gold Flake cigarettes he'd taken to and returned to Woodbine. Her only consolation at his rare appearances was that he was probably too busy to take out any girls at all. Lillian had made some derogatory remarks about him lately and Iris had said it was because he was no longer dating her. Not, of course, that his private life was anything to do with her.

A telephone was installed in *Hats by Laura* and the expense was proving worthwhile. She had grown to know some of her customers' preferences and was now used to receiving calls.

Lady Mallender would phone: 'Laura, is that you? I need a headdress for a houseparty in Windsor. Something light to go with a new heliotrope gown. Such a difficult colour to match, but I'm sure you can do it. I'd like the headdress to be of satin ribbon and small feathers. Send one of the girls round with some colour swatches.' Lady Mallender seldom said please, or thank you, and she expected everyone to run after her as if she were a queen. But Laura couldn't afford to offend her. So she would despatch Violet, at fourteen, the elder of the two apprentices, to the big house on the Downs.

Ralph and Adrian between them had taught her how to drive and she was able to visit her outworkers when necessary. It was strange, but Ralph, usually so good-humoured and courteous was always abrupt with Adrian. He said nothing derogatory about him, but Laura knew her brother didn't care for him. Yet he clearly liked Nancy. More than liked her, Laura feared.

She drove herself to Kingswood, where the new shop was in a road just off Regent Street. It had one window which was filled with hats, gloves, stockings, scarves and necklaces. Face powder, hand and face creams, a few lipsticks and bottles of scent were displayed on black velvet, along with a glittering paste brooch.

Dolores was obviously proud of her window. 'Is it exactly right, Laura? I remembered what you told me to put in.'

'You've done it perfectly.'

'I thought of the kind of things I can afford and went on from there,' said Dolores.

Iris appeared from the small kitchen behind the shop. She had decided she would like to work for her sister who was delighted to have her. Iris's good sense and strong loyalty gave Laura a feeling of security. Granma, and especially Ralph, had sown a doubt in her mind about Dolores. However, so far they

252

had been proved wrong. The new shop, open only four weeks, was doing splendidly.

Dolores asked diffidently, 'I wonder if you could do me a favour, Laura. Well, really it's for my sister, Millie. Do you remember her?'

'Of course. She's in accessories in Gregory's store.'

'Not any more. That awful Arthur Gregory accused her of stealin' and all because she slapped him when he tried his usual games with her.'

'But she's only thirteen. Still a child.'

'Fourteen now,' said Iris, 'like me.' Iris's small face was very serious and Laura looked affectionately at her. 'Fourteen, of course,' she said.

'They sacked our Millie on the spot,' said Dolores. 'Of course, she's got no references. I wondered if you could give her a job.'

Laura was reluctant. She had worked out her budget very carefully. Although she wouldn't admit it to anyone she was nervous about how much money it had taken to open up the Kingswood branch. Trade was good, but it took a great many inexpensive hats to make enough money for rent, heating, lighting, and wages and, so far, *Hats by Laura* was subsidising the new place.

'She won't ask much, Laura,' begged Dolores. 'She needn't stay long, either. It's just so as someone'll give her a reference.'

Remembering her own struggle and the weeks in the tobacco-stripping room Laura nodded. 'All right. She can begin straight away.'

Dolores beamed, but Iris didn't looked pleased. Was she afraid of being dominated by Dolores and her sister? Perhaps, but she need have no fears. Laura was watching Iris's progress closely. She believed that one day she would be fully capable of managing a shop.

When Laura got back to *Hats by Laura* Rick was waiting for her. He wore a dark suit. 'You're looking smart –' she began, then stopped. His tie was black, his face sombre. 'Rick, what's happened?'

'It's Mum,' he said flatly. 'She died.'

'Oh, I'm so very sorry. When did it happen?'

'Yesterday. She's had to miss work several times lately because she felt too ill to go out.'

'I wish I'd known. I would have visited.'

Rick continued as if she hadn't spoken and she realised with pain that he was controlling terrible grief. It reminded her that his mother had been the only parent he'd known. 'She was sent home yesterday because she was ill and had a heart attack in the night. She was dead before the doctor arrived. He said he'd told her she'd live longer if she rested. She wouldn't, though. Poor Mum. She had a stinkin', rotten deal.' He was agonising over his mother's betrayal in the past, over her proud struggle to rear him and Laura dared not offer comfort for fear of saying the wrong thing.

'Will you come to her funeral, please, Laura?'

She nodded, her heart warming to him. 'Of course.'

The funeral was short and sparsely attended. The minister did his best to give a eulogy, but 'Mrs' Merriman had been a quiet, mouse-like creature, whose one lapse from morality had affected her whole existence. Afterwards Laura returned to the flat in Hotwells with Rick and Aunty Mabel and drank tea and ate ham sandwiches. Rick just smoked, lighting one cigarette from the stub of another.

'You'll miss her,' said Laura softly to Aunty Mabel.

'That I shall, my dear, that I shall. Of course I'll have Rick to keep me company. That's if he decides to stay in Bristol.'

Laura hadn't thought of this aspect of Rick's mother's death. Well, what odds did it make if Rick went or stayed? They hardly ever saw one another. And, besides, she had Adrian now.

'I'll be spendin' more time in London,' said Rick, 'but I'll need to come back to check the cinemas. I was goin' to give Mum a softer life when I had some money. I could have if I hadn't spent it all on tryin' to make more.'

Aunty Mabel chided him. 'She was proud of you, Rick. Prouder than you realise. She talked to me a lot over our household jobs. You were the best thing to happen to her.'

Rick turned his head sharply to stare from the window at the steep hill. Laura could sense his misery. She wished she had the right to put her arms around him and comfort him. Aunty Mabel half rose, then sat down again, shaking her head. Rick got up and walked out and moments later they saw him climbing Brandon Hill, kicking his way through the rain-soaked grass, his head bare.

After work that night Laura's doorbell rang. She half expected Adrian and was surprised to see Rick standing outside. 'Can I come in, Laura?'

'Of course.'

There was so much she wanted to say to him, but she remained silent. For a while he just sat by the fire and smoked. He accepted a cup of coffee.

After a while she said gently, 'When did you last eat, Rick?'

'I don't know. Last night, I think.'

'You'll be ill. Your clothes are still wet, too. And your hair's plastered down with rain.'

'I don't care.'

'Where's your hat?'

'I don't know. For God's sake Laura, it really doesn't matter.'

'But it does! What would your mother say if she knew you were neglecting yourself? She thought the world of you. She'd hate to think you were sacrificing yourself to grief.'

He looked up angrily. 'Is it wrong to grieve?'

'Of course not. She was a good woman. She deserves the compliment of grief. She also deserves to have you look after yourself.'

Some of the tension drained from Rick's face and he gave her a small smile. 'You remind me of her. What do you suggest?'

'I've got some soup left.'

'All right,' he said. His answer was ungracious, but he ate the soup and his face became less haggard.

'Laura, I left it too late to give Mum a few luxuries. Don't ever make my mistake.'

'My family wants nothing much from me. Even Enid's all right now Jack's working.'

255

Rick's brows narrowed over his dark eyes. 'I can't believe they'd refuse your help. Their livin' standards are poor.'

'The boys will take anything I offer, but Mum takes my money grudgingly. She and my sisters resent me.'

'You're too touchy.'

'I am not! It's true. Iris is the only one who really loves me. And maybe Joyce, but she –'

'Joyce is sweet.'

'You don't need to tell me that, but I don't see her these days.'

'Why not? What's happened?'

It seemed that Joyce's situation had been contained within the family. 'She and Freda have moved north to live with Gran and Gramps Palmer – my mother's parents.'

'Why? Your whole family adore Joyce.'

'Mum thought a change would do her good. Gran and Gramps Palmer have never seen enough of her, and Freda goes everywhere she goes.'

'You'll miss them.'

Laura nodded. 'And now you'll be going to London.' A stab of anguish managed to pierce her attempt at nonchalance. 'When will you leave?'

'As soon as the new cinema is redecorated and ready for openin' I'll be travellin' to London more often, but I can't afford another manager so I won't be away for long spells, not at first, anyway. However good a manager may be he's lookin' after his own interests first. Don't forget, Laura, you should never be too trustful of your employees. I had a look in the Kingswood shop. I see you've got Dolores Handley in charge.'

'What's that supposed to mean?'

'She's a bit flighty, baby. I wouldn't want to see you go under.'

'How did you know it was my shop?'

'Ralph told me.'

'Oh! Well, you've no call to criticise Dolores.'

'I wasn't. I was just tellin' you not to get too complacent.'

'You and Ralph have got it in for her.'

'So Ralph thinks the same as me?'

'Let's change the subject, Rick, please. I couldn't bear to

256

quarrel with you. Not today. Tell me how the agency's getting on.'

He began hesitantly, but his voice grew stronger as he described some of his acts. 'There's a magazine just for jazz lovers, Laura. It's called *Melody Maker* and it's great for learnin' about musicians. Through the ads. I've got a chap who can play red-hot syncopated rhythm on a trumpet. He does a hat-muted solo.'

'Am I supposed to understand that?' she laughed. 'It's like a different language.'

'It's a different world.'

'If it isn't a stupid question, what kind of hat?'

'A bowler. If he holds it over the end of the trumpet it changes the sound.'

'So I should imagine. It's funny, Rick, but we're both using bowlers to do something they weren't meant for.' She explained and was gratified to see him smile. There was another ring on the door-bell.

Rick jumped up. 'You've got a visitor. Were you expectin' someone? I'd better go.'

'No need. It's probably Iris, or Dolores. I'll be getting a telephone in the other shop as soon as I can afford it. It'll save us a lot of running about.'

Adrian stood outside. His eyes were stormy, his voice was a shade too hearty. 'Hello, darling. I just had to come and see if you were all right after the funeral. Such grizzly things, funerals. Ought to be abolished. When I go I'd like to be put on a boat and pushed out on the sea in flames. That would be a real climax to one's life. Aren't you going to ask me in?'

Laura stepped back. 'Of course. Sorry.'

When Adrian and Rick saw one another their hackles rose. 'They were just like a pair of fighting dogs,' Laura said afterwards to Noreen and Miss Morton. 'I can't think why. Rick's only a friend and Adrian doesn't usually get heated over anything.'

Rick left abruptly and Adrian threw himself into a chair and said moodily, 'Is he a boyfriend?'

Laura, leaning on the mantelshelf, said coolly, 'No, he isn't, but if he was it would be none of your business.'

'Don't be cross with me, darling. I couldn't bear it tonight.'

'What's upset you?'

'Oh, nothing. Well, yes, it's Mummy. She can be so damned autocratic at times.'

'I thought she gave you your way in everything.'

'Most things. She's a good old girl, really, but if she's got a bee in her bonnet there's no holding her.'

'And she's got one about you?'

'Yes.'

'But you're not going to tell me about it.'

'It would bore you dreadfully, darling.'

'No, it wouldn't. I'm interested in anything that hurts you, but of course you don't have to tell. It isn't my business.'

Adrian stood up so suddenly that Laura sloshed her coffee into the saucer. He grabbed it from her and plonked it on the table. Then he put his hands on her shoulders and shook her gently, but firmly. 'Anything that concerns you is my business, Laura. Just because I'm not one of those pushy chaps doesn't mean I don't have feelings.'

Laura stared into his blue eyes that had grown dark with anger. 'You care about me?'

'Of course I do, old thing.' He sat down again and reached for his coffee and drank it.

Laura composed herself and sat down opposite him, waiting for his next words. He was clearly restless and anxious.

She watched Adrian who was staring into the fire. His mouth was as sensitive as a woman's, his skin perfect. His looks and his silky hair were totally unlike Rick's broad face and springy curls. Adrian really was handsome.

'Laura, you like a peaceful life, don't you?'

She was surprised at the earnestness of his tone. 'Yes, I suppose I do. It's the way I was brought up.'

'Ah, yes, Granma was strict wasn't she, and a stickler for manners?'

'Yes. I didn't appreciate it when I lived with her. Now I see she was right – about some things, anyway. I don't know much about society, but at least I can behave properly towards my customers.'

Adrian left his chair and knelt at Laura's feet. 'Laura, you would always behave properly in any situation. You're what's known as a born lady.'

'Thank you, sir.'

'Don't mock me, darling. I'm serious. I like you tremendously. In fact, I really rather care for you. Surely you've noticed.'

'You're most attentive. I enjoy your company.'

'More than that, I hope.'

'Perhaps, but Adrian, we've never got really close. You don't even kiss me. Not properly.'

'I'm afraid I was brought up not to show my feelings.'

'So was I, but that doesn't apply to – to lovers.'

'Darling Laura! Is that how you see us? As lovers?'

Laura flushed. 'Sorry. That was forward of me.'

Adrian put his arms around her waist and held his head close to her breast. 'No, my love, I was only teasing. It's the way I see us, too.'

Laura smoothed her palm over his head and down his neck to his shoulder. He moved uneasily. 'Don't you like me touching you, Adrian?'

'Of course, darling, but I don't believe in love-making before marriage.'

'Well, you'd be called old-fashioned today. The way my clients talk about love and sex, quite openly in the shop, makes my hair curl. And I wouldn't call what I just did love-making.'

Adrian looked up sharply. 'Does that mean you've allowed a man to –'

'No, it does not!' Laura was over-emphatic because she knew she would have given Rick the freedom to make love to her. The thought of Rick's passion started the blood rushing through her. This was all wrong. She should be thinking only of Adrian.

'Kiss me,' she said.

He was startled. 'Kiss you?'

'Why not?'

'No reason.' He rose, frowned, then laughed. 'No reason at all, my love.' And he pulled her up to face him and slid his

259

arms around her. His mouth touched hers, delicately, and moved gently upon it. Laura felt paroxysms of need convulsing her body. She held Adrian's face between her hands and deepened the kiss, opening her mouth slightly and touching his lips with her tongue. He lifted his head, flushing. 'Don't do that, Laura,' he rasped.

She was hurt. Was she destined always to be rebuffed? She sat down suddenly, confused.

Adrian knelt again and held her hands. 'Don't look like that,' he begged softly.

'Like what?' Her voice was bleak. 'I can't believe you really want me.'

'Oh, but I do, I really do. It's just that I don't want to make love until I'm married.'

'Have you anyone in mind?' she asked abrasively.

'I thought I'd made it clear.'

Laura stared at him. He was serious. 'You mean it. How is it possible? Your mother would destroy me. I've not met your father, but I can guarantee he'd be none too pleased. I bet your mother has had someone planned since babyhood for you. Someone with pots of money.'

'She hasn't Laura, honestly.'

'Well, she won't want me. Adrian, don't look so miserable. I do care for you, but you must know my family would shock yours.'

'You shouldn't be ashamed of them.'

'I'm not. I love them all. But they simply don't behave like yours.'

Laura couldn't afford to offend Lady Mallender. She must discourage Adrian, though it hurt her. She realised she cared a lot for him, that she loved him in a quiet, steady way. She drew a breath. 'Adrian, listen to me. My younger brothers drag a barrow to the boot factories and bring home what work they can get. My sister Freda was a machinist in a corset factory; at the moment she's working in a factory near Manchester. My parents,' she paused, hating to run them down, 'my parents get drunk on Saturday nights and weave their way home, singing loudly. Then they drink more beer until they stagger up to bed and wake with a hangover on Sundays. My –'

'Enough!' said Adrian. 'I'm not courting your family.'

'Courting? You really do mean it!'

'Most certainly. I want to marry you, Laura, and if you agree nothing shall prevent us.'

Laura felt a warmth spreading through her, dissolving the stony lump of hurt sculptured by years of rejection. 'I want to marry you, darling, but you must understand that I shall go on working. I intend to be financially independent. And I've no intention of cutting loose from my family.'

'Fine. I like loyalty. And I'll never interfere with your work, I promise.'

Laura sighed. 'This is ridiculous. Your mother won't let you near me once she discovers what you want to do. Do you realise she has the power to ruin me? If she cared to use her influence in no time her friends would stop patronising my shop and the Kingswood branch isn't breaking even yet.'

'You've proved you're not afraid of life, Laura. Show some courage now. Come out to dinner with me next Saturday night.'

'What will that prove? We've had dinner together before.'

'Yes, we have.' Adrian paused. 'But only in rather ordinary places.'

'They didn't seem ordinary to me.'

'You're sweet, Laura. So honest. No pretensions at all, but I've never taken you where I'd meet my friends or family. We'll go to the latest thing in night clubs in Bristol. My chums will be there, people who know me and my family. That will prove to you I'm serious.'

Laura drew a deep breath. 'Next Saturday night? All right, I accept.' She felt she was taking a long step into uncharted ways.

'Good.' Adrian was suddenly brisk. 'I shall pick you up here at eight o'clock.' He kissed her lightly on her forehead and went down the stairs whistling *Anytime, Anyday, Anywhere* as lightly as a bird.

Laura lay awake for a long time that night. Mrs Adrian Mallender. Lady Mallender. If she married him she would one day become a real lady. The thought shook her. It could never happen. Adrian was a dear, but he would soon realise that his family and friends would look at a marriage between them at best, as a joke, at worst, a disaster. She felt sad. She'd like to be married to Adrian. He would give her such support. She would belong to someone at last and know she was the centre of another human being's life. And they would make love. The burning passion that Rick had brought to life and whose fires she'd had to dampen down could enjoy wonderful release.

Chapter Seventeen

It was April and the shops were displaying the spring fashions. Waistlines remained obstinately low at hip-length, but Laura was selling many hats with wider brims.

Adrian had led Laura into a different world. It began with the dinner. She dressed carefully for it, deciding finally on a simple apple-green silk crêpe dress with three rows of grey silk tassels near the hem. It fell straight from her shoulders to her knees. Her stocking were of fine grey silk. Anita, as usual, had sold the clothes to her at cost and had presented her with some delicious underwear in exchange for a model hat. Laura's camiknickers, she had long ago discarded the elastic-legged knickers advocated by Granma, were peach-coloured georgette. Laura loved the light airiness of them, but she was very much aware that only a thin strip of material caught the front and back hems between her legs. She couldn't command her imagination, couldn't ignore the sensuous caress of the silk. There were times lately when she cursed the day she'd met Rick who had awakened her sensual nature, then denied its fulfilment. But, she admitted ruefully, if she hadn't met him she would certainly still be under Granma's domination, maybe even engaged to Reggie Prewett, destined to live her life in a white apron behind a grocery counter. She shuddered, then laughed aloud. She would never have accepted him. Never.

Adrian called for her in the Daimler. 'I believe you're even slimmer,' he said, looking at her admiringly. 'You're positively boyish.'

'I'm not surprised. I never stop moving. Does it matter? It's still the fashionable shape.'

'I know, darling and on you it's good, very good. I admire it.

You're so elegant and your eyes look even larger. They're your chief beauty, you know.'

Laura was gratified. The word 'beauty' was not one that was usually applied to her. She sank into the soft luxury of the car and stared at the chauffeur's back. 'Why aren't you driving me yourself?' she asked in a whisper.

'It's all right. He can't hear through the glass screen. There's a speaking tube here if I need to give orders. I'm not driving because I want to concentrate all my attention on you. You really do look wonderful.'

'As a matter of fact, so do you.' Adrian's white tie and evening tails were faultless. 'You look very handsome,' she informed him.

'Thank you, my lady.' He lifted her hand to his lips and she glowed with pleasure. She was still convinced that Adrian would never be free to offer her a future with him, but she wished to keep their friendship alive. She must tread very carefully, though probably if Lady Mallender knew of their association, she would smile indulgently at a son who was amusing himself with a member of the lower orders. Again the shop talk had educated her there! Only last week she had burned with indignation as a flapper had said maliciously, 'My brother's taking out a girl who works in a chocolate factory. Mummy is furious, but Daddy says the boy must have his fling.' The others had responded with hen-like cackles of appreciation. No, Adrian would eventually remember his future role in society, but meanwhile she was having a little fun.

She said suddenly, 'Adrian, would your mother be angry if she discovered our friendship?'

She expected an evasive answer and was surprised when he said, 'Absolutely not, old thing. She's ever so nice when you get to know her.'

Laura couldn't prevent the tinge of disbelief in her voice. 'Is she really? Er, have you actually told her about me?'

Again he surprised her. 'After tonight I won't have to. The chauffeur will tell the staff and it'll reach Mummy through her maid. The postal services could learn tips from the servants!'

The car drew up outside a large building in Clifton. It looked very much like a private residence from the outside, except for a discreet sign which announced The Purple Fanfare. Inside everything was charming. The decor was light, the hall filled with flowers. A dress-suited man greeted them with a bow and directed Laura to a maid who showed her to the ladies' cloakroom. In there Laura saw several girls who had bought hats from her. She wasn't sure if they recognised her as she took powder and lipstick from her vanity bag and applied more make-up. She tossed her head casually and her earrings danced gaily, but her thoughts were chaotic. This certainly was one of the exclusive clubs; here they were bound to meet Adrian's friends.

He was waiting for her in the hall and greeted her with a small, accomplished bow that delighted her, then escorted her into a large, carpeted room filled with tables. A band played on a stage next to a ridiculously small space left clear for dancing. They sat at a reserved table for two and waiters materialised. The menu was in French and Laura thanked heaven that her schoolgirl variety plus some tuition from Anita enabled her to understand enough to order. She noted the look of pleased surprise Adrian couldn't keep from his face and was inwardly gratified.

As they ate the food and drank the continually flowing wine, they talked. Or rather Laura talked. Adrian mostly asked questions. He seemed fascinated by every aspect of her life, but chiefly the hat shops. No one had ever shown so much interest in her and, her senses lulled by wine, her vanity flattered by his gentle attention, she became expansive. After a while she felt he must know as much about the business side of her life as she did. Maybe more. He seemed to understand about the falling gold standard and said it had almost ruined some people. She made a vow to learn about financial matters. She had no intention of becoming a helpless little woman who left big decisions to a man.

A chatter of noise exploded at the entrance and Adrian groaned. 'Oh, no! My cousins! I thought they were going to the Blue Room. That's the end of our peace.'

Thelma and Daphne Charlton were with a party of young men and women who seated themselves at a large reserved table, shrieking loudly to friends at other tables, who yelled back. A young man with Thelma, his hair so slicked back it looked polished, threw a bread roll across the room. It was returned with interest. The head waiter hurried to the noisy table. He was smiling, but Laura felt he looked strained.

She was astonished. 'Do they always go on like that, Adrian?'

'No!' He grinned. 'They're frequently much worse. In fact, they're sure to get thoroughly obnoxious tonight. It's Thelma's birthday. She's twenty. I sent her a scarf and some beads I bought from your shop.'

Laura sampled Adrian's Egyptian cigarettes which he kept in a gold case, and there was comparative peace for a while as Thelma's party ate and smoked and danced their way through their meal.

Then Thelma wove her way rather unsteadily between tables towards the cloakroom and caught sight of her cousin. 'Adrian,' she shrieked, 'you swine! You turned my party down because you had a previous engagement. I thought it was important, but it was only a date.' She peered at Laura. 'Haven't we met? Good God!' Her voice surely reached all four corners of the room? 'It's the girl from the hat shop. Laura! How *utterly*! Listen chaps and girls, Adrian is here with Laura. Of course you know her. Well the girls do anyway. *Hats by Laura.*'

Laura felt everyone staring at her. 'At least she's giving me some free publicity,' she muttered under her breath to Adrian.

'That's my girl,' he said, squeezing her hand. 'For heaven's sake, Thelma, go and pee, or whatever it is you have to do.'

Thelma screamed with mirth and walked on, but she hadn't finished with them. On her return she dragged a chair from another table while its occupant was dancing and sat close to Laura. 'Fancy going out with Adrian. My dear, *too*, too mirth-making.'

Adrian coloured angrily and Thelma pouted. 'Now he's cross with me. Don't be cross, cousin darling.'

A man from her party appeared and took her by the arm.

'Come along, sweetheart. Enough's enough.'

'God damn it, let go of me, Paul!'

Paul tightened his grip. 'You're with me, remember?'

'Take your bloody hand off me!'

Laura was startled. She hadn't supposed ladies swore in so public a place. She hadn't supposed, either, that ladies got drunk and made scenes. Joyce had said that the swells were not much different from themselves. Clever, tragic Joyce. Laura evidently still had a lot to learn.

Paul was watching her with a deprecating smile. 'I'm afraid she's had a little too much to drink. She's not always like this.'

'Only often,' grated Adrian.

'You must introduce us one day, Adrian,' said Paul. 'When I haven't got my hands full.'

Paul was tall, over six feet, yet fine-boned. His eyes were almost black as he looked admiringly at Laura.

'I'll not go until Adrian and Laura come and join us,' Thelma declared.

The band stopped playing and people returned to their tables.

'If I might have my seat,' murmured a nervous-looking man.

'You might have it, old thing,' cried Thelma, 'then again, you might not. It depends entirely on my bootiful cousin, and his bootiful girlfriend.' She clung to the back of the chair.

'Oh, for God's sake join us,' begged Paul. 'She'll go on until you do.'

Adrian rose and offered his arm in a courtly gesture to Laura. 'It doesn't have to be for long, darling.'

'Oh, yes, it does, *darling*,' cried Thelma. 'You *must* celebrate my birthday.'

Room was found for Adrian and Laura at Thelma's table, after which she appeared to lose interest in them as she launched into a story. 'Gather round, chaps and girls. As I was saying, Freddy Simons asked us to this *perfectly* doomed party, promising me I'd meet the *most* divine man, but the most *utterly* foul thing happened. You all know the Hon Jenny, of course you do, a *positively* foul woman, and she's been having *glands* and thinks she looks *quite* fifteen years younger. Of course she doesn't at all, but have you ever noticed that people seem to believe what you want them to believe and the divine man – and my, dears, he was *simply* the most divine thing I've seen for a century – *utterly* adulated her, and the *crowning* climax was that poor little me had to dance with the *most* hydraulic bore –'

Laura's mind drifted away from Thelma's inane ramblings. Was this high society? It wasn't something she yearned to join. She felt like standing up and shrieking, 'Thelma, you are the *most* awful female and *too*, too utterly vulgar.' She grinned to herself. Help, she'd almost giggled. The wine had reached her knees. If she didn't watch out she'd turn into another Thelma!

The band began to play a dreamy tune and Adrian asked her to dance. They swayed together – there wasn't room to do much else – and Adrian sang softly in her ear. He had a light tenor, so different from Rick's voice. Go away, Rick! Leave me in peace! She was afraid she had spoken aloud, but Adrian continued to sing and she joined in. She suddenly felt comfortable in his arms, happy and carefree. Life with a man like this one, mild and undemanding, could be good. She knew she was tipsy, but she couldn't resist an impulse to lean further into him. He pulled back very slightly. 'Not here, sweetie, rather public.'

For a moment she felt rebuffed again, a little humiliated, before accepting his reproof as just. She mustn't behave like an alley cat on a public dance floor, though now a very drunk Thelma was dancing and openly kissing someone she called Boy. She surrendered again to the music and relaxed in Adrian's arms. Happy.

Miss Morton and Noreen approved of Adrian and when Laura was so overloaded with work that she was on the edge of illness they added their persuasion to his to go somewhere with him in his large, opulent car, if only for a simple drive. On a sweet, still, sunny afternoon Adrian drove her across the Clifton suspension bridge to the countryside where she breathed in the soft air which blew kindly over the wild daffodils.

'Are you completely ready with the spring fashions, darling?'

Adrian asked. He was always willing to discuss the shops.

'Of course, thanks to my wonderful staff. I wouldn't be much of a business woman if I weren't. We showed the new hats in January, remember? Tonight we're re-decorating the windows. Iris will do the Kingswood branch. She's showing real talent. I really shouldn't be here, you know –'

'Nonsense. Miss Morton and Noreen agree you must keep a reserve of energy. You spend hours after they've gone home drawing and matching colour swatches. You could have been an artist if you hadn't chosen millinery, though I suppose it is an art.'

'Art was one of the things I was good at at school. One of the few things. I hated most of it. Perhaps I should have paid more attention. I might have understood the country's finances better.'

'Oh, forget them. An artist like you needs all her faculties for creation.'

'You're so sweet, Adrian.'

'I'm glad you think so. Will you come to my home to dinner next Saturday night?'

Laura was jerked out of her restful mood. 'What?'

'Heavens, darling, it's not such a bizarre request, is it?'

'Is the invitation from you, or –'

'Mummy suggested it. She wants to meet you.'

'That's silly. She knows me well.'

'No, she does not. She's only seen you as a milliner, not as a person.'

'In my world boys and girls only ask one another home if their intentions are serious,' said Laura lightly, trying to diffuse the build-up of tension his words had created in her.

'Is that so?'

Laura looked at Adrian sharply. He wasn't joking. 'Does that mean that you – that I –'

'It means, darling Laura, that I truly am rather serious about you. How do you feel about me?'

Laura leaned back and stared up into the canopy of trees, their buds bursting with the pale green of spring. Sunlight dappled over her face. She knew she must answer Adrian. This could be the most vital decision of her life.

'I like you a lot,' she said.

He looked disappointed. 'Only like me? I hoped for something more.'

'But I never know how far to go with you. You're wonderful to be with and I love it when you take me places, but you so often draw back when I –' she continued slowly, 'when I want to show you affection.'

'I thought we agreed that love-making was for marriage.'

'But even our kisses are not – not at all passionate. Oh, Adrian, I have so much love to give! I feel sometimes I might burst with it.'

He pulled her to him. 'Dear, sweet Laura. I am lucky to have met you.' He kissed her forehead, then traced her face with his lips. For the first time he really kissed her, his tongue exploring the soft crevices of her mouth. He stroked her, his hand smoothing over her hardened nipples, past her waist, to her leg. It crept up until she moaned with desire, her flesh aching, burning to be touched. Then he gently removed his hand and replaced it about her waist. The shock was so great she wanted to scream at him.

'Adrian,' she gasped hoarsely. 'Don't play games with me.'

'Games are the last thing on my mind, my love.'

She lay back, breathing hard, feeling cheated.

'So, will you come to dinner?'

'What? Dinner? Oh, yes. Are you sure your mother hasn't mistaken me for someone else? When I worked in Gregory's she treated me –' She stopped. She couldn't run down Adrian's mother to him.

He smiled. 'Treated you harshly. Oh, I know what Mummy can be like. She does knows who you are. After all, you've been supplying her hats for months. She sees you differently now that you own the business.'

Laura thought of meeting Lady Mallender as a prospective bride for her only son. It just couldn't happen. 'Maybe she wants a few free models,' Laura said lightly.

'That's not funny,' Adrian really did sound hurt.

'Sorry. That wasn't nice.'

'No!'

'All right, I'll come to dinner, though I'm not sure I'm wise.

Miss Morton says it's a bad policy to mix business with pleasure.'

'Miss Morton is a dear, but she's old-fashioned. The world's changing. People are more broad-minded.'

Laura didn't agree with him.

Adrian touched her full red lips with one finger. 'Passion-flower,' he teased. 'I'll call for you at seven thirty. We dine at eight.'

'Just one thing, Adrian. You haven't mentioned your father.'

'No. Daddy takes very little interest in me. He prefers Nancy.'

Laura was shocked and deeply sympathetic. She knew all too well how much that could hurt. 'Poor you.' She held her hand to the side of his face. 'It's painful, isn't it?' For the first time she could talk to someone who suffered rejection. How surprising that it should be Adrian.

He only shrugged. 'I gave up caring ages ago.'

'That's so sad, but it's better than suffering. I suppose,' she added bleakly.

He slid his arm around her waist. 'But you don't really think so. Inside you're wounded.'

She turned to him, warmed by sudden happiness.

Laura changed her dress three times before the dinner party. In the end she phoned *Anita Fashions* for advice. Anita was crisp. 'For a private family dinner wear something simple. Your black crêpe tiered dress will be perfect with a single chain of pearls and small earrings.'

Laura had never felt so ill-at-ease as when the Daimler delivered her to the front door of Mallender House with Adrian. So short a time ago she'd been treated here as a servant – or lower – and she could not rid herself of the fear that Adrian was being over-optimistic. She was wrong. The butler led the way to the dining room and announced, 'Mr Adrian is here with Miss Laura Blackford, m'lady.'

As soon as Laura saw Lady Mallender she was thankful she had followed Anita's advice. Her ladyship wore a modest beige silk-knitted suit and Nancy, who rose at her entrance, a navy jersey dress.

Laura walked to Lady Mallender who held out a languid hand for her to shake. 'I'm happy to receive you, Laura. Sir Hugo will be down presently.'

Nancy greeted Laura with a kiss that sent Lady Mallender's eyebrows climbing; she could not know how often the two girls met.

Sir Hugo was tall, extremely thin, grey-haired and stooped, with watery blue eyes with which he regarded everyone in a disinterested way. Except when he looked at Nancy. They showed animation then.

'Daddy, this is Laura,' said Adrian.

The baronet made a small, stiff bow. 'Welcome,' he said, in a voice that would have cracked ice.

Laura had the impression that she was living in some kind of dream. Not exactly a nightmare, but the kind of dream where values and impressions shift and change from moment to moment until everything grows increasingly chaotic.

Dinner was delicious, served by soft-footed, quiet-voiced servants. Their muted movements added to the surrealist atmosphere. Laura ate little. Outwardly the scene was tranquil. Beneath the surface there were currents that tied her stomach in knots. Sir Hugo's attitude towards Adrian was aloof and chilly. To Laura, he was coolly courteous. Didn't he really want her there? Maybe Lady Mallender dictated the rules, just as Granma and Phyllis did in their spheres of life. Indeed a number of her clients spoke of their husbands, or parents, for that matter, as if they were mere ciphers, living simply to pay bills.

Lady Mallender asked, 'How is business, Laura? Still paying well?'

Laura was astonished. Granma said that well-brought-up folk never discussed money. '*Hats by Laura* is prospering, thank you, Lady Mallender.'

'You sound dubious,' her ladyship boomed.

'No, no, business is very good. It's the Kingswood shop –' Laura didn't want to discuss her worries here.

But Lady Mallender had no reservations. 'What about it? Adrian was telling me that you cater for the poorer members of the populace there.'

'That's right. I thought it would be a profitable thing to do, but the returns are disappointing.'

Her ladyship frowned as servants removed the fish and produced a sirloin of beef. 'You must find out why and remedy the matter. There should be good money to be made out of the lower orders.'

'Many of them don't have much money,' said Nancy.

'What do you know about it?' demanded her mother.

Nancy flushed and Laura saw a flash of sympathy between her and Sir Hugo.

'The lower classes are always whining about their hard lot in life,' Lady Mallender continued, 'but they fill the public houses and smoke as much as the well-to-do and go off for outings on those dreadful charabancs. It's nonsense to say they need to be poor. You, my dear Laura, must hustle around and make the Kingswood shop pay.'

Laura was almost overcome by embarrassment at hearing the way her ladyship talked in front of her servants, though she supposed they must be used to it. And anyway their lives were probably quite easy compared with many.

'There's a great deal of unemployment,' said Laura.

'I don't see what that has to do with it,' retorted Lady Mallender. 'Prices are stable at the moment. In fact, some have gone down.'

'But wages have gone down, too, and the unemployed don't get given enough money to live properly.'

'You are not one of these blasted communists, are you?' asked Sir Hugo belligerently.

'No, Sir Hugo.'

'That's a bloody relief. They're at the bottom of most of the insubordination in Britain today.'

Laura wished Rick was here to argue. She remembered some of the things he'd said and quoted him. 'The influence of the communists is exaggerated. It's poverty that makes people so angry. And what's worse,' she continued firmly, 'some of the people, especially the older men, are so disillusioned because they just can't find work they're beginning to see unemployment as inevitable for the rest of their working lives.'

'They are lucky to have the dole,' said Adrian in his mild way.

Laura felt a flash of anger. He was no different from the others. Then she subsided. It occurred to her abruptly that she was making herself unpopular with his parents. She struggled with her conscience, but antagonising her customers wouldn't help. She said quietly, 'I don't have much time to study these matters.'

She caught Nancy's eyes and saw disappointment in them. Damn! She liked Nancy. But Ralph would have approved of her capitulation. 'Get level with them, Laura, as far as money's concerned, then argue with them.'

The exchange renewed her uneasy feeling that there was more wrong with the Kingswood shop than local unemployment would account for. She had tried various ways to make the place more attractive. Her young brothers had painted the interior a soft ivory, she had put advertisements in the newspapers and her family had assisted by posting leaflets through doors. She had even, for one week, given away a pair of fine lisle stockings with every hat. Still the money hadn't come in. And Iris was working too hard. She looked skinny and pale. Millie hadn't yet found another job and Laura couldn't really afford her wages. She and Dolores were full of reasons and excuses for Millie's inability to get a job. Some were valid; others were not.

Her ladyship hadn't finished. 'Most of the unemployed are a feckless lot! There's work if they bothered to look for it. And they could emigrate. Go to Canada or Australia or some such place.'

'Many do,' said Nancy. 'It's hard to be parted from the people and places one loves. For ever, if they can't earn enough money to travel home. I admire their resolution.'

Lady Mallender decided to ignore her, but Sir Hugo smiled for the first time at his daughter's pacifying words. He could look quite attractive thought Laura. Why didn't he care for his son? It was so at odds with everything one heard about men, the aristocracy in particular. If Sir Hugo had not sired a son one of his nephews was in line for the baronetcy. Adrian would keep the title in the immediate family, yet instead of appreciating him Sir Hugo appeared to despise him.

As soon as dinner was finished Sir Hugo disappeared. 'My husband is not fond of social intercourse,' pronounced Lady Mallender. 'I have asked some young people to join us for coffee and drinks.'

The young people turned out to be her nieces, Thelma and Daphne, and an assortment of their friends, including Paul.

He walked immediately to Laura's side. 'How do you do, Miss Blackford. We meet again, though I don't believe we were properly introduced. I'm Paul Harrington.'

'I'm happy to meet you,' said Laura, smiling.

Paul glanced over at Thelma. 'She's sober tonight – so far, anyway.'

Laura smiled distantly. She scarcely knew him and, although she couldn't like Thelma, she refused to be a party to his criticism. Thelma was, after all, Adrian's cousin. Paul seated himself beside her. 'You're the most elegant woman I've seen in a long time.'

'Thank you.'

'But you're not very talkative.'

His dark eyes were full of gentle mirth and Laura felt more at ease. She laughed. 'What would you like to discuss?'

'I hear that you're one of Bristol's leading millinery designers.'

'What? Who told you that?'

'Do you mean it isn't true?'

'I doubt I've become so elevated. I certainly design exclusive models and have them made up in my own workroom.' Laura heard her own words with surprised gratification. She really did own a going business. She had been too busy to appreciate the extent of her accomplishment.

'Your fame is spreading,' said Paul. 'You must be an expert because Arthur Gregory hasn't a good word to say about you.'

Laura said, 'Oh! What is he saying?'

'That you're taking his father's business from him.'

'Am I?' Laura's brows rose. 'How – gratifying.'

Paul gave a bark of laughter and Thelma's head went up

sharply. 'He says you were dismissed by his father for a breach of honesty.'

Laura frowned. 'That's slanderous!'

'Perhaps you should sue him.'

'I don't have that kind of money.'

'Just as well. Never go to law unless you must. Arthur Gregory is generally disliked and few pay any heed to him. What actually did you do?'

'I provided Lady Mallender and her nieces with purses privately, instead of selling them from Gregory's.'

'Clever girl.'

'Unfortunately my employer didn't think so. I was sacked.'

'And look where it's got you. Perhaps you should send them a thank-you letter.'

Laura laughed.'Maybe one day I will, but I still think it's an exaggeration to say I'm a leading milliner.'

'Well, you've got under Gregory senior's skin and that can't be bad.'

'I take it you don't like the family.'

'Nouveau riche, my dear. Dreadful upstarts.'

'Like me, do you mean?'

Paul seemed imperturbable. 'No, not a bit like you. Some people will always be upstarts. Others are different from the moment they're born.'

'Is that how you see me? Different?'

'Most definitely.'

'Different from what?'

'From the ordinary girls one meets.'

'My parents thought so, too,' said Laura impulsively. This Paul Harrington had a way of drawing confidences.

'Don't sound so sad. Didn't they understand you?' His voice was tinged with a mixture of mockery and sympathy.

'No, and they still don't. I've learned to put up with it.' That was a lie. Their rejection still hurt. It would always hurt.

'What are you two talking about so earnestly,' shrilled Thelma, walking over to them, clutching a glass of wine. 'Such delicious sherry, Aunty Maud,' she called over her shoulder. 'Bristol cream, Laura – the dear old city's home-brewed.'

'Thanks for the information,' said Laura drily.

Paul sighed. 'Thelma, one does not apply the term 'home-brewed' to the nectar of the gods and I believe Laura already knows about her city's wines.'

'Oh shut up, Paul. And you're not to monopolise Laura. We want her over with us. Laura, you must have oodles of gossip to tell us. I bet your clients talk endlessly about one another. Come on, dish up the dirt.'

There were many speculating eyes upon her and Laura rose and strolled across the large drawing room to where the others were draped over chairs and sofas. She felt like running away when she saw the malicious gleams in those eyes. Nancy was the only one who looked sympathetic. In her plain dress she looked like a small hen in a farmyard of brightly feathered cockerels.

Laura seated herself and said, 'What would you say if I did tell you all I know?'

There was a clamour of voices. 'Do tell, darling. Tell all! We won't breathe a word.'

'But if I do you'll never trust me and then you'll stop gossiping in my shop and I'll learn nothing new.'

'She's right,' said a girl in an electric-blue dress which barely reached her knees.

'Be quiet, Poppy. Who's side are you on?'

'Nobody's,' said Poppy, putting a hand to her mouth to conceal a yawn. 'God, I'm tired. I was at Bobbie Tindale's party till nine this morning. *Such* fun. We went to the kitchen and cooked eggs and bacon for breakfast.'

'Not fair,' complained the one called Boy. 'I wasn't asked.'

'Well, if you will get drunk and smash the ancestral ornaments you can't expect to be invited back.'

'It was only a vase. A frightful thing.' He shuddered. 'Absolutely sick-making.'

Laura suddenly felt tired of the inanities. She also remembered a pile of hats in *The Hat Shop* for which she still had to design original embellishments.

'I must leave,' she told Adrian.

'Nonsense!' said Daphne. 'We're all going on to a club.' She

277

glanced at Nancy. 'You'd better hurry and change your frock. You can't go out looking like that.'

'I had thought of staying in,' said Nancy.

Lady Mallender's voice boomed across the room. 'Stay in! At your age! Go and put on your pale-pink chiffon with the embroidery.'

Nancy sighed and rose, 'Yes, Mummy.'

Daphne turned her attention to Laura, 'Do come, darling, it's going to be an absolute winner. Rick Merriman's playing and he's got a new singer he's brought from London. She's so pretty and she sings jazz. *Too* exquisite. Poppy is *madly* jealous, aren't you, darling?'

'Shockingly!' agreed Poppy. 'I'm mad about Rick. He's so – so *manly*. Not at all handsome, of course, but *so* exquisitely male.'

Laura's heart had jumped at the sound of Rick's name and Paul, who seemed to have an uncanny way of reading people, said, 'A friend of yours?'

'Yes.' Laura's voice gave no encouragement for further questioning. She was trying to define the unpleasant sensation inside her. It couldn't be jealousy. Could it? She seldom saw Rick these days. It was Adrian who filled her mind now.

Adrian said loudly, 'If you wish to hear Rick Merriman and his girl I'll be happy to take you, Laura.'

He sounded annoyed and Laura impulsively took his hand. 'No, thank you. I truly must get back. I've work to do.'

'Work?' shrilled Thelma. 'My God, don't you ever stop?'

'Not very often. Thanks for the offer, Adrian.'

When she said goodnight Paul said, 'I'll be seeing you,' as if he meant it.

In the car Adrian sulked. Laura was at first surprised, then amused, and finally annoyed. 'What's the matter, Adrian? If you don't tell me I can't do a thing about it.'

'You were very pally with Paul Harrington.'

'I've only met him in your company. Would you expect me to be rude to your friends?'

'He's no friend of mine. He doesn't like me.'

'Why not?'

Adrian shrugged one shoulder. 'How the hell should I know?'

Laura sighed. 'Does it matter?'

Adrian had one of his swift mood changes. 'No, old thing, of course it doesn't matter. You're so sensible. And so wise not to go on to the club. Thelma and Daphne and their crowd will make their usual appalling racket. But wouldn't you have liked to hear the new jazz singer?'

'I haven't time.'

'They say Rick Merriman's smitten with her. She really is pretty.'

'I hope it keeps fine for him,' said Laura.

As she worked into the night thoughts of Rick and the singer kept intruding. She worked on until she was too tired to think of anything but sleep.

The following afternoon Millie came from the Kingswood shop with the latest figures. They were a disaster, worse than any of the previous ones. Ralph had worked out the average income she could expect to make each week. The shop would cater for women with money to spend on medium-priced clothes, the wives of shopkeepers, accountants, doctors. The cost of the hats was kept at a tempting level. The offer to decorate a hat exclusively had caught on and Laura, assisted by Noreen whose creativity grew daily, had been kept busy. Most women used make-up, if only a little, and the mark-up on these was high. Accessories were always stocked to match the hats. The policy was sound and should be working. Laura expected to clear between ten and fifteen pounds a week, but the latest figures showed a net profit of only five. She left Noreen in charge and drove to Kingswood, a silent Millie in the seat beside her.

Dolores looked surprised to see her – more than surprised. There was a furtiveness in her manner that made Laura's heart sink. There was definitely something wrong. Iris offered her a cup of tea. She was more timid than usual and for a terrible moment Laura wondered if her young sister was implicated in some kind of dishonesty.

Laura called Dolores into the small back office, opened the

ledger and went through the latest figures with her. The first pages had been neatly kept, then they became untidy with crossings out and alterations. It gradually became obvious that goods had been delivered and sold, but that not all the money had gone into the till.

When Laura had finished she looked at the white-faced Dolores. 'I want an explanation.'

'Business hasn't been as good as you expected,' blustered Dolores. 'The customers crowded in when we opened, but lately –' Dolores's voice dwindled beneath Laura's ruthless scrutiny. 'I'm not good with figures, Laura.'

'Don't lie to me. I worked with you in Gregory's remember? You can work out quite complicated sums in your head. And the figures for this shop are straightforward. I supply goods, I pay the overheads, you sell the goods and put the money in the till. Only you haven't, have you? Now, do you want to tell me, or must I get someone from outside to question you?'

Dolores cried, 'The police, do you mean?'

'I wonder why your mind leapt to the police?' Laura's voice was thick with anger.

Dolores's shoulders slumped. 'All right, I've been using your money. I only took a bit at first and meant to put it back, but somehow I couldn't, and now it's reached a point where I'll never be able to repay you.'

'How much have you taken?'

'I'm not absolutely sure –'

'Approximately how much?'

Dolores said miserably, 'We've been open just over twelve weeks and – just like you said – we've been makin' between ten and fifteen pounds a week profit.'

'But since the second week you've been handing over much less. Eight pounds has been the highest figure.'

Dolores reached into the back of the desk drawer for an exercise book which she handed to Laura. It contained a list of names with varying amounts of money, sometimes shillings, sometimes only pence, beside them. 'I couldn't help it, Laura, honestly. All those women are friends of my family – a couple are my relatives – and they're so poor. My aunty got me to let her have some stuff on credit to be paid back weekly. I told her to keep quiet, but she didn't and in the end I was lettin' stuff go –'

Laura had been scanning the figures. 'Some haven't paid more than one amount. They still owe the rest.'

'I know. They said their husbands were out of work, or had some other excuse – new shoes for the kids, or somethin', and – God, I'm sorry, Laura. I've let you down.'

'You have! And furthermore you're not even telling the truth now. This still doesn't account for all of the missing money.'

Dolores swallowed. 'No.' She looked bleak. 'Laura, I've given the rest away. I've got a cousin, Agnes – well, she's more like a sister, though she's a few years older than me. She used to be in the dressmakin' trade, but she went to Wales when she married. Andy, her husband, is a coal-miner. He was thrown out of his job at a minute's notice. He'd done nothin' wrong. They were just cuttin' down. You know how badly the miners were treated after the general strike. Andy lost his job months ago. He walked miles tryin' to get another, but there's a terrible depression in Wales. He got desperate. He felt so humiliated. In the end he was hardly speakin' to anyone.'

Dolores paused to wipe the tears which were spilling from her eyes and Laura waited.

'At first he got dole money – fifteen shillin's for himself, five for Agnes and a shillin' each for the kids. There's eight of them, two girls and six boys. Agnes dressed them from jumble sales, but the boys' boots were a problem. They had to go barefoot when they weren't at school.' Dolores paused again, staring into some black hole of misery.

Laura's wrath was yielding to pity. 'Go on,' she encouraged.

Dolores said, 'It's awful on the dole, worse in some places than others. Andy had to prove he was lookin' for work before he could get his money and the officials were really nasty. They'd reduce it because they said he'd not been diligent enough in searchin' for a job. Or they'd find some other pretence. Anything to stop givin' them money. Then the fifteen weeks were up and Andy wasn't entitled to the dole any more and it was the Board of Guardians for them. In the end there was never enough food in the house and two of the boys had to go to school barefoot. Kids can be cruel, Laura. Some of them were mockin' and the boys came home cryin'. Now the doctor says one of the girls has got consumption and needs lots of good food. Andy couldn't bear any more.' Dolores paused, then said in a cracked whisper, 'He hanged himself.'

Laura was too deeply shocked to speak.

Dolores glanced up at her with tormented eyes. 'They brought in a verdict of "suicide with evidence of depression from unemployment and illness". I know he shouldn't have done it, Laura, but he was such a proud man. He loved Agnes and the kids and felt he'd let them down.'

'And you've been sending your cousin money from the till?'

Dolores nodded. 'I sent as much as I could from my wages, but Mum can hardly manage at the moment. Dad's just lost his job as a clicker – that's a pattern cutter in a boot factory –'

Laura nodded. 'I know what they do.'

'The boss said he was sorry to get rid of Dad and he can have his job back when the orders start comin' in again.'

'But that's no help at the moment.'

Dolores stared, a flicker of hope in her eyes. 'You understand.'

'Of course I do. Dolores, why didn't you come to me? I would have done what I could to help.'

'What would that have been? Sorry, I didn't mean to be rude, but you've got your own worries, your own family to look after.' She added slowly, 'And anyway, you're different.'

'Different?'

Dolores said hesitantly, 'You're always in a hurry these days. You never speak to us about anythin' except work? And now you're mixin' with the nobs. I thought you wouldn't understand.'

Laura was aghast. 'I didn't mean to put a distance between us.' She rose and began pacing. 'I didn't realise, Dolores. I vowed never to get like the Gregorys and it seems I've become one of them without knowing it.'

'No, you haven't, you could never be like them. Not really.'

'God, I hope not. I'll watch it in future.' Laura sat down and called Iris to make some tea. 'Did you know what was going on, Iris?' she asked when her sister carried in the tray.

Iris glanced at Dolores and said, 'I know Dolores has been givin' credit to customers. I should have told you, but then her cousin's husband killed himself and I hated to upset her any more.'

Dolores said, 'She knows nothin' about the money I took. I do the books.'

Iris's eyes opened wide and Laura explained briefly. 'Leave us now, dear, we've got to talk.'

Dolores said, 'It's all right, Laura. You don't have to tell me. I'll pack up and go.'

'And who would run the shop? I depend on you.'

Dolores's eyes opened wide. 'You mean – you'd trust me after this?'

'I mean exactly that. This has been partly my fault. You're right. I've not been approachable.'

'But I must have upset all your money plans.'

She had. Laura was interested in a small place on Park Street in the right area to tempt the wealthy, with upper rooms that stretched over the shop next door. She needed bigger workrooms.

'I'll pay back every penny,' cried Dolores.

'How?'

'I don't know. I'll get a job cleaning on top of my work here. I'll do it somehow.'

Laura poured them a second cup of tea. 'You can owe me the money for now. I presume your cousin can sew well if she was in dressmaking.'

'She can and she's wonderful at embroidery.'

'Will she be coming back to Bristol?'

'Yes, her mother and my mum are goin' to have half the family each until they can get a place of their own.'

'Then she'll be glad of a job.'

Dolores's eyes lit up. 'Laura, do you mean – ?'

'I mean if she's as good as you say she can come to work for me. The money isn't as high as I'd like, but it'll be better than poor relief. And Dolores, if I get above myself again you have my permission to tell me.'

Dolores took Laura's hands in hers and her eyes were moist again with tears. 'You'll never have cause to doubt me again. Never! Never!'

Laura was thoughtful on the way home. When Adrian visited that evening she told him the terrible story.

He was uneasy. 'But they're only one of many, Laura. You can't let Dolores get away with stealing.'

'Is that all you can say?' asked Laura coldly.

'I'm thinking of you, darling. All your lost plans. The shop in Park Street would have raised your prestige and brought in lots more money. I'm sure of it.'

'I can't get rich by stamping on others weaker than myself.'

'Everyone else does.'

'Not everyone. There are some charitable companies. G B Britton, the bootmakers give boots to any child without. And look at Fry's Chocolate, the owners are Quakers and they look after their work people.'

Adrian said sulkily, 'They can afford to. You'll be able to when you're really rich. In the meantime you should look out for yourself. You know how – fond – I am of you, Laura. I can't bear to think of all your plans going to waste. It upsets me.'

He was genuinely distressed and Laura softened. She touched his cheek gently and he seized her hand and pressed a kiss to it. 'Dear Laura, I'm not really so mean. I got carried away. You must work things out in your own good time.'

Laura felt a surge of happiness. It was wonderful to have Adrian caring for her whole-heartedly. They were sitting on her sofa near the fire and she moved a little closer to him. His arm slid round her waist and abruptly all worries faded as a wave of desire swept over her.

'Adrian, my love,' she murmured. She pulled his head to her and kissed him full on the lips. For a moment he seemed reluctant, then he put his arms around her and held her close, and their tongues met in a dance of pleasure.

She leaned back on the sofa, still holding on to him. He gazed into her passion-filled eyes. 'Wonderful Laura,' he murmured. 'I believe you care very much for me.'

'You must know I do. Oh, Adrian, I've so much to give you.'

'I know.' He disengaged her arms. 'But not now.'

'But when?' His rebuff was torment to her.

'I've told you, old thing, I don't approve of sex outside of marriage.'

Laura slumped. 'Where does that leave us?'

'Still courting,' said Adrian, almost primly.

'Courting? Is that what we're doing.'

'Certainly it is.'

'Well, aren't you the old-fashioned one!'

'I thought you'd never made love to anyone.'

'No, I haven't.'

'But you've wanted to.'

'I want to make love to you.'

'What about Rick Merriman?'

Laura held her emotions in check. 'What about him?'

'I believe you thought a great deal of him. In fact, I sometimes wonder if you still do.'

'What nonsense!'

'There's a different quality in your voice when you speak of him.'

'I hardly ever see him.'

'It's said that no one ever forgets their first lover. That nothing else is ever as good.'

'Is that so?' Laura was getting angry. 'I wouldn't know because I've never had a lover.'

She got up. 'Would you like some coffee?' And strode into the tiny kitchen. When she returned with the coffee she had simmered down. It was not until Adrian had left that she wondered if his show of jealousy had been simply a ploy to cool her down. She felt suddenly ashamed of the way she was throwing herself at him. She must remember that he was the old-fashioned kind.

Dolores's cousin, Agnes, was extremely thin, but her soft brown eyes shone with gratitude when she accepted Laura's offer of work. The children wore holed and shabby clothes, but they looked much more healthy than their mother. Except for

285

ten-year-old Olwen whose eyes looked enormous in her sunken cheeks. Laura was alarmed. She asked Agnes where Olwen would be living.

'In St Paul's,' said Agnes. 'Thanks to you I can keep the children with me. I've got a nice big basement room.'

'She needs food, rest and fresh air,' said Laura.

'She'll get the food she needs and the rest, but I don't know about fresh air. There's nothing I can do about that. I'll just have to pray hard.'

Laura decided to help Agnes's prayers. She visited Rick's aunt in Hotwells.

Aunty Mabel looked exactly the same. She welcomed Laura with a big kiss. 'Rick tells me you're doin' well, my love. Do you see much of him these days?'

'No, we're both too busy.'

Aunty Mabel looked mournful. 'That's such a shame. He's an idiot to neglect a sweet girl like you.'

Laura smiled ruefully. 'I'm not that sweet. Not any more. Business is awfully tough, you know.'

Aunty Mabel's eyes twinkled. 'You sound like one of *them*, but you never will be, not in your heart.'

Laura laughed and sank into the ease she always felt with Aunty Mabel. 'Does Rick still live here?'

'No, he's got himself a flat in Cotham. A woman comes in to clean. I told him he was wastin' his money, but he said he couldn't expect a woman of my age to wait on him. Rubbish, of course. He knows I love lookin' after folk. I suppose he wants his own place to be a man in.'

Laura was startled. 'What?'

Aunty Mabel smiled. 'Men will be men, won't they? He probably takes a different girl there every week. He'll not get too thick with any one, though. I wonder if he's cut out for marriage.'

Laura drank the strong tea and nibbled a cake. 'I came for a special reason.' She told Aunty Mabel about Olwen. Before she could go further Mabel cried, 'I'll have her here, if her mother will allow it. Oh, I would love to take care of the poor little creature. We get air sweepin' up the Avon right from the sea and Brandon Hill is always breezy. I'll make her well and strong again and I'll be glad of the company.'

'I knew you'd say that.'

'Bring her mother to see me. And I hope you'll visit more often, Laura.'

'On one condition. That you come to tea in my little flat.'

'It's a bargain. Rick tells me there's a small place to rent on Park Street. He thinks it would just do for you. He's surprised you haven't already snapped it up. He thinks you're very clever, Laura. He says you'll succeed. Just as he means to.'

Chapter Eighteen

Rick breezed into *Hats by Laura*, his snap-brim tipped to the back of his head. He wore a light-weight suit and a pearl-grey tie. His dark hair had been expertly cut and was more controlled, though it still displayed a tendency to defy the taming hair cream. His eyes were bright, alert, his manner confident. He had a presence, an assuredness that Laura admired, yet in an odd way, resented. He was building his confidence on his exploitation of others. But wasn't she doing the same? She charged much more for her model hats than they cost to make. And then she felt even more irritated because he made her face the reality of her success.

'What blew you in?' she asked, still fiddling with the arrangement of a pair of lavender gloves.

'Is that a nice way to greet me after so long apart?'

For an instant every detail of their association flashed into Laura's mind and she wanted to yell at him, to order him not to be facetious.

'It's nice to see you, Rick,' she said, matter-of-factly.

'I expected a more enthusiastic welcome, especially as I've come to offer you somethin' good.'

She was curious, yet still the resentment lingered and she refused to question him.

'I've been hearing *tophole* things about you.'

Laura had a job to keep her face straight at his 'bright young thing' expression. 'Oh?' She arranged a scarf and carefully placed three enamelled powder compacts on it.

Rick picked one up and examined it. It was white with a gold and red design. 'I like this. I'll buy it.'

Laura wrapped it carefully in tissue and reached for a bag.

Rick said, 'You've learned a hell of a lot in a short time, baby. I like it.'

'Fancy.' Laura could not prevent a flash of annoyance at his calling her 'baby', yet to say so would only make her look childish.

'The compact is perfect for a friend of mine.'

'Would that be your new ladyfriend, the jazz singer?'

'As a matter of fact, it would. And while you're about it you can wrap up the scarf too. I know just the lady that would suit.'

'Your life is so full of ladies.'

'Yes, thank goodness. I'm fond of them.'

'You make that only too clear. And, of course, there's safety in numbers.'

'You never said a truer word, baby.'

Rick took out a cigarette – Laura noted he had abandoned Woodbines again and returned to Gold Flake and assumed that business was good. She frowned at him and he grinned and put the cigarette back in its plain silver case. 'OK I give in. No smoking.'

'*OK*! What sort of talk is that?'

'American, baby. I heard it in London. It means all right. It's good, eh?' '

'You like everything American.'

'Well, they certainly move fast. That suits me.'

'Can I get you anything else?'

'Want to be rid of me?'

'Don't be daft, Rick. I'm busy, that's all.'

'You're always busy. You shouldn't work so hard. If you get thinner you'll disappear when you stand sideways.'

'Thank you. For goodness' sake, if you've come to tell me something get on with it.'

He grinned again, reached once more for his cigarette case, and returned it to his pocket. 'I've just come from Aunty Mabel's.'

'How is she?' asked Laura, looking up.

'Happier than she's been since Mum died. And she's got you to thank for it.'

'Are you serious? All I've done is give her a problem.'

'Are you referring to Olwen as a problem?'

'You've met her? Is the poor lamb any better?'

'Aunty Mabel says the doctor's pleased with her progress and Aunty looks ten years younger. She was born to mother people. It's a pity she never got married.'

'Trust a man to say something like that. There is life outside marriage, you know.'

Rick grinned infuriatingly. 'I also met Olwen's mother. She can't praise you enough. And Aunty told me how kind you've been to Dolores.'

'My God, I hope people aren't talking about her. She's miserable enough already.'

Laura reached for a cream straw with rosebuds and placed it carefully on a shape.

'Laura, you're swell, you really are.'

'I suppose "swell" is another of your Yankee words.'

'A good one, too. All right, you don't want praise. But I think you're an absolute *brick*. In fact, *too*, too awfully sweet.'

Laura giggled helplessly. 'You've got the accent perfect.'

'You're doing rather well yourself, old girl.'

Laura laughed outright.

'That's much better, honey. Laura, I was surprised you hadn't taken the Park Street shop. It's a marvellous site and quite near Anita. Now I understand where your money's gone and I'd like to help.'

The conversation was halted by the entry of a customer, a large woman, who glared at Rick.

'You'll find Mr Blackford in his shop, Mr Merriman. It's just next door,' said Laura firmly.

Rick gave a small bow which almost broke Laura's calm and went whistling out.

He returned half an hour later when the customer had gone. 'Baby, I must talk to you and I can't do it while you're continually bein' interrupted.' He glanced towards the street from which came the loud chatter of giggling girls. 'I suppose that lot will be comin' in next.'

'I hope so,' said Laura loftily.

'What time do you finish?'

'Tonight? About midnight I should think. We're already preparing for the July sales.'

'In May? Well, you know best. But you must stop to eat.'

'Of course. Adrian's taking me to a small restaurant.'

'Adrian Mallender.' Rick scowled.

Laura felt annoyed. 'Yes, he's wonderful to me. So courteous and gentle.'

'I see. Well, could you spare me a little of your precious time? It'll be to your advantage.'

Laura softened. 'Adrian won't come in tonight. Have coffee with me about nine thirty.'

Rick arrived at exactly nine thirty carrying a box of chocolates and a posy of flowers.

'There was no need to bring anything, Rick,' she protested. 'We're only friends, not' – The word 'lovers' stuck in Laura's throat – 'not anything else,' she finished weakly.

'This is how I like to treat my friends.' He looked round the flat. 'Does Adrian bring you presents?'

'If we're not to quarrel you'd best stay off the subject of Adrian, especially with the tone of voice you're using. I don't know what you've got against him.'

Rick opened his mouth, then closed it. 'All right. What you do is no business of mine.'

'No, it isn't,' said Laura crisply, and marched to the kitchen to fetch the coffee.

'I've got a bit of spare cash,' said Rick, biting into one of Iris's home-made biscuits appreciatively.

'Already? You've hardly begun.'

'Yes, already. And, if you're willin', I'd like to invest it in you.'

'Me? What do you mean?'

'I mean I'd like to help you open another shop. In Park Street.'

'Rick!' Laura felt pleased. Then she subsided. 'Are you doing this out of gratitude because I've cheered up Aunty Mabel?'

'You must think I'm a fool if that's what you suppose.'

'No, you're not a fool.'

'You bet your boots I'm not. You're on the road to success, Laura, and if it hadn't been for Dolores you would have taken the shop, wouldn't you?'

'Well, yes, I would.'

'So it's just as well I've done it for you.'

'Well, of all the bloody cheek –' Laura smiled broadly, 'Oh, Rick, have you honestly?'

'Yep! Paid a month's rent in advance in your name.'

'My God, if people hear that I'll have no name left.'

'It's OK. I've told the estate agent that we're business partners.'

'You don't change, do you. You just go barging ahead. I don't want a partner.'

Rick was unperturbed. 'OK. If you say so. But you are glad I've taken the shop for you, aren't you?'

'Yes,' she admitted.

'I'll get my lawyer on to the legal formalities at once.'

'You don't waste time, do you? Be sure you make it clear you're only lending me money. I'll pay you back as soon as possible.'

'If that's what you want, though I would have enjoyed workin' with you.' His eyes glowed.

Laura felt his magnetism eating insidiously into her defences. 'How are the cinemas doing?' she asked.

He smiled. 'The first two are still playin' to packed houses. People seem to have a never-endin' appetite for melodrama. That's somethin' over-acted and –'

'Thank you, Rick. I do know what it means. My childhood was filled with melodramatic Victorian books. They lent them out at Sunday School. I wept buckets over most of them.'

'Poor Laura,' grinned Rick. 'My customers don't mind how old the films are and it suits me because they're cheap to hire. Last week it was Lillian Gish in *Sold for Marriage* and a gangster film called *Reggie Mixes In* with Douglas Fairbanks. And they love the pictures showing the nobs. I can't think why they enjoy spectacles of the wealthy when all of them are poor and some only live on bread and spuds. Another sure-fire draw is a comic picture. Harold Lloyd always has a queue stretching for miles.'

'Aren't you ever going to show something modern?'

'Ah, now you're talkin'. You must come and see the new place, Laura. We serve afternoon tea in the matinées. The place is full of well-off folk who get bored during the day. They like quite naughty pictures. Gloria Swanson in *The Affairs of Anatol* did a roaring trade. And *Three Weeks* was a runaway success.' Rick grinned. 'When I showed it a deaf woman who could lip-read wrote to me and complained that when Conrad Nagel was carrying the heroine in his arms she said, "If you drop me, you bugger, I'll break your neck".'

Laura laughed. 'And was she saying that?'

'I reckon so. Of course that'll all end when the talkies arrive.'

'If they arrive.'

'They will. The nobs also enjoy a good laugh like Mack Sennett's *Three and a Half Weeks*, which was a send up of *Three Weeks*. By the way, that's a book –'

'– by Elinor Glyn,' said Laura. 'I read it. At the time I thought it was wonderful, but it's nothing like real life.'

'Who the hell wants a night at the pictures to learn about real life! People go to forget their troubles. That's the way I operate, anyway.'

'So we're both making money out of the idle rich.'

'Yes, and a bloody good thing, too.'

Laura stood up and stretched. 'I must get back to work.'

Rick rose. 'A kiss to seal our bargain.'

Laura drew back, her uncontrollable heart thudding. 'Save your kisses for your girlfriends.'

He laughed, raised a hand in salute, and in a moment was gone and Laura heard the revving of his car engine. She peeped from the window and saw that he had not come alone. The car was open-topped and the evening was cold, but waiting in the passenger seat was a girl swathed in a fur cape. Poppy! So she'd got her sharp little claws into Rick. Was the scarf a present for her? She must be aware that Rick had brought flowers and chocolates for another girl. What excuse had he given her? Whatever it was Poppy was obviously prepared to accept it.

Rick was altogether too charming, too plausible for her taste, she assured herself. She went downstairs and plunged into work.

She was awakened before seven by a frantic ringing and banging on the street door. She pulled on a dressing gown and ran down on bare feet. Outside Iris was shaking and weeping. Clearly something really dreadful had happened. Iris tried to speak, but her words were lost in sobs. Feeling cold with terror inside, Laura took her sister's arm and led her upstairs and poured a drop of brandy and forced it between her lips. Iris choked and coughed, struggling with her first experience of spirits, and with her overwhelming emotions.

'Laura, I can hardly say it – I don't want to believe it –'

'For God's sake, Iris!'

'It's our Joyce.'

Laura's heart seemed to contract with horror. 'What about Joyce?'

'She's had her baby –'

'Has something happened to it?' Laura asked, a distant part of her praying that it was the fate of the child that had so stricken Iris, not the mother, no, not the mother.

'No, it's a boy. Healthy. And big. Too big.' Laura waited barely breathing. 'Too big for our Joyce. Laura, she – died.' Iris broke into frantic wailing.

Laura sat down heavily, feeling sick. It couldn't be true – it couldn't. It was some obscene trick. Joyce, beautiful, childlike, trusting Joyce could *not* be dead.

Iris looked up and saw Laura's frozen, staring-eyed horror and tried to control herself. She lifted the glass of brandy and ordered Laura to drink. 'I'll make a cup of tea,' she said brokenly.

Laura sat still until Iris returned with the tea, sweet and milky, so that they could drink it at once.

'How did you hear about it?' asked Laura numbly.

'Gran Palmer wrote. Our Joyce had been dead nearly two days before we even knew about it.' Iris stopped, her throat choked by her weeping. She swallowed hard and went on, 'Gran didn't ask the police to let us know she said because of keepin' the secret of the birth from everyone.'

'I can't believe it! Not Joyce. My poor sister. I wonder if she knew what was happening. I wonder if she ever knew.'

'Gran said she kind of understood, but talked of the baby as if it was a new doll. Gran said she died peacefully, as if she was just fallin' asleep.'

'Falling asleep? Oh, Iris! What about Mum. How's Mum?'

'One of the boys has gone for the doctor. She looks like death itself.'

Laura's numbness was pierced by anguish and she began to cry. Great tears, laden with grief, rolled unchecked down her face.

Iris, weeping again herself, said, 'Don't cry, our Laura. Don't cry. Remember what they say at chapel. Joyce is in heaven now with God. She'll be whole again, like she was meant to be.'

'Damn God!'

'Laura!'

'Damn a world where a man can murder my sister.'

'It wasn't murder!'

'It was, it was! If some stinking, rotten brute of a man hadn't put his filthy hands on her she'd be alive today.'

Iris said bleakly, 'Even Dad cried. I never knew men cried, Laura.'

'Poor Dad.'

'I – we – must tell Ralph.'

'Yes. I wonder how Freda is?'

Iris began to tremble. 'I'm afraid to think.'

The days had to be got through somehow. It was given out that Joyce had died of flu. Phyllis insisted that her body be brought home and laid out in the front room which was swept and scrubbed and turned into a bower of fragrant carnations, the dead girl's favourite flower. Adrian had stripped his mother's hot-house of all the pink and white blooms she loved best.

Freda accompanied her sister home. There had always been an angry streak in her, latent, but ready to explode at any slight, real or fancied, directed towards her sister, and Phyllis had been dreading her recriminations, and her reproaches for permitting Joyce to go out to work, but there were none. Freda said almost nothing. Whatever she felt was locked inside. Only her burning eyes gave a hint of the frantic rage and sorrow which possessed her. She made up a posy of lilies of the valley and forget-me-nots and placed it over Joyce's death-ivory folded hands, and sat all day beside the coffin as neighbours and family filed in to pay their last respects, and slept on a folding bed beside her sister at night. Joyce looked ethereally beautiful.

Freda spoke once to Laura, 'She's too pretty to bury.'

Gran and Gramps left the baby with friends to attend the funeral. Gran said that Joyce wanted him christened Andrew and that had been done. He would stay with her for now.

Phyllis insisted on placing a notice in the Bristol newspapers and messages of sympathy and flowers arrived and were added to the others. A wreath came from Joyce's former employers and after staring at it for a long time Freda ripped it to shreds, tearing her hands heedlessly on the thin florists' wire.

Phyllis said wearily, 'Our Freda's livin' in hell. She's rememberin' every word anyone ever said about Joyce that might have been a bit unkind. She's full of hate. Oh, Laura, death wipes out the past. It does, doesn't it? There is a heaven, isn't there, where my Joyce will be whole again, like she was meant to be? I wish I could pray, but sometimes I feel as full of hate and anger as Freda.'

It was the closest Phyllis had ever got to letting Laura see into her mind, but when Laura tried to put her arms around her mother she was shaken off. 'Leave me be. I've got work to do.' Yet she wept in Enid's arms.

Laura worked through it all. The cold wet summer didn't deter the eternally optimistic British ladies who continued to buy hats for outdoor pursuits. Coco Chanel had decreed that a suntan was fashionable and a white hat showed it off beautifully. Laura had both straw and felt, trimmed, if desired, with colours to match madam's favourite beach pyjamas, sundress, or bathing costume. She went through the motions like an automaton. Most of her customers knew nothing of her personal tragedy, and if they had, she thought bitterly, they would not have been concerned. A simple-minded girl had died. What of it?

When she said as much to Ralph he frowned. 'Laura, you've no right to make such a judgement. Not all the rich are nasty. Take Nancy, for instance. She's sweetness itself.'

'One girl out of all of them.'

'There must be others like her.'

'I've not met any.'

'What about Adrian?'

'Yes, there's Adrian.' She didn't want to speak about Adrian's reaction. He had been horribly awkward when he had heard the news and it was clear he couldn't cope with death but, as well as supplying the flowers, he had written a kind letter of sympathy to Phyllis and William. He told Laura he would leave her in peace until after the funeral.

'I wish I knew who'd got her pregnant,' said Ralph, standing up, moving about restlessly, his face filled with impotent fury. 'I wish I knew.'

'What would you do?'

'I don't know.' Ralph struck his fist into the palm of his other hand, his usual calm destroyed. 'I think I might castrate him.'

'You wouldn't.'

'No, I suppose I wouldn't. But a man like that should get punished. Somehow.'

Rick had come to Laura as soon as he had heard. He had pulled her into his arms and let her sob out her grief, smoothing her hair, kissing her tears. There was no passion in it. He was unutterably tender.

He attended the funeral and offered sympathy to Phyllis and William in a simple and genuine way. A strange woman and a tottering old lady also arrived for the service, both dressed expensively in black and furs, the older woman supported by a nurse and a chauffeur.

'Who are they?' demanded Freda through white lips after the coffin had been lowered into the ground.

Phyllis looked at her nervously. 'That's Mr Goodwin's wife and old Mrs Goodwin, his mother.'

Freda's head snapped up. 'Is that the bitch who got Joyce out of the kitchen to run her errands?'

Phyllis nodded, afraid to speak, afraid of what Freda might do.

Freda made no move towards the two women. 'Her!' she snarled. 'The bloody cheek of her! I'd like to kill them both, just like they killed my Joyce.'

'They couldn't help what happened,' said Phyllis desperately. 'And they needn't have come. The old lady looks as if she's about to drop. Don't make a scene, our Freda. Not here. Not now.'

'What d'you take me for? I'll never tell anyone about what happened to Joyce. Her memory's got to stay pure. She was pure. But I'll hate that family until the day I die. If they'd kept a proper eye on her –' Freda choked on her words and great tears she had not shed before filled her eyes and streamed down her face. Her nose began to run. Laura held out a handkerchief, but Freda knocked it aside. Her monumental sorrow rose far above care for her appearance and Laura caught her breath. She suddenly hoped that Freda never would discover Joyce's lover. There was no telling what she might do.

'A beautiful ceremony,' said Granma Blackford, back at the house. 'And so many flowers. She was a well-loved child.'

Laura held her breath when she saw Phyllis's face. Everyone knew that Granma had cared no more for Joyce than for her daughter-in-law. Less, probably. She had no hesitation in deciding that people who weren't right in the head should be hidden in the proper places, lunatic asylums. Now Granma was pretending that Joyce had been perfectly normal.

Granma and Grampa left with the other visitors, Granny and Gramps Palmer went to bed and Phyllis and William started drinking and continued until they could barely stand.

The July sales were successful. Laura had little time to mourn as she travelled between her three shops.

The new place in Park Street was also called *Hats by Laura*. Again her young brothers were helping and the familiar Laura colours of silver, gold and white were transforming what had been a dingy place into an airy, summery attraction. This shop would definitely be exclusive to the rich; prices would ensure that. And Laura had decided that she would allow customers to open accounts, as many of them already did in the big stores. Ralph was dubious.

'You're a stick-in-the-mud at heart,' Laura said. 'I don't know how you ever got the ambition to get a shop of your own.'

'I dislike being bossed around by other people,' said Ralph grinning.

'How is business?' asked Laura. 'You've not said much lately.'

'No, neither have you.'

There was a brief silence and Laura knew that Ralph's deepest thoughts, like hers, were with Joyce. 'Business is going well,' he said. 'I've engaged a fellow to help. He's been working as a picture restorer in London, but prefers to be in Bristol where he was born. Dad's turned out to be quite good at sitting in the shop, but he's as likely as not to doze over his paper, or reduce a price if someone is insistent. When I go to auctions and house sales I need someone I can rely on who knows the value of the merchandise and can hold his own against a bargain hunter. And when Alfred and Harold are done with you they can help me. The van could do with a lick of paint.'

'I wish we could employ them all the time,' Laura said. 'The outwork is hard and so badly paid, and the shed is freezing in winter. Alfred gets terrible chilblains.'

'Maybe the day will come,' said Ralph. 'Perhaps one of them will turn into a millinery designer.'

'Or a restoration expert.'

They laughed and realised it was the first time since Joyce's death. Laura turned her face away, her laughter overtaken by tears.

'Grieving won't bring her back,' said Ralph gently, but his voice cracked.

Adrian called more often than ever. He shied away from any mention of Joyce's death, but otherwise he was tender and gentle. Laura knew he was expressing his sympathy in the only way he could. She grew easier with him every day. He was a good companion, a man she could be comfortable with. It would be wonderful to belong to someone so soothing.

The opening of the Park Street shop was also a success. Laura, with the help of her family, and Adrian and Nancy, turned the new large workroom into a show place for the day.

This time Dolores joined Anita and Laura in the mannequin parade and Iris was recruited to wear the cheeky little berets that were becoming so popular. Millie looked after the Kingswood shop. Laura had decided to keep her on. She was quick and clever and would be an asset. Nancy Mallender gave the commentary in her soft, cultured voice, having learned by heart the script written by Laura.

Lady Mallender had given her permission. 'These days, Laura,' she said, 'it seems to be quite the thing for ladies to indulge in the fashion business. One knows quite smart people who do it.'

She was horribly patronising, but Laura was too busy to feel offended. She was simply grateful for all the help she could muster, especially if it was voluntary. Money was moving through her hands and her bank, but there was little left over.

She introduced a new range. Anita was assiduous in passing on Paris predictions. Her mother had been a mannequin with the great Paul Poiret and now held a senior position in the workrooms of Jean Patou. She was too loyal to give away his secrets, but her nose for fashion was invaluable and as soon as he had shown his new collections she wrote to Anita telling her about the latest designs she felt would catch on. Hair would still be short, hat brims were to be more defined, the helmet shape would be carried down on to the face and hats must suit the new, slightly fuller skirts. *Arts Decoratifs* was still the rage and jewellery and accessories continued to follow its abstract lines. The applause for Laura's show was prolonged and genuine. Accounts were opened, Lady Mallender being the first name in the book.

That night Laura sat with Adrian in her flat. 'I've engaged more girls for the new workrooms,' she said, her nerves still quivering after the apprehensions and triumphs of the day.

'What about the old ducks who work at home?'

'Oh, I'll still use them. They've come to depend on the extra money and they've been so good I'll let them go only when they want to.'

'It must be a nuisance having to drive round delivering and collecting stuff.'

'No, not all all. They're dears and they've helped me a lot. And I don't do it all now. Dolores has learned to drive. She's great. I never thought she'd turn out so well.' Laura paused and smiled ruefully. 'Actually, nature is providing a solution for my old ladies. Three of them have died.'

Adrian shuddered. 'Don't! I hate talking of death.'

'It's part of us, darling. We all go the same way.'

'Well, I'll face that when I have to. I've something far more pleasant I want to talk about. A question to ask. I think you know what it is.'

Laura waited breathlessly for Adrian's next words. He took her hand in his. 'Such a pretty hand. Who'd guess that it works so hard? Will you give it to me?'

'Give it to you?' Laura laughed nervously. 'Like in the old fairy-tale books?'

'Don't make fun of me. I'm serious.'

'Are you? You used such an old-fashioned expression. Are you asking me to marry you?'

'Will you, old girl?'

'Delighted, old chap,' said Laura lightly, though her heart was thudding so hard she felt she must be shaking.

'You're determined to be flippant. I mean it, you know. I care for you.'

'Sorry. It's just that you're so – calm about it.'

'Did you expect a knight in armour to sweep you off your feet?'

'Something like that,' said Laura, 'but you'll do in the meantime.'

He took her in his arms and Laura leaned against him feeling incredibly safe. She raised her face and he kissed her. She hugged him to her and her lips moved beneath his in a silent appeal for love. His kiss deepened and his hands moved over her shoulders, down past her slender waist to her hips. They stopped there.

'You're trembling,' he said.

'I want you,' breathed Laura.

She felt his almost imperceptible physical withdrawal, but his words were soft and tender. 'I know, dearest. And soon

301

we'll be together. Come out with me tomorrow and we'll choose the ring. And in the evening you're invited to dinner.'

'Where?'

'At home, of course. The first celebration of our engagement. I shall announce it formally.'

Laura drew back. 'Do you mean your parents don't know?'

'Daddy doesn't yet. Mummy does – and approves.'

'Are you sure? I can hardly believe it?'

'I fail to see why not?'

'You must see, Adrian. My background, my occupation, everything about me. Surely she's looking for someone like your cousins, someone as gently bred as Nancy, as a wife for you.'

'Not at all. Mummy thinks Thelma is dreadfully vulgar, though Daphne's not quite so bad, and she gets awfully fed up with Nancy's timid ways. She admires someone like you who can fend for herself.'

Laura wasn't convinced. As she worked that night she recalled Lady Mallender's attitude towards the girls in Gregory's, to her maid, to herself.

The ring was a modest half-hoop of small diamonds and sapphires and Laura felt proud and happy to wear it. To see it gleaming on her finger almost convinced her that marriage with Adrian was a possibility.

Anita stared at it, her dark brows almost meeting. 'I don't understand you, Laura. Fancy getting married when you're financially independent. It'll be a terrible drag on you.'

'It won't. Adrian says I can go on working.'

'Oh, bully for Adrian! So he'll allow you to work, will he? Where's your spirit gone? It was what drew me to you.'

Laura was indignant and a little hurt. 'Does that mean you would prefer our association to cease?'

'Don't get pompous with me! We're of use to each other, you and I, and if I find you slacking off I'll have something to say about it.'

'Will you come to my wedding?'

'I don't know.'

Laura got ready for the dinner. Since Joyce's death she had

worn quiet colours, as did the other members of the family. Freda dressed only in black. She had returned to work in the corset factory, bitter and morose, and never went anywhere frivolous. Instead, she walked for miles until even her prodigious energy was depleted and she could sleep.

Adrian fetched Laura once again in the Daimler. She wore a simple honey-beige silk dress with a fine-pleated skirt with a belt at the hips. Her earrings were pale yellow studs.

'You look just right,' approved Adrian, 'but that's only what I expect of you.'

Laura sensed tension in the air when the butler took her wool wrap. She could have sworn there was something different about the expression in his eyes. Adrian said servants knew everything. Were they already discussing their young master's odd choice of a wife?

'You can go,' Adrian was irritable towards Renton and Laura knew that he, too, felt the strained atmosphere. He ushered her into the drawing room where Nancy and Lady Mallender waited.

Nancy jumped up and hurried across the wide expanse of carpet. She kissed Laura. 'We're to be sisters. I'm so very happy.' She didn't look happy. In fact, she looked decidedly uneasy and her eyes wouldn't meet Laura's.

Lady Mallender greeted her with a determined affability that unnerved her more than ever. Sir Hugo arrived as dinner was announced and the five of them seated themselves at one end of the dining table.

Dinner began. Laura barely touched the different wines which were poured into glasses of the most delicate crystal. Sir Hugo spoke little. He waved away the home-made vanilla ice-cream and ate a welsh rarebit. Then the table was cleared and fruit and nuts were brought, after which the servants withdrew. While they were present there had been only formal conversation. Now Adrian fetched a magnum of champagne which had been cooling in an ice bucket on the sideboard.

Sir Hugo's brows rose. 'I enjoyed dinner, my dear' – he raised his glass of port to his wife with a noticeable air of mockery – 'and now champagne. Is there something of significance about to happen? Do please enlighten me.' His eyes flickered over to Laura.

Adrian opened the bottle with expertise and filled five wide glasses with the bubbling wine. 'I think you've already guessed, Daddy. Laura and I are engaged to be married.'

'Indeed!' Again Sir Hugo looked at Laura. His eyes held no warmth. Then he lifted his glass, 'Congratulations – to you both. I hope you will be very happy.' The words were spoken in a well-bred manner, but there was scorn in Sir Hugo's tone, in his eyes. Her head went up proudly. So a baronet didn't care for a working-class girl marrying into his family. Well, Adrian loved her and she loved him, and her ladyship was on their side.

Lady Mallender proposed a toast, 'To the happy young couple,' she said, her voice and demeanour more like someone declaring the winner of a prize fight.

Sir Hugo raised his glass a couple of inches and held it to his lips. He didn't drink the wine.

Shortly afterwards Lady Mallender announced, 'We'll leave the gentlemen to their port.' Turning at the dining room door she said, 'I shall dispense coffee in half an hour, my dears. You'll have time for a talk.' Neither man looked pleased at the prospect.

Conversation in the drawing room was awkward at first. Then Nancy asked how business was and Lady Mallender became interested, and it was obvious that her interest was genuine. Her sharp eyes were fixed on Laura's face.

'The Park Street millinery must be doing well,' she said. 'One hears it mentioned by one's friends all over the place.'

'Plenty of hats are going from the shop,' said Laura. 'Now I'm waiting to see if people pay their bills at the end of the month.'

'I'm not sure if credit is a good idea,' said Lady Mallender. 'It may be better to ask for cash from some people. Families who have always been wealthy in the past have found their incomes from foreign investments horribly depleted lately. They have had to dismiss some of their servants. Sir Hugo believes the government has made some foolish decisions. Britain's share of the world trade has gone down disastrously.'

Lady Mallender owed more money to Laura than anyone else and Laura wondered if her strictures included herself. The monthly payment on her car was due and if her ladyship paid up there would be no problem. Laura followed the world monetary situation, though she failed to see what the average person could do about it. Her chief aim was to keep her business profitable enough to pay wages, produce a variety of stock, and have some money left over. All three women were preoccupied and conversation dwindled and it was a relief when Adrian and Sir Hugo entered. Sir Hugo sat in a chair near the window looking out morosely over the Downs. His only sign of animation was when Nancy carried his coffee to him.

'Thank you, darling,' he said quietly. The words held a world of love and Laura's happiness, always precarious, was eroded a little more. She would give a great deal to have William speak to her like that. Sir Hugo took his coffee and announced he was going to his study to write letters and, with a brief nod at Laura, he left. She felt insecure, humiliated.

Nancy said breathlessly to Laura, 'The poor darling isn't usually so abrupt. He has business problems. Just like so many others,' she added nervously, as her mother glared at her.

'What nonsense!' said Lady Mallender. 'Sometimes, Nancy, I despair of you.' She took a slim cigarette from a silver box on an occasional table and put it between her lips. Adrian leapt up to light it for her. His mother was a picture of elegance; she was impeccably gowned in black and grey, small sleeves covered the tops of her arms, the neck was almost high – not for her the exposure of elderly flesh favoured by some modern matrons. 'One could hardly call Daddy's preoccupations problems,' she said, blowing out a cloud of smoke.

'Well, I think he might have shown my fiancée more of a welcome,' said Adrian, as he lit Laura's cigarette. Nancy was the only one not smoking. 'He can be impolite at times.'

Lady Mallender reached over and patted Laura's hand. 'You will become accustomed to my husband's quiet nature, my dear. He is a trifle absent-minded, that's all.'

'I didn't know Sir Hugo was in business,' said Laura.

'Good heavens, girl, he isn't!' The shock in her voice revealed that her ladyship had forgotten for a moment that Laura was a working girl. 'Not business, as you understand it, my dear,' she said, backpedalling hard. 'His family have invested in foreign ventures for years. Our broker deals with all that, but Sir Hugo takes an interest.' She turned to Nancy. 'Play for us, please. I'm sure Laura would like to hear you. She can sing, too, Laura. She has a sweetly pretty voice.'

'I've a voice like a corncrake,' said Nancy, 'and Laura plays much better than I do.'

Lady Mallender didn't trouble to conceal her astonishment. 'You play the piano?'

Laura could not resist it. 'Even the lower orders are permitted to take music lessons.'

Her ladyship pressed her lips together, then smiled thinly. 'You must not pay any attention to me, my dear. I have welcomed you into our family, but I need time to – to understand your background.'

Laura felt she had been ungracious. 'I'm sorry. Of course I'll play.'

She seated herself at a gem of a baby grand piano and ran her fingers over the keys. 'Something old, or modern?' she asked.

'Something in between,' said her ladyship.

Laura played softly as she sang the words of a song popular a few years ago. *If you were the only boy in the world, And I was the only girl.* She followed it with *Love's Old Sweet Song* and, to her amazement, Lady Mallender walked over to the piano and joined in with a pure contralto voice. When the song was over she actually needed to dab at her eyes. 'So foolish of me – please excuse it – the song brings back such memories to me –' She hurried from the room.

Laura looked aghast at Adrian and Nancy. 'I've upset her.'

Adrian said gently, 'No, you haven't, darling, that was beautiful. So sweet of you to sing an old song for Mummy. I'll just go and see if she's all right.'

He left and Nancy said, 'Don't worry. Mummy loved it. It's difficult for you to believe that she can get quite emotional at times.' She wandered restlessly about the room, picking up a

306

small ornament and setting it down, examining a photograph. 'Laura, you do love my brother, don't you?'

Laura was taken aback by the earnestness of the question. 'Of course I do. I wouldn't have promised to marry him without love.'

'Are you absolutely sure?'

'Of course I am. He's so gentle, so kind. He treats me better than anyone ever has before. I know I'm going to be happy with him.'

Why should Nancy look so relieved? This family had the oddest reactions. Laura wondered if she would ever understand them. Maybe not, any more than they would ever understand the noisy family chaos that prevailed in her parents' home, or the intensely religious element in Granma and Grampa's house.

'You look very pensive,' said Nancy.

'I was just wondering if human beings ever truly get close.'

'But you're close to Adrian.'

'Oh, yes, though there's still a reserve I must break through. I suppose it's our different upbringing. Once we're married we shall belong completely to one another. I'm so looking forward to it.'

'I'm glad for you, Laura. Being in love is marvellous, isn't it?'

'Are you in love? Oh, that's not my business.'

'It is now. We'll soon be sisters, remember. Yes, I'm in love, but nobody knows it yet except me and – my man.'

The revealingly passionate way she said 'my man' gave Laura a jolt. She loved Adrian, she knew she did, and he loved her, but there was something in Nancy's attitude that she felt was lacking in her own.

Adrian returned with his mother who had recovered her composure. She seated herself on a couch and leaned back. 'Laura, Adrian tells me that one of your sisters has died. I did not know. Please accept my commiserations.'

'Thank you, Lady Mallender.'

'Of course, one is always sad at the passing of a dear one, but it's a blessing when one of your sister's kind die.'

'What?'

Adrian said quickly, 'I told Mummy how Joyce was backward and would never grow up.'

'Such a tragedy for your poor parents,' said Lady Mallender. 'I understand she was the prettiest in the family. But it must be such a relief to you all not to have to worry about her any more.'

Laura was sick with anger. 'We didn't see my sister's death as any kind of blessing,' she said in low tones that vibrated with her fury. 'On the contrary. We all adored her.'

'Of course you did.' Lady Mallender's voice was honey-smooth. 'But her beauty must have put her in particular peril. A friend of mine had exactly the same situation to contend with. Fortunately she was able to incarcerate her daughter in a place where she could be perfectly safe. As far as I know, she is still there.'

Nancy twisted her hands nervously. 'Joyce was very much loved, Mummy. Her mother is desolate and her twin sister is very angry.'

'Angry? It's of no use getting angry with the will of God,' stated Lady Mallender.

Nancy's eyes met Laura's briefly, but meaningfully, and Laura wondered if Nancy knew how Joyce had died.

'No, of course not, Mummy,' said Nancy. 'Freda is just angry with – with fate.'

'An equally pointless exercise. One must accept what life brings. I don't say we should not try to change our lives if we can but, on the whole, we must accept what we are sent.'

Laura couldn't take any more. She rose. 'I must get back. I've a lot of work on hand.'

Lady Mallender held out her hand. 'Of course, I quite understand. It would not do for you to neglect your shops. Such a success you are, my dear, and still so young. I am convinced that you have a great future.'

Laura was silent on the drive home. Adrian slid his arm around her and moved close, pulling her head to his shoulder. 'Mummy keeps putting her foot in it. You'll have to forgive her, darling. She'll love you so much when she gets to know you that she'll forget you've not always been one of us.'

Laura jerked away. 'Do you realise what a damned insulting remark you've just made?'

'No, probably not.' Adrian sounded sad and resigned and Laura melted.

'I've a lot to learn, too. I'm sure it'll all work out well in the end.'

'I'm sure, too. Mummy isn't quite so well born as she appears. Daddy's the one with the family tree as long as a monkey's tail.' The oblique allusion to Darwin's theory of evolution made Laura smile. 'Mummy's father was a northern factory owner. Rich, but not classy, as they say. She was educated at the best schools, and finished her education in Switzerland. Old photographs show her looking very attractive and more aristocratic than the aristocrats – I think it's got something to do with her nose.'

They both laughed and Laura felt comfortable again.

She turned and kissed Adrian's cheek just before the car stopped outside her flat. Adrian saw her safely upstairs, and she waved from the window as he was driven away.

Ralph rapped on the communicating door and came in. 'How did it go, love?'

'Fine – I think.'

'You're not sure?'

'Lady Mallender was nice to me and Nancy, of course. She's such a dear girl. But Sir Hugo – Ralph he looked as if he despised me.' Ralph looked angry. 'I don't mind,' Laura hastened to assure him. 'I expect I'll win him over in the end.'

'You do love Adrian, don't you, Laura?'

'Of course I do. You sound as worried as Nancy. Why?'

'And he loves you?'

'Yes, he does, definitely.'

Ralph nodded. 'How did Nancy look?'

'As pretty as usual. She's different from the others. The odd thing is that her father seems to dislike Adrian, but to adore her. I always thought that the aristocracy revered boys. After all, Nancy can never give him an heir and if Adrian doesn't produce one the baronetcy goes to a cousin's line.'

'Fathers often care more for their daughters.'

'Do they? Ours didn't.'

Ralph sat by her and put his arm round her shoulders. 'You've had a rotten time, haven't you?'

His tender sympathy almost made her cry. She took a deep

breath. 'Living in the past is useless. I'm going to have a wonderful time from now on. Marriage to a really good man, my own business – there's no question of my giving it up – babies in due course, everything a woman could want. I only hope you have the same luck.'

'I probably shall.' Ralph stood up and stretched. 'I've got some restoration work to do for a customer who's in a hurry and I know you've plenty to get on with. It's a wonder we keep going the way we do. We hardly ever sleep.'

On the following Sunday Laura told her family of her engagement. Granma and Grampa were astonished and not altogether pleased. Grampa feared she wouldn't be happy marrying a man from so different a background. Granma was concerned about her soul.

'Are they a chapel-going family?' she demanded.

'They attend church quite regularly.'

'Church of England? Well, I suppose it's all right, but I'd still have been better pleased if you'd picked a chapel man. God seems nearer in a chapel than in one of those big churches with their fancy gewgaws. Some of them even use incense and candles.' She couldn't have said fire and brimstone with more distaste.

Phyllis and William took the news calmly. It seemed to Laura that everything she did was now too far removed from them to make sense.

William said, 'You'll have plenty of money to put into your business, chick.'

'Surely you won't go on workin' after marryin' one of *them*!' said Phyllis.

'Of course I shall. They're modern, enlightened people.'

'Are they? I'd have said they were bloody mean makin' you work.'

'I want to, Mum, can't you see that? I want to be independent.'

Phyllis sighed. 'You always were different.'

Laura bit her lips to stop from making the terse reply that sprang to them. The boys came charging through and heard the news with roars of mirth. 'Our Laura – Lady Laura – do you hear that, Lillian. Our Laura's goin' to be a real lady.'

Lillian went first red then pale. 'Don't be daft. She's havin' us on, Laura. What swell would marry you, Laura Blackford?'

'Adrian Mallender,' shouted Alfred. 'I've seen him hangin' about our Laura. He came and watched us paintin' one day. He said, "Jolly good, chaps".' Alfred and Harold rolled around with laughter, shouting, 'Jolly good, chaps.' They were joined by Val, now a precocious seven-year-old, imitating his big brothers whenever possible. The little girls laughed and shrieked, and Laura felt like running away. Freda came in and was told the news. She scowled and said nothing and Laura was again frightened by the expression in her eyes. Freda believed that Joyce had been defiled by one of the upper crust. She probably saw Laura's engagement as a stab in the back.

Enid redressed the balance. She was genuinely pleased and so was Jack. His job was safe with Rick and the little house was cosy with good furniture and a new rug. A vase of flowers stood in the exact centre of the table, a crocheted mat protecting the shiny surface. A piece of white knitting lay to hand. Enid was five months pregnant, able to stay at home, and clearly happy.

'Fancy, one day you'll be Lady Mallender and swan it over the likes of us.'

'Never!' declared Laura. 'You'll always be my family.' Even as she spoke she knew it was going to take a magical balancing act to keep on terms with her family and her future husband's.

Chapter Nineteen

The following evening Adrian suggested a visit to the cinema. 'Let's try Rick Merriman's new picture palace. They say it's wonderful and they're showing Tom Mix in *The Lucky Horseshoe*. It's a cowboy film. I just adore cowboys, don't you?'

'No,' said Laura, 'but I'll come with you if you promise that next time we can see something I choose.'

'It's a bargain.'

Laura had been curious about the new cinema and welcomed the chance to visit it, especially with the man she was going to marry. She wondered if Rick was off somewhere working on one of his deals. His name appeared more and more frequently in the Bristol newspapers as having promoted some top quality artiste, or for having brought a new film to Bristol for the first time. He also had a growing reputation for his ability as a performer. Not so much now in public, but at private parties to which he was invited. He was going up the social scale, just as she was and she was glad he was a success. Just as she knew he would be happy for her.

The *Premier Picturehouse* was impressive. It had been a concert hall and boasted a balcony which was more expensive to sit in and Laura looked down over the edge to see the lesser mortals below. They weren't as noisy as the audiences she was used to. Perhaps they were slightly over-awed by the grandeur. Rick had clearly decided to offer the Bristol people interesting entertainment from the moment they set eyes on the building. The exterior was painted in gleaming white with red woodwork. Big, coloured posters outside were rivalled in the sumptuous foyer by the smaller, but far more lavishly coloured, lobby cards on easels. The fact, as Laura discovered later, that the scenes in the silent black-and-white film bore little resemblance to those depicted on the posters appeared to bother no one. The foyer also abounded in red and the cinema interior echoed the arrogant colour in the plush seats, the carpets and the enormous heavy velvet curtains. Everywhere were signs proclaiming *This Cinema Is Ready For Sound. Watch This Space.*

A three-piece band played before the performance and between films. There was also a singer, Jenny, the girl Rick had introduced to Laura what seemed like an age ago. She was more decorously dressed tonight and was enthusiastically applauded. Rick knew exactly how to gauge his patrons.

After the film Adrian took Laura to a small restaurant for supper. She ate with pleasure, cocooned in the memory of the picture house, the happiness of being alone with Adrian and the quality of the food and drink set before her.

As she sipped a last glass of wine and smoked a cigarette she sighed, 'What a lovely evening, Adrian. Thank you.'

'No, I have to thank you, old girl. You liked the cowboy film?'

'More than I expected.'

Adrian beamed. 'Tom Mix is wonderful, isn't he? Do you know he fought in the Boer War and the Mexican Revolution, and was a Texas Ranger and a United States marshall before he went into films?'

'No I didn't know. Evidently a man of action.'

'Yes. I love that kind of man, don't you?'

'It depends,' said Laura smoothly. 'After all, I love you.'

'You're teasing me, darling. All right, I know I'm not one of your heroes, and I never shall be but that doesn't stop me liking them. And you said Mix was great in the part.'

'His horse was good, too. What's its name?'

'Tony! Oh, you're doing it again. Pulling my leg.'

'Do you know everything about Tom Mix?'

'Of course not, but I like to read articles about the stars.'

'You should talk to Rick. He's as crazy as you about films.'

'He wouldn't want to talk to me. I don't think I care for him and I'm sure he doesn't like me.'

313

Laura laughed. 'Well, you're very different from him.'

'Different nice, or different nasty?'

'Don't be a goof! How could I love you if you were nasty?' Adrian kissed her hand. 'Angel!'

'Of course,' said Laura reflectively, blowing out a stream of smoke, 'the heroine wasn't bad. I mean, without her Tom needn't have performed all his wonderful deeds of derring-do. What was her name?'

'I don't remember.'

'It was Billie Dove.'

'Thanks.' Adrian grinned boyishly and Laura laughed.

'I should be praising the men and you the women,' she said.

'Not necessarily. We both see the good points of our own sex. That's not a bad thing. It must help you to understand your customers.'

He kissed Laura goodnight at her door and she went up the long flight of stairs, suddenly weary, aware of her disappointment that Rick hadn't appeared in his cinema. She would ring him and congratulate him on his new picture house. Of course, he would have to call it *Premier Picturehouse*. Nothing but the best for Rick.

An August wedding was decided upon. 'Bristol's absolutely empty,' said Lady Mallender, 'so it won't be difficult to keep the ceremony small. You won't want a lot of fuss so soon after your bereavement, Laura.'

Laura had learned that unless the town was filled with friends of the Mallenders it was designated empty. She now shrugged off such statements.

'Now,' said her ladyship, her silver fountain pen poised over thick cream paper, 'for the guest list. Who will be attending from your side, Laura? You were brought up by your grandparents – a highly respectable couple, I believe. And there will be Sir Hugo, myself and Nancy.'

'Won't anyone else from your family be invited?' asked Laura, astonished and annoyed.

'My dear, *everyone* is in Cannes, or precious Venezia. I could be in Monte Carlo were it not for the wedding preparations.'

Laura resented Lady Mallender's whole attitude. 'If you would prefer to go abroad I've no wish to stop you. I can wait a while to be married.'

'Now, now,' her ladyship wagged her finger playfully. 'But I excuse you, Laura. You have pre-wedding nerves. I suffered badly from them myself. They make one so irritable.'

Laura subsided. Trying to get under her future mother-in-law's guard was like trying to prick a hippopotamus's skin with a blunt pin.

She said, 'The Charlton girls are still around. They could come.' Laura no more wanted them than did her ladyship. Only sheer perversity led her to mention them.

'Well, my dear, if you say so. And one cannot invite them without their parents. I'll add them to my list. Have you decided on your guests?'

'Granma and Grampa, of course, and my parents, my brother Ralph, three of my sisters and my brother-in-law,' Laura said recklessly.

Lady Mallender wrote down their names with tight lips and Laura immediately wished she had been opposed. She thought of William and Phyllis exposed to free booze, of Jack's clumsiness, of Lillian's sulks. Thank God, she hadn't demanded the presence of the little ones; or Harold and Alfred, with their pudding-basin hair-cuts and permanently grimy nails. Freda's name was on the list, but Laura knew she'd refuse. Since learning about Adrian she had behaved as if Laura didn't exist.

Laura told Adrian about the scene later. 'And the awful thing is I feel worried now in case somebody shocks your family and I wish I hadn't been so dogmatic. Your mother made me cross.'

Adrian laughed and hugged her. 'You're an absolute poppet. Mummy means well, but of course you must invite whomever in your family you want.'

Small wedding or not, Laura was determined to look her best. She bought a gown from Anita, of soft ivory chiffon with handkerchief points, over a satin slip. Her shoes, stockings, hat and gloves were also ivory. The only touches of colour were to be her pink lipstick, the small pink and blue silk flowers which

315

were part of her modest head-dress and a posy of real flowers in the same colours.

Adrian's best man had been abroad for months, but was expected back for the wedding.

'What about bridesmaids?' Adrian asked.

'I thought Nancy and one of my sisters.'

Adrian nodded. 'That sounds excellent.'

Laura drove home to deliver the invitations herself. As she had expected, Freda tore hers up and threw it on the kitchen fire, her face dark with anger. The others worded acceptances as dictated by Laura.

She said hesitantly to Lillian, 'Would you be a bridesmaid? Adrian's sister is one. I should like you for the other. After all, you're the prettiest sister I've got.'

Freda got up and walked from the room, carefully closing the door behind her.

'She's changed,' said Phyllis. 'D'you remember how she used to bang about? Now she's quiet. It's as if she's livin' a different life from the rest of us. She never makes any noise. She reminds me of a cat.'

'I shouldn't have referred to Lillian's good looks. Freda can only remember Joyce as beautiful.'

'No!' said Phyllis worriedly. 'That's where you're wrong, our Laura. Her biggest memory is of the baby bein' born. Just after the funeral she told me about Joyce's confinement. It's the only time she's mentioned it. Joyce clung to her all the way through the birth. Gran Palmer said her hands and arms were black and blue after. It was a bad birth and she saw everythin' that happened, all Joyce's pain, her screams, her bewilderment, the blood –' Phyllis gagged on the words.

'Don't, Mum,' begged Laura, herself near to tears. 'I thought Gran Palmer said Joyce died peacefully.'

'So she did, but only after she'd been through hell.'

'Oh, my God. Why should it have happened to Joyce?'

'That's a question that'll never be answered,' said Phyllis in bleak tones. She spoke sharply to Lillian, 'Well, you heard what Laura asked. Will you be a bridesmaid, or won't you? You're lucky you got asked after takin' her money.'

Lillian tossed her head, 'When I can get a word in edgeways I will. Yes, I'd like that. What shall I wear?'

'Nancy's dress is to be pink and yours is to be blue,' said Laura. 'That will pick up the colour of my flowers. Blue always suits you. And you'll have a lovely chiffon hat of the same colour.'

'Who's payin' for all this?'

Laura hoped that Lillian would behave more graciously at the ceremony. 'I am, at least for our gowns. The Mallenders will pay for the reception.'

Dad appeared from behind his paper, 'Just as well, chick, we couldn't have given you a slap-up do.'

'Our Enid had a lovely wedding,' said Phyllis indignantly.

'A slap-up do,' agreed Lillian.

'She did, Mum,' said Laura, trying to blot out the memory of the drinking and singing which continued far into the night until the neighbours had yelled that enough was enough. 'It's the Mallenders who must have everything posh, Mum. They don't understand anything else.'

'I wonder they asked us at all,' said Lillian.

'You surely don't imagine I'd think of getting married without my family there?'

'Not the boys, though!'

Laura evaded the statement. 'Ralph's coming. It's to be a small affair. Because of Joyce.'

'Where will you be livin' afterwards?' asked Phyllis.

'Above the Park Street shop. The third floor used to be living quarters once, but they've been very neglected. Until the place is ready I imagine Adrian will join me in my flat.'

'Not very grand for such a *grand* gentleman,' observed Lillian, but Laura was relieved that the malice had gone from her voice. She was clearly delighted to be taking a prominent part in the wedding.

The marriage announcement appeared in the Bristol papers and *The Times*, in London, and a few presents arrived.

'Good,' said Lady Mallender. 'I was afraid that no one would send anything since we are not asking people to the ceremony. Only invited guests are obliged to send something, Laura.'

Laura kept silent. More and more she was having to bite her tongue to stop reacting to Lady Mallender's patronising ways. There was no use resenting it. Her ladyship just couldn't help herself.

She looked forward to the day when she and Adrian would move into the flat. Ralph had fetched her tin trunk from Granma's. She had never collected it after she had been ordered to leave. Ever since she was eleven years old she had been filling it. Yards of material had been converted into pillow slips, cushion covers and tablecloths which she had spent hours embroidering, dreaming of the future. She had managed to save for a pair of cotton sheets, and Granma now gave her three pairs of heavy linen ones of immaculate quality.

'They were my own dear mother's,' said Granma. 'I've never used them, but you're getting so grand they'll be just right.'

The day of the wedding seemed to speed closer. Laura worked frantically to enable her to take off the two weeks that Adrian demanded for the honeymoon. They would stay first in London, then visit Paris.

Anita was pleased. 'I'll write to *Maman* and she'll arrange for a visit to Monsieur Patou. You'll be so impressed. Everyone is.'

Laura had no time to feel nervous. The days had been fraught with arguments. Her parents had taken it for granted that she would be married in the chapel she had attended since an infant. The Mallenders insisted on a Church of England wedding and Phyllis had eventually, reluctantly, accepted it.

Then Phyllis had suddenly become stubborn about the reception. 'This house was good enough for our Enid and it's good enough for you.'

Laura sighed. 'Mum, you know we can't come here. There isn't enough room.'

'There's plenty at Christmas. I never heard you grumble!'

'The Mallenders aren't like us. They aren't used to being squashed up.'

William and, unexpectedly, Lillian, had sided with Laura and persuaded Phyllis that the Mallender house was more suitable. Phyllis capitulated so abruptly that Laura suspected her protest had simply been a need to vent her inner feelings on someone. No matter what Laura was doing it was Joyce who was in her mother's mind. There was an atmosphere of suppressed misery in the house these days and not all of it caused by Freda. William and Phyllis had been to see Joyce's little son. They said he was beautiful and thriving. Freda never mentioned him.

Laura was surprised at Lady Mallender's reaction when she mentioned that the work on the Park Street flat was going ahead rapidly. 'My brothers are doing a lot of it,' she told Lady Mallender. 'It'll be ready for us in good time.'

Her ladyship stared at her incredulously. 'You surely don't expect to live over a *shop* after you are married!'

Laura quelled her irritation for Adrian's sake. She was doing so a lot lately. 'Why not?' She managed to keep her voice equable. 'It's good for me to be near the workroom. I often have to work very late. And the new flat is quite spacious.'

'It's not the size I'm thinking of!' snapped Lady Mallender. Abruptly she changed her tactics. 'Laura, my dear, Adrian is used to living here.' She swept her arm around. 'Just look at his home. Large rooms, plenty of light and space, lovely things all around him, servants. My boy would be miserable with anything less.'

'You're not doing him justice. Adrian's wants seem simple enough to me.'

'Yes, Laura dear, I quite agree with you that the dear boy is moderate in his living, but what will he do with himself all day while you are working?'

'Do with himself?' Laura hadn't given any thought to the matter. In her world men worked if they had a job and if they hadn't they met their mates and passed the long idle days with them.

'What has he been doing up to now?'

'He has his interests. And he loves reading, often in his bedroom. You haven't seen it, Laura. Come, I'll show it to you.'

Adrian's room looked almost as large as the total space of the flat, and overlooked the beautiful green Downs. The decor was unexpectedly delicate and all the furnishings had been lovingly matched. There was an exquisite Persian carpet, the surrounding light oak floors were highly polished. Laura was furnishing her flat with pieces picked up at house sales by Ralph and hadn't even considered that they must match. Even Granma had some odd pieces except in the front room where the pride of her possessions was the three-piece suite.

Lady Mallender ran her hand along the top of a dressing table. 'Light oak, Laura, as is all the furniture. Do you like the curtains and bed cover? William Morris. The designer, you know.'

'Yes, I do know. I learn a great deal from my brother.'

'Your brother? Ah, yes, Ralph. A pleasant young man. I'm sure he will prove successful one day.'

There was a fireplace with a fire laid ready. Antique ornaments were arrayed along the mantelpiece. Ralph was teaching her the value of such pieces and she recognised that these were good. Four delicate watercolours were hanging on one wall. They were of the same scene during the four seasons.

Laura, always interested in art, walked over to them and read the artist's name. 'Rex Lorimer! But he's the best man.'

'That's right.'

'Adrian didn't tell me he's an artist.'

'Rex is a professional. The small oil near Adrian's bed is one of his. He does pastels, too.'

The oil was a pastoral scene, similar to the others, and just as accomplished.

'I shall look forward to meeting Rex,' said Laura. 'I enjoyed art at school.'

Lady Mallender looked puzzled. 'Hasn't Adrian told you he himself is a water-colourist?'

Laura shook her head. 'No. I had no idea.'

'Naughty boy, but he's always modest about his work. He *must* be allowed to continue with it, Laura. Rex is his teacher as well as his friend.'

'I'm glad he'll have an occupation,' said Laura, her tone acerbic. In spite of her efforts to stay calm, resentment was building inside her.

Her ladyship sank into a fireside chair. 'This is so comfortable. We shall bring another one in here exactly the same for you, my dear. You will have your own little domain and no one shall enter without permission.'

'But a newly married couple should live alone,' said Laura, struggling against the tide of relentless goodwill that was swamping her. 'I won't interfere with Adrian's pastimes, any more than he will stop me from working.'

'Dear Laura, you don't understand him yet.' Lady Mallender pulled a small stool towards her and patted it. 'Sit down, please.'

Laura unwillingly sat. The low stool meant that she had to look up to her future mother-in-law who said, 'That's much better, and far more friendly. Adrian is a sensitive soul. A move from familiar surroundings could upset him dreadfully. He might not pick up a paintbrush for ages.'

'Surely you don't propose to keep him here for ever!'

'You must not be cross, Laura darling! Of course I don't, but when he leaves me I must know that he will be in appropriate surroundings. And a flat over a shop, however tastefully decorated, cannot match his home. This furniture belonged to his great-grandfather. And the sweet little writing desk –'

'Is Georgian. Yes, I recognise the period.'

'Do you? Do you really? What a comfort to know that my dear boy is to marry a connoisseur. One who will readily understand his nature. The writing desk belonged to an ancestor.'

Lady Mallender led Laura along the landing and opened a door to a bathroom. A proper one with a plumbed in bath and everything else that was needed for cleanliness and comfort. 'Do you like it? I believe the amenities at your present dwelling are somewhat crude.'

If you think they're crude you should try visiting my parents, thought Laura, but she kept her tongue still.

'Are you having a proper bathroom put in at your new flat?' enquired Lady Mallender sweetly – too sweetly.

'Not yet. I shall later.'

'Ah!' The retort was small, but held a world of meaning.

As Laura walked through the front hall where Renton waited to open the door Lady Mallender's maid, Gardner, passed her.

And Laura was so startled by her she was outside before she could gather her thoughts. The maid had given her a look full of loathing. It didn't seem a good omen as to how she would fare in her husband's home. Sir Hugo had scarcely spoken to her even now and still seemed to dislike her. And Lady Mallender had no intention of relinquishing any part of her hold over Adrian. Laura's thoughts were turbulent. She drove straight to the Park Street shop and climbed the staircase to the flat. Workmen were checking the electric lighting. Plumbers were fixing a small room with lavatory and wash-basin. A hip bath hung on the wall. It had seemed luxurious to Laura and she had enjoyed picturing herself and Adrian in the flat, learning more about one another, making love. Lady Mallender had cheapened it all.

Adrian was as astonished as his mother when she told him what had happened. 'Good heavens, darling, of course we'll live with Mummy and Daddy. I'm afraid I took that for granted.'

'But you knew I was having the Park Street flat completely renovated.'

'Yes, but I assumed it was for one of your employees.'

'Apparently we both assumed too much.'

'Does it matter? Oh, Laura, you'll be so happy at home. I always am. I love it. And you'll enjoy having servants to do all the housework and cooking.'

'I haven't neglected my home or food!'

'No, of course you haven't, but sometimes you've been too tired even to talk. How can we be happy together if we can't even talk?'

'I had thought of employing a cleaning woman.'

'But it's not the same. And where could I have my studio? At home I use an attic with a north light.'

'You could return to it during the day, and Adrian, you've never even mentioned your painting to me. Your mother says it's important to you.'

'It is! Very! But I've been busy telling you other things.' He pulled her into his arms. 'That I'm the happiest man in the world to have won you.'

Laura leaned against him. What did it matter? She would continue to spend most of her time in her shops and workrooms anyway. She was loved, that was the vital thing.

She was touched to discover that her employees had banded together to buy her a dinner service with no less than sixty-seven pieces. It was white with a fruit border on a dark blue background.

'That's a Battersea design,' said Ralph. 'Not original, but pretty expensive none the less. Your girls must think highly of you to have collected so much money.'

The dinner service was taken to the Mallender house for display at the reception. Her ladyship produced a pair of pince-nez. 'Pretty,' she pronounced. 'Battersea. Reproduction, of course. It will not be needed here. We have plenty of real china.'

Laura felt an almost overwhelming impulse to box her lady-ship's ears. She cheapened everything connected with Laura. 'Why do you want me to marry Adrian when you seem to like nothing about me?' Laura heard her own voice with amazement. The words seemed to have sprung from her outside her will.

Lady Mallender looked hurt. 'Dear child, what a question. He wants you. That's all that matters.'

'Have you always given him everything he wants?'

'Whenever I could.'

Her ladyship looked suddenly bleak and turned away.

Laura touched her arm, the first sympathetic gesture she had ever made to Lady Mallender who did not encourage intimacy. 'I'm sorry. I didn't intend to upset you.'

'Upset me? Whatever can you mean?' Lady Mallender moved away. 'Cook has finished the wedding cake. It's a two-tier one. More would be ostentatious for such a small reception. She is to decorate it soon. Have you any wishes in the matter?'

'No. I'm sure she'll do it well. Everything is done well here.'

'How sweet of you. *Too* kind.'

As the date of the wedding grew nearer Laura almost panicked. The dresses were ready, the flowers ordered, the vicar prepared. Laura faced the day with a mixture of hope and trepidation. She was giving up her freedom. She would have to leave her shops for two weeks. How would they fare without her? She told herself she was being a fool. Trade was slow at present, Dolores was proving an excellent manager and was moving to the Park Street shop while Laura was away and Iris and Millie were quite capable of running the Kingswood branch for a short time. Noreen had lately been running the first *Hats by Laura* in Redfield. She preferred the workroom and one of Laura's first considerations when she returned would be to find another manager.

Laura had insisted on one guest from outside the family; Miss Morton, who had helped her so generously to achieve success, who had taught her her trade and thereby opened doors into a prosperous future, could not be left out.

The actual day dawned bright, a hot sun beaming from a cloudless sky. Perfect, thought Laura. A perfect day for a perfect ceremony. By this time tomorrow she would be married, she would have yielded her body to a man for the first time, she would have experienced at last the longed-for joy and wonder of love, of belonging body, heart and mind to another human being.

Chapter Twenty

Miss Morton arrived at lunch-time to help Laura dress. She was sparkling with excitement. Her outfit, a mid-blue gown with lacy collar and cuffs, a small brown felt hat and white gloves, suited her well.

She kissed Laura and persuaded her to eat a little. 'It wouldn't do to faint at the altar, love, now would it?'

The food tasted like chaff, but Laura managed soup and a slice of bread and washed it down with tea.

The ivory satin underdress was a perfect fit, sliding over her body like a caress. The chiffon gown was as soft and transparent as a cobweb and the handkerchief points floated round her legs with every movement. The posy of flowers arrived, sweet and fresh and the half-opened pink rosebuds scented the room. Laura went downstairs to the shop where there was a full length mirror.

Dolores, already installed, clasped her hands. 'Laura, you look beautiful. Really lovely. Your headress matches those gorgeous roses perfectly.'

Laura contemplated her reflection. Her skin was as flawless as her ivory dress, but she was so pale. It made her eyes look even bigger. Perhaps she should have added a little rouge as Anita had advised. She decided against it.

Anita had been invited, but had refused. 'I'll not come and gawp at you shackling yourself to a man, *and* I'll be watching carefully in future to see if you waver one iota from your business responsibilities.'

'Don't worry, I won't.'

'I've heard that before. I've known extremely clever women get perfectly torpid after marriage. I suppose you'll be having babies next and all the ghastly mess that goes with them. You'll probably even want to suckle the darn thing, too, and have to wear frightful dresses that button up the front. And you won't be giving full attention to work and –'

Laura had laughed. 'For goodness' sake, Anita, let me get married first. And I can assure you that I won't be a mother until, and if, I choose.'

Anita's finely plucked brows rose. 'Well I never! Thank God you're going into marriage educated in the important things.'

Unexpectedly she had kissed Laura. 'For luck,' she said, 'not because I approve of this marriage. You're too young. You don't know enough about the world and bugger-all about men.'

'Well, I'm about to learn. And I only want one man. Adrian is enough for me.'

Anita sighed. 'I wonder if you realise just what you're letting yourself in for.' She paused, seemed to be about to speak, then paused again. 'Oh, Laura, I hope you won't get hurt.'

'You're kind to care, but I'm sure Adrian and I are going to be happy.'

Again Anita had hesitated before she said, 'It's a different world that the Mallenders live in, but they're customers of both of us and you must have some idea of what they're like. There's nothing like a gown shop, or milliner's to see a woman at her worst. Unless you're a corset-fitter!'

'Were you ever one?'

'Don't remind me. Heaving handfuls of flesh into a corset, dragging at the tapes, breaking my nails on steel fasteners. I mean to say, one understands the poor things wanting to look slimmer, but really!'

'I promise not to fit corsets,' said Laura gently.

Anita grinned, then she became solemn. 'Remember, no matter what happens, or where Adrian takes you, walk proudly and act as if nothing surprises you.'

'Thanks for the advice, Aunty Anita,' said Laura. She had frowned worriedly. 'I'm expecting a delivery of hats from the wholesaler to *The Hat Shop*. Iris will tick them off on the invoice. She has a list of customers who are ready to pay for exclusive trimming. Noreen and Miss Morton will see to that. Iris is very capable, but she's so young –'

'Unlike her big sister who's so old.'

Laura ignored the flippant interruption. 'I'm going to engage an office clerk when I get back and –'

Anita had put her long slim fingers gently over Laura's mouth. 'For God's sake, just get married. One would think you're indispensable. There are plenty of people to look after your interests, and you've got a marvellous workforce. Everyone of them thinks you're a wonder. Including Nancy. I don't understand how she came from such a toffee-nosed family as the Mallenders – whoops! – sorry, Laura!'

Laura had chosen to ignore Anita's remarks which inwardly she agreed with. She said, 'I wanted Nancy to look after the new shop while I'm away so that Delores could spend more time in Kingswood. Nancy wanted to but Lady Mallender refused permission.' Laure smiled ruefully. 'She said that she would prefer her daughter not to engage in trade, though if Nancy did work all the important clients would be personal acquaintances, and the others didn't matter!'

'Stupid old cow,' Anita had said. '*Everyone* with money to spend matters. However, I'll concede that only the well-heeled will dare to come into the Park Street shop, or anyway, to stay there once they've seen the prices.'

The hired car arrived bearing William who stepped out to hand his daughter in. 'You look pretty, chick.'

'You look good yourself, Dad.'

William wore a new grey suit, a new white shirt and a dark-grey tie. Even his shoes were new, and his hair was brushed to a shining smoothness. He was quite distinguished and Laura was proud of him. Perhaps on this special day he would say something she could hug to herself through the years.

'Your mother, Enid and Jack will be in the church by now with Granma and Grampa, and Lillian will be waiting at the door. Ralph's been ferrying them.'

'Nancy will be there, too,' said Laura. 'And Thelma and Daphne Charlton and, of course, Sir Hugo and Lady Mallender.'

The words suddenly sounded odd on her tongue. What was she, Laura Blackford, the unwanted member of the Blackford family, doing sitting in a large expensive car being driven smoothly to church to marry a member of the upper crust? It all seemed fantastic and somehow far away. Perhaps all brides felt like this. She should have asked Phyllis and Enid.

'I didn't expect to be nervous,' she said shakily.

'You'll be fine, chick. You always land on your feet.'

Laura turned to stare at him. He was looking ahead, leaning back as if he owned the car. His face was bland and serene. He had no idea that his words, delivered so pat and complete, with no account taken of her struggles to survive, were devastating to his daughter. Laura closed her eyes for a moment, disappointment flooding her. Nothing about her, it seemed, could dent William's iron-clad tranquillity. Thank God she was on her way to marry a man who would put her first, who would give her the love she so wanted. To be first in someone's life was essential to her.

They were at the church and there were the bridesmaids. Lillian had blossomed into real beauty and Nancy looked very pretty. She smiled, her blue eyes shining, 'Laura, how wonderful you look. She does, doesn't she,' she said, turning to Lillian.

'Yes, very nice,' said Lillian stiffly, and Laura knew that her sister was unbearably envious.

The church was empty save for the verger, the organist, the vicar and the tiny number of guests. The organ played as Laura walked down the aisle on William's arm. Adrian, looking handsome and solemn, was waiting. By his side stood a man Laura had not met before. This must be Rex Lorimer, the artist friend. He turned with Adrian to look at her and she had a shock of surprise. She had expected that Adrian's best friend would look as gentle as he. Rex certainly didn't. He was over six feet tall and muscular and emitted an air almost of aggression. His eyes were deep-set, dark-blue, and his reddish-brown hair was thick and wavy. He could not be called handsome, but when he was present in a room he would be noticed.

William relinquished her to Adrian who intoned the responses as quickly and quietly as Laura. The vicar gave a blessing, and she was returning to the sunshine on the arm of her husband. As she emerged into light too brilliant after the cool dimness of the church Laura felt joy bound within her. She and Adrian were man and wife and soon they would be one – one flesh, the bible called it. Adrian was a good man; he had kept his desire firmly under control. She presumed he was as virginal as herself and soon they would taste the fruits of perfect love together.

A photograper waited, his tripod set up, and the small crowd of women who always grouped for a wedding gave 'ohs' and 'ahs' as the bride and groom appeared.

Lady Mallender was assiduous in arranging people for the photographer who eventually gave up and allowed her to organise everyone. It wasn't until later, when Laura had time to think, that she realised that her whole family had been allowed to pose only once. Then it was back to the Mallender residence. Laura had dreaded the moment when the two families met and talked, but Phyllis was too overwhelmed by the large house, the dignified butler and busy maidservants, and all the panoply of riches to talk much. She, too, had on a new gown, a beech-coloured marocain, with a brown felt hat and gloves to match. Laura couldn't remember her looking so smart. Phyllis's almost emaciated body was up-to-the-minute fashionable and she avoided laughing so that the gap in her front teeth stayed hidden.

Twice Laura had given her the money for dental treatment, but each time Phyllis had spent it on one of the children. There was little to spare yet from the profits of the shops, most of which had to be ploughed back into stock or handed out in wages and bills, but when Laura visited her family she usually took a little money. She would hold it out and invariably Phyllis gestured towards a cracked vase on the mantelshelf and Laura dropped the cash inside. But there could not possibly have been enough to pay for all the new clothes and Laura realised that her family must have gone into debt. She felt half angry, half proud that they had complimented her in so extravagant a way.

In spite of his new clothes, Jack looked as scruffy and ill at ease as ever. His tufty hair was plastered in hair grease which smelled as cheap as it was. His suit hung on him, fitting only where it touched and he didn't know what to do with his feet and hands. Enid was trying to conceal her five-month pregnancy. Lillian was over-reacting, making a poor attempt to match her speech to the Charlton girls who were staring at Laura's family as if they were beings from another planet. Granma and Grampa were dressed in their inevitable black, he carrying his walking stick, Granma having relinquished her umbrella reluctantly to Renton. She was watching Laura with so odd a mixture of pride and bewilderment that she almost laughed. She guessed that the doughty old lady could not understand why Laura, who had broken away from her discipline and committed so many sins, should end up here among the rich and titled. She should have been weeping with repentance by now.

The food was delicious and tastefully presented. Laura had unwittingly become used to such things, but her family regarded everything with amazement. Food to them was something which was slapped on the table and eaten as fast as possible so as to get seconds on the rare occasions this was possible. It never consisted of bite-sized triangular sandwiches, squares of toast spread with pâté de fois gras, savoury mixtures in pastry cases, several dozen fancy cakes. William and Phyllis drank deeply of claret cup. It was quite weak and they stared into their glasses in disgust. Granma didn't hold with fancy cooking, and certainly not drinking, and she glared around as Turkish and Egyptian cigarettes were produced and the room took on a smoky blue haze. There was food left over and Phyllis looked wistfully at it. Laura prayed that she wouldn't ask for a bag to take some home for the kids. In Phyllis's world giving a guest something to take home for the kids was a routine procedure.

Sir Hugo wandered around the room, occasionally speaking to one guest or another, not troubling to hide his gloom.

Adrian whispered in Laura's ear. 'Take no notice of Daddy. He's had to travel from Scotland and miss some of the shooting.'

Lady Mallender was ineffably gracious, while Nancy did her best to put everyone at ease.

When the cake had been cut, the toasts drunk, Rex strolled over to Laura and Adrian. 'Congratulations, old chap. You're lucky to have won so charming and clever a bride.' He bowed to Laura. 'I look forward to seeing more of you when you return from your honeymoon.'

He smiled affably and Laura held out her hand. 'It's a pleasure to meet you, Rex. I love your paintings.'

'You do? Delighted! Perhaps you'll allow me to present you with one when you move into your new home.'

'Hasn't Adrian told you we're residing with his parents?'

Adrian's mother called him away and Rex said quietly, 'I get the strongest feeling that you would prefer not to live with the Mallenders.'

'Not at all,' replied Laura loyally, 'I'm just a bit nervy today.'

'Understandable.' Rex lit another cigarette. 'I'm going to be absolutely honest and say that to live in close proximity to her ladyship would drive me potty. And Sir Hugo looks like a caged beast who hasn't been fed for a week. His heart is in the highlands. He thinks he's stalking.'

The description of the restless Sir Hugo was so apt that Laura laughed.

'How pretty you are when you laugh, Mrs Mallender. You should do it more often.'

Laura was taken aback. First by Rex's compliment, secondly by hearing her new name for the first time. Even Adrian had not thought to say it on their way from the church. But most by her sudden awareness that she seldom laughed with Adrian.

Laura and Adrian caught a train to London. Their luggage was piled up in the rack above their heads, natural hide cases, with a special vanity bag for Laura and a dressing case for Adrian, all monogrammed with their entwined initials. They were a present from Rex whose taste appeared to be excellent, though Laura marvelled at the costliness of his gift.

When she remarked upon it to Adrian he just shrugged and said lightly, 'Oh, Rex is rolling in money.'

Laura leaned forward and stared from the window as they steamed out of Bristol and into the countryside. She sighed.

'Don't sound so mournful,' said Adrian, smiling.

'I wasn't, darling, far from it. I'm happy. I feel so cared for. And I've never been in a first-class carriage before. In fact, I've hardly ever been on a train, especially for such a long journey. Granma and Grampa took me to Weston sometimes in the summer, but it was nothing like this.'

'You're so sweet, but it would be better if you didn't reveal your inexperience to others.'

Laura felt rebuffed. 'There's no one but us in the carriage,' she pointed out. 'But I will behave well, I promise,' she added hastily as Adrian's brow creased in a frown.

His irritation vanished immediately. 'I know you will. You're such a clever girl. Oh, by the way, I was handed an extra present to give you. It's from my mother.' Adrian took out an oblong parcel wrapped in white paper from his dressing case.

'How kind of her.' Laura undid the silver thread and revealed a large dark blue book. She read, *The Book of Etiquette* by Lady Troubridge.'

'What is it?'

Laura handed it to him silently, fuming.

He laughed. 'Oh, isn't Mummy absolutely sweet.'

'Sweet? Is it sweet to imply that my manners need mending and get you to hand me such a book just as we're setting off on our new life?'

'Surely you don't mind! Why, I believe you're cross. Why should you be? Have you any idea of how to act in a big hotel, for instance? Or how to greet the people we may meet in Paris?' He riffled through the contents page. 'It's all here. Mummy has done you a great kindness. You must see it that way.'

'If I'm so ill-bred why did you marry me?'

'Because I love you.'

The reply completely disarmed her. 'Oh, Adrian, and I love you. It's so marvellous to think we belong. And I'm going to London for the first time, and then to Paris.'

Adrian said tentatively, 'Darling, I hope you and Mummy

are going to be friends when we live at home.'

'Your home, not mine!'

'Laura! Sweetheart!' He paused and leaned forward to take her hand. 'Do you realise we're teetering towards the verge of our first disagreement?'

Laura subsided. 'Sorry, darling. I'm tired. There was so much to arrange before I left the shops. When I get back I must engage a new manager, and organise a more profitable contract with a wholesale firm. After that –'

'Do you mind not talking about your business?'

'What? You usually like hearing about it.'

'Not today. There's a time for everything.'

'Sorry.' She seemed to be apologising for everything. She'd read Lady Mallender's damn book and act like a duchess if that's what they wanted. She wondered, not for the first time, what it would be like meeting her customers socially. Would it be beneficial? Or a disaster? She closed her eyes. The day had been wearing and she slid into a doze. Faces and voices drifted through her mind. Phyllis, William, who hadn't said the fatherly words she had longed for, her sisters and brothers, Dolores, Anita, Ralph, Rick. She woke with a small cry to find Adrian watching her from the window seat opposite.

'Did you have a bad dream, old girl?'

'I don't think so. Sorry I fell asleep.' Damn it, she was apologising again. Perhaps she'd better read her new book and find out what ladies did, or did not, do.

An elderly couple took their seats at a stop and Adrian immediately became aloof. The couple clearly accepted this as correct and the train roared on with scarcely a word spoken. Laura remembered the time she had been on a train with her family. Years ago. The memory had all but faded. Herself, a small girl clutching her sandy bucket and spade, in her pocket a tuppeny stick of rock, on her head a straw hat with bright red and yellow shiny berries, on her way home from Weston. A Sunday school outing, a day on the wide, warm sands, with the tide creeping closer over the mud flats, filling her sand-castle moat with grey water. Phyllis and William, Ralph, Enid, Lillian and herself, the twins, and her mother grown fat. She must have been big with Iris. They were crushed into a compartment with two other families, the children sitting on laps, running to the lavatory, racing up and down the corridors like little animals let out of cages. Everywhere was noisy, with Phyllis chatting to everyone in sight, known or unknown to her, while William fell asleep, his mouth dropping open, emitting gentle snores.

Laura looked around her, the sensation of unreality invading her once more. Four people behaving with cold propriety. She thought of the Charltons and their friends. She was going into a crazy world. If you had not been introduced you acted as if no one was there. If you had, you shrieked and drank too much, talked constantly about sex, played pranks, gossiped cruelly, threw bread rolls. She wondered if she would ever fit in.

They took a taxi to their hotel. Adrian tipped everyone, the cheerful railway porter who loaded the luggage into the vehicle, the taxi driver, and the bellboys who carried the cases to their room. Laura had never tipped anyone in her life. Another thing she must learn about. Adrian was slightly lofty, and the recipients touched their caps gratefully, all in an approved pattern of manners.

She had never entered even the lobby of such a place as this. The entrance was between lofty pillars supporting a turreted roof where plants grew. A striped canopy ensured that no one got wet walking from car to door.

Laura was thankful that she had acquired a good trousseau. Her hats were all designed by herself and already female heads had turned to look at her. She was excited to realise that sophisticated London women thought her creations worth more than a first glance. She wore a pale-green knitted silk jumper suit and a head-hugging green straw hat with a scarlet feather. Her stockings were of silk, her shoes white buckskin with a louis heel.

They were shown into a suite of rooms, a sitting room with elegant furniture, comfortable chairs, a sideboard, a writing desk supplied with headed paper, pens and ink and a blotter. There was even a vase of flowers. Laura walked swiftly across the carpet and opened doors. One led into a bedroom equally sumptuous and her gaze lingered for a moment on the double bed, another into a warm bathroom.

'Do you like it?' asked Adrian.

'Like it? It's absolutely wonderful.'

'Yes, it's rather nice, isn't it? My family always use The Connaught. We love its homely atmosphere.'

'Homely! You call this' – she swept her arm around the room – 'homely! It's not like any home I've ever been in – except yours,' she added.

'Exactly. They pride themselves on having the atmosphere of a well-run country house. I've ordered dinner, by the way.'

'Good, I'm starving. I ate almost nothing of the food your mother provided. I was far too excited.'

'I didn't eat any,' said Adrian.

'Nothing? Were you too filled with happiness, too? Darling' – Laura sped across the room and flung her arms around his neck – 'isn't everything *too*, too blissful.'

She had given a passable imitation of Thelma and Adrian grinned, before he removed her arms from his neck. 'I think I'll take a bath before dinner.'

Laura felt a little chilled. They were here in a private suite, newlyweds, and in spite of her hunger and weariness her body wanted to be loved. *She* wanted to be loved. She sighed. Adrian was so formal; he obviously wasn't a man to get to his honeymoon hotel and leap straight into bed. Well, she could wait. It wouldn't be long now before they were tucked up together with no fear of interruption. There was a knock and a bellboy carried in a tray of champagne and glasses. 'Ordered by your husband, Mrs Mallender.'

'Oh, how lovely!'

The boy stood waiting and Laura looked at him, then realised with dismay that he was expecting his tip. She nervously took half a crown from her purse and handed it to him. His eyes opened wide, then he smiled and left.

When she told Adrian he was astonished. 'Half a crown for carrying up a tray. Sixpence would have been ample. Good God, woman, I hope you don't throw your money around like that all the time.'

Laura felt irritable. 'I don't have enough to do that. I just didn't know –'

'It's all right, darling.' Adrian rubbed his wet hair with a voluminous towel and his voice came muffled. 'I reckon we must both be worn out. I've never been married before. It's very wearing.'

His remark was clearly intended to be humorous and, as he emerged from the towel, his hair sticking up in spikes, Laura giggled. 'Oh, Adrian, life will be marvellous and in the next two weeks we'll have such fun, so much happiness.'

'We shall, indeed. Now, how about having your bath and putting on one of your prettiest frocks to confound the other diners. I'll call a maid and valet to finish unpacking and iron anything that's creased.'

'Is there anything they won't do here?' Laura said, laughing, but inside she felt a stab of disappointment. In all the novels she had read honeymoon couples dined alone.

However, it would be fun to enter a room on Adrian's arm, as his wife. She must accept that he was conventional.

The dinner was excellently chosen and beautifully served to the music of an orchestra, the lights were soft. It was so hushed it reminded Laura of a church. Tranquillity reigned, but Laura suddenly wasn't very hungry.

'You must eat, darling,' persuaded Adrian. 'If you don't the chef may come out of the kitchen to ask why?'

Laura was startled and Adrian laughed. 'Just a joke. At least, I hope it is.'

There were arrays of pill boxes and bottles of medicine ranged on a few tables. Adrian gestured towards them. 'Some people keep a suite here permanently and always have the same table.'

'Does your family?'

'Not now. We used to. Mummy and Daddy used to bring us to London quite often, especially at Christmas, but we haven't bothered just lately. Laura, you look awfully pretty tonight. Is that another of Anita's gowns?'

Laura looked down at her silky peach-coloured gown with its

slightly darker peach stripes. 'Yes, she chose it for me. She says that horizontal stripes make me look shorter.'

'Was she referring to my lack of inches?' Adrian was annoyed.

Laura said hurriedly, 'I'm sure she wasn't. She says I need to choose clothes with care because I'm so tall and thin, but that's the advice she gives to many of her customers. In any case, love, you're not short.'

'Five feet nine inches, that's all I am. Just an inch more than you. I thought I'd be tall like my father. I think the time he decided he didn't like me was when he realised I wasn't going to grow any more.'

'That's absurd. Surely –' Laura stopped. Who was she to argue? 'Well, I love you the way you are. I always will.'

'Always?' Adrian was regarding her with speculative eyes.

'Always,' she repeated firmly.

'Your shops must be making a lot of money if you can afford to wear silk.'

'I thought you didn't want to talk business.'

'I didn't, so soon after the wedding, but now we're settled for a few days, I don't mind.'

'It isn't silk. It's Celanese. Artificial and much cheaper. Women are buying it in droves, Anita says.'

Gradually Laura's stomach muscles unknotted and she enjoyed the delicious food, and the wine which they both drank in moderation. That was another good thing about Adrian; he was no toper. When they had finished a waiter poured coffee, another brought liqueurs.

'I expect you're surprised to have coffee at the table,' said Adrian.

'No more than I am at everything else.'

'No. Well, ordinary hotels serve coffee in the lounge, but The Connaught brings it to the table because they don't wish diners to think they're being hurried away.'

'I see.' Laura didn't see really. It seemed a trivial point to her, though Adrian sounded quite supercilious about it.

He had been waving discreetly to people all through the dinner and passing remarks. 'There's one of Mummy's friends – or perhaps I should say one of her friendly rivals. And old General Charters. He'll tell you anything you want to know and a lot that you don't about the Great War and the Boer War, too. If he looks our way I'll pretend I don't see him.

'Look at the Smithson lot. All as fat as butter. I wonder why they're here today. Their usual time is mid-week for visiting their corsetière or gunsmith and the like. I wonder who that is over there. I don't know him. Never seen him before.'

Laura smiled. 'You sound as if he's a gatecrasher in your own home.'

'Do I? Well, that's how it seems when a stranger appears here.'

'I'm a stranger.'

'Yes, but you're with me and that makes all the difference.'

'Why doesn't anyone stop for you to introduce me?'

'Good gracious, no one would dream of such a thing. They'd consider it an invasion of privacy. But don't judge other hotels by this one. This is unique.'

They lingered over their liqueurs, smoking and talking in a companionable fashion that Laura found delightful. Adrian suggested a walk before retiring and they strolled in the still-warm air to St George's, Hanover Square, into the old grave-yard with inscribed benches and a drinking fountain.

'Don't you mind being here?' asked Laura.'

'What? Oh, the graves. No, not at all, do you?'

'I don't, but I thought you hated anything to do with death.'

Adrian look vaguely at the tombstones. 'I hadn't thought of that. These graves don't concern me at all. They're so old. Too old to care about.'

They seated themselves and listened to the frenzied chatter of starlings roosting for the night under the eaves.

Laura caught Adrian's hand. 'I'm so happy.'

Adrian gripped her fingers so tightly her rings hurt her. 'Are you? Are you really?'

'Don't you feel the same?'

'Of course. Sorry, old girl, I'm not much of a one for flowery speeches.'

'That doesn't matter as long as you love me?'

'Can you doubt it when we're sitting here, married?'

When they finally reached their rooms Laura was relaxed and happy. She bathed in the deep bath filled with deliciously perfumed water – as much hot water as she wanted, for the first time ever – and put on a nightgown, a pale-blue silk with pink and white bows. She brushed her hair until it shone, dabbed scent on her wrists, throat and knees – the last being Anita's advice – and slipped into a flower-patterned satin dressing gown and dainty slippers.

Adrian was reading the evening paper. 'Laura, how very pretty you look. I shall take my bath now.'

Laura sat on the edge of the bed. She was feeling more and more nervous. If only her husband was as passionate as she felt, as demanding as Rick. This was all so slow, so formal. It should, perhaps, heighten her desire. Perhaps it did for Adrian. Maybe that was it. Probably he enjoyed expectation as much as gratification. Jaw-breaking words, Rick would say. Keep out of my bedroom, Rick, especially on my honeymoon! She slid out of her wrapper and slippers and climbed into bed. It was wide, the acme of luxury, the sheets and pillowslips snowy white and ironed to perfection. She wondered if the Charlton girls ever noticed the linen when they went to bed. They had never seen their mother, red-faced and exhausted, pushing a hot iron over yards and yards of material.

The bathroom door opened and Adrian came in wearing a pair of yellow silk pyjamas, the trouser bottoms of which she could see beneath a brown and yellow dressing gown. She was almost as startled by a man wearing silk as by realising that he was about to climb into bed with her. Grampa wore thick striped flannel and so did Dad. The boys went to bed in their vests and shirts.

Adrian walked over to the bed and looked down at her and she was touched to see that he looked as shy as she felt. 'Do you want anything else, darling? I can have it sent up.'

'I want only you,' said Laura simply.

Adrian took off his dressing gown and tossed it on to a chair, kicked off his slippers, and paused, before climbing gingerly into bed with her.

Laura laughed. 'I won't break, you know.'

Adrian laughed, too, but so nervously that his voice was a croak.

They lay back on the pillows and stared into one another's eyes. She put her arm around Adrian and after a brief hesitation he slid an arm under her, and slowly began to stroke her. His hand slid over the silky nightgown, over her breasts which ached for his caresses, and down the length of her body, and stopped.

'Don't torment me,' she gasped. 'We're married, remember? Make love to me – please.'

Adrian gave a small groan. He dragged off his pyjama trousers, rolled over and pulled up her nightdress. She was on fire with her need and his fingers on her bare flesh were a sweet torment. She wanted him to go on touching her, to tease her until his passion overcame him. He pushed her legs apart and moved his body close to hers. Then he slumped back on his pillows.

'Sorry, can't be done.'

'What do you mean?'

'I mean, darling, that nothing is happening to me. I believe it must be weariness. Not to worry.' He gave a small laugh. 'Maybe later, when I've had some rest.'

Laura lay awake, listening to her husband's even breathing. Was ever a honeymoon begun with such a fiasco? If only there was someone she could ask. The only people she knew who had phones were Lady Mallender, Dolores in the Park Street shop, and Anita. Oh, and Aunty Mabel. Rick had insisted on installing one. But all were unmarried, except her mother-in-law, and to speak to her on the subject of sex was unthinkable.

Perhaps she should phone the Hotwells' flat. Aunty Mabel's down-to-earth sense might help. What if Rick was there and answered? What would she say? 'Hello, Rick, old pal, I'm on my honeymoon, my husband just tried to make love to me and couldn't. What's my next move?' She twisted restlessly, her body's hunger still strong. She murmured Adrian's name, hoping he would wake. She pushed her hand beneath the bed-clothes, her fingers itching to touch him, to caress him into a need to equal her own. But what if he awoke and was still cool? She couldn't face another rejection. That was probably the wrong word. Weariness, excitement could easily combine to exhaust one. So why hadn't it happened to her? She fell into an uneasy doze.

She awoke with a cry as she felt his hands upon her. He had been right to wait; she was shuddering with passion, her voice hoarse, words unintelligible, as his hands moved over her. She could never have imagined such exquisite torment when his fingers began to stroke the intimate softness of her body.

Abruptly he raised himself above her, his elbows each side of her breasts, kneed her legs open and thrust his hard penis into her. It hurt. It hurt like hell. She tried to cry out, but he stopped her mouth with a kiss as his body moved convulsively on hers, driving deeper and deeper into her and as her pain became unbearable he gave a loud cry and sank upon her, his weight pinning her down and robbing her of breath. He stayed still for a moment, then pulled himself away.

'Thank you, darling,' he said and climbed out of bed and went to the bathroom and Laura heard water rushing from the taps. She lay very still, anger and anguish mingling within her. Was that sex? Was that all it was for a woman? She couldn't believe it. Books and films and poetry said otherwise. Surely they hadn't lied. In spite of her terrible soreness she was quiv-ering with the power of her unassuaged desire. Adrian walked back, drew on his pyjama trousers, and climbed in beside her, yawning. He closed his eyes.

'Are you going to sleep?' she asked, her voice as sharp as her disappointment.

He seemed not to notice. 'Of course. Aren't you tired?'

'Yes, but, Adrian, I don't feel as – happy as I expected. I mean, is that all that happens?'

'All?' He actually sounded supercilious. 'Wasn't it enough?'

'You hurt me a lot and left me –' Laura stopped because she didn't know how to go on. What was she supposed to feel? She had assumed that love-making was as wonderful for a woman as for a man.

'I thought you knew nothing about sex,' said Adrian. He actually sounded sulky.

'I don't really.'

'Then how do you know what's supposed to happen?' Adrian's voice was suddenly as acerbic as hers had been.

'I don't, of course, but surely love is supposed to be more than just pain for a woman.'

Adrian sat up and reached for a cigarette. He offered her one and she shook her head, then changed her mind. Perhaps smoking would cool her nerves. 'This is only the first night of a whole marriage, Laura. I told you I've never made love to a woman before. I suppose I'm not very skilful. I'm sorry, darling.'

She sighed with relief. 'It's all right. You do understand.'

Laura awoke early, her body still yearning for fulfilment. She reached for her boudoir cap without which, said *Vogue*, no lady would ever be seen in the morning and glanced at herself in a small hand mirror. In spite of its being a few yards of ribbon, a touch of net and a sprinkle of forget-me nots, it reminded her of the mob cap Granma wore when she dusted the ceilings. She giggled.

'What's so funny?' Adrian's eyes were open.

'My cap.'

He yawned. 'I think it's rather sweet.'

'Do you?' She leaned over him and kissed him. She had meant it to be a good-morning peck, but, unintentionally, her lips opened on his and her tongue touched his mouth.

In one movement he pushed her off and sat up. 'You're incredible,' he said, amusement in his voice.

'You think I'm funny!'

'No, my love, I think you're adorable.' He glanced at his travelling clock. 'Breakfast will be served in five minutes. We wouldn't want the maid to catch us at anything, would we?'

'No-o. Don't you feel – don't you want to make love? I do.'

'My God, I had no idea I was marrying such a passionate female.'

'Do you wish you hadn't?'

'I keep telling you, I love you,' he said reproachfully.

They ate a delicious breakfast of bacon and egg and toast with coffee in bed, Laura feeling odd. She had never eaten in bed except when ill and it seemed like the height of indulgence. They raced one another for the bath and Laura got there first.

'Cheat,' yelled Adrian.

'I'm not. Why don't you come in with me?' The words were out before she had time to think.

'I prefer to bathe in private, thanks.'

Outside the hotel Adrian waved down a taxi and the next two hours were enchanting as they were driven to the places Laura had only heard of: Buckingham Palace; the Tower of London; Hyde Park. The taxi was dismissed at Madame Tussaud's and Laura gazed with awe at the wax replicas of so many famous and infamous people. She left the Chamber of Horrors quickly, hating it. Adrian laughed at her.

'I suppose you've seen it all before,' she said.

'Of course. My nurse took me everywhere, but it's wonderful seeing it again through your eyes. Like being a child again.'

'And you'd enjoy being a child again?'

Laura's words were rhetorical, but Adrian grew serious. 'Sometimes I think I would. Life was beautifully uncomplicated then. I had Mummy and my nurse. Even school was easy. Mummy wouldn't let me go away to a boarding school. Daddy was furious, but she was right. I couldn't have stood up to the life.' He shuddered. 'I've heard about it from friends. Too ghastly!'

'I would never want to experience my childhood again,' said Laura slowly.

'Wouldn't you, darling? That's sad.' Adrian whistled as a taxi drove past and they were whisked back to The Connaught where lunch was waiting. 'Steak, kidney and mushroom pie,' said Adrian without looking at a menu.

'How do you know? Did you order it?'

'No. They always serve it on Saturdays. I could tell you their luncheon for every day of the week. Such delicious nursery food.'

'Have I married a man or a boy?' asked Laura teasingly.

'A bit of each I think. What are you?'

'Just a woman, I believe. I can't find much child in me.'

'What a shame.' Adrian had stopped listening to her again and was waving discreetly to a couple on the other side of the restaurant.

The week in London was, for Laura, a mixture of pleasure and frustration. The days were filled with enjoyment. Kew Gardens, a proper look at the Tower, walks in the parks, and, oh, the shops! Harrods took her breath away with its grandeur and beauty and Bond Street, Oxford Street and Regent Street were pure pleasure. She bought an exercise book and jotted down details of clothes and hats and drew swift sketches. Adrian was patient and never seemed to mind waiting. He was co-operative when it came to her artistic work and she thanked heaven for it. It would make life easy.

In the evenings they went to a theatre, always in the best seats in the stalls, where Laura could display her slender arms and neck in her trousseau dresses. Adrian introduced her to a few people, but explained that almost everyone was out of town at this time of year.

'London looks pretty full to me,' said Laura, the next day, as they stood in a doorway to let a crowd of gesticulating tourists pass.

'You know what I mean,' said Adrian. 'All my friends are abroad, or enjoying themselves on their country estates. Tennis, swimming, that kind of thing. You'll meet them in time.'

Laura revelled in London entertainments. No wonder Rick was so impressed. They saw *The Squeaker*, a play by Edgar Wallace. 'It's his afternoon edition,' whispered Adrian as the curtain went up. Laura was too enthralled to wonder about his remark until the interval.

'It's just a joke,' Adrian explained. 'Mr Wallace writes so many books and things that *Punch* talks about them as if they were magazines or newspapers.'

Not so long ago Laura had never heard of *Punch*, but she now knew it to be a satirical magazine read by 'everybody who is anybody, my dear'.

She wept over a play about a shell-shocked soldier with amnesia, though Adrian said it was a bore and took her the next day to a farce about a frustrated spinster. But while Adrian laughed, Laura, recalling little Miss Morton and Aunty Mabel, didn't find it very funny. However, during supper in a small restaurant they could giggle together at their dissimilar reactions.

They went to see a western film and Noel Coward's *The Vortex*.

At supper that night Laura said, 'A friend of mine told me that on stage in *The Vortex* the hero says, "Mummy, will you give up lovers, if I give up drugs?", but a film censor changed it to, "Mummy, will you give up going to teas and dances if I give up cigarettes and aspirin?" Somehow that sounds rather ridiculous, don't you think?'

Adrian shrugged. 'I saw the play. I suppose Rick Merriman is the friend.'

'Yes.'

'Laura, you'll need to be careful in future about your acquaintances. It won't do to get too chummy with the lower orders – with more humble people. You'll be mixing in Bristol's top society, and London's, too, I dare say.'

'If I give up knowing the lower orders I shall have to stop seeing my family,' said Laura furiously.

'You know I didn't mean that. Of course one owes loyalty to one's chums and especially one's family, but there is such a thing as discretion. You must think of me, darling.'

Laura sighed. 'I'm sorry. I'll do a superb balancing act, you'll see.'

To round off the week they saw Charlie Chaplin in *The Gold Rush* and found no point of dissension there. They both loved it.

The days were absorbingly joyful. It was the nights that were bad. The routine never varied. Bath, bed, sleep, woken in the night, Adrian thrusting himself into her and getting his satisfaction fast, leaving her hurting, yet quivering with a tortured feeling of incompletion. So much for the pretty camiknickers, the silk stockings, the cheeky garters, the nightgowns she had chosen with such care, with such a thrill of anticipation. Two nights before they were due to leave London she felt so miserable after Adrian's assault – the word occurred horribly to her – that she couldn't sleep. She switched on her bedside lamp and actually began to riffle through Lady Troubridge's *The Book of Etiquette*. What do you do, your ladyship, when your husband seems to have about as much perception of a woman's needs as the stone lions in Trafalgar Square? There was nothing to tell her that, but by God she'd know how to address an ambassador and how to dress for court or send out an invitation to a tennis party.

The following night when Adrian woke her she yielded to his caresses, but when he made a move to roll on top of her, she twisted away.

'What's up?'

'Nothing. I'm not ready.'

'What!'

'Dearest Adrian, please give me a little longer. Be gentle. There has to be something better in lovemaking for a woman.'

She held her breath as she waited for his reaction. Would he sulk? He had a propensity for sulking. Would he get angry? That would be preferable. She was immeasurably relieved when he sighed and murmured, 'All right. I'll do my best.'

His wooing was short but just enough. His mouth moved over her face, down to the pulse in her neck, to her breasts where he licked each nipple, while his fingers caressed and stroked her until she felt she had become nothing but a vessel of supreme aching longing. Next time he moved above her she accepted him, but put her hands down to her stomach and forced him to enter carefully. It was still sore, but easier.

'Slowly, darling, slowly,' she murmured, and he obeyed, gasping out his own need.

She held him close as wave after wave of pleasure beat into her senses until her hunger was satisfied in an explosion of sensation. From a distance she heard Adrian cry out and her own half scream mingled. Tears forced themselves beneath the lids of her closed eyes and rolled down her cheeks.

'Laura! Are you all right?'

She opened her eyes. 'All right?' she breathed. 'Of course, my love.' She pulled his head down and kissed him. His face and neck were slippery with sweat. 'It was wonderful, wonderful.'

On their last night Adrian controlled himself again and once more she was able to share his passion with him.

'Life is going to be heaven,' she told him. 'Work that I enjoy through the days and you, beloved, at night. I'm so lucky.'

'So am I, though we won't always be able to make love.'

'No, there are a few days when we can't, but apart from that –'

'I mean when you get pregnant we shall have to stop.'

'Pregnant! You've not mentioned that before.'

'Well, it's hardly the thing to talk about before marriage, is it.'

'I suppose not. Wouldn't you rather wait a while to have a child? Surely we need to learn about one another first.'

'No!' The exclamation was so loud she jumped. 'No,' he continued more softly, 'I don't want to wait. Why should I? Surely you feel the same. Women want babies, don't they?'

'Of course they do and I shall love to give you one. You took me by surprise, that's all. I hadn't realised that a man could want a child so much.'

Laura lay awake that night feeling inexpressibly guilty. A week before her marriage she had visited a clinic which specialised in advising women about contraception and had been fitted for a vaginal cap, a device which would prevent Adrian's seed from reaching her womb. Before she considered childbed she must get her shops flourishing. She had meant to tell him, but there was an odd streak of prudery in him that had inhibited her. Now she was glad she had remained silent.

Before leaving London Laura telephoned Ralph, Nancy and Dolores who all assured her that everything was running smoothly even though she was absent. There was affectionate humour in Ralph's voice, soft assurance in Nancy's. Dolores, still unused to the telephone, shouted so loudly she made Laura's eardrum ring, but she said that business was steady and much as could be expected in August. The new shapes had arrived in the Kingswood branch, Miss Morton and the workforce were busy steaming felts ready for stitching and Noreen and an assistant were dealing with the straws.

'I'll have to move most of the work to the bigger workrooms

as soon as we get back,' she told Adrian. 'They're very cramped at the Redfield branch. I need a clerk, too.'

Adrian, for once, looked faintly bored with her business talk. 'I know nothing of office work and don't wish to.'

'Sorry, love. It all means such a lot to me. I've created it from nothing.'

Laura said no more. The balancing act between home and business might prove more trying than she had anticipated. Thank heaven she had made sure of not having a baby before she was ready. She was cheating Adrian and she felt guilty, but clearly he would never understand.

On Saturday they caught a train at Victoria Station on their way to Paris. The crossing was quite calm, but Laura's old enemy, travel-sickness, struck her. Adrian brought her a bowl with cool water and a sponge, then disappeared to find a stewardess.

'You'll be better soon, old girl,' he muttered as he left.

The stewardess smiled, 'Men are no good at all when it comes to this kind of thing, are they, dear?'

I knew one who was, thought Laura. The memory of Rick's tenderness disappeared in a fresh wave of nausea.

When the boat docked she recovered quickly and Adrian was apologetic. 'Sorry, old thing. I just hate illness. I always have.'

'It's not important. The stewardess was sweet.'

'Did you remember to tip her?'

'Of course.' Laura was indignant. 'I gave her five shillings. Was that too much?'

'Not enough for what she did. Ten would have been better.'

Laura sighed. 'I'll get it right, I promise, though ten shillings is such a lot of money. It's as much as some of my outworkers earn in a week.'

Adrian frowned. 'What's that got to do with it?'

'Nothing,' she said hastily, retreating before Adrian's frown.

Her love for him was more strongly rooted now his love-making made her happy. Surely he was everything a husband could be? She was lucky to have him.

348

Chapter Twenty-One

Paris was hot, but enchanting. Adrian derived as much pleasure as Laura from window shopping, seeing the names of the famous couturiers, milliners, jewellers.

'Anita's mother works for Patou,' said Laura. 'She's written to her about me.'

Madame Rodrigues lived at the top of an old house in a narrow street. The concierge greeted them suspiciously, then smilingly when Laura explained who they were.

'Madame – she expects you – please, up to ze top.'

Anita's mother was an older carbon copy of Anita, though her sleek dark hair owed much now to artifice. 'Welcome, come in, come in, *mes petits*. I delight in young lovers. A honeymoon. How well I recall my own. It is vivid in my mind as if it happened yesterday. We went to Cannes – it was summer – in those days *les Anglais* and *les Americains* visited Cannes only for the winter sun and it was quiet – so quiet, and so romantic . . .'

Adrian's attention was wandering. He got bored quickly, especially when people were talking of themselves. Madame Rodrigues was perceptive and stopped her reminiscent flow.

'Can I offer you cocktails? It is the cocktail hour – *oui*? Would you like a Chicago – an import from America – or perhaps Charlie's After-lunch invented right here in France by a barman of the Pavillon Henry IV at Saint Germain?'

'The French drink would be delightful,' said Adrian.

Madame Rodrigues smiled, showing white, even teeth. 'You choose well. Suitable for honeymooners – champagne, Cherry Rocher and Grand Marnier.'

They toasted one another in the knee-buckling mixture and

Madame filled their glasses again. 'Drink up, *ma petite*,' she urged Laura. 'This is the best time of your life. Enjoy it. My Anita writes all the time about you. She is a great admirer. She is so confident that your hats will become all the rage.'

Laura flushed with pleasure. 'I trust her judgement. She helps me to dress well. I value her advice.'

'Ah, she has the talent, though she learned much from me. I began life as an *arpette*, with Jacques Doucet, picking pins from the floor. The great Poiret came to work for him at the same time. He went on to greatness and I became his *deuxième main* – a second hand.' She sighed. 'Then along came Senor Rodrigues and whisked me to London. I was happy with him and I had my beloved Anita, but now he is gone – phut!' Madame made a gesture with finger and thumb. 'And I fly back to my beloved Paris and work for Monsieur Patou because I am enchanted by his designs and he has made me his *première main*. Such a life I lead. He is so droll, different from everyone. In 1924 he advertised for American mannequins. What a sensation! Paris talked of nothing else. Why not Parisians, it was asked? Monsieur was clever. He knew that people would talk about him. He looks first at ankles and feet. He will adore yours, Madame Mallender. He makes clothes for the young and the women who love the sports – he made the boy-girl look famous. He dresses Suzanne Lenglen, the champion of tennis. And famous actresses and duchesses and even princesses come to him for original clothes.'

'Most interesting,' said Adrian. Laura was embarrassed by his cool tone. 'Thank you for the cocktails. *Too* delicious, but we have a lot to do and it must be goodbye.'

'*Mais non*, my little Anita says you want to visit the salon of Monsieur Patou. I have arranged it.'

'You have?' Adrian snapped back to attention. 'When?'

'Tomorrow afternoon. It is a great honour. So it is only *au revoir*.'

Adrian was clearly delighted and once more Laura felt a surge of pleasure at his interest in her life, though she was puzzled by the way he vacillated.

'Why did you get bored with Madame Rodrigues?' she asked him as they strolled in the sun.

'She went on too long. I dislike women who gush. Thelma and Daphne are terribly gushing and I keep out of their way as much as possible. You never gush.'

Laura was pleased by the compliment.

For the visit to Patou Laura wore a simple pale-green frock, with a tiny yellow satin rose on her left hip. She chose her hat with great care, knowing Patou's flair for millinery, a green felt with a brim which just touched her face at the sides and shaded her eyes. It bore a single large yellow satin rose with a small, glowing crimson medallion at its centre. Her shoes, gloves and purse were of the same pale green as her dress. They met Madame Rodrigues at noon in the rue de Tivoli. She exclaimed at Laura's elegance, then guided them along the narrow little rue Saint Florentin until, on their left, they reached an eighteenth-century building with a double carriage arch. Set in one side was the single word: Patou. The inside was breathtaking with its huge salons leading one into another, romantically decorated, said Madame Rodrigues, by the architect Louise Sue, and the designer, André Mare. Accompanied by Madame Rodrigues they were allowed to wander almost everywhere. The atmosphere was permeated with couture: everyone breathed it, lived it, loved it. Laura was infected immediately and was greedy for knowledge. Of course, the new season's fashions were denied to her, but she saw at first hand the famous shining white satin sheaths, black slipper-satin petticoat chemises, beach clothes, bathing costumes in jersey with designs after the dominant cubist painters, guaranteed not to shrink, all original creations.

At the end of the visit they met Monsieur Patou himself. He was cooling down after one of his short, but violent rages. Neither Laura's schoolgirl nor Adrian's slightly more accomplished French were sufficient to understand his rapid speech.

Madame Rodrigues interpreted his diatribe. 'Poor man, he has been hours with a *grande horizontale*, trying to persuade her to conceal her fatness, while she wanted to wear red satin. Of course, Monsieur won, but it makes him very angry when a client won't obey him.'

Patou's more than six foot lean frame fitted elegantly into

one of his famous grey wood and cane chairs. On a pale-wood table was a bottle of wine and he poured some into four crystal glasses.

He spoke rapidly, gesturing towards Laura. 'Monsieur admires your hat,' said Madame Rodrigues. 'He wishes to know if it's your own invention.'

When Laura said that it was Monsieur Patou kissed the tips of his finger and thumb and blew the kiss to her.

'He likes the way you look. He says that you understand that clothes must not dominate the woman, but always the other way round. He tells you never to forget.'

Laura left reeling with the delight of it all, still glowing from the compliments from the great man himself.

'Madame has the figure and walk of a mannequin, and oh, such beautiful feet. I would like to employ her.'

Smilingly, Laura had thanked him. 'Perhaps one day I shall be as famous as Monsieur Patou himself.' He had laughed and called out and a little *grisette* came trotting forward holding a bottle which he presented to Laura. Without waiting for her reaction he rose and bowed, kissing her hand.

Outside Laura said in awe 'It's Joy! He's given me a bottle of Joy, one of his most famous scents and terribly expensive.'

'Good, I like scent.'

Laura asked, 'What is a *grande horizontale?*'

Adrian grinned. 'A prostitute, but one who makes a rich living from selected lovers.'

'Oh! Don't women like that care if people know what they do?'

'Not here. In London they are discreet. In Paris people accept it, though it isn't discussed in polite society, not publicly anyway. It's merely understood. I particularly loved the satin gowns, didn't you, Laura?'

'I loved it all, the clothes, hats, everything, and the décor – and the huge bevelled mirrors – one day I'll have a place like that.'

'I'm sure you will. I'll help choose the decorations. You can have a nursemaid so you won't be interrupted.'

Laura swallowed hard, then pointed to a woman across the

street. 'Look, Adrian,' she breathed, 'A Schiaparelli sweater. There's no mistaking it. Black and white. They've made her famous.'

'Don't point,' said Adrian mechanically, but he was diverted from the subject of babies and Laura breathed easily again. His repeated references to having a child disturbed her immensely. She couldn't face childbed yet, with the inevitable disturbance it would bring to her world. She had seen too much of bearing babies and its aftermath to have any illusions. She was as tender and womanly as anyone in her view of children and would like one of her own – one day – in her own time. She was not yet twenty, for God's sake! She should be firm and tell Adrian what she felt, but she held back. There was an undercurrent of something in him that she had only discovered since their marriage. She could not define it, but she sensed it was there and instinct warned her not to thwart him openly. She pushed it to the back of her mind. She was happy with her husband, she was young, healthy, energetic and imaginative. And the great Patou had liked her hat.

That night Adrian took her to the Casino de Paris to see Josephine Baker. The jazz music with its wailing saxophones reminded her of Rick and the time they had first met. It seemed an age ago, yet it was not so long. So much had happened. Laura forgot everything when the star appeared. Josephine Baker, coffee coloured, was all but naked in a fringe of feathers around her hips and sang in a high, little-girl voice, then danced without a trace of inhibition, with a blissful certainty of acceptance. The audience loved her and so did Laura, and when the singer and her band began to clown the laughter and applause was prolonged.

'She's wonderful,' Laura said. 'Just wonderful. Can we see her again tomorrow?'

'No, I think not. We'll visit the Revue Nègre at the Théâtre des Champs Élyseés.'

Laura didn't argue. She wanted to keep Adrian in a good mood. She felt guilty when they made love, supposing that every time he must be hoping she would conceive. Perhaps he'd promised Mummy to bring her home pregnant. And it would, of course, have to be a son.

353

One night Adrian didn't wake her. Laura already had her eyes open, waiting for the moment when his hands began to touch her body. She become aroused very quickly now for love and Adrian had seemed glad of that, though she couldn't be sure if his relief was for her or himself.

This night he slept peacefully. She moved restlessly, hoping to disturb him, then she began to touch his body. Her hand moved over him in long, caressing strokes and, when this had no effect, she touched him intimately. At last he stirred, awoke, and at once pushed her hand away. 'No!'

'Adrian! What – why – ?' she stammered.

She switched on the light and he half rose and stared at her as if she were a stranger.

'Don't look at me like that, Adrian. It frightens me.'

He sank back against the head of the bed. 'Sorry, love, you startled me.'

'You were deeply asleep. Were you having a bad dream? You stared at me as if you'd seen a ghost.'

'Did I, darling?' He reached for the cigarettes and lit one for each of them. She snuggled beside him. 'Sorry,' he said. 'I think all the excitement has caught up with me. I'm exhausted. Aren't you?'

'I don't know. No, I'm not, really. Perhaps it's because I'm used to working such long hours. And even if I was exhausted I should still want to love you. I do now.' She twisted round and kissed him. 'Make love to me.'

'I can't manage it every night.'

'Oh! Is that usual? I mean, do all men feel that way?'

'I can't answer for all men. I only know that I'm bloody tired and I wish you were.'

He was snappy and she felt suddenly vulnerable, exposed. 'Sorry. It's just that I love you.'

'And I love you, but don't forget a man does all the work making love. You just lie there.'

She felt as if he'd thrown ice-cold water over her and her desire died. 'Is that how you see me? Just lying there. Don't you sense the response in me?'

'I don't know. Yes, I suppose so. It's all so different for men.'

He took her cigarette away and stubbed both out. 'Let's go back to sleep. We have the rest of our lives. What's one night?'

'Nothing, sweetheart, nothing. Goodnight.'

He had already turned from her, his head was half buried in the pillow and he grunted. It took her a long time to get back to sleep.

The day after his rejection she had hurried about, sightseeing in a frenzy of activity, insisting on dancing until late.

The following day Adrian complained, 'You're like a whirling dervish. I'm going to take advantage of a continental custom and have a siesta.'

'With me?'

'No, not with you. I'll never get any sleep.' He was laughing at her, his brown eyes teasing, and she managed to laugh, too.

'I'll look at the shops,' she said.

'Don't you ever get bored?'

'Bored? In Paris? How could I?'

'I wonder if you'll ask that in five years' time. Now go and enjoy yourself and I'll sleep.'

The afternoon rest did him no good at all. He seemed less inclined than ever to make love and grew tetchy when she tried to persuade him. When she returned to England she'd pay another visit to the discreet clinic and ask a few questions about male and female love-making.

It wasn't until two nights later that Adrian made love to her again and Laura had begun to feel she was shamefully oversexed. She didn't know now how to react. Should she contain herself, hide some of her rapture? She was so tense her body resisted Adrian's advances and her eventual climax was disappointing. Adrian didn't notice.

The next day he took her to a little café on the left bank. They reached it through narrow cobbled streets that twisted among the hills and flights of stone steps. It had darned tablecloths and an elderly dog lay in one corner.

'This is a special part of Paris,' said Adrian. 'Everyone should pay a visit to the left bank to see the artists and writers. They come here from everywhere, but mostly from America. The franc's weak and the dollar strong, you see.'

They ordered simple, tasty food and drank a country wine. Adrian told her which of the diners were writers, and which were artists. She watched them, seeing their animated faces, listening to the jumble of their conversation. She felt relaxed.

'This is gorgeous,' she said. 'Better than anywhere. Why did you leave it so long?'

'Because, my dear, one tries to keep the best till last.' His eyes were constantly roving round the room and he looked up each time someone entered. 'Fascinating place, isn't it, I –' He stopped abruptly. 'Look at that man who just sat down outside. I think I know him.'

Laura glanced between the red-and-white checked curtains. Several groups were enjoying their food and wine in the sun. 'I can't tell –'

'Of course you can! The man with his back to us sitting alone – that's Rex, I'm sure it is.'

'Your best man? What's he doing here?'

The glance Adrian gave her was impatient, almost scornful, and she felt shaken by it. Without a word he rose and went outside. The man turned. It was Rex. He took Adrian's hand and shook it, then placed his other over it in a warm gesture of welcome. Adrian gesticulated towards the café and Rex turned and saw Laura. He waved. Adrian spoke rapidly to him, he shook his head at first, then got up and strolled inside, while Adrian hovered about him, reminding Laura of a dog frisking around its master after an absence.

'Laura,' said Rex equably, 'how delighted I am to see you. Please forgive me for intruding on your honeymoon. I tried to tell Adrian that it would be bad form, but he persuaded me to join you. However, I shall refuse unless I have your firm assurance that you want me.'

He was smiling and Laura smiled back. His eyes were charmingly diffident. She hurried to put him at his ease. 'Of course you must lunch with us. This is a wonderful place. It's our first visit, but I'm so interested in the left bank.'

'Are you, indeed? Adrian should have brought you here before and you must come back tonight and dine with me in my studio.'

Rex had a knack of putting people at their ease and he amused them with stories of his life in Paris. It was late afternoon when they parted.

'It's hardly worth going away,' said Adrian.

'I'm afraid you must,' replied Rex. 'I've work to do. A client expects to take a watercolour back to America with him. Don't come before nine.'

Adrian seemed restless and distant when they left the café. 'We'll walk by the Seine,' he said.

Laura, as usual, fell in with his plans. She was beginning to comprehend that Adrian's mild manners concealed a will as strong as his mother's and if he was thwarted he brooded and sulked. Freda was the only one in Laura's family who shared this trait and Laura had never been able to bear it. Thoughts of Freda brought memories of Joyce. She mustn't allow herself to dwell on her sister's miserable death. She would always mourn her in her heart, but she had to fight on. But pity for Freda flooded through her.

'What's up?' demanded Adrian. 'You look bloody miserable. Don't you want to go to Rex's for dinner?'

'Of course I do. I was just thinking of Joyce.'

'That's not a very good idea on our honeymoon. Really, darling, you must push it out of your head. After all, as Mummy said, it's not as if she'd ever have been any use in the world.'

Laura was filled with cold rage. She stared at him. 'Don't ever say that to me again. Never, do you understand?'

He capitulated. 'No need to get so touchy.'

He had given way, but Laura felt no sense of satisfaction. Joyce's death had no meaning for him at all, any more than it had for his mother.

To visit Rex she wore a bronze crêpe de Chine dress with bronze earrings and a brown velvet wrap. When he opened the door a strong smell of turpentine and oil was wafted out.

Adrian sniffed it like a dog who scents a meal. 'Delicious,' he breathed. 'How I adore painting smells.'

Rex wore wide-legged trousers and an open-necked shirt. 'You're elegant, but so formal,' he said to Laura.

'I didn't know –'

'Adrian did. He knows we never dress for dinner here.'

Adrian was in a fawn summer suit with a yellow shirt and cravat. He said, 'Sorry, old girl, I didn't notice what you had on. Anyway, it doesn't matter. If she gets paint on her she's got plenty more clothes.'

For a moment Laura fumed with anger. It had taken the combined skills of herself, Miss Morton and Noreen, and Anita to get her trousseau together. They'd repaired damaged goods, added interesting ornaments to hide flaws, working together in their few spare moments and still keeping up with their day-time tasks. Then she sagged inwardly. What use was there in resenting Adrian's remarks? He didn't know anything about the frenzied sewing and he would never discuss money with her, saying that he just didn't understand the stuff. 'I know how to spend it, that's all,' he had said early in their honey-moon and she, smiling indulgently, had not heard the alarm bell that sounded louder now.

Rex led the way through his studio to a room containing comfortable furniture and a dining area. Through the window Laura could see the darkening roofs and crooked old chimneys. 'It's lovely here,' she exclaimed.

'It is, isn't it?' Rex said, taking her wrap from her. 'I'm so glad you like it. Adrian doesn't.'

Laura turned in surprise to her husband. 'What's the matter with it?'

Adrian glared at Rex whose smile didn't waver. 'I was disappointed when he decided to move from London to Paris,' he said. 'The place is all right.'

'Thanks,' said Rex laconically, and Adrian's face set in the mutinous lines that Laura hated.

Rex ignored him completely and looked at a half-open door through which drifted delicious aromas of food. He called, 'Pierre, bring in the wine.'

'*Bien sûr*, monsieur.'

A tray of wine and glasses was carried in by a boy of about sixteen. His fair hair was long and brushed the collar of his striped cotton jumper. He smiled shyly at Adrian and Laura. His teeth were white against his perfect sun-tanned skin and his eyes deep blue. He was the most handsome youth Laura had ever seen and she watched him in fascination as he poured three glasses of wine and returned to the kitchen, muttering something to Rex as he went.

'Pierre says he needs help,' said Rex. 'Aren't his looks heavenly? I sometimes use him for female poses as well as male. Make yourselves at home, friends.'

Laura sat on the window seat. 'Come and look at the wonderful view, darling.'

'To hell with it! I've seen it before!'

Laura looked round in surprise. Adrian's eyebrows were knitted with his frown. 'Adrian! What's the matter?'

'I wish we hadn't come. We'd have done much better to dine in a restaurant alone.' He drew a deep breath. 'We shan't have much time alone together when we get back to Bristol. You'll be working all hours, I suppose.'

Laura jumped up and went to him. 'Oh, darling, that's the first time you've said anything like that. Will you really miss me?'

'Of course.'

Laura kissed him. 'I knew this marriage was right, even though Anita was dubious.' She mentally cursed herself; she'd made him angry again.

'Have you been discussing me with her?'

'No, no, darling. Please – she seems to be against marriage to anyone.'

'She hates me.'

'No, you're mistaken. She wished us well.'

'Wished you well, more like. Not me. She wouldn't care if I dropped dead tomorrow. Neither would anyone else. Except Mummy. She'd weep for me.'

'Adrian! What a terrible thing to say. If anything happened to you I'd be devastated.'

He looked at her unseeingly for a moment, then rubbed a hand over his head. 'What am I burbling on about? I think excitement's overwhelmed me. My nurse always said I got jumpy before a birthday party. And this – our marriage, I mean – is a lot more than a party.'

Rex walked in and Laura wondered if he'd overheard them. His smile was still expansive. 'Come, *mes petits*, we eat in the kitchen. Pierre is fraught with impatience. The omelettes will be ready in one minute from now. We musn't keep him waiting.'

Pierre cooked perfect omelettes which he served with a pale-gold, cold white wine, fussing round the diners until he was satisfied they had everything they needed before he joined them. Laura complimented him on his cooking, but he just smiled and shook his head at her. Rex said something rapidly in French to him which made him smile again shyly.

'He speaks only his native language,' Rex said. 'He's delighted by your compliment.'

Delicious bread and a variety of cheeses were served with more wine, and coffee. They lit cigarettes and Laura felt replete and content and almost wished she could lead such a life as this for ever. Pierre refused any help with the clearing up and she heard him singing as he clattered dishes. Her mind drifted as Adrian and Rex talked about mutual friends.

She was brought back to reality when Adrian asked, 'What time does Pierre leave?'

'Oh, my dear chap, he doesn't.'

'But you've only one bedroom!'

Rex laughed. 'Pierre curls up anywhere like a dog. Actually he lies on the couch here. It's luxury for him. When I found him he was practically living on the streets. He's only just sixteen, you know, I can't kick him out at night. Besides, he's very useful.'

They left at almost midnight. Tomorrow they were travelling home. Now the advent of Mallender House was close Laura wished desperately they were returning to her flat over the Park Street shop. The workmen had almost finished on her wedding day and already it had looked light and attractive.

'When shall we see you again?' Adrian asked Rex who shrugged and spread his hands in a Gallic gesture.

'Who knows, my dear chap. I'll probably be in London fairly soon. You'll always be welcome here, and you, too, Laura, my dear.'

'Thank you,' said Laura, smiling. She liked him. He was firm and knew what he wanted and how to get it. 'It's been a lovely evening, Rex. Please visit us when you're in England.' She stopped abruptly, remembering that she would be living in Adrian's home.

Rex lifted her hand to his lips and pressed a kiss on it. 'A pleasure and an honour to have you, Laura. I look forward to our next meeting.'

As Adrian and Laura began the walk back to the hotel Adrian said, 'Damn! I've left my cigarette case behind. Stroll on slowly, darling, I'll catch you up.'

'Don't leave me –'

Adrian had gone. She wandered on, pausing often to look at paintings displayed in lighted windows, dreamily listening to the animated conversations between men and women inside and outside the many cafés which had their doors thrown open in the heat. At one small tree-shaded square she paused, not quite sure of her way, and a man approached her and spoke to her, lifting his hat.

She smiled and shook her head. 'I don't speak French. At least, not very well.'

'And I do not speak English well, mademoiselle. It need not matter.'

Laura flushed. There was no mistaking the way he was looking her up and down. He thought she was selling herself.

She held out her hand with its new wedding and engagement rings. 'I am married, monsieur. *Je suis* –' she was searching for the word married, but her mind went blank as the man seized her hand. '*Tres jolie*'. He turned to a group of men outside a café and said something which made them laugh. Then he stepped closer to her. A woman strolled by, her face heavily made-up, and scowled and Laura realised that she was one of the prostitutes who ranged Montparnasse and presumably assumed Laura to be trespassing on her territory. Where was Adrian? To her immense relief he appeared, hurrying towards her, and the stranger dropped her hand hastily.

'What took you so long, Adrian? That man –'

'My case had slipped down the side of the couch,' said Adrian. He was offhand and gloomy.

Laura felt suddenly furious. 'You've been here before. You must have known I might be molested if I walked about alone at this time of night.'

'What? Was that man annoying you? Well, he's gone now.'

'Not a word of apology?' demanded Laura. 'Not a single word? Anything could have happened to me.'

'Now you're being melodramatic. You must learn to curb yourself.'

Laura was silent, but it took her the remainder of the walk to regain her balance. Adrian made no attempt to break her silence. She thought he hadn't really noticed it.

As the train drew near to Bristol Laura felt she could hardly wait to get back to her shops. She wondered if her honeymoon would be counted as a good one. How could she tell? She had never heard one discussed. She was slightly sad as she recalled the past two weeks. There had been moments of great joy, but too often she had been puzzled and made unhappy by her husband's moody nature. Thank God she had work to do and wasn't expected to live a life of idle boredom.

Late that night they were received in the hall of Adrian's home by Lady Mallender, the butler and a couple of maids who welcomed them.

'This is Stevens,' said Lady Mallender, introducing the taller of the two maids. 'She will be responsible for keeping your room clean. If you need any little service, Laura, you may call on her. Or, of course, on Renton.'

Stevens dropped a curtsey which embarrassed Laura. She had no problem when it came to dealing with her workforce. She knew exactly where she was with them, but Stevens, slender and attractive, and so deferential, was going to be a different matter. As for telling the stately butler to do something – that seemed beyond her.

She had to admit that the bedroom was beautiful. Everything shone and sparkled with cleanliness and there was a vase of carnations, sweet peas and pink roses on the table.

'Oh, aren't they heavenly,' Laura exclaimed. 'How thoughtful of your mother.'

'Thoughtful?' Adrian sounded vague as he wandered around stopping to gaze at the paintings. 'I expect Stevens did the flowers.'

'Well, I think your mother must have told her which to use. They're the same as my wedding posy.'

'Are they?' he said distantly. 'What were they?'

Laura stared at the back of his head. 'If you look at the table, you'll see.'

'Don't get cross with me,' said Adrian coolly. He threw himself into a chair and stared moodily at the fire that gave out a welcome warmth. It was only the end of August after a good summer, but at night there was already an autumn chill in the air.

A small glass-topped oval table with a three-way mirror and a small gilt chair had been added to the room. Laura felt sure that Lady Mallender was trying to make her welcome.

'Are you happy to be home, Adrian?'

'Mmm. How about you?'

'I'm looking forward to beginning work.' She picked up the new number of *Vogue* which she now took regularly. 'Waists are rising, and here's a sweater by Schiaparelli, a *trompe l'oeil* –'

'That's a type of painting. It's got nothing to do with clothes.'

'Well, here's a picture – see for yourself – of Mrs Somerset Maugham wearing one.'

Adrian stared at the magazine in an almost hostile fashion, then became interested. 'I see! The scarf round her hips is an illusion, but there's a matching striped bow which is actually there. Clever.' He began to look through the pages. Laura felt irritable at him taking over the magazine, but controlled her impatience. Adrian in a good mood was so much better than in a sulky one. He'd been morose all the way home.

She slept well that night and when she went downstairs at seven, leaving Adrian asleep, she had to admit that it was pleasant to find a good breakfast awaiting her and Stevens ready to serve.

'Am I the only one up early?'

Stevens smiled. She really was pretty. 'Yes, ma'am.'

'I must be making extra work for the staff.'

Stevens looked surprised. 'Not at all, ma'am. We're here to wait on you.'

Laura felt crestfallen and munched through a roll and marmalade.

Stevens said, 'If Sir Hugo was home he'd be up, too. He's gone back to Scotland.' She was smiling in a definitely friendly way. Laura smiled back. She had no idea if she should and at that moment she didn't care. She supposed she must make time to read the book of etiquette. It wouldn't do to make mistakes in public. She had no wish to let Adrian down.

'Is Miss Nancy still asleep, too?' she asked.

'Gracious no, ma'am. She's been living in the flat over the Park Street shop ever since you left.'

'What? Are you sure?'

'Yes, ma'am.' Stevens brought a fresh cup of tea. She coughed, 'Her ladyship wasn't altogether pleased, but it seems there was a problem and Miss Nancy said someone you could rely on had to be there.'

'I wonder what went wrong. I phoned from London. Nobody said anything to me.'

Laura was really musing aloud, but Stevens said, 'No ma'am. They didn't want to upset you on your honeymoon.'

'I see.'

Again Laura felt lost. Should she have reprimanded a servant for gossiping?

'I hope you won't object to my saying so, Mrs Mallender, but I've been to look at your shops and I think your hats are just beautiful.'

Laura smiled. 'Thank you.'

She left the Mallender house thankfully, yet somewhat cheered to know she had two allies in Nancy and Stevens. How ridiculous she was being. It sounded as if she was fighting a war. She took a taxi straight to the Park Street branch, let herself in and called Nancy who came running down the stairs.

'Welcome back, Laura. Was Paris wonderful?'

'Absolutely! But why are you here? What happened to Dolores?'

Nancy led the way upstairs and talked over her shoulder. 'Poor Noreen just couldn't cope with running the Redfield shop so Dolores went there to sort things out and I took over here.'

'That was kind of you. I do appreciate it. Is everything going smoothly now?'

Nancy pushed open the door to the flat and Laura looked round delightedly. 'They've finished. It's beautiful. Just as I pictured it. I've disturbed you at breakfast.'

'That doesn't matter. Sit down and have a cup of coffee and talk to me, please. Oh, Laura, I've felt so happy here on my own. I wish –' Nancy stopped, flushing. 'Tell me about Paris.'

'It was marvellous. And so was London. We went to theatres in both cities. I've only ever seen pantomimes before and very few of them. And I actually met Monsieur Patou. You look different, Nancy.'

'Do I? Are you surprised? For two whole weeks I've been living – actually living – as opposed to existing in the ghastly social round. Oh, how I hate it! Now I'll have to go back.'

'I'm sorry. I would love to keep you on, but I can't offer suitable wages.'

'Do you mean that? I wouldn't mind working for nothing. My grandmother left me some money. It brings in enough to buy my food and pay a share towards the fuel bills. Oh, Laura, if only you'd let me work for you –' Nancy clasped her hands, her fair skin rosy, her blue eyes sparkling with hope.

Laura poured herself a fresh coffee. 'That wouldn't be fair to you. You're supposed to circulate and find yourself a husband.'

'It's degrading! It's like being trotted out at a livestock show. You met Adrian through your work. That could happen to me, you know.' There was an almost exultant note in her voice. 'Oh, Laura, damn being fair! Daddy wouldn't object, I'm sure. Mummy might be a bit sticky, but she can't lock me in my room.'

'Wouldn't life be rather a misery if you defied her?'

'I'm used to that! I don't suit her idea of a daughter. I never have.'

'But if I make her cross Adrian won't like it.'

'Oh, darling, how selfish of me! I can't expect you to put up with Mummy's displeasure, or Adrian's.' Nancy looked regretfully around. 'It's so cosy here, Laura. I've just adored it.'

It really is a nice place, thought Laura. She and Adrian could have been happy here. There were two rooms, a box room big enough for a small spare bed, a kitchen and lavatory. It should be enough for anyone, except perhaps a member of the pampered rich.

'You could visit as often as you like, Nancy, and give us the benefit of your ideas.'

'I don't have ideas. I'm not the type. I just love being here.'

'How did you get round your mother to let you come?'

'Er, I didn't exactly. As soon as I heard that Dolores needed help I announced I was going to keep an eye on the Park Street shop for you.'

'And just how did you happen to get the news?' Laura asked, but her tone was equable and Nancy smiled.

'I just happened to drop into Ralph's shop and he told me. When I said I would help out he was really pleased. He trusts me, as I do him.'

'I see.' Laura looked at Nancy's animated face and wondered if her bubbling happiness was entirely on account of her brief break into independence. She and Ralph got along very well indeed.

'Mummy almost had a fit and phoned Daddy,' said Nancy, 'but he said I could go ahead. I think they had a row about it and I felt conscience-stricken, but Laura, I have to live my own life sometime. I just have to.'

'I quite agree,' said Laura quietly. She wondered if she was about to be embroiled in a tussle between Nancy and her mother. If she was she would back Nancy, no matter what the consequences. She had been too long a prisoner of Granma to back away from such a challenge.

Nancy bit into a roll with butter and honey.

'I'm grateful to you,' said Laura gently, 'but it wasn't strictly necessary for you to sleep here, was it?'

'No, I know. Oh, darling, don't be cross with me. I so wanted to get away from home for a little while.'

'I'm not cross. How could I be? Weren't you lonely here? Park Street at night isn't exactly a hive of activity.'

'Ralph came in every evening to see if I was well. And Dolores kept an eye on me. She thinks you're the most wonderful person on earth. You should hear the way she talks about you.'

'Best not. I might get conceited.' Laura dipped a teaspoon in the honey pot and licked it. 'Mmm, delicious. Don't you adore honey?'

'Don't change the subject, Laura. Miss Morton came a couple of times with Dolores and she sings your praises, too.'

'It must have sounded like a revivalist meeting,' said Laura drily.

Nancy grinned. 'Not quite, though the paean of praise got louder when I joined in. Oh, Laura, how glad I am that you've married Adrian. I always wanted a sister just like you.'

'Happy to fill the bill.'

There was a long ring on the doorbell and Nancy's eyes lit up and she hurried downstairs, returning with Ralph who looked more attractive than ever. Prosperity was doing wonders for him. He looked the perfect young business man, though he still kept a pair of overalls to use for restoration work and rooting about in dusty old houses and junk shops, always searching for a good piece of antiquity.

Laura's heart jumped when she saw Ralph and Nancy together. They were in love. Their eyes met often and as Nancy handed Ralph a cup of coffee their hands touched and stayed together a fraction longer than necessary. Nancy went to the kitchen and returned with cereal, hot toast and marmalade. 'Ralph's been having his breakfast here,' she explained. 'I hope that was in order.'

'Of course. Far be it from me to see my brother starve – or keep you two apart.'

Nancy blushed. Ralph ate cereal in a dedicated fashion though the tips of his ears were pink. Laura stopped her teasing. Ralph was a deeply thoughtful man who didn't make big decisions in a hurry. But at least he made them. At least he would be willing to commit himself to a lasting relationship. Unlike Rick.

'How's Rick these days?' she asked, surprising herself. She

hadn't meant to mention his name. The words had just slipped out.

'All right, I think,' said Ralph. 'He's been in London for about a month, but he's due back next weekend. Jack keeps me up-to-date.'

'And Enid?'

'Perfectly well. The midwife says the baby's kicking like a footballer.'

'I'll visit them all during the week. Nancy, could you stay for today? I must check on the other shops.'

'Delighted, darling.'

Laura left Ralph finishing his breakfast and borrowed Nancy's almost brand-new Austin Seven to drive to Redfield. It was five to nine and Dolores was preparing to open up.

'Welcome home, Laura!' She yelled up to the workroom and Miss Morton, Noreen and the others came clattering down the stairs, surrounding Laura with smiles and questions about London and Paris.

'All in good time,' she said, laughing.

'Iris has done splendidly,' said Miss Morton. 'And Dolores has driven about to make sure everything was running smoothly.'

Laura gave Dolores a warm smile. 'Thanks, love. I knew I could depend on you.' Dolores looked almost as if she might weep and Laura said hastily, 'I see you've got the new autumn hats well displayed. Do you like the wider brims and the face-hugging shape? I had a good look round at the Paris fashions and we're on the right track. I'll come back later and get up to the workroom.'

Iris was proud of herself as she showed Laura the figures. 'We made twelve pounds profit the first week and fourteen the second. The shop is ever so popular. I've taken orders for seven specially decorated hats, too. And I hope you don't mind, Laura, but a traveller came round showin' some pretty scarves and I ordered a dozen. This is a sample.' She held out a long silky scarf of mingled red, white and yellow. 'He said bolder colours are all the thing and it's the fashion now to sew a scarf to the neck of a dress, though I don't know if that's true.'

'It is.' Laura took the scarf and slid it through her fingers. 'Artificial silk – very pretty. How much are they?'

'They should retail at one and sixpence each and I've got them for five and six a dozen. They should be six shillings, but the traveller said I'd save sixpence if I ordered a whole dozen.'

The scarves were good value and Laura smiled at her anxious sister. 'That's good, dear. We'll make a little extra profit there. And the price is exactly right for our customers.'

'Mr Arnold – that's the traveller – said we should stock turbans for sporty women, but I told him that they were a summer line – at least in Kingswood. I dare say your posh customers will wear them to play tennis and things abroad in the winter, won't they Laura? He tried to sell me some fur tippets, but I said he must see you about them, too.'

'You've done really well, Iris.'

'Dolores helped me, but I couldn't get in touch with her about the scarves.'

'The telephone will be installed here at the end of this week. Then we can all keep in touch.'

'That's good, though I wonder how I'll get on with it. I've never spoken on one.'

'There's nothing to it.'

'It made Noreen hysterical and she said she couldn't go on.'

'But she spoke to me when I called from London.'

'I know and it upset her. She's refused to touch a telephone since.'

'What? No one told me that.'

Iris put her hand over her mouth in a familiar little-girl gesture. 'Drat my silly tongue. Dolores told me not to worry you with trivial things.'

'Don't fret. Noreen's far too valuable in the workroom for me to want to lose her. You've all done splendidly between you.'

Laura slipped happily and easily back into her working routine. She might never have been away if it were not for returning to the Mallender house and sleeping with Adrian. And it was only sleeping, most of the time. His inclination to make love grew weaker, while hers grew stronger. The only antidote to her terrible frustration was to work like a demon. She tried to discuss her needs with him, but he refused to speak to her on the subject. She grew angry and that night he drank more than usual and made love to her quickly and without finesse. She felt cheated, despoiled. What was the matter with her that her husband could only make love when his senses were a little deadened by drink?

Lady Mallender treated her with cool courtesy, but as she treated Nancy in exactly the same way Laura assumed it was her normal behaviour. With Adrian she was different; she could not hide her adoration.

After arriving home unavoidably late for dinner on the third consecutive night and receiving a reprimand, Laura announced that she would dine in her own flat. Lady Mallender set her lips angrily and Nancy looked stricken. Adrian simply accepted her decision.

The winter parties and dances began and invitations poured into the house. 'We shan't be able to accept them all, of course,' said her ladyship, 'but we must attend a selected few. I shall let you know when you are needed, Laura.' Laura thought she sounded as if she was speaking to Stevens. She shrugged. The shops were thriving, she was making more money, gaining more of Bristol's well-heeled customers. She was a success and she intended to keep climbing. She would attend as many society functions as she could for Adrian's sake, though sometimes she wondered whether he cared if she was with him or not. He'd changed so much since their marriage he often seemed like a different person altogether. The tenderness of their courting days was only a memory. When she tried to revive it he grew impatient, then annoyed. She had grasped at the love she'd so longed for and it had faded like an illusion.

'Why did you marry me?' she asked bitterly one night after he'd turned his back on her again.

'Because I thought we'd be happy,' snapped Adrian.

'And you're not?'

'I would be if you'd stop making your everlasting demands.

Damn it, Laura, you were fun when we just went out together. Can't we be friends again?'

'Friends? Sometimes you look at me as if you dislike me.'

'That's nonsense. Go to sleep.'

He refused to speak again.

Chapter Twenty-Two

Sir Hugo returned home one evening two weeks later. He walked into the drawing room looking gloomy. His wife greeted him laconically. 'Back so soon, dear? I hope you enjoyed yourself.'

'Not much. Shooting was bloody abysmal.' He smiled at Nancy then looked without enthusiasm at his son. 'You're back, too, I see. How was Paris?'

'Lovely, as always, Daddy.'

'And you?' Sir Hugo demanded of Laura. 'I believe it was your first visit.'

'My first to London, too. I loved both cities.' Sir Hugo continued to stare at Laura from beneath frowning brows and she felt that more was expected of her. She said nervously, 'A friend of mine arranged for us to visit the great designer, Monsieur Patou. We were thrilled, weren't we, Adrian?'

Adrian grunted his agreement and Sir Hugo's frown grew fiercer. Laura stumbled on, wishing Adrian would help. 'Adrian showed me lots of beautiful things in Paris. We went to theatres. And right at the end I was able to meet an artist in his studio on the left bank.'

'Ah! Rex Lorimer.'

'Yes, of course, you know him. His home is so attractive. He has a studio, a living room and a bedroom and –' Laura stopped. She couldn't continue to ramble beneath the acerbic gaze of her father-in-law. 'Well, it was all very nice,' she finished.

'I see,' said Sir Hugo, and disappeared behind *The Times*.

Lady Mallender smiled a tight smile, but her eyes held annoyance. She said to Laura, 'My husband is somewhat cross because his shooting was interrupted.'

The newspaper was slapped down. 'I am no such thing. I shall read in my room. There is clearly not going to be any peace here.' He flung Laura a final look which held more than a little disgust and marched out. They heard him stamping along the hall to his library.

Lady Mallender's smile reminded Laura of the crocodile's in *Peter Pan*. She tutted. 'Now he'll be in a foul mood for the rest of the week.'

'When is he anything else while I'm around?' drawled Adrian.

Nancy had remained silent, but now she said, 'Mummy, it might have been better if you had allowed Laura to live in her flat.'

'Mind your own business!' snapped Adrian.

'I trust you are not suggesting, Nancy, that my son should be turned out of his own home because his father decided to be cantankerous.'

For the first time Laura saw Nancy look angry. She opened her mouth, made as if to speak, then closed it, and turned away. Laura was sure she was hiding eyes that were bright with tears.

The following morning Laura picked up her folio of drawings and left the house thankfully, feeling sorry for Nancy who had to remain behind. She could have saved her pity. As she parked her car and climbed out, Nancy's drew up beside her.

'I've escaped,' she said. 'Darling, please let me stay with you today?'

Laura nodded. To hell with her ladyship. Nancy needed relief. She happily took her place in the shop, leaving Laura free to go upstairs to the workroom. The builders had used wood and glass to partition off a small office with a drawing board and desk for her and she sat down and got on with next year's spring creations. The winter hats were already being made. Next Sunday Ralph was going to move the equipment needed for the felt hats to Park Street, leaving the Redfield place free for making the straws. Every entry point for the rats had been blocked and the rat-catcher made regular visits. Laura shuddered still when she recalled the horror of that night.

Anita poked her head round the door. She had been in London for two weeks attending trade shows, prowling around the big stores.

'Welcome home to the happy bride,' she said, failing to keep a sardonic tone from her voice.

Laura was used to her now and just grinned.

'You don't exactly look like a blissful bride,' observed Anita, sitting on the edge of the desk and swinging her long, silk-clad legs.

Damn, thought Laura. Anita was altogether too observant and always said exactly what she thought. 'I'm fine,' she lied. 'I'm catching up on work. Two weeks are a long time to miss out on designing.'

'*Maman* said you got to see Patou. Apparently you made a hit with the great man. He's mentioned you since. He took a fancy to your narrow feet. He judges everyone by feet. An odd creature in many ways.'

'But charming.'

'Oh, he's that all right. There are many women who can tell you so. He goes through lovers like a hot knife through butter.'

Laura shrugged. The deeper she got into the fashion business the less surprised she was at its vagaries. The whole world must be filled with odd facts she'd never encountered in her sheltered upbringing. Who cared? She would push steadfastly ahead in spite of those around her.

'What's up, *ma petite*?' Anita's voice was surprisingly sympathetic.

'Nothing, thanks.'

'Sorry you got married?'

'For God's sake, leave it alone.'

'Righto.' Anita never took offence. She looked at Laura's drawings. 'You're right on line for the winter season. Congratulations. You have what *Maman* calls the perception. I have it, too, which is why my shop's a success. Poor *Maman* doesn't have it, but she was acute enough to know it early on and made her living in the world she loves in a different way. What theme are you using this time?'

'Adrian took me to the art galleries in Paris and I saw pictures of the French Impressionists for the first time. I'm going to try to reproduce the atmosphere of light for spring, using their colours as much as possible. I particularly like Renoir with his soft hues against black. I shall use spring greens, yellows and violets.'

'Sounds like a good idea, but will the demand for stronger colours have died?'

'Oh, I shall make sure I have some of those, too, but they won't suit all types of skin.'

Anita nodded. 'Waists are rising ever higher. Next year, or maybe the one after, I think they could be back in their proper place. Then perhaps hats will get bigger.' She paused. 'Laura, you're looking tired. You can't go on doing all the designs yourself. Have you thought of engaging an assistant?'

'I've thought of it, but where can I find a designer?'

'In the art schools. Go and look at some of the final year students' work. See if there's anything you like. Find out if anyone would welcome a career in fashion.'

'That's a good idea. Meanwhile Noreen is proving excellent at thinking up hats for the lower end of the market. When I say lower, I *only* mean as regards income.'

Anita's eyebrows rose. 'You sound pretty miffed. Life with the Mallenders not proving cosy?'

'Are you laughing at me?'

'Not at all. I don't think they're at all funny. Does Adrian protect you?'

Laura paused. She felt disinclined to discuss Adrian. She said slowly, 'It's not a question of protection. I just don't fit in. I think Sir Hugo hates me. Why, I can't imagine. Perhaps it's his way. He's really bad-tempered, except with Nancy.' Then she put an end to the painful subject by throwing down her pencil and leaning back, flexing her shoulders. 'Coffee?'

'Of course. And a cigarette.'

'Upstairs then. Smoking is forbidden here.'

'I know. If only one could stop the silly cows of customers lighting up in the shop. If I didn't cover the clothes with cellophane bags they'd need fumigating.'

Laura climbed the stairs to her flat. 'They all smoke so much they probably expect everything to smell of tobacco. Anyway, who are we to talk?'

'Just the bloody owners, that's all. The ones who do all the work and take all the knocks so that society bitches can flaunt themselves at Ascot, or the boat race, or Henley, or some damn great ball in London, where they talk of their little dress-designer, or their little milliner. Haven't you heard them?'

'Not yet, but I've a nasty feeling I'm about to. Mother-in-law informed me that I should soon have to go out and about in society.'

'God! Poor you!'

Laura put the kettle on to boil. 'Adrian said the Mallenders once kept a suite in the Connaught Hotel in London. I wonder why they stay so much in Bristol now.'

Anita shrugged. 'There's plenty going on here. I suppose they find that enough.'

Laura reluctantly left her desk at seven fifteen. She had promised to be at a dinner party that night given, said Lady Mallender, in honour of her marriage. She was met in the hall by Stevens who said anxiously, 'Thank goodness you're home, Mrs Mallender. Her ladyship has been having kittens wondering if you'd forgotten. I think she's been telephoning the shop for the past ten minutes.'

Laura hurried upstairs and met Lady Mallender's maid Gardner on the landing. Gardner definitely loathed her. She made no attempt to hide her black looks and frowns. Laura had given up trying to understand why. It seemed she had only to exist in this household to be disliked by some of its members.

'M'lady was wondering whether you'd forgotten the dinner party,' said Gardner, her voice bordering on insolence. 'I said you might not have since it's being given in honour of your marriage to Master Adrian.' Her voice softened as she spoke his name. Good God, surely she wasn't jealous? She must be fifty. 'M'lady suggested I might help you dress.'

'Stevens can do that.'

Gardner cast up her eyes in disgust. 'If you say so. She hasn't trained as a lady's maid, but I don't –' The rest of the sentence was muttered and Laura ignored it.

Stevens ran her bath and she stepped into the scented water and out into a large bath towel held by the maid. 'You're so thin!' Stevens exclaimed. 'Just right for the fashions, but I wonder how you stand up to all the work. And now you're going to be sociable, too.'

'It's all part of my life,' said Laura, patting Coty's foundation cream on to her fine skin. Increasingly she found Stevens a comfort and was beginning to treat her as much as a friend as an employee. She powdered her face, pencilled her lids and touched her eyelashes with brown, and painted her lips dark red to match her wine-red watered silk gown. Over her shoulders went a tiny pale-blue velvet cape fastened with a gold-coloured clip. Her red and gold earrings almost touched her shoulders and swung against her slender neck with every movement of her head. Her hair was brushed into a shining silk cap. Adrian had a dressing room next door and appeared in his evening suit.

She smiled at him. 'You look handsome, darling.' Now that she was ready she was actually looking forward to an evening not working.

'Do I?' Adrian spoke perfunctorily. 'And you're very fine. Is the gown one of Anita's?'

'Of course. I've promised to advertise her clothes and she's promised to wear my hats.'

'Good idea.' Adrian held out his arm and they went downstairs.

When Laura entered the drawing room she was surprised to find at least twenty guests who looked her up and down as if she had been a mannequin in one of her own shows. Some she had met either briefly with Adrian, or in the shop. Thelma, Daphne and Paul she knew and there was Poppy, Rick's girlfriend. She wondered if he'd ditched her by now. She returned look for look, smiling as graciously as she knew how and eyebrows which had been raised dropped. As she said to Anita later, 'I think some of them expected a char-woman in a wraparound apron and her husband's old cap on back to front.'

Anita replied languidly, 'Perhaps you should have appeared like that, darling. You might have set an entirely original fashion.'

Lady Mallender, in a grey gown which made her look singularly unattractive – she appeared to have no sense of colour at all – introduced Laura, her nose knifing the air as if to threaten any who behaved with the slightest sign of condescension to her daughter-in-law. No one did. Beneath that piercing gaze, no one dared.

Cocktails were served. 'So fashionable,' said Lady Mallender, 'but if anyone wants sherry do please say.'

The tray was proffered by Renton, while a nervous little maid trotted behind him with a tray of canapés.

Dinner was announced and they filed informally into the dining room, ladies first, gentlemen bringing up the rear. Paul Harrington was seated on Laura's right; on her left was a plump man who reminded her of Reggie Prewett. Except that Reggie would not be wearing a monocle and talking in an exaggeratedly upper-crust accent. Laura tried to imagine Reggie here and let out a small chuckle. Those cocktails had been strong. She glanced quickly at Paul who grinned sympathetically.

'Cocktails are more powerful than you'd suspect,' he smiled. 'They've got such innocuous names too: White Lady, Sidecar. One tends to forget that they contain quite lethal potions.'

Laura felt comfortable with Paul whose dark good looks and immense charm soothed her. 'I never once had an alcoholic drink until I was almost eighteen,' she confided.

'So late in life.'

'You're laughing at me!'

'No! Well, maybe, just a little. You're so sweet.'

She had read nothing in Lady Troubridge's book to tell her how to react to a compliment from a comparative stranger. She said, 'Thank you,' and was rewarded with a smile that showed Paul's teeth white against his continental tan and lit up his eyes. Yes, he certainly was attractive.

The soup was served and Sir Hugo tapped his sherry glass with a spoon. The party fell silent. 'This dinner, as you know, is the first we have given since the marriage of my son to Laura.' He rose and the others, except for Adrian and Laura (thank heaven now for Lady Troubridge!) followed and toasts to their happiness were drunk.

When they had settled again Paul said quietly, 'You looked surprised. Doesn't anyone confer with you on social engagements?'

'Not usually,' said Laura, 'though I knew about this one. I wasn't expecting Sir Hugo to propose a toast just then, that's all.' She paused. 'Actually it's my fault they don't always tell me things. I'm scarcely ever in the house. My work is increasing so much. I intend to enlarge my workforce, but I can't afford many new extra people – yet.'

Paul laughed outright. 'Yet! A woman of determination. And so young.'

'I know of women younger than me who are married with a baby.'

'An accomplishment scarcely difficult,' said Paul drily.

She laughed again. She was reminded that Adrian and she almost never shared a joke.

Adrian had Lady Marjorie on one side, slurping soup as fast as possible and downing a couple of sherries with it. On the other sat Nancy who was struggling to hide her boredom. Adrian's gaze flickered to Paul and back to his wife. He was scowling as he crumbled a bread roll on to his side plate.

When Renton made to serve Laura another glass of wine she shook her head and asked for water.

Course followed course.

Thelma's voice stabbed the air. 'Have any of you read *The Well of Loneliness*? What a lark. *Too*, too unkind of the Home Secretary to ban it.'

Sir Hugo asked, 'Is that the book by that wretched woman, Radclyffe Hall?'

'Yes, what did you think of it?'

'Think of it? I did not read it, miss, and neither should you.'

'Oh, but Sir Hugo,' pouted Poppy, 'we had to know what the fuss was all about.'

Lady Marjorie said through a mouthful of beef, 'That's the woman who dresses in men's clothes and wears her hair very short, isn't it? Peculiar creature. Prefers women to men.' She looked around. 'Not that she's got the monopoly on short hair. Excellent beef, Lady Mallender. I always said you have a fine cook.'

'No one's answered my question,' complained Thelma.

'We shall talk of something else, dear,' said Lady Mallender icily.

'We most certainly shall,' said Sir Hugo. 'I do not care to have my niece mention such a subject.' The look he turned on Thelma would have blistered Laura, but Thelma seemed oblivious.

'Righto, Uncle Hugo. How about our darling Prince of Wales? I hear he's going to tour Africa soon. A semi-private visit, so Lady Furness will no doubt join him.'

'The dear little Princess Elizabeth can already curtsey,' Lady Mallender informed her guests. 'Such a graceful, charming child and such wonderful parents. Never a breath of scandal about them.'

'And consequently tedious to Thelma,' whispered Paul in Laura's ear.

'She's got a mischievous tongue,' said Laura.

'She's a first-class, one-hundred-per-cent bitch,' said Paul. 'Watch out for her.'

The conversation had been successfully turned and Thelma sulked. After dinner the ladies retired to the drawing room.

'How's the shop going, Laura?' asked Lady Marjorie.

'Well, thank you. It's shops now. I've opened two more.'

'We're all so proud of her,' said Lady Mallender, honey in her voice.

'Times have changed,' said Mrs Charlton. She wore a brown crêpe de Chine dress and looked dismal in it. She was as colour-blind as her sister. 'In my youth ladies did not work in shops.'

'Good gracious, Clara!' exclaimed Lady Mallender loudly. 'That's a very old-fashioned notion. Lady Rhonnda is a company director, Lady Boot is said to be the driving force behind Boots the Chemist –'

'That's not the same as serving in a shop,' persisted Mrs Charlton. Her daughters giggled.

They need an etiquette book more than I do, thought Laura. She wished Paul were here to share the joke. Not long ago she would have cringed inwardly at such a conversation taking place about her. Now she found she didn't care much. Her shops were becoming the most important thing in her life and if any stupid women didn't like the fact she could go and jump in the Avon.

But Lady Mallender minded. 'Mrs Dudley Coats opened a scent and handbag shop in Davies Street – London, of course – and no one can say she isn't a member of top society. She didn't scorn to advise her customers.'

Mrs Charlton drew in her chin indignantly. She spoke in mellow tones, 'My dear Maud, I never meant to imply that there was anything disreputable in shop-keeping.'

Nancy said, her voice a little desperate, 'Who has seen the film *The Singing Fool*? An actor – Al Jolson – actually speaks and sings in it. His voice comes right out at you – it's quite amazing.'

Daphne yawned, 'Thelma and I have. It's been on in more than one place. We went to The Premier. *Too* priceless. It was afternoon and they served tea.'

'I was there, too,' put in Poppy. 'In the interval someone sang on the stage and there were some dancers.'

'And the manager gave us a little speech about how the arrival of the wonderful talking pictures would put an end to the silents.'

'It was the owner, Rick Merriman.' Poppy sounded irritable. 'Have you seen it, Mrs Charlton? You like the cinema, don't you?'

'I certainly do and I accompanied Thelma and Daphne. I am not altogether sure I cared for the noise. One shudders to imagine a full-length talking film.' She turned to Laura. 'How did your honeymoon go?'

Laura was aghast. No one in Mum and Dad's circle of friends would have asked such a question, at least not in quite so blatant a way. The men nudged and winked and laughed at one another. The women whispered secrets that made them giggle. That was all. 'Very well, thank you,' she answered, only a slight tremor in her voice betraying her agitation. Try as she might the fear that her marriage was a mistake plagued her. 'London and Paris were lovely.'

'Did you happen to bump into Rick Merriman in town?' asked Poppy. 'He's been there recently. I heard he'd got several acts at the Hammersmith Palace.'

'No. We went to theatres nearer the centre and we spent a lot of time in the art galleries. And I was able to wander round the marvellous shops and look at hundreds of fashions. Harrods is like a palace.' Who had said that to her? Rick.

'Not many husbands would want to spend time in fashion departments,' said Mrs Charlton.

'No,' agreed Laura. 'But Adrian is interested in my work.'

'How cosy,' said Thelma. 'I do hope my cousin squired you well. Did he enjoy his honeymoon, too?'

'Perhaps you had better ask him,' said Laura in such a frozen tone that even Thelma was taken aback.

There were male voices in the hall and Lady Mallender said, 'Ah, the gentlemen are joining us. I think we must have some music.'

The plump young man with the monocle came straight to Laura. 'I say, Mrs Mallender, that's an awfully jolly outfit you're wearing. I gather you're an expert at fashion.'

'Ladies', not men's.'

'Oh, no, I wouldn't for a moment dream – I mean we have men to tailor for us. But I know you design simply splendid hats. My mother and sisters all buy them. They're dying to know what you're like –' He stopped and his face became a fiery red.

Laura could have finished for him. What you're like in quality society. She could hear them, 'Does she use the correct cutlery? Does she know which glass to drink from?' 'You'll be able to tell them I don't eat my peas with a knife, won't you?' She said it so gently that it took a moment for it to sink in. He went even redder. 'Here, I say – I didn't mean – I think I'm wanted over there.' He scampered across the room and Laura smiled acerbically.

Paul spoke politely to one lady and another as he drifted to Laura's side where he overheard the end of the conversation. He took the vacant chair beside her. 'I fear you've upset poor Monty.'

'Good.'

Paul laughed. 'What an unexpected joy you are. Did you have a happy half hour with the tabbies?'

'My lips are sealed,' said Laura.

'Fair enough. I think our hostess is signalling to you.'

Laura sighed. 'She wants me to play the piano. I'm not very good.'

Unexpectedly Paul followed her. 'I'll sing. I'm not very good either. Between us we might make a splendid whole.'

Laura laughed. She played *Only a Rose* from *The Desert Song* and managed to get her fingers round the faster tempo of *Fascinatin' Rhythm*. Paul sang the first song with her, but when she skipped into the syncopated beat Thelma and Daphne tripped across and leaned on the piano to join in.

Sir Hugo boomed, 'Must you play that ghastly stuff? Give us a good old tune. Adrian, go and join your wife.' It was an order, not a request. Adrian walked silently across the room.

Laura was so surprised by Sir Hugo's sudden attention she wavered and forgot everything she knew.

'Stand up,' said Adrian brusquely. He opened the piano stool and produced a pile of sheet music. 'Here, try *Love's Old Sweet Song*.'

When Laura had thankfully left the piano Daphne and Thelma played a duet and sang *Yes, Sir, That's My Baby* in little-girl voices. Laura could hear Sir Hugo's snorts clear across the large drawing room.

The party broke up at eleven, to Laura's deep relief. She could get a decent night's sleep and be ready early for work tomorrow. She had a bath and returned to the bedroom. Adrian was sitting, still dressed, in an easy chair.

'You were very friendly with Paul Harrington tonight.'

'He was a guest. And I like him.'

'You don't have to spend the entire evening clinging to him.'

'I did no such thing!' Laura was angry. 'Don't tell me you're jealous,' she taunted.

'Of him? I should say not.'

'Then what's up with you?'

'I don't want my wife getting so friendly with another man.'

Laura hesitated, irresolute, praying for the inspiration to do the right thing. She walked to her husband and knelt in front of him. The firelight flickered on his face and gleamed in his brown hair. 'Sorry, darling. I didn't think I was flirting, but perhaps it looked that way.'

'It's humiliating for a man to know that people are sniggering about him and his wife.'

'Who did the sniggering? Don't tell me. Your horrible cousins. Someone should have drowned them at birth.'

Adrian laughed. 'That's what Daddy says and for once I agree with him. You don't get on awfully well with him, do you?'

Laura shook her head. 'It isn't my fault. I don't know what he's got against me. He's not very nice to you either. It isn't as if he opposed our marriage, yet he treats me as an interloper.'

'You're exaggerating.'

Laura let the remark go. She had more important matters on her mind. 'Darling, don't you think we might do better if we lived in our own place in Park Street?'

'Oh, don't start that again! This is my home. I'm happy here and comfortable. You'd never have time to look after me properly.'

'Oh, Adrian, what's happening to us? We've had such a short time together, but –'

'But what?'

'Our marriage seems wrong – incomplete. I do love you, I do. I want you to love me – in *every* way.'

'That again! You're obsessed by sex.'

'I'm not. I just want to feel close to you.'

'We make love.'

'But so seldom.'

Adrian stared down at her. 'Why don't we do it now?'

There was about as much romance in his manner as there was in a factory chimney, but Laura had learned to ride over what she couldn't smooth. 'Yes,' she said, 'now.'

It was all over quickly, but Laura felt happier. Did Adrian? She couldn't tell. He rolled away from her immediately afterwards and lay still and quiet. She was sure he wasn't asleep, but she didn't dare risk his temper by testing him. She needed her energy, both physical and emotional, for work and any reproach, even a hint of dissatisfaction could degenerate into a quarrel.

* * *

On the following Sunday Laura was to visit her family. As she walked along the landing Gardner confronted her. 'M'lady wants a word with you.' She turned and stalked away and, although she was irritated by the maid's insolence, Laura felt she had no choice but to follow.

Lady Mallender was sitting on her day bed, fully dressed. After dismissing Gardner, she patted the couch. 'Come and sit by me, Laura, my dear.'

Laura did so and waited.

'Are you happy here, Laura? Of course, you must be. Such a lovely old house and servants to wait on you. It's a blessing that you'll have so much more energy to devote to your work.' She paused. 'Are the shops doing well?'

'Yes, thank you, though there are always improvements to be made. I must engage another designer. And I need more work-room staff.'

'Splendid. Customers must be flocking to you. Your darling hats are becoming quite famous.'

Laura tried to keep from looking as amazed as she felt. Surely her ladyship hadn't called her in so early for a friendly chat. She hadn't. 'So it will be no problem for you to contribute to house-hold expenses,' she said.

Laura stared at her mother-in-law whose eyes were fixed firmly ahead. 'Do you mean you want rent?'

'No, no, I wouldn't put it like that, but certainly every member of the family must pay their way.'

'Oh, and what does Adrian give you?' Laura's voice shook. 'He certainly has nothing to spare for me, indeed he keeps asking me for money. My car is falling apart and I need another one, but he hasn't offered a penny to help me.'

'But he doesn't earn anything and you do.'

'He has his allowance. It's more than most men earn after slaving for a week.'

'I'm afraid Sir Hugo has had to cut it down. The fact is, Laura, we have been badly hit by the economic situation. You may not know it, but we usually spend a good deal of our time in London. We couldn't do that this year, or last. Sir Hugo has had to curtail his sporting activities. Of course, we shall rally in time, but meanwhile each of us must pull our weight. Nancy contributes out of the income left to her by her grandmother, and I expect you to do the same.'

'No one ever left me any money,' Laura snapped. 'I have to work hard, damned hard for every penny I make –'

'There's no need for bad language.'

Laura got up and paced across to the window where she turned and stared at her mother-in-law. 'How did Adrian manage to afford to take me on such an expensive honeymoon? Or are you waiting for me to pick up the bills for that?'

Lady Mallender pushed out her chin. Her nose seemed extra-sharp. 'Laura, moderate your tone. Of course we don't expect anything of the kind. Sir Hugo gave him a sufficient sum.'

'I can't think why. He doesn't like me, that's obvious.'

Lady Mallender sighed. 'I don't think he likes anyone at the moment.'

There was a tone in her voice which made Laura simmer down. She returned to the couch. 'Are things really bad with you?'

Lady Mallender nodded. 'We've got rid of two housemaids and a kitchen maid. I may have to dismiss more servants, but I can't turn out the old ones. Some have been with my family, or Sir Hugo's, for almost a lifetime.'

Laura felt ashamed. Of course the elderly servants must be protected. 'I'm sorry I was so hasty. What income has Adrian?'

'None, except what we can give him.'

'But Nancy –'

'My late mother favoured her.'

'Forgive my plain speaking, but I understood your father to be a wealthy man.'

'He was. He left most of his money to my two brothers. It seemed right since I was married to a rich man, but times have changed.'

Laura frowned. 'Yes, they have. And financiers are predicting worse to come.' She felt a frisson of fear. She mustn't lose her business. Many had failed. She must not. 'Adrian and I could live cheaply over the Park Street shop. You haven't even been to see it. It's very nice.'

'No! He can't! I won't have it!'

The stubborn note was back and Laura sighed. 'I'll go through my accounts and give you as much as I can.'

Laura drove to Kingswood, thinking over the astonishing scene with her mother-in-law. She and Adrian could have had a far less expensive honeymoon, but she had enjoyed it. It was a memory for life. And Adrian had not neglected her this week. He was no great lover, but at least they were on a closer basis and that was a relief. She'd managed not to yield to temptation and point out to her mother-in-law that she owed *Hats by Laura* over thirty pounds. And some of the other grand society ladies were no quicker in paying. As soon as she had more help she'd make sure they were sent another of her invoices, her name and addresses in gold and silver lettering on thick white paper, but with the account marked clearly in black.

She wondered, as she had many times, why Adrian had chosen her to marry. There were plenty of rich girls from his own background he could have proposed to. She was still puzzled about why Lady Mallender had unexpectedly approved their marriage and even Sir Hugo had apparently not protested. Perhaps Adrian had insisted on marrying her. Surely that must mean he loved her. She felt her spirits soar. As long as she was loved she could put up with a great deal.

First she dropped in on Granma and Grampa. The house was always exactly the same and to her surprise Laura appreciated it. Nothing in her life was durable; this place had begun to seem like a haven.

She produced her gifts, carefully chosen so as not to annoy Granma's sense of propriety or economy. She had even bought them in London knowing that Paris was regarded by her as a city of sin. Granma's present was a box of lawn and lace handkerchiefs from Harrods; Grampa received six Dickens novels, identically bound in dark red and tooled with gold lettering.

He turned them over and over in his hands, caressing them. 'Laura, I don't know what to say. I'll have such a grand time reading them.'

'And he'll have plenty of it,' said Granma. 'He's been sacked.'

'What? That's terrible! Why?'

'They're cutting down staff again,' said Grampa. 'Times are getting harder.'

'But you've been there all your working life,' said Laura. 'How cruel they are.'

'You can't depend on the rich,' said Granma in tones almost of satisfaction. 'They don't know about our sort, or care.'

'If you need help –' said Laura.

Granma gave her a long look. 'Thank you, but we can manage. We've been thrifty and Grampa will have his unemployment pay.'

'But that's so little.'

'I've always made a little go a long way.' Granma's voice was strong. She wasn't asking for a vestige of pity. 'It's a disgrace that others can't follow my example.'

Laura knew she was referring to Phyllis. She resented it, but let it go.

'It was good of you to think of us,' said Grampa. 'Granma will enjoy using the beautiful handkerchiefs.'

'And Grampa will pass pleasant hours reading the books,' said Granma, surprising them both. She'd often said she considered 'sitting with your nose in a book' a waste of valuable time.

Driving on, Laura felt betrayed. There was no security anywhere. The only way to be safe in this world was to make money, plenty of it, to have it between you and disaster. It was a necessity almost equal to love.

Her parents' house was in its usual state of noise and disorder. William lowered his sporting paper. 'Hello chick. Had a nice holiday?'

'It was my honeymoon, Dad.'

'Still a holiday, eh? I remember I took your mother for a week to Weston. We were as happy as larks. Still are. She's through in the kitchen.'

He raised his paper. It was the longest speech he'd ever made to her. He and Phyllis had loved one another through years of struggle and misfortune. She had never thought she would envy them, but in spite of the past weeks she still didn't feel truly close to Adrian and she was the one who made all the compromises. Perhaps that applied to Phyllis, too. Who could tell what another person's marriage was like, even a child of the union? So much depended on what happened behind the closed bedroom door.

Phyllis was in the scullery peeling potatoes to add to the stew which was bubbling on the kitchen fire. Enid, big now with the baby expected next month, was seated a foot from the table scraping carrots. She gave her sister a welcoming smile. Enid never forgot Laura's kindness. Iris was there, stirring a cake mixture.

'You look well, Enid,' said Laura. 'Hello, Mum.'

Phyllis turned briefly and nodded. 'I can't say the same for you. You're as thin as a rail and look tired.'

Well, you got the truth from Phyllis, reflected Laura.

'Oh, Mum, she's fine,' protested Enid. 'God, I only hope I get my figure back when this one's born. Laura, I like your dress.'

Laura sat down opposite her sister. 'Baby still all right? It must be. You look really happy.'

'I am. Jack's got a steady job with Rick and he's determined not to lose it. Rick's a good boss.'

'Have you come to stay to dinner?' asked Phyllis.

'I thought I would, if that's convenient.'

Phyllis snorted. 'Convenient! There's enough, if that's what you mean.'

Lillian walked in. 'Well, well, the wanderer returns. What was life like in the big city? Oh, I should say cities. Fancy goin' to Paris for a honeymoon. Did you see any naughty shows?'

'That'll do,' snapped Phyllis. 'If you can't think of somethin' better to say clear out.'

Lillian held out her left hand and waggled it. On the third finger was a ring with a small green stone.

'You're engaged!'

'Give a prize to the lady in the hat.'

'Congratulations. Do I know him?'

'Shouldn't think so. His name's Victor Sherwood. He's in the same line as our Ralph.'

Phyllis looked up sharply. 'He's not like our Ralph, though.'

'Just because he still drives an old van! Ralph started with a wheelbarrow.'

'Ralph's an honest man.'

Lillian went red. 'So's Victor.'

'Maybe, maybe not. He gets hold of some pretty fancy stuff to sell. I'd like to know where his money comes from.'

'He's thrifty. He doesn't drink much and only smokes a bit. And, anyway, you never say anythin' when the boys pinch leather to burn.'

'They don't pinch it. It's offcuts.'

'Some of those offcuts are big enough to make a bloody pair of boots.'

'They're good boys.'

'Oh, all your boys are good. Pity you don't care as much about your girls.'

Laura's eyes opened wide in surprise. It had never occurred to her that her sisters might also feel a lack of caring in Phyllis.

'You're a liar! I love all my children.'

A first-class screaming match was developing and Laura said very loudly, 'I'd like to meet Victor.'

Lillian swung round on her. 'Is that a fact? You amaze me. I should have thought you were too used to toffee-nosed nobs to want to meet a man who has to scrabble for a livin'.'

Evidently Lillian's temporary truce for the wedding had been terminated. 'I'm no different from what I was,' said Laura.

'No different! You come here in a bloody crêpe de Chine dress that must have cost the earth and a black straw hat that looks as if you're off to a bloody garden party and say you're no different –'

Phyllis's patience snapped. 'Shut your soddin' mouth, our Lillian, or I swear I'll come over and shut it for you.'

'You and who's army?' But Lillian moved hastily away and went into the front room and jazz music swung through the house.

'Bloody row,' muttered Phyllis without malice.

'The dress is part of my trousseau, Mum,' said Laura. 'Noreen and I made it from a *Vogue* pattern. And the hat's one I turned myself.'

Phyllis glanced up. 'You're clever. Have been since you were born. You used to give me the creeps the way you stared at grown-ups and listened to their conversations.'

Laura was amazed. Was her child's curiosity, her thirst to learn, all a part of what had made her mother reject her?

'Lillian's that jealous,' said Phyllis. 'Always was. I don't know why. We've given her exactly the same as we gave all the others.'

Including love and a home, thought Laura. She blanked out the memories. She was a grown woman now and should forget the bad experiences of childhood.

Freda came in. She barely nodded to Laura. Her mouth was drawn down at the corners, her eyes held darkness that Laura found disquieting, frightening.

Lillian's temper had cooled and she was quiet at the dinner table. Not that anyone would have heard her speak if she'd wanted to. The room as usual was hot, noisy and even more crowded now Jack had joined them for Sunday dinner. Laura ate the rather greasy stew with hunks of bread and managed a piece of suet pudding and syrup. She had become used to far lighter food. Even Granma's now seemed over-rich with the ingredients which she insisted built up strength. Laura's insides protested at the onslaught of so much fat, sugar and starch, but she dared not let her feelings show by the flicker of a muscle or Lillian would store it up and make an issue of it later.

After dinner she fetched a big bag from the car and handed out gifts. She'd chosen with care; she'd not had much money to spend. There was a scarf with Paris printed on it for Phyllis who laughed raucously. 'I'll wear it to the pub on Saturday. That'll give the neighbours somethin' to shout about.'

William got a cravat. 'Men-about-town wear them now, Dad.'

William grinned. 'Mum and me'll look like a couple of peacocks.'

The little girls got dolls, Val a tin motorcar. Alfred, Harold and Jack whooped over chocolates and Enid was delighted with a pretty glass fruit bowl. Lillian opened her package and if she was pleased with her delicate hair ornament she managed to conceal it.

'The hair styles are changing,' explained Laura. 'Some women are having a ringletted permanent wave.'

'A what?'

'The hair's still quite short, but wavy and curly. Hair ornaments are becoming fashionable.'

'I haven't seen anyone lookin' like that,' said Enid.

'It's starting in Paris and is sure to arrive here.'

'Oh! Paris!' sniffed Lillian.

Iris had already had her present of a taffeta workbag and Ralph, his pipe. He had recently given up cigarettes saying, with a laugh, that customers liked a man with a pipe in his mouth. It gave an air of steadiness.

Freda stared at her gift of an onyx brooch, then stuck it on the mantelpiece.

Enid and Jack left and others wandered off to their various pursuits.

'Will you be stayin' on till tea time?' Iris asked hopefully.

'I'd like to, but I can't.'

'I suppose you'll be workin'.'

' 'Fraid so. I can't keep the workroom girls waiting for the new spring designs.'

'Spring,' said Freda abruptly. 'Spring.' Her voice was low and bitter and permeated the room with menace, silencing the others. She got up and walked out and Iris hurried after her, leaving Laura with Phyllis and William.

'Freda seems no better,' said Laura.

'She's worse,' said Phyllis flatly. 'Sometimes I think she's goin' crazy. Perhaps she was injured at birth, just like our poor Joyce, and we've never seen it before.' Phyllis stared at Laura who felt sick inside. Was she now to be blamed for Freda, too?

'How's Joyce's baby?' she asked.

Phyllis's face twisted. 'He's comin' along a treat, Granny Palmer says. I just wish he was home.'

William puffed at his pipe. 'She does, Laura. She says so every day.'

'You said you'd wait until talk of Joyce had died down.'

'Yes. Not that anyone knows what really happened. Anyway, now they've got a woman in the next road to talk about. They say she's havin' an affair with the milkman. Her husband beats her every Saturday night when he's got a skinful. If he finds out he'll kill the poor bitch.' Phyllis looked bleak. 'Just two months since Joyce left us. I miss her so much. I'm longin' to have little Andrew here, but I'm worried about Freda.' She stared into some dark inner vision. 'When I said to Dad the other day we'd soon be able to fetch Andrew home she stared at me somethin' horrible. Her eyes were like – like black coals. I thought for a minute she was goin' to attack me.'

'But surely she'll love Andrew for Joyce's sake.'

'That's what I thought, but I'm not sure. I never understood our Freda very well and now I don't at all.'

Laura let herself into the Park Street shop. The road was quiet in the autumn sun, only a few window-shoppers in their Sunday best and the occasional passing car breaking the silence. She walked through the shop, looking with pride and a sense of achievement at the hats and accessories waiting to be sold. All of it, everything here and in the other two shops were the creation of her brain and hands. Every day she was gaining more customers who were drawn by her originality. She'd had several requests for a hat to outdo a special friend, or rival, and she designed what the women wanted. It wasn't her business to be critical over their behaviour. All her thoughts must be directed to one end – towards success.

Rick walked into the shop a week later and was sent upstairs by Nancy. He looked round the new workroom where six girls were busy. A new apprentice, Lottie, was steaming felts, another, Daisy, was picking up pins and returning them to pincushions. Daisy was quick and biddable, with a ready smile. Lottie was slower and sometimes looked resentful at being given orders. They both spent two mornings a week with Miss Morton, learning their trade.

He stuck his head round the office door and whistled softly through his teeth, 'Baby, you're coming up fast.'

'Rick!' She couldn't keep the delight out of her voice. She quickly subsided. 'It's nice to see you. What have you been doing? Getting more acts together?'

'You're looking pale, honey.'

'Stop calling me honey, or baby. I'm a married woman.'

'So you are.' He got out his cigarettes, then stuck the case back in his waistcoat pocket. 'How's married life?'

'Fine, thanks. How's everything with you.'

'Fine, thanks.'

They laughed and Laura called to Daisy to bring some tea.

'Rick, you look different.'

'Nice or nasty?'

'Neither. There's something about you; you're just different.' She knew what it was really. His face was set in sterner lines, his eyes were bold, but watchful, like a prowling cat's. He looked bigger, taller, and he exuded male dominance and a force of power which intrigued her.

'Find any nice girls in London?'

He shrugged. 'A few. Some were naughty and that was nice, if you see what I mean.'

'I do, thank you very much.'

'Don't play the prude with me. I know you're not one.'

Her face flamed. 'Don't say such things. What if someone should overhear?'

'I'll take care that no one ever does.'

'I asked you if you'd found some new acts.'

Rick perched on the edge of a tall stool, took out his cigarette case and, at Laura's frown, returned it to his pocket again. 'Better than that. I heard about "dropsie".'

'I thought that was a disease.'

'Not in theatre parlance.'

'Your accent is almost like Adrian's.'

For a split second he looked furious, then he said calmly, 'Think so? I'm glad. I've been taking elocution lessons. And

I've become a booking manager. That's a better proposition at the moment than an agent, though I'm still keeping the acts I've got. I like to hold open all channels. Remember I told you how the middlemen make the money. A booking manager stands between agents and their ability to get good parts for their clients. Many an agent's book falls open where a few pounds have been left. Hence, dropsie. There's nothing like money for greasing the wheels. It spurs me to find work for their clients.'

'Is that honest?'

'It's not dishonest.'

'How are Aunty Mabel and Olwen?'

'Aunty seems to be getting smaller, but she's as bright as a button. Olwen's looking pink and healthy.'

Laura glanced down at her drawings. 'I'm sorry, Rick, but I must get on. The girls have got to get everything ready for a show soon after Christmas.'

'It's only October yet.'

'I know and it leaves us little enough time. There are the wholesale hats in *The Hat Shop* with lots of orders for original decoration. The straws are in the Redfield shop. Noreen's very capable, but she needs guidance. She's no confidence in herself.'

'And Miss Morton?'

'Not quite so spry. She works part time and mostly supervises now.'

'What about the army of wrinklies?'

'Another died in the summer. Dolores and I still take work out to the others. They depend on it not just for the money, but for the interest it gives them. They love hearing about the shops. It all takes up time.'

'Why don't you leave all the running about to Dolores?'

'They've become personal friends. They want me.'

'I can't blame them for that.'

'What's that supposed to mean?'

'For heaven's sake, baby, you're as jumpy as a flea. I mean that the old dears have got fond of you, they admire you, their vanity is flattered to have the boss visit them. I bet they boast to the neighbours.'

Rick got up and stretched. She stared up at him, remembering suddenly the way those muscled arms could embrace, the way his body had so swiftly reponded with passionate desire, and wished with all her heart that Adrian was more like him.

The weeks up to Christmas raced by. Laura had engaged a girl straight from art school. She was twenty-one, short, plump, with a pasty complexion and frequent spots, but she was full of good new ideas and was capable of seeing them through.

Laura was obliged to attend society functions which bored her more and more. No wonder Nancy loved working. Now they had even more in common as they chatted over coffee, groaning over long tedious dinner parties, bitching pleasurably about Thelma and Daphne and their friends.

Ralph listened to them, grinning. 'Oscar Wilde says that only those who can't get into society pretend to despise it.'

'Well, that's not so in our case,' said Nancy. 'We're trapped in it and want to escape.'

'Laura enjoys dancing.'

'I do. It's about the only part I do look forward to. D'you know, Ralph, next week there's to be a fancy dress ball and we all have to go disguised as some furry animal. Such nonsense.'

'You're beginning to sound like some old stick-in-the-mud.'

'She is not,' protested Nancy.

He only laughed louder at them.

The dance costume took time to make and Laura grudged every second of it. Noreen and the others giggled when they saw her in a cat's outfit with furry head and tail.

'I can't think what possessed me to choose fur. I'll roast,' complained Laura.

'It'll be like a Turkish bath,' grinned Noreen. 'You'll sweat so much that when they open up the costume there'll be nothing inside.'

Adrian revelled in the preparations. He had chosen to go as a mouse. 'You can chase me in your cat costume, Laura.'

She was pleased to see him animated and happy. He had tried to quarrel with her when she expressed surprise at his mother's demand for housekeeping money. Laura had given up mentioning it. A peaceful marriage was worth more than a few pounds, however hard she had to slog to make them.

Chapter Twenty-Three

Laura gazed down at the baby she cradled in her arms. Enid's daughter was a month old, born on time without difficulty, a lively child whose intelligent bright blue eyes were fixed on her aunt.

'I thought babies couldn't focus their eyes until they were six months old,' said Laura.

Enid looked vague. 'Can't they? Mum never said that. Glory can definitely see –'

'Who? Glory? Is that her name?' Laura was startled.

'Yes, lovely, isn't it? I read it in a book. I've had time to do a lot of readin' these past few months. It's really wonderful Jack havin' a job with Rick. I shan't wait too long to have another baby. Then my children can grow up together. Thanks to you, there won't be any more after that. Two's plenty and my Jack won't ever earn a lot of money, but a kinder man never lived.'

Laura couldn't argue. Enid didn't have dreams of the impossible. She accepted what she'd got. Better than that, she was happy with it.

Glory whimpered and Laura rocked her in her arms singing, *Go to sleep my baby, Close your pretty eyes, Angels watch around you*. As she sang, gently swinging the sweet weight of the child a sudden yearning filled her. She wanted a baby of her own. She wanted to carry it in her womb, nurture it in its dark, secret cave of flesh for months, bring it forth and love it.

Enid flipped out a breast and held out her arms, taking her daughter and holding her close. Glory's head twisted, open-mouthed, from side to side before she found the big nipple and sucked. The sisters laughed at the sound of gulping.

'She's lovely,' said Laura.

Enid looked up at her sister who leaned close. 'No sign of a little one with you yet?'

Laura shook her head.

'That's a shame. Or is it? You won't ever have a child you don't want, will you?'

Laura only smiled.

Driving home she couldn't forget Glory. She still felt the softness of her skin, smelled the wholesome aromas of infancy, baby powder, and wind-dried garments. Surely she could work while expecting a baby? Many women had to keep on far more gruelling jobs than hers. It would make her mother-in-law happy too. Laura grimaced. Lady Mallender had stopped hinting about an heir and had said straight out that she hoped she would not have to wait much longer for Sir Hugo to have a grandchild to hand on the title to. Laura resented it, yet felt Lady Mallender had a certain amount of right on her side. Even Phyllis had remarked on the length of time Laura had been married and the non-appearance of a pregnancy. She'd fallen for Ralph the first time. Laura still kept the secret of her vaginal cap from Adrian. She had a writing desk in the bedroom with one locked drawer. In it were a few personal papers, and underneath them the precious appliance which prevented conception. Perhaps soon she would leave it there.

She told Adrian she had seen Glory.

'Good God, what a name for the poor brat!'

'I don't know. People often grow to suit their names. She might be beautiful, talented, an actress maybe.'

'And she might end up like Freda, or that ghastly new woman you've got working for you. What's her name?'

'Pansy Henderson,' supplied Laura.

Adrian shouted with mirth. '*Pansy*! She doesn't exactly bear out your theory. I've seldom seen such a pudding of a girl. I don't know how you can bear to have her around.'

'Pansy is a talented designer, especially clever at putting original finishing touches to a hat.'

Adrian shrugged. 'It's your business. Far be it from me to interfere.'

'You give me the freedom I want,' said Laura, slowly, 'but I'd be glad of help from you sometimes. Especially if – if we should have a child.'

Adrian's head jerked up, his eyes filled with hope. 'Are you – ?'

'No, not yet, darling. You'd really like one, wouldn't you?'

'A man always wants an heir.'

'I couldn't guarantee a son.'

'No, but we've got a fifty-fifty chance. And we don't have to stop at one.'

'You are truly fond of children?'

'I would be of ours.'

Laura laughed and Adrian pulled her towards him and held her close. His heart was thumping hard. She felt remorseful.

'Adrian, we should make love more often to be sure.'

'Then we will. Tell me the very minute you know, won't you, Laura.'

Laura sat down at her dressing table and applied the eccentric make-up needed for her costume for tonight's party. White skin and round pink cheeks with an exaggerated cupid's bow mouth. This time the guests were to go as babies. Ironical, she thought, or maybe prophetic. She had managed to dodge quite a number of engagements, but not this one. It was being held in the Mallender house.

'You'll give something towards the cost, won't you, Laura,' Lady Mallender had said. 'We can't afford to entertain on a lavish scale, but we must have a party here after accepting so many delightful invitations. A buffet supper with dancing will be much less expensive than a grand dinner and ball.'

Laura had coughed up thirty pounds, and watched it disappear into her mother-in-law's bag with a sense that someone had amputated one of her limbs. She was hoarding money, building up a credit balance in the bank, winning their confidence in her. She wanted to buy the shops as soon as possible and she had other plans.

She flatly refused to go to the party in anything totally

idiotic. Instead she had got the workroom girls to run up a chintz nightgown – white with pink and blue flowers and a ruff round the neck and wrists. With it she wore pink slippers on which were sewn little rabbits' heads made by Pansy. Laura had watched her tie tiny bows of ribbon around their necks, her sausage-like fingers handling the thin satin as delicately as if it were porcelain. Since joining Laura she had cosseted and massaged her hands until they were soft and smooth. In fact, decided Laura, her fingers looked like uncooked sausages which was worse. She had thanked Pansy who looked at her handiwork, shook her head and grunted, 'Stupid bloody idiots.' She made no attempt to hide her contempt of the idle rich and rejoiced whenever some wealthy society woman paid well for a model hat she had trimmed for a few pence.

The party started at nine o'clock and might go on till dawn. Laura groaned. She'd feel gruesome tomorrow. She and Adrian received the guests in the hall. Sir Hugo and Lady Mallender would appear among them later. Sir Hugo seemed to grow more morose daily, and his language regarding the theme of the fancy costumes would have blistered a stable-lad's ears. 'I suppose they'll do those bloody jungle dances!' was the mildest thing he had said.

Paul arrived, managing to look manly in an Eton uniform made to measure. He bowed and kissed her hand. 'Charming, my dear. Quite charming. May I have the first dance?'

'Certainly not. That's Adrian's, but you may have the second.'

The last guests were arriving and Laura was surprised to see Rex among them. 'I thought you were in Paris!'

'I was until yesterday. Adrian telegraphed an invitation to me, didn't you, dear boy? I'm afraid I had no time to prepare a suitable fancy dress.'

'I wish I could say the same,' said Laura.

Rex's brows rose. 'You look charming, but do I get the impression that you find the whole business rather infantile?'

Laura was saved from answering.

'Rex, why aren't you properly dressed?' Adrian looked peevish.

Rex looked down at his evening tails and immaculate white shirt and tie. 'I was under the impression that I was.'

'You know what I mean. You must find something here. Gardner's a great one for fixing up fancy dress. She used to do Nancy's and mine when we were children. You know where to find her. She'll be in the housekeeper's room.'

Rex shrugged and walked away.

In the drawing room the carpet had been rolled back, a small jazz band engaged, and the dancing began. Adrian led Laura on to the polished floor and others joined them.

At the end of a one-step Adrian thanked Laura with a smile. 'Phew! I need a breather. Would you excuse me for a moment, darling. I'll nip out to see if Rex has all he needs. He'll try to get out of dressing up if he can.'

'Do that, Adrian. I'll be here when you come back.'

Laura felt relaxed. Whatever problems she had she could forget them in the rhythms of the Charleston, the Black Bottom, the Shimmy. Paul watched Adrian leave and immediately claimed her. In spite of the lack of room the dancers kicked and whirled, recklessly ignoring the fact that their shoes came into painful contact with ankles and shins. Nothing mattered; only the dance. The room was throbbing with the sound of jazz, the dancers moved in a haze of tobacco smoke. The cocktails were strong. Everyone was worshipping the dance, Laura with them and she didn't lack partners.

The band struck up a slow foxtrot and Laura looked round for Adrian. The mood had seized her, the wine had excited her. Surely tonight, when they lay together in the comfortable double bed in the soft, enveloping darkness, she would conceive. Getting babies came easily to the rest of the family. Neither her mother nor Enid had any problem there; quite the other way, in fact. Nor had Joyce. She wondered suddenly if one of the men enjoying the Mallender's hospitality had fathered Joyce's child. She pushed the thought away. Tonight she wanted only harmony in her mind. Her baby must be started in an atmosphere of sweet accord. It would be welcomed by everyone. Even Sir Hugo.

Paul approached her again. 'You look positively doe-eyed.'

'Do I? I was hoping to dance with Adrian.'

'With such an expression? That handsome husband of yours doesn't deserve you. Dance with me, please. It's a pity to let a good foxtrot go to waste.'

Laura slid into his arms. Paul was a good dancer – better than Adrian.

'You still have that look of – trustful innocence,' he said.

'Good lord, do I? It sounds fearful.'

Paul's arms tightened. 'Don't flirt with me, darling, or I might just be tempted –' He paused. 'Where *is* Adrian?'

'Don't exactly know,' said Laura dreamily. 'He may be in the housekeeper's room fixing Rex a fancy dress. Rex is probably proving stubborn. I haven't caught sight of Adrian for ages. But he'll be back soon.' She lifted her head and for a moment her eyes looked straight into Paul's. What she saw there made her gasp. He wanted her. She was no longer an innocent miss who couldn't read the signs.

She lost her footing, apologised, recovered. Paul bent his head to her. 'Do you know I've never seen a woman change as much as you have in so short a time. You're more than beautiful. You look like a flame among a crowd of cigarette ends.'

Laura giggled.

'That's better. I knew you'd laugh.'

'So you didn't mean what you said?'

'I meant every word.'

Laura held herself as far away from him as his enclosing arms allowed and looked around. Nancy was nearby, managing to look winsome in a knitted silk outfit of leggings and jumper. Her partner was a young socialite in a ridiculous napkin with an enormous safety pin and little else. She caught Laura's eye and made a tiny grimace.

There was little doubt in Laura's mind now that Nancy loved Ralph. Her brother's business was flourishing and he was fixing up a lovely flat over his shop. When it was ready Laura was sure he would propose. Nancy's parents could scarcely object after the way they had accepted Laura.

The bandsmen went to the kitchen for refreshment and Renton and the maids served the guests in the dining room with a feast of delicacies. Laura wondered if she would ever get used to watching the rich stuffing themselves with lobster, pâté, mousse, smoked salmon, ham, beef, chicken, a dozen different salads, fresh fruit and fruit salads with jugs of thick, yellow cream, and drinking fancy cocktails, while so many folk thought themselves lucky to get a scrag end of mutton for a whole weekend and some men could scarcely afford a glass of beer.

Sir Hugo and Lady Mallender arrived in the drawing room and her ladyship said, 'You see how economical the buffet is, Laura, dear.'

'*Economical?*'

'Yes, indeed. It was all prepared in our own kitchens. So much less expensive than going to a hotel, or employing caterers. Of course, one has to engage a couple of extra women for the washing up, but that costs very little.'

Laura thought of the women coping with the dishes, putting up with orders from the cook and butler and any other servant who felt bad-tempered, thought of their varicose veins, their weariness. She doubted she'd ever fit into the Mallender mould; she could never forget the people who worked at the bottom of the social scale.

The butler rapped on a small tray for silence.

'Good evening, everyone,' Lady Mallender said graciously. 'I hope you're all having fun.'

Sir Hugo managed a smile. 'I'm sure you are.' He muttered. 'Make enough bloody noise about it.' His voice was not one designed to be used quietly and his words were perfectly clear to the guests who treated them as a huge joke, laughing and applauding, before they returned to their eating, drinking and gossiping.

Laura asked, 'Have you seen Adrian, Lady Mallender?'

'What? No, I haven't.'

'He said Gardner would fix Rex up with fancy dress. He said he was going to find them.'

Lady Mallender turned. 'Gardner was in the hall a moment ago. Don't worry, Laura. The dear boy is probably enjoying a talk somewhere. He's none too keen on this kind of party.'

'Then why have it?'

Lady Mallender's brows rose. 'Fancy dress parties are all the rage. I'm following fashion. I would have expected *you* to approve of that. Adrian won't be long, I'm sure and it's your duty to entertain your guests until he returns.'

Sir Hugo frowned and walked off. Laura followed him from the room and saw him stomp into the library. A footfall sounded behind her.

Gardner said, 'If you're looking for Master Adrian I believe you'll find him in his studio.'

'Are you sure?'

'Pretty sure, madam. He was always a shy boy. Such a dear, shy boy. When he was younger he would try to escape from his birthday parties. He used to go to the attics and examine all the old stuff stored up there. Now that one of them has been converted to a studio he still finds solace there.'

Solace! What an odd word to use. And why was Gardner being so helpful all of a sudden? She didn't believe a word of what she said. She would find it amusing to send Laura all the way to the top of the house on a wild-goose hunt. She began to walk back to the drawing room. Then she stopped. Gardner might have been telling the truth. Damn it, she wanted to dance with her husband.

She climbed the wide stairway to the bedrooms, past the pictures of Mallender ancestors engaged in various forms of hunting, then the narrow stair leading to the attics, carpeted with drugget, and walked along the landing to the studio. Her slippers made no sound; in her long chintz gown she might have been a ghost. She pushed open the studio door and heard someone speaking. She stopped. Someone spoke again. Adrian. His voice was too low to make out his words. He was probably showing his work to a guest. Then he said clearly, 'I'll have to get back to the damn party. I've hardly spoken to Laura all evening.'

Laura felt encouraged to push the door open fully and look into the room.

She thought her heart would stop beating. Beneath a dim light, on a couch sat Rex. Adrian was curled up at his feet. As Laura watched Rex smoothed Adrian's hair, allowing his hand to rest for a moment on the nape of his neck. Adrian looked up at Rex and his voice was filled with a passion Laura had never heard from him. 'You don't know how I've missed you, how I've longed for you every day.'

'I do, dear boy, I do. You're the one who decided to get married, remember? How do you think that makes me feel?'

Big childish tears rolled down Adrian's face. 'You've got Pierre and all I've had is Laura. A woman! Who wants her? Who wants any bloody woman?'

Rex laughed softly and the sound made Laura shiver. 'Pierre is nothing to me. I intend to get rid of him. The little swine steals my paints and sells them. Any time you want me I'll be waiting for you.'

No one, not even one as unsophisticated as Laura, could be deluded. The two men were lovers and so engrossed in each other they hadn't sensed her presence. Adrian twisted and lifted his face. Rex leaned forward and brushed his lips in a gentle kiss.

Laura had been as transfixed as a wax dummy in a museum, but at last she managed to move. She must get away, leave this room, leave this house, leave her travesty of a marriage. As she turned her foot caught a long piece of drapery on which stood the ingredients for a still-life Adrian was painting. She tried to extricate herself and her frantic efforts brought down the fruit, the inkwell, the books and a china vase which smashed. Both men's heads jerked towards the door. They stared at Laura who was suddenly motionless, held by their eyes like a rabbit with a snake.

Adrian's eyes held shock, resignation, but above all, relief. 'So now you know,' he said.

Rex's were mocking, amused, as they travelled over her rabbit-adorned slippers, her baby's nightie, her foolish make-up. 'Sorry, darling. We didn't mean to spring it on you this way. You're supposed to breed first.'

Laura came to life then and ran. She raced down the stairs, along the landing and into her bedroom – *their* bedroom and slammed the door, locked it and stood leaning against it, breathing in great gulps. She scurried to the window and threw it open. Early December misty air drifted through and she drank it in, its promise of winter cooling her limbs, blowing softly against the sweat that had broken out on her.

Now she understood so much that had been hidden from her. The sly looks, giggles and innuendoes. She had thought girls were jealous! Oh, my God! She must be the laughing stock of Bristol, of London, everywhere that society folk gathered. No wonder Adrian hadn't tried to marry one of his own class. If the young ones didn't know what he was their fathers would. The Mallenders had needed a brood mare, preferably one with an income, and she had been their choice. She wondered how many people believed she knew of Adrian's true nature and had married him for position and a title. Did Sir Hugo? Was that the reason for his hostility?

She sank to her knees and rested her head on the sill, her world crumbling about her. Her marriage was a sham. She wondered if Adrian had met Rex on the afternoon in Paris when he'd said he wanted a rest. She rose and walked about the room, her pain and humiliation too horrible to bear. She bit her knuckles savagely. She wanted to experience physical hurt that might take her mind from her emotional agony. She wished she could weep, but she was frozen. Oh, God, to think of her first lover having to force himself to take her body, hating it, but doing his duty by his family. The gross degradation of it! She felt soiled, unclean. No wonder Adrian had been overcome by impotency. He wasn't sexually cold. He was revolted by her woman's body.

Thank God, oh, thank God, she had discovered what he was tonight instead of tomorrow by which time she might have been pregnant.

She must get out of here, out of this disgusting house whose mistress had deliberately wed her to a man who would never be a proper husband to her. Where could she go? If ever she needed a friend she needed one now. If she couldn't release this excruciating dam of horror she would die. She grabbed a coat, raced down the stairs and across the hall. As she reached the front door she heard Gardner's laugh.

She flung open the wide garage doors and climbed into her battered car, swinging through the open gates so recklessly that she heard a scrape as stone met metal. She drove fast around the Downs roads, trying to blank out what she had seen. What Gardner had meant her to see. That's why she was jealous of Laura; a male lover could never hold her darling boy like a wife.

She left the Downs and drove without thought and found herself in Whiteladies Gate.

Rick had a flat near by. He had left his new address at the shop with a scribbled note. 'If you need me you know where I am.' Instinct had brought her here; she was past reasoning. She found the tall house where he had a flat and pushed her finger against his doorbell, keeping it there so that it trilled on and on.

'Shut that noise!' yelled someone in the house.

Then there was the sound of footsteps hurrying down the stairs and the door was flung open.

Rick was in his dressing gown, his hair tousled. 'What the hell – ?'

Laura cowered back. What if he had been in bed with some-one? 'S . . . sorry –' she stammered. 'I'll go –'

'My God! Laura.' Rick stepped out and grabbed her arm. Her legs felt weak and he supported her upstairs, kicking his flat door open. He helped her gently to a couch, lit the gas fire and turned up the jet on the lamp. He fetched brandy which he forced through her shaking lips. He asked no questions, just made little murmuring noises of comfort, stroking her hair, soothing her, until she stopped shaking.

Then he slid an arm around her shoulders. 'Do you want to tell me, Laura?'

'I must. I've got to talk to someone.'

Rick kept silent as Laura spoke. As she explained she felt the muscles of his arm clench. When she had finished the silence was broken only by the flickering hiss of gas.

Then he said softly, 'Poor kid. That was so damned brutal. You really didn't know, did you?'

'Of course I didn't! Did you? Rick, did you?'

'Men can sense these things.' His lips twisted. 'It isn't difficult.'

'No one told me. Everyone kept it from me. So did you!'

'It wasn't my place to interfere. I assumed you'd made your choice. Either you loved him enough to put up with him, or you accepted what he was so that you could carry on working from a position of strength.'

'You believed that of me?' Her voice was a whisper of horror.

Rick pulled her close. 'Baby, I wasn't judging you. You've had a tough deal. I would never blame you for trying to make it the easier way – with money behind you.'

'Money! They don't even have that. I have to pay housekeeping, and I gave a contribution to the party. I'll never live in that place again. I suppose everyone thinks I'm nothing more than a money-grubbing little tart.'

'My, haven't you learned some fancy words.' He was teasing, yet so gently and with such compassion it didn't hurt.

She leaned back on the couch. 'I have to be at work tomorrow. I'll be a wreck.'

He lifted her and carried her through to his bedroom, placing her carefully on the bed amid his rumpled sheets. They were still warm and smelled a little of soap and tobacco. 'There's a lavatory and washbasin through that door.'

'Where will you sleep?'

'On the couch.'

'Don't leave me, Rick, please, I shall go crazy.'

She clutched his arm and he stared at her. 'I can't spend the night with you. I'm not Adrian.'

'No, you're not Adrian. You love women. I'm a woman, Rick, a cheated, unhappy, needful woman.' She dragged him close to the bed. 'Don't leave me, not tonight.'

'Laura, if I stay I shan't be able to keep my hands off you. I've never stopped wanting to make love to you.'

'Oh, say that again. What glorious, wonderful words.' She was more than a little drunk. 'Beautiful, darling words. Love me, Rick. I need to be loved.'

'You're not in your right senses, baby. It's shock and the brandy talking. I can't take advantage. Tomorrow you'd regret it.'

She sat up, tearing off the stupid dress, sliding out of her camiknickers so that she lay naked before him.

Rick gasped. 'Oh, hell! Laura, I want you.' He threw off his dressing gown. He was naked beneath it, he was muscular, his arms and legs rough with hair, a dark mat on his chest. The evidence of his desire was clear. Her eyes drank in every detail of his body.

'I ain't no purty picture, honey lamb.'

'You're beautiful. You're a man. A real man. Not a travesty of a man, a kind of half woman, or whatever it is that *he* is.' She held out her arms.

He knelt beside Laura. He kissed her, softly, sweetly, beginning with her forehead, smoothing back her hair with a tender hand. He explored her body with his mouth, his lips caressing her face, her ears, the long column of her white neck, her shoulders, her breasts. She began to writhe beneath the exquisite torment. He took each nipple in his mouth and teased it and waves of hot hunger flooded through her. She cried his name as his mouth moved down to her flat stomach, to the dark triangle of hair, and arched her body in intolerable need, but Rick continued to tease her.

'Not so fast, my love,' he murmured. 'We've waited a long time for this. Let's enjoy it.'

He traced paths down her legs and over each of her narrow feet. Then swiftly he moved upwards and Laura cried out as his lips found the throbbing most intimate place of her body. She could never have imagined such intense pleasure.

'Rick, please –' she gasped, 'please, love me – love me –'

He entered her slowly, with infinite care, tantalising her still more until her body began to move of its own volition, reaching up to him in an age-old rhythm.

It was Rick's turn to gasp. 'God, Laura –' He moved faster and she matched him, stroke for stroke, until together they reached a climax so powerful their hands gripped and pulled on flesh as if to anchor themselves as they were swept upwards on a tide of ecstasy.

Chapter Twenty-Four

Rick lay beside her, and Laura gently pushed her fingers into his dark hair. 'I never knew – never dreamed –' she said softly.

'What, baby?'

' – that love could be like that.'

'You're happy?'

'That's a mild word for what I feel. I've never known –' She stopped. In spite of Adrian's betrayal, to discuss his unimaginative performance in bed was beyond her.

Rick put his hands gently on each side of her face and kissed her. 'You're a wonderful girl, baby. You deserve better than you got.' Tears forced themselves beneath her lids and trickled down her face and he kissed them. 'Don't cry, my sweet.'

'I – can't help it.' She had almost said *I love you*, but that wasn't true. They were lovers, physical lovers, friends but not in love.

Rick reached out for a handkerchief and dabbed her eyes. 'You've had a wicked deal, Laura.' He turned and lay on his back, but one hand still smoothed her. 'You've got beautiful skin.' He reached down and pulled the covers over them, then picked up a pack of cigarettes, lit two and handed her one.

They smoked for a while in silence. 'I imagined you understood about Adrian,' said Rick at last. 'As I see it, marriage is strictly between two people – others don't have the right to interfere.' He paused. 'I left my new address at the shop for you, just in case you needed someone. I was afraid for you. You're such a sweet innocent.'

'I was grossly deceived by the Mallenders. I know now why they didn't oppose our marriage. They wanted an heir desperately and I came along, young, healthy, making a respectable

412

living and so damned ignorant they walked all over me.' She had a sudden thought. 'Nancy!'

'What about her?'

'She surely knows what Adrian is.'

'I reckon she does. She's not daft.'

'I thought she was my friend.'

'I'm sure she is. She's a nice kid.'

'How do you know?'

'Ralph and I are good mates. I see her with him. They're in love, Laura.'

'I know.'

'Are you doing anything to warn her that it's hopeless?'

'What do you mean? The Mallenders won't oppose her. Why should they? They didn't oppose – Adrian and me,' she finished slowly. 'Oh, my God, I see what you mean. They didn't care who Adrian got as long as there was a baby in it for them, but it'll be different for Nancy. Poor girl, poor Ralph.'

'The point I'm making is that you didn't warn Nancy.'

'But I didn't realise all the circumstances, not until this minute.'

'Exactly,' he replied gently. 'And Nancy didn't understand yours and Adrian's. What are you going to say to her now?'

Laura drew smoke in and breathed it out in a long stream. 'I don't know. You're right about not interfering. Nancy adores Ralph.' She was silent a moment. 'Of course, her case isn't like Adrian's. Ralph is all man. If she can get over her parents' opposition she'll be happy. Well, Lady Mallender's actually. Sir Hugo lets her do what she likes. He didn't mind at all when she came to work in the shop.'

'It isn't the same,' warned Rick. 'He probably sees her work as a little hobby. Marriage is a very different proposition.'

'I suppose so.'

'Buck up, old girl,' said Rick in affected tones and laughed. 'We're all getting so posh. You and Ralph and I. You'll put this disaster behind you and get on with your life.'

'I shan't live with Adrian any more. I'll move to the flat, and if he tries to get in I'll have him thrown out.'

'That's the stuff!' Rick tossed his half-smoked cigarette into the small empty grate and followed it with Laura's. He turned and slid his arms around her slender waist and drew her close. 'Now I've got you at last I'm going to make the most of it. You've sobered up now. D'you want to make love, honey pie?'

'Rick –' she protested, smiling at the silly voice he put on. But there was nothing silly in his face when she pressed close to him and opened her mouth for his kiss.

The night was euphoric, but it had to end and in the morning Laura was again depressed.

'Cheer up, love,' encouraged Rick. 'Don't let the buggers get you down. That's always been my motto.'

'Bit different from Granma's,' said Laura.

'You escaped from her, didn't you? Let's see a smile. Don't despair, you'll manage.'

'I won't despair. I promise, I won't, but it's not going to be easy. I can see awful difficulties. What a fool I was to get married when I was doing fine without a husband. Now he's nothing but a complication in my life. I thought Anita was cynical, but she's got a lot of sense.'

The horrific picture of Adrian in Rex's arms suddenly rose in her mind and she moaned. 'I'll never forget what I saw. Never. Oh, Rick, why?'

'That's the question we all ask about life and there's no answer, love.'

'What Adrian does is horrible, disgusting.'

'Not everyone sees it that way. You've had a particularly nasty experience. Homosexuals are not all as deceitful as Adrian.'

'Do you see a lot of them?'

'You have to in show business. I don't mind what they do with their private lives, it's their choice, but I despise the ones who pretend to be ordinary and get married so as to appear respectable. Often they put their partners through hell.'

'Adrian's purpose was different.'

'Whatever reason he married you for, Laura, it was wrong and he knew it.'

Rick left for work, telling her to help herself to anything she needed. She filled a deep basin with hot water and found a flannel and washed herself from head to toe. She would clean her teeth when she reached her flat. There were bruises on her legs where Rick had entwined himself around her, and on her arms where he had clutched at her. He probably had some, too, she reflected with a kind of grim satisfaction. Then she went cold with sick misery. Rick wasn't her lover in the true sense. He was still only a good friend who had lifted her out of despair by filling her body with passionate joy.

Adrian had a lover. Rex loved him, though not, Laura suspected, as much as Adrian cared about Rex. She surprised herself by a tinge of sympathy for her husband. It seemed there were all kinds of different hells attached to love.

She drove herself to Park Street. Nancy had already opened the shop and the first customer had been fitted with a hat and was examining a scarf and gloves to match. Nancy gave Laura a quick embarrassed glance as she hurried by with a muttered good morning. Laura walked past the workroom door, averting her face from the glass panel behind which sat Pansy and the other girls. When she saw herself in the mirror in her bedroom she saw she had black shadows beneath her eyes and that she was very white. She set to with make-up and created a face for herself to cope with whatever came next.

Downstairs, Dolores was waiting with half a dozen headbands for her approval. 'Were you very late last night?' she asked, peering at Laura concernedly.

'Mmm,' Laura said noncommittally. 'Who decided to make headbands for *The Hat Shop*, and whose idea was it to use spangles?'

'Iris both times. We've been asked for somethin' pretty for evenin' wear. Do you approve?'

'Yes, I do. I'll congratulate her when I see her.'

'Good,' said Dolores. 'Er, how did they look in their baby outfits?'

'Bloody silly mostly. Dolores, are the hats ready for the three Miss Dobsons? They telephoned to say they'll be in later.'

Dolores grinned. 'Miss Morton says they'll be on time. I'll ferry them up for the three Miss Dobsons. They sound like a musical comedy act.'

'Don't be disrespectful about our valued clients,' said Laura.

They both laughed and Laura felt better. The Misses Dobson were on the wrong side of forty and dressed too young. All tactful efforts to get them to wear attractive hats that became their years were unavailing.

Laura went up to her office, greeting the girls, stopping here and there to look at what they were doing.

Pansy was making a gathered rosette, instructing Lottie and Daisy in her gruff voice as she worked. 'This rosette will be two and a half inches in diameter so we'll need a yard of ribbon an inch in width. Cut it for me, please, Daisy. Thanks. Now Lottie, hand me the foundation. Remember how we did it yesterday? Two-fold muslin wired round the edge and covered with thin silk. Always begin with the ribbon from the outside, working from right to left, pleating and stitching it evenly and neatly. When we reach the centre the pleating will have graduated off and the end must be drawn well down. Now, Daisy, let's see how you do it. Lottie, cut the ribbon for the bow I shall work on next, then steam press the black felt.'

Lottie walked away, her face sulky, her mouth mutinous. She muttered something and Pansy called her back. 'If you've anything to say to me I'd like to hear it.'

'Why is it always Daisy who gets to do the best things, while you give me borin' things like ironin'?'

'You must try harder. As soon as you're able I'll give you plenty to do, never fear. And even if the damp pressing is boring, it's extremely important. Remember, the finished shape of the hat depends upon it.'

Lottie slouched over to the ironing board. Laura watched her as she thumped the iron down amid clouds of steam.

'Come into my office, Lottie,' she said.

Laura closed the door and spoke quietly. 'Don't you like working here?'

'Not much sometimes, Mrs Mallender. I think Pansy has favourites. Daisy's one.'

'Who are the others?'

Lottie stared down at her feet. Her shoes hadn't been cleaned for days by the look of them. She shrugged.

'Don't you understand, Lottie, that materials cost money? They're the precious tools of our trade. They have to supply quite a large number of people now with a living and we simply can't afford waste. You must do as Pansy tells you, or I shall have to speak to your parents and explain that we can't employ you any longer.'

Lottie stared at her, opened her mouth, then closed it again. She was pretty, thought Laura, with her clear skin and blue-grey eyes, or would be, if she didn't scowl so perpetually. 'You'll have lines before you're old if you frown so much,' said Laura. 'And please make sure your shoes are clean before you come to work again.'

'Yes, Mrs Mallender.'

Lottie left the office, her whole body expressing resentment, and Laura sighed. She did her best to make her employees' lives pleasant. The sales staff earned commission, and the workroom girls were paid a little extra if they passed their daily quota. Noreen's wages were up to two pounds weekly, the same as Dolores's and Miss Morton's. The elderly lady had protested, saying she did a much shorter working week these days, but Laura had refused to listen. 'If it weren't for you, dear, I don't know where I should be. Yes, I do. Sitting at a bench stripping tobacco.'

'Nonsense! You'd have made something of yourself whatever you did.'

'But I wouldn't have had any skills without you.'

Miss Morton had given up arguing. She spent quite a few weekends with her friend in Weston-Super-Mare these days and was looking happy and well.

Nancy worked steadily through the day, unwilling to meet Laura's eyes, speaking only when she couldn't avoid it. She looked deeply miserable. Neither she nor Laura felt inclined to talk of last night.

After everyone had finished work Laura went upstairs and made up the bed. Daisy had been out shopping for her and she ate a simple meal of cheese, rolls and fruit. She hadn't felt hungry since the scene at the party. She had time to think of it now, and of what had followed. She and Rick had made love and she gloried in it still. Even thinking about it stirred her to desire, but she was not under any illusion that their night of passion indicated Rick's settling down, though she was sure that what had happened meant more to him than a passing whim. She was wiping up dishes when the ring came on the front door. She wondered who it was. Adrian? Rick? Ralph?

Laura walked downstairs, taking her time, and opened the door to be confronted by Lady Mallender.

Laura stared at her angrily for a moment, then turned without a word and led the way up to the flat where her ladyship looked around her with a contemptuous expression.

Laura seated herself opposite her mother-in-law and waited.

'Have you nothing to say?' demanded Lady Mallender.

'About what?' asked Laura flatly.

'About your disappearance from last night's party which, I must remind you, was held for you.'

'Just for me?'

'And for Adrian, naturally. Laura, your behaviour was outrageous! How do you suppose I was able to account for your sudden withdrawal?'

'How did you?'

'I made the usual type of excuse. I said you had developed a dreadful headache.'

'Poor me! Did Adrian say I had a headache, too?'

'Of course.'

'Then he did finally leave his studio.'

'His studio? I don't know what you're talking about. He danced enthusiastically for most of the night.'

'Did he? And what about Rex?'

'Rex?' A wary look crept into her ladyship's eyes. 'What has he to do with this?'

'Don't you know?'

'Stop fencing with me, young lady!' Lady Mallender cried angrily. 'Your action was disgraceful and all you can give me now is insolence.'

'Insolence. That's a word you're fond of, isn't it? You use it about servants, and shop girls, and any other inferior you're forced to deal with.'

Lady Mallender stood up. 'I find your mood most odd. We shall talk together after dinner tonight. It will be served as usual at eight o'clock.'

Laura remained seated. To hell with Lady Troubridge's book of etiquette! What advice would she give to a woman who had witnessed a scene like last night's? 'I shall come to the house after dinner to fetch my clothes and toilet articles. They are mine, all paid for by me.'

Lady Mallender paused, then reseated herself. 'Laura,' she said in wheedling tones, 'I assume you have had a quarrel with Adrian. Now, my dear, all young couples quarrel. It's part of marriage. Making up will be delightful. Do please forget your wrath and come home.'

'Home! Will Rex be there, too?'

Her ladyship's chin drew back sharply. 'You keep bringing his name in. What has Rex to do with you and Adrian?'

'Last night I went looking for Adrian. He had been gone so long from his own party, you see.'

'There's no need to take that sarcastic tone with me. I'll remind you that we welcomed you, humbly born as you are, into the kind of life you could never have dreamed of.'

'How right you are. I suppose every girl dreams of marrying a decent man, but I certainly could never have imagined someone like Adrian.'

Her ladyship would have said more but Laura held up her hand and said quickly, 'Don't let's fence over this. You love your son, in spite of everything; I admire you for that –'

'In spite of –!'

' – but it was very wrong of you to inflict him on me – on any woman. He prefers men, doesn't he? And last night he most definitely preferred Rex. I saw them together – in the studio. I don't think you want me to describe the scene.'

Lady Mallender seemed to shrink. Her over-bearing attitude collapsed. She licked her lips nervously, 'Forgive him, my dear. You love him, don't you? Love is forgiving. Accept him as he is, as I've done. You'll find happiness with him, I'm sure. He's weak, but he's gentle. And when the babies come along –'

In the face of her mother-in-law's distress Laura's answer

was far more mild than she felt. 'I'm sorry, Lady Mallender, but there won't be any babies. Not by me. If Adrian wishes to divorce me for desertion I shan't put obstacles in his way.'

'Divorce! Such a disgrace! We've never had one in our family. That's typical of someone from the lower class. A well-born girl would keep a brave face and make the marriage work.'

Laura lifted her head. 'Oddly enough, divorce is considered quite a disgrace by the lower classes, too. In fact, I may have to divorce Adrian. The reasons will look marvellous in the newspapers, won't they?' Lady Mallender went so white Laura rose to her feet. 'Are you faint? I'll fetch water –'

Lady Mallender waved her hand imperiously. 'Be silent! I want nothing! I am deeply disappointed in you, but I tell you this, if you try to make a scandal around my son – around my family – you will be sorry. You'll find no witnesses ready to help you, I can assure you of that. The Mallenders are well known and respected, whereas your family –' She paused, her lip curling. 'Who will take the word of a girl from such a background as yours?'

'Might you not find it difficult to explain your consent to my marrying Adrian?'

'I think not. I am well known for my charity.' She stood. 'I shall advise my friends not to enter your shops again.'

Laura felt a deadly anger. 'If you do I shall tell people exactly what I saw, and that I was tricked into marriage and, above all for your materialistic world, I shall expose the fact that your rich living is all sham. I imagine I'm not your only creditor.'

Lady Mallender glared hatred and walked out stiffly. Laura heard the heels of her expensive shoes tapping down the wooden stairway. She sat down abruptly, exhausted by the scene. It was degrading. She recalled her threats with disgust. Malicious gossiping wasn't in her nature.

That night she drove to the Mallender house at nine o'clock and rang the bell. Renton opened the door and didn't quite manage to conceal his gleeful anticipation. Laura wondered if he disliked Adrian, or her, or just enjoyed a bit of spicy scandal. It didn't matter. After tonight she wouldn't enter this place again. She went up to her bedroom and began packing her clothes. She folded her trousseau, her lips pressed tight as she recalled her anticipatory joy when she'd made them. She left the few presents given to her by Adrian, including the engagement ring. She was finished when the door burst open and Adrian rushed in.

'Laura, don't go. Darling, please, I love you, I do truly, I –'

'Don't lie to me! You disgust me.' Her words came out in a near scream, all her pent-up misery exploding. 'You revolt me!'

'I can't help it.' To her horror Adrian began to cry, knuckling his eyes like a child. 'Mummy's terribly cross with me. It's making me feel awful.'

'Stop it. They're just crocodile tears. Stop crying, will you?' she said harshly.

'Laura, please stay. I'll try to be a good husband to you. I can't help what I am.'

'It's not that. I suppose the Lord puts different sorts on earth, but you lied to me, you cheated me, you made me believe I was marrying a whole man!'

'I made love to you. You enjoyed it.'

Laura almost cringed at the memory. 'You made love to Rex as well.'

'I didn't mean to. Honestly, Laura, that man's got a hold on me. He makes me do these things. I love you, Laura. Please stay.'

He stepped towards her and she backed off. 'You're a liar and if you touch me I'll scream blue murder.'

He stood aside as she walked out, carrying her case. In the hall Sir Hugo waited. 'Please, Laura, will you step into the library and grant me the favour of a few words.'

The library was lit by a single lamp over a desk. The smell of leather-bound books was pleasant.

'Please sit down. Over here, by the fire. The nights are getting cold. It will soon be Christmas again.'

It was the first time he had spoken kindly to her. Laura waited. She wondered if he was about to appeal to her on his son's behalf.

'This house has been in turmoil today. I gather that last

night you witnessed a scene that distressed you.'

'Yes.'

'Am I to understand that you had no knowledge of my son's – er – proclivities prior to that?'

'If you mean did I know he was a homosexual, the answer is, no.'

'I see.' Sir Hugo sat opposite her, his long hand resting on a small table, his fingers tapping. After a while he said, 'I misjudged you. I thought you had traded your self-respect for a place in society.'

'You were wrong.'

He looked into her face. 'I see I was. I must beg your forgiveness for what we have done to you. Does anyone in my family owe you money?'

'No,' said Laura firmly.

'We probably do, but I won't plague you. The sooner you forget us, the better. I suppose you'll divorce Adrian.' He couldn't keep his voice from cracking. 'There will be hideous publicity, but it's what we deserve.'

'People already know about Adrian.'

'Yes, society people do, but not the others.'

'By the others I take it you mean the general public.'

'Yes. The newspapers – our name will be tainted. It has always been an honourable one.'

Laura pitied him. 'Sir Hugo, I'll forget divorce for now if Adrian will undertake to leave me alone. I just want to make a success of my business. And if you could prevent Lady Mallender from blackening my name among her friends – I need their custom.'

The baronet frowned. 'Is that what she threatened? I'll speak to her. But, Laura, I don't know if I can prevail upon her – she is a strong-willed woman – I can't be sure she won't gossip.'

It must have been painful for him to confess to her that he had no real control over his wife. Laura felt sorrier than ever for him.

'I can't stay here, Sir Hugo, you see that, don't you?'

'I see very well. You're dealing kindly with us, my dear, more kindly than we have a right to expect.'

The following morning Nancy turned up at eight o'clock, an hour before the shop was opened. She still had her key and Laura heard her light footsteps as she walked upstairs. She entered the flat. She looked as if she hadn't slept. 'Have you left Adrian?' she asked. 'I can't get a reply from anyone.'

'I've left him,' said Laura grimly, 'and nothing anyone says can make me go back.'

'I can't blame you. Adrian shouldn't have married you.'

'It seems everyone was in the secret, except me.'

'Forgive me, please, Laura. I couldn't speak against my own brother. I hoped so desperately that marrying you would change him.'

Laura sighed. 'Well, it didn't. Our marriage is over. I suppose you'll not want to work here any more.'

Nancy hugged her. 'If you'll have me, Daddy says I can work full time. Mummy was absolutely beside herself with rage, but Daddy stood firm.'

'I'm so glad,' Laura said, 'you're a tremendous asset.'

'Oh, thank you. Our family doesn't deserve such generosity. You saw Adrian with Rex, didn't you? It's all rather sordid.'

'How do you know what happened?'

'Daddy told me. The servants know, too. I can tell by the way Gardner smirked at me.'

Gardner! Laura had forgotten her. She had known what was happening in the attic and had meant to strike a lethal blow at Laura's marriage. She had succeeded.

Chapter Twenty-Five

If Laura had been nursing any fears that her customers would reject her once they discovered she had left Adrian she was utterly mistaken. During the next weeks they came in droves. Both *Hats by Laura* shops did booming trade and she was kept busy helping Nancy to serve, which meant she had to stay up very late to concentrate on her designs and the clerical work. The presence of Adrian's sister in the shop was an added titillation, it seemed, and even in Laura's dreams the high-pitched, gossiping, questing voices echoed. Laura was disdainful. They must suspect the truth, but they never stopped hinting, doing everything but ask outright what exactly went wrong.

Daphne and Thelma Charlton were leaders in the prying, just as they were leaders in Bristol's young society.

'Adrian's really quite a darling,' said Thelma, as she twisted and turned, peering into the mirror in front of her and the one which Laura held behind her head. 'I like the colour, but do you think the brim quite suits my face? Let me have the other one again. The poor lamb is quite distraught.'

Even the gentle Nancy got angry. 'Nasty-minded tabby cats,' she said.

Ralph, as always, backed his sister. He said little, but she sensed his sympathy. It was a different matter with her other relatives.

Laura knew it couldn't be long before her family heard the news. Lillian was the first to find out. She was at home with Victor, her fiancé, on the first Sunday Laura was able to visit. Her eyes were alight with mischief, 'Hello, Mrs Mallender. Well, that little jaunt went wrong pretty damn quick, didn't it?

Discovered you don't like the nobs? You should have got married to someone like my Victor here. Meet Laura, my sister. Laura, Victor Sherwood. We shall be walkin' down the aisle soon.'

Victor grinned and flexed his arm muscles. 'I'm a better man than a toffee-nosed nob any day, aren't I, Lill?' He grabbed Lillian and pulled her on to his lap, holding her tightly, his hands clasped under her breasts, while Lillian squealed and Phyllis frowned.

'What happened, chick?' asked Dad of Laura, returning immediately to his reading, making it all too evident that he didn't want to become embroiled in explanations. Not that Laura intended to offer any.

Mum sighed. 'I don't hold with what you've done, but he's not our sort.'

Freda sat eating her tea, silent, her heavy jaws munching. Her eyes seemed almost opaque, as if she had imprisoned herself in a world which no one could enter. She left and went walking as soon as her meal was finished.

Phyllis said, 'I don't know about our Freda. Dad and me are fetchin' Joyce's baby next week and I'm worried. You don't think she'd hurt little Andrew, do you, Laura?'

'Surely not. She'll grow to love him. He's all we've got left of Joyce. Mum, if you need any help with the train fare –'

'Put it in the vase.' Phyllis took the money grudgingly, as if she couldn't abide benefiting from the daughter she had rejected.

Enid was still locked into happiness. Little Glory was a picture, dressed to perfection in pink and white. Laura held her close to her fast-beating heart. So much for her dreams of being a mother. Enid was unravelling a white jumble-sale jumper. 'There's enough wool to make Glory a winter set. Some people must have more money than sense the stuff they chuck out. Look, I got this one, too.'

'Blue? That's for a boy.'

Enid smiled broadly. 'The next one might be. I'm expectin' again. Six weeks gone.'

'So soon after Glory?'

'Why not? I'm healthy, we've got a nice little house and no worries.'

As Laura drove back to Park Street Enid's words ran through her brain. No worries, no worries. Lucky Enid. But by the time she reached her office she had forgotten everything but the need to complete the designs for her new collection. The hats must be ready in time for the show to be held when the sales finished. From now on she would devote her whole life to work. Love was an illusion. Making love was different. Perhaps when she was successful she would take lovers. She wondered how Anita managed about sex.

Anita had been more amused than anything by the break-up of Laura's marriage. 'So your wits have returned? Thank God you had enough sense not to get pregnant.'

Laura flinched. 'Has it ever occurred to you not to be so rough with someone's tender feelings?'

Anita blew out a cloud of smoke. She had taken to using flat Egyptian cigarettes which had an exotic aroma. 'No,' she said simply. 'The world's a hell of a place. If you've got tender feelings the best place for them is locked away deep down inside where no one ever suspects them, never mind sees them.'

'Well, that's cynical.'

'It's practical though.'

'Has someone hurt you? Is that why you're afraid to show what you feel?'

Anita laughed. 'Forget it, my sweet. There's no burning misery in my soul. I was still a child when I decided that if I ever married it would be to someone of my choosing who would let me live my life and not his. So far I've never met the man. Quite the opposite. The ones I've been attracted to in the past have so far put me off for life. Bastards! I think perhaps it's the influence of a French mother. The French are realists. They arrange their marriages for practical reasons. Love is something you get as a bonus.'

'What about making love?'

'Sex, you mean, don't you? That can easily be taken care of. There's always someone around to help. Male – or female.'

Laura stared. 'You don't mean – that you're the same as Adrian.'

426

'No, but sex is sex, as far as I'm concerned. Adrian's a bloody fool to let the world know what he is. If he'd had any sense he would have kept you and enjoyed his other pleasures quietly.'

'That's horrible! I don't know how you can talk like that!'

'Simmer down, Laura. Face the world as it is and not as you would like it to be.'

'Why are you telling me this? How do you know I won't gossip about you? What would your customers say?'

'You won't, and they wouldn't care. They'd relish the idea. It would give them so much scope for delicious chit-chat.'

Her words forced a laugh from Laura. Anita could always get under her defences. 'That's better, darling. Now let's have a little drink together to toast your freedom and a further step in your education.'

Rick had gone to London the day after the party. Some time later he walked into the Park Street shop as Nancy and Laura were tidying up at the end of a busy day.

'You look tired, Laura.'

'Thanks. That's a nice way to greet me. It gives me such a thrill.' She met his eyes and they held such knowledge, such teasing charm that she had to look away, thankful that Nancy was present. 'How was London?'

'Wonderful, as always. There's a lot of talk about a new American company called Shenandoah. Goldman Sachs and the Financial and Industrial Securities Corporation have launched it just to buy and sell shares. They've already got assets of two hundred and fifty million dollars. Think of that!'

'I'll try,' said Laura drily, 'but meanwhile I'll attempt to rub along with my three little shops. I don't understand stocks and shares.'

'You may have to one day. You mean to make it big, don't you?'

'Make it big! Every time you come back from London your language sounds different.'

'And talking pictures are going to make it even more different. But I'm quite glad to be back. Bristol has its own particular charms. I've signed up some good stuff for the Empire Theatre.'

'What as, an agent, booking manager, or cinema owner?'

'Bit of each. I like to spread my talent around. Two of the acts are going to appear at the Premier between films.'

'How are the cinemas doing?' asked Nancy.

'Very well. Did you see *The Jazz Singer*?'

'Yes,' said Nancy. 'It was amazing.'

'No,' said Laura, 'I didn't have time, but I've heard all about it.'

Rick grinned. 'You still don't believe the talkies will catch on, do you, but I'm taking business away from some of the oldest cinemas that didn't think sound had a future.'

'That's like stealing,' said Laura in a perverse wish to annoy him.

'I hear you've taken trade from Gregory's, as well as other stores,' he said amicably. 'Is that stealing?'

'Definitely not!' She was equally amicable. 'Rick, I'm glad things are going well, but I have a show to plan for and we've been so busy I've had to be in the shop for most of the days lately, and –'

Rick threw up his hands. 'All right, baby, I hear you loud and clear. When, *if*, you ever stop work I'll make sure you see a talking picture. How about *Uncle Tom's Cabin*?'

Laura was impressed, in spite of herself. 'I've read the book. Do you mean I'll be able to see it, like a play?'

'Sure you will. See it and hear it. I'll take you.'

'That's a date,' said Laura, without thinking. She turned away to hide a blush. Would Rick imagine she was asking for another night with him? She recalled Anita's words. Why the hell shouldn't she make it clear? Her body had got used to love. It craved fulfilment. Even Adrian had been better than nothing. And Rick – she caught her breath at the memory. His lovemaking had lifted her to ecstasy she had never dreamed of. She turned and looked him full in the face and he grew suddenly serious. Nancy had gone upstairs and Rick said, 'Not me, baby. Don't look at me.'

'What are you talking about?'

'Don't pretend, Laura. You must find a husband worth

428

having, someone who'll value you for the dear girl you are. I'll never settle for marriage.'

Her face flamed. 'Marriage? Who the hell's talking about that! I'm still hitched to Adrian, remember?'

'Don't be angry with me, honey, I'm trying to be honest. You respect honesty.'

'Do I? I'm not so bloody sure any more.'

'Don't swear.'

'Oh, go to hell!'

Rick shrugged, smiled ruefully, touched his hat and sauntered out. She felt like hurling something after him.

The workrooms were up to date with the shapes for spring. Everyone was working hard. Even Lottie had lost her peevish expression and smiled and hummed as she went about her duties and took a much deeper interest in all that was happening. Laura congratulated herself that she had reprimanded the girl at the right time.

In Redfield Noreen and Miss Morton dealt with the straws which were large floppy affairs destined to flower on sunny foreign beaches. Suntans were all the rage and beach suits and bathing costumes were cut to show as much skin as was decently possible or, in the opinion of some, indecently disgraceful. The felt brims were broadening a little, too, and hats would not be quite as spartan as in the past few years.

Women were to have breasts again, waists were returning and corsets were on sale with brassière tops. Fashion was making one of its periodic upheavals and Laura spent hours when her problems receded studying magazines, listening to letters written to Anita by Madame Rodrigues, and poring over her sketches and colour swatches. Many of her new shapes were in a soft black, the trimmings would reflect the soft pastel shades beloved of Renoir.

Noreen still managed the Redfield shop, though Laura had promised to relieve her as soon as she found someone suitable to take over. Millie assisted her; she had no fears about using the telephone.

Laura was feeling tired and irritated by her inability to fight it off. She seemed to be waking as weary as when she went to bed.

'It's not surprising,' said Miss Morton severely, 'when you get about six hours' sleep a night and often not that. You'd best be careful, Laura, or you'll fall ill and then where would we all be?'

Laura bought herself a tonic, Parrish's Chemical Food, which Granma had given her as a child. It seemed to help a little.

Rick called occasionally. He was, as usual, outspoken. 'You look like a raccoon,' he told her.

'Never having seen one I can't know what you mean,' said Laura brusquely, as she draped a length of black velvet in the window. 'Look at this, Rick, I'm putting an assortment of cigarette cases, jewellery and make-up on the velvet. I'm trying to make it look like a garden of flowers. Does it work?'

Rick went solemnly outside and inspected the window. 'It looks all right,' he reported.

'Does it look like a garden?'

'From a distance – a short distance,' he amended hurriedly as she lifted a block threateningly.

'A raccoon,' explained Rick, 'is an animal with dark fur round its eyes.'

'I see. Thanks. Do you like this?' She held up a black lace dress sent down by Anita. 'I'm going to display it against a white velvet backcloth.'

'I'd like to see you in it.'

'I'm not asking for stupid flattery. And you just told me I look like a raccoon.'

'You should rest more.'

'I'll rest when my shops are ready for it. And you can't talk. I hear you're back playing piano at fashionable parties on top of all your other activities.'

'I'm a man.'

'Huh! A woman's as good as a man any day.'

The exchange with Rick had exhilarated her, unlike the wearing arguments she'd had with Adrian and his mother. They pestered her constantly to return to the family home. 'If only for the sake of appearances,' begged Lady Mallender.

'Surely you love me a little,' whined Adrian. 'I promise not to see Rex again. I sent him away after you left and we've completely lost touch.'

Since Laura had seen the two of them dining *à deux* one evening when she'd gone out to dinner with Ralph, Nancy and Rick, she gave no weight to this claim. She couldn't be bothered to argue. She just wanted him to go away. She must have been crazy to fall for a miserable, whimpering weakling like him. She began to think longingly of divorce – when she had time she would do something, she promised herself. Time was what she needed as the days flew by.

One evening as she sat in her flat eating a light supper the bell rang.

Dolores was outside. 'Come on in,' said Laura.

Dolores followed her upstairs and accepted a cup of tea, but refused a cheese sandwich.

'Is that your meal?' she asked.

'Mmm. There's plenty of goodness in it.'

Dolores was silent and Laura said, 'Surely you didn't come here at this hour to talk about my supper.'

'No. I didn't. I've been wonderin' how to say what I've been asked to.'

'This sounds serious.'

'It is. The fact is, Laura, you're goin' to have a revolt on your hands. Maybe even a strike.'

'What! You're joking.'

'Would I joke about such a thing?'

'But why? I pay the girls good money. They all get extra for overtime which is more than Gregory's ever gave us, and I've made their working conditions as pleasant as possible. What earthly reason have they got?'

'You're pushin' them too hard.'

'How, for God's sake?'

'Think about it. You've got this show comin' up and you're loadin' the girls with tons of extra jobs. You seem to forget that they've still got their everyday tasks to get on with. Business is good, very good, and it's as much as they can do to keep up with it. And the apprentices aren't gettin' the teachin' they should and that's upset Miss Morton.'

Laura was angry. 'And where do you come into it? You've only the wholesale hats to deal with? And am I supposed to have exploited the shop staff as well?'

'We've had a meetin' –'

'We! Who's we?'

'Laura, please don't be angry with me. I'm only tryin' to help. All of us met one evenin' in my shop. They said it was neutral ground.'

'*All* of them. Do you mean that? Even Miss Morton!'

Dolores hesitated, biting her lip. 'Yes, and Noreen and Pansy. *All* of us.'

Laura sprang up. 'And you let them meet at Kingswood? How could you be so disloyal?'

'I'm not, Laura. You know I'd do anythin' for you. I thought if they met there I could keep an eye on things for you.'

'And the others sent you to speak to me!'

'Yes.'

'Does Iris know about this?'

'Yes.'

'My own sister let this happen without warning me?'

'She was asked not to. She's miserable about it, but it was decided that I should speak.'

'So I'm working them too hard! Don't they realise how hard I'm pushing myself? I get up at dawn sometimes and go to bed long past midnight just to make sure we all have jobs.'

'The girls know that, but they can't see it exactly your way. They like and admire you, they want to work for you, but they've begun to feel you're aimin' mostly at your personal success. They say they can't go on takin' such a load. The workrooms are open far too long after hours, and the shop staff stay behind to help in pricin' and storin' the hats for the show.'

Laura stared. 'And what do you think?'

'That you should treat this carefully. The last thing I want is to see you fail and that's not just because I should lose my job.'

Laura sat down and faced Dolores who stared at her anxiously. She thought over the past weeks. She was far more obsessed with work since the break-up of her marriage. She had substituted success for love. She was driven by fear. If she was to end up alone she didn't intend to be poor like Miss Morton and so many others.

'What do they want?' she asked.

Dolores sighed with relief at the more tolerant tone. 'Not much. The workroom staff want their hours to be more clearly set out and their Saturday half-day closin' properly enforced. At the moment they never leave at lunchtime and sometimes go on into a full day. The sales' girls need their half day, too. Nobody minds doing reasonable overtime, but you're givin' them too much.'

Laura was silent for a while, then she said slowly, 'I feel disgusted with myself, Dolores. I'm worse than Gregory.'

Dolores laughed shakily. 'No, you could never be that, love.'

'Thanks. Ask Pansy, Noreen and Miss Morton to see me after hours tomorrow. We'll decide upon a proper working schedule. I'll also advertise for more girls. To be honest, I'm feeling the strain myself. I can't seem to cope with serving and working upstairs.'

'You haven't been lookin' too well lately.'

'So Rick Merriman kindly told me.'

'Rick's a scream.'

'One long hoot from beginning to end,' agreed Laura drily.

Once the staff understood that Laura was sympathetic the meeting was amicable, with everyone intent on doing what was best for the business and the people who earned their living by it. Laura listened to their grievances, realising with rueful clarity that she had been losing touch with her employees. She promised them changes. She engaged more girls who were grateful for the work, and she asked her senior staff to let her know in future of even a hint of unrest.

The changes made inroads into her capital, but she was still amassing a respectable sum. After the spring sales she felt she might be able to make an offer to buy the Park Street shop. She still needed someone reliable to serve alongside Nancy and that problem was quickly sorted out. Nancy told her that Stevens, the Mallenders' maid, had been sacked. 'Rex said something about a maid involved in betraying him and Adrian to you.

433

Mummy has decided it was Stevens. Of course she didn't tell her that was why she must leave.'

'It was Gardner,' said Laura.

'I guessed.'

'Couldn't you tell your mother so?'

'I tried to. She wouldn't listen. She would never risk upsetting Gardner. They've been together too long.'

'So poor Stevens is the scapegoat.'

'To do Mummy justice, there's more to it than that. They're cutting costs again. I feel sorry for them. I know they've treated you badly, Laura, but I can't help loving them. They're my family.'

'Oh, Nancy, I understand that only too well. I admire your loyalty.'

Stevens was duly interviewed and engaged and Laura was able to devote her days to designing and fashioning the hats. She was also getting more rest. Everything was running smoothly when Laura had a visitor. Everyone had left for the night and she was surprised to find Miss Pringle at her door.

'How nice to see you. Come in quickly out of the cold. Have you just finished work? I'm sure you could do with a cup of tea.'

Upstairs Laura looked at Miss Pringle sympathetically. 'You don't look at all well. You should be at home.'

'I do feel unwell. I'm sick with anger. Laura, I was in Mr Gregory's office this afternoon and he was called away. I sat and waited for him and my eye was caught by some designs on his desk. They looked interesting, but ordinarily I wouldn't have touched them. It was just that the style looked so familiar – exactly like yours.'

'What?'

'It's as distinctive as your handwriting. I examined them closely and opened a folio beside them. Let me guess at your next season's fashions. Soft black with pastel shades for trimmings. Floppy straws, bigger brims –'

She broke off as Laura rushed for the lavatory where she was violently sick. When she returned, shaking, she looked very white.

Miss Pringle was horrified. 'Laura, my dear! I should have broken the news more gently.'

'There isn't any way you could have told me that in a gentle way. I've not been feeling up to much all day. How could Gregory's have got hold of my designs? Only my top assistants have any idea of what they are.'

'Do you leave your office for any length of time with the door unlocked?'

'Not so much now, though I did sometimes when I served.'

'And were the girls allowed in the office?'

'They weren't forbidden, but they had no reason to use it. And no one could have got in without Pansy seeing them. It can't be her, it just can't.'

'It isn't,' said Miss Pringle slowly. 'Young Mr Gregory has a new girlfriend. They've been seen together. She works for you. It's Lottie, your apprentice.'

'That child! I can't believe it. Even Arthur Gregory wouldn't stoop to taking out a child. Lottie's only fourteen.'

'He would if he and his father wanted to know which way they could destroy your credibility at your next show. We're putting one on, as usual, but the date hasn't been set which is definitely *unusual*. I think they're waiting to hear about yours and will choose the day before.'

Coming on top of what Laura saw as Adrian's treachery this new blow seemed impossible to bear. For weeks she had kept misery at bay by immersing herself in the new designs, working long hours, striving to make sure the new collection would be a triumph. Her art was all she had left. And it had been stolen from her.

She felt a physical pain at the idea of one of her well-cared-for employees behaving in such a way. She still felt nauseous and shaky.

Miss Pringle looked sad. 'I wish there was something I could do, Laura.'

'Thank you, but you've done all you could.'

'I'm so sorry I had to be the bearer of bad tidings, but I'm sure you'll fight your way out of this setback.'

Laura nodded. She said, 'Yes,' but her voice was so

dispirited that Miss Pringle, who had risen to leave, sat down again. 'Laura, it may not matter. Your shops are considered far more exclusive than Gregory's.'

'It isn't enough. I vowed I would have an original collection twice a year and that's a vow I mean to keep.'

After Miss Pringle had gone Laura considered the consequences of Lottie's behaviour. She would have approximately one month to find a new theme and get the hats made in time and it would have to be done during the hectic January sales. She lifted her calendar from the wall and checked on the exact dates. Just about four weeks. Then she peered closer. There was the red dot indicating her time of the month for December. There should have been one for January. She sat quite still thinking, her heart thudding, wondering if she had simply forgotten, though she knew she hadn't. She never did. No wonder she felt so tired and off-colour; no wonder her stomach was so temperamental. She knew with complete clarity of mind that she was pregnant. By Rick. She was carrying his child. She panicked. She hadn't meant to have a child until she was well established. How could she continue to work at the frantic pace needed? Then came relief that Adrian was not the father. If she hadn't discovered him with Rex she could so easily be having his baby. Thank God she wasn't. It was Rick's, conceived in that wild night after her discovery of her husband's perversion. Laura hardened her resolve. No one need ever know the truth. Everyone, including Adrian, would assume that the baby was her husband's. The thought gave her a pang of self-disgust, but she must protect the child. Rick's life had been soured by the circumstances of his birth. Their child must be born within the sanctity of marriage, even a broken one such as hers. She wished she could tell Rick. He always understood her dilemmas, but this was one secret he must never know. She groaned and held her head in her hands, dreading the coming months. She even wondered if Granma had been right all along and that God was punishing her.

The following day, after speaking to a horrified Nancy, and telephoning the other shops she drove Pansy to meet Dolores, Miss Morton and Noreen. They were aghast at her disclosure.

'What'll you do?' asked Miss Morton. 'You're already working too hard. You look quite peaky, in fact.'

'That's as may be,' said Laura, 'but there *will* be a show in *Hats by Laura* after the sales and that's a promise.'

'Good for you,' cried Pansy. 'I'll give it all I've got.'

'The hours will be long,' reminded Laura.

Dolores looked solemnly at her workmates. 'Laura's thinkin' of our protest.'

'As far as I'm concerned that'll be forgotten for the emergency,' said Noreen.

The others agreed vociferously.

'Nothing of this must leak out,' warned Laura, 'or Gregory's will copy me again. And you'll be paid for every minute of overtime.'

Miss Morton was quietly determined, her lined face solemn. 'It's up to all of us seniors to make sure she's got the backing she needs.'

Laura ran her hands over her hair and massaged the back of her neck which was beginning to ache. 'The trouble is I haven't thought of a new theme, though I've been up half the night. My brain seems to have done a temporary bunk. At least, I hope it's temporary.'

'Why not try Bauhaus?' Pansy suggested.

The others looked blank but Laura said, 'I've read about them. The ultimate in machine-age aesthetics. It's connected with the theatre and seems to be all cubes and jagged lines and odd designs. Hoops, masks, metallic shapes –' Laura laughed at the blank faces and the ease of tension made her feel better. 'I think Pansy's hit on a brilliant idea. It's totally opposite to the soft colours I had in mind. The hats can keep the basic shapes. We'll need to produce some really different finishes.'

Laura drove Pansy back to Park Street, where she called Lottie into her office.

She didn't waste words. Lottie stared, then her eyes filled with tears. 'Please, Mrs Mallender, don't sack me. My Dad'll murder me and if he doesn't my Mum will. Don't send me away.'

'I notice you don't ask what you're supposed to have done,' said Laura.

Lottie sniffed. 'It was that Arthur Gregory. He wormed the secrets from me.'

'You knew you were doing wrong. You must have sneaked into the office when Pansy's attention was diverted. No one suspected you, unfortunately.'

'I'll never do it again. Let me stay.'

Laura shook her head. 'I can forgive a great deal, but I won't employ a girl I can't trust.'

Lottie shouted, 'You mean, spiteful cow! You're just upset because your husband doesn't want you any more!'

Pansy walked into the office. 'Shut your hysterical mouth, you traitorous bitch. Get out of here before I forget myself and hit you.'

Laura held up a protesting hand, but Lottie scurried away, bawling.

'Good riddance to her,' said Pansy. She told the other workroom girls that Lottie had been dismissed for extreme misbehaviour and the atmosphere was subdued for the rest of the day.

'Don't worry, Laura,' said Pansy cheerfully. 'They're really quite glad to see her go. She's a born troublemaker.'

Laura told Iris the truth. She listened with huge indignation. Iris was growing up. Not that she'd ever seemed much of a child. In that turbulent home in Kingswood she had always been hurrying about in the background, baking, sorting out the young ones' problems, trying all she could to make life easier for her parents. 'Lottie is wicked,' she said. 'She'll not find it easy to get another job.'

'No, she won't.' Laura frowned, remembering how she had been sacked by Gregory's for 'stealing' a customer.

Iris said quietly, 'Sackin' Lottie has upset you, hasn't it.'

Laura nodded. 'I'm remembering how I ended up stripping tobacco.'

Iris touched her sister's arm tentatively. 'It isn't the same, love. What Lottie's done could have ruined you.'

Laura laughed shakily. 'I wonder. I hope not quite ruined.'

'That horrible Mr Gregory is capable of anythin'. If our show had gone ahead like you first planned it he would have told people that you'd stolen his ideas. You might never have recovered.'

Anita listened to Laura's story with a frown. 'That's disgusting. She should be whipped. But you say you have another idea.'

'It's Pansy's.'

'She's a wonder. It amazes me how such delicate work and such a clear mind can inhabit so unattractive a body.' She offered Laura a cigarette and when Laura refused lit up one for herself. They were sitting in Anita's one-room flat over the shop. It was furnished with modern stuff: Corbusier tubular steel chairs and a glass-topped table designed by Eileen Gray, a sofa upholstered in red and black stripes, a scarlet tubby basket chair. There was a slender vase with one flower, and a Lalique ornament, a dancing girl whose movement had been captured in spectacular glass. There was even a radio, a wooden table-top model which was playing music.

'That's coming from the Savoy Hotel in London,' said Anita. 'The Savoy Orpheans.'

She blew out a cloud of smoke and Laura caught a whiff and abruptly her stomach churned. 'I need the lavatory,' she gasped and hurried away. She tried to vomit quietly, but Anita stared at her when she returned. She had put out her cigarette.

'Are you ill?' Her eyes sparkled with an almost malicious curiosity.

Laura stared at her. 'I'm pregnant,' she said flatly.

'Oh, my God! You stupid idiot! So Adrian got his way after all. I thought you knew how to protect yourself.'

'I did. I do, but – that time I didn't use it!'

'Rather you than me,' said Anita.

'Well, you don't have to sound so bloody triumphant about it!'

'It's no good getting miffy with me.'

'I know. Oh, damn it, Anita, I hate myself.'

A flicker of sympathy showed for a moment in Anita's dark eyes. 'Have you thought of getting rid of it?'

'An abortion? No, it's too risky. And anyway –' Laura stopped, amazed by the protective feeling which was flooding through her. The idea of aborting Rick's child was an anathema to her. Rick's child. The realisation hit her with force.

Anita was staring at her with raised brows. ' "And anyway", you were saying.'

'I couldn't kill it.'

Anita shrugged; what others did with their lives was their business. 'I like you, Laura, and it's not often I can say that to someone, but you've got guts. I think you're crazy to go on with the pregnancy, but I'll help you if I can. In a professional way,' she added hastily. 'I don't want anything to do with kids.'

It was impossible to keep her condition secret. Laura felt nausea much of the time. She couldn't face tea or coffee or cigarettes. As she grew thinner and more pallid her senior workforce was horrified.

Dolores summed up their feelings. 'You'll have to go back to your husband, won't you?'

When Laura shook her head Dolores said, 'How are you going to manage the work for a new show?'

'I'll do it, if it kills me,' said Laura, gritting her teeth against the sickness that threatened to overwhelm her.

During the next weeks the response of her workers proved her ability to choose the right people – apart from Lottie, of course. Miss Pringle told Laura that Lottie had run straight to Gregory's with the news of her sacking, but they were complacently sure that Laura and her staff would never get another show ready on time. Among her other staff all grievances were forgotten and they worked long hours to repair the damage done. Nancy kept a record of their overtime and took on much of the clerical work, assisted by Iris after work. She made no attempt to persuade Laura to go back to Mallender House. She said very little at all about what had happened and never imputed blame. Ralph was his usual supportive self. He and Nancy had settled into a comfortable relationship in which words were often superfluous. They sensed each other's wishes and feelings. Their relationship transcended any need for display, at least in public. They went out together whenever they had time which wasn't often.

Pansy and Laura worked each side of Laura's desk, sketching, discussing, occasionally arguing. In the end they produced ideas which satisfied them. Christmas and the sale had passed in a kind of blur for them both. Pansy lived with her family, but ran her life independently of them. 'They're a load of loonies,' she informed Laura cheerfully. 'They think I'm mad and I feel the same about them.'

Rick called and Laura felt a devastating embarrassment in his company. 'Hey, simmer down, kid,' he murmured, making patting motions in the air with his capable hands. Laura stared down at them, remembering the way they had wandered over her body, and through all the discomforts of early pregnancy she still felt a wave of desire for him. 'I can feel the turmoil from here,' continued Rick. 'I came to tell you that Jack's had an accident. It's not serious. He's broken his leg and is hobbling round in plaster.'

'Not serious! But he won't be able to do his work properly and Enid's baby is on the way.'

'No, he can't do much at present, but I'm still giving him his wages. I can't risk having you jump on my neck again. Besides I like him and Enid – and most of your family, if it comes to that.'

Rick was kind as well as passionate. Laura dragged her emotions into order. 'How did Jack hurt himself?'

'In a typical Jack way. His bicycle wheels got jammed in the tramlines.'

Laura burst into a peal of laughter and Rick joined her. 'Jack's such a fool. I can't think why our Enid loves him so much.'

'He's a nice chap. Helps anybody any time and always with a smile. The trouble is he's short of brains. How's life with you, baby?'

'I'm so busy, Rick.' She told him of Lottie's treachery and he swore. 'I'm really sorry, honey. What a stinking little hellcat. I'd like to wring her neck.'

'You and Pansy have got something in common.' Laura's pale face broke into a smile.

'You don't look well.'

'I'm fine,' she lied.

Three days later he returned after the shop was closed for the night. Laura's heart beat fast as she led him upstairs.

'You're a rotten little liar,' he said amicably, when he was seated in front of the fire with a glass of whisky. He'd brought his own, knowing that Laura kept only sherry.

'Thanks, *honey*.'

'It's no good trying to get smart with me. You told me you felt fine and you don't. You're having a baby, aren't you?'

Her heart thudded. 'Have they put it in the paper now?'

He grinned. 'Glad to see your spirit isn't broken.'

'You make me sound like a horse. How did you find out?'

'Iris told me.'

'What? I'll have something to say to her.'

'Why? How long was the secret supposed to be kept? It's one that gets obvious. She said you were very unwell. She told me from the best of motives.'

Laura was glad that Rick knew, yet dreaded what he might say next.

He was right on cue. 'Laura, I didn't mean to speak of the time you ran from Adrian, but is there any chance – I mean, after that night – I didn't – I'm not –'

'The baby is Adrian's,' said Laura angrily, glad that he'd touched a raw spot with his semi-flippant tone, so that she was able to hide the trouble in her heart.

'Does her ladyship know?'

'What?'

'Lady Mallender. Your mother-in-law, remember? That family is desperate for an heir.'

'I've said nothing to them.'

When asked the next day Nancy said, 'I haven't told them. They'll find out soon enough and be down on you like an avalanche. I'm hoping you'll get the show over first.'

The hats were ready on time and Laura sent out her invitations. She'd decided to hold the show in Ralph's shop. His stock was improving as he invested most of his takings. He had begun to specialise in porcelain, bone china and coloured glaze ware produced by the Wedgwood potteries, small pieces, easily transported, needing little room for display, picked up in country house sales where they could often be overlooked or disregarded by the big buyers.

'There's so much to learn, Laura,' he said. 'Wedgwood have done so many different things. Cameos, for instance, Egyptian, Roman, famous philosophers and illustrious men. And they've made practical pieces that can be used every day. Jugs and pots and bowls and all sorts of other things. And there's the creamware with beautiful coloured designs, and jewellery and hair ornaments, scent bottles and –' He stopped and grinned. 'Don't mind me.'

Laura was delighted to see him so absorbed, but he never forgot his sister's plight and eased her life as much as he could.

As soon as Gregory's got word that Laura's invitations had gone out they arranged their show for the day before.

'I'm still nervous,' Laura confided to Pansy. 'Perhaps the women won't want to come to another show the next day.'

'Don't talk tosh! Of course they will. Most of them are idle and are desperate for something to do, and no one will want to miss anything you come up with.'

They had decided to use black with strong colours, brilliant reds and pinks, emerald green and azure blue, and almost strident yellow and burnt orange. Pansy had contacted an art-school colleague who made costume jewellery, which was now wildly popular, and whose prices as a beginner were modest, and the hats were trimmed with metal cubes holding geometric diamond-like stones, marcasite hoops, glittering cut glass rectangular shapes, metal hands with fingers curled around a soft feather, or spread like an oriental dancer with angular metal bows supporting tiny Japanese enamelled faces.

The little gilt seats filled quickly and there was a general buzz of conversation in which the name Gregory could be overhead. The customers sounded as if they had been impressed. '*So* pretty,' declared one girl. 'I could *see* the impressionist paintings. I ordered three hats.'

Laura clasped her hands together. She had worked like a demon, through times when she felt desperate with nausea, through backaches, headaches, indigestion, hunger, and – she smiled grimly to herself – heartache. Now she was to be tested.

She sighed with relief when the front door was closed and Lady Mallender had not appeared. Thelma and Daphne, however, were lounging in the back row, escorted by a couple of men.

Anita had agreed to act as a mannequin, with Dolores and Laura. The others tried to dissuade Laura. She was adamant. 'I'm going to do it and nothing you say will change that. We need three models and the baby doesn't show yet.'

The mannequins wore black-satin dresses with belts and buckles to match the shining embellishments of the hats, grey stockings and black shoes. Ralph gave the commentary and Nancy played the piano. As Ralph's mellifluous voice welcomed everyone to the 'important' show of *Hats by Laura* the chatter died. The first few minutes were devoted to hats similar to the ones displayed by Gregory's the day before. The customers moved uneasily, two or three patted back yawns, murmurings were heard, but Laura had deliberately chosen to begin this way to point out the contrast. Anita wore the first of the daring creations. She moved imperiously along the improvised catwalk, her pale complexion, black eyes heavily made up, black hair just peeping under the crown a perfect foil for a deep-brimmed crimson straw decorated with an miniature electric blue guitar around which was twisted a plait of bottle green satin ribbon. There was a gasp and someone broke into spontaneous applause. From then on the audience were in Laura's hands as hat after hat appeared, stunning in their originality. Finally the three girls waltzed down the catwalk together in three enormous straws in blue, yellow and orange, all covered with silk cobwebs of black with a metallic spider in their centres.

The customers behaved as outrageously as any poor woman fighting in a jumble sale as they pushed and shoved to buy. Several spoke of Gregory's show in scathing terms, expressing relief that they hadn't spent much money, and the girl who'd boasted three hats looked furious.

'Gregory's were somewhat similar to the ones you displayed at the beginning,' said one lady, 'but even they lacked your magic touch, Laura.'

Lady Marjorie agreed loudly. 'They did, indeed. Your hats are too delicious for words, dear.'

'Everyone wants the credit of being first to recognise your genius,' whispered Ralph.

'Genius,' Laura laughed. 'Hardly that, brother dear. And anyway it's Pansy you should compliment for the original idea.'

'She told me she thought of the work of the Bauhaus group and that you came up with the brightest ideas based on that.'

'I'm too happy to argue.'

It was almost a sellout and it was clear that from now until autumn the girls would have as much work as they could handle. More, in fact, because by then there would be the autumn show. Laura was surprised to find that the idea exhilarated her. She had expected to feel dreadful, but at some point during the day the nausea had lifted and she was tingling with life. She felt as if she had returned after a long illness.

Paul Harrington surprised her by calling and asking her out to dinner.

'Certainly not! I'm a married woman.'

'Don't try that one on me. You've left Adrian, haven't you?'

'Yes.'

'Doesn't surprise me. I was astounded that you married a man like him.'

Laura looked coolly at him. 'It's hardly your business.'

'No, you're right. Laura, I'm only asking you out for a meal. Do say you'll come. It will do you good.'

'No, thank you.'

Paul looked genuinely disappointed and she was sorry. She liked him and she liked his looks. He had a thin, clever face, with sharp planes that created lights and shadows, his dark eyes were deep-set beneath black brows, his black hair slicked back. He was a good dresser, too. Conservative without being stodgy. 'The truth is, Paul, I haven't been getting enough sleep for weeks and I'm not terribly well. It's probably overwork.'

Paul's eyes flickered over her. 'If you say so, darling.'

The inevitable day arrived when Lady Mallender marched through the shop door and demanded to speak to her. Laura left the workroom and climbed the stairs to the flat, followed by a puffing Lady Mallender who sank on to the couch and with an obvious effort produced an ingratiating smile.

'Laura, my dear, I hear you have good news for us. You are expecting my first grandchild. Is that correct?'

Laura felt uncomfortable at her mother-in-law's piercing gaze. 'Who told you that?' she answered evasively.

'Gardner. She knows someone who's a relative of one of your workforce. You can't keep a piece of good news secret, my dear.' Her ladyship wagged a finger roguishly and smiled. 'Not that kind of good news.'

'No.'

'Now, Laura, you must not be cross with me. Of course, you'll return home. We shall take great care of you and the dear little one. Adrian agrees with me.'

'Does Sir Hugo?'

Lady Mallender frowned. 'Of course he does.'

'Are you sure?'

'Laura, you are being deliberately provocative, but I won't let you rile me. Expectant mothers are easily upset. As a matter of fact, Sir Hugo is abroad, but he will agree with me when he returns.'

'I'm sorry, but I'm not coming back to your house.'

Lady Mallender's good humour was wiped out. 'But you must! What will people say? And it's your home, too, you know. Our first grandchild must be born there.'

Laura felt an almost overwhelming urge to tell the truth and rid herself of this domineering woman for ever, but the words stuck in her throat. She remembered Rick and his unwillingness, or inability, to give unstinting love. The child must come first.

Lady Mallender tried again. 'My grandson must see the first light of day in the house where his father and his ancestors were born. He must!'

'No, I shall never live under the same roof as Adrian again.'

'Will you come back if I send Adrian away?'

Laura was shocked. Adrian was a young god to his mother. She must be desperate. 'There's no need to do that. Even if you do, I shan't return.'

A stream of words broke from her ladyship, pleas, appeals to Laura's sense of right and dignity, threats. Nothing moved her, she would never forget the humiliation, the horrified anguish of the moment when she had discovered the truth about Adrian and Rex.

'I won't leave it there,' cried Lady Mallender before she departed. 'I shall make sure that my grandson is not left to a girl like you to bring up. And in such a place.' She looked round Laura's sitting room as if it were a rubbish dump, then swept out.

The following day an obviously reluctant Adrian arrived to make an appeal. When he put out his hand to touch her Laura moved back quickly.

'I'm not a leper,' he said. He sounded like an indignant child. 'I can't help the way I am. I didn't ask for it. It's not my fault.'

'No, I suppose not,' she agreed quietly. 'I'm not being prudish. How others run their lives is up to them, but I'll never forgive you for involving me in yours.'

'Mummy made me.'

'Yours was the final choice. You could have resisted.' Laura loathed the whining tone Adrian had lapsed into.

'She kept on and on. I do care about you Laura, honestly I do. You're the first girl, the only girl –'

'Stop it! Go away! Nothing you can say or do will make me change my mind.'

'I told Mummy how it would be. If you belonged to our social sphere you'd return for the sake of form, my child would be born in its rightful home and you would pretend that everything was all right.'

'It's a pity you didn't marry one of your society girls then you'd have had no problem, would you? Though only an ignorant idiot like me could be taken in by you and your scheming mother. As a matter of interest, do you want me back only for the baby, or because of the money I could bring you?'

'You're damned insulting.'

'Oh, am I? Everything you've given me, every action you've taken with me, everything you've ever said to me, every time you've touched me' – her voice broke and dropped to a harsh croak – 'every time you made love to me was damned insulting.'

Adrian stared at her in amazement, then changed his method. 'I'm sorry, old girl, I shouldn't have said that. *Do* please come back. Life's horrid at home. Daddy will be back soon and he's always angry nowadays because his overseas shares are losing their value. Mummy has cut down my allowance again. But that isn't why I want you,' he said hastily. 'And you must admit, however hard up we are, our lives are a lot more, well, genteel, than yours.'

'I've yet to find anything I covet in your world, Adrian.'

His lips thinned in a malicious grin. 'All right, but you'd best watch out. Mummy always gets her own way in the end. She'll put lawyers after you and then we'll see who wins.'

Laura sank into a chair when he'd left, wondering what the next months would bring. It seemed that the best thing she could hope for was that her baby would be a girl.

Chapter Twenty-Six

One Saturday evening Laura sat working on her accounts in the quiet of her new flat in Park Street. It was May and the weather cool and unsettled, but as usual the ladies went on buying hats and clothes with unabated enthusiasm. Anita had extended her shop to encompass the one next door in which she sold ladies' classic suits, raincoats, coats and umbrellas. Their mutual arrangement to display each other's goods was working better than ever. Customers could now rely on *Hats by Laura* and *Anita Fashions* to produce a whole outfit for any occasion, except a really grand ball.

Laura shifted her position as the baby moved. She glanced down at herself. She had not increased much in size, although her condition was now evident. Just my luck, she thought, to be pregnant when fashionable clothes were definitely showing signs of a waist. Not that it made much difference to her as she seldom went anywhere. The early distressing symptoms of her pregnancy had mostly gone, but she tired more easily and once the day was over wanted only to sit and work out designs for next season's hats.

Paul had called again soon after she knew she was pregnant and asked her for a date. He was a difficult man to resist, with his dark good looks, his air of dominance which was partly his personality and partly the stature acquired by men as wealthy as he. His fortune was a family one and he had proved an excellent custodian.

'I'm expecting a baby,' she said simply.

Paul had frowned. 'And you've left Adrian.'

She nodded. The discovery of her husband with Rex was still too recent for her to think of it without emotion.

Paul said gently, 'Will you make up your quarrel?'

'Never!'

'You must have fallen out over something very important.' He paused, waiting.

Laura hadn't meant to tell him, but the power of his dark stare was mesmeric. 'I saw Adrian – and Rex –'

She had no need to proceed further. Paul had drawn a sharp intake of breath. 'You poor girl.'

The sincerity in his voice moved her deeply. 'You sound as if you really care.'

'You were deceived by the Mallenders! Laura, you need someone to look after you. Let me at least take you for a drive.'

Laura laughed shakily. 'Sorry, that's absolutely out. I can hardly bear driving myself at the moment. I've always suffered from travel sickness and now –'

'As if you hadn't enough to put up with. How about a theatre visit? We could easily walk as far as the Hippodrome.'

'No, Paul. You're very kind, but I dare not be seen with another man. The Mallenders are trying to force me back to Mallender House. I'll not give them anything that would add power to their arguments.'

'You mean her ladyship wants you. I'd bet a thousand pounds that Adrian doesn't care – sorry, my dear, if that hurts – and Sir Hugo, though he's a grisly curmudgeon, would quite happily let the baronetcy go to his cousin's line.'

'How do you know?'

'Sir Hugo has never made a secret of his disgust for his son.'

'I see. I suppose there's a lot of gossip.'

'The Charlton wenches are opening their mouths at every opportunity.'

'Of course, they would. You do understand that I must be very circumspect.'

Paul shrugged. 'I'll accept that. But one day I shall take you out. You're a girl with spirit and I like that.'

Paul's visit and compliment had given Laura a lift from gloom.

She started when she heard steps on the stairs, then identified them as Nancy's. She had given several people a key to her front door to save herself negotiating the stairs too often. She smiled at Nancy who looked content and serene and always did Laura good. 'Come and sit down,' she said. 'I'll make us a cup of tea.'

'No, you won't. I shall do it.'

Laura grinned. Nancy was lovingly bossy. Laura prayed nightly that she and Ralph would get married. She sipped her tea, her feet up on a stool as recommended by the doctor. Nancy sat cross-legged on the floor in front of the small fire. 'Ralph's gone to a sale in a village near Gloucester. He asked me to go with him. He always does.'

'Why don't you?'

'Because he may need to stay overnight. Mummy would have a fit, though the silly thing is that Ralph would never dream of taking advantage of me. But even Daddy would draw the line at my going, and he's a pet.'

Laura smiled, one eyebrow raised and Nancy laughed. 'All right, he wasn't so much of a pet to you.' Her face grew serious. 'He respects you, Laura.' She paused. 'Has Mummy been bothering you again?'

'Not for two weeks now. I think she's giving me time to think, though I've made myself perfectly clear.'

'It's an unhappy situation – for you both.'

'I agree. I wish with all my heart that my marriage had been different. Adrian calls every so often and begs me to come back, but it's perfectly obvious that he's just obeying orders. Sometimes I almost feel sorry for him.'

'He's weak, not bad.'

Laura didn't answer. The scenes with Adrian, who begged, threatened, sometimes wept, left her exhausted. The threat of legal action had been an empty one. No one could force Laura to return to Mallender House and, in any case, the Mallenders feared the publicity a legal wrangle might bring.

'Once he brought Rex with him.'

'What? How could he?'

'I don't know. Would you believe, Rex gave me a long lecture on the sanctity of marriage and my duty to the Mallenders.

If I hadn't been so disgusted I think I should have laughed. Imagine! Rex Lorimer invoking the sanctity of marriage.'

Nancy stirred the fire with a brass poker and the flickering light from a small flame danced over her. 'Adrian's very miserable. He pretends to Mummy that it's your fault, but I've heard him on the telephone arguing. He's worried that Rex is having an affair with that boy Pierre.'

Laura shrugged. 'I just can't get interested, Nancy. I seem to have become almost bovine.'

Nancy laughed. 'Not you. You still dash all over the place in your car.'

Laura had bought another car, bigger than the Austin Seven to allow room for her increasing girth, and with an electric self-starter to avoid strain. 'It's funny,' she said, 'but my weariness falls off me like a cloak when I have interesting work to do for the shops. It's only the drudgery that makes me tired. Housework and balancing the books, for instance.'

'I wish you'd let me do more.'

'I won't impose on anyone.'

'Must you be so hard on yourself? After all, and however much you dislike it, we are sisters, kind of.'

'I love having you as my sister. It's the only thing about my marriage that is good. I'm sorry, Nancy. I shouldn't have said that. They're your family.'

'I can't defend them. Not Mummy or Adrian, and even Daddy' – Nancy paused – 'even Daddy was too compliant. He let the others ride roughshod over him. He's deeply sorry now.'

'Has he said so?'

'Not exactly, but he always asks after your health when no one else is about and yesterday he told me to be sure you were eating properly and getting enough rest.'

'Sir Hugo said that?' Laura was amazed and felt a rush of appreciation – one couldn't call it affection – for the proud baronet.

The next day was Sunday and Laura drove out to visit her family. On an impulse she went first to Granma's and stopped a little way along the road, wondering if she should try again to see them. When Granma had heard about the break-up of

Laura's marriage she had been first disbelieving, then a little patronising and amused, telling Laura that all married couples had tiffs, but soon made them up. Since then she had realised that Laura was not prepared to live again with Adrian and was angry and refused to let her into the house.

Laura climbed out of the car and tapped tentatively on her grandparents' front door. It was opened by Grampa whose eyes widened.

'Who is it, Wilfrid?' Granma's voice, as imperious as ever.

Grampa opened his mouth to speak, closed it again and a determined look spread over his mild countenance. He beckoned Laura in and she obeyed, her heart beating fast.

'Who is it?' called Granma, impatient now.

Grampa took Laura's light loose coat and hung it with her hat in the hall, then threw open the kitchen door. 'It's our Laura come to see us.'

'What?' Granma rose to her feet and stuck out her chin. 'Out you go, you hussy! As for you, Wilfrid, I'll speak to you later. You know my views on such behaviour as Laura's.' Granma marched to the kitchen door and flung it open. 'Out!'

Disappointed, Laura turned to obey her. The last thing she wanted was a quarrel. The advice from her doctor had been to work when she must, but try to make sure that the rest of her life was tranquil. She wished she hadn't come. Granma's eyes were stony, her whale-boned bosom beneath her dark dress heaving angrily.

Grampa put a detaining hand on his grand-daughter's arm. 'You're to stay,' he said quietly.

Granma and Laura were united in their astonished disbelief.

' "To stay!" ' repeated Granma. 'I said she was to leave and leave she shall.'

'This is my home, too,' said Grampa, 'and I want our Laura to visit me. I want to see if she's well. And when my great-grandchild is born I want to hold it. If you don't want those things then you must go and sit in the front room.'

Granma glared at him, then marched into the front room and closed the door. They heard a chair creak as she settled into it, then silence.

Grampa looked so like a small boy who has just successfully performed a naughty deed that Laura couldn't resist the need to giggle. She held her hand over her mouth and tried to control herself, but the harder she tried the more helpless she got until the giggles turned to hilarious mirth. In the end she was forced to bury her head in a cushion. Grampa was affected by her mirth and seized another cushion to stifle his guffaws. When they emerged, red-faced, eyes streaming, they were chagrined to find Granma standing over them, glaring.

'S . . . sorry, Amy,' said Grampa. Then he was overcome again by laughter and fled upstairs. They could hear him yelping all the way up to the bedroom.

Granma said testily, 'Well, don't just stand there. Sit down and take the weight off your feet. I'll get a cup of tea and you must have a slice of chocolate cake. If it wasn't for that –' her head nodded to Laura's stomach – 'your ribs would meet.' Laura felt a mixture of relief and discomfort as she munched her cake in silence. She would have preferred to refuse it, but she was as subdued by Granma's order to 'eat it up to the very last crumb' as she had been as a child. Grampa eventually returned, slid into his chair and accepted cake and tea.

When Granma spoke both Laura and Grampa jumped. 'Reggie Prewett is engaged to be married to Sally. You remember – Sally Whiteley? – the girl next door?'

'Yes, of course. I'm sure she'll have a good life with Reggie.'

'So am I. A very good life. He's a God-fearing man who takes responsibility at chapel. He carries round the collection box now and never misses a service, as well as attending prayer meetings during the week.'

'You must tell me when Sally marries. I'll write and wish her well.'

Laura caught Grampa's eye once during Granma's little speech, but looked away hastily, before they disgraced themselves by collapsing with mirth again. Poor Reggie Prewett had always been a secret joke between them.

Laura got up to leave. She bent to kiss Granma's cheek, expecting her to move away, and when she didn't she kissed it a second time. 'May I visit again?'

'*He* seems to want you to.'

The reply was ungracious, but it was an opening and Grampa did a little dance of triumph in the hall, his rubber-soled boots squeaking on the highly polished lino.

'I hope you're not leaving black marks on my floor,' said Granma.

'No, love.' Wilfrid kissed Laura who hugged him. 'I'm so glad to be back,' she said.

As she drove to her parents' home she pondered on Grampa. He had always been her friend, helping her when she'd got into mischief, slipping her a bit of bread and butter when she'd been denied her supper for being naughty, but she had never suspected that his sense of humour was quite so puckish. What a lot of joy had been lost in the past.

Lillian was getting married in two weeks' time. She was dressed gaudily in a cerise dress with shoes to match and was swaying round the front room in time to *Moonlight and Roses*.

'Oh, it's you,' she said, as Laura peeped in. 'D'you like my new gramophone? Victor bought it for me. He gives me lots of things. He says it won't be long before we can afford a house with a bay window and I can furnish it any way I like. No more second-hand rubbish for me.'

'I'm happy for you,' said Laura, 'I hope everything is wonderful for you.'

'Well, it's bound to be better than the mess you've made of your marriage.'

Laura walked away into the kitchen where tea was being laid.

Phyllis greeted her with a smile. She was much kinder to her since her pregnancy. This was one place where they shared equal ground. 'Sit down. We'll get you your tea. You must feel tired doin' all that work. I know I always do.'

Iris brought tea and bread and jam. The china was new. White, decorated with roses. 'Victor gave it to us,' said Iris, without enthusiasm. 'He gives too many presents.'

'Hark at you, grumblin' about a generous man!' said Phyllis. 'You think he steals things.'

'I used to,' said Phyllis firmly, 'but I've changed my mind.'

The kitchen filled with the family, including Jack and the pregnant Enid.

'If any more of my sisters expects a baby we shan't be able to get in the kitchen,' said Harold.

He reeled from a resounding clout from Phyllis. 'I'll not have that kind of talk in my house.'

Harold rubbed his ear, and grinned.

William said, 'It's not a laughing matter, Harold. Your mother's quite right. A gentleman never refers to these things in public.'

Whenever William referred to himself as a gentleman Harold and Alfred creased themselves laughing, but silently. Phyllis was perfectly capable of fetching a wooden boiler stick to beat them. Val began to laugh with them and slid under the table and the little girls clamoured to join him.

'Shut up, the lot of you,' shrieked Lillian. 'It's like a pig farm. I'll be thankful to get a place of my own.'

Phyllis flashed a look at her. 'Let's hope all your dreams come true.'

Lillian flushed at her mother's sarcastic tone.

Phyllis looked tired and harassed and, as Laura ate her tea, she wondered what it must be like to have parents you needn't pity. Parents who were strong and vital. She vowed her child would never need to be sorry for her.

The sound of a baby's wail came from upstairs and Phyllis moved to the door fast. 'Our Freda's asleep. If little Andrew disturbs her –' The rest of her sentence was lost as she hurried away.

A moment later Freda came stumping into the kitchen and shoved her way to the tea table. Val jumped up and gave her his seat, more from fear than courtesy.

'Bloody racket,' said Freda, spreading jam liberally on a hunk of bread she cut clumsily, dropping crumbs all over the tablecloth and floor. 'I knew how it would be with the brat here.'

'Andrew doesn't cry often,' said William. 'He's as good as – as –'

'Say it, why don't you? As my Joyce was. You always used to

tell us how Joyce was the happy one and I was the bugger who woke you in the night.'

'Language,' said Phyllis, coming through the door with Andrew in her arms.

'You can talk!' muttered Freda, as she continued to eat, stuffing her mouth and slopping tea into her saucer. Her brothers and sisters watched her in fascination, wondering why she should be allowed to behave in a way that would get them a whack. They were nervous in her presence. When she reached for things they cringed back and if she turned her clouded gaze upon them they looked away.

Phyllis seated herself with Andrew on her lap and fed him fingers of bread and jam. He munched away with his tiny white teeth and regarded the others solemnly from Joyce's beautiful eyes. He resembled her uncannily in looks and drew admiring stares wherever he went. No one knew how many of the neighbours had noticed the likeness. The subject was taboo.

Freda had hoped he would look like his father. 'We'd get a clue to the bastard who killed her then.'

She glared at Andrew and he shrank back against Phyllis, grabbing her wraparound apron. She sheltered him with her arms. If she reprimanded Freda it would end in a quarrel of horrifying proportions and Freda would scream loudly enough for the people at the end of the row to hear. Everyone was relieved when she finished her tea and walked off.

Phyllis clutched Andrew as if he were in danger. 'I really thought she'd grow to love him, but I think she hates him. Her own sister's boy. You'd think she'd be grateful to have somethin' of Joyce. I know I am.'

'If it wasn't for Andrew Joyce'd still be here,' pointed out Alfred.

'Don't be stupid,' said William.

'She blames Andrew for Joyce's death,' said Lillian. She spoke matter-of-factly.

Phyllis frowned. 'I don't know about you either. You don't show much feelin' for your nephew.'

Lillian shrugged and examined her nails. 'Damn! The polish

is chippin'. I'll have to do them again. Ask Victor to wait if I'm not down.'

'Bossy pig!' said Harold.

'Hold your tongue,' snapped Phyllis. 'Criticisin' your sister at your age!'

William raised his eyes from the racing page he was studying. 'He's not a child any more. He's sixteen. That's a man.'

The family listened with awe. When William spoke, thought Laura, it was as if Moses had descended again from the mountain. The irreligious thought made her want to laugh. What was the matter with her? Her emotions swung from side to side these days. It must be pregnancy.

Phyllis nodded. 'You're right, Dad. I forget how the years pass, what with bein' so busy and one thing and another.' She sighed and looked at Laura. 'Lillian's not strong-minded like you. She's a bit silly and easily led. I dare say she loves Joyce's baby really, though she doesn't show it.'

Victor arrived driving a large open-topped car.

'He's here,' yelled Val. 'Come on, Lill.'

'Don't call me Lill! I'm ready, Victor. No need to come in.'

The boys followed her to the front door and Laura peeped from behind them.

'From wheelbarrow to car in one easy jump,' muttered Harold.

'Shut up, our Harold,' hissed Lillian as she passed them. Then she beamed brightly at Victor. He was out of the car and slid his arm round her waist. He wore a pair of green tweed plus fours in the new baggy fashion, draped over brightly coloured socks, a dark coat and a motoring cap.

'Ain't we grand,' murmured Val and ran back in to hide his mirth, recalling all too vividly the strength of Lillian's hand if she caught him a good one. He couldn't hit back. William had decreed that no gentleman ever hit a lady.

'I want to say hello to your parents,' said Victor, 'and any more of the folks that are around.'

Lillian pouted, her dark-red mouth puckered in what she believed was a film-star way, but Victor only pushed her in front of him through the front door and removed his cap revealing a heavily hair-creamed head of brown hair.

'Hello, Ma,' he greeted Phyllis who gave him a wry smile.

'Hello, Pa!'

William nodded and puffed his pipe.

'And the two mothers-to-be,' said Victor heartily. His light brown eyes were shining with pleasure. 'Laura, I'm always hearin' about your shops and I've been to have a look at them. You're a very clever girl, better than many a man, and I don't care who hears me say so. As soon as the infants are born Lillian must tell me and I'll make sure I've somethin' in the car to make their ma's' eyes light up.' He patted Lillian on her bottom. 'Weddin' won't be long, old girl. It's in two weeks. You'll come, of course,' he said to Laura.

'Thank you,' Laura said. 'I shall be delighted.'

'We're havin' a grand do afterwards. A proper sit-down meal – none of your fancy society pickin's-on-a-plate affairs. And there'll be drink in plenty. All sorts.'

When they left Victor opened his car door for Lillian to get in. She sat staring ahead of her, ignoring the curiosity of the neighbours and the catcalls of the children. No car of such size had ever been seen in the road before. The couple drove away and Alfred, Harold and Val staggered back and forth imitating Victor, patting each other's rumps and saying in affected tones, 'Won't be long, eh, old girl. Eh! Eh!' They ignored Phyllis's mild reproof after they caught her lips twitching.

Chapter Twenty-Seven

Lillian's wedding was, as Victor put it, a proper riot. They were married in church, Lillian in a billowing white gown, long veil, six bridesmaids dressed in pink satin, and two pages in black velvet with large white collars. Victor insisted on Iris being a bridesmaid.

'She's such a dear little soul,' he boomed, crushing any possible protest. He seemed incapable of speaking in a normal tone. 'It's only right an' proper for one of your sister's to be a bridesmaid. I'd insist on Laura, but she can't at the moment.' The remark was accompanied by a large wink and a leer in Laura's direction. She wondered how Lillian would fare. Victor was like an over-sized puppy frolicking and bumping into everything around him, but he seemed to love Lillian. Val had been approached with a view to his being a page, but his look of horror and bawled refusal had convinced even Victor.

Afterwards there was 'a slap-up do' in a local hotel, with food and wine loading the tables. The joyful couple drove off for their honeymoon at a secret destination with Victor expansive in a dark double-breasted lounge suit, a white shirt, a bowler hat and a large cigar. He wore white and black buckskin leather shoes. 'Co-respondent shoes', as they were known and 'not at *all* the thing, my dear', as Thelma might say. Lillian was in a black and red voile dress sent to her by Anita and a matching straw hat presented by Laura. She looked very pretty and suddenly vulnerable as they drove away and Laura found herself praying that Lillian would find happiness in her marriage.

After the wedding there was the usual feeling of let-down and Phyllis asked Laura to come back for a chat and a bite to eat. Laura wouldn't have refused whatever she had planned.

Her mother's gestures of kindness, small though they were, soothed away some of the ache in her heart. Sometimes she lay awake at night, unable to sleep because of the kicking baby, thinking about her life. She still felt she belonged nowhere.

William produced beer and wine 'to toast our Lillian again' and he and Phyllis settled down to an enjoyable bout of drinking. Iris got tea and Laura nursed Andrew. If her own baby was half as adorable she would be satisfied. The way he looked at her through her dead sister's eyes was uncanny. He also had her colouring, her sense of fun, her sweet nature, and added to it all was a lively intelligence. It was as if Joyce, in leaving them, had sent them a beautiful reminder of what she might have been. Phyllis worshipped him and his sunny nature, and the memory of his beloved mother made it impossible for anyone, even little Greta, at three the youngest in the family, and sturdy, to be jealous of him. Laura kissed the top of his silky head and he gurgled with delight, patting her face with his chubby hands. He was passed from one to the other, always keeping his serene composure and during tea was given anything he wanted from the table. All the rules about eating bread and jam before cake were forgotten. He pointed and his wish was gratified.

'I hope you won't spoil that child,' said William from his armchair, but there was no real reproof in his voice.

'How could we do that, Dad?' asked Priscilla, clutching her nephew and letting him lick the cream and jam from her yellow shop-bought cake. Priscilla was seven and didn't understand what spoiling a child meant.

Laura drove Iris back to the Kingswood shop and returned to Park Street. There were several customers who all turned to stare with high-bred careless curiosity at her, their lashes, heavy with mascara, sweeping up and down as they surveyed her figure.

'How soon will the little one be born, Laura?' asked one woman surrounded by yellow felt hats.

Laura marvelled again at the blatant expressions of curiosity of the upper classes who were far more outspoken in many ways than her own kind.

'Not for quite a while yet, Mrs Brownlow,' she replied

suavely. She stepped forward and removed a hat from Mrs Brownlow's head. 'Not pale yellow,' she said firmly, 'not with your colouring. I'm sure I've warned you before.'

Mrs Brownlow was gratified as the other ladies turned to stare. It was becoming fashionable to boast about how Laura had forbidden one to wear such and such a colour. '*Such* a scream, my dear, and she *insists* on one buying a different colour.'

Laura studied Mrs Brownlow's face intently, though she knew its sallow complexion, washed-out blue eyes and rather drooping mouth perfectly well. 'What outfit are you trying to match?'

Mrs Brownlow sighed. 'You and Anita are a pair of *frightful* bullies. She made me take a navy-blue dress and I wanted something to brighten it. I thought a hat – yellow's such a summery colour – it's for a garden party in June.'

'I see, an out-of-doors occasion. Why not wear a straw?'

'I haven't for years!'

'They're fashionable now for quite formal engagements. Try this.' Laura picked up a navy plaited straw and placed it firmly on her customer's head. 'At the moment it has yellow daisies on it, but I shall remove them and use a much deeper yellowy-brown colour to add the brightness you want. Will you call for it, or shall I have it delivered?'

'Laura, you're *dreadful*.' Mrs Brownlow still basked in the attention. 'Send it, please, and put it on my account.'

Laura rejoiced inwardly. Mrs Brownlow was a good payer.

'And while I'm at it I may as well take stockings and that dear little navy purse in the window. Oh, and new gloves. I suppose you insist on navy for them, too.'

'I most certainly do. Here's a pair in your size in French piqué suede at only six and elevenpence. You will look charming in your ensemble.'

Mrs Brownlow left looking ridiculously smug and Laura fled, leaving Nancy and Stevens to cope. Mary Stevens was proving an ideal assistant, with her tall good looks and her knowledge of how to behave with the customers. Laura was getting a good name among clients for employing superior people, paying fair wages and overtime. Some shopkeepers didn't approve. They expected their staff to work on a Saturday for no extra pay until the last customer had finished. Laura hadn't forgotten the times when, before Christmas, she had reached home just before midnight after being on her feet all day.

She was thankful that tomorrow was Sunday. On the insistence of her doctor she was taking Sundays off, using them to drive to the Downs and walk for a while, or just to sit by the fire and read, something she'd missed since becoming one of the bosses.

Consequently she was irritated when her front-door bell rang insistently the next morning. She checked her clock. Only nine. She groaned and rolled out of bed, slipping into her dressing gown and tying the cord round her expanding waist. She looked down at herself. 'You won't give me peace during the night,' she told her baby, 'and they won't leave me alone on Sundays. What a life.'

Opening her door she was surprised and then angry to see Adrian standing there. Then she took in his ravaged face. 'Come in,' she said quickly. 'No, don't explain here. We'll go up to the flat.'

Adrian threw himself into an armchair. 'You've got to come back to me, Laura. My life is ruined!'

'Don't be melodramatic. And if you only came here to ask me to return –'

He burst into tears. Not manly tears, but the slurping sobs of a small boy, producing copious tears that rained down his face.

'Adrian, please don't.' Laura placed her hands on her stomach as if to reassure her child that it mustn't get alarmed. Or was it for the comfort of herself, her reassurance that one person in the world, for a few months at least, belonged to her and she to it and that between them there was total harmony? No one could ever take this wonderful experience from her. 'Adrian, please don't,' she said again.

He still wept and she handed him a large handkerchief and left him to make some coffee.

He took it with a shaking hand that slopped the drink into his saucer.

'For goodness' sake, you'll scald yourself.'

463

'I wouldn't care! I don't care about anything any more. Since you went away my life's been dreadful with Mummy going on and on at me to get you back. I keep telling her you're as stubborn as a mule. Oh, Laura, couldn't you live at Mallender House, if only until our baby is born? It would keep Mummy quiet for now.'

'What about later?'

'I don't know. Something might turn up.'

'You sound like Mr Micawber.'

'Who?'

Laura sighed. 'No one you'd know.' Adrian was not a reader. 'Do *you* want me back?' asked Laura.

'You're my wife!'

'That's no answer.'

'Yes, of course I do. I – miss you.'

'Liar,' said Laura. 'Adrian, why aren't you honest with me? And why weren't you honest enough to stick to your beliefs in the first place?'

'I don't know what you mean.' Adrian blew on his coffee and sipped it, looking like a sulky boy reprimanded by his nurse. She had seen him with exactly such an expression before, even before their wedding, and wondered how she could ever have been so naïve as to imagine he was man enough for marriage. She'd never make such a mistake again. That is, if she ever got the chance, or found someone she wanted to marry. Thoughts of Paul and Rick flickered briefly in her mind.

She said, 'Adrian, why are you so particularly upset today? Has your mother – ?'

'It's Rex!' he interrupted.

She felt coldly angry. 'How dare you disturb my rest day to tell me about that man.'

He caught her hand, 'Don't be cross, Laura. Everyone's cross with me. You, and Mummy and Daddy – though *he* always was – and now Rex. I can't bear it!' Tears spilled from his eyes again. Laura disengaged her hand from his. She suddenly pitied him, but still she didn't want his touch. Not ever again.

'What has Rex done?'

'He's having an affair with that boy, Pierre, I know he is. He won't admit it and it's driving me mad. He used to love me. He said I was the only one he'd ever care for and he's lied to me.'

'Where is Rex?'

Adrian looked up eagerly. 'You understand, don't you? Will you see him for me and –'

She was appalled. 'No! Never! Are you out of your senses?'

'Then what did you mean?'

'I just wondered if he was in Paris.'

'No, Bristol. He's got a small pied-à-terre in Clifton. He says that Pierre is in Paris, but the last time I visited the flat I found a blue voile scarf, not at all the type of thing Rex would wear and it's Pierre's favourite colour and I know he likes that filmy sort of stuff. I've visited twice when Rex didn't expect me and I'm sure Pierre was hiding in the bedroom. I could swear I heard him giggling. Rex was so cool with me and asked me to leave because he had work to do. I couldn't push him out of the way. He's bigger than me and stronger.'

'I see. There's nothing I can do to help.' Laura felt as if she was in one of the surrealist pictures that were so fashionable. The whole situation was crazy, normality turned upside-down. Her husband asking her to help him become reunited with his male lover. 'Adrian, please leave now. I need my rest. The doctor advised me –'

'It's all right for you!' Adrian turned his misery into anger against her. 'You've got your business and money and friends and everything, even a baby. And it's my baby, too! I've got a right to say what should be done about it and I want it born in my home.'

'As yet,' said Laura grimly, 'the child is still a part of me and you can't force me to live anywhere.'

'After he's born I'll take him home and you'll have to live with me again. Any court would say so.'

'You think so, do you? What will any court say after I've told them about you and Rex and Pierre. It might be a different story then.'

'You wouldn't!'

He was right, of course. She would never do anything to taint her child's life, but she was damned if she'd let Adrian know. 'A mother will do a great deal to protect her child,' she said, a feeling of desperate weariness creeping over her. 'Now, go!'

She let him out through the front door and made her way slowly upstairs. Her heart was thudding and her back ached. She lay on her bed, grew chilly and crept into the living room and lit a fire and wrapped her arms around her body. The warmth was comforting and gradually her tension eased. She dressed and decided to drive out into the country and walk somewhere quiet and peaceful where she might be able to gather her thoughts together.

When her door bell rang again she felt as if she were being persecuted. If that was Adrian – she didn't quite know what she would do. Damn Rex and his infidelity! After splitting her marriage asunder it seemed he was tired of his prize.

She was taken aback to see Lottie with her parents. She had met them once before when she had engaged the girl as an apprentice. Lottie looked mutinous, her parents pleading.

'Mrs Mallender,' said Lottie's mother, 'I'm really sorry to bother you on a Sunday, but in the week I know you'm busy an' that, so Dad an' me thought perhaps you'd give us a minute today.'

Laura looked into the woman's troubled face and capitulated. 'Come in, Mrs Gage. And you, Mr Gage.'

'No need to make you walk all up the stairs, Mrs Mallender, not in the circs' – she glanced once at Laura's girth then away. 'If you'd give us the favour of a word here.'

Laura sat in one of the customer's chairs and waved Mrs Gage to another. Her husband preferred to stand and looked uncomfortable as he twisted his Sunday hat in his hands.

'It's our Lottie, Mrs Mallender. She's been out of a job since you – since she behaved so badly –'

Lottie gave a half sigh, half grunt and Laura's impression that she'd been brought here unwillingly was reinforced.

'You didn't give her a reference, you see. I know she don't deserve one –'

'She don't,' said Mr Gage, his face and ears reddening.

'That's what I said, our Perce,' said Mrs Gage. 'We was wonderin' if there was any way you could take her back.'

Laura hated to disappoint them, but to allow her workforce to believe that someone could get away with treachery could lose her the good discipline she had. To be a successful designer meant keeping secrets. She had learned this lesson only too well. She could never employ someone untrustworthy.

She explained this as gently as she could to the Gages. They were clearly deeply disappointed, but Mr Gage said, 'I knew we shouldn't 'ave come, Mother. Mrs Mallender was let down proper by our Lottie. She don't deserve to be took back.'

'Don't want to come back here,' snapped Lottie. 'I hated it.'

'You're a wicked, ungrateful girl!' said her mother. She turned to Laura. 'Mrs Mallender, did Lottie do her work right?'

'She did quite well. I should have been pleased to keep her if only –' her voice dwindled. These people were too nice to be badgered unnecessarily.

'Well, could you write a few lines sayin' that?' begged Mrs Gage. 'It wouldn't be a lie, would it. You could say she was willin' an' able, but didn't suit the work.'

Laura thought for a moment. 'Very well, but if anyone asks me the truth about why she left I can't lie.'

'No, no, we wouldn't agree with makin' you tell lies,' said Mr Gage. 'We're chapel people. We believe in the truth.'

'Mrs Mallender d'know that,' reproved Mrs Gage. 'She d' go to Zion Methodist like her Gran and Grampy, Mr and Mrs Blackford. That's so, isn't it, Mrs Mallender?'

Laura nodded. 'I'll write the reference and send it to you,' she promised.

She kept her promise, but a week later the Gages returned, this time on a Saturday.

'Lottie's run away, Mrs Mallender. She left a note sayin' she was fed up with everythin' an' everybody in Bristol an' she'd look out for herself from now on. We wondered if you had any idea where she might have gone.'

Laura said regretfully, 'None, I'm afraid, but if I do hear, I'll let you know and I'll ask a friend who travels around a lot to keep an eye open for her.' She made a note to speak to Rick, and maybe Ralph could help.

As Laura's girth increased her freedom was curtailed. She still fitted herself behind the wheel of her car and drove resolutely to her other shops and once to visit the three 'wrinklies' who still worked for her. All were widows whose children had long ago left home and they were full of advice. She should drink raspberry tea to make the birth easier, she should sleep as much as possible 'because you won't get much after', she should wear a good strong binder after to keep her figure. Laura had been so preoccupied with work that she had not given much thought to the actual process of giving birth, but these old ladies with their earnest faces and memory-filled eyes brought it home to her. She knew pitifully little about childbed. Phyllis said she was always glad when it was over and the less said about it the better. Enid said vaguely that you soon forgot the pain.

Laura was sitting in her parents' home one Sunday when Freda stalked in. She stared at her two sisters and their swelling bellies.

'Rather you than me,' she growled.

'Leave them alone, our Freda,' said Phyllis wearily. The strain of caring for Andrew and distancing herself from Freda's venom was telling on her. She had confided in Laura and Enid that she wished Freda would go away and inflict herself on someone else.

'She never stops thinkin' about it,' Phyllis said. 'She never mentions Joyce's name, but I can see everythin' in her face. She still walks around Bristol in her free time, especially the posher parts and tries to catch a sight of some man who might look like little Andrew. She even applied for a job as maid in the Goodwins' house, but they turned her down. I'm not surprised. Most of the time these days she looks like she's been dragged through a hedge backwards.'

Today Freda was in an odd mood, possibly brought on by the sight of her fruitful sisters. She plonked herself on a chair and stared at them, hostility sparking at them from her eyes. 'I was with Joyce when she had her baby,' she said suddenly. 'She screamed a lot. There was a lot of blood, too. Much too much, the nurse said.' Freda held out her hands; they were broad, rough and strong. 'They were covered in bruises. Joyce did that. It hurt so much it covered me in bruises. She screamed and screamed.'

'Freda, for God's sake –' begged Phyllis weakly.

'Don't they want to know how their sister died? I know. I think about it all day and dream about it all night. It was the screamin' –'

Enid burst into tears and Laura put her arms round her, though she felt like weeping herself. She wanted to weep for Joyce, for Phyllis whose face had gone grey, for Freda who was going mad with the torment of her memories. And she wanted to weep for herself and the innocent child she carried. She held back her tears. They only weakened you.

William came in. He'd been for a Sunday morning drink. He sat himself in his chair and looked at his womenfolk. 'You all look like you lost a shilling and found a farthing. Cheer up. What's for dinner, Phyllis?'

Even Freda wasn't proof against her father's impregnable self-interest. She stamped out.

'Tears, chick?' William said to Enid. 'No need for tears, surely? Is Jack coming to dinner?'

Enid shook her head and wiped her eyes. 'He's got some work to do for Rick. They're doin' up the St George cinema and gettin' it ready for sound.'

'What's happening to the one in Old Market?' asked Laura, dragging herself back to normality.

'Don't know.'

'I dare say Rick's got plans for it,' said William. 'He's a clever chap. Mmm, is that a beef stew? I'm starving.'

The birth was imminent when Lady Mallender put in another appearance. Adrian was with her and courtesy demanded that Laura invite them upstairs. Her ladyship looked around the small flat, her blade-like nose lifted as if over a bad smell. 'My grandson cannot be born here,' she stated, as if with her autocratic words Laura might pack her bags and depart for Mallender House immediately.

'My child will be born in a nursing home with a doctor and nurses in attendance,' said Laura. 'I am as anxious as you that it should have all the care possible.'

'I see. Adrian have you nothing to say? You sit there mute while your wife defies the conventions recognised by all decent people.'

Laura felt anger begin to burn within her. 'How can you talk to me like that?' she asked in low tones. 'You and your son enticed me into marriage with lies to be nothing but a vehicle for breeding.'

'Such indecent talk!'

'Indecent? You are the indecent ones. I'm sick and tired of the way you badger me. I'm never going to return to Adrian. *Never*! Can you understand that, or must I go on and on repeating it?'

Lady Mallender sat straight-backed. 'I shall not accept it.'

Laura spoke with slow deliberation. 'Lady Mallender, Adrian is a homosexual. I am not condemning him, or criticising him for his way of life, but what I can't forget is the conspiracy to drag me into a sham of a marriage.'

'It's a better one than you could ever have hoped to make.'

'Oh, no! That I won't accept! I wanted marriage with a man who could behave to me as a true husband should. What I got was a travesty of a man.'

'You see, Mummy, I told you it was useless to see her.'

His mother glared at him.

'I want to go home,' wailed Adrian.

Laura felt sick at his infantile behaviour. 'Go! Please go!' She tried to control the begging note that had crept into her voice, but she felt she couldn't endure any more.

Lady Mallender abruptly changed her tactics. 'Laura, my dear, I won't press you to live in Mallender House, but there is a solution which would answer. Adrian could come and live here. It would silence the gossips.'

'But I don't like it here,' said Adrian.

'Be silent,' snapped his mother. 'If Laura is willing to take you – after all, your behaviour is not above reproach –'

'Not above reproach!' Laura was astounded. 'He was – he

470

was –' She struggled to find the words to express her shame and horror. 'He and Rex –' She felt suddenly too ill to go on and leaned back in her chair, her face white.

'You see,' said her ladyship triumphantly. 'You're not as strong as you think. You should be with us where you will be properly cared for.'

'Go away,' said Laura. 'Go away!' She closed her eyes.

There was a light tap on the door and Nancy entered. She took in the scene and fetched a glass of water and a damp flannel from the kitchen. Laura sipped the water, then Nancy wiped her face and hands with the cool flannel.

'Mummy, it's so bad for Laura to be upset like this.'

'Oh, of course, you'd take her side,' said Adrian.

His sister stared at him. 'I've no wish to fall out with anyone, but you really must leave. I'm going downstairs to telephone for the doctor.'

Lady Mallender looked alarmed. 'She's all right, isn't she? The baby –'

Nancy said, 'I promise to let you know what he says. You'd much better leave.'

Adrian lingered in the doorway as his mother descended the stairs. 'Laura, I don't like the way Mummy goes on at you. I would leave you completely in peace if you'd only come home. It's horrible without you.'

'Out!' said Nancy, and went to the telephone.

Doctor Jameson came at ten o'clock. It had taken him an hour to arrive. He apologised for the delay. 'Had a patient I couldn't leave.'

Laura said, 'I think I'm in labour.'

'And how would you know?' Doctor Jameson sounded stern, but his eyes were kind.

'I've had pains in my back quite low down.'

'How many?'

'Two!'

'Two, eh? How far apart?'

Laura stared at him. 'I don't know.'

'Into your bedroom, young woman. Let's have a look at you.'

His hands were gentle. 'Yes, you're right. The best place for you is in the nursing home. Normally I would advise waiting at home, but there isn't anyone to care for you here, is there?'

Nancy was standing by the bedroom window, her fists clenched with tension. She turned, 'I'll look after her. Just tell me what to do.'

Doctor Jameson looked at her wide, scared eyes, and smiled. 'I think not. You can go with her if you like. Do you drive? Have you a car?'

'Yes, to both questions. Do you mean I'm to take her?'

Nancy was excited and fearful at the same time. Laura had packed a small case weeks before and Nancy added clean nighties, toothbrush, soap, flannel and sponge bag. She folded Laura's dressing gown on top and closed the lid.

Halfway down the stairs Laura stopped and gasped, supporting herself on the walls of the narrow stairway, bending over, biting her lips.

'Is it bad, darling?' asked Nancy.

'I don't know,' Laura managed to say with a weak laugh as the pain subsided. 'I've never done this before.'

They both giggled nervously, but once behind the wheel of the car Nancy became calm. She carried the case through the double front doors of the nursing home and was instructed by a well-starched nurse to say goodbye. She left with a final wave, her face anxious.

Laura was bathed, her bodily hair removed, an experience she found embarrassing, an enema administered and another examination made.

'You've a while to go yet,' the senior nurse said. 'Try to get some sleep.' She snapped off the main light, leaving one with a faint blue glow. 'There's a bell by the bed. Press it if you need me. My name is Nurse Graham. I'll look in quite often.' She relented. 'Don't worry, Mrs Mallender. We deliver babies here all the time.'

Don't worry, Laura thought. Another pain gripped her and she stifled a groan. This wasn't at all what she'd imagined. Pictures of infants and mothers in advisory books were always of light and smiles and happiness. They said nothing about a dim blue haze, a hard white bed, and lonely suffering.

Surprisingly she did manage to doze between contractions until they reached proportions that forbade rest. At some point during the night she was removed to the delivery room, a glitteringly sterile place with glass cupboards holding fearsome looking instruments from which she averted her eyes. The contractions were now close together and she cried out, then stuffed a corner of the sheet into her mouth to stifle the noise.

During the long hours Nurse Graham had changed from a stiff and starchy nurse to a humane and kindly fellow-woman. 'It's getting bad, isn't it, dear?'

'Getting bad,' gasped Laura. 'My God, it's been bad for centuries.' She wondered fleetingly how her mother had been able to undergo such torture so many times. 'Someone has rung your doctor,' said the nurse.

Laura wondered what good that was, but then he arrived and murmured the words 'twilight sleep' and something was administered that distanced the worst of the pain.

'Push now,' said Doctor Jameson. 'You're ready, Mrs Mallender, push.' No wonder they called it labour. Finally she was allowed to float away on a wave of anaesthesia and when she heard the cry of a new-born infant could not immediately connect it with herself.

'A boy,' pronounced the doctor with as much satisfaction as if he had done the whole thing himself.

'A boy,' echoed Nurse Graham in Laura's ear. 'You've got a lovely, healthy son, dear. Not long now and then I'll clean you up and you can sleep.'

Wonderful, blessed sleep. And she was the mother of a son. She drowsed as she was moved again and awoke in the morning to find herself in a ward with three other mothers who congratulated her on a successful birth.

'This is a good nursing home,' said an older woman, mother of five. 'They're kind here. I could tell you tales of some –'

Her voice dwindled as a day nurse entered and frowned. 'Now, then, dear, no horror stories here, if you please. We want our ladies to be happy and look forward to the next time.'

The next time? Oh, my God, thought Laura, never again.

How on earth had Mum survived? How did Enid face a third birth apparently without a qualm?

Nancy brought an enormous bouquet of flowers. 'From all of us,' she said, smiling. 'The whole workforce chipped in, even the apprentices, and I'm to tell you that no one is slacking.'

Laura lay back as Nancy arranged the brilliant summer blooms in vases supplied by a nurse. She felt like a queen.

Her euphoria was abruptly dissipated when Adrian and his mother were shown in. A wide-eyed junior nurse said, 'Here's Lady Mallender and your husband to see you, Mrs Mallender.'

Her ladyship bent and pressed her cool cheek to Laura's and Adrian kissed her hand. They were far too well-bred to mention anything controversial in public, and the conversation followed a normal pattern.

'I've brought you a gold locket on a chain to celebrate the birth of our son,' said Adrian, stressing the word 'our'. His voice was hoarse and he looked ill. She felt a tinge of pity for him, imagining how he was being treated at home.

'My first grandchild,' said Lady Mallender. 'The heir to the baronetcy.' She hadn't intended others to hear, but it never occurred to her to lower her customary autocratic tones and the words boomed round the ward. All conversation ceased for a moment. Neither Lady Mallender nor Adrian noticed, but Laura saw the amazed expressions of her companions in childbed.

She saw more than that. When the ward was darkened for the night she had to face just what she'd done. Inside her body her baby had been a part of her, a human being, yet not possible to visualise. Now he was born, he had a name, Lady Mallender and Adrian could see him, and they claimed the right to direct his life. She had given them that right by her deception. The future looked frightening.

Laura's strength returned quickly. 'And you're so thin,' marvelled Nurse Graham, 'but you must be very wiry.'

After two weeks she was driven home by Nancy, her son cradled in her arms and for the next two weeks revelled in her child and forced herself to ignore any kind of work. All her senior girls visited her, bringing presents of hand-knitted garments, fluffy toys, rattles.

Miss Morton was the first. She held the baby tenderly and looked down at him with moist eyes. 'Laura, how thankful I am that you came into my life. It's almost as if –' She stopped.

'Go on,' said Laura softly. 'Say it.'

'As if I had a grandson. Or perhaps,' Miss Morton corrected herself with a little laugh, 'a nephew. What name have you given him?'

Laura had thought deeply on the subject. She couldn't call him after Rick and she certainly wasn't going to choose a Mallender name. In the end she decided on David. It was a good plain name and as far as she knew no one in either family bore it.

It displeased Lady Mallender who stood looking down at the sleeping child. 'He should have a family name. You made no attempt to consult us.'

Laura stared at her, tall and imperious, the sharp contours of her profile outlined against the pale wall. She seemed impervious to rebuffs. Laura had to quell a stirring of fear. What if this woman with so much strength and influence should try to take David from her?

'How is Adrian?' she asked, more for something to say than a desire to know.

Her ladyship turned cold eyes upon her. '*How* is Adrian? Don't you mean *where* is Adrian? Or has my son been here without me?'

'No! I thought he looked unwell when he came to the nursing home.'

'Unwell! I'm not surprised! My son is – a fool.' She seated herself on a chair near the bed. 'A fool, Laura. He has made you suffer and now we must have these continual disagreements over his son. I wish things had been different.'

Laura was alarmed. This abrupt confidentiality was a new line of attack.

'I wish so, too,' she said.

'Did you love my son?'

'I wouldn't have married him otherwise.'

'No, I don't believe you would. You don't care at all for position, do you?'

'Oh, yes, I care, but our ideas on what makes a good position are different. I've realised that your world is very different from mine. To me an honest marriage, love and friendship are more important than wealth and position.'

'The latter carry influence!'

'Yes. I'm sure they're useful protection against interference in one's life.'

Lady Mallender frowned fiercely. 'That remark is meant for me, isn't it? And here I am trying to make up our quarrel.'

Laura shifted in the bed, where she was trying to take the afternoon rest prescribed by Dr Jameson. 'I don't want to quarrel with you.'

'So you will return to Mallender House where my grandchild can be brought up as his future position in society demands?'

Laura was angry. She was weaker than she'd realised and in no fit state to cope with being badgered in this way. 'I can't talk now,' she said. 'I need rest.'

'But I haven't finished –'

'Yes, you have, Mummy.' Nancy had entered quietly. 'Can't you see you're upsetting her. How is she to feed little David if she loses her milk? Dr Jameson said she was to have peace and quiet.'

Lady Mallender rose. 'You haven't heard the last of this.' She marched out, her back as rigid as a guardsman's.

Laura said, 'Nancy, how can I go on resisting? Surely, they'll wear me down in the end.'

Nancy said briskly, 'I'm going to fetch you a drink of malted milk. That will serve two purposes. It'll help your milk and soothe you.'

Laura laughed. She and Nancy were closer than ever.

Her parents made an obligatory visit and stayed to drink tea, sitting stiff and awkward as Nancy served them, unconsciously intimidating them with her air of gentility and her 'plummy' voice.

Grampa kissed his great-grandson, uncritical as always, but Granma joined battle on the side of the Mallenders, persuading Laura that now she had a son she *must* go back to Mallender House.

Pansy took a special liking to David, touching his soft skin with her thick pink finger, smoothing the down on his head. Laura wondered if she wanted a child of her own. She said little about her life outside the shop, working long hours and apparently having no other interest.

When Anita came Laura was in the living room knitting, the crib standing beside her. Anita looked down into it at David who lay awake, his month old eyes fixed on her.

'He's going to be handsome,' she said. 'I didn't come before, Laura, because I can't abide the look of new-born infants.' She strolled to a comfortable chair and relaxed into it like a cat, lighting up one of her Egyptian cigarettes. 'You realise you've now given a hostage to fate, don't you?'

Laura nodded. 'Yes. I hadn't thought about it before his birth. But yes, I'm vulnerable now. How do you know?'

Anita tapped off ash and smiled. Now she looked like a satisfied cat. 'I just know. If you love *anybody* you're handing fate the winning cards and a child is the worst of all.'

Sir Hugo brought her a silver tankard engraved with David's name and Laura felt guilty when she accepted it. The baronet had not troubled her since their talk in his library. 'Nice little fellow,' he pronounced. 'I like the name, too. Good, solid one. Don't spoil him, Laura. Don't indulge him. Make him into a man.'

Paul called when David was six weeks old. He was shown up to the workroom where Laura was bent over her desk, David lying sleeping in the cradle by her side. Her eyes often left her sketching to watch him as he slept, his face working, his mouth making tiny sucking movements.

'I waited until you were back at work,' said Paul. 'I thought a visit from me any earlier might add to the gossip.'

'Gossip?'

'Of course. What did you expect? There's Adrian looking like death, you here with the Mallender son and heir, Lady Mallender behaving like a tragedy queen with tears behind the smiles and Sir Hugo more morose than ever. Everyone's intrigued.'

Laura frowned. 'To hell with them!'

Paul laughed softly. 'You're wonderful. You'd take on the

world, wouldn't you? I congratulate you on producing a fine child, my dear. Have you engaged a nurse yet?'

'No. I dislike the idea of handing him over to another woman. I want to care for him myself.'

'But?' he asked, sensing her indecision.

'But it won't be possible. I can't give either David, or my work, the amount of attention they need. The thought of looking for a woman I can trust utterly is daunting. David is so good. Nothing must upset him.'

Paul looked down at the baby again. 'His face already shows strength. He's nothing like his father.'

'If that's all you have to say I'd prefer it if you kept your thoughts to yourself.' Laura spoke resolutely, but inside she quivered. There were times when she saw Rick in David so clearly she was amazed that no one had commented upon it. But of course they assumed that Adrian was the father. They looked only for his features. 'I suppose he must take after your side of the family,' said Paul. 'Now about the question of the nurse. I can recommend one. She looked after me and she's had charge of my cousin's children for years, but the last one is ready for Eton and there are no more babies in the family.'

'How old is she?'

'Young enough to care for David.'

'I don't think so, thank you. How can I ask her to share my flat with me? She's used to grand houses.'

'That's true, but she's no snob. Why not just see her and then decide? She'd be far better than some young, untried girl.'

Nanny Allan turned up the following week. She was thin, her grey hair strained back into a bun. She wore a black coat and hat and Laura found her daunting until she smiled. Then her face lit up, her eyes became warm and she radiated goodwill. She lifted David who gave her one of his best smiles. Laura showed her around the flat. 'I must be honest and tell you that this is Mr Harrington's idea. I told him you wouldn't like it here –'

'I decide what I like,' said Nanny Allan, 'and Master Paul knows that. Master David is a beautiful baby. Where shall we sleep?'

Laura felt as if she were on a fast flowing tide. Nanny Allan's authority was supreme. 'I shall turn my bedroom over to you as a nursery and take the box room.'

Nanny Allan nodded. 'Good idea. When would you like me to start?'

'You'll come?'

'I've just said so, haven't I?'

Laura had a fleeting regret for the quiet, private life she'd enjoyed in her flat. Now she would never be alone. The box room was tiny. She thought of how Anita would tease. But she would never regret having her son.

Laura had seen so many people since David's birth, but one hadn't come. Rick was in Bristol. Ralph had sold him a pair of gilt cupids with round stomachs and bows and arrows for the St George cinema. They were heavy, though not valuable, and he had bought them along with a mass of other stuff.

'They look great in the foyer,' said Ralph. 'You should see the new place. Rick's keeping the name Palace of Delights and he's turning it into a proper palace. Nancy says it's vulgar and she's right, but it'll draw the crowds. He's got the common touch, has Rick.'

She longed to ask Ralph if Rick had mentioned the baby, but didn't dare. And anyway, why would he?

She had given up expecting him when, soon after Nanny Allan began work, he called on her on a Sunday night.

Laura introduced them. Nanny rose and retired to the room she had made into her own and David's.

'It's completely different here,' whispered Laura. 'She got Ralph to bring up a big screen and covered it with blue cotton stuff and put it round David's crib. She sits in the room under the dimmed gas light knitting and sewing and reading.'

Rick grinned. 'You look fine,' he said. 'Having a baby evidently did you good. You're not so skinny. There's something different about you.'

'I suppose it's being a mother.'

'Maybe. Or maybe it's the air of success. I like it. I hear the Mallenders have been at you.'

'Lady Mallender has. Not Nancy, or Sir Hugo, or even Adrian lately.'

'I saw him the other night with Rex Lorimer. They were eating supper in The Premier before the final show. Did you know I've got a restaurant there now? It's so popular you have to book tables well in advance. Lorimer and Adrian were all smiles when they got there, but by the time they'd finished they were at it hammer and tongs.'

'Arguing?'

'I'll say! Arguing, calling each other names – at least Adrian was doing the name calling. Not loudly, he's too much of a gentleman for that, but the waitress overheard. Lorimer just leaned back in his chair and sneered at him. At one point we thought Adrian was going to pick something up and smash it over Lorimer's head. I've never liked Adrian, but I actually felt sorry for him. Rex Lorimer is a swine. In the end he walked out without seeing the film and Adrian trotted after him. Pity. It was a good picture. John Gilbert and Catherine Dale Owen in *His Glorious Night*. All-talkie.'

Laura didn't want to talk about Adrian and Rex. The subject still had the power to make her feel sick with humiliation. 'You were right about the talkies,' she said.

'I know.'

'Well, don't sound so smug.'

Rick laughed. 'Which is your favourite so far?'

'I still haven't had the time to see or, rather, hear one.'

'It's incredible! You just don't know what you are missing.'

Laura laughed at Rick's expression. 'There are other things than talking pictures. Some people still don't think they'll last. I read an article in *Punch* that was really satirical about them.'

'*Punch*! What do they know? And if you've got time to read magazines you've got time to go to the pictures! Oh, of course, the baby. Sorry, honey, I almost forgot. Look, I brought the little blighter a present. It's a ball.' Rick looked round the room. 'Daft sort of thing to buy him, I suppose. You haven't got a garden.'

'No, and he's not exactly playing football yet, but I'm going to have to think about that. We can't stay here for ever, it's far too cramped.'

'I wish you well in your move. I'll come and visit you when I get back.'

'Is it London again?'

Rick's dark eyes blazed with sudden excitement. 'America! I'm going there at last. I've got good managers in the two cinemas and I've placed all my acting clients with another agent and put someone I can trust in charge of the Booking Agency. I was right, Laura, it's the middle man who comes off best and I'm making real money. Now I intend to spend a bit and see just what's happening over the other side of the world.'

The other side of the world. Laura felt chilled. The thought of thousands of miles between them disturbed her. That was crazy. They were still only friends in spite of that magic night when he had comforted and consoled her with his body and his tenderness.

She shivered. 'When are you leaving?'

'I'm taking the overnight train to Southampton and sailing tomorrow. Just think, Laura, in a few days I'll be in the States. It must be the most brilliant country in the world. Money is flowing like water. Even ordinary men and women are investing all they've got in holding companies and investment trusts, mostly Goldman Sachs – they're experts who invest other people's money. As my American friends put it, they're riding high.

'I'm going to see some New York shows then take a train to California where they're making the talking pictures. They say the air's so sweet and clear you can see for miles. That's why they make films there.' Rick's enthusiasm dampened Laura still further. She had been prone to bouts of depression since David's birth. 'Quite natural,' Nanny Allan had assured her, but they were difficult to deal with none the less.

'You look a bit down, honey,' said Rick suddenly.

'No, not really. I – shall miss you.'

'Will you?' Rick looked astonished. 'We hardly ever see each other these days.'

'No.'

'I've left the name of my solicitor with Ralph. I'm hoping to rent out, or to sell, the Old Market cinema. It used to be a factory so maybe someone will find some use for it. Ralph is empowered to act for me. Now, am I going to be allowed to see the baby?'

Laura led Rick into the big bedroom on shaking legs. It seemed odd to have to tap before entering. Nanny Allan cautioned them to silence by placing her finger on her lips. 'Master David's had a tiny little touch of wind. He's only just gone to sleep.'

Rick tiptoed to the crib and looked down. Laura stared at him. His face was shadowed by the screen and she couldn't read his expression. She felt cheated. A woman should see the face of the father of her son when first he looks on him. Rick left soon after and Laura sank into the chair he had used, touching the arms, pressing her head into the back. Her depression grew deeper and she felt bewildered. Rick was nothing to her now, but perhaps he would always have the power to affect her. After all, he had been the one who had awakened her girl's body to life. Adrian had continued what he had begun but Adrian was a poor lover and Rick had completed her education. Their night of passion, wild, tender, sweet, lived in her and always would. She wondered if she would ever again know such joy.

Laura had worked hard before David's birth and she and Pansy had produced a collection of hats for the autumn show. Hair was longer and Laura had allowed hers to grow past her ears and had it permanently Marcel-waved, sitting as patiently as she could while the necessary heat was applied for hours. It had cost her a shocking five pounds.

A large number of people attended the show and Ralph was hard put to find room and most of his stock had to be carried into the workshop at the back. He now employed two men full time on restoration work.

'Some of the stuff is so restored it's practically new,' he told Laura.

'Don't the customers mind?'

'I tell them the truth and show them a picture of the original. They seem to think it's amusing. Every darn thing's amusing to them.'

'I know. And in my shop every darn thing's gossiped about no matter how personal.'

Laura had gone this time for autumnal colours. Pansy's jeweller friend had copied her designs, mostly leaves and flowers, but keeping to the still popular abstract shapes. She also commissioned tiny enamelled car models for the few who would want to be different, who retained their boyish way of standing and speaking. Not many now. Femininity was returning with interest. Suddenly it was fashionable to look curvy and women who had spent the past few years starving themselves fell upon cream and chocolate with whimpers of joy. 'At this rate,' Laura told Pansy, 'I'll have to pad myself out.'

'If you'd stop pushing yourself so hard you might gain weight,' said Pansy. 'You should delegate more.'

She was right, as she so often was. Laura began to plan ways of relieving herself of much of the donkey work.

Anita Fashions was up-to-date with the new style clothes. The shoulders must be broader, the waists nipped in, the hips a soft female line. Instead of falling from attenuated or rigidly-corseted breasts silk and satin were cut on the cross and allowed to cling to bodies displaying womanly charms. This season Anita stocked winter sports clothes, too: trousers, and wool jumpers she bought from Scottish hand-knitters, and Laura complemented her stock with tight wool caps and hair bands.

Pansy said, 'You two should amalgamate.'

Laura frowned. 'I want my own business. I like Anita, but I'm sure we'd fall out all the time.'

'She's right,' said Nancy. 'They're both much too bossy.'

Nancy was one of the few people who could get away with remarks like that. She came to look at larger flats and sympathised when Laura decided she couldn't afford to move. Nanny Allan's wages were quite high, the bills for the nursing home and doctor had to be paid and the paraphernalia surrounding a baby seemed never-ending. What spare cash there was must be ploughed back into the shops. It represented security for David as well as for Laura.

One evening as Laura was about to eat there was a ring on her doorbell. Nancy was outside. She looked ill and haggard.

'For heaven's sake, what's the matter?' asked Laura. 'Have you driven here in that state? Sit down. Tell me –'

Nancy got no further than the shop where she sank into a chair. 'It's Adrian,' she said hoarsely. 'He went driving. He's had an accident.'

'Oh, no! Is he badly hurt?'

'He's – dead!' Nancy burst into a storm of weeping. 'He's been killed. Oh, Laura, I know he behaved badly to you, but he was my brother.' She sobbed, almost losing control of her voice.

Deeply shocked, Laura led her upstairs. Nanny Allan brought a cup of tea.

Nancy said, 'We had such good times together when we were little. And I've been so unkind to him lately. I wish I hadn't.'

'It doesn't help to talk that way,' declared Nanny. 'We all feel like that when someone we love dies. Calm yourself Miss Nancy, and think of Mrs Mallender here. He was her husband, no matter if –' She stopped. 'They *were* married.'

'Sorry, darling,' said Nancy brokenly to Laura who felt guilty.

'I'll drive you home,' she said. The thought of going to Mallender House and meeting Adrian's mother appalled her. Apart from that she seemed frozen inside. She could feel nothing. Not grief. Not regret. Not even shock. Maybe that would come later.

Chapter Twenty-Eight

The sight of Gardner's ravaged face did nothing to help. She had clearly been weeping. She glared hatred at Laura. 'It's your fault! My Master Adrian! Such a sweet boy. You married him. You should have loved him for what he was.'

'Be silent,' said Nancy harshly. 'How dare you speak to Mrs Mallender like that!'

'I dare!' Fresh tears poured down Gardner's face as she struggled to form more words. 'I can't tell you! I can't say it!' She hurried away her words floating back to them like a dirge. 'All her fault.'

Laura was bewildered. 'I don't understand. How can an accident – ?'

Lady Mallender walked out of the drawing room and stopped in the hall. Her face was grey and filled with anguish, her eyes staring. 'So you've come. You and my daughter. *His* sister who gave him no support.'

'Mummy,' said Nancy, 'please –' She seized Laura's arm and pulled her into the drawing room where both girls sat side by side on a sofa. Lady Mallender stood over them. 'You know he's dead! But you don't know how!'

'An accident,' said Nancy. She seemed calm, but the quiver in her voice betrayed her. 'That's what Daddy said on the phone.'

'It was *not* an accident. He killed himself.' Lady Mallender wailed the last words and her voice went on, keening, rising and falling in a weird song of despair.

Laura watched her, pity and horror mingling. At last she asked through lips that felt stiff. 'How? *Why?*'

'How? In his car. Why? You know the answer to that. You are to blame.'

Laura's horror and pity were suddenly replaced by anger. 'I am not! First Gardner, now you.'

'*She* loved him. You didn't.'

'I did – I tried –' Laura paused. 'Please, must we talk about that? For God's sake tell me exactly what has happened?'

Lady Mallender walked unsteadily to the bell rope and pulled it, then half fell into a chair. When Renton came in she asked him to pour her a glass of brandy. 'And you'd better give some to the young ladies.'

'Not for me,' said Laura quietly. 'It wouldn't be good for David.'

'Nor for me,' said Nancy.

'You don't need it,' said her ladyship. Her words were an accusation. There was silence while Renton gave her the brandy. She dismissed him, swirled the drink around the glass and watched it as if mesmerised, then she sipped.

'You don't need a drink. Neither of you need help to recover from the shock. Why should you? You didn't really care about him.'

Nancy gripped Laura's hand. Laura felt demeaned, but pity for the woman before her held her still.

'There are no words to wrap up neatly what has happened,' said Lady Mallender. 'Adrian killed himself by driving his car deliberately into a tree. He died instantly.'

Nancy wailed, 'No, oh no, he couldn't.'

'He left a note.' Lady Mallender's hand was shaking as she took a piece of crumpled paper from her pocket and handed it to Nancy who read it aloud, her voice breaking: '*Dearest Mummy, I can't bear not being loved any more. My life is ruined. I'm going to end it all. Please don't mind. Love, Adrian.*'

Even in the midst of her distress Laura was astonished. The note was like a child's scribbled defiance. How could a grown man have departed the world leaving only an immature scrawl as his dying testament?

Tears trickled down Nancy's cheeks. 'He must have been so unhappy.'

'He was desperate,' said Lady Mallender in a frozen voice. 'I've seen it in his face. He was slowly starving for love. May

God forgive you, Laura. You have much to answer for.'

Laura stared at her mother-in-law. 'You know that isn't true. I'm not the one he wanted. It was Rex. That horrible man and his affair with his pretty boy Pierre are what destroyed Adrian.'

Lady Mallender gasped. 'Watch your tongue! I will not permit you to say such a thing. What would the newspapers make of it? They would drag my boy's name through the mud. No, we must let people believe that it was for love of you that he died, Laura. You owe him that much.'

Laura sat silent, outraged, trying to make sense of her thoughts, endeavouring to visualise her position if she took the blame. One thought came uppermost. It was David who mattered. What would be best for him? What would be worst? She could brand herself as a callous wife; or she could brand his father as a sexual deviant. When he became a man what would give him the deepest pain? Adrian wasn't his father, but David must grow up believing the Mallenders to be his family, that he had been conceived and born within a proper relationship or he would suffer as Rick had suffered. She had allowed the living lie to be perpetrated, turning away from the dictates of conscience. Now she and David were irrevocably caught up in it. What a mess she had made of everything.

She looked at Adrian's mother whose face crumpled as she wept. 'Laura, please, for Adrian's sake, don't talk to anyone about Rex.'

Again pity swamped Laura. She herself was now the mother of a son. She took a deep breath and said, 'I don't think I owe anything to Adrian but, for David's sake, I won't speak of Rex Lorimer or Pierre.'

'But Laura,' cried Nancy, 'you'll be crucified. The press will make all they can out of it.'

'Let them. I can't take any other course, you must see that.'

'She is right,' cried Lady Mallender. 'You should be supporting her in her decision.'

Nancy looked at Laura's set face. 'Does anyone outside of this house know about the note? Surely we can keep it between ourselves and let people think Adrian had an accident?'

'Gardner knows, so does Renton.'

'That's still inside Mallender House,' said Nancy. 'They loved Adrian. They wouldn't talk.'

'No, but he wrote to Rex Lorimer. No doubt he, too, will keep silent, but the Charltons also have a note. My sister has telephoned already and I dare say Thelma and Daphne are busy spreading the news. I don't know how many others he wrote to. It seems as if my poor boy wanted to shout his misery from the rooftops.'

That was typical of Adrian, thought Laura. Granma had always taught her that it was wrong to speak ill of the dead. Laura hadn't understood why. If people were bad dying didn't make them good and Adrian was self-centred to the end. Granma's indoctrination succeeded in making her half ashamed of her thoughts. She felt like a calculating bitch, but her mind was her own. Why didn't she feel grief? Surely it would come? Surely she should feel more than this? She had laughed with Adrian, slept with him, made love to him. But still the numbness held her.

The inquest was a nightmare and the newspapers had a feast of scandal. Before Adrian was buried there were headlines proclaiming *Adrian Mallender's sadness* and the story following began: *The man who died because he wasn't loved.* No direct accusation could be made, but the clever juxtaposition of the facts with the news that Mr Mallender's wife and son lived apart from him made certain that readers' thoughts were manipulated just as the writer wished.

If Laura experienced any form of sadness for her dead husband it was stifled by the activities of the reporters who photographed her shops, her car, her hats, herself whenever she made an appearance, David and Nanny, Ralph, his shop. The details of her life were dwelt upon. It was discovered that her younger sister had died tragically young, though thankfully no one had delved deeper than that. There were pictures of Phyllis and William, and anyone else in the family who took the press's fancy during the few days between the inquest and the funeral. The difference in social standing between her dead husband and her own upbringing was speculated upon and it was subtly hinted that she had fled from the grander life in Mallender House because she was not up to it. It was learned that her grandparents had reared her and her family were badgered with questions as to why. Not that any newspaper was likely to discover that, thought Laura. She wondered how Phyllis had dealt with the reporters and a wry, almost humorous smile twisted her mouth.

Somehow no one got a photograph of Granma and Grampa. Laura discovered later that they had remained locked in the house until the furore died down. The girl next door had done their bits of shopping. The London papers carried the story, too. It was kept to an inside page with few photographs, but it ensured that the Mallenders' friends and acquaintances all knew what had happened.

The verdict was grist to the sensation: *Suicide while the balance of his mind was disturbed.* Then, two days later, an enraged husband killed his wife's lover and the Mallenders were abandoned in favour of the new compelling drama.

Adrian's funeral was a private affair. Laura stood at the graveside, her head bent. Only once did she raise her eyes to see who was there. It shocked her to discover Rex Lorimer. For an awful moment she looked for Pierre, but of course Rex had probably shipped him hastily back to Paris. Rex looked grieved. And so he should. He was the one who should be pilloried by publicity. The Charltons were there, Thelma's and Daphne's eyes, bright with malignant speculation, fixed on her. Phyllis and William and Ralph represented her side of the family. Her mother looked ill and Laura knew she was remembering another day, another grave into which her beloved Joyce had been lowered. Ralph supported his sister, his arm encouragingly through hers and Laura watched as the coffin was put into the ground. Lady Mallender stood unnaturally straight; not a vestige of emotion showed. Laura walked out of the churchyard. There was to be no gathering afterwards. Even if there had been Laura couldn't have attended. She could bear no more. She went straight to her flat, trying to come to terms with what had happened. She had ended by loathing Adrian, but she grieved for his lost youth, his despair; and for Nancy who mourned her brother.

Anita called on her later. 'So that's that,' she said. 'Now forget it.'

Laura looked helplessly at her. She was unbelievably self-contained. Did she never permit herself to feel emotional? Oh, if only Rick were here. He would comfort her. He understood grief and tenderness. 'I wish I could forget. I keep remembering the evil things said about me. I keep remembering how I behaved to Adrian. God, Anita, perhaps he did kill himself because of me.'

'If you're going to talk bloody nonsense I'm leaving. He was crazy about Rex Lorimer and you know it.'

'Do you think many other people think that? Perhaps not everyone blames me.' Laura looked up hopefully.

Anita shrugged. 'Adrian's sexual activities haven't been exactly the world's best kept secret, but it can't be proved and no one would dare print a story about it. It's easy to get at you so the tabbies will keep gossiping.'

'I've been made to feel like scum. And soon I'll have to get back to the shops. I don't know if I can stand it.'

'You're determined to talk bloody rubbish. Darling, believe me, you'll do more business than ever. Everyone adores a bit of scandal and they'll pour into the shops. Business will be great, I promise you.'

Laura managed a shaky laugh. 'Anita, you're gruesome. Have you no scruples?'

'None whatsoever. Why should I? No one else has. Take what life offers if it's good and throw it back if it isn't. Where business is concerned publicity is everything. The reporters were only doing their job. Good stories sell newspapers. You couldn't have got so much advertising if you'd paid out a fortune. *Hats by Laura* and the background of your aristocratic customers have been mentioned dozens of times in the past weeks and *The Hat Shop* got in a few times. Watch out for a deluge of women clamouring to be served. You'll have to descend to the shop and help.'

'I shall do no such thing.'

'Business is business. And talking of business, now would be a good time to think about developing the underwear and make-up side of ours. It'll take your mind off your worries, too. What do you think?'

Laura was half shocked, half exhilarated by Anita's visit. She knew that Anita talked a lot of sense. She must put the past behind her and get on with the present and future. Money would protect David so money was what she must have.

Anita was correct, of course. More hats were sold than ever before. Accessories went so fast Laura had to make special journeys to get more. Scarves, gloves, stockings, everything saleable vanished from the shelves and, of course, Laura had to serve.

Gradually the rush died down, but it left Laura with more customers, many of whom had come to gloat and stayed because they were impressed.

Her business was thriving, David grew stronger and more beautiful every day and Laura could see Rick in him sometimes when he smiled, or when he looked at her in a certain, quizzical way. She went to visit Aunty Mabel. Olwen looked bonny and healthy. Her mother missed her, but was content to take the doctor's advice and leave her daughter with Miss Merriman and Laura happily watched them cement a friendship of the kind that could sometimes spring up between a child and an elderly person. Miss Merriman was not as spry these days and Olwen delighted in helping her, and the little flat in Hotwells was filled with content. Laura loved the atmosphere, though sometimes she wondered if she would have visited so often if Rick had not been at the back of her mind. It was said that a woman never forgot her first lover, that he always reigned supreme in her being. That wasn't true. Adrian had made love to her first and she had very few happy memories of him and none connected with sex, but perhaps the saying was right, after all. Rick had been her first true lover. She seldom indulged herself with such daydreams. For one thing she hadn't time; for another, more cogent reason, she feared that at the end of such dreams there lay a private sorrow that she couldn't face. Whenever she found herself becoming entangled in ungovernable thoughts she did something that would take up all her physical and mental energy.

Aunty Mabel had received two letters from America. The first said everything was swell – another of the new expressions culled from the talkies. New York was apparently more swell by far than London. Rick was meeting musicians of all nationalities; there were even women bands. There was so much money around that buying and selling shares seemed to have become the national sport. There were a few voices crying woe, but the influential and knowledgeable *Wall Street Journal* was advising people that it was patriotic to go on dreaming, presumably of a nation where everyone was rich. He sent his best wishes to everyone but he didn't mention Laura specifically. Aunty Mabel said she had sent a letter telling him of Laura's dreadful tragedy, but she wasn't sure of Rick's movements after New York. The second letter said he'd soon be moving to California to see the talkie sets and he might travel south to hear the jazz musicians he loved.

Miss Merriman said, 'Do you understand about the money, Laura? There's been a lot about it in the papers, but it's double-Dutch to me.'

Since Rick's letters there had been a terrifying change in the American stock market. In New York on Wall Street on 22 October six million shares had been sold and a market slide began. On 29 October there were reports of a monetary crash, of previously eminent business men, unable to face ruin, leaping from skyscraper windows to their deaths.

Laura said, 'Only up to a point. It sounds dreadful and it seems to me it's all to do with gambling on paper with money that doesn't really exist.'

Paul left his card with a scribbled message asking if he could call on her. The small courteous gesture soothed her. Try as she might she couldn't rid herself of the picture of Adrian climbing into his car, driving faster and faster, the Bentley screaming along the country roads until it was steered into a thick tree, hurtling to its doom, thrashing itself around the trunk and tearing his body to bloody shreds. She knew the details because Lady Mallender had related them to her, trying to exorcise her torment by unloading it on to another.

Laura remembered Adrian's horror of death and couldn't

relate it to suicide. When he killed himself he couldn't have been in his senses. His madness must have masked his fear.

Lady Mallender called several times to visit David, panting as she climbed the stairs, disapproval in every line of her body, every expression of her face. Thank God Paul had produced Nanny Allan. Even Lady Mallender could not fault a woman who wore navy dresses buttoned to the neck, starched white collars, cuffs and aprons, navy wool stockings and flat leather shoes, whose grey hair beneath its stiff white cap was strained back into a merciless bun and whose every nuance proclaimed her to be a nanny of the old school.

Her ladyship said little. She sat and nursed David, staring down at him, her face a mask of suffering. Laura dreaded the visits and lay awake at night in her tiny bedroom, staring at the stars which were framed in the roof window, her only source of daylight, and wondered if she should tell the truth about her son. Granma would have nodded with satisfaction had she know of Laura's torment at her fearful deception.

When Paul called he took both her hands in his in a warm gesture of sympathy. 'My dear, you look so wan. How long is it since you had a good breath of fresh air?'

Laura shook her head. Foolishly his kindness had brought her nearer to tears than anything.

'Dear girl, don't cry. Please don't be sad.' He led her to a chair and seated her in it as if he had been the host. 'I brought some sherry. I know you like it. Good old Bristol Cream, matured in the cellars beneath the streets of the city.' His voice had taken on an air of declamation reminiscent of an advertisement and Laura smiled.

'Do you know that there's talk of the cinema advertisements being put out in sound?' Paul asked.

'Is there? I gather that words are quickly overtaking mime.'

'You should know. Your friend, Rick, is one of the leading talkie exponents in Bristol.'

'I haven't seen much of him for a while and now he's in America. He always longed to go.'

'He writes to you, I suppose.'

'No. Why should he?'

'Then there's nothing between you?'

Laura was taken aback. 'I was married to Adrian.'

Paul seated himself opposite her and leaned back. Seated one each side of the fireplace Laura thought they must look like an old married couple. She was grateful to Paul. He offered warm, soothing friendship and never made any attempt to embroil her in an emotional situation she knew she wouldn't be able to deal with. He seemed to read her well. He was also straightforward.

He said softly, 'Laura, darling, let's you and I be honest with one another. We both know that Adrian was crazy about Rex Lorimer. Left to himself he would never have got married. His mother pushed him into it. His biggest sin was weakness.'

Laura stared at Paul, at his thin, clever face, his almost olive skin, his dark eyes expressing only understanding and wonderful sympathy that was like a soothing healing ointment on a burn. She felt herself relaxing in its beneficence.

'Lady Mallender blames me,' she said.

'She would! She's like an animated monument to motherhood.'

Laura laughed, and Paul looked pleased. 'You're wonderful when you laugh. I love to look at you.'

'Don't tease. I'm no oil painting.'

'I wonder how you got that impression? If you mean you're not pretty in a shallow way, or attractive as some women are in a facile way that will fade with time, you're right.'

'Thanks.' Laura tried to sound flippant and failed.

Paul's eyes were hypnotic. 'You have a beauty of bone and form and skin texture that will never leave you, only get clearer and more brilliant with the passing years. You have elegance, grace, charm, and any woman with those qualities is far beyond mere beauty.'

Laura was astonished. Paul sat looking at her, sipping his sherry calmly. He didn't realise that in two brief sentences he had demolished years of her being told that she was plain, skinny, unattractive. She wondered briefly what Lillian's reaction would have been to Paul's declaration. She wanted to speak, but couldn't find words.

Paul said, 'May I take you for a drive?'

'What?' The commonplace question seemed incongruous.

'A drive, darling –'

'You mustn't call me darling!'

'But darling, everyone calls everyone darling.'

Laura gave a small laugh. 'Maybe, but you shouldn't. I mean, you're here alone with me –' Her voice dwindled off as he surveyed her with amusement.

'Yes?' His voice was soft.

'You keep teasing me.' She felt colour rise to her cheeks.

'You see, you're already looking better and so far we've only *discussed* fresh air. Also, I'd like to point out, I saw Nanny Allan taking David for his walk. She could return any time and if she thought for one second that I was misbehaving she's quite capable of boxing my ears.'

Laura grinned. 'I do get fresh air, Paul, on the Downs on Sundays when I take David out. Nanny actually trusts me on my own with him.'

'How do you get on with the old girl?'

'Wonderfully well. I can't thank you enough. Not only does she look after David like a second mother, but I'm sure she's the only buffer between Lady Mallender and me. Her ladyship can't accuse me of not looking after my son when she sees Nanny Allan.'

'Just as I thought.'

'Do you mean you saw this far ahead?'

'Of course. Won't you let me take you out?'

'But if we're seen together! The newspapers –'

'Were doing their job. Forget it. They've forgotten you. The people close to you understand. Those who don't aren't important. And your shops are going great guns.'

'How do you know?'

'I don't. I guessed. People adore a melodrama. They always have.'

Laura laughed outright, but shook her head, although she felt herself opening out, releasing some of the hurt. 'I can't go out with you.'

'Why not?' Paul lit a cigarette.

'Adrian's death was so recent –'

'I'm not suggesting a passionate night in Paris, darling. Just a small drive in broad daylight. To Weston, perhaps. The air there is particularly bracing. Or so all the posters tell me. I prefer Cannes, or Monte Carlo.'

Nanny Allan returned with David and beamed her pleasure at the sight of her former nursling. 'Master Paul,' she exclaimed, putting him firmly in his place. 'How nice to see you.' She sniffed at the smoke. 'I shall remove David to the nursery where the air is purer. He was good, as usual, Mrs Mallender. It'll be bath time in half an hour, Master Paul, so I'm afraid you'll have to leave. Mrs Mallender enjoys helping with bath time. Then it's supper time and beddybys.'

'You don't change,' grinned Paul. He had risen at Nanny Allan's entrance, a courtesy Laura observed with pleasure, and he bent over and planted a smacking kiss on Nanny's cheek. 'I've been trying to persuade your mistress to take a drive with me.'

'An extremely good idea! Next Sunday then. Weston will be the best place. Whenever one of my babies had an illness we always went to Weston to recuperate.'

She marched out carrying David and Paul laughed. 'So that's settled.'

'I don't appear to have an option,' said Laura drily, but she was gratified. It was so easy to have a decision made for her. Easy to slide into the plan made by Nanny and Paul, both of whom appeared to look upon her as a woman to be cherished.

Chapter Twenty-Nine

The outing to Weston undoubtedly improved Laura's well-being. She forgot her problems for a while as she and Paul walked along the wide sands.

'When I was a child,' she said, 'I thought Weston was the most marvellous place on earth.' She laughed lightly. 'In fact, for all I know it still is.'

'What? Have you never visited any other seaside town?'

'No, but I don't feel deprived.'

She had a joking note in her voice and Paul smiled. 'You must have been a sweet-natured child.'

The darkness of her childhood momentarily blotted out her pleasure. She drew a breath of the cool, slightly misty winter air. 'I don't think I could have been. I wasn't – wanted.' It was an effort to say the words. Paul had a way of drawing out the truth, however much it hurt.

'I find that difficult to believe.'

Laura was silent for a while, staring down at her shoes making imprints in the sand, imprints which were immediately washed out by wet sand which slid beneath the incoming tide. 'My parents sent me to live with my father's parents. Their reason was good at the time, but – they never fetched me back.'

'You were not happy as a child.' It was one of Paul's flat statements. She had no need either to confirm or deny.

'I was happy in Weston,' she said dreamily. 'When I was very small I was brought by Mum on a Sunday school outing. That was great fun. I've just remembered,' she added, surprised, 'Mum rode a donkey and paddled.' She fell into another silence which Paul didn't break. 'When I came with Granma and Grampa they sat in deck chairs all day. Grampa dozed with

497

a newspaper over his head. Granma read the *Christian Herald* or a book by Annie S Swan – she's a writer who brought God into her work a lot.'

'Do you believe in Him?'

Laura was surprised at the question. Paul smiled crookedly, 'I was reared in a Christian family, like you. Church every Sunday, choirboy –'

'A choirboy? You?'

'Why such astonishment? Do I look like a sinner?'

Laura glanced at Paul. Had she offended him? It seemed not. He was grinning at her in a companionable way that soothed her feelings, so badly lacerated over the past weeks. 'You are – you seem such a man of the world.'

'I'm gratified to know that my sartorial and social efforts are not in vain.'

'You're teasing me again.'

'A little. You're delightful to tease. But there's more to me than you may believe.'

'I'm sure there is,' said Laura fervently. 'Like most of us.' She tried to imagine the suave man at her side, in his tailored clothes and beautifully tended nails and hair, as a choirboy.

'I haven't been to chapel for ages,' she sighed. 'Granma used to chide me for it.'

'Used to?' Paul asked gently.

He had caught her regretful note. 'Since Adrian's death I haven't seen her. I called and Grampa said she wouldn't have me in the house. He was upset about it, but she was adamant. She blames me for what happened, like everyone else.'

'Not everyone.'

'No. Not everyone. There are a few –' The conversation had broken through her temporary euphoria and the thick dark unhappiness and regret which had enveloped her from the day she had heard of Adrian's awful death swirled round her again.

'I'll soon have to go to church for David's christening. That will make Granma even worse. She looks upon the Church of England as only slightly less idolatrous than the Roman Catholics. All the Blackfords must be christened, married and buried in Kingswood church.'

'Except those who gave their lives in some distant part of the British Empire,' said Paul.

'Oh, you know about them.'

'Most families have some relative thrashing the poor natives on to immense efforts to grow something when all they want to do is grow just enough to eat and sit in the sun.'

'No one in my family spent time abroad, except those who were sent to fight wars. And didn't come back,' she added, remembering family reminiscences.

'I gather you disapprove of war.'

'Don't you?'

'Sometimes they're necessary to prevent a greater evil.'

Laura stopped for a moment to look at a sand castle built by some child holidaying late in the year. The Bristol Channel water was already licking at it and causing a landslide. That's how the devil picked at people was what Granma would have said. Give him an inch and he'll take all of you.

She remembered Paul's earlier question. '*Of course* I believe in God.'

'There's no of course about it.'

'I suppose not. And you do?'

'Sometimes. Like today, for instance.'

'Why today?'

'Because the sun is shining through the mist, the air is pure, the sand is soft, and I'm with a friend.'

Laura's heart was warmed; a little of her depression lifted. 'You are the dearest man –' She stopped, catching her breath.

Paul looked sideways at her, his eyes humorous. 'The *dearest* man?'

'I should have said the dearest friend.'

'That will do – for now.'

His tone sent a pleasurable shiver up her spine.

They took tea in a large hotel overlooking the sea, paper-thin sandwiches with delicious fillings, cakes that melted in the mouth, and lots of delicately flavoured tea to drink. Laura poured, thankful she'd had practice in public, and wondered if she'd ever get used to hotels like this. Later, Paul drove her home.

'Do you want to come up?' she asked.

'You don't really want me to, or you would have phrased your question differently.'

Laura's cheeks burned. 'That sounds discourteous of me after all your kindness.'

'Not at all. Kindness be damned! Let there be honesty between us.' He raised her hand and touched it to his lips. 'I'll see you again quite soon.' Then he left.

She thought of him that night. He was different from anyone she had ever known. One never felt dominated by him, yet he always got his own way, in a sweet and gentle manner perhaps, but he got it. Beneath that smooth and mannerly exterior she was beginning to sense a certain ruthlessness. No, not quite that, determination was a better word. She talked of him to Nanny Allan who was pleased to discuss her former charge with someone who liked him.

'Master Paul? He was a *very* naughty little boy, I'm afraid. Sometimes he was so disobedient I had perforce to report him to his Papa. Then he got whipped. Mr Harrington would stand for no nonsense.'

'Didn't you mind him getting whipped? You loved him, didn't you?'

'That was why! Spare the rod.'

This was a new aspect to Nanny's character. 'I don't want David chastised.'

'Of course not. He's far too small.'

'Not ever.'

Nanny smiled. 'I think you may change your mind when he's grown into a rollicking boy. A whipping now and then never did Master Paul any harm. In fact, it prepared him for going away to school. He got a lot of beatings there. All the boys did. And not only from the masters. The prefects had canes and the authority to use them. He, being so wilful, found school difficult.'

'Poor little boy!' Laura was horrified.

'He soon grew up and became a prefect himself.'

'I hope he was kind to the small boys.'

Nanny laughed. 'By that time he had come to recognise that

500

boys are all the better for discipline. He gave them a good share of beatings.'

'I can't imagine Paul doing that.'

'If it made Master Paul into the man he is today, how can you believe it's wrong?'

Laura didn't know the answer to that. She only knew that the idea of physical violence was anathema to her. She still carried the emotional scars of the perpetual canings administered by Granma 'for the good of your soul'.

She gave David his late-night bottle and he sucked enthusiastically.

'He's a strong-willed little soul,' said Nanny, half admiringly, half admonishingly, and Laura shivered at the idea that anybody might try to tame his spirit with a whip or cane.

Laura's customers kept referring to the American stock-market crash.

Thelma Charlton declared, 'It's *too*, too ridiculous. Daddy said there were eleven thousand millionaires there – twice as many as before the war.'

'That *was* perfectly true,' agreed a florid lady who spent much of her winters in the hunting field, as a frowning Laura forcibly removed a cerise-coloured hat from her clutching hands. 'You're still a dreadful bully, Laura. Motherhood hasn't softened you at all. How is the darling baby?'

'In good health, thank you, Mrs Tomkinson,' Laura refused to be drawn by any references to her private life – such as she had left.

'What colour will you let me wear?'

'The same as always – cream, black, or any other dark shade, or you may wear grey, except dove-colour. I have the perfect hat here to suit you.'

Laura placed a clear-grey felt trimmed with a claret feather on the customer's head. 'You see how the shades tone down your complexion? And I happen to know that Anita supplied you with a lovely tweed suit of grey and claret. As a matter of fact' – Laura bent confidentially forward – 'I was hoping you would buy your hat from me and was keeping this especially for you.'

Every lady's ear bent to hear this intimacy and, as Laura had not lowered her voice too much, knowing that Mrs Tomkinson would revel in being singled out, every lady heard.

'You're both bullies,' complained Mrs Tomkinson genially, choosing a grey bag and gloves.

Laura called on her banker. Mr Russell had smiled somewhat patronisingly at her when she had opened her first account with five pounds. His smiles now were of genuine welcome and respect.

'I've decided to expand again,' Laura told him. 'With your co-operation, naturally.'

'Another shop? Or are you hoping to buy one of your existing premises?'

'Not yet. I want to rent somewhere where I can set up a large workroom and make hats for a bigger market. That way I can keep *The Hat Shop* supplied at reduced cost, and sell wholesale to other places.'

Mr Russell frowned slightly. 'Are you sure you're ready for such a venture?'

'Absolutely,' declared Laura. 'I must have much more room for the straws. There are so many materials which need to be stocked to give a full range: Italian straw, Yedda plaits from Japan and Chinese grass, raffia, wool, horsehair, cotton, paper, even wood shavings – they and many other materials are needed to make a comprehensive selection.'

'I had no idea.' His eyes narrowed. 'I have faith in your business ability, Mrs Mallender, you know that, but I wonder if you're wise to deplete your reserves at such a time. There is so much unemployment and it's rising. And some wage rates are falling.'

'But the cost of living is also falling, though more slowly at present,' she reminded him. 'And standards of living are better than ever for those in full-time employment. I don't need to remind you that most of my customers are financially sound.'

'Some have been quite badly affected by the American crash.'

'Yes, but it doesn't seem to stop them buying hats. There's a great gulf between the so-called hard up among the rich and the real poverty of the poor.'

'*The Hat Shop* could be affected. Your clients there aren't rich.'

'Many are the wives of professional men, teachers, doctors, factory managers, skilled workers who make good money and no woman would be seen in public without a hat. And all of them enjoy buying a new one. I intend to keep my prices low in *The Hat Shop*.'

Mr Russell looked relieved. 'I just wanted to reassure myself that you have things in perspective. I should have known you always keep up-to-date with financial matters.'

'As far as they affect me I most certainly do,' said Laura. 'Later, I'm going to start a line of cosmetics and perfume. *Anita Fashions* will stock my products and I shall increase my display of their lingerie and some gowns.'

'But surely you won't have room.'

'When I have my girls in a factory I shall open up the present workrooms as sales areas,' said Laura calmly.

Mr Russell laughed, showing his slightly buck teeth and removed his spectacles and polished them. 'Have you premises in mind?'

Laura nodded. 'Rick Merriman owns a place in Old Market and my brother has the authority to rent it out. Mr Merriman ran it as a cinema, but it was a shoe factory before that. It's a one-storey building with plenty of light. At least it will have when all the windows have been unblocked and polished. I intend to make a place that girls will clamour to work in, with proper facilities, a pleasant airy atmosphere, and decent hours and fair wages.

'My brother, Ralph, has promised to help – do you know he's in demand now as an adviser in interior decorating? – and so will my other brothers, Alfred and Harold. They're getting almost no outwork these days and need jobs. All my senior staff are excited at the idea and will work to settle us in. I plan to have everything ready for the next spring show. Of course, I shall need an overdraft.' Laura smiled at Mr Russell, throwing the words at him as a kind of afterthought.

'An overdraft? Without collateral? Your shops are rented and cannot be used as security.'

'No, but I can get the factory for a very modest yearly figure. I'm asking you to trust my business acumen. One day I shall own everything. I've never let you down yet, have I?'

Laura got the assurance of an overdraft. It was less then she had hoped for, but by careful management she would make it do. Ralph had agreed with her that the time was right for expansion. She respected his views. He was cautious without being cowardly; he waited until the propitious moment before making moves to increase his trade. He bought cleverly, restored expertly, was honest in his dealings and people were ready to pay him well for consultation over the furnishing and decorating of new homes.

Laura's victory in the bank lifted her spirits. She picked up David and swung him round, then kissed him ecstatically. He gurgled with laughter, but Nanny Allan was indignant.

'Madam, he'll have to be calmed down before he has his milk.'

'Yes, Nanny,' said Laura, feeling like one of her infant charges.

The reorganisation began well, but underlying everything Laura did was the fear that the future held a menace. Lady Mallender called once a week and sat holding David, her back stiff, her eyes unforgiving. Laura couldn't believe that she would allow her son's son to be brought up apart from her and when Gardner telephoned to say that Lady Mallender would make an unplanned call after church Laura waited nervously.

Her ladyship seated herself on the sofa. Paul had said that Sir Hugo enjoyed a flutter on the Stock Exchange and had been hit by the Wall Street crash. 'Of course, he'll pick up in the long run,' said Paul. 'He's got old money behind him.' If Lady Mallender was worried about money it certainly didn't show. Nanny Allan had retreated into the bedroom with David who grew lustier and more handsome every day. 'I'll wait, Mrs Mallender, until you summon me,' said Nanny. 'Her ladyship will want to see her grandson.'

Lady Mallender smiled graciously on Nanny, then said in a voice she was keeping determinedly business-like, 'Now then, Laura, we must discuss dear David's future.'

Laura waited.

'You've nothing to say? Well, there is little you can say. You are a clever girl and understand perfectly well that the future Sir David Mallender must get to know his family home.'

'That's reasonable,' said Laura. Sir David Mallender. She was shocked once more by the maelstrom of lies she had stirred. But when David was born Adrian had been alive and he hadn't cared at all for the coming child, even though he believed himself to be the father. It had all seemed so far away. After his father he would be Sir David but not for years and years. The future had stretched far into the distance.

A look of relief flickered in Lady Mallender's eyes. She was by no means as calm as she pretended.

The knowledge gave Laura a small lift of confidence. 'I'll make sure that Nanny brings him to visit you every week,' she promised.

'That will not do!' Lady Mallender's voice boomed out harshly. 'There is absolutely no reason for you to live in these dreadfully cramped quarters when we have a beautiful home just waiting for its new young master.'

Laura tried to speak, but her ladyship simply raised her well-bred voice. 'The nurseries have been redecorated and I have delegated one of the servants to wait on Nanny and David. Fortunately you have made a wise choice of nurse. She positively oozes old-fashioned sense. What day would suit you for the move?'

'I told you,' said Laura, in low shaking tones, 'I will not live under your roof again.'

Her ladyship's eyes were piercing, her voice menacing. 'I care nothing for where you are. David must and shall come home. Remember your late husband. Show some respect for what his wishes would have been.'

Laura almost shook with frustration. 'You deliberately twist everything to suit your own ends. Adrian never wanted to marry me. He cared nothing for an heir. It's you who are the ambitious one. I don't think even Sir Hugo minds.'

'My husband is –' Her ladyship paused, clenching her hands. 'Sir Hugo has no choice. David is the heir.'

Laura was being drawn deeper and deeper into the vortex of

lies. If only she could talk to someone, ask advice. She stared hopelessly at Lady Mallender, seeing things through her sharp eyes. If their positions were reversed she surely would be sitting there, demanding a proper upbringing for the child she believed to be her grandson. Laura wondered what would happen if she blurted out the truth. She knew the answer. Lady Mallender would simply not believe her. In David she saw a continuation of the Mallender line through the Mallender blood and her body. Sir Hugo considered he only held the baronetcy in trust for the next legal inheritor, be he his son, or a cousin's, and was content to allow events to take their course. Adrian had taken after his father in his disinterested attitude to life. Sir Hugo would find that deeply insulting, but it was true.

Lady Mallender had been silent, watching her face. She said now, 'Laura, you know I'm right.'

'I know nothing of the sort. David will stay with me in my home. You will be welcome to visit him, and later invite him to stay – if he wishes to. I can go no further that that.'

'I see.' Her ladyship tightened her lips. Then she rasped, 'May I see my grandson?'

Laura called Nanny who brought the baby in and handed him to her ladyship and stood a little distance away to await further orders. What a blessing that Paul had produced a woman used to the ways of society.

'He's beautiful,' declared Lady Mallender. She touched David under his soft chin with a tender finger and brought a smile to his face. He stared up at her, trusting, welcoming, entirely charming. 'I see Adrian clearly in him. He was exactly the same as a baby.' She fingered his gown, his hand-knitted matinée jacket, his soft shawl. All were spotlessly white. She lifted him to her shoulder and pushed her aggressive nose into the soft part of his neck and sniffed at the delicate scent of good soap and talcum powder, then pressed a kiss to his forehead and handed him back to Nanny. 'Congratulations. You look after him beautifully.' There was an aching wistfulness in her tone that touched Laura, even while it frightened her. Beneath all her bombastic vigour Lady Mallender really cared for David and love was a very strong weapon.

'Thank you, my lady. Does your ladyship want me to remain in the room with Master David?'

Nanny was dismissed with a wave of the hand and a slight smile.

'Laura, please, I *must* have him,' said Lady Mallender. 'Don't cross me in this. We could bring him up together, amicably. I beg you, don't be stubborn.'

Laura shook her head. 'I'm sorry. I won't return to Mallender House. I can't. I can never forget the shock, the humiliation – Adrian and that man – the deceitful way you treated me.'

'Be silent! I won't listen! If you refuse to be reasonable you must argue it out with lawyers. I shall see mine in the morning. I shall take you to court and say you are an unfit mother.'

'In what way?' Laura was deadly calm now, her eyes as hard as her former mother-in-law's.

'You work, you leave the child for hours at a time –'

'In the care of an excellent nurse as any lawyer would accept.'

'You keep him cooped up in this dreadful flat over a common factory workroom –'

'That won't last for ever. And Nanny takes him every day to the Downs.'

'My son killed himself over you. That will weigh heavily with any court.'

'We both know you're lying. Will you lie in court, under oath?'

'I'll do and say anything to get David where he belongs.'

'And suppose I tell the court what Adrian really was, who he really loved, the true reason he died?'

Her ladyship's face was a mask of twisted victory. 'You will not, though, will you! You kept silent before, and you will again. We both know what such a revelation could do to the boy as he's growing up. At school he would be taunted. Children are the cruellest creatures in the world, and don't forget that the boys he grows up with will be the men he will one day meet in society, perhaps work with. He will never know what they say behind his back, what their speculations might be, but he'll know they exist. You won't risk that for your son.'

Laura had no answer and Lady Mallender rose and stared at her 'I'll leave you to think it over. I won't hurry you too much, but David *will* move to Mallender House. Nanny Allan, of course, will be welcome.'

In spite of Lady Mallender's overhanging threat, Christmas was a happy one for Laura. It was her first with David and she bought a tree so large that it took both Ralph and Paul to haul it up to the flat. They caught their breath, grinning at it.

'I hope you've got enough tinsel,' said Ralph. 'Or would you like me to fetch another hundredweight?'

'And lanterns,' said Paul. 'What about more lanterns?'

'Don't encourage her,' said Ralph, 'if she gets any more she'll not need the lights on at all.'

Laura had gone out with Paul several times since the trip to Weston and he visited her quite regularly. He made no attempt to touch her. They just talked and she felt warm and cared for in his company, though sometimes she caught him looking at her, with eyes so intent they seemed to be trying to seek out her soul.

When Nanny brought David in he held out his arms and crowed to the tree and when the decorating was finished, the lights lit and the presents placed beneath the pine-scented branches, Laura felt thrilled, as she discovered a state of childhood she had never known.

Granma had grudgingly allowed a very skimpy tree in the front-room window, more for the neighbours' sakes than for the family's. Great preparations had to be made and paper spread everywhere so that no pine needles should stick into the rug or scratch the shining polish on the lino. It wasn't even pretty paper, just the brown stuff used for parcels. Presents were kept small and handed out solemnly after breakfast, before chapel. Laura had hung one small sock at the foot of her bed and received an orange, an apple, a few nuts and a gift, a colouring book and crayons, or an exercise book and pencil. Granma liked presents to be practical. Laura had never had any illusions about who put the things in her sock. Granma said

508

that to pretend that a kindly old gentleman came down the chimney was a lie.

Laura vowed that David's socks and his shoes, too, would be filled to the brim with gifts chosen and bought in love. And he would believe in any of the wonderful childhood fantasies that gave him joy. She went shopping and returned with bags of rattles, a silver teething ring, cuddly toys including an enormous teddy bear and rag books. Next year she'd have far more scope. Next year! She had a feeling of dread as the thought of Lady Mallender intruded. Would she have David to care for next year? Lady Mallender had not yet proceeded with her threat of a legal claim, saying in a condescending manner which infuriated Laura that she was prepared to give her time to come to her senses. She visited regularly and each time asked Laura if she had made the decision to move back to the house on the Downs. On the last occasion when Laura shook her head she had grown coldly angry. 'I've given you a fair chance to bring David to his rightful home on your own terms. I warn you, Laura, you may find yourself excluded from Mallender House and parted from David.'

'No one would give you that authority!' cried Laura.

'You think not?'

'One day I shall move to a home with a garden,' burst out Laura.

'I don't believe you! Why haven't you already done so? Because you have no time! You never have time to give to David. That's what a child needs most. I devoted my life to my children.'

'Is that a fact?' cried Laura angrily. 'As far as I can see Nancy never sees much of her mother and you made a fine mess of Adrian.'

Lady Mallender's face drained of colour. 'You wicked woman! I'll never forgive you for that! I loved him. I loved my son – how much you'll *never* know –' Her voice broke and tears filled her eyes.

Laura was horrified. 'Please, I'm sorry –'

'You will be sorrier, that I promise you.' Lady Mallender dashed away her tears and strode out.

Nancy was distressed and apologetic. 'I've tried to talk to her, Laura, but claiming David has become an obsession. She seems to see him as a replacement for Adrian.'

Laura went cold. 'Nancy, what was Adrian like as a boy?'

'As a boy? He was normal, I suppose. He loved riding and hunted regularly until he fell off and broke his arm. Then Mummy wouldn't let him hunt any more.' Nancy said more slowly, 'He enjoyed all kinds of sport, rugby, cricket, skiing, skating –' She paused. 'Mummy stopped what she called rough games, fearful that he might be hurt, and gradually replaced them with books and painting. She took him to art galleries and the theatre. It was a worry to her when he learned to drive, but he sulked until he got a fast car. She emasculated him. I'd never thought of that. I suppose I just got used to him and I did love him.'

'I know. Forgive me, but I can't permit David to be brought up by your mother. The idea terrifies me.'

'I agree with you.' Nancy sighed. 'I asked Daddy for help, but he says he won't interfere with Mummy's plans. I get so angry with him these days. He used to be stronger, but now I think he'll do anything for a quiet life. He doesn't look well, poor man, so I can't keep badgering him. It's odd, Laura, he couldn't bear Adrian's way of life, yet now he's dead I think he genuinely mourns him. Or perhaps he mourns the son he wished he'd had.'

Nanny took David to visit Sir Hugo and Lady Mallender on Christmas Eve. Laura had meant to go, in spite of her assertion that she would never enter Mallender House again. Maybe a visit would exorcise the shocking horror of her betrayal there. She had no chance to find out. There was a rush of last-minute shoppers and the shops remained open until nearly ten o'clock which even then was not as late as many, including Gregory's. She slipped upstairs briefly to kiss David goodnight.

'Her ladyship fed him with all sorts of sweetmeats which aren't good for him,' said Nanny crossly. 'I tried to stop her. I hope he's not sick, that's all.'

Laura kissed David's flushed face. She heard later that he had vomited all the sweets and chocolate over his clean bedding and Nanny had had to bath him again and change the whole cot.

'Master Paul's parents always listened to me,' Nanny said indignantly, 'and so did all my other Harrington mummies. We can't have Master David going to live under *her* roof.'

Laura said nothing. It was inevitable that Nanny would know what was going on. In so small a place it would be impossible to hide it from her. Not that Laura had tried. The older woman was stolid, dependable, and Laura relied on her good sense and bossy friendliness.

David awoke on Christmas Day, recovered and smiling. He threw all the cuddly toys out of his cot, including the ones brought by the staff, waved the rattles and tasted the teething ring and threw them after the toys. Then he ate his breakfast and went to sleep.

Laura and Nanny leaned over his cot and admired him together before they toasted one another in sherry. Laura gave Nanny a box of hand-made lace hankies for show, rather than use, and Nanny gave Laura a soft wool scarf she had knitted herself. Lady Mallender sent over a parcel for David with two complete pram sets and a teddy bear far larger than the one Laura had bought.

Rick sent a card from America. It showed a picture of New York with its incredible skyscraper buildings. The message was scant.

Laura took gifts to Aunty Mabel and Olwen. Aunty Mabel was fast growing frail and relied on Olwen who was content to be the old lady's helper and friend. They were delighted with warm hand-knitted jumpers and a large box of chocolates.

Aunty Mabel held David in her arms and rocked him back and forth and he stared back at her wonderingly. There was an immediate affinity between them and when Aunty Mabel looked at Laura her eyes were knowing. 'He reminds me of Rick,' she said. 'He's gone to look up some of his favourite jazz singers in a place called New Orleans. He got my first letter telling him I'm well, but apparently the others are following him around still.'

'So he knows nothing of what's happened to me?'

'Not so far as I can tell.' Aunty Mabel's voice expressed deep regret. She had never stopped hoping that Rick would find in Laura a quality that would make him settle down.

This year the whole family had been invited to Lillian's for Christmas Day. She had asked Granma and Grampa who had refused. Laura had sent them a carefully chosen card, but had not received one from them. This time it seemed there was to be no forgiveness and Laura felt she could hardly blame them. Granma's carefully cherished life had been turned upside down by the scandal.

Nanny was to spend the day with her sister in Bedminster and Laura drove her there before going to Lillian's house in Fishponds. Nanny had given her several dozen instructions regarding 'Master David'.

For an angry moment Laura had considered refusing her sister's invitation. At the time of the scandal Lillian had posed for the newspapers as often as she had been asked, appearing above legends such as: *Mrs Lillian Sherwood, wife of the well known Bristol business man Mr Victor Sherwood. Mrs Sherwood is the sister of Mrs Adrian Mallender whose husband died recently in tragic circumstances. 'I thought my sister and Adrian were happy together,' said Mrs Sherwood.* Laura had shrugged off her resentment. It was Christmas, the time of good will, of forgiveness. A pity Granma couldn't feel the same.

Lillian had a little skivvy to do her housework. Maureen was undersized, but cheerful, with a wide grin, and Lillian and Victor were kind to her in their own brash way. They had given her a new best frock for Christmas and Laura brought a perky straw to match. Maureen was delighted. 'I've never had such presents before, Mrs Mallender.' She had been reared in a children's home and this was her first job.

Lillian had put on weight. She wore a red satin dress that did nothing to hide her curves. Sapphires adorned her neck and ears. Her hair had been tinted a lighter shade and was marcelled into rigid waves and little sausage curls. She welcomed everyone into her four-bedroomed house with *double* bay windows as graciously as a queen.

'Isn't she lovely?' Victor demanded as he handed round

drinks. 'And next year she'll be lovelier than ever because she'll be holdin' our baby in her arms.'

'Victor! I was goin' to tell them myself.'

'Well, I've beat you to it, darlin'. I'm the proud daddy and have as many rights as you over our baby.'

'Huh! That's all very well, but I'm the one who has to carry it for months an' then have it.'

'Sorry, love, I can't do it for you. Not that I'd want to, eh?' Victor nudged Ralph in the ribs so hard he almost spilled his drink. 'How about you, mate?'

Ralph just grinned and shook his head. 'Nice wine, Victor,' he said.

'Got a job lot. I can always get stuff cheaper. Just let me know what you want.'

'He can,' said Lillian, looking at him proudly. 'Anythin' at all. Sit down, our Laura. Give me the baby.' She pulled David from Laura's arms and cuddled him. 'Who's goin' to have a little cousin, then?' she cooed. David eyed her wonderingly, then reached up and tugged at her necklace.

'Now then,' said Lillian. 'Watch what you're doin'.' She handed him back to Laura. 'He's lovely. He really is.'

She could afford to be magnanimous. Laura might have shops and a reputation for designing millinery, but she had made a complete mess of her personal life while Lillian had a fair-sized house, a loving husband and plenty of money without having to lift a finger for it. She had no need to press the point. It was in her eyes and voice.

Laura asked her mother where Freda was and Phyllis grimaced. 'God knows! She said she wasn't havin' a Christmas without Joyce and slammed out. She'll walk for miles and come back sweatin' and stuff bread and cheese in her mouth, then go to bed. I tell you, Laura, I think she's definitely goin' round the bend.'

Laura thought of Freda, walking alone on the special day of the year when families rejoiced in the birth of a son to another family two thousand years ago. 'Nothing can bring Joyce back, Mum. Can't she see she's making it harder for you all?'

'She doesn't care.'

Babies were swapped around. Laura cuddled Joyce's son for a while, though he refused to remain on anyone's lap for long, but chased about the house, smacking at balloons and blowing a tin trumpet. His early likeness to his mother had faded and he resembled no one in the family. Supposedly, he took after his unknown father in looks. He still had Joyce's good humour, which seldom failed.

Jack and Enid arrived with Glory and their second child, a son, always called Jacko and as contented as his sister. The house was filled with warmth, movement and happy noise all day. The Christmas tree dwarfed Laura's and gifts were piled up beneath it. They were opened with cries of gratification and Maureen almost vanished behind the welter of coloured paper which she shoved into a sack as she exclaimed over her gifts. No one had forgotten her and her pinched face was red with excitement. Dinner was enormous and lasted for hours and no sooner was it cleared away and the dishes washed by a perspiring Maureen, helped by Enid and Iris, than a huge decorated cake was brought in with tea. Afterwards there were games. Silly, family games that were fun and made Harold and Alfred and the little ones yell with mirth. Laura put David down for his nap and stayed with him, afraid that he would roll off the big bed. She was glad of the respite; she was tired after the long hours in the shops.

Lillian came to see where she was. 'Come on down, Laura. He'll be all right.'

'I'll stay with him, if you don't mind, Lillian. He may fall.'

'O' course he won't! Look, we'll push the bed to the wall and shove the chairs up against it. We're goin' to have "Spinnin' the Platter" and you've got to join in. Or don't you want to? Perhaps you think it's all a bit lowbred for you.'

'God, no, I don't. It's a wonderful party.'

Lillian was mollified by her obvious sincerity. 'That's all right then. You stay here if you like,' she added generously. 'I'll tell them you need a rest.' She paused by the door. 'You really do look a bit washed out. I suppose it's all been a strain. How's old Lady M these days? Is she still tryin' to get hold of David? You stick to your guns. Don't let the bitch have her own way.

514

Just because you and Adrian didn't hit it off! He was an idiot to do what he did. Catch me! I'd like to give that woman a piece of my mind. I will if you like. Victor would come with me gladly.'

'No! No, thank you, though it's good of you to offer.'

Laura lay back, watching her sleeping son. Lillian had meant what she said and if a gleam of triumph had shone in her eyes she could hardly be blamed. Then Laura tried to imagine her sister and Victor confronting Lady Mallender and she laughed softly, a laugh which ended in a sob, before she drifted into a doze.

By the end of February Laura had moved her entire workroom staff into the new factory near Old Market. She had gone to great lengths to ensure that her girls should have all the facilities possible, electric light, proper steamers, a pleasant, airy cloakroom. She picked up some second-hand sewing machines at an auction and more members of staff were engaged, eager girls who longed to be part of the fashion scene; pathetic women who had searched in vain for work for months. Laura's heart was heavy as she was forced to turn many away. Unemployment figures were still creeping up. When Laura passed Clackers' Corner nowadays in her car the numbers of men, dejected and hopeless, who stood there talking for hours, increased daily in number.

The old workroom beneath her flat had been renovated and redecorated in her colours of white, silver and gold. Only the most expensive and exclusive hats were available there, a fact which encouraged the wealthy to climb a flight of narrow stairs; *Climbing Laura's Stairs* indicated money to those in the know.

The hats for the spring show were ready. Laura had decided to produce a collection in the colours of Vlaminck, a painter she had always admired. The basic hoods were still mostly stubbornly head-hugging and the interest must lie in hues and trimmings. Old rose and moss green, wheat yellow and poppy red, veridian green and pale orange, were mingled on the felts and straws. The emphasis was on romance and there were little cakes ready with pink icing hearts to serve with tea, or wine.

Harold and Alfred had constructed a raised catwalk which

could be assembled quickly and Ralph had found her a narrow gold carpet which could be stretched along its length like a strip of unpolished topaz.

Laura and Anita were to share a show this time.

'You're lucky,' said Laura, examining Anita's new stock. 'Gowns have changed style. I have to use all my skill to make my hats look attractive and different.'

'Stop whining,' said Anita. 'They won't be able to keep wearing the cloche much longer. Hair is being allowed to grow. Here's a picture of a film star – Jean Harlow – look, quite long blond hair with waves and curls. I can't imagine customers with styles like that being content to shovel it under a small hat.'

The show was the biggest success yet. There were gasps of pleasure at the new-style dresses that flowed in graceful lines reaching mid-calf, with waists pulled in by clever stitching, or belts, displaying more feminine curves.

Laura and Anita had collaborated in a collection of underwear in materials guaranteed not to crease or run, in peach, pink, mauve, and daring black, all with nipped in waists to suit the clothes. There were exclusive transfers, designed by Pansy, featuring birds and butterflies which could be purchased if madam wished to embroider her underwear. They showed the new style elastic belt with suspenders and crocheted brassieres. Men had been excluded this time from attending!

'We shall be showing underwear and the models are not strip-tease artistes,' Laura explained smilingly to an entranced audience before she went backstage to change. The older, more conservative women had not been overlooked. For them there were attractive petticoats with built up shoulders, their somewhat dowdy image relieved by vandyked hems and ribbon insets. Nancy gave the commentary. Anita stayed behind the screens to make sure each girl wore exactly the right ensemble. Once or twice Laura overheard her jabbering in French and was sure she was swearing. She drove herself and others hard.

Ralph had organised a three-piece band of piano, violin and harp whose repertoire included love songs, dreamy ones like *Moonlight and Roses*, and cheeky ones, such as *Lady Be Good* while the girls modelled underwear. Laura felt a surge of regret that there was no smoke-roughened voice to sing the words.

Several of Laura's new workers had been trained to stalk the catwalk and they looked down upon the customers as proudly as a bevy of duchesses. Not all the models were thin. Dolores's cousin Agnes, now a full-time employee, had been delighted to help show the styles more appropriate for older, somewhat larger women.

The audience clamoured to give orders and both Anita and Laura were delighted.

Mr Russell rubbed his hands over the money that Laura banked. 'At this rate your overdraft will be cleared in no time.'

Laura was gratified, but at the back of her mind was the incessant worry of Lady Mallender and her activities. Her ladyship had seen a lawyer and put her case to him. Nancy brought her the news. 'He wasn't all that hopeful at first,' she said. 'Mummy started by saying that David's health could suffer by being cooped up in the flat.'

'Nonsense! His health is perfect.'

'She made a great deal of your abandoning Adrian. She says you're an immoral woman.'

'What? How dare she! And what possible grounds can she have? I consider I've been remarkably discreet.'

'So do I, darling.' Nancy looked miserably at her. 'Laura, she's had a private detective following you. I know it's dreadful of me, but I eavesdropped when I heard your name. He says that Paul Harrington spends time at night in your flat.'

Laura stared open-mouthed. 'Now that is too ridiculous. Paul does come up sometimes. We talk, we have a drink, that's all.'

'That's not what Mummy says you do.'

'Nancy! I'm sorry to have to say this, but your mother has a wicked mind.'

'She'll do anything, say anything, to get David from you.'

'I shall produce Nanny Allan in court and explain that she's always been in the next room when Paul calls. They'll take one look at her and the case will be laughed out of court. After all, most rich people hand their babies over to nannies.'

'It isn't that simple.' Nancy spoke diffidently. 'Laura, did you spend a weekend with Paul in Weston?'

Laura felt as if someone had punched her in the stomach. 'Why, yes, but it was perfectly innocent. Do you remember I had flu? I wasn't getting over it and Paul insisted – he practically kidnapped me – on three days of sea breezes.'

'He stayed at the same hotel.'

'Yes. Why not? We didn't share the same room. We didn't even share the same floor, for God's sake. Paul was adamant that there must be no breath of scandal.'

'Did you take David?'

'No. Paul and Nanny insisted I needed complete quiet and it was time he was weaned.' Laura fell silent. Then she said, 'She can't make anything of such an innocent weekend!'

'Maybe, maybe not, darling. But how will you feel defending your character in public – after the terrible things that were hinted about you when Adrian died?'

'Is your mother really willing to rake them all up again?'

'I'm afraid she will. She's obsessed now with having David. She can't see anything beyond that.'

Laura confided in Paul whose face went dark with anger. 'She's mad! All that bloody family's mad! I hear that Sir Hugo rarely comes out of his library now. Nancy is the only sane one.'

'Do you think she's got a case, Paul?'

'I doubt it, though one can never be sure about courts where children are concerned. Damn my stupidity in staying at the same hotel as you! I should have booked in miles away. Or, better still, have returned to Bristol.'

He paced the confines of her flat, his dark eyes stormy. 'Somehow you must be rescued from this.' He came to sit beside her. 'Laura, my dear, I had every intention of leaving you alone for a year at least after Adrian's death. For the sake of form, you understand, not because I think you mourn him. How could you?'

Laura looked at him, her heart beginning to pound. He was unusually solemn, his narrow face set in sombre lines.

'Laura,' he said, 'you must know how I feel about you –'

'Don't!' She put out her hand.

He left his chair and knelt at her feet. 'Darling girl, don't be afraid.'

'I'm not – I'm not –'

'I think you are. Men haven't exactly been good to you so far, have they?'

She was startled. 'Men?'

'I believe you once cared for Rick Merriman.'

'How do you know that? I mean, it isn't true –'

'Honesty between us, that's what we agreed. I know you so well, darling. There's a different note in your voice when you mention Merriman. You did love him, didn't you?'

'I thought I did.'

'You feel nothing for him now?'

'It's all long dead.' Laura was lying. Rick was always somewhere in her. Surely Paul could tell. He was frighteningly percipient.

He chose to leave the subject. 'And you also loved Adrian.'

'I loved what I believed was Adrian.'

'And now?'

'Disgust. Pity at the way Rex treated him. I hated him for a while, but I see that he was as wronged as me.'

Paul raised his hand and stroked her hair. 'Do you love me?'

Laura was hesitant. 'I don't know. I may do. I haven't allowed myself to think about it.'

'Please do so now, my love. I'm asking you to marry me. I'll give you a little time to consider, but you may not have much. Lady Mallender will strike soon, I think.'

'But if I'm not sure I love you?'

'Marry me anyway.'

'Are you proposing marriage to keep David safe?'

'Don't be a silly girl. I love you and your problems are mine. David will be safe with me. There's never been a breath of scandal in the Harrington family. Well, not since a Georgian member ran off with a nubile schoolgirl. Even he married her in the end.'

Laura laughed shakily. Her nerves were settling. She leaned back and a glorious mixture of emotions flowed through her. Relief, happiness, and a blissful warmth and trust that must surely amount to love. She did care for Paul. 'I don't need time to think, Paul. I'll marry you.'

'Dearest, you've made me so happy.' His kiss was gentle at first, then grew deeper as his tongue found hers. Their passion soared together and they were breathless when they broke away. Paul stared down into her wide eyes. 'My lovely Laura. My beautiful, wonderful, ardent creature. Let's not wait too long.'

Chapter Thirty

Paul wouldn't wait. Laura, still scarred by the shock and scandal of Adrian's death was nervous about courting publicity again. It wouldn't be possible to hide from the newspapers. Paul was a prominent socialite, rich and newsworthy. He was a superb sportsman, a tennis player of Wimbledon standard, a polo enthusiast, a cricketer, a golfer. He was also a lover of music and art, attending concerts and gallery openings regularly.

He held Laura close. 'Don't worry, darling. Whatever happens, whatever anyone says, I'll be here to stand between you and the problems. Trust me.'

'I do. But eventually I shall have to face my customers again.'

Paul had agreed that Laura should continue to work at the occupation she loved as long as she gave her husband the time he considered proper.

Paul smiled wrily. 'More publicity for your shops, darling. Oh, I despise the prurient as much as you, but one has to accept facts.'

The coming marriage was not publicised by Paul and Laura, but the newspapers got hold of the story. Paul just shrugged. 'It was inevitable.'

It was easier for him. He came out clean in the various articles. He had had plenty of women friends, but this was the first time he had been involved even remotely in scandal. He had no immediate family alive, but his numerous more distant relatives appeared to have led exemplary lives for generations. Laura was fair game. She winced at the wounding words: *Mrs Laura Mallender is to marry distinguished Bristolian, Mr Paul Harrington. Mrs Mallender's late husband, Mr Adrian*

Mallender, died in tragic circumstances only six months ago. His body was found –

Laura hurled the paper angrily to the floor. She was in Anita's flat and took the cocktail she produced, sipping it through shaking lips. She fitted a cigarette into the long amber holder given to her by Paul and breathed out a stream of smoke, watching morosely as it curled to the ceiling. 'Bloodsuckers! Bloody parasites, that's all they are, battening on to people in trouble just to sell a few more copies!'

Anita stretched. She lay on her sofa, as elegant and smooth as a cat. 'You ask for it, darling.'

'What? I only want to get on with my life. Surely that's why we're all here. To get on with life.'

'Yes, but some of us seem to get on a lot louder than others, if you see what I mean!'

Laura stared angrily, then slumped, and smiled wrily. 'Damn it, you're right! But I never meant all these things to happen. They just seemed to, well, happen.'

'Nonsense! You could have stayed single and prospered. You don't need men.'

Laura smoked thoughtfully for a while. Anita waited; she was cat-like in this, too – she was prepared to wait patiently.

'Don't you ever long for someone close, someone of your own?' asked Laura.

'No.'

'I do. I suppose I'm just a weak idiot.'

'My God, you really should curb this tendency to talk trash. I wish you could see yourself in business. You remind me of a sword, sharp, flashing, ruthlessly cutting away anything that impedes you.'

'That's me?'

'Wide-eyed little innocent, yes, that's you. If only you could forget men. Or better still, take a lover now and then. Why do you have to get so bloody involved?'

'I don't know.' Laura did know. She wanted love. She needed it like a man lost in a desert needs water. Her first taste of it had been through Rick and the sorrowful ache of her heart had been assuaged by him for a few glorious weeks. She had been deceived into believing that Adrian would cure her barren loneliness. Now she had Paul. He was different. *Definitely* different. He combined the good qualities of both previous men. He was gentle and artistic, like Adrian; he could be strong and masterful, like Rick.

'This time it'll be different,' she said.

Anita rolled her dark eyes. 'I've heard that one before.'

Laura shook off Anita's cynicism in the warm glow of Paul's love. Even the public raking up of the old wounds got lost in his deep, abiding care.

He had made all the arrangements for their honeymoon without consulting her. A few days before the wedding she asked, 'Please tell me, where are you taking me for the honeymoon? I need to pack the right clothes.'

'Paris.'

'Paul, no! We can't!'

He looked gravely at her, his thin face expressionless, his eyes watchful. 'Why not?'

'You know why not. Adrian took me there.'

His expression changed and his eyes darkened with anger. 'I happen to love Paris, especially in the spring. I would be making my usual visit there anyway. Now I look forward to enjoying it with you. You surely can't be comparing my sort of Paris with anything that decadent little swine, Adrian Mallender, showed you. Can you?'

She felt a frisson of – not fear, that was impossible, rather of trepidation at his cutting tone. She wanted everything between her and Paul to be perfect, without conflict. 'No, darling, of course not. It's only that –' She stopped. Paul was getting angrier. 'Sorry, darling,' she said. 'I was taken aback. Paris has bad memories for me, but I'm sure you can change that. After all, I have to get used to going there. One day I intend to visit the fashion shows.'

He pulled her into his arms, his hands caressing and soothing her. 'Darling Laura, please forgive me. I can't help being jealous. I sometimes try to imagine what you must have been like as a girl. It infuriates me to think that someone else had the privilege of bringing your dormant passion to life, especially someone like Mallender.'

'I love you,' she said. 'Only you.'

'Then we will conquer Paris together. We'll do touristy things. I bet Adrian didn't take you up the Eiffel Tower, for instance.'

'No, and I was disappointed. How did you guess?'

'He was terrified of heights. We were guests at a country-house party years ago – he was about eleven – I was older, one of the boys, don't you know?' Laura laughed at his assumed silly-ass accent. 'There was a folly in the grounds, a kind of tower overlooking an ornamental lake and, late one afternoon, all the young people became involved in a dare to climb to the top. It was not too difficult. The place had been built looking deliberately ruined, but was actually stable and there were plenty of foot- and hand-holds. Everyone climbed, except Adrian. In the end we forced him up –'

'Forced him? How?'

'We gave him the usual schoolboy tortures – Chinese burn, pushed his head under the water and held it there, that kind of thing. He went up and got stuck at the top. He begged someone to help him.'

'And did you?'

'Don't look so tragic, darling. We all had to go through the same kind of thing at some time. It's what makes men of us.' His voice again took on overtones, this time of a cinema hero, but Laura couldn't laugh.

Paul's eyes flashed briefly with annoyance. 'No, we did not help him. We left him there with his eyes and nose running. Just before dinner a couple of the girls rescued him. *Girls*! I ask you?'

'Some people can't help being scared of heights.'

'Boys must conquer such fears if they're to grow into men. But of course, as we both know, Adrian didn't. I wish I'd had him at school when I was a prefect. I'd have beaten sense into him.'

'I wouldn't want my son beaten.'

'Our sons won't need it. They'll be strong and fearless.'

'Sons? Yes, I hope we have sons, and daughters, too. But I was speaking of David.'

'Of course. I shall care for him like a father. One can tell by looking at him that he's got the makings of a fine man. He must have much more of you in him than his sire.'

His remark effectively silenced her, as any reference to David's parentage always did.

Laura was satisfied that the shops and factory would proceed efficiently while she was away. She had installed bright electric lighting in the factory so that no woman need ever end up with sore eyes, her back permanently bent like Miss Morton's from years of crouching beneath a flicker of light.

Pansy, promoted to overseer of the factory and having her wages raised to four pounds a week, raised her heavy eyebrows, nodded and grunted, 'Thanks.' She was never communicative and she knew she was worth the high wage.

Miss Morton, offered the same sum, refused indignantly saying she only did a short week. Laura kissed her, 'You're the corner-stone of the business. Please let me repay a little of what I owe you.' Miss Morton had been unable to refuse such a request but she looked near to tears.

There were now ten girls, plus four apprentices who were paid only a nominal sum for the privilege of learning their trade at *Hats by Laura*. All clerical work was undertaken by a Miss Prewett, who was quick and excellent with figures. She was a cousin of Reggie, older, but with a certain resemblance. She said that Sally Whiteley, now Reggie's wife, served behind the counter at his father's grocery store. That could have been me, thought Laura, shuddering. Miss Prewett's first task was to engage a typist-filing clerk of just fourteen, a pretty, cheerful girl with a dusting of freckles on her nose and across her cheeks.

Nancy managed the Park Street shop and Mary, the Redfield branch. Dolores had gained a surprising assistant in *The Hat Shop*. Harold, now eighteen, had developed a deep interest in fashion and shop work and was encouraged by Laura in the face of criticisms from most of the family, including the sixteen-year-old Alfred, who couldn't believe that he was to lose the continual companionship of a brother who had been almost like his twin. However, after a lot of teasing, during which words like 'cissy' and 'girlie' were hurled at Harold's impervious head, Alfred accepted the fact. He bought himself a second-hand motor cycle and hired out his services to Rick's picture houses working alongside Jack, or anywhere else he could pick up a few shillings. He was often useful as a messenger when Laura was too busy to motor between the shops and promised to make himself responsible for carrying the takings and relevant papers to Miss Prewett while Laura was away. He reminded her a little of Rick. She hoped he had his flair for success. She'd had only the card from Rick since he sailed to America and couldn't deny that his indifference still had the power to wound her.

The wedding was even quieter than her first. No one from either family was invited, a fact which enraged Phyllis. 'What's up with him? Too bloody proud, is he?'

'Now then, love,' admonished William. 'We know what's what. They don't want to make a fuss in the circs.'

'Make a fuss! Havin' her parents to watch her get married. Huh! It's a funny carry on, if you ask me.' Since David's birth Phyllis had reverted to her former remoteness and it hurt Laura even more after she had happily basked in a motherly glow, however faint. She swore that no matter what children she bore, under whatever circumstances, she would love each one, always. She was soothed a little by her father's championship, though it hadn't lasted long. He was soon back behind his paper.

Lillian was visiting. She looked plump as well as pregnant, both developments appearing to please her adoring husband. 'More to cuddle', had been his expressive phrase. Lillian looked suitably smug. She seated herself near the fire, her fox fur still round her neck, heavily adorned with jewellery and wearing one of Laura's hats. 'Only the best is good enough for my Lill,' proclaimed Victor. 'And *Hats by Laura* is all the rage these days. Clever little thing, aren't you?' He had nudged Laura in the ribs. She hated being touched like that, but she forced a smile.

'Not so little.'

'Well, no, you're tall, but by God, you've not much meat on you.'

Lillian drank the cup of tea Phyllis handed her. 'I must say I agree with our Mum, Laura,' she said smugly, in her adored role of pampered wife. 'I don't see how you can have a proper weddin' without guests. What about presents, and all the lovely clothes you'd have worn? I wouldn't have missed mine for anythin'.'

'Neither would I, love,' said Phyllis.

'Of course it's nice to have presents,' said Laura placatingly. 'I shall be wearing just a two-piece outfit. Nothing fancy.' Paul would probably not accept the kind of presents that would be given by her family. His house, into which she was to move, was Georgian, and almost everything in it had to be commensurate with that age. There were a few modern exceptions, such as a Picasso drawing and a small blue painting by Monet and Ralph had provided a few pieces of good quite modern furniture. Laura was surprised to discover a painting by Rex. She was startled into a comment. 'I didn't think you would have one of his works in your home.'

'Oh?' Paul said coolly, 'I'm not as short-sighted as you appear to think. The man is a bounder; I loathe him and his way of life, but he paints well and the value will increase. I have no difficulty in separating emotion from practicality.'

Granma asked Laura to call; she approved of this marriage. 'The Harringtons are a good family,' she said, 'a very good family. No scandals *there*.'

'Amy –' protested Grampa.

'I can only hope that this will prove a turning point in your life, Laura. We must try to forget the past and look to the future. The Harringtons.' She rolled the word around her tongue. 'Church-goers, but nobody can be perfect. You've done well for yourself, I have to say, better than you deserve.'

Laura clenched her tongue between her teeth.

A reporter and photographer turned up at the wedding and pictures later appeared of Laura looking proudly indifferent as she walked to the chauffeur-driven car. There were more of her and Paul together after the ceremony. The pictures were

527

accompanied by the inevitable resumé of the past. She and Paul were driven to London, the big car cruising smoothly over the roads. Paul had asked her to have her luggage packed and ready for shipment to Paris, promising her a surprise. It seemed a curious thing to do, but when Laura discovered what the surprise was she understood.

'*Fly* to Paris. In an *aeroplane*.'

'The aeroplane will be necessary, darling. It's impossible to take to the air without it.' Paul's voice was teasing, his eyes filled with laughter.

Laura, nervous, but excited, put on the clothes secretly purchased by Paul. Fur-lined suede jacket and trousers trimmed with mink, and a tight-fitting helmet to match. She exchanged her dainty shoes for soft, puttee-like boots and pulled on thick gloves.

'It gets cold up there,' explained Paul.

She understood the clothes and the remark when she realised that the plane was an open two-seater and that Paul was going to fly it himself.

'You trust me, don't you?' he asked, grinning at her. He looked aggressively masculine in leather as he gave her a hand into the plane. She pulled on a pair of goggles similar to his and the plane bumped slowly along the airfield, getting faster and faster. It made little jumps as if gathering its strength. Laura hung on to the sides, breathless with a mixture of fear and exhilaration, and then she realised they had left the ground.

'Like it?' yelled Paul, above the engine noise.

'It's w – wonderful.'

He laughed exultantly. 'I knew you were a sport.'

At the large hotel in Paris their trunks were waiting for them. Laura was still dazed. Everything seemed unreal. In their room she suddenly felt alive, deeply aware of herself. She had actually married again. She was about to take another man to her bed. She had left David, reluctantly, but assured of his welfare in Nanny Allan's hands.

Paul slid his arms round her. 'Any doubts, my darling?'

She hugged him. 'No, not at all. But it's all been like a dream.'

'I know. It's the same for me. Laura, I've watched you and wanted you from the first moment we met. And now you're mine. All mine. For life.' His voice held deep significance.

They dined in their room. When fruit and champagne were served Paul dismissed the waiters and they drank the sparkling wine, toasting one another, their eyes meeting above the rims of the glasses. This is how it should be, thought Laura. This is a real honeymoon. She bathed and put on a satin pale eau-de-nil night-dress, trimmed with lace over her breasts. With it she wore a matching negligée and fur slippers. She brushed her hair into gleaming waves. She had let it grow longer and a few curls clustered in the nape of her neck.

Paul was waiting for her, already bathed, wearing brown silk pyjamas and a short dressing gown. He was smoking and when she appeared got up and opened another bottle of champagne.

He was incredibly gentle with her, behaving as if he were her first lover. When his fingers began to roam over her body as he plundered her mouth with searching kisses, she reacted immediately. Her body arched and stiffened and her long-stifled desire came to vivid life and coursed through her like a torrent. She put out her hand and touched Paul. Beneath the silken smoothness of his pyjamas he was deeply aroused, but as soon as she stroked him his whole body became rigid. It was not passion that tautened him. He stopped moving, then removed Laura's hand. 'Be still,' he murmured. She lay quietly by his side, outwardly passive, inwardly quivering, hungry for love, holding back words which would reveal her desperate need.

When he finally kicked off his trousers and entered her she couldn't suppress a groan of satisfaction. He stopped moving again, holding himself above her, deep inside her, torturing her senses. She stared up at him, knowing she must be revealing her longing in her eyes. His were almost opaque, commanding, revealing no inner need. He smiled, then bent his head and kissed her gently, moving his hips in slow rhythmic strokes that drove her crazy with frustration. Her passion rose in waves of heat until she gained her release and a wild cry of triumph and joy broke from her. Paul took his own satisfaction immediately, then pulled himself from her and lay back on the bed, breathing hard.

'You're happy!' he said. A statement, not a question.

'Yes,' said Laura, but she wished he had not withdrawn so abruptly. She raised herself on one elbow, aching to hold him close, to revel in the aftermath of bliss, to kiss him tenderly, but he pushed her gently away. He had given her pleasure as intensely as Rick, but his act of love had been coolly, almost scientifically performed.

'I'm a little cold, Paul,' she said. 'I would like to pull the covers over me.'

Instantly he was contrite. He climbed out of bed and tucked her in as gently as if he had been her nurse, then lay beside her quietly. His breathing told her he had gone to asleep. It was a long time before she was able to follow his example. He had given her sexual release. But had he made her truly happy? The two did not necessarily go together, as she knew only too well. Deep joy was being held tenderly after the act, lovers using their own intimate language as their bodies relaxed. If Rick hadn't made love to her she wouldn't have known how good that could be. My God, Rick was intruding into this honeymoon, too! She must forget him. She would coax Paul into understanding her needs.

The days that followed were good ones. Paris, as yet unaffected by the financial disasters that were terrorising much of the western world, was like a woman gowned in silks, bright with jewels. From the Eiffel Tower Laura saw the whole of the lovely spring-time city spread in a panorama. The Seine flowed beneath the famous bridges, the ancient streets of the left bank climbed the hill to where the Basilica of the Sacred Heart stood in dominance. She wished briefly that Paul would permit her to visit the artists' quarter again. He was odd, inconsistent; he displayed one of Rex's paintings, yet hated the man. He could bring her to Paris, yet could not endure the idea of his wife even approaching any place where she had been happy with another man. But she forgot her disappointment in the arrangements Paul had made for her delight. They were welcomed in private homes where she enjoyed sumptuous meals in genuinely old-world surroundings. It seemed that the revolution hadn't managed to destroy all the aristocracy.

The Louvre was a particular joy. And the theatres, all different from those visited with Adrian. Paul questioned her meticulously on such points. He took her one night to the Folies Bergères where she looked with astonished appreciation at the perfect, silken, naked bodies of the show girls. Once she leaned forward, startled.

'That's Lottie!'

'You mean you are acquainted with one of *them*!'

She calmed down at his critical tone. It was all right to look, but not to know. 'She's a girl I was forced to dismiss from my employment. She was dishonest.'

Paul nodded. 'Quite correct, my dear. Obviously destined to come to a bad end.'

'But the girls here are respectable.'

'Who told you that?'

'Anita. She knows some of them.'

'In future, my darling, you will be guided by me in such matters.'

She felt the now-familiar frisson of – not fear, of course, not fear – merely a touch of surprise at his autocratic attitude.

They were welcomed to the showrooms of Coco Chanel. 'She claims to have been reared in an orphanage,' said Paul, 'though her background is obscure. What was certain is that she began her brilliant career by making hats. Just like you.'

He bought clothes for Laura without regard for cost. 'Chanel's serene simplicity was designed just for you,' he said. He chose simple black gowns and three pairs of trousers to be worn on the beach. 'I shall introduce you to Deauville, darling, you'll love it there. All the women wear trousers these days, and bathing costumes, too. We must take some for you. And some of Chanel's lovely pleated skirts and soft jumpers and cardigans. And, of course, a supply of her wonderful scent, Chanel No 5.'

At Schiaparelli Laura acquired tweeds, the skirts fastened with the new zipper.

Paul ruled out Molyneux. 'Too flowery,' but they visited Vionnet, 'the genius who invented the bias cut.'

Laura was dazzled by the wealth of colour and textiles. Paul showed the same enthusiasm for clothes as Adrian, but there was a vast difference. Adrian loved them for their own sake, perhaps even seeing himself in them. Paul bought them for his wife.

His wedding present had been a double necklace of glowing pearls with drop earrings. Family jewels, perfectly matched. Now he supplemented them with a diamond necklace and bracelet, a brooch holding a glorious opal and a mass of brilliant fake jewellery, now de rigeur in society, designed by Chanel. 'Lots of them are copies of her own collection,' Paul said.

If only the nights had been as good. Paul's lovemaking was tender, gentle, exquisite, yet it was spoiled for Laura by his insistence on her passivity. She had tried to talk to him about it, telling him how much she longed to caress him. He listened in silence, his face becoming grim, his eyes icy.

'I thought I made you happy?' he said, clipping his words.

'You do, darling, but I want to touch you as you touch me. I want to kiss you and –' She had stopped, brought up sharply by his expression. It startled her. It surely couldn't be distaste?

'It is for me to lead you into the act of love, Laura. You must follow my way. If ever I cease to satisfy you, you are at liberty to tell me.'

'I see.'

'I suppose you crawled all over Adrian Mallender.'

Laura was shocked, both by his crude words and the bitter resentment in his voice. 'I made love to him, yes! Why not? Damn it, I was married to him!'

Paul had seized her arm in a grip that hurt. 'Nothing that happened between you and him will ever be the same with me.'

'Is that the only reason for your – dictates?'

'Dictates! That isn't a word I care for. And no, as it happens, that isn't the only reason. I prefer love-making my way.'

'What about me? Have I nothing to offer?'

'You have everything.' His voice softened. 'Darling, bear with me. It is, after all, only a small thing. We are happy together, aren't we?'

'Yes, Paul. We are happy.' Most of the time, she added silently, yielding to his implacable will.

They returned to Bristol after two weeks and Laura found a personal maid waiting for her in her new home. Harrington House, like Mallender House, named after the family. She wondered what caustic comment Rick would produce about this display of egotism. It was a tall three-storied elegant building with a flight of graceful stone steps to the front door which was flanked by two pillars. It was situated only two miles from the Mallenders', though it was a world away in charm for her. Laura liked it even though she was somewhat awed by its uncluttered perfection. She wondered how a child would fit in among the delicate porcelain, much of it Chinese, brought to Bristol by Harrington ancestors in sailing ships, and displayed on tables and alcove shelves, and antique clocks which marked the passing of time with melodious sound. Already David, at eight months, could pull himself up and stand sturdily by clinging to furniture.

Laura needn't have worried. Paul had no intention of allowing David to get near his treasures. He was brought downstairs by Nanny Allan only when sent for and rigidly supervised by her.

Laura was delighted when she found Nanny and David had already been installed in the old nurseries on the top storey.

She kissed Paul quickly when he told her and raced up the stairs to arrive breathless, not knowing exactly where David was. She called, a door opened, and a young girl poked her head round.

'I'm Mrs Harrington,' announced Laura, and Nanny's voice floated through the crack.

'Betsy! Open the door, you silly girl. It's David's Mummy.'

Laura seized her son and held him close. He smelled delicious and looked handsome in a blue romper suit. 'Oh, my baby, I've missed you,' she crooned, kissing his round, smooth cheeks and his silky hair.

David submitted for a few moments, before pushing her away and turning to Nanny Allan.

Laura went cold.

'Don't worry, Mrs Harrington,' soothed Nanny. 'Children forget dreadfully quickly. It's a mercy the Lord's granted to them. He'll soon be your own little boy again.'

'Yes, of course –' Laura stood watching uncertainly when the young nursery maid said that Master David's bath was ready and Nanny carried him through. The nurseries were spacious, a day room, two large bedrooms for children, and two smaller for the staff. There was a central living room with enormous cupboards into which Betsy began stacking toys, most of which Laura had never seen before.

'Mr Harrington ordered them,' said Betsy, wide-eyed. 'He said Master David must have everything of the best.'

Laura wanted to help with the bath. It was impractical of her to be disappointed in her son's reaction. David must learn to be without her if she was to continue working, and she should be grateful – was grateful – for Paul's thoughtfulness, for the presents he had provided, but she felt a sudden chill as it seemed that once again she was being ousted from the affection of someone she loved.

Nanny almost purred her content. 'This was my home for years, Mrs Harrington. It's wonderful to be back again, with another budding family.' Her eyes flickered over Laura in an obvious hope that her young mistress was pregnant by 'Master Paul'. Laura hoped she was not. She wanted her shops on a more secure footing before she had to take time off for mother-hood. She had meant to explain this to Paul, but he was so easily moved to anger and on their first day in Paris he had made it absolutely clear that he wanted children. It wasn't fair. A woman should be mistress of her own body. Guiltily she was again forced to hide her contraceptive in a locked jewel case, another Harrington possession and a treasure itself.

In the drawing room Paul was waiting. He spoke with barely suppressed irritation. 'Laura, please don't ever behave that way again.'

'What have I done *now*?'

There was a flash of fury at her response. 'There's no need to be rude to me. I am merely telling you that I'd prefer it if you did not behave like a hoyden in front of the servants. Racing upstairs, yelling like a fish-wife, is not behaviour expected of a Harrington lady.'

'A fish-wife! Surely not!' Laura, too, was furious, but she took a deep breath to calm herself. She so enjoyed basking in Paul's goodwill, which could only be maintained by gaining his approval. 'I'm sorry, Paul. I was so happy to see David again. Thank you for having him here waiting for me and for all the lovely toys. It was good of you.'

Paul was mollified. 'I'll forgive you – this once,' he said, bending to kiss her cheek. She reached up for him, but he moved swiftly away. 'Save it for tonight.'

Not in front of the servants, thought Laura. It was an expression she had read, but its force had never registered until now. After she and Adrian had married he had scarcely shown affection behind the bedroom door, let alone anywhere else. Yet there were haunting similarities in her situation. Both men made use of her when it suited them.

Paul rang the bell and sherry was brought by the stately butler, Claypole.

Laura suddenly felt petrified. She had not given a thought to the management of a grand house. At Mallender House Lady Mallender had taken care of everything. After Claypole left she said so, tentatively, because she was never sure of Paul's reaction.

He smiled tenderly at her. He liked her submissive, hesitant, dependent on him. 'It won't be difficult for you. Mrs Claypole is our housekeeper. If you give her instructions she'll see they are carried out.'

'That's a relief. I shall be busy at the shops and factory,' reminded Laura.

'Render unto Caesar,' said Paul lightly. 'You will soon work out how to divide your time suitably.'

This statement proved to be impossibly optimistic. Laura rose the next morning at seven, anxious to see what had been happening to her shops in her absence. She had crept out of bed leaving Paul asleep and didn't ring for Hawkins, her maid. She glanced in her mirror before she went downstairs. The new skirt length, the subtle curves and graceful lines suited her. She carried a beautiful tweed coat trimmed with leopard fur over her arm and wore one of her own hats, a draped turban in black and gold, after the style of Reboux. A surprised housemaid brought her tea and toast. Laura ached for a sight of David before she left and, after eating a little, she went swiftly to the nurseries. Nanny Allan stared at her so indignantly she felt like an interloper, but David smiled, showing his first teeth, white against the pink of his mouth. He held a spoon which he hurled to the floor.

Betsy picked it up. Nanny Allan said, 'Master David is about to eat his breakfast, Mrs Harrington. Your interruption is undoing my teaching. He had almost stopped throwing down his cutlery.'

Laura nearly apologised. Then she felt deeply annoyed. 'I'm here to kiss him goodbye before I go to work. You can expect me each morning.'

She kissed her son and smoothed his soft cheeks with hands that longed to hold him to her. Downstairs she was about to let herself out when Claypole appeared.

'Mr Harrington requests your presence upstairs, madam.'

Laura stared at him. Words trembled on her tongue. She wished she dared send a message back to Paul, but it would not do. She smiled instead. 'I left him sleeping.'

'Yes, madam.'

She sighed and walked up the carpeted stairs, feeling Claypole's eyes boring into her back.

Paul was sitting up in bed eating a breakfast of fruit juice, poached eggs and bacon, toast and marmalade, and coffee which his valet, Skidmore, had carried to him. Hawkins hovered in the doorway.

Paul smiled as he dismissed her. 'Your mistress will ring when she needs you. Thank you, Skidmore, lay out my navy worsted, then send Mrs Claypole to the morning room. Mrs Harrington will be there directly to discuss the menus.'

'Yes, sir.' Skidmore's face was impassive as he withdrew.

Laura watched Paul as he unconcernedly spread a piece of toast with butter. She glanced at her watch. 'You sent for me,' she said flatly.

'Please don't glare at me. And be seated. You appear to be somewhat put out.'

She remained standing. 'Put out! Yes, I am. I want to get away early.'

'Just where were you thinking of going?'

She stared in disbelief. 'You know! You must know I was – *am* – going to work. We agreed –'

'We agreed that you should divide your time. So far we have not discussed the measure.'

'Then we'd better do so right now.' Laura looked at her watch again. It was small, the band studded with tiny jewels. Another of Paul's generous gifts, and it brought her up short. She sat down. 'Please, darling, let's not waste time.'

'You consider time spent with your husband as wasted?' Paul tackled his toast with vigour.

'Of course not –' Laura stopped, confused. 'Paul, I'm sorry I reacted badly just now. Please, darling, tell me what engagements we have for this evening and I'll make sure I'm home in good time to change.'

'We have engagements right through the day.'

'That's impossible! I have an appointment with a young chemist who's agreed to produce a new perfume for Anita and me. I must be there to help with the decision. He has several mixtures ready.'

'How do you know?'

'Anita left a note with Claypole. He gave it to me last night.'

'I see. You must telephone Anita, and tell her to defer the appointment to a time more suitable for you. I cannot have my bride jaunting off to work when she is expected to begin morning visits to my friends. People who will become your friends, too, Laura, my dear. The parents and grandparents of the children David must get to know one day.'

He had a knack of disarming her by playing on her love for her son. Did he really care for David? 'Tomorrow, please, darling,' she begged. 'Let's make our calls tomorrow.'

'Today!' said Paul, eating steadily, as if the issue was settled. As if, she thought resentfully, she was a child whose minor pleasure trip had been altered. 'Now you must go to the morning room and interview Mrs Claypole. We shall be giving a dinner party one week from today and she likes to be prepared several days ahead. She will advise you. Today we are lunching out.'

Laura stood up. Paul had slid his bed-tray away and was getting up. Last night they had made love with heated passion. She was beginning to gain control over her wilful body, forcing it to enjoy his in passivity. Paul looked lean and powerful in dark navy silk pyjamas. His thin face was pale, his dark hair a little tousled. He was so seldom anything other than immaculate that this small dishevelment made him seem more approachable as he walked towards her.

She tried again. 'Paul, please darling, let me go to work just for this morning. I'll get back for lunch. You knew when we married how important my shops are to me – and now there's the new factory.'

'You have efficient staff in charge.'

'Yes, but I should be there. I must be there –' She stopped abruptly, her head reeling. For a moment she thought she had suffered a brief blackout. She staggered against the bedrail, clinging to it. Paul stood over her, his eyes sparking fire, his hand still poised over her.

'You hit me,' she whispered. 'You hit me!'

'I chastised you,' he said, coldly. 'I will not have my wife arguing with me. I am your guide as to behaviour in society and you will obey me.'

'You hit me!' she said again, dazed by shock. She sat down heavily on an ottoman at the foot of the bed. Her hand went to the back of her head which was throbbing.

'Have you bathed yet?' Paul asked as equably as if he had not just dealt her a blow which had not only hurt her physically, but had shattered her self-esteem.

'Not today – not yet – last night –'

'Have your bath now,' said Paul.

'You've bruised my head.' It was such an inadequate remark.

'It won't show. Wear your pale-grey suit this morning, and your green afternoon dress and jacket for tea. Tonight your maid will lay out the georgette evening gown with the cape. She will advise you on suitable jewels and hair style.'

'I don't need her advice,' said Laura hoarsely. 'I'm a fashion designer remember?'

Paul's eyes were still heavy with his inner fury as he advanced on her. He had turned into a stranger. She forced herself not to shrink. She knew instinctively that to do so would make him despise her and bring more violence.

He stopped. 'Nevertheless, Hawkins will advise you, as she has other Harrington ladies. Oh, yes, by the way, the book presented to you by Lady Mallender – the one on etiquette – is very good. You must study it.'

'I showed that to you as – as a joke!'

'Etiquette is far from funny, as you will learn. We shall be making frequent visits to London and mixing with people the Mallenders cannot at the moment afford to see. Now, hurry my dear, and take your bath.'

Laura's dressing room with her private bathroom led off the bedroom. Paul's similar suite was on the other side. She sat down on the edge of the bath, still dazed by what had just occurred. No one had struck her since Granma had wielded her cane, and never any man. She felt besmirched, tarnished, and deeply, deeply ashamed and utterly bewildered. Paul had always been kind. She tried to think back. Had there been signs unnoticed by her? Had she wilfully ignored anything about him in her desperate attempt to keep David safe? This was something she could never disclose to a living soul. She was undressing when Hawkins walked unceremoniously into the bathroom.

Laura said angrily, 'I'll ring when I want you.'

'Mr Paul sent me, madam,' said Hawkins, as if this settled everything. Of course, it did. Laura hadn't liked Hawkins when she had been presented to her. She was plump, elderly, with a poor complexion and steel-grey hair strained beneath her white cap. Her dull black dress emphasised her sallow skin. She had maided several Harrington ladies and, like all the servants Laura had met so far, she deferred to Paul. None of this would have mattered if she showed any warmth towards her mistress, but she didn't.

Laura lay back in the bath water whose sweet-scented steam

reminded her of her appointment. Mr Driscoll, Anita had said in her note, was young, and enthusiastic at the idea of helping to market a new perfume. It might make his name. He and Anita had toyed with a brand name for their range of scent and the cosmetics they were to produce and Laura had looked forward to being with them, to enjoying the thrill of accomplishment that her successful business brought her. Paul promised, he promised! The words spun in her brain like a child's roundabout, discordant music shrieking the memory of his violence.

Laura phoned Anita, keeping her voice light. 'Sorry I can't be there today. I needs must visit Paul's closest friends. A bride's duty, don't you know.'

Anita didn't laugh. 'Bloody stupid rot! Tony Driscoll's a busy man. He's a pharmacist and had to get the morning off to see us. God knows when he'll be able to do that again.'

'Can't we see him one evening?' asked Laura. The anxiety in her voice was tinged with something else. A note of panic she couldn't control.

Anita didn't answer for a moment, then she said quietly, 'I'll arrange it. Tony's a nice bloke. He'll understand.'

Laura spent the day in a daze. She met people, talked nonsense, answered questions about her impressions of Paris. Once, she almost spoke of something she had seen with Adrian. Paul had become as watchful as a beast of prey and she must keep a constant guard over herself.

Lunch was taken with an elderly couple. There were several people there, including the Charltons and the man they called Boy. He and Thelma were engaged.

'How was Paris, darling?' asked Thelma. 'Ah, gay *Paris*! *Too*, too wonderful for words, especially in the spring. Shall we be seeing you at Deauville this summer? So *utterly* lovely. Sunbathing, an occasional swim. Boy and I will be there, won't we, darling?'

Paul and Laura returned to Harrington House for the second time that day to change for dinner. Laura put on the evening gown ordered by her husband. Her head ached quite seriously now and she couldn't endure an argument. When she felt better she would tell him positively that she would not permit him to strike her. It wasn't difficult to be firm in her dressing room, but when she saw Paul impeccably dressed in a superbly cut dinner suit, a lightly frilled shirt and black bow tie, his powerful presence overwhelmed her. How could she have known him for so long and not sensed his aggressiveness? She had believed he was like Rick, but he was nothing at all like him. Rick would never use his strength against a woman. He was tender and loving. She drove him from her thoughts. Paul might sense what was going through her mind.

She acquitted herself well at the dinner party. Many of the people she had met at lunch were present. She passed the hours of gossip by checking to see how many of the guests wore one of Anita's model gowns, how many were sporting one of her evening head-dresses. A satisfying number.

Paul's voice broke in on her thoughts, smooth, calm, laughingly teasing. 'Laura, darling, Lady Marjorie is speaking to you.'

Laura flushed. 'I beg your pardon. I'm afraid I was dreaming.'

Lady Marjorie's loud, hoarse laugh was enough to shatter the delicate wine glasses. 'I said I hoped you would go on designing your darling hats. We ladies need you.'

There was a general laugh and murmur of agreement.

Laura felt suddenly angry, perverse. 'You had better ask Paul. I must defer to my husband.'

Her reply brought a volley of approval from the men and humorous protests from the ladies.

'Darling, you're *priceless*,' cried Daphne. 'Isn't she priceless?' she demanded of her sister.

'*Too*, too mirth-making,' agreed Thelma stonily. Boy seemed more intent on drinking himself into a stupor than paying attention to his fiancée.

That night, after undressing and putting on her nightdress, Laura dismissed Hawkins, then eyed the slender day-bed in her dressing room, which was as large as Granma's best front room. The window overlooked the garden. She longed to be able to open it for air, then lie down alone and seek oblivion. She lingered, lassitude creeping over her.

Paul knocked. 'May I come in, darling?'

She was amazed. His voice was honey-sweet. She opened the

door and he came to her and pulled her close, smoothing her hair, covering her face with kisses. 'My love, I was a brute. Please, forgive me. I can't think what came over me. Yes, I can. I was jealous. Can you imagine that? Jealous of your business and the time you must give to it?'

A glorious wave of relief spread through Laura. She put her hands each side of his face and drew his lips to hers, lassitude gone, the gentle pardon of her generous heart expressed through her kiss.

'I was so afraid,' she whispered.

'Of me? Oh, God, what a swine I was.' Paul picked her up and carried her to the bed. He removed her nightgown with care, tracing a path over her body with hands and lips, with infinite delicacy, sweet finesse, before he entered her and gave her release.

He always slept almost immediately. She lay awake, thankful that his lapse into abuse had shocked him as much as it had her.

Early the next morning she called first on Anita who said drily, 'And how's our social butterfly this morning? Did you enjoy the day with the nobs?'

Laura shrugged. 'I prefer work.'

Anita lit her second cigarette of the day and Laura smoked with her as they sat in Anita's flat, drinking coffee.

'You didn't visit *Maman* this time,' said Anita.

Laura blew out a plume of smoke. 'I hadn't time. Paul seems to know everyone in Paris.'

'Everyone in the upper echelons, you mean. *Maman* isn't good enough for him.'

'That's not true! Honestly, Anita, we did so much –'

'Spare me. I've made an appointment to see Tony Driscoll at seven o'clock this evening. He'll drop in after his work.'

Laura went swiftly over Paul's plans. Dinner tonight was with another of his friends. Thank God it wasn't served until nine. She could get back in time to bath and change.

She toured her shops, beginning with *The Hat Shop*. Iris was delighted to see her. At first Laura was almost inclined to laugh at Harold. He had invested in a dark suit, an off-the-peg thing that barely fitted his lanky frame. His shirt was snowy, his grey tie tied in the Windsor knot made fashionable by the Prince of Wales. But her amusement turned to respect when he began to speak. He kissed her. 'You look great. Wait till you see the figures for last week. I arranged a small show. Well, not a show exactly. I sent invitations out, sayin' that our upstairs room would be opened for chosen customers.'

'What upstairs room?'

'The one you use as extra storage space. Ralph lent me a big screen and we shoved all the stuff behind that. Iris scrubbed the place and I washed the windows and paintwork. It's in quite good condition. We put a few chairs around, Iris made some little cakes and scones and the ladies flocked in. We did great business.'

Iris was beaming at her brother, obviously not at all jealous that he had taken charge. She was so sweet. Utterly loyal and dependable. Laura was amazed by the figures and said so. Her brother clearly had a flair for business.

Dolores had done well, too. 'I think the news of the weddin' brought in lots of customers,' she said drily. 'Some of them asked the nosiest questions.'

'What did you answer?'

'I was really servile, and chatted a lot, but they got nothin' out of me. Not that I know anythin',' she added cheerfully.

The Park Street shop had done even better. Nancy greeted Laura with a kiss. 'Are you well, darling?'

'Fine,' lied Laura. She had another headache, caused as much by lack of sleep as by the blow.

In the factory she was greeted by cries of welcome and some-one sang 'Here comes the bride –'

Laura sniffed joyously at the mingled odours of stiffeners and varnish, of bolts of materials stacked on the shelves, of the steamers emitting soft clouds through the pipes fitted to the sides, the unmistakable smell of felt being steamed beneath a hot iron.

Pansy barely waited to greet her before diving into business. 'Come and see this bolt of cloth, Laura. They're tryin' to sell it as silk velvet but it's cheap stuff. I've not sent the invoice to Miss Prewett.'

'Quite right,' said Laura, fingering the material. 'They must think we're mad. Who are the suppliers?'

Pansy told her. 'The new one we tried.'

'Send this back and strike them from our list.'

Miss Morton was instructing two of the apprentices. 'Cleanliness is essential. Most of our blocks are wooden and very expensive. They can split if they're dropped, but will give us years of service if cared for properly. A light scrub with soap and water and a soft nailbrush, slow drying, *never* in heat. That's the way. Gently does it.'

The apprentices glanced at Laura then quickly away. They were nervous. They made her aware, more than anything else had done, that she was the boss, one of the ranks of the well-to-do who had power over others. She resolved anew never to abuse it.

Noreen had the other apprentices standing with her at a work bench. 'A hat should never weigh more than two or three ounces. Even four ounces isn't desirable. It could give a woman a headache. Remember that some of our hats will be worn for many hours at a stretch. Now watch me carefully as I block this espartie. It's a very light material, but I shall use it as sparingly as possible. This is an important part of your training. It's the foundation of the finished shape and if the foundation is wrong then everything else will be wrong.'

Laura wanted to stay. This was her domain, she loved the colours, the textures, the pressing pads, the blocks that stood with hats in varying stages of completion, the ranks of silk and cotton and mercerised thread. A sad regret came over her at the knowledge that she must now spend much of her life in pursuits that bored her. She had to remind herself that it was for David's sake. And of course she loved Paul.

She had discovered that both Thelma and Daphne coveted his wealth and no doubt they and many others failed to understand what he saw in her. In Paris, in the first flush of joy and trust, she had asked him. He had looked at her, his dark eyes studying her. 'You have the most determined spirit of any woman I've ever known. I look forward to taming it.'

They had both laughed.

Chapter Thirty-One

Tony Driscoll was twenty-seven, tall and thin, his wrists sticking out of his blue serge suit like a growing schoolboy's. His skin, hair, eyelashes and brows were fair, his eyes blue, adding further to his young look, but he was a clever pharmacist and there was nothing immature about his work.

He talked fast and at length about 'one-drop perfume concentrates, benzyl benzoate, vanillin, syn musk solution, amyl salicylate –'

Laura had expected to hear about flowers petals, wafting scents, something delicate and sweet. When she said so Tony was not in the least taken aback.

In fact, he grinned. 'All right, Mrs Harrington, violet, lemon, patchouli, oils of geranium, lavender, rosemary, thyme, clove. You'll be here all night if I try to tell you everything I know about making scent.'

'Perish the thought,' drawled Anita. 'Mrs Harrington has to get back to an important dinner party. She's doing her duty as a new bride.'

Tony looked startled, then again he grinned. 'Sorry, I should have offered my congratulations, Mrs Harrington. I get so enthusiastic over my work.'

'I'm glad you do. Please call me Laura, and just keep talking.'

'Righto, Laura. All the ingredients can be used in soap, too. You and Anita could market a whole range of toilet items. Face creams, hand lotions, nail polish. Do you know, I could even produce the scent of new-mown hay?'

'I think not,' said Anita. 'We might give our customers hay fever.'

Tony laughed in a rather abstracted way. 'Just as you say. What shall I begin on?'

Laura had been considering this for some time. 'If Anita agrees I thought we might produce two perfumes to begin with – and soap to go with them. We should have a sultry, sophisticated scent for Anita and something to suit me –' She paused.

Anita gave a somewhat derisive leer, but Tony looked seriously at Laura. 'Yours will be sophisticated, too, yet light; sweet, but not too sweet, something with a hidden tang –'

Anita interrupted with a shout of laughter. 'He's got you summed up, Laura, me love.'

Laura's flush was no redder than Tony's. 'She enjoys tormenting me,' she said. 'Go ahead, Tony, and produce your ideas. Contact us when you're ready.'

His flush grew deeper. 'I already have them here. Just the essential oils, you understand. They could soon be prepared ready for marketing.'

Laura was surprised. 'How on earth – ? You've never met me.'

'Anita told me a bit about you and I saw –' Tony stopped.

'Yes,' prompted Laura, 'you saw – ?'

'Your photograph in the newspapers several times.'

'I see.' Laura said. 'Let me smell the oils.'

Tony fumbled in his nervousness, but managed to produce a small leather case from his pocket. It contained two glass phials and Laura and Anita held out their wrists for a couple of spots to try.

'Yours is perfect,' pronounced Anita, 'but I'm not sure about mine. It's not quite – um – deep enough.'

Tony nodded. 'I'll make it more sultry.'

'I'm happy with that,' said Anita. 'Are you, Laura?'

'Fine. What about the practical side?'

Tony said eagerly, 'I've set up a laboratory at home. I live with my parents and they've given me quite a large room. Mum is excited about the thought of my designing exclusive toiletries for fashion houses. Dad's not so keen. He would prefer it if I was manufacturing something a bit more masculine, but he'll be delighted when I'm a success.'

'Hitch your waggon to ours and become a star!' cried Anita.

'When this takes off you'll need to leave the pharmacy and give us all your time.'

'Glad to. I can't wait. What name will you market the scents under?'

Laura said, 'I thought of two likely names. Lanita or Laurita.'

'Laurita,' said Anita at once. 'It's got a good foreign sound. Women like to think they're getting something imported.'

The meeting had been held in the Park Street shop. Laura glanced at her watch as she let Anita and Tony out. A quarter to eight. She should go. It would take her a good hour to bathe, make up, have her hair dressed by Hawkins. The longer styles took more time. Laura wore hers waved across her well-shaped skull and curled tightly in the nape of her neck. She was due for another permanent wave and the ends needed to be tamed with a hot curling iron. But still she lingered. David would be asleep by now. Paul would be waiting and he'd be annoyed if she was late. She shivered as she remembered the way he had struck her. It had been quite a heavy blow. Her head still felt tender. But he had been sweet and loving in his remorse. Just one last look round the shop, then she must leave. She gazed at the white, gold and silver bower she had made by her own efforts. One day she would buy it, but already it was hers alone, the product of her own brain and hands. She started as she heard the shop door open, and swung round.

Rick was standing there, leaner, sun-tanned. He grinned, took off his hat and bowed. His curls had been clipped and were, for once, under control.

'You are real,' breathed Laura. 'I thought – I mean, you're supposed to be in America.'

He walked swiftly to her and stopped a couple of feet away, looking at her intently. 'Hello, baby. I came back.'

'That's obvious.'

'Aren't you glad to see me?'

'Of course. You're a friend.'

A friend, that's all he was. Then why was her heart pounding in her ears? Why had her mouth suddenly gone dry? Why did she want so desperately to touch him?

'Haven't you got a kiss for me then?'

547

Laura stepped back. 'Did you have a good time in America?'

Rick's eyes narrowed. 'Wonderful,' he said quietly. 'You must go there some day. Of course, not everything about it is good.' He began to pace up and down and his voice grew louder and more animated. 'Prohibition's given awful power to men who'll stop at nothing to make money. They make and sell booze mostly. Some of it's terrible stuff. It's also produced speakeasies – illegal clubs, where you can drink as much as you like and get good entertainment.'

Rick stopped and grinned at Laura. 'Not boring you, am I?'

She could only shake her head as she tried to sort out her feelings.

'New York is a wonderful, crazy city. It's full of music, Laura. Sometimes I hardly went to bed at all. Louis Armstrong plays there now. I saw him – and heard him. God, what a man – what a player! He was born for jazz. He's got the right lips, an open throat and loose vocal cords, and he's as strong as a horse. And Fats Waller makes a piano dance. I shook his hand. It was like holding a bunch of bananas. How he tickles those ivories the way he does, I'll never know. And the shows. I spent every night at the theatre or cinema. I made good contacts, agents, impresarios, angels –'

'What?'

'That's what they call the people who put up the money for the theatres. They can make fortunes, or go broke. I went to California and watched them making talking pictures. I was right. The silents have gone for ever.

'Then I made a trip to New Orleans. That's the home of jazz – it's where Louis Armstrong came from. I heard Bessie Smith sing the blues, and Ethel Waters. I brought some of their recordings back too. Oh, and I met Bix Beiderbeck. What a guy!'

'A guy?' Laura was mesmerised. It was as if the past three years had been wiped out and she had met Rick Merriman for the first time. She had forgotten how powerful were his vitality, his bounding zeal for living, his devastating sexual vibrations.

'I'll play all my new gramophone records for you, baby. Wait till you hear *Sweethearts on Parade*. It's sheer genius.' Rick's voice stopped and he looked at Laura in a way that made her feel weak-kneed. 'Hark at me going on!' His voice became gentle. 'You've had a tough time, kid.'

Her mind on Paul's sudden descent into cruelty, Laura said, startled, 'How do you know about it?'

'It's no secret. I gather the newspapers were full of it.'

'What are you talking about?'

'Adrian's death, of course. What would I be talking about? Aunty Mabel's letter telling me about it followed me around and caught up with me when I got back to New York.' Rick paused, began to speak again, hesitated, then said, 'Laura, I met a woman out there.'

'Don't tell me,' Laura said harshly, trying to come to terms with the sudden sick feeling inside her.

'I *must* tell you. Please listen, Laura! Please! Just give me a few minutes and you'll understand.'

Laura waited, tight-lipped, angry.

'She travelled with me –'

'And I suppose you slept together.' With a huge effort, Laura had gathered together her emotional forces and managed to sound almost flippant. 'Well, that's Rick, the great lover, for you!'

Rick continued as if she hadn't spoken, watching her intently. 'I wasn't in love with her –'

'Well, of course not!'

'Auntie Mabel's letter was a shocker! In more ways than one. Reading about how you'd been suffering, while I was living it up miles away, brought me to my senses. Laura, I was attracted to the woman because she reminded me of you! I didn't know it until that minute. I realised suddenly what I'd thrown away. All I wanted was to be with you.'

Laura stared at him with dilated eyes as he went on, 'I took the first passage I could back home, got straight off the boat and hired a car and here I am. My poor baby –' He suddenly reached out and pulled her close to him. She should push him away, but she couldn't. He took off her hat and smoothed her hair. 'My poor baby. Those swines of reporters. You must tell me what really happened, but not until after –' His mouth came down hard on hers and he kissed her like a man slaking a long and desperate thirst. Laura melted into him. This was how he had comforted her when she had fled to him. She had borne his son. David! Paul! She was married to Paul.

She pushed Rick away, savagely this time, almost hating him for the way he made her feel. 'Stop it! You left me for months without a word, now you return and expect to find me waiting – What arrogance!'

'You don't mean that, do you? God, I've been such a fool! I love you, Laura. I love you like no woman's been loved before. I just want us to get married and I'll spend my life making you forget all the things that have made you miserable.'

'No. Oh, no.' Laura's voice came out in a moan. 'Rick –' She walked to a chair and sat down heavily. His words had released a flood of sensations. Sensations that she realised she had been inwardly denying. Love for Rick rushed up to overwhelm her; it filled her mind, her heart, her whole body. 'You should have kept in touch, Rick.' Her voice was raised in a wail that startled him. 'I needed you – now it's too late.' Then anger replaced her despair. 'It's all your bloody fault! You and your trips to America. Speakeasies! California! New Orleans! Jazz! You should have been here when I needed you. Now it's too late.'

'What's too late? What in hell are you talking about?'

She shook her head.

'Damn it, Laura, *what's too late*?'

'Stop yelling at me! Everything! You are! Lady Mallender tried to take my son away. She said I wasn't a fit mother. So I married Paul Harrington.'

'What? *The* Paul Harrington? The *rich* society playboy?' Rick's voice was jagged with anger.

'Don't you presume to judge me! It was the only way I could protect David.'

'Do you love him?'

'Who, David?' she asked dazedly.

'No, you stupid bitch, Harrington!' Rick's fury had risen to meet hers.

'Don't dare to call me names! Yes, I love him. Well, I thought I did. I do! He's given me a fine home and he's willing to let me go on working. But the most important thing is he's saved David from going to that ghastly woman, Lady Mallender.'

'How bloody noble! You sacrificed yourself to stop a baby going to live with his grandmother. What's wrong with that?'

'David's my son. I want him with me. And, if you'll cast your mind back, I'm not likely to be in favour of a grandmother bringing up a child.'

'Not all older women are like your Granma. My Aunty Mabel did a hell of a lot for me.'

'Lady Mallender isn't like Aunty Mabel. From what Nancy tells me she emasculated Adrian. How could I let my son suffer the same fate?' Her voice went on echoing through her head. *He's your son, too, Rick. Your son. If you'd only come back sooner. If you hadn't gone away, we could have brought up our child together.* 'Paul's provided a good home for David.'

'Well, ain't that grand of him!'

Rick's face was filled with scorn and she was scorched by the intensity of her fury. She leapt to her feet, her fists clenching and unclenching. She wanted to punch him. She wouldn't, of course. Violence was terrible. Only savages tried to appease their feelings with violence. And Paul.

It was all she could do not to sob in her rage and regret. 'Get out,' she stormed. 'Get out! I should be leaving.' Suddenly horrified, she looked at her watch. A quarter to nine.

'My God, I'll be late. Oh, no, no.'

Rick stared at her. 'Does it matter that much?'

'Out! *Get out!*'

'Some marriage you must have!' said Rick angrily. She pushed him out and locked the shop door and without another look at Rick leapt into her car, a zippy sports model, yet another gift from Paul, and shot off towards the Downs, leaving Rick standing on the edge of the pavement, staring after her.

Paul was seated in the bedroom, looking handsome in evening dress, smoke from his cigarette wreathing about his head.

'You're late,' he said. His voice was almost conversational, but Laura was sensitive to the underlying steel.

'I'm so sorry, darling. I was detained. The scent man –

Tony Driscoll – it took ages to decide.' She raced into her dressing room where Hawkins waited, a mocking smile downing the corners of her mouth, her eyes heavy with disdain. 'Your bath's ready, madam.'

'I've no time –'

'You *must* bathe, madam. A Harrington lady would never go out to dinner without bathing. I've laid out your gown. As you weren't here I asked Mr Paul and he said the russet-gold panne-velvet with the short tiers over your hips. So flattering to madam's thin shape.' Laura scarcely heard her. She soaped herself with desperate concentration, then Hawkins wrapped a large white bath towel around her. Within moments she was in her silk underwear, holding up her arms for the maid to drop her gown over her head. While Hawkins applied the curling-tongs to her hair, she put on a fresh coat of make-up. She was ready at nine-fifteen.

Paul helped her on with the matching coat, trimmed with soft fur. 'Charming, my dear,' he said, in tight, controlled tones that made her shiver. He said nothing on the drive to the dinner party and she remained silent and still.

Their host and hostess were graciousness itself as Paul apologised. 'My wife had urgent business,' he said, laughing affectionately at her.

'Paul, darling, you're so kind to let her work,' trilled a fair girl in white satin who had never done a stroke of work in her pampered life. 'I wish my husband would be as accommodating. I positively *ache* to serve in a *scrumptious* shop like Laura's, but he never lets me out of his sight.'

'Except when I go to my club,' amended her husband, a monocled young man. 'And when she visits her dressmaker, shoemaker, hairdresser, beautician –'

'Do be quiet, Charles,' trilled his wife. 'Nancy Mallender is permitted to work. I don't see why any lady can't do the same.'

Paul led the hostess into dinner and Laura was given the arm of her host. As newly-weds they were guests of honour, a fact which Paul had not mentioned and Laura felt all the more mortified at arriving late for a carefully planned meal. Paul said that unpunctuality was a social solecism of the worst order, yet no one seemed really to mind that they had been a little late. Only Paul, whose eyes she found upon her many times during the course of the evening.

On the way home Laura tried to talk about the party, but Paul didn't answer and she fell silent. He drove fast and steered the car with an iron grip that threw them round bends.

'Please,' she broke the silence. 'Please, Paul, drive a little slower. After a long day and a large dinner I can't take all the swinging about.'

He ignored her completely and she felt splinters of resentment and animosity grinding over her, tearing her nerves to shreds. By the time they reached their bedroom she was dizzy and half sick. 'Please ring for iced water for me,' she said.

'It's two o'clock. I told the servants not to wait up.'

'I see. I'll make do with water from the bathroom.' She filled her toothmug and sipped. The water was almost warm, but it quietened her queasy stomach. She pulled off her clothes and dropped them on to a chair. Let Hawkins see to them. That's what she was paid for. She brushed her teeth and almost fell into bed, utterly weary. Paul came from his dressing room. He wore deep red silk pyjamas. The colour suited him.

'You look handsome,' she said.

He moved to her side of the bed and stood staring down at her.

'Is that what you told Merriman?'

She gasped. 'What?'

'Merriman. Your erstwhile lover who you received in the shop. Your present lover, for all I know.'

'Paul, how can you? You're so wrong. He's been in America since before our marriage. He was – is – a friend.'

'You told me you went to meet Anita and a pharmacist –'

'I did!'

'It made a good excuse for being out late, didn't it? But you soon got rid of them –'

'Our business took a lot less time than I had anticipated.'

'Then you waited for the real assignation. Rick Merriman.'

'No, Paul, no!' Laura tried to sit up and he thrust her back. She lay, fear building up inside. 'I was terribly surprised when

Rick turned up. He said he'd come off the boat, hired a car and driven straight to Bristol.'

'To see you.'

She was handling this wrong. She should have lied. She should have told him that Rick was driving past and happened to see the shop light. Her tongue was paralysed as Paul's eyes took on the same dead look of the previous night.

This time she saw the first blow coming. He punched her chest, her arms, her stomach, her thighs, punched and struck until she cried for mercy. Cried in a voice she kept low for fear of being overheard. The pain was less than the humiliation. She lay motionless and terrified as he took off his clothes.

'No –' she moaned. 'No, not now, please –'

She knew her appeal was useless. He took her body swiftly, unable to maintain his control, clearly exhilarated by his cruelty.

Later he explained calmly that he had sent Hawkins to check on her. The maid had driven quickly back and reported that she had seen Mrs Harrington and Mr Merriman embracing.

Laura said tonelessly, 'He didn't know I was married to you.'

'I warned you,' said Paul. 'I am jealous, very jealous and I expect obedience. As long as I obtain it I shall not find it necessary to chastise you. If you break my rules you know what to expect.' He yawned. 'God, I'm tired.' He turned over and within minutes was asleep. Laura moved as far from him as she could and lay awake, her body aching. David was asleep upstairs. Nanny Allan was near him. Nanny and Paul believed in whipping children. When Laura thought of the future she shivered.

Again Paul had not struck her where the bruises would show. Laura worked next day, forcing herself to be pleasant, showing patience when Pansy erupted with irritation because the eldest apprentice had ruined a piece of wool felt.

'Best quality and the hat half made,' stormed Pansy. 'She had no business touching it.'

'Why did she?'

'She says she saw a bit that she thought needed more steaming. Of course it went limp and the scarlet satin flower that I'd stiffened so that it stood out was ruined. The work's to be done again.'

Laura spoke to the weeping apprentice and calmed Pansy, though she could have joined either of them. She could have wept until she had no more tears. She could have raged until she was exhausted.

She was to have seen Anita, but telephoned her instead. She couldn't hope to fool her. 'What's the matter?' asked Anita. 'Your voice sounds wrong.'

'I'm tired. The dinner party finished late.'

'I see. Tony says he'll soon have the first sample of scents ready for us to judge. Can you see him during the evening?'

'No! That is, I may not be able to. I've lots of engagements.'

'I hope you're serious about the cosmetics, Laura, because if you're not –'

'I am, oh, I am. Truly. Could Tony meet us on Sunday afternoon at your place? I'll have to check with Paul, but I think it'll be all right.'

'Bring him along,' said Anita. 'If he's interested,' she added drily.

That night when Laura returned well in time for dinner Paul was waiting in the bedroom. She had difficulty in not flinching when she saw him.

He hurried to her and enfolded her in his arms, kissing her mouth, her eyes, her forehead.

'Forgive me, my darling, please, forgive me. I get a devil in me. I can't help it. I'm crazy with love for you.' He pulled up her sleeve and pressed his lips to a livid bruise above the elbow.

Laura looked down at his sleek dark head. 'Love should be kind, Paul, never violent.'

'I am violent at times. It's the way I've always been. You must try to understand.' He led her to the deep couch set by the fire and they sank into its softness together.

'Laura, bear with me, I beg of you. Don't go against my will.'

'How can I promise you when I don't know what makes you angry. You assured me you didn't mind my working, then you said you were jealous of my work. And you actually set Hawkins to follow me, a servant. I wasn't born into this kind of life, but I know that to urge a maid to spy upon her mistress is wrong.'

'Hawkins grew up in this family. She's not like an ordinary maid.'

'Maybe not to you, but she is to me.'

He slid his arm about her waist and she winced. 'Darling, did that hurt? Did I strike you there? Oh, Laura, my love, I'm sorry, so sorry.'

He reached into his pocket and pulled out a black velvet case. 'This is a token of my repentance.'

She opened the case to reveal a necklace and earrings of deeply green emeralds set in gold. 'They're beautiful, Paul. Lovely.' She looked at them for a moment, only half seeing them, knowing that each time she wore them they would remind her of the way his fists had beaten her, the way he had taken her body, raped her.

As they were going downstairs to drive out to dinner they heard a commotion in the hall. A woman's voice was raised in anger and to Laura's horror she realised that Freda was there, yelling like a lunatic.

'What the devil?' Paul's frown was black.

'It's my sister,' said Laura briefly and ran down. 'Freda! It's all right, Claypole. This is Miss Freda Blackford. Come into the drawing room, dear.'

Freda wore an old coat that was torn in several places, her stockings were wrinkled and her shoes hadn't had a lick of polish for months. Phyllis had tried to smarten her up, but given up in the face of Freda's hostility. 'Poor little cow,' Phyllis had sighed. 'It's a pity she couldn't have been took with our Joyce. She'll never be happy again.'

'I've walked here,' said Freda. 'I walked very fast. I'm hot.' She was, and she smelled. She had almost given up washing.

Paul appeared in the doorway. To Laura's relief he looked more curious than annoyed. 'What does she want?'

'I came to see if any of the nobs were here. I spend a long time lookin' at the nobs. I'll find him one day.'

'Find who? What does she mean, Laura?'

'I'll find the man who hurt her,' said Freda. She got up. 'You goin' out, our Laura?'

556

Laura was relieved that Freda hadn't gone into one of her storms of anger against her sister who had married one of 'them'. 'Yes, but have a drink first. A long, lemony one, the kind you like. We can give you a lift home. We can, can't we, Paul?'

He looked lazily at his watch. 'We've just time if we leave now.'

'Don't trouble yourself,' grated Freda. 'I'll drink water when I get home and I'd rather walk. I might see *him* somewhere. I'll come back again.'

Paul opened the front door for her and watched as her short thick figure took itself off down the drive. 'What a curious creature,' he said lightly. 'Still, most families have a nutcase, though they usually keep them out of sight. Who does she hope to find?'

'Someone who once upset her,' said Laura, keeping her voice even. 'Poor Freda isn't well.' She resented Paul's half humorous, half contemptuous dismissal of a girl whose hell of grief and loneliness had driven her senses from her.

Chapter Thirty-Two

By the time 1930 gave way to the new year Laura was commanding a great deal of money in her own right. *Hats by Laura* in Park Street and Redfield were hers, or would be when she had finished paying off the loans, but this caused her no difficulty. *The Hat Shop* held on to its distinctive clientele.

Four perfumes had been successfully launched. Tony Driscoll had begun to work full-time for Anita and Laura, and Laurita cosmetics were increasingly popular.

Paul had offered to assist Laura's business financially, but she had refused. The shops and factory were hers alone and had become her refuge, her way of escaping for a while from insoluble problems at home. Paul's behaviour had not improved. She felt as if she was walking on the edge of a deep, black pit, never knowing when she would slide into a welter of blows and abuse. It had become a hideous routine. Violence because of some fancied flirtatious glance at another man, followed by remorse and pleas for forgiveness, always accompanied by an expensive gift.

Through Paul she entered doors which remained closed to any but the élite. Her home was a museum, filled with treasures, beautifully decorated, never a thing out of place, but it was a gilded prison. Sometimes she despaired. What a mess she had made of her life! Two husbands, both cruel in their different ways.

Anita had quickly sensed her unhappiness, though she knew nothing of the beatings. Laura couldn't bring herself to tell anyone about those shaming episodes.

'You make mistakes in choosing your men because you've never had a proper male figure to look up to,' was Anita's diagnosis. 'Your father's a nice guy,' Anita had taken swiftly to the new idioms brought to Britain by American films, 'charming, but so wrapped up in himself I doubt he'd notice the house was on fire unless your mother told him. Then he'd probably expect her to carry him out. You should read Freud. He's got explanations for everything.'

Laura had laughed, but it wasn't funny. At least she had been able to make Phyllis's life a great deal easier. There was no longer a need for her to take in washing, or to mind other people's children. She had actually put on a little weight and some of her former prettiness had returned. She never refused the financial help Laura offered, but she still didn't show particular pleasure. Enid would only accept traditional gifts at Christmas and birthdays. She had no big ambitions and was happy with her two children Glory and Jacko, and her Jack who earned a respectable sum these days.

David grew sturdier and more handsome every day. Laura adored him, but never saw enough of him. Once, she had brought him down to the drawing room without Nanny Allan. While she answered a phone call he had broken a fluted Chinese vase. Laura had paid for this lapse in pain and humiliation. David was too young to be punished – yet. Her fears for the future with Paul grew greater.

She saw Rick fairly often. It was inevitable in Bristol, where his increasing success brought him invitations to many of the houses she and Paul visited. She was careful to treat him with only simple civility, but just the same had received blows from Paul because he said Rick had spent the evening following her with his eyes. It was probably true. Whenever she caught his glance it said more to her than words. She ached with regret. As the days passed her love for him grew and, do what she might, she couldn't damp it down. Prosperity had been good for him. His muscular figure now set off clothes cut in Savile Row, his manners were impeccable, his diction clear without being affected. He was actually regarded by some upper-crust mothers as a good prospective partner for their daughters. He took out many girls, but no one had yet succeeded in leading him to the altar, though Daphne Charlton had tried her best and he still escorted her to various functions. Laura wondered if habit and friendship would eventually lead them into marriage. The idea was unbearable. Her dreams were invaded often by Rick and she awoke, sweating with terror in case she had talked in her sleep.

The morning of the Kingswood Whitsuntide walk dawned bright and clear, an oasis in a dull, wet summer. Laura was taking David to Kingswood to watch the procession, unaccompanied by Nanny Allan. She had fought Paul for this concession and won. He was amused in a condescending, sneering way, but even he couldn't imagine his wife getting up to any mischief at such an innocuous event. At least, Laura prayed that he couldn't. She would know the answer when she returned. It was important to her to have David to herself whenever she could. Nanny Allan figured far too largely in his life to please Laura. She had to admit that he was well cared for. He was healthy, rosy-cheeked and had a sweet nature. After the early down on his head had been rubbed away his hair grew in a mass of black curls. 'I can't think where he gets them from,' was one of Nanny's constant remarks. 'The Mallender hair has never been like it.'

Laura knew only too well the origin of those bounding curls. Sometimes she saw Rick so clearly in their son that she trembled inwardly with the fear that Paul might see it, too. She had even come to be glad that David was brought to the drawing room only at set times. It gave Paul less chance to study him. He made sure that the child's material needs were generously, even lavishly catered for, but held no affection for him.

Laura hated her husband. It was a hatred that had taken root and grown with fiery speed. Sometimes she wondered why he didn't sense it flowing out of her in a molten river as he took his fill of her body. She remained mute beneath his abuse, but her soul was consumed by contempt and loathing.

He still said he loved her. His last gift of reparation had surprised her. After the usual apologies he said, 'See what I've got for you, darling.'

She had handled the bundle of papers curiously. 'Shares, my love,' said Paul with pride. 'Gregory's are hard hit by the depression. Old man Gregory fancied himself a financial wizard in the stock market. He's a fool. He's had to sell shares to private buyers and I've acquired a large block for you. Through my solicitor, of course. Gregory doesn't know that the girl he once fired now holds enough shares to make her voice felt.'

Paul smiled at her, waiting for her praise, his triumph making his eyes gleam maliciously. To be able to gloat over any man who had held power over his wife was a source of great satisfaction to him.

'Thanks,' she managed. 'If Mr Gregory knew it would make him very angry.' She put the shares in the safe in her dressing room, placing them on top of the red, black, navy and bottle-green velvet boxes that held the magnificent jewels which were Paul's attempts at atonement. Then, that evening, she wore a trinket she had extracted from her stock at the shop.

Paul had frowned, then smiled. 'That's a pretty piece. An enamelled butterfly. French, isn't it? I like that turn-of-the-century style.'

She looked at him wonderingly. He could act so tenderly and lovingly; then change in a second to a brute. In the first days of their marriage she had accepted his apologies and tried harder to please him. Now she took each day, each moment as it came, stifling fear of physical pain in the pleasure she got from her work, pushing her sense of degradation to the back of her mind. Lady Mallender visited David and he was taken to Mallender House on occasion, but he was safe from the woman who might create of him a man like his supposed father. That was what mattered. She tried not to look too far into the future.

The iron control she was forced to exercise over her emotions spilled into her business life. She had developed a second skin which enabled her to meet men on their own level and bargain and fight for what she wanted. She was impervious to the kind of veiled insult handed out by the Charlton sisters for their amusement. Thelma was sour these days, though her husband was well-to-do and followed her like a lap dog. She treated him like a slave.

'He asks for it,' was Anita's candid remark. 'He's a sap. He feels guilty because he lost money in the 1929 crash and lets her take out her spleen on him.'

'Do you mean they are poor?'

'Not really, but Thelma wants to be a society leader, in London, as well as Bristol. She can't hope to compete with real wealth like Laura Corrigan's – eight hundred thousand dollars a year' – Anita rolled her eyes – 'or Emerald Cunard. She lost money in the Wall Street crash – it sometimes seems like everyone in the world did – but she's still a society lioness.'

Laura shrugged. 'I've met both of them. Their way of life fascinated me at first – all that underhand fighting, but they soon bored me.'

Anita gave a shout of laughter. 'Laura, you're priceless! What does Paul say when you tell him things like that?'

Laura changed the subject. She tried to keep all thoughts of her husband away when she was out of Harrington House.

For months now, after he had made love to her – that's what he called it, she had another name – he always asked in a soft tone which made her shiver because of its integral menace, 'Is there any sign yet of a child?'

The answer was invariably no, and would continue to be no. When she discovered her husband's true nature, and thanking God that she had avoided pregnancy so far, Laura had secretly visited a clinic during one of their visits to London and been fitted with a new contraceptive cap that was as safe as anything could be. She knew the risk she was taking. If Paul discovered it he would react in the most terrible rage, but the thought of having his child made her feel sick.

She spent more time in London than she liked. 'Doing the Season,' it was called, but there was plenty there to interest and amuse her. Paul didn't expect her to live in London for the few months of the spring parliament, as many others did, but they travelled up quite often, first class in the train, a car always to meet them, and luxury in the hotels.

It was impossible to feel miserable all the time. She enjoyed visits to the pictures, sighing over *Journey's End*, the first film which revealed to the shocked and horrified audience the gruesome truth of the futile suffering and fatalities of 'the Great

War'; to theatres, private parties, balls where more decorous dances were pushing out the Charleston and Black Bottom in popularity.

The long bean-feast of the twenties was passing away, its gaiety stifled by the slump, lost in the shuffling of men on hunger marches, drowned in their shouting pleas for work and the suffering of their women and children. Not that Paul and his like seemed to notice what was happening to millions of their fellow countrymen and women. Laura often felt angry with them.

Once, at a large dinner party, Thelma said, 'Last week Boy and I went slumming in the east end of London. *Too*, too dreary, my dears. It used to be fun to visit the Elephant and Castle, but all we got were dirty looks. It's all the fault of the ghastly Labour government.'

Laura said, 'The Labour government hasn't yet had a fair chance to put things right.'

It was as if a bomb had dropped in the elegant dining room. 'My dear,' shrilled the hostess, 'don't say you are one of the new radical reformers!'

'No, I don't think so, but anyone who cares about the working man must surely vote Labour.'

'I always knew it was a bad day for Britain when women got the vote at only twenty-one. They're mere schoolgirls,' said a bucolic colonel.

'And are men of the same age mere schoolboys?' Laura asked sweetly.

The colonel's face had grown an unhealthy shade of puce, but Laura was prepared to stand up for her beliefs. That night Paul tormented her until she promised to vote Tory. She made the vow, knowing that she'd break it. She'd cut off her hand before she'd vote against the socialists. Women hadn't suffered and died for her to use her vote at a man's dictates.

Leaving the house Laura lifted David into the back seat of her car, a pretty cream and burgundy Swallow, a saloon so that he couldn't fall out. He beamed up at her and her heart lifted with love. She parked in a side street and carried him to the place by the sweet shop where her family always stood for the

Whit walk. They were there, even Dad, in a straw hat and a spotted bow tie. Phyllis grinned at her, displaying the new false teeth Laura had paid for.

'It's like havin' a bloody dinner plate in your mouth,' she'd complained, but she wore them.

Ralph took David and hoisted him high on his shoulder and Nancy looked up at them, yearning in her eyes.

'Come to see the fun then, chick?' said Dad, not listening to the answer.

'Aren't you walkin'?' asked Lillian sarcastically. Since Laura's marriage to one of the richest men in Bristol her attitude towards her sister had reverted to jealous envy. If only she knew! Victor, resplendent in a new check suit, supported his little daughter on his shoulder, his large hand holding her safe. He had removed his hat so that she could clutch his hair and he was apparently unconcerned about the ice cream that was dripping down a cone she waved in her fat little hand. Angela was plump and dimpled, she licked her ice cream, gurgling, her rosy cheeks stretched in a grin. She wore a pink satin dress with flounces and a sun bonnet to match, and a knitted silk jacket. Her feet in white socks and white kid shoes kicked a tattoo on her father's chest in time to the first of the bands. Victor adored her as much as he adored her mother. Nothing was too good for either of them.

Val, now a tall eleven-year-old, had joined the Boys' Brigade with the sole object of learning to play the bugle. He was ruthless in his wish to master a musical instrument and impervious to the jeers of some of his friends, his will as strong as ever. Not once had he answered to any name but Val since the day he'd decided to change. He blew enthusiastically, his cheeks puffing in and out, not even a glint of a smile appearing as his brothers and sisters yelled his name. Priscilla cheekily shrieked, 'Oranges, our Val, sucked lemons.' He marched past, not a note out of place.

Iris was walking and waved. She was with several of the factory girls who all greeted Laura with smiles. Alfred and Harold, who had allowed his new business image to slip for the day, whistled and clicked their tongues at the pretty ones and ducked, grinning and pretending to cringe as Phyllis's hand swept towards their ears. She laughed at them, her adored boys.

Granma and Grampa were in their usual place with Zion Chapel, wearing their uncompromising black, swinging umbrella and walking stick. They looked neither to the right nor to the left.

Laura was taken back to her girlhood, it seemed centuries ago, to the time when she had played truant and sat with Rick in a sun-warmed field and drank wine and kissed. Her throat constricted. If only Rick had loved her then. David reached down from Ralph's shoulders and tugged at her hair to attract her attention and she smiled into his eyes, as dark as his father's. He clapped his hands in time to the music.

Afterwards they all went back to the crowded family house. All the children were passed around, as always, examined, admired, thrown into the air and caught, and fed food too rich for them. When Enid's youngest was suddenly sick in the easy way of small children it was cleared up with a minimum of fuss to a crescendo of laughter. Then the younger ones took the babies to the front room. Thanks to the boys' wages coming into the house and help from Laura and Ralph it was no longer a place of bare boards and broken chairs. There was lino from wall to wall with a good carpet square. A sideboard held a bowl of fruit and a pair of gilt candlesticks. There was a table with a lace cloth in the window and a plant in a pot.

'Come and see what I've bought Phyllis,' said Victor to Laura, pulling her unceremoniously to her feet and following the others. He pointed with pride to a new gramophone where a dance record was already playing *Dancing on the Ceiling*, the beautiful song from *Evergreen* which Laura had seen on the London Stage falling, like everyone, under the spell of Jessie Matthews.

'Hurry and roll that carpet back, boys,' ordered Victor. 'I'm going to give my sister-in-law a whirl.' He grabbed Laura as if she had been a sack of flour and began to sing as they circled the floor, his voice gruff and unmusical, his breath already smelling of the beer produced by Phyllis. *He dances overhead, On the ceiling near my bed.* Victor was brash, loud, pushy and condemned once and for all by Granma as 'common'. He was also kind, thoughtful and loving and Laura liked him. She obliterated the wish that she had been in Rick's arms, while he sang to her.

'I suppose you've got a dozen gramophones in that swanky house of yours,' said Victor.

'Three, I think. The servants have got one in the basement, Paul's is in his study and there's one in the drawing room. I enjoy listening to music.'

'That's money for you!' said Victor.

But she was too matter-of-fact for him to take offence. Not that he would. His good nature seemed endless. 'I bet you have posher stuff than this, though. Classics and opera and ballet. I don't like it meself. Especially opera. All that screechin' in foreign languages.'

'Some of it's lovely,' said Laura, 'but I'll never stop enjoying a good song with a catchy tune.'

Victor beamed approval, then stepped on her toe as Andrew ran across the floor and collided with them.

'Bloody hell,' said Victor, 'Oops, sorry, love. Shouldn't swear in front of a lady, nor the children neither. God they sprout up here like cabbages in a wet summer. I can't think why ma-in-law had to adopt another. That Andrew is a handful and what a temper he's got. One minute he can be as cheery as my Angela, the next, woosh, he's yellin' and tearin' into someone. I like a boy with spirit, but he'd best not go for my Angela or I'll give him what for, Phyllis or no Phyllis.'

Laura said nothing. Evidently no one had told Victor the facts of Andrew's birth.

Freda walked in as they were all having tea, crushed together 'like sardines' said Victor, who enjoyed the noisy family fun. She stared around, her eyes as watchful as a cat's, until they stopped at Laura.

'There you are then. Why d'you let her come here, Mum? She's married *another* of *them*.'

'Now, love,' chided Phyllis gently. A tantrum from Freda was something to be avoided. 'Would you like some tea?'

'No. I'll get my own when I want it.' Perversely she took a slab of cake from Harold's plate and he hastily gave her his fender seat.

'That poor girl should be put away,' muttered Victor to Laura, kindly but unwisely.

Phyllis overheard. 'I'll thank you to keep such opinions to yourself, Victor Sherwood.'

For a moment an unpleasant situation loomed as Lillian bridled and opened her mouth for a retort, then Val arrived, still in his uniform, his bugle tucked beneath his arm and the moment thankfully passed as attention turned to him. He was deluged with teasing and obliged with a good 'blow on the bugle, lad' requested by Dad.

Freda didn't follow her usual custom and slam out of the room. She said, breaking through all conversation, 'Do you ever see the two Goodwin bitches, Laura?'

'The Goodwin girls?'

'You know who I mean. The two who drew men to their house like dogs after bitches in heat –'

'Freda!' expostulated Phyllis weakly.

'Them that brought a man to our Joyce?' said Freda relentlessly.

Lillian glanced at Victor nervously. 'Time we were leavin',' she said, getting to her feet, smoothing down her dress stretched over her ample stomach.

'Not yet, love,' Victor protested.

'Angela's worn out. Can't you see that? And I'm tired too.'

Victor immediately gave in.

'Lillian hasn't told him about Joyce,' said Phyllis to Freda after they'd gone.

'Well, our Laura,' said Freda, ignoring her mother, 'do you ever see them?'

'Not often. They stay in London for the season, that's during the first part of the year, and then they go to the south of France. In the winter they ski. That's what a lot of society people do.'

'Have you found out yet what men were in their house when Joyce worked there?'

'Of course not. How can I ask them something like that? What reason could I give?'

'I'd have found out – somehow. Did your husband ever go there?'

Laura was startled. 'I don't know.'

'Well, you could start by asking him. Perhaps he could tell you a few names.'

Laura stared at her sister. Freda's eyes burned into hers with the fire of fanaticism. If it took the rest of her life she meant to discover the man who had betrayed Joyce.

In the following morning's paper there was an announcement of Ethel Goodwin's engagement to the younger son of an earl. In the post was an invitation to a celebration party for the following week.

'She's been angling for him for months,' said Paul, sardonically. 'The Goodwins love titles.'

'Have you known Ethel and her sister long?' asked Laura, casually.

'Since they were children.'

'Were you ever one of their admirers?' Laura carefully concentrated on spreading a piece of toast with marmalade.

'For a while. It became a kind of fashion to woo the Goodwin girls. Their mother kept a lavish table, but it was their father's wine cellar that drew me.' He looked at his watch. 'I'll have to be off. I'm due at the golf club in half an hour. I'll see you at seven. Don't forget we're dining with Aunt and Uncle Charlton.'

Laura hated to cut short her working day for a boring dinner with relatives. She had hoped to keep an appointment with a young woman who had offered to demonstrate her make-up skills with a view to private sessions with customers, but she knew she would have to be present at the Charlton dinner table. Anita would handle the business, along with some derisory remarks about Laura's 'subjugation to a man'.

Ethel Goodwin was looking very pretty in a Jeanne Lanvin gown of silk lamé. She greeted her guests, waving her left hand about to show off a very large diamond solitaire engagement ring. Her sister, Irene, equally resplendent in scarlet was endeavouring to appear unconcerned at her sister's good catch.

'Irene's got her eye on a French viscount,' said Paul in Laura's ear. 'She'll probably get him and she and Ethel will spend the rest of their lives in rivalry.'

Laura smiled with the reserve she now showed habitually towards Paul. He had been in a good mood for over two weeks. Sometimes he had such stretches. In the beginning they had lulled Laura into believing that he had reformed but, sooner or later, he lost control and threw her back into despair.

Both Goodwin girls, along with all the other young women, stared at Laura in not-quite-concealed hostility. She wore a floor-length black silk gown with a low neckline and tiny cape sleeves. It moulded itself to her slender figure and made her look even taller than she was. Paul's gift of a diamond necklace and earrings, worn at his express wish, were gleams of colour as they flashed and sparkled. Her hair brushed into chestnut-brown satin was coiled simply in her neck; her large hazel eyes, lustrous beneath long lashes, surveyed the room with an unconscious touch of hauteur, induced by her ever-present need to keep her marital fiasco hidden from the world. Her face held more than beauty. She made other women, those with true classical beauty, wealthier, higher born, more expensively gowned, feel dissatisfied with their appearance, yet she was so good-humoured, pandering so sweetly to their whims and fancies in her now acclaimed fashion shops that they couldn't quarrel with her.

'Play something jazzy, Rick,' begged Irene. Laura was glad and sorry that he was here. His presence at a party made her ache with regretful longings; his absence diminished any lingering pleasure she obtained from going out and about with Paul. She heard the strains of the piano as Rick's expert fingers caressed the keys.

'You're a wizard,' called Ethel to him. 'Isn't he a wizard, everyone?'

Rick just grinned and shrugged as he played.

'He's every bit as good as any of the Yankee jazz players,' said the young, newly captured fiancé.

569

'Don't burble rubbish, fathead,' declared Ethel.

'Don't rubbish me, you young blister,' returned her fiancé equably.

'My God, the latest slang!' muttered Paul.

He and Laura seated themselves on a couch near a velvet-draped window. 'I haven't been here for ages. The place doesn't change much. The Goodwin seniors lead pretty stagnant lives. However, their daughters make up for that.'

Laura, her heart beating fast, asked 'Has there always been competition for their favours?'

'Yes, a good deal.'

'Including yours.'

'Including mine,' he agreed, 'but there's no need for you to be jealous, darling.'

Laura marvelled at the way his voice could sound softly teasing. To outsiders he must seem the perfect husband, usually close to her side, displaying open affection.

She said coolly, 'What happened before you met me is none of my business.'

Paul gave her a sharp look, then he leaned back and looked across the room to where Rick was still playing the piano. Rick began to sing and several of the girls joined in.

Paul's lip curled. 'Look at them, drooling over a man who climbed out of the gutter. Oh, but I forgot, you like him, don't you, darling? He's your sort.'

He lit a cigar and leaned back, taking a long drag and easing out the smoke in a series of rings. Laura waited, motionless with dread. She could sense his bitter jealousy.

Paul spoke with an air of amused condescension which failed to mask the latent menace. 'I soon dropped out of the running for the Goodwin girls. I found easier and more – luscious game.'

'Where? Here?' Laura managed to make her voice as humorously sardonic as his, though her heart was racing.

'Yes, here. They had an old witch of a grandmother. Locked her upstairs. She was as batty as hell. There was a nurse.'

'A nurse. Pretty, was she?'

'God, no, as ugly as sin. But there was a girl who came up

from the kitchen. She ran errands. The grandmother took a fancy to her and made a pet of her. The old hag sent her running round the house with messages. The Goodwins didn't mind. They'd have done anything to keep grandmother quiet. The girl was the prettiest thing I'd ever seen and pliable. Oh, yes, very pliable.' His voice softened, his smile grew warm.

Laura waited again, her nerves jumping. She felt like screaming, tearing at his throat to force words out. Yet a part of her wanted to stop the conversation for ever, wanted to run away and not hear what she dreaded was coming.

'I gave her a few presents. Beads and things, nothing of value, and told her to keep our friendship a secret. I said if the grown-ups found out they'd stop our meetings.'

'Grown-ups –' Laura actually managed to infuse a hint of laughter.

'She was a simple girl – in the ancient sense – beautiful, but witless.'

'I see.' She mustn't appear too eager. If Paul got the slightest hint that she was more than casually curious he would clam up. He found it amusing to irritate her. She took her cigarette case from her bag, noticing with amazement that her hand wasn't shaking. She felt as if she were turned to ice, remote, as if she were a spectator watching herself in a play.

Paul held a light for her and she inhaled, breathing out smoke before she said casually. 'Meetings?'

'She used to slip out of the house at night and I'd wait for her in the garden. There's a rose arbour there. I dare say some of the guests will end up in it tonight. It's beautifully secluded and sheltered.'

'Laura!' Ethel cried, 'you used to sing with Rick in public. Come and sing now.'

Laura was consumed with frustration. She felt Paul's cold anger rising in him as Rick waited for her. What did he expect her to do? If she refused to oblige her hostess she would appear ungracious, yet her acceptance would stoke his hot jealousy.

He gestured benignly towards the piano. 'Hurry, darling. You can't disappoint our newly engaged hostess.'

Laura walked to the piano, her head up, drawing admiring

glances even from girls who envied her deeply. She had everything. Striking looks, money, an adoring husband, a son, a lucrative profession and freedom to pursue it.

Rick glanced up at her and nodded and Laura prayed that Paul hadn't seen the yearning in his eyes. He began to play a medley of tunes drawn from their particular favourites, letting them trickle through his fingers like beads on a rosary. Laura leaned on the piano for support. Rick wasn't trying to torment her. He wasn't that sort. He was lost for a moment in his own dreams. He strayed into the opening chords of *My Heart Stood Still*. 'D'you know this one, Laura?'

Every eye in the room was on them and she nodded, thinking ahead to the words, knowing that every syllable would add to Paul's fury. She couldn't deny knowing the song. Paul had bought her the record after they had enjoyed *One Damn Thing After Another*: the show it came from. Rick was watching her as he swung into the tune, keeping the tempo slow: *I took one look at you, That's all I meant to do, But then my heart stood still.*

'Join in, Laura,' clamoured the guests and she blended her voice to Rick's. She was transported into the past, to the days when they had played and sung together in the cinema, the days when she had fallen deeper and deeper in love with him and looked forward to their happy future. Unconsciously her ache of longing and regret metamorphosed into melody, investing her voice with a hint of tragedy and loss, and even whispers tailed off as people leaned forward to catch the heartbreaking sound. Rick became suddenly aware of the atmosphere. He began to jazz up the song and Laura followed him as if they had rehearsed. They finished to a storm of applause and Rick played *I can't give you anything but love, baby*, sinking his voice to the gravelly tones of Louis Armstrong, removing sentiment while Laura strolled back to Paul.

His eyes met hers and her stomach churned. She made a tremendous effort and said lightly, 'I read somewhere that the song was based on a girl who said "my heart stood still" when she almost had an accident in a taxi.'

'Is that so? Such a triviality to produce so sentimental a piece.'

Laura's voice cracked as she laughed. She accepted a cocktail offered by a maid carrying a tray and sipped. 'God, what's this ghastly stuff? It tastes like turpentine.'

She had to get back to the conversation that Ethel had interrupted. If she worded her question in the right way Paul would respond. 'You were telling me an amusing story, darling.'

'I was?'

'Yes, the reason why you discarded the Goodwin sisters.'

'Ah, yes.' He was pleased. She had flattered his vanity by using the word discarded about two pretty girls.

She took another sip of her cocktail and grimaced. 'I think I'll hide this behind something,' she said, desperately trying to sound casual. 'What was her name?'

'Whose name?'

'The girl who took your attention from Ethel and Irene Goodwin.'

Paul looked vague and slightly annoyed. 'Oh, I can't recall much about her now. It was insignificant, though amusing at the time. She'd never had a man before me. We enjoyed a short but sizzling little affair until one day she just didn't come back to work. Just as well. I was beginning to tire of her.'

'I thought your memory was unfailing. You once said you never forgot the names of women you admired.'

He was stung by her critical amusement. 'She was a maid, a nobody – why should I remember – wait a tick, I do recall something – Jane? – no – Jenny? – it was definitely something beginning with a J. I've got it! Joyce! That was it. You see, darling, My memory is infallible.'

'Congratulations!' she managed.

'Yes, I remember. She was a delicious little armful with a lovely face and body.'

Laura had learned to hate him. Now a new seed took root in her. She despised him. She had wondered what kind of man could take advantage of a girl who was still a child in mind. Now she knew and the knowledge was agony.

Everything became unreal. She couldn't be sitting here, listening to inane chatter about how the Woolworth heiress, Barbara Hutton, had been presented at court. That the Duke of

Connaught had had an operation on his nose. Not when the man responsible for Joyce's pregnancy and indirectly for her death was sitting beside her. Her husband. She was married to her sister's betrayer.

At home, she bathed and pulled on her nightgown, shivering at the idea of sleeping beside Paul.

He was waiting for her in the bedroom. 'You and Rick Merriman looked at each other like a hungry dog and bitch,' he said almost pleasantly.

She said nothing, just stared at him steadily, making no effort to hide her hatred and contempt.

'Don't look at me like that! You think that by defying me you'll escape your just punishment for your exhibition with that man. You won't.'

Laura made no reply. He advanced on her and she took his blows, pain half obliterated by the revulsion that had sent her into an almost trance-like state. She walked to her dressing room and lay down on her daybed, ignoring his command that she should lie with him, just looking up at him, her eyes enormous in her white face. For once he left her in peace. Perhaps he was tired.

She lay awake for most of the night. She could no longer stay with Paul. Ever since she'd realised he was a vicious bully, a wife-beater, she had known that one day she must leave him, or lose her self-respect. Always the thought of David had held her. There would be more scandal. And there was Lady Mallender to think about. She seldom went into society these days, but if she was ever in the same room with Laura her malevolent eyes followed her, and Laura knew that she would strike at the first sign of weakness and try to get custody of David.

The fact that Laura had created her terrible dilemma for herself was an even greater cross to bear. Whichever way she turned it seemed that David was the one who would eventually be hurt.

Her torment didn't abate through the following day as she visited the shops and factory. She talked, advised, praised, sometimes admonished, putting up a fine act. She had no engagement for that night. Paul was going out to dinner with some friends from his university days. Some kind of reunion. He wished her a pleasant evening in his most honeyed tones, kissing the cold cheek she turned to him.

She visited the nursery where Nanny Allan was stitching the hem of a coat for David and the nursery maid was ironing. They looked at her as if she were an intruder. She leaned over David's cot and watched him as he slept, wishing that she shared more of his life. Even when she cut short her hours at work Paul made it difficult for her to give time to her son. His jealousy intervened in every aspect of her life.

Downstairs she turned the pages of Pansy's drawing book containing sketched ideas for next season's hats. It was impossible to concentrate. Joyce's face blotted out everything. She couldn't rid herself of the picture of Paul seducing simple, trusting Joyce who had died a cruel death in childbed.

She wandered restlessly from room to room, touching the beautiful ornaments, smoothing her hands down the silk brocades and velvet of curtains, the shining furniture. At ten o'clock she could stand it no longer. She had to talk to someone. Not Rick. Not this time. This was a family matter.

She drove to Kingswood, her agony of mind now so intense that she *must* share it. The only one she could think of, the only one she wanted, was her mother. It was as if the years between had been wiped out and she was a small girl again running to Phyllis with a raw wound.

Thank God the little ones were in bed and the others out. William looked up in surprise. 'Hello, chick. Not at one of your parties tonight?'

Phyllis was knitting a baby's shawl and listening to a programme of dance music on the wireless that was Victor's latest gift. She glanced up, saw Laura's face and put down her work. 'I've got to put our Enid's sheets in to soak. Enid's not very well,' she said to Laura, jerking her head towards the scullery. 'Ate somethin' that disagreed with her.'

Phyllis carefully closed the scullery door and she and Laura faced one another in the stone-flagged comfortless room.

'What's happened, Laura?'

Now she was here, face to face with her mother, Laura was suddenly bereft of words. She stared, her mouth working.

'For God's sake,' said Phyllis. She dragged a wooden stool from the wall. 'Here, sit down.'

Laura sat down heavily, 'Mum –'

'No, wait.' Phyllis went back into the kitchen. 'William, could you walk along to the pub and get some cigarettes. I thought I had some, but I can't seem to find them.' There was the clink of coins. 'Have a pint or two while you're there.'

William's lazy protest was stilled by this largesse offered during the week.

As soon as he had left Phyllis led the way back to the kitchen. Laura was shaking and her mother poked the fire. The embers shifted, ash drifted up, and a waft of warmth enveloped them. Phyllis had begun by sounding impatient, but her voice softened. 'What's happened? You look awful.'

'Are you sure everyone's out?'

'Except the kids. They're in bed. Oh, and Freda. She's asleep upstairs. She was out all night again. She looked terrible this mornin'. She was covered in mud and her hair – you'd have thought she was a tramp.'

'You're sure she's asleep.'

'When I took her up a cup of hot milk she'd already dropped off, but I'll go and check.'

She returned quickly. 'She's well away. The draught took the door out of my hand and it banged, but she didn't move. Now what's happened?'

'Mum – Paul and I went out last evening. Oh, God, this is terrible.' Laura's voice broke. 'We were at Ethel Goodwin's engagement party.'

Phyllis looked at her intently. 'Yes?'

'Paul started talking about – about a maid who once worked there. Mum, he was talking of our Joyce.'

'Tell me about it,' Phyllis kept her voice even.

'Mum, he said he never bothered much about the Goodwin girls because there was someone prettier there. A girl who waited on the old grandmother. Our Joyce. It was him. He's the one who made her pregnant. He used to take her to the rose arbour in the garden. He made a joke about it. He thinks it was funny.'

Phyllis was very white, her eyes starting. 'The bastard! The dirty, filthy bastard! Does he know she was your sister?'

'No, I suppose he doesn't. Mum, I'm married to him!' Laura's voice rose in her anguish. Phyllis's face was close to hers and Laura saw horror spread over it. Her mother's arm went round her. 'You poor little sod.'

For a moment Laura felt a deep relief as her burden was shared, then Phyllis stood up, suddenly remote. 'There's nothin' we can do about it,' she said coldly. 'Why did you have to tell me?'

'What?'

'Like you said, you're married to him. And now I'll have to meet him, knowin' what he's done and never be able to talk about it to him. He'll go unpunished. It's worse than before. Much worse. Oh, my God. Laura, why did you come here?'

Laura's sense of rejection was more bitter than ever before. 'I'm sorry.'

'You're sorry! What good's that?' Phyllis began to weep, holding her apron to her eyes and rocking back and forth on the balls of her feet, wailing, weeping, railing at fate, at the wickedness of it all, at Laura.

Laura turned and left the house, climbed into her car and drove. She didn't want to return to Harrington House. She never wanted to set foot in it again, but she couldn't abandon David. There was no one to turn to, nowhere to go, but back to Paul's house.

She slumped in a chair in the bedroom, her face in her hands. She had dismissed Hawkins, who flounced out, and given orders that she was not to be disturbed again that night. How could she continue to live with Paul? Was it possible to divorce a man for cruelty? The idea of standing in a court room speaking of her humiliation was sickening. And there was David. How could she inflict any more bad publicity on him? Once she thought she heard a sound outside in the corridor, and she tensed, wondering if she had lost herself in a doze and not heard Paul's return. When he didn't come in she slumped back.

She drifted into an exhausted doze. The next thing she knew there were the sound of a slammed car door, voices of the chauffeur and Paul, followed by unsteady footsteps climbing the stairs. The door opened and the light was switched on, flooding the room with brilliance, illuminating her.

Paul was drunk. She had never seen him the worse for drink before. Men seemed to regard reunions as a reason for swilling their senses away. He pulled himself up when he saw her, weaved his way across the carpet and offered her a clumsy bow.

'Goo' evenin', my dear. Waitin' up for me like a duti – dutiful wife. Come to bed, my darlin'. I'm even better when I'm drunk.'

She drew back from him, her eyes flashing hate. He laughed. 'You've got sp – spirit. That's what I love. A girl with spirit.' He reached out and jerked her to him. His wiry strength seemed unaffected by the drink. He dragged her to the bed and threw her back on it, unbuttoning his evening trousers. She squirmed away and he fell on her, pulling up her skirts.

'No, you won't, you swine,' she gasped. 'You horrible filthy swine!'

Paul's weight pinned her down. He hiccuped. 'Now is tha' a nice way to talk to your lovin' husband? You weren't like that when we married. You enjoyed me, didn't you?' His hand moved up her leg and he caressed her. 'See, you want me. My sweet little passion-flower who stays still when she wants to wriggle.'

Laura made a tremendous effort and twisted beneath him, forcing his hand away. 'Get off me.'

'No! I w – want you and I'm goin' to h – have you.' He knelt over her, one hand pressing down on her breasts. With the other he ripped her nightdress to the waist, then dropped his head and took a nipple in his mouth.

'Lie still, you bitch,' he mumbled. 'Lie still. You know you love it.'

'Not this time, Paul!' She grasped his hand and bit deep, drawing blood.

'Bloody hell! Is tha' how you want to play it tonight? Well, it makes a change.' His hands were on her again, in a moment he would have forced himself between her legs.

'Joyce was my sister,' she shrieked.

'What?' He stopped moving, poised above her. 'Who the hell's Joyce?'

'The girl you seduced at the Goodwins'. She was my sister.'

'Well, I'll be damned!' An amused smile spread over his face. 'I'd almost forgotten your plebian roots. Whatever happened to Joyce?'

'She – she died.'

'Pity. But that's p – past history. Just now we're goin' to make love.'

'No!' Laura tried to avoid his fist, but it crashed down on her shoulder, half paralysing her arm. He struck her again between her breasts. She cried out in pain and anger and drove her clenched fist into his face. It landed painfully on his nose.

His grip loosened and she dragged herself free and ran towards her dressing room. He followed her, caught her and spun her round and for the first time aimed a blow at her head. She jerked to one side and the blow landed behind her ear, she staggered and fell against the door jamb, striking her head again and sliding to the floor where she lay half stunned and helpless. He bent to her, his face a mask of fury, and yanked her up. Then, unexpectedly, he dropped her with a curse. Everything seemed to Laura to be moving slowly. Freda was there, her face contorted almost out of recognition, her hair hanging down, unkempt, shaggy, like a beast.

Chapter Thirty-Three

Paul stared at her in disbelief. 'Good God! How did you get in? Godammit, you kicked me.' He moved to the servants' bell.

Before he reached it Freda sprang at him. Laura, unable to move, watched in horror as she produced Phyllis's long, sharp bread knife from beneath her tattered coat. Clutched in her hand it rose and fell, rose and fell, each time finding a target. If he hadn't been drunk Paul might have saved himself, but even his sharp wits were blurred. On its first descent the knife sliced through his hands as he tried to protect himself, then it plunged into him.

'This is for Joyce! This is for Joyce!' screeched Freda over and over, through teeth bared like an animal's. 'You got to know why you're dyin', Paul Harrington. This is your just punishment for killin' my Joyce. She died havin' your brat.'

Paul let out a series of strangled screams, after that he only gurgled.

'Joyce! My Joyce!' Tears began to rain down Freda's face which was distorted by grief and fury. 'Joyce! Joyce! Joyce!' The knife slashed into Paul's body long after he had stopped moving and moaning and Freda's shrieks grew louder. The door burst open and servants rushed in. Freda didn't even try to resist them. She stood still, her head hanging, breathing hard as the petrified servants stared. Hawkins bent over Laura, looking genuinely horrified at her condition. Laura knew it must look as if she, too, was injured. She tried to explain that it was Paul's blood that was sprayed over her, but her tongue wouldn't obey her.

She was lifted and carried out of the red-stained room, away from the smell of violence and hot blood, and into a bathroom where Hawkins cleaned her while a housemaid supported her. The maid exclaimed over the bruises. Hawkins was silent.

'Concussion,' the doctor said as Laura lay in bed in a guest room. 'Keep her quiet. I'll see her tomorrow. What a dreadful thing! She's badly shocked.' He gave her something to drink, something that sent her floating out into the darkness where nothing could reach her.

Laura was in bed for two days during which she was permitted only two visitors.

Nancy was her first. Freda had been taken into custody and charged with Paul's murder, she told her.

'Why did she do it, Laura? She just stays mute.'

Laura put up a hand to her aching head and Nancy was contrite. 'There will be time enough for questions. Ralph says to tell you your mother will be here tonight.'

When she arrived Phyllis stared down intensely at her daughter. Her voice was low and bitter. 'Will there never be an end to the trouble you bring us?'

'What about me? I'm suffering, too,' gasped Laura.

'Why shouldn't you?'

Laura fought back tears. 'What made Freda turn up here? She must have overheard. But you said she was asleep.'

'She must have been pretending and came here and waited for Paul. My God!' Phyllis's voice rose. 'Couldn't you have stopped her? It's hellish. There are newspaper reporters everywhere.' She twisted her hands, her face was drawn and white and there were black shadows beneath her eyes.

Laura pitied her. 'I'm sorry, Mum. I couldn't do anything. I was practically unconscious.'

'Yes, they say you were injured, too. Did she attack you before she killed Paul? She hated you for marryin' him. Oh, my God, if only you hadn't!'

Laura was shrivelled inside with hurt. 'Freda didn't touch me. It was Paul, Mum. He was like that. He was cruel to me right from the start. I wish now I'd had the courage to break away. Mum,' she cried in anguish, 'Freda looked like a mad woman.'

'Don't say that!' Phyllis groaned. 'I can't bear it.'

'But don't you see, no one will punish her if they declare her mad. If we tell them about Joyce and how Freda worshipped her –'

'No! Never! Freda won't say a word. She'll die first. She'll never betray Joyce and you mustn't either. If you do her sufferin' will all be for nothin'. She wanted to avenge Joyce and she's done it. Leave it there.'

Laura half sat up. 'But you *can't* stay quiet. Mum, they'll *hang* her. They'll hang our Freda!'

Phyllis looked at her daughter, her eyes steely. 'You said Paul's been hittin' you almost from the first. Didn't you ever try to defend yourself?'

'Yes, but he only got more violent.'

'So you put up with it.' Phyllis said scornfully. 'You could have left him. Some poor bitches have to stay with violent men because they've got no money, but you've got plenty of your own.'

'I put up with it because of David. There was always Lady Mallender lurking around like a bloody wolf, waiting to steal him from me. But I wasn't going to put up with it any more. Not after I heard about Joyce.'

'Bit late, wasn't it? Well, we must stick together and tell the same story,' said Phyllis. 'Between us we might be able to help Freda.'

'How?'

'We can say she overheard you tellin' me about the way Paul beat you and she came here to defend you. Everyone knows that Joyce's death unhinged her mind. They'll believe us when we tell them she came to your rescue.'

Laura sank back. Pictures played across her mind. Herself in a courtroom, standing in a witness box, relating Paul's vicious treatment of her for all to hear, talking of the hidden bruises, perhaps having to relate details of his love-making. Lawyers spared no one.

'I can't, I can't,' she said. 'There must be some other way.'

'There's no other way,' hissed Phyllis. 'It's up to us.'

The nurse engaged by the doctor bustled in. 'Mrs Blackford, my patient is flushed. What have you been saying to her?'

'Nothin',' said Phyllis. She looked resentfully at the white starched figure. Then she marched out and Laura sank back, her heart aching as if she were a child again, longing for her mother's love.

Paul's funeral was attended by as many people as could cram themselves into the church, and those members of the inquisitive public who couldn't stayed outside, trampling over graves, destroying flowers and shrubs. There were many distant relatives who returned to the house afterwards and Laura dispensed sherry, coffee and sandwiches. Without exception they regarded her with suspicion and dislike.

She overheard remarks.

'She has a very low-class background.'

'She'll have his money, it's not fair.'

'I shouldn't wonder if she's glad her sister . . .'

Finally most of them left and Paul's will was read. There were bequests, some small, some generous. Laura inherited what remained. She returned to work, somehow functioning, while a never-ending film was screened against her eyelids, of Freda, her eyes crazy, her face contorted, attacking Paul. His blood-soaked body was forever falling, the sound of his choking was a ghastly dirge in her ears. And when she slept the horrible sights and sounds invaded her dreams.

The newspapers were restrained, as they must be before the case was brought to court. Laura had fatalistically accepted that she would have to help Freda in the only way she could and talked to the defending counsel – she could afford the best for Freda – and told them the story demanded by Phyllis.

The lawyer was solemn. 'Your sister does not seem to care if she lives or dies, Mrs Harrington. In fact, I think sometimes she would prefer to die. But we must save her. It is our duty. One day she will thank us.'

Laura doubted that.

'She hardly ever speaks. She says she is guilty and does not wish us to defend her. We must do so, of course. The plea will be "Not guilty by reason of insanity".'

'Insanity! Does that mean they won't hang her?' asked Laura.

The lawyer pursed his lips. 'Talk of hanging is defeatist, Mrs Harrington. Of course there can be no doubt that she committed the crime, but we must hope that our plea is accepted.'

'What will happen then?'

'She will be committed to an asylum.'

'Oh, my God. She'd be better off dead.'

'That's not the way to think, Mrs Harrington.'

'You don't know Freda. She's been like a wild animal since her twin died.'

'So I understand.'

'You can't shut her up in an asylum. You just can't.'

'Not I,' said the lawyer, smiling in a determinedly sympathetic manner, though to Laura he looked like a shark. 'The court will decide.'

The weeks passed and Laura went daily to her work, performing her tasks, immersing herself in customers' wants and fancies, bolts of cloth, trimmings, as if they were the most important things in the world, and all the while the thought of Freda, locked in a cell, tormented her.

Rick came to the shop in Park Street one night after closing. He brought Nancy with him. 'A chaperone,' he said briefly. 'The newspaper guys are watching.'

Nancy waited downstairs while Rick and Laura went up to the flat. He held out his arms and she went into them. His heart beat hard as he held her close. 'I had to see you, my love,' he said. 'I had to tell you you're not alone. I love you. Never forget that. One day, when all this is over –'

'When it's all over? Rick, I can't bear the thought of what Freda must be suffering. And if they say she's mad, they'll lock her away –'

He smoothed her hair and kissed her forehead with gentle lips. 'I know, darling, but from all accounts her mind really has gone. She just obeys every order she's given and doesn't show any emotion at all.'

'Oh, God, it's horrible. I keep thinking it's my fault. If I hadn't run home to Mum . . . Rick, I'm dead inside. I've nothing to give any more.'

'Just remember I'm yours and always will be.'

'I'll remember.' But she watched him go without emotion and wondered if she could ever feel love for a man again.

Laura drove herself home. Home was still Harrington House. It was even more museum-like, the only life seeming to exist in David's nursery. Nanny Allan was still in charge. She was kind to David and he liked her, but her eyes were filled with deep resentment when she looked at his mother. One day, when this nightmare was over, Laura would find another nurse.

She was consumed with guilt. It had many faces. If she hadn't involved Phyllis – if she'd shown enough courage to refuse to submit to Paul's violence – if she'd left him – if – if. And the most terrible thing of all was her relief that Paul was dead and she no longer had to face being beaten and hurt.

Anita accepted what had happened with her usual practicality. 'Poor old Freda's done you a favour.'

'Anita!' Laura was shocked, but Anita's cold reasoning helped. She could even take some interest in her fashion talk.

'Madam Vionnet is the thing this autumn, especially for evening wear. She's using material cut on the bias and stitched so that not a wrinkle or gather appears anywhere. At least, they don't in the slim women. As usual, there will be the overweights who insist on the latest gown and will look hideous, but that's nothing new.'

'Anita, you're so unkind.'

'Unkind be damned! I offer them gowns that suit them, cut to the proper size, but they turn up their noses. Pah!' she said, in a French fashion no doubt learned from her mother, 'they think we can fulfil their dreams, when all we can do is to cover their grisly bodies.'

'The gowns are gorgeous,' said Laura. But her animation had deserted her and her voice held such sadness that even Anita was moved to pity.

'Don't be unhappy, Laura, *ma petite*.'

'It's Freda –'

'I know, but anyone can tell she's been batty for months. They'll let her off.'

'The lawyer says if they do she'll have to be shut up probably for life.'

'Lawyers! Forget them and try to see Freda as she is. She's living in a world of her own. Nothing anyone does will touch her. Now tell me if your hats will be ready to show with my clothes. Life must go on, you know.'

'They'll be ready, though there are a limited number of ways to decorate an upturned bucket.'

'Laura! Sacrilege!'

The show took place as usual and was crowded. Late comers had to be turned away. Laura gave the commentary, dressed in black, her head high, her voice not showing by a single quaver that tragedy and violence were taking a terrible toll on her. Afterwards orders poured in and voices were raised complimenting her on her designs and also on her courage.

'My dear, such a dreadful calamity,' said a woman whom Laura hardly knew.

Bloody cheek! Laura wanted to shout. Keep your bloody opinions to yourself! But she accepted everything that came and parried the barbed words with a smile, a brief nod, a quick turn of the head, a deprecating wave of the hand.

Afterwards Ralph and Nancy took her out to dinner in a quiet place with private booths.

'Ralph and I are engaged,' said Nancy.

'Oh, I'm so happy for you. But what about your family? Your mother already loathes me and when the trial takes place it's going to be dreadful.'

'I know. Mummy is absolutely livid with me and says she'll never acknowledge me again if I marry Ralph. I hope she doesn't mean that, but it isn't going to stop me. Daddy was surprised, but he gave us his blessing. Poor darling. He's had all the stuffing knocked out of him.'

Laura had kept up a good face, but that night when she was alone in her bedroom – a new one, the other had been closed up – she wept. She hadn't shed tears for so long, not for herself, but now they rained down her face. Alone she wept over the trap she was in, the deceit that had begun so innocently, when she was a seventeen-year-old creeping out to meet a boy. She could see no way out of the maze and it involved everyone she knew, everyone she loved.

The trial opened. The public gallery was full, every prominent newspaper in the country was represented. Evidence was given as to how the murder had been discovered. It was established that Freda had crept into the house through an open window and that she had carried a knife brought from her mother's kitchen.

The housemaid testified to bruises on her mistress's body. Hawkins gave similar evidence. The doctor confirmed that Mrs Harrington had suffered concussion, but no knife injuries.

Phyllis's bread knife was produced, an identifying tag hanging from it, and the police doctor described the number and nature of wounds found on the deceased's body. It made sickening hearing and there were gasps of part-horror, part-relish from the gallery.

It was Laura's turn on the witness stand.

'Mrs Harrington, please describe to the court exactly what you saw –'

Laura stumbled over her words as she relived Freda's terrible attack.

'Please tell the court what you confided to your mother on the evening before the murder.'

There was a swift rustle, then silence and everyone listened intently as Laura was drawn to reveal the catalogue of Paul's brutality, his attempt at forced love-making on the night of the murder, his blows, the struggle. 'How many times has your husband beaten you?' 'For what reasons?' 'What injuries did he inflict?' 'Why did you tell no one before?' On and on went the questions and Laura heard her voice setting out the humiliating background to her marriage.

She thought she had suffered until the prosecuting counsel took over. Then the torment reached new depths. 'Were you never happy with your husband?' 'Surely if the cruelty you allege had been true you would have sought a separation?' 'Why didn't you?' 'You have a business and money. You were not bound financially.' 'What drove you to tell your mother on that particular night?' 'Did you really tell her?'

She went on answering, hearing whispers that rippled around the courtroom in a sibilant coil.

At last she was ordered to step down and Phyllis took the stand. She gave her evidence firmly, without faltering. No one was going to get at Joyce through her. Laura was to be the sacrifice.

Freda sat still and mute, her eyes occasionally wandering round the courtroom as if wondering where she was. Twice she got bored and stood up and attempted to leave, and was restrained by wardresses. To Laura's relief, they were quite gentle. When she was questioned she answered randomly, haphazardly, until the presiding judge stopped the proceedings.

Doctors were called, psychiatrists gave their informed opinions. The jury was directed and returned the verdict: '*Guilty, but insane.*'

Freda was sent away to be locked up and her family returned to their homes to face the future as best they could.

Chapter Thirty-Four

Now at last the newspapers had the freedom to go ahead and print their stories. They mused and speculated, distorting the truth.

Beneath the headlines the legends were related, the facts given their aura of sensationalism: *Mrs Harrington is a woman of tragedy. Adrian Mallender, her first husband, died horribly in a car smash.* No detail of this was omitted, including, of course, the fact that he'd committed suicide. Somehow they'd got hold of the list of his injuries, something which even Laura had not known. The reasons for his suicide were dissected. Her second marriage, a society affair, they called it, was documented. *Mrs Mallender married the deceased six months after her first husband's death. Mrs Mallender spent two honeymoons in Paris and both husbands have died in dreadful circumstances.* This was mulled over at sickening length. There was speculation as to her reasons for returning to the scene of a former honeymoon with a new husband – as if she'd had any choice, thought Laura bitterly. Violence within marriage was the subject of many articles; most writers applying it to the working classes and drunken husbands. It was never admitted that such a situation could apply to a well-bred woman. Old photographs were resurrected from the newspaper vaults and reprinted side by side with new ones. This time they managed to get a picture of Granma and Grampa. There were photographs of the hat shops and articles about their success. There was even a piece extracted from Arthur Gregory about how Laura had been dismissed from his father's store and why.

Laura felt as if she was being skinned slowly. She was raw, every nerve racked. Granma once more refused to allow her in the house. When she visited her parents the atmosphere was unwelcoming. Lillian said regretfully that although she and Victor didn't blame Laura they'd best wait until the scandal died down before she called on them again. 'We've got our position to keep up,' said Lillian. She dismissed her sister with a disdainful sniff and a hint of malicious satisfaction.

Enid and Jack never turned her away, but they were so wrapped up in themselves and their children that they unintentionally excluded her and Laura turned aside from their happiness, afraid that she might spoil it as she seemed to have spoiled everything else.

Nancy and Ralph, too, were so enamoured with their joy, so busy planning their future, that they made her feel like an outsider.

Her workforce was kind. Too kind, too understanding, too ready to jump up and bring her coffee, to run her errands, to offer assistance. In the end they unnerved her almost as much as the newspaper reporters.

Anita accepted her as she had always done, but Anita's sympathy was hard and fleeting. She never dwelt on the past, or suffered regrets, and had no patience with anyone who did.

Lady Mallender visited. She seated herself in the impeccable drawing room in Harrington House and stared round.

'You've done well for yourself,' was her opening remark.

Laura shook with anger. 'That's not how I feel.'

'Really? You surprise me.'

'You've read the newspapers. You *must* know that my life with Paul was dreadful.'

'So *you* say. Paul seemed nice enough to me and you apparently took great pleasure in showing yourself off in public. One wonders what you did to upset him so much.'

Laura rose to her feet. 'If you came here to insult me you've achieved your purpose. Now you'd better leave.'

Lady Mallender remained seated. 'I came here, as well you know, to see my grandson, but before I do, I must tell you that I intend to apply for his custody. There will be no Paul Harrington to shield you this time.'

Laura said coldly, 'I shall fight you every inch of the way. I'm no longer a poor milliner.'

'No, indeed. You have profited very nicely from your sister's wicked crime.' Lady Mallender raised her voice to drown Laura's angry retort. 'I can't believe that anyone will think you a fit woman to raise the future Sir David Mallender.'

'On what grounds will you say such a thing? My poor sister is proved mad. That's hardly my fault.'

'Hardly your fault! I suppose nothing that has happened is your fault! I suppose none of the misery that surrounds you is your fault!' Lady Mallender stood up and thrust her face close to Laura's. Her eyes blazed hate. 'I suppose you can't be blamed for my son's death. And according to you, Paul simply beat you for nothing. That's what you claim, isn't it? I don't believe it, and your wicked tattling to your mother led to his death. You can't *truthfully* go on claiming you are just a victim. Everyone connected with you has suffered in some way.'

Laura didn't need this woman to tell her that.

'You'll never see anything from my point of view,' she said tonelessly.

'And the same applies to you,' said Lady Mallender bitterly. 'Adrian –' She stopped, her voice breaking. 'My son –' Again she stopped, her mouth quivering.

Laura was appalled. Pity swamped her. She half rose and her hand went out to Lady Mallender who drew back, staring at Laura's hand as if it was a deadly snake. 'I don't want your sympathy,' she grated. 'I want only one thing from you and that I intend to have. David will live in Mallender House, where he belongs.'

Laura thought of much she could have said, accusations she could have made, but she didn't. 'This conversation is pointless,' she said.

'I quite agree. Now may I see David?'

Laura stared at her for a moment, then moved to the fireside and rang the bell. 'Please ask Nanny Allan to bring Master David to the drawing room,' she said to Claypole. He obeyed all her orders without question, but his resentment was in his eyes, as it was in the eyes of many of the Harrington servants. Apparently it didn't matter to them that their master had seen fit to torture his wife. She wondered if Paul's father had been equally inhuman. Perhaps the soft-footed, sharp-eyed servants were keeping dark secrets long hidden from the world.

'I would much prefer to see David in the nursery, as usual,' declared her ladyship.

Laura didn't doubt it. She was sure that Lady Mallender had a great time exclaiming over David's virtues and hinting broadly to Nanny Allan of his mother's faults. She probably went no further though. Even under these extreme circumstances Laura couldn't imagine Lady Mallender unbending with servants.

Ralph said that Rick was in London. He had become a member of the Film Society and was mixing with people like Bernard Shaw and HG Wells. Not content with owning cinemas he was thinking of pushing forward and upward into film-making itself. 'He isn't committing himself,' said Ralph, 'until he sees what money might be made.' He became thoughtful. 'Though our home-grown entrepreneur is so hooked on the cinema, he could be willing to take a chance.'

'It wouldn't be the first time,' reminded Laura. 'He began with nothing, remember?'

Ralph nodded. 'Just as you and I did.'

Laura lay awake at night wondering if she was destined forever to bring tragedy to those she loved. Where had it all begun? Why had she made so many mistakes? She writhed in her bed, desperately seeking answers, wondering if she was doomed to live without love, to cause unhappiness until the end of her days.

She had blundered into marriage with Adrian. She had been used by him and his mother. Then Paul had offered his protection and she had gone blindly into marriage again. Both times she had believed she was acting sincerely, but perhaps a girl from Adrian's own society would have tiptoed away from the scene that had so horrified her, and maybe Paul wouldn't have abused a woman of his own class.

Laura wondered if Rick would keep his promise to stand by her? Or had the latest events proved after all too much for him to stomach. He was so successful he could so easily forget her. Well, she could stand alone, run her business efficiently. She'd become a power in the world of fashion and to hell with men and the disturbing sickness of love.

A week later Rick returned unexpectedly from London. He phoned and asked Laura to meet him in Ralph's place.

As soon as she saw him, Laura knew that she had been deluding herself if she thought her love for him was dead. The ice round her heart melted and when he held her she put her arms round him, hugging him close, pressing her face to his, murmuring her welcome as he kissed her.

'Laura.'

She let him go, a sense of shame filling her as she recalled the stories of her humiliation at Paul's hands.

He lit their cigarettes and they sat down. 'Have you missed me?' he asked.

'Of course.' Her cruel embarrassment made her sound stilted.

Rick stared at her for a long moment before he leaned back and dragged on his cigarette. 'I've made some good contacts in London.'

'Yes. Ralph told me a little of what you've been doing.'

'I've met some interesting people. I've never been much of a one for reading, but I bought a couple of books. Do you know the work of HG Wells?'

Laura nodded.

'Yes, you would. I should have known.'

They were silent. She must get away. If she stayed she'd break down.

'I must go home,' she said, standing. Her voice cracked on the word home and Rick looked up sharply. In a moment he was beside her, tossing his cigarette into the fireplace and following it with hers.

His arms went round her and he said gently, 'Laura, don't leave yet. I've missed you.'

'Oh, Rick –'

'I wanted to come back at the time of the trial but I thought the newsmen might make capital out of it. They knew we sang and played piano together. I managed to fend off the few curious ones who lay in wait for me in London. They decided I wouldn't make much of a story. They had far better material. *I'm* still alive.'

Laura flinched.

'Damn, that was clumsy! I meant that I wasn't what's known as newsworthy.'

'I know what you meant,' said Laura, dispirited.

Rick tilted her face with gentle fingers. 'My Laura, you've been through hell. The last thing I want to do is make you feel worse. What I do want is this.' He bent his head and kissed her mouth, his lips sweet and caressing. 'My Laura. You are still mine, aren't you?'

'If you want me.'

'If I want you! Can you doubt it?'

Relief coursed through her. 'I love you, Rick,' she murmured against his searching lips. He kissed her again and his arms held her tighter.

He stared into her eyes. 'I love you, my darling. I'll always love you. If only I'd asked you to marry me when we first knew each other –'

'But you didn't love me then –'

'I think I did. I didn't want to admit it, even to myself. I have to shoulder some of the blame for all the misery you've suffered.'

'No –'

'We'll not quarrel about that. There are more important matters to discuss. Will you marry me?'

'Oh, I want to, I do, but I'm afraid! Lady Mallender said I brought disaster to men.'

'That bloody woman talks bloody rubbish,' said Rick. 'Adrian and Paul were victims of their own natures. Say you'll marry me, Laura.'

'Yes, oh yes, please, darling Rick.'

'We'll have to wait.' He cradled her chin in his hand and kissed her tenderly, massaging her neck with his thumb. 'Let the furore die down and we'll slip off somewhere and get hitched quietly.'

'Quietly. That sounds exactly right. Nothing in my life has been quiet for a long time.'

Ralph had left a bottle of wine on a side table and Rick poured two glasses. 'To us.'

'To us,' said Laura.

'And to David,' said Rick.

A shock jolted Laura. In her exquisite happiness and relief she had actually forgotten David. Rick had to know the truth. How did one find words to make such a confession?

She took a deep breath. 'Rick, there's something you must know. Remember the night I discovered Adrian with Rex and ran out of the house and came to you –'

Rick smiled. 'As if I could ever forget.'

'I don't know how to say this – there was a consequence to our lovemaking.'

His head went up sharply. 'What?'

'Rick –' She swallowed hard. 'David is your son.'

He frowned at her. 'No! It's not possible! You denied it.'

'*He's yours*! Rick, I swear it! You've got to believe me.'

He said slowly, 'By God, you mean it.' He began his familiar pacing. 'My son – *our son*? No! You can't possibly be sure. You were married to Adrian. Weren't you sleeping together?'

'I used a contraceptive. I didn't want to get pregnant at once because of my work. He didn't know.'

'Laura –' Rick held her at arm's length, his fingers digging into her with unintentional force, and stared into her face. 'My God,' he said softly, 'You're telling the truth. David is my son. My son!' He resumed his pacing. 'You should have told me. You should have, Laura. I asked you outright. You denied it,' he said again.

She was angry at his accusatory tone. 'When you asked me if there'd been a consequence of our night of love, you were being flippant.'

'I didn't feel flippant.'

'How was I supposed to know that?'

'You should have told me!'

'Don't keep saying that! What if I had? I was married to Adrian. You'd made it clear on every possible occasion that you weren't cut out to be tied down by a family. All I could think of was my baby born safe in marriage.'

'But David would have inherited a title! Damn it! He's still in line. That's cheating, that's *really* cheating.'

'All right, so I cheated, but by God, I've paid a heavy price for it.'

Rick swung round to face her and his anger died. 'Yes. Yes, you have. What an opinionated, selfish swine I've been. You should have been able to come to me. The Mallenders will have to know, of course.'

'Lady Mallender won't believe it. She'll think it's just a plot to keep David from her. She says she's going to sue for custody. She threatened to when Adrian was killed, but when I married Paul –'

'Did you marry him just to keep David out of her clutches?'

'No! I don't know! I suppose it could have been part of it. I thought I loved him.'

'Hell, what a mess!'

Rick sounded grim and Laura said, 'I couldn't possibly foresee what would happen.'

Rick's face softened. 'No, that's true. Poor Laura. You've been through so much alone. Does anyone else know?'

'I've never spoken of it – but I think Aunty Mabel guesses that David's yours.'

'She would.' He drew her to him again. 'Honey, you really did keep quiet to protect our son, didn't you? And I've been gallivanting across the world leaving you to carry the burden. The sooner we're married the better. You need protecting from yourself.' His voice suddenly became jubilant. 'My son! I've got a son! *We've* got a son.' He gave a shout of laughter. 'What a hell of a way to start a marriage!'

'I want David to know who his father is!'

'Don't worry, he will.'

'How are we going to stave off Lady Mallender?'

Rick gently tugged her down to sit on the couch beside him. He traced the outline of her features with a tender finger. 'I'll

596

need time to think about that. Meanwhile –' He pressed her back on the cushions. 'Meanwhile – Laura, I'm starving for you.'

'Ralph – ?'

'Won't come back until I phone him. He's taken Nancy to a club.'

'Rick, I've wanted you so.'

They said little. There was no need for words. They moved swiftly and Laura gave and received love in full measure, knowing that for the first time she was joined in one flesh to a man who loved her just as she was, whose love encompassed her mistakes, who gave himself wholly to her. Her passion soared, and her body was aflame as the blood coursed through her veins, her heart leapt in ecstasy. Together they reached a climax that held them in one another's arms long after the act of union was finished, murmuring tender endearments, sweet promises for the future.

Rick and Laura went to Sir Hugo and told him exactly when David had been conceived.

'I'm deeply ashamed and sorry for the way I've deceived you,' said Laura. 'Events just overtook me.'

'I know how that feels,' said Sir Hugo with feeling. 'I deplored Adrian's behaviour. You were badly treated. My son –' He paused, his face twisting in a spasm of distress. 'I shall speak to my wife.'

'She won't want to believe it,' said Laura.

Sir Hugo picked up a framed photograph of David from his desk. He looked at it searchingly, then at Rick. He nodded. 'I see. Yes, I see. She will believe it, I promise you. There will be no more scandal, no more lawyers and court rooms. And no more of her intrigues.' He flushed and gave a small dry cough. 'She's my wife –' He stopped and coughed again.

'She's very concerned about the succession,' said Laura gently.

Sir Hugo smiled faintly at her. 'There is no need. The heir, my nephew, is a fine boy. I'm happy to know the title will go to him.'

Rick helped Laura into his car.

'You've got your Rolls Royce at last, Rick.'

'I told you I would.'

'I've happy memories of your first car, and of the motor bike and sidecar.'

'So have I, baby. I haven't given you much to remember with pleasure, have I? But that's going to change. And of course there's much more room in the Rolls if we decide to stop in some quiet spot.'

'Can't you get your mind off sex?'

'Sure, honey, but not for long.'

'You may not have many hours to spare for me. You've an empire to build, remember?'

'And so have you, Laura, my love, but I reckon we'll find plenty of time in between for us.'

Laura could see no flaw in this.